HER FIRST LESSON IN LOVE

The April sun was shining warmly upon Gerard's bare head as he came toward

Mavreen

"So you have come!" he said, "I was in torment all night fearing you would not do so."

"But I promised I would be here, Gerard. Nothing could stop me."

"Ah, Mavreen!" he cried, taking her fiercely into his arms. "I have dreamed all night of kissing you…"

She raised her mouth to his with the simple eagerness of a child. But it was not as a child that her body responded as his mouth came down on hers.

He kissed her until she could scarcely breathe. His voice was filled with the urgency of a young man's passion as he said:

"If you but knew how greatly I desire to teach you the ways of love."

"I have learned much already!" she answered.

"It is but a beginning!" he told her…

Mavreen

A Novel By
Claire Lorrimer

BANTAM BOOKS
TORONTO · NEW YORK · LONDON

*This low-priced Bantam Book
has been completely reset in a type face
designed for easy reading, and was printed
from new plates. It contains the complete
text of the original hard-cover edition.*
NOT ONE WORD HAS BEEN OMITTED.

MAVREEN

*A Bantam Book / published by arrangement with
Arlington Books Limited*

PRINTING HISTORY

*First published in 1976 by Arlington Books
in Great Britain*

Bantam edition / January 1977

2nd printing

ISBN 0-553-10208-7

Published simultaneously in the United States and Canada

PRINTED IN THE UNITED STATES OF AMERICA

FOREWORD

Sussex, in the south of England, was the obvious choice of county for the country background for *Mavreen*. Not only was it a center of smuggling for more than six centuries, but because of the Prince of Wales's building of the Pavilion in Brighton, it was also royally fashionable during the period of my story. I am, therefore, much indebted to E. V. Lucas for the considerable amount of information I have been able to acquire from his book, *Highways and Byways In Sussex;* not least for information relating to the Sussex dialect. A short list of words used in the story and their meanings is given below.

It may be of interest to American readers that many students of the old Sussex dialect have remarked upon the similarities to words in common usage in America as, for example, "the fall" for autumn; "guess"; "reckon"; "disremember"; and of phrases such as, "You hadn't ought to do it"; "Be you" for "Are you". One cause may be the two hundred Sussex colonists taken over to America by William Penn who was one time Squire of Warminghurst in West Sussex; although in the opinion of the American writer Mrs. Phoebe Gibbons, the peculiarities of the Sussex dialect more closely resemble those of New England than of Pennsylvania.

So far as I have been able to ascertain, the historical events referred to in this book are correct. Obviously, however, this adherence to truth does not apply where fictitious characters are involved with historical persons.

CAST OF CHARACTERS

PART ONE 1779–1796

Sir John Danesfield (*Mavreen's father*)

Druscilla, Lady Danesfield (*his wife*)

Prudence and Selina Danesfield (*their daughters*)

Mavreen (*Sir John's natural daughter*)

Letitia Ashworth (*Mavreen's mother and Governess to the Danesfield children*)

Clarissa Manton (*Sir John's mistress*)

Vicomte Antoine de Valle (*deceased*)

Vicomtesse Marianne de Valle (*his wife*)

Vicomte Gerard de Valle (*their son*)

Jules (*manservant to Gerard*)

Master Thomas Sale (*farmer, Mavreen's foster father*)

Mistress Agnes Sale (*wife of above*)

Dickon Sale (*eldest son of above*)

Patty, Anna, Henry, Edward Sale (*Sale's other children*)

Gilbert, Lord Barre (*Sir John's friend*)

Baron von Gottfried (*Austrian card cheat who dishonoured Antoine de Valle*)

Arthur Glover (*Mavreen's Sussex tutor*)

Marquis de Guéridon (*friend of the late Vicomte and the Vicomtesse de Valle*)

Hon. James Pettigrew (*Gerard's Eton school friend*)

Hon. Anne Pettigrew (*James' sister and friend of Gerard*)

Herr Mehler (*Austrian music teacher*)

Marquis de Faenza

Donna Mercedes de Faenza (*daughter of above*)

Baron von Eburhard

Baroness Lisa von Eburhard (*wife of above, school friend of Clarissa Manton*)

Baroness Helga von Heissen (*Gerard's one-time mistress*)

Rose (*Clarissa's maid*)

PART TWO 1797–1799

Percy Lade (*Anne Pettigrew's fiancé*)

Clarence Barre (*cousin and heir to Lord Barre*)

Thomas Spray
George Pring
Will Bennett
Spencer Collinson } (*smugglers*)

Tamarisk (*Mavreen's child*)

Prince Monte-Gincinto

Princess Isabella Monte-Gincinto (*his wife*)

Donna Faustina Monte-Gincinto (*daughter of above*)

Donna Torina (*Faustina's duenna*)

PART THREE 1803–1812

Sister Marie-Therese

Thomas, Emma, Harry Lade (*Percy and Anne Lade's children*)

Luther (*Mavreen's butler*)

Gideon Morris (*alias Peregrine Waite*)

John Ward

Thomas Creevey

Miss Payne (*Tamarisk's governess*)

Baron Stern
Baroness Stern

Georg (*Baron von Gottfried's manservant*)

Professor Spiegel (*Austrian surgeon*)

Nikolai Kuragin (*Gerard's captor and servant*)

Richard Fortescue (*Tamarisk's tutor*)

Sir Frederick Morris (*Gideon's father*)

At the age of thirty-six, Sir John Danesfield was in the prime of life. He was a tall man of great physical strength, enormous energy, and superior intelligence. He was also immensely virile and passionately susceptible to women's charms.

On the evening of December 4, 1779, he sat alone in the library of his home, Wyfold House, Piccadilly. He was sated after a vast dinner eaten alone in the big dining room but far from satisfied in all his bodily appetites. If he so wished, he could call upon a quite exceptional number of ladies of his acquaintance who would be happy to open the doors of their bed chambers to him. Rich, titled, aristocratic and by any standards a handsome man, he seldom lacked the female company he constantly required, but somewhat unusually for him, he now found himself in the unfortunate position of desiring one particular female—and she, to his ever increasing frustration, was resisting his every advance.

Sir John finished a second glass of brandy and became even more uncomfortably aware of the fire in his blood. His conscience was at war with his determination to seduce the girl under his roof whom he could summon to his presence by a mere pull upon the bell rope.

Restlessly, he rubbed a hand up and down his hawklike nose, dark eyebrows drawn down in a scowl as he pondered his moral scruples. Upstairs lay his miserable wife Druscilla, and in the nursery wing, his two young daughters. As usual, all three were in ill health, coughing, sneezing and snivelling in what appeared to be their permanent condition every year when the chills of winter attacked them. Robust himself, Sir John found any kind of sickness distasteful. He had never loved his wife and, of late, he found himself more and more often resenting his marriage, despite the financial advantages it had brought him. He was thankful that following upon the difficult birth of their second daughter, Selina, their hitherto dutiful cohabitation had ceased by unspoken, mutual agreement.

Sir John reflected that his wife had never shown anything but the greatest distaste for this side of her married life; and this being the case, his conscience need not trouble him if he found his pleasures elsewhere. Unfortunately, his conscience could not so easily be set aside in relation to the young woman he now desired most urgently to bed.

Letitia Ashworth had come to his house a year ago as governess to the five-year-old Prudence, his eldest daughter. His wife had engaged the girl, the daughter of a Derbyshire parson. He, himself, had barely noticed the quiet fair-haired girl in her unobtrusive grey gown with Quaker collar and cuffs of starched white linen.

Occasionally, this past summer, he came upon her walking in the garden with the child. She bobbed a curtsy, kept her eyes down and her hands folded and answered his dutiful questions as to the child's welfare in a voice so quiet he had to strain to hear her replies. If he felt anything at all, it had been a faint irritation because her downcast lashes, Quaker primness and convent-like demeanor reflected, so it seemed to him, his wife's obsession with the life *religieuse*. His own nature demanded color, vitality, laughter, activity and although he appreciated a feminine woman, his preference was for the voluptuous, the flamboyant, and passionate.

She had first come to his attention one day last summer. He returned home unexpectedly one afternoon to discover her quite alone in his wife's powder room. She was dressed in one of Druscilla's most lavish and seldom worn ball gowns, beautifully coiffed powdered wig upon her head, pivoting with obvious delight at her reflection in front of the mirror.

The girl did not observe him as he had stood staring in silent astonishment. He was intrigued and amused by this transformation of his prim young governess. The lace ruffles of the dress fell delicately off the beautiful creamy roundness of the girl's shoulders and rose even more tantalizingly over the tender curve of her breasts. The embroidered bodice of the gown enhanced the taut uplift of the young bosom and narrowed excitingly to a waist so tiny that he would have had no difficulty in encircling it with his hands.

But it was not her figure alone which prompted a sudden upsurge of all-too-familiar desire. Letitia's green eyes were sparkling with excitement, her oval face tilted provocatively to one side as she admired herself and her hands moved over her body outlining its curves with an unmistakable sensuous pleasure. He knew instinctively that she was imagining a man's hands were touching her, and his desire to be that man was so violent that he caught his breath.

She swung round and saw him. The color rushed to her cheeks and she caught her little red tongue between her teeth as she gasped in guilty dismay at having been discovered.

A kindly man, Sir John had at once sought to dispel her fears.

"Do not worry, my dear!" he said, as he took a step into the room toward her. "I have no intention of telling your mistress about your little escapade." He knew very well, as the girl herself must have known, that Druscilla would instantly have dismissed the young governess from her service had she known of this. "In truth, you look so charming, I regret you cannot more often attire yourself in such fashion."

Letitia looked upon the point of tears, the blush fading from her cheeks as she stammered out her apologies. She was in such pitiful confusion that he decided to make his retreat and allow her to collect her wits and remove her borrowed finery in peace.

From then on, the girl blushed whenever she chanced to meet him in the house or garden. Keeping her eyes downcast, she would answer his amused questions in monosyllables. But having glimpsed that other woman with fire and passions half awakened, he knew she needed only a lover's touch to ignite the conflagration. And Sir John Danesfield wanted to be that man.

That Letitia was now as aware of him as he was of her, he had no doubt. Her very avoidance of him betrayed her fear of him. As the summer days passed to autumn, he sought her more and more often, finding a dozen pretexts for summoning her to his presence. She, in turn, did her best to evade any encounter with him. She remained always either in the company of her young charge or of his wife. Sir John had little doubt this self-imposed chaperonage was deliberate and though he was enormously frustrated by it, he was by no means displeased that she should feel afraid to trust herself alone with him. Sir John was not particularly conceited but his life long successes with women left him in no doubt that they found him attractive. He was, therefore, a self-confident lover in pursuit of a new quarry.

But this girl presented a serious problem for him. Her virtue, by nature of her upbringing and class, was of utmost importance to her and any kind of liaison with a man would preclude her ultimate hopes of marriage. It was not his habit to dishonor virgins. There was yet another reason why he hesitated to pursue his attentions further. As a man of honor, he had essayed to be a dutiful husband and afford his sickly spouse the respect due her as his wife and the mother of his two disappointing daughters. He had tried not to show too obviously his resentment that she had failed to give him a son and built a life for himself outside his home, enjoying his various sporting activities, pastimes and women apart from his family, leaving his wife free to run his home in the convent-like atmosphere she seemed to approve. It was not, therefore, his habit to indulge his baser appetites beneath his own roof.

But these moral scruples had become insidiously weakened in the last six months, during which time he had grown more and more frustrated as his awareness of the girl increased his thwarted desires. The girl, herself, was now as obviously aware of him. She was unable to control the trembling of her hands when he spoke to her, nor the delicate blush on her cheeks if he passed her on the stairway and their bodies touched.

This evening, his scruples were finally overcome. The

brandy which he had drunk in order to bring about a degree of insensibility had merely inflamed his desire. Moreover, with the children long since abed and his wife confined to her sick room, he knew that tonight Letitia would be without the protection of their company. The servants would not go up to the nursery quarters unless summoned.

Letitia was sitting at the nursery table, correcting sums when, unannounced, he opened the door and found her.

To Sir John the nursery lit by firelight seemed warm, intimate and welcoming after the austere masculinity of his book-lined library.

Letitia rose awkwardly to her feet, eyes downcast as usual, cheeks aflame. She waited for Sir John to speak but he remained silent and she felt herself forced at length to look up at him. He was standing in the open doorway staring at her. There could be no mistaking the expression on his flushed face and her blush deepened. For a long moment, they stood there, eyes locked across the distance between them. Then Sir John closed the door behind him.

She had imagined this situation so often both in her dreams and hours of waking that now there came a feeling of unreality as the tall dominant figure moved toward her. She was both afraid and desirous of his approach. Many times in the past few months she had faced the reality of her situation and knew very well that a girl in her position was frequently at the mercy of the gentlemen in the house, as were all the lower echelons of the household staff. Her mother had warned her of these dangers and cautioned her about the terrible consequences, but she had not warned her that her own body's needs might betray her or spoken of the feelings a young girl of twenty might experience were she to fall in love.

Letitia's heart, mind, and body were in a turmoil almost equal to that of her employer as the handsome Sir John pursued her relentlessly throughout the long hot summer. His eyes were forever demanding a response she knew she must not give, requesting an encouragement that could only bring about her downfall. Her strict parsonage upbringing left her in no doubt as to the sinfulness of her romantic thoughts about her employer. Her father would consider Sir John to be a wicked man, and Letitia was confused by the certainty that he was far from wicked. Living as she did in Sir John's house, she was aware that there was no love in his marriage. Lady Danesfield made no attempt to hide her revulsion at her husband's presence. She sighed with relief when Sir John left the house, complained continuously about the obnoxious smell of his tobacco fumes, of his untidiness, his very maleness an affront to the shadowy cloistered silence she endeavored to maintain in the house.

Letitia herself was oppressed by the colorless unsmiling austerity of Druscilla Danesfield's preferred way of life and although it was not unlike her own austere home where her father believed in rigorous discipline and adherence to God's teachings, at least there had been some warmth in her mother's soft voice or in the way her eyes rested fondly upon her husband. Letitia had been aware of the loving relationship between her parents and even felt, at times, excluded from some magic circle enclosing them and longed for the day when she would find some man who would love and marry her and with whom she, too, could experience this privileged unity.

She had not thought of herself as beautiful or desirable until Sir John had discovered her dressing up in Lady Danesfield's ball gown. He had come upon her when she was in the process of learning there was a very different aspect of her nature than that of the prim, demure girl her mother had carefully encouraged her to be, and one far more in keeping with her most secret feelings. If the sight of her reflection had not been disturbing enough, the look in Sir John's eyes was sufficient to bring the truth frighteningly home to her—that the love of God was not, as her father had promised, sufficient to sustain her throughout life.

Letitia stood up, her green eyes returning Sir John's gaze as if mesmerized by his proximity. He hesitated. The chase was over and the quarry at bay. But somehow he could not bring himself to take that last irrevocable step. The girl looked so terrifyingly young and helpless, so frighteningly vulnerable.

He put out a hand and laid it with clumsy gentleness on the soft silkiness of her hair.

"Letitia!" he said, his voice husky with urgent desire for her. "You know why I have come to find you, don't you?"

She nodded.

"You wanted me to come to you, did you not?" he insisted.

Her eyelids closed over her eyes in momentary confusion.

"Yes, sir. I suppose I did. And yet . . . ."

He turned away from the despairing look and said with an anger that was not so much directed at her as against his own weakness, "My name is John! Call me by it!" This was no time to be feeling sorry for her, he told himself.

"Yes, John!" she said so softly he barely heard her words.

Her shyness delighted him and intensified his desire for her. He sat down on the chair she had vacated and taking her hands, pulled her toward him. Through the thin fabric of her dress, he could feel her trembling.

"I'm not going to force you, my dear. You are at liberty to say nay, if that is your wish. You have no need to fear violation from me."

Suddenly, she found her voice.

"It is not my wish to refuse you, sir . . . John," she corrected herself. "But I am afraid. Not exactly of you. But because this—this is wrong."

He felt a moment of triumph. He had been right in his assumption that she was by no means averse to him as a man. Only her moral scruples stood between him and what he had wanted for so long.

"Is it your fear of committing a sin that has caused you to avoid me so cruelly?" he asked, half-seriously, half-teasing. When she did not answer him, he drew her closer against him and said harshly, "Can you really have no idea how such behavior has tormented me? Never a glance, never a smile from those pretty eyes of yours! Was it your intention to drive me to despair?"

Her breath came now in short gasps. She could feel the

heat of his body through her dress and it seemed as if every nerve in her own body had come to the surface, and awaited the touch of his hand upon her.

"I did not know you were so affected!" she said in a low voice. "I hoped that if I were to keep myself from your sight, we might both think less about our sinful longings!"

To her surprise, a smile spread over his face at her puritanical choice of words.

"Sinful!" he repeated. "Maybe so! Yet somehow I doubt the need men and women have for one another was ever intended by God to be a matter of sin."

"I do not know any more what is right or wrong!" she cried. "I know only that my conscience tells me it would be wrong. And that I—I love you!"

He could feel her trembling. It inflamed him. Fighting hard to control his excitement, he said, "So, 'tis love you feel for me! And yet you gave me no sign of it all this summer long."

Her cheeks colored.

"Maybe because, sir, you gave no sign of love to me. Indeed, I did not expect any, for you are a married man and not free to give love to another."

"So it is love that you are seeking rather than your salvation from sin!" he said. "Would then my declaration of love make the difference to your 'yea' or 'nay'?"

Her hesitation was not feigned. Her eyes were very serious as she said slowly, "I think that it would—even though it cannot lessen the sin of wrongdoing. Love, methinks, is a powerful emotion and as such, offers at least an excuse for breaking the Commandment."

"Thou shalt not commit adultery?" he asked. "No, not that, my charming little preacher, for you are unmarried and it is only I who would commit adultery. And for that sin I have no conscience nor ever had, and I think you well know the reason, Letitia."

She nodded.

"Leave me to my sinning!" he said quietly. "It is you and not my sins I have upon my conscience for though I might love you, I cannot marry you, as well you know."

Her eyes now widened in tremulous surprise and happiness.

"I was not aware that you felt love for me!" she said. "How could I have presumed so much from a man of your years, your position, your experiences. Why should you love me? You know nothing of me but that I am from a simple parsonage background and that I am your children's governess. Of my character and intelligence you can know nothing, nor of my true nature or beliefs. How then can you be sure you love me?"

The logic and directness of her thinking came to him as a sharp rebuke for his deception. He had not intended to make a declaration of love, but he knew that if he withdrew it now, he must lose her. With her slender young body trembling between his thighs, he was not strong enough to resist the advantage she had so innocently given him.

"All that I have observed about you since you came to live in my house, I have learned to love and respect!" he said. At least this much was true. "And I suspect that were I to know you better, my feelings of affection could only increase. Letitia, do you know what I am suffering? Before God, I need you. I pray you, do not deny me longer!"

His hands moved swiftly upward to the soft swelling of her young bosom. Beneath the flimsy material of her gown, he could feel the sharp outline of her hardening nipples and with a cry, he buried his face against her. Her long sweet-smelling hair tumbled about his flushed cheeks and the swift rise and fall of her bosom seemed already in unison with his own fast breathing.

For months he had secretly dreamed of seeing her naked. Now he knew he had only to unbutton the fastenings of her dress and she would be revealed to him. His heart beat even faster with an excitement that increased twofold when suddenly she lifted her arms to assist him while he struggled with the tantalizing buttons. The dress fell to the floor in a heap about her feet. Impatiently, he began to tear away the rest of her garments. She made no protest at his feverish fumblings, but helped him as best she could.

When at last she stood naked before him, he could not take his gaze from her. No woman had ever seemed more

desirable, her small perfectly formed young breasts peep-
ing between the modest coverings of her small white fingers. His hands feverishly encircled the tiny waist, ran
down the gentle curve of her hips, over her stomach and
the light gold triangle of hair, and gripped the long slim
legs.

"You are in truth a Venus in miniature!" he said hoarsely, and releasing her began to tear at his own clothing.
"Help me!" he commanded, but need not have done so
for now she was as eager as he for the touch of his naked
flesh against hers. She had never seen a man's body and
curiosity mingled with desire. When he stood before her,
proud and unashamed in his manhood, she lost the last
traces of modesty and reached out to hold him, her eyes
burning with impatience.

Sir John curbed his longing to take her quickly and
cruelly. Many years of possessing women had taught him
that the rewards were always sweeter when passion was
reciprocal. Some women offered their bodies for a man's
pleasure but themselves found no delight in the union. It
was true that reciprocation was not expected of them but
when a man found a fire to match his own, its very rarity
increased the power of the flames.

He kissed and fondled Letitia until her soft sighs gave
way to low moans of pleasure. They were lying where
they had undressed one another on the thick carpet before
the fire. He would have lifted her and carried her to one
of the bed chambers but was afraid if he did so, her ardor
might cool and reason reassert itself. He knew that although he was not acting against her will, he was nonetheless seducing her. But his conscience was quickly enough
deadened by her unabashed delight in him. Now she was
discovering the fierce needs of her body so carefully in-
hibited by her parents' teaching for the past seven years,
and allowed them free expression as she cast off one by
one the chains of her upbringing.

When at last Sir John could endure the waiting no
longer and he thrust himself into her with a wild cry of
delight, she flinched only once with pain before her hands
clenched against his back, pressing him even more deeply

into her. It was as if she were as eager as he for her own deflowering.

Sweat poured from their bodies as they lay locked together before the fire. Like a little animal, Letitia put out her small pink tongue and licked his glistening skin. Much moved by the sweetness of this loving gesture, he kissed her parted lips and spoke words of love to her that brought a happy smile to her lips.

"I love you with all my heart, dearest John!" she declared. "I cannot feel that we have been bad in what we have done. Tell me again you do not think we have sinned."

He closed his eyes, unwilling that she should see the uneasiness in them. She had not sinned. But he had. She had been totally innocent and he had no justification for changing her from virgin to mistress. Yet that must be the outcome of this night's pleasure. He could not keep away from her now. He would unquestionably desire her again and yet again. The girl had but started out upon the road of discovery and with each experience would find new ecstasies and pleasures as her innately sensuous nature burst into full bloom. From such beginnings, who could put a limit upon the delights they would now share! He was aware of them before she could do more than suspect them. He could not leave her now.

He stopped her questioning with kisses and reassurances of his love and regard for her. As to her future, he did not allow himself to contemplate it.

Up until Christmas, Lady Danesfield complained ceaselessly to Letitia that her husband was spending more and more time at home. He was forever underfoot, impossible to ignore, disrupting the quiet of the well-ordered nursery where he over-excited little Prudence with his hearty laughter and boisterous play.

"Let us hope he will cease this charade of paternal concern once the festivities are over!" Druscilla moaned. "For to be sure, my head is aching with all the noise."

Such remarks filled Letitia with ever-increasing remorse and guilt. She was the reason why Sir John no longer left his home for the pleasures of the gaming rooms. Since the night when they had first expressed their love and need for each other, there was no halting the tidal wave that followed. There was no secluded shadowy corner of the great house where they had not stolen kisses, touched one another hungrily; barely a single night when he had not come to her bedchamber and spent the long hours with her in an abandonment of loving. And she, far from discouraging him as she knew was her moral duty, desired him as often and feverishly as he desired her.

Letitia tried, ineffectually, to voice her reluctance to go on living in such a manner in his house where she must daily face the wretched woman they were deceiving. But Sir John overruled her objections with the simple argument that Druscilla had no love for him. As to Letitia's receiving delights that were his wife's by right, she must understand that a man's body was as distasteful to Druscilla as it was welcome to her.

Letitia might have found resistance easier if Sir John had proved an unkind or thoughtless man. But he remained remarkably patient with his ever-complaining and sickly wife, as he also did with his sniffling daughters. Prudence approached him only when he held out some sweetmeat to her and then struggled from his arms if he attempted to pet or fondle her.

He was ever kind, attentive and loving toward Letitia although she had begun to doubt now that he loved her in the same degree as she loved him. She would happily have died for him had he demanded it. She would, if he so wished, have left his employ and become his mistress, accepting the open admission of her lost virtue, the inevitable rejection by her family and the end of any hopes she might have entertained for marriage.

He stressed that he found this new passion in his life perfectly satisfying in every respect and was unhappy that she, too, did not find it so. So she became silent, keeping her fears, misgivings and remorse to herself; she resolved that she would bring their relationship to an end. By giving in her notice and leaving the house forever, she would place herself beyond the reach of temptation.

But each determination was undermined by the far

stronger need for her lover. He had but to glance at her across a room to set her blood raging. She feared that she would never find the strength of mind to leave him.

December sped by. The New Year began with a bitterly cold January. Letitia now had other worries upon her mind. By February she was no longer in doubt that she was with child.

Had she known of it a month earlier, she might have told Sir John of her predicament. But throughout January it became terrifyingly plain to her that his love for her was cooling. He was once more absenting himself for long periods from Wyfold House. For two long weeks, he disappeared to the country game-shooting. Her body ached in protest at this sudden curtailment of their loving. When he returned, she knew that he had scarcely missed her. He came, as usual, to her bedchamber, but his attentions were less ardent and he departed long before the night was over. Once she found a woman's lace handkerchief in the pocket of his night robe and guessed, correctly, that he had not been faithful to her. It caused her unbearable anguish.

So by the time she knew she was carrying his child, she knew also that he no longer loved her. Fiercely proud, she kept her agony of mind to herself. She had very little money and no friends in London. She would have to find work to support herself and her coming child but knew no one unconnected with the Danesfield family who might wish to employ her as a governess. She was untrained for any other work except that of a domestic.

Then she learned from one of the servants that casual labor was easily come by in Sussex. There was fruit picking, hop picking, dairy work, and in Brighthelmstone, servants wanted by the gentry who were beginning to open residences there now that the Prince of Wales was making the town fashionable. Nor were too many questions asked with labor in short supply.

Letitia counted her meager savings, packed a portmanteau, and departed Wyfold House silently and unobserved by its inhabitants.

Seven months later, ill, starving and alone, she was

given refuge by a kindly Sussex farmer and his wife, and Sir John Danesfield's hapless bastard was born. The infant, determined upon survival, fought her way with the greatest of difficulty into the world.

Letitia called her Mavreen.

PART ONE
1779-1796

CHAPTER ONE
1788

The June sunshine beamed fiercely through the open door of the hayloft. It formed a square golden carpet on the piles of dried meadow grass. On this warm sweet-smelling bed a small girl lay spread-eagled on her back, coarse linen smock pulled up to her thighs. She was watching with rapt concentration as a yellow butterfly, wings folded, perched on her bare brown knee.

Mavreen knew it would be cooler in the orchard where the geese and goats grazed and the heavily laden apple trees cast patterned shadows on the grass. But the child was in hiding from Mistress Sale, the farmer's wife, who, if she saw her would most certainly call her indoors to help with the ironing. The heavy flat irons made her thin arms ache and although she quite liked the steamy smell of freshly laundered linen, domestic tasks were not little Mavreen Ashworth's favorite occupation.

The butterfly's wings quivered as it prepared for flight. It rose into the tiny particles of dust circulating in the sunbeams.

Mavreen sighed. She wished momentarily, that she, too, was a butterfly. Or perhaps a swallow. The beautiful little birds had nested, as every year they did, in the roof of the loft, flying in and out with food for the fledglings, darting gracefully to and fro. Later, when the summer was nearly over, the youngsters would be strong enough to migrate with the adult birds far away from England to another land. Mavreen wished she knew where they went but Dickon, the farmer's eldest son, who was twelve years old and knew nearly everything about animals and birds and insects, alas, lacked any knowledge of foreign places.

If she were a swallow, Mavreen thought, she could fly away and explore the world. She could go to the continent

of Australia where Captain Cook had discovered a vast
new country. Dickon said that one day he might become a
sailor and go exploring and Mavreen decided that if he
went away she would go with him. But Dickon said girls
could not become explorers.

Mavreen sat up, pulling wisps of hay from her thick
honey colored hair. She sighed again, fine straight brows
drawn together over wide hazel green eyes, her small
mouth, red as a Kent cherry, puckered in disapproval.
There was no doubt in her mind—God had made a mistake when He had decided she should be a girl. Even more
than she wanted to be a butterfly or a swallow, she wished
she were a boy. Girls had to do dairy work, laundry work,
house cleaning, fruit preserving, baking, cooking, washing
dishes. They had to wear long trailing skirts and petticoats instead of breeches. They could not ride horses and
climb trees, go fishing and hunting.

Her small face broke into a mischievous smile. She
could, in fact, do all these things. Ever since she could
remember, and she was now eight years old, she had been
Dickon's shadow. Whenever they were far away from the
farmhouse and out of sight of Master and Mistress Sale,
she could hitch up her skirts and forget she was a girl.
Dickon did not really approve her behavior but she had
only to plead with him to get her every wish and demand.
He loved her very much and she loved him in return.

She was vaguely aware that he was less quick-witted
than she was, slower in his speech and in his understanding
of anything new. But he more than made up for this by
never forgetting anything he learned. He was totally dependable, totally reliable, unchangeable and to the small
girl, whose nature was multifarious, Dickon's consistency
was the perfect antidote. His natural caution counter-
acted her impetuosity.

The sound of a horse clattering over the cobbled yard
below brought Mavreen to her knees. Curiosity ousted all
other thought. She knew that Bessie, the cart horse, was
down in the turnip field with Farmer Sale, clip-clopping at
a slow steady pace.

A visitor to Owlett's Farm was a rare event. Excitedly,
Mavreen leaned out of the loft, craning her neck to see

round the side of the barn to the yard beyond. Directly beneath her, flies swarmed and buzzed around the pile of dung Dickon had newly cleared from Bessie's stable. It steamed in the noon heat.

Now she could hear voices. Dickon's soft and familiar Sussex dialect was clearly audible as he explained that his father was down in the turnip field but that his mother was certainly in the house, that he would run instantly to fetch either one his lordship desired to see. The second voice, deep, resonant, and cultured replied authoritatively, "Stay here and mind my horse, boy. And don't touch him. He can be uncommonly spiteful and dangerous with strangers."

Overcome with curiosity, Mavreen leaned even further forward, lost her balance and somersaulted through the air, landing eight feet below on top of a pile of manure.

Stunned but uninjured, Mavreen lay still, waiting for the buzzing in her head to subside. She recovered her senses fully when Dickon lifted her up from the pile of dirty straw and dusted her down with the sleeve of his rough smock.

"Whatever be you doing, Squirrel!" he remonstrated, his freckled face beneath its cap of curly red hair a comical mixture of concern and reproof.

He had given her the nickname years ago when she first began to follow him about the farm, asking interminable questions and storing the answers in her head the way a squirrel stored nuts.

"I fell out of the loft!" Mavreen replied simply. "I was trying to see the visitor, Dickon."

"Curiosity killed the cat!" Dickon broke in predictably.

"And satisfaction brought it back!" Mavreen retorted. "But Dickon, who has come visiting? Has he gone to see Mam? Why is he come here?"

The boy was well accustomed to Mavreen's habit of running one question into another. Usually he waited patiently for her to stop talking and then he would reply to the questions one by one. But now he was anxious about the big black horse he was supposed to be minding. With a last look at Mavreen to make certain she had not broken any bones, he took her hand and led her round the big haybarn. For the first time she saw the stallion hitched to the oak gatepost.

Mavreen stared at the great black beast, her eyes widened in wonder, her tumble quite forgotten. Not even in Alfriston had she ever seen such a magnificent creature. He was all of seventeen hands in height, every line of his body proclaiming he was a thoroughbred.

The little girl edged forward, pushing aside Dickon's restraining arm and slowly reached up with her hand, standing on tiptoe so that she could touch the horse's soft velvet muzzle.

"You're so purty!" she crooned.

The stallion's ears pricked forward at the strange voice, his eyes flickering nervously as he felt the gentle touch on his nose. His lips curled back, revealing huge yellow teeth.

Dickon held his breath—and his voice. He was terrified that the horse would bite Mavreen, or worse still, rear up and trample upon her.

But Mavreen had no such fear. Speaking soft endearments she continued to stroke the animal until he relaxed, though still alert, and had settled back into a waiting posture.

"I'm going to ride him!" she announced, turning a grubby, shining face to Dickon.

"No, you don't do no such thing!" Dickon forbade, but Mavreen was already climbing the fivebar gate, talking all the while to the stallion.

Once again the boy was afraid to move lest he frighten the animal out of its apparent passivity. Heart in mouth, he watched Mavreen hitch up her dirty, dung-spattered skirt and ease herself from the gate onto the stallion's back.

His ears flattened instantly. He began to prance, his hoofs clattering on the cobblestones, his eyes rolling as he pulled against the restraining reins. Mavreen clung to the saddle and laughed softly.

"Be still, you great silly. It's only me. Don't be afraid. I'm not going to hurt you. Hush now, don't be frightened!" The horse once again accepted her and settled back into a resting position.

They had quite forgotten the animal's owner who now

appeared walking down the path from the farmhouse toward them, Mistress Sale following a pace or two behind him and looking hot and flustered. It was too late to remove Mavreen from the stallion's back, Dickon realized. She had been seen already by Sir John Danesfield.

His face was suffused with anger. He was hot, tired, and disappointed by what had turned out to be a wasted journey. Now, to add fuel to his ill temper, he had come upon one of the farm brats astride his horse. Sir John's eyes darkened and he beat his riding crop against his boots as if he were already giving the farmer's lad the lesson he deserved for daring to mount his precious Raven.

His expression changed to one of astonishment as he came near enough to see that the lad was no lad at all but a maiden, an urchin sure enough, filthy from head to foot, but with dancing curls and merry eyes. She was laughing down at him, not one whit ashamed of her audacity.

"And who gave you permission, Missie, to stride my horse, may I ask?"

The haughty tone, the unsmiling face of their aristocratic visitor were enough to daunt poor Mistress Sale and her son, Dickon. But Mavreen, blithely unaware of any transgression, smiled back at her interrogator and patting the stallion's neck, said, "Why, *he* did. He doesn't mind at all, do you, my beauty!"

Sir John's expression changed once more from severity to surprise. The child's cultured voice was as unexpected in this farmyard as a nightingale in a rookery.

Enlightenment dawned. He turned to the farmer's wife and raised his thick bushy eyebrows.

"Is this the one, Mistress?" he asked bluntly.

Mutely, she nodded.

A grin not unlike the mischievous smile of the child herself, softened the hawklike features of the man. He looked almost handsome.

"So you've made friends with Raven, have you?" he addressed Mavreen. "He is a damned ill-tempered brute, you know! He once near trampled one of my grooms to a pulp for daring to put his toe in the stirrup. It's a wonder he hasn't sent you flying back into the dungheap you came from, I warrant!" he added, wrinkling his nose as he drew

near enough to Mavreen to sniff the odor of horse
manure.

Quick as always in Mavreen's defense, Dickon spoke up
bravely, "She don't ornery smell like that, sir. Her done
tumble out of the hayloft a-looking to see you."

To Dickon's relief, Sir John laughed.

"I'm relieved to hear it!" he said, his humor now fully
restored. He looked up at the child with a curiosity that
matched her own as she returned his stare.

"So you like horses?" he asked.

Mavreen nodded, her eyes wide and serious.

"One day, when I'm growed really big, I shall have a
horse like this all of my very own!"

Sir John grinned.

"Will you, be damned. A mount like Raven would cost
you a pretty penny. But no doubt you're a rich young lady."

Mavreen nodded solemnly, unaware of his teasing.

"I reckon he would be costly," she agreed. "And I'm
not rich, sir, but . . ." her smile quickly flashed again . . .
"I shall marry a rich man and he can buy a horse like
Raven for me. Perhaps I'll even marry the Prince of
Wales!"

"M'vreen!" hushed Mistress Sale in alarm. She was afraid
the fine gentleman might think such a statement near to
treason. But Sir John was laughing again.

"I wouldn't put it beyond you to marry whom you
please!" he said, bowing with mock gallantry. He had not
failed to notice, and he had an experienced eye for wom-
en, that the child might if scrubbed and dressed, be
very pretty indeed. Not that pretty was the right word for
her. She had that indefinable *je ne sais quoi* with which
some women are born but none can acquire. This little
girl had what was needed to captivate a man's heart.

Sir John had desperately wanted a son, not just as an
heir but as a companion on the occasions when he could
indulge in one or another of his favorite pursuits. Standing
now in the sunshine of the farmyard, he remembered the
letter in his coat pocket. Its contents had sent him riding
posthaste from London in the hope of finding the son he
so earnestly desired.

The letter, written over a year ago, had been waiting for him on his return from India. When he had gone there in the spring of 1787 he had expected to stay only a few months, but unfortunately, within a few months of his arrival in that vast, mysterious country, he contracted an unidentified fever which brought him near to death. His convalescence was long and slow. He had, therefore, been unfit to travel home before the late spring of 1788 and then to find the past had caught up with him.

Fortunately, the wax seal on the letter had not perished with time and seeing it was unbroken he had been greatly relieved to learn that his wife had not discovered his past misdemeanors.

The letter, dated 1787, was from a young woman he had all but forgotten, one Letitia Ashworth, former governess to his two daughters. Her handwriting, befitting a governess, was neat and perfectly legible.

. . . After leaving Wyfold House with an abruptness which must have astonished you and Lady Danesfield, I made my way home to Derby. I had hoped that my father would offer me sanctuary for I found myself to be in that most distressing of feminine conditions, and not wishing to be a burden or a scandal to you, sought the only refuge I could.

Alas my father turned me away and I travelled south once more, finding employment where I could, the details of which I will not now recount, since I have little strength left for holding my pen.

I was taken ill on the road to Lewes and would have died but for the kind intervention of Master and Mistress Sale, a farmer and his wife, who befriended me then and have continued so to do. My child was born prematurely and would, I believe, have died on birth but for the nursing and care of Mistress Sale. Thanks be to God and to her, we both survived.

I would not be writing to you now but for the fact that I have contracted an illness from which I shall not recover. It being likely that I shall have left this world by the time this letter is in your hands, I feel impelled to inform you that my child will shortly be

> *orphaned. Good people though the Sales be, they have no obligation or responsibility to one not of their own flesh and blood and it would greatly ease my troubled mind were I to know that you could offer some assistance, albeit at your discretion.*
>
> > *Your Obedient Servant,*
> > *Letitia Ashworth.*

His first reaction was one of dismay. Although he had suspected the reason for Letitia's sudden departure in the middle of the night, without notice either to his wife or to himself, not having received any request for financial assistance during the ensuing months, he had put any thought that he might have got Letitia with child far from his mind.

But following his dismay, he was struck with a sudden hope. There had been no mention in the letter of the child's sex. If, by good fortune, Letitia should have given birth to a boy, he might well decide to acknowledge his bastard son. Fired with an ever-growing impatience to find his son, Sir John waited only long enough for the doctor to pronounce his health sufficiently restored to enable him to ride, before setting off on horseback for Alfriston without delay.

His first glimpse of Owlett's Farm and young Dickon Sale somewhat dimmed his excitement. He had given no thought to the fact that his son, reared on a farm, might prove more akin to a yokel than a gentleman. Forgetting that the boy could be but eight years old, Sir John surveyed Dickon's broad freckled face beneath its untidy thatch of ginger hair and nearly turned his horse toward London without further ado. But he was not a man to refuse at the first hurdle and at Dickon's direction, he went to speak to the farmer's wife.

The ultimate disappointment came when the buxom Mistress Sale informed him that Letitia's child was, in fact, a girl. He was relieved to learn she was somewhere about the farm for he had no wish to see her. But nevertheless, he told the good wife that he was a distant relative of the dead woman, and left with her a substantial purse of gold sovereigns.

He eased his conscience with the thought that the child's

bastardy would doubtless go unnoticed in these primitive surroundings. Having known no better way of life, she would not fare too badly at the farm.

Now, however, he was face to face, not with the son he had wanted, not with a country bumpkin, nor yet with a thick-limbed country lass, but with a little porcelain figure of a maid, dung-bespattered it was true, but with the unmistakable delicate bone structure of an aristocrat, a delightful melodious voice that would be a credit in any London drawing room, and the intelligence, courage and determination that were so forceful a part of his own nature.

He lifted the little girl from the stallion's back, his nose wrinkling again in disgust at her odious smell. Standing beside him, she reached only to his thigh. She fingered the hem of his coat.

"It is a fine cloth," she said. "I like it."

So she has good taste, he thought.

"It should be. It cost me a pretty penny! Tell me, child, where did you learn your speech?"

Mavreen's face clouded with a half-forgotten sadness.

"My mother used to teach me. But then she died. And since then I ask Dickon when I need to know something."

For the first time, Mistress Sale found her tongue.

"Her mam learned her reading and writing and counting, too. And I dunnamany other fancy things she teached. She were a knowledgeable young woman, m'lord. M'vreen only disremembers such like embroidery which she don't care for nohow. Master Sale do reckon she'd make a fairish boy. She doesn't like woman's work like her mam did."

"M'vreen knows a tidy lot more'n other maids of her age," Dickon spoke, scarlet-faced. "She done learned all us children reading, and my Da too. He can read the Bible now, all by hisself."

It was rare for Dickon to utter so many words in public and he did so now only because his instinct told him that in some way, this stranger's approval was of importance to Mavreen.

Sir John surveyed the lad with some amusement. It was clear his small daughter already had a staunch knight errant.

"Go fetch your father, boy," he said to Dickon. "I would talk with him. Meanwhile," he added, turning to the farmer's wife, "may I suggest you put this young scarecrow in a tub of hot water and scrub her clean? Then, perhaps, I shall enjoy her company better." He glanced down at Mavreen and seeing the laughter in her eyes, he smiled at her. "Put on your very best gown," he told her. "If you look as pretty as I anticipate, I might take you into Alfriston to sup with me at the Star. Would that please you?"

Mavreen's small white teeth bit into her underlip and her eyes rounded in excitement.

"You mean I can ride with you, sir, on Raven?"

Now Sir John laughed aloud.

"It was the meal I intended as a treat!" he chided her. "Not a ride on Raven! Now be off with you, or you'll have neither."

Mistress Sale took the child's arm and tried to hasten her away but Mavreen hung back, a strange look on her face.

"Well, what is it? What now?" Sir John asked.

Mavreen tilted her head sideways and gave him a quick glance. She reminded him of a sparrow searching for crumbs.

"It's that word, sir. The one you spoke just now. Anipate? Please, sir, what does it mean?"

"I'll explain its meaning whilst we sup," he promised, now completely captivated. This extraordinary offspring was proving one continual surprise and delight to him. Mavreen might not be the son he had so ardently wanted but damn it, she was the next best thing.

He laughed softly to himself. Marry the Prince of Wales she would never do but it was not beyond the realms of possibility that in due course the child could become one of the prince's favored mistresses. A little influence at court might serve Sir John well and the young prince was very susceptible to pretty women.

Sir John caught himself up at this point. As so often happened, his imagination had run away with itself. The child was only eight years old. For the time being she would have to remain where she was. Before returning to

London he would make arrangements to have her educated. If he was ever to have her with him in London, she would need to know more than the rudiments of reading and writing. She must be taught history and geography. The social graces could come later. There must be, he thought, some local parson willing to tutor the child, glad, no doubt, of the extra money it would bring in.

There were compensations to living in London; he was closer to his mistress, Clarissa Manton, for one. He was able to spend as much time in her home as in his own. There were his many friends, too, not to mention his clubs and the gaming tables. His love for gambling rivalled his love of the outdoor sports. But now, in this pastoral setting, far away from the over-crowded city streets with their endless passage of coaches and people, the dirt, the smells, the poverty, he felt a reawakening of his love of a rural life. This was by no means an unattractive place for his small daughter to live. She had fresh air and freedom, all nature at her door. She could remain unspoiled by social pressures, develop as sweetly and naturally as had her poor mother in her Derbyshire parsonage.

He would have no regrets leaving the child here for a few more years. His only regret was that he would have to return to London without her.

Unaware of it, Sir John Danesfield had already become as securely ensnared by Mavreen's charm as had Dickon, who he'd humorously dubbed her Knight Errant.

CHAPTER TWO
1788

If Sir John had any lingering doubts as to his desire to adopt the small daughter he had so impulsively invited to dine with him, they were speedily dispelled before the day ended.

Mavreen looked quite enchanting when she presented

herself to him following the bath he had prescribed for her. She curtsied as she awaited his approval of her Sunday dress, a lavender-sprigged muslin. With her white stockings and buckled shoes, her newly washed and shining hair curled into ringlets and tied with a lavender ribbon, she looked as fresh as a garden daisy.

He returned her curtsy with a courtly bow which produced a ripple of laughter from her, crinkling her straight little nose, widening her rose-red mouth.

He drained the pint-sized pewter mug of home-brewed cider and handed it back to Farmer Sale, a huge ox-like man with the ginger hair inherited by his five offspring. The Sale children, unlike his self-possessed little daughter, had been over-awed by his presence in their humble kitchen, and remained mutely staring at him in uncomprehending surprise.

His evening in the company of Mavreen held no tedium. She prattled tirelessly, enlivening the journey into Alfriston as she sat behind him, her small arms reaching as far as possible around his waist. One minute she was pointing out landmarks, the next plying him with questions. How fast did Raven trot? Could he gallop faster than twelve miles an hour? Did he eat the same fodder as Bessie? How old was he? Did he live in London? Was he married? Did he have children and what were their names?

She quieted only to eat. Content with the repast, Sir John enjoyed watching his guest fill her small frame to the brim. He was gratified to see that while she ate a great deal, she did so daintily, with fine manners, no doubt instilled by her mother during her earlier years.

He was further amused by her occasional lapses into the Sussex dialect. At times it seemed her more genteel vocabulary failed to provide the exact meaning she desired to convey.

Occasionally Sir John was startled by flashes of resemblance to her dead mother. Letitia had not involved him in her disgrace and now guilt, such as he had not felt at the time, made him momentarily uneasy. But he was not a man to cry over past mistakes and he salved his conscience by vowing that he would do what he could for the child.

Careful questioning of Mavreen revealed that she had no knowledge of his relationship with Letitia. She believed her father to have been a naval officer who died at sea. One day, Sir John thought, he would reveal to her the truth of her parentage, but not until she was old enough to understand the ways of the world. He considered it was better to leave her in ignorance for the time and was quite satisfied with Letitia's choice of fictitious husband for herself.

Mavreen's love for her mother was intense. Despite the fact that Letitia had died more than a year ago, the child clung to all her edicts. It was Mama who desired her always to speak the way she'd taught her, Mavreen informed Sir John, her face composed and grave; Mama who begged her never to forget her manners: to study good books and to improve her writing; to keep herself neat and clean as befitted a young lady from what seemed to be her humble origin.

Mavreen laughed as Sir John raised his eyebrows at the remark. "I am as well aware as you, sir, that I was neither neat nor clean when you first saw me!" and sighed as she added, "And to my sorrow, I find keeping myself tidy the most tedious of all the promises I made Mama. I fear Mistress Sale is justified in her complaints that I am less neat even than Patty or Anna and they are a good deal younger than I."

Sir John was amused by her honesty. Seeing that he did not intend to remonstrate with her on her shortcomings, she added the further confidence that in her opinion the Almighty had made a grievous mistake in creating her female.

"Which comment I most heartily endorse!" he said, as much to himself as to her. "Now tell me why *you* should think such a thing."

His daughter tossed her head in a way that was purely feminine. Her brows drew together into a scowl.

"Girls cannot have adventures as boys may do," she said. "They may not become soldiers or sailors nor smugglers. They may not wear breeches and must ride sidesaddle, which . . ." she gave an even bigger sigh . . . "is vastly tedious. They must do women's work about the house and when they marry, they must obey their husbands whether or not they wish to carry out his commands. Moreover, they are forever with child or birthing children or suckling them." She paused, her eyes thoughtful. Finally, she said simply, "Girls are not free as boys are."

"We might as well cry for the moon as expect the Creator to rectify his mistake," he told her. "And who can say, m'dear, but that He has some great purpose in mind for the woman you will one day be."

The child's eyes widened with interest.

"You really think that might be so, sir?"

He had only intended consolation but now his imagination took hold.

"I see no reason why not. You will be pretty enough, I'll warrant. But the few really important ladies in history have had a deal more than looks to their credit. They had knowledge and the wisdom to use that knowledge wisely."

He knew that the little girl did not fully understand him but he was warming to his ideas.

"I shall arrange for you to have the same education that I would have provided for my son—had I been blessed with one," he added. "I will have you taught not merely the lessons of the schoolroom, but politics, mathematics—and yes, why not? Archery, gunnery, too, if you so desire. Then you will be able to converse with any gentleman you meet and know as much as he does. What say you, child?"

Mavreen did not understand the full implication of his words but she realized that he was opening a door for her into a world far beyond Owlett's Farm.

"You are the first fine gentleman I have conversed with, and if others are as fine as you I should enjoy it vastly."

Naturally he was pleased with her reply. The thought struck him that such instinctive desire to please presaged well for her future in society should the time come for her to make her debut.

"Tell me," he said. "What particular subject do you most wish to learn, Mavreen?"

She regarded him thoughtfully. "I think that most of all I long to be able to play a musical instrument. Upon occasions I have heard Rob, the blacksmith's son, playing the fiddle. Once he played especially for me so that I could dance."

"So you dance, do you?" Sir John commented. On a sudden impulse he clapped his hands for the landlord.

"Know you where to find Rob, the blacksmith's son, who plays the fiddle, my good man?"

The rubicund landlord nodded eagerly.

"Indeed, sir, yes! The smithy is not far from here. I can send my lad to fetch him at once if it please you."

"Then do so!"

Mavreen listened in silence. This was her first taste of the power that riches could wield. Sir John had only to command and his wishes were instantly obeyed. He was a magician who could wave a wand and acquire anything he desired. Her heart beat faster with excitement at the thought of Rob being summoned to play his fiddle so that she, Mavreen, could dance.

Within minutes the landlord's son returned with Rob. He was a gangling youth with tow-colored hair and hunched shoulders, an unattractive, awkward boy, but when he tucked his fiddle under his chin and drew his bow across the strings he played tunefully and with a natural ear and skill.

Anticipating the piece of silver that must surely come his way, he played with increased enthusiasm. Mavreen, showing no sign of self-consciousness, spread out her lavender-sprigged frock, kicked off her shoes and began to dance in harmony with the music. At times she was awkward but for the most part her movements were entrancing. Sir John watched her intently as she turned this way and that, her small face rapt and glowing.

Suddenly she tripped and fell full-length upon the floor. Rob dropped his fiddle and went to pick her up, but Sir John was there before him. He lifted the child into his arms. There were tears of disappointment trembling on her lashes—or so he thought.

"I should not have fallen!" she said in a small furious voice.

He laughed and setting her back upon her feet, patted her cheek.

"You did well, Sweeting. Life is full of unexpected tumbles and you will come to little harm if you learn to take them in good heart."

He threw Rob a coin and the boy departed, delighted to be paid so handsomely for so little work. While Mavreen was recovering her breath and her composure, he roared for the landlord who was hovering in the background and demanded to be notified at once if any learned man lived in Alfriston or nearby.

Happy to be able to oblige his illustrious guest, the landlord beamed and nodded his head vigorously.

"Happen we do have an unaccountable clever gentleman in these parts. A lawyer he were when he were younger. Master Glover is his name. A very sing'lar old gentleman, very sing'lar indeed."

Sir John interrupted his loquacious host to ask where the learned old gentleman lived.

"Twixt Simson and Alfriston, m'lord. 'Tis not but six miles from here."

" 'Tis even less from the farm," Mavreen said. "I have been there once with Dickon. 'Tis below the hill."

"Then bring me more cognac, landlord, so that we may drink to our good fortune!" Sir John said, well pleased. "And a mug of apple juice for the child."

He glanced out of the window and said regretfully, "Then we must bestir ourselves to get you back to the farm, m'dear. 'Twill soon be dark."

"Maybe we shall hear the nightingales!" Mavreen said, content with the world at large and with the anticipation of the long ride home on Raven's back. She hoped she could keep awake, for she was beginning to feel uncommonly sleepy. As on all farms, the Sales were out in the fields by four in the morning and abed soon after sundown. It had been a long and exciting day and now her eyelids were so heavy she could scarce keep them open.

Sir John looked at the little form, wilting like a thirsty flower against his side and was assailed by tenderness—an emotion new to him. Sportsman, man of action that he was, softness of any kind was abhorrent to him. He had avoided love, taking his pleasures with women, behaving dutifully to his wife and daughters, but in no way was his heart moved by them as it was now by his natural daughter.

He lifted her onto his lap and allowed her to nestle against his shoulder. Within seconds, she slept. Once again he felt tempted to take her back to London with him. But common sense prevailed, and when the landlord suggested the little girl be put to rest on a truckle bed in one of the guest chambers and taken home on the morrow, Sir John readily agreed. He, too, had had a long day ending with a very substantial meal and several glasses of his host's excellent brandy and he did not relish the thought of more riding and in the dark, too, when the countryside abounded with robbers and cutthroats.

Would the Sales worry if the child was not brought back that night? He thought it would be foolish of them to do so, since they knew she was in his charge. When the landlord's wife came to remove Mavreen to her bed, carrying her away against her ample bosom, the child remained soundly sleeping, unaware that a new life for her had begun.

There was but a mile between Selmeston and Alfriston, and the grange where Arthur Glover lived was halfway between them. From there it was a scarce three miles to Owlett's Farm. Every morning, no matter how hot or cold the weather, Mavreen walked, and in the late afternoon, she walked home again, tired but perfectly content. She had found what she most needed—someone who could and would answer all her questions.

Arthur Glover was a strange, scholarly old man approaching his seventies. He was stooped, with little more than a few wisps of grey hair springing from his egg-shaped head. His brown-spotted hands were gnarled, his eyes faded and watery. At first Mavreen believed him to be a wizard materialized from some story book. Now she knew better. He was, purely and simply, a wise man; a man who for sixty-odd years had soaked up knowledge and retained everything he learned in his remarkable memory.

Perhaps the first important lesson Mr. Glover taught her was the sobering fact that she could not, as she had expressed the wish, ever learn everything.

At first she thought that he was casting aspersions on her ability to absorb knowledge, but he quickly reassured her, with the wry comment that it was not that she had too few brains but that there was too much to learn. In one hundred lifetimes there was not time enough to know everything, he said.

"I will help you all I can," he smiled. "I will teach you Latin, Greek, Hebrew, rhetoric, logic, poetry, natural philosophy, and mathematics," he promised with hidden amusement as he watched the child's lips trying to form the words after him. "Also cosmography, astronomy, geography, theology, physics, navigation, calligraphy, drawing, heraldry, history, French, German, Spanish. Russian, too, if you so desire. Will that satisfy you?"

Her frown of concentration gave way to her quick smile.

"It will do for a start, sir!" she laughed.

The old gentleman was both charmed and delighted with his pupil. He had heard the curious background of her birth, parentage and subsequent life on the Sales farm, but Mr. Glover had no reason to suspect Mavreen of mental powers such as she showed. Young and uneducated though she was, within a few days he realized that she had a remarkable intellect and the makings of a true scholar. As her father and Mavreen herself before him, he regretted that such a mind was in the body of a female. Nevertheless, it was not long before he stopped thinking of her as a girl and began to feed her hungry mind as fast as she could absorb the knowledge he offered her.

Her ear for languages was remarkable. Suspecting that with this ability went an ear for music, he introduced her to his pianoforte. He played for her the music of Johann Sebastian Bach and Handel, Haydn, and the young Wolfgang Mozart. She was captivated. At her own request the art of playing the pianoforte was added to her lessons.

Current affairs were introduced to the timetable when Mavreen demanded to be told about Parliament and how laws were made; why the poor people in Paris were starving and was it true King George was ill? In the market square last week, she said, people had been talking of the terrible harvest in France this summer and were saying that because of it two men had been brutally torn to pieces by the people of Paris. What had they to do with it?

Patiently, Mr. Glover answered her questions. The king was indeed ill. The Parliament was debating whether he was mentally fit to rule or whether the Prince of Wales should rule in his place. He showed Mavreen a copy of the Morning Post which gave an account of the two murdered men, a M. Berthier de Sauvigny and his father-in-law, a M. Fouillon de Doue, and explained that they had been killed because people were blaming them for the shortage of food in Paris, M. Berthier being the official of the area.

Mavreen's quest for information was limitless and as the summer gave way to winter, the old man found himself regretting that with the shortening hours of daylight, her time with him was curtailed.

It had never occurred to Arthur Glover before Sir John approached him, that he might pass on to someone the treasure trove of knowledge he had so painstakingly accrued, else everything he knew would die with him. Now he suddenly discovered the great pleasure and reward to be had in watching a mind develop entirely under his direction. He felt a genuine excitement at the quality of the child's intellect, recognizing a replica of himself at the same age.

In all the years he had lived, Mr. Glover never thought of himself as a lonely man, but now he felt sad when it was time for Mavreen to reach for her cloak and bonnet and bid him goodnight at the end of the day. He would wake early in the morning, his first movement a look to the sky to reassure himself that the weather would not prevent the child's journey to him. Perhaps it was as well for Mavreen that the arrangement was for her to return to the farm each night. In the presence of her tutor, her mind was in a constant state of stimulation. Still not yet nine years of age, she needed the rest from her lessons, for while with him she demanded and soaked up all he imparted like rain falling on thirsty soil.

Not that her mind was at rest at the farm unless she slept, which she did deeply and soundly. Even on the Sabbath, after church, she was exercising her brain when she played what she chose to call her "game". This, quite simply, was a reversal of her rôle with her tutor. Encouraged by the farmer and his family, she would stand upon a chair in the kitchen to give her the necessary height of authority, and proceed to further their education as best she could by passing on a little of what she had been taught. With a sharpened goose quill and ink and paper presented by Mr. Glover, she formed the letters of the alphabet for them all to copy. She read them simple stories from books borrowed from the old gentleman's library. Soon, to her foster father's delight, she had him signing his name so that he need no longer put a mark against it in the merchants' ledgers when he went to market. Thanks to the money Sir John had given them the Sale family had greatly improved their circumstances. There was now a hired laborer, paid at the rate of nine shillings a week, new implements—a pitch prong, a speen spud, a dung drag, a turnip peck, a sneath and hog form, an iron turnwrist plow, four juts and a zinc skip. A list of these purchases, together with their cost, was neatly written down into a new ledger Mavreen kept for the farmer.

Dickon was the only member of the household who was not entirely content with the way the wind was blowing. As winter approached, he noticed more and more that Mavreen was fast growing away from him. There was no time now for their long hours of shared companionship. He no longer told her if he had discovered a fresh badger's earth or seen a sparrow hawk for she was all day away at Glover's grange. He missed her questioning little voice beside him for now she asked the old gentleman everything she wished to know.

He loved Mavreen and for her sake, he tried to be content in the knowledge she so greatly enjoyed her new life. But at times, lonely for her bright presence beside him, he wished that Sir John Danesfield had never come from London on that hot summer day. In no way did his family's bettered conditions recompense Dickon for the loss of his little companion. The only compensation he had was Mavreen's radiant face as she set off each morning for the grange, and her tired but satisfied air when she returned.

Mavreen, in fact, found pleasure not only in the hours spent with her tutor but in the journeys to and fro, her affinity with nature not lessened by her growing understanding of the arts and sciences. She was never lonely on her long walks, for even in winter there were birds to chatter to her. One owl in particular seemed to wait for her in the twilight on the last lap of her return journey to the farm, calling a soft *twit-twoo* as if he were bidding her goodnight.

Dickon had taught her how to hold a blade of thick grass pressed between her thumbs, small fingers arched into a hollow so that she could imitate the hoot of an owl almost to perfection.

"You be near as good as Bird Man," Dickon complimented her upon one occasion.

The Bird Man was well known in the area, although he was seldom seen by anyone. He lived in the beech woods, poaching rabbits for food and was said to be not quite right in the head, but Mavreen had often longed to meet him because he was known to be able to perfectly imitate the calls of all the birds.

When one late November afternoon she finally confronted the hermit, she saw the shadowy figure of a man appear from behind the big beech tree in which her owl lived; she knew no fear, only curiosity. He wore a roughspun habit like that of a monk, the fullness gathered at the waist by a plaited rope girdle in which was stuck a short bladed knife. As he sidled closer toward her, she noticed that beneath the long dirty tangle of hair, one eye was distorted by a squint; he regarded her intently with furtive interest. His face broke into a crooked grin. He opened his mouth as if to speak but from his lips came such a perfect imitation of an owl's call that Mavreen clapped her hands in delight.

"Why, you must be the Bird Man!" she cried. "I can imitate an owl but not nearly so well as you."

He did not speak but stood still, barring her way along the wooded track, staring at her. For a moment Mavreen wondered if he were deaf and dumb like the idiot boy in Alfriston but that seemed unlikely since he could make bird sounds.

"My name is Mavreen and I live at Owlett's Farm," she said. She took a step toward him so that now she was close enough to see the grimy wrinkled face, matted beard and broken dirty fingernails on the hands fumbling at his waist.

Without warning he lifted his habit. Mavreen stared at him in utter bewilderment. Why should this man wish to reveal his nakedness to her? He looked grotesque standing there and she felt a sudden quiver of fear and revulsion as the smile upon his face seemed to change into a menacing leer.

He took a step toward her and for the first time she sensed danger. Fear exploded into terror. She darted forward in an attempt to pass him but equally quickly his arm shot out and caught her. She twisted and squirmed like a trapped animal but his grip only tightened.

"Let me go! Let me go!" she shouted at him.

With extraordinary strength he lifted her off the ground with one hand and held her at arm's length in front of him. The indignity of her position evoked her anger and thereby lessened her fear. Mustering her last reserves of strength she kicked out violently and found herself hitting the ground with a thud as the Bird Man, his hands clutching his groin, doubled up in agony.

Dignity forgotten, Mavreen took to her heels and ran. She did not stop running until she reached the farm.

"Lawks a'mercy, what has befallen you?" Mistress Sale asked as Mavreen stood panting for breath in the kitchen doorway. For the first time in her life Mavreen hesitated to give a straightforward reply. Without understanding why, she felt degraded, humiliated, as if the Bird Man had defiled her. The mere memory of his hands clutching her body sickened her. She could think of no reason why he should want her to see his nakedness nor, indeed, why he should have rejected her friendly overtures in such an unaccountable manner. Perhaps, she thought more calmly, he was truly deranged and not to be judged as other, sane men, were.

Nevertheless, the experience was something she could not bring herself to talk about, so she invented a story that she had been frightened by a ghost and was comforted by Mistress Sale who hugged her to her ample bosom and shushed her, promising that in the future Dickon would come to meet her so that she need not walk through the woods alone again.

But as it happened Dickon's services were not needed. The winter of 1788 was long and severe. There were days when the snow piled in drifts against the farmhouse and barns and blinding white storms swept across the weald, making Mavreen's visits to the grange impossible, but her tutor, anticipating the weather, had given her books to carry home to cover such an eventuality. So her studies continued in the big farm kitchen, uninterrupted but for the cheerful singing of Mistress Sale as she baked and ironed and cooked; and the cries of the younger children playing on the kitchen floor. Mavreen sat at the long scrubbed wooden table near the range, which sent out welcome heat. Laboriously she read *A History of England,* or traced a map of the world, or made careful lists of words she did not understand so that when she journeyed across the fields to the grange, her kindly old tutor could explain their meaning.

Eagerly she scanned the sky each morning for signs of better weather. Unknown to her, Mr. Glover was doing the same. Not without some knowledge of meteorology, he was afraid the severity of the winter was unlikely to abate quickly. Frequently he found himself wondering anxiously whether Mavreen was studying the books he had lent her or if, away from his supervision, she had found other distractions.

Sir John Danesfield had told him in strictest confidence that the child was his natural daughter. The Danesfields, as Mr. Glover well knew, were of the nobility, their family history traceable to the days of William the Conqueror, but the old man knew nothing of the background of Mavreen's mother. When Sir John omitted to mention her, he had supposed her to have been some country wench of no consequence. But now Mr. Glover doubted it. Though Mavreen was as rosy-cheeked and sturdy as any farm lass, she had the delicate bone structure and fine skin, the slim ankles and small straight nose of innate good breeding. She did not physically resemble Sir John, but she had his determination.

The old man sighed. Sir John spoke of taking Mavreen to live in London when she was twelve or thirteen years old. By then he himself would be into his seventies. Doubtless he would be dead before Mavreen grew to womanhood, a thought which irritated rather than saddened him. He had the same insatiable curiosity as the child and would so much like to live long enough to see the grown woman Mavreen would become.

CHAPTER THREE
1789

The boy was out hunting in the Forest of Compiègne. It was his thirteenth birthday and he carried his birthday present in the crook of his arm: a double-barrelled flintlock sporting gun. It had been made especially for him in Bordeaux and he was very proud of it. It had silver mounts, a stock inlaid with silver wire and silver-plated locks. It had proved today to be deadly accurate. His servant carried three brace of woodcock, a rabbit and a wild duck to prove it.

Wonderful though the day's sport had been, his arm was aching now and he was ready to go home.

It was as well that the young vicomte, Gerard de Valle, was making his way back to the Château de Boulancourt, his servant Jules thought, as they walked slowly homeward through the forest. His mother, the vicomtesse, worried these days whenever her son was out of his sight. Had it not been the boy's birthday, doubtless she would have refused him permission to leave the château.

But Vicomtesse Marianne de Valle could trust him, Jules thought proudly. Even in these troubled times, she could have no doubt that Jules would gladly lay down his life for his young master.

The summer of 1789 was proving as hot as the winter had been cold. But for the shade of the great oak trees, the August afternoon would have been too sultry even for the keen young sportsman. The man eyed the boy thoughtfully. Thick wavy hair clung damply to the smooth forehead. His curls were the chestnut color of a horse and shone with health. Wide, dark-brown eyes fringed with extraordinary long lashes revealed the same Latin physiognomy as that of his Italian-born mother. But he had the fair skin and slightly arched nose of his father, the late vicomte de Valle, in whose service Jules had spent the fifty-eight years of his life.

Jules' devotion to the family sprang from the heart; he respected them deeply, honoring them not only for their high birth but for their integrity, their care for and consideration of their servants, even the most humble peasant. Jules knew that few aristocrats showed this same humanity toward those who served them. The queen herself, so gossip had it, cared nothing for the poor and the king was said to be weak and under her influence. He did nothing to prevent the nobles from levying such heavy taxes upon the peasants that sheer survival was fast becoming an impossibility.

Jules shifted the weight of the game he carried and sighed deeply. Fearful stories were rife. It was rumored that there were as many women as men, and children too, among those who stormed the Bastille last month. Even the very old men were said to have faced the muskets of the Swiss soldiers. Armed with little more than staves and paving stones, they had bravely made a human shield for those behind them.

Jules shuddered at what was happening in the capital. Who could tell what would be the outcome? Revolution! The word itself was terrifying. Compiègne, his beloved native town, was but eighty-four kilometers from Paris—not five hours' ride on a good horse. Two weeks ago the vicomtesse had despatched a messenger to the city to ascertain the safety of friends who lived there. But the man had not returned. Only the *bon Dieu* knew if he had been killed, imprisoned or, most unwelcome suspicion, decided to join the ranks of the revolutionaries.

Jules' grim reflections were momentarily diverted as the vicomte shouldered his gun and took aim at a squirrel. To Jules' surprise, the boy suddenly laughed and lowered the gun.

"I cannot kill an *écureuil!*" he said shamefacedly. "See, Jules, how charmingly it sits upon its haunches, head on one side as if it is asking me 'Why should you kill me? I am doing you no harm!' See also its feet? Like two little hands!"

His servant made no comment. The young vicomte had always shown a great affection for animals and birds. His two hunting dogs, spaniels bred in the Noailles kennels, seldom left his side; he had such a vast menagerie of pets that it required the services of one man just to keep them fed and clean. Yet the boy would hunt and kill wild animals for sport although making sure at all times that his prey did not suffer.

The vicomte was no weakling. The untimely death three years previously of his father, Antoine, the late vicomte de Valle, had forced the responsibilities of manhood early upon his son.

Having been accused of cheating at cards, the vicomte had been killed defending his honor. The terrible aspect of the affair was that all but his closest friend, the marquis de Guéridon, who were in the card room in Paris at the time of the alleged offense, were unwilling to testify upon oath that the vicomte de Valle was innocent.

No one in Compiègne or on the vicomte's estate who had known him believed him guilty. It was inconceivable that a man of proven integrity could stoop so low as to cheat at cards. People preferred to believe the story upheld by the marquis de Guéridon, that the Austrian Baron von Gottfried, a visiting foreigner, had successfully performed a sleight-of-hand with the deliberate intention of disgracing the vicomte. The marquis was unable to offer an explanation as to the motive for such dastardly behavior since the two men were unacquainted. He was unable to prove the baron was a *tricheur*. The rogue had disappeared from Paris within hours of the duel and no trace of him had been found.

This event had had a momentous effect upon the de Valle family. The beautiful chestnut hair of the vicomtesse, who was still only in her thirties, within a month had become streaked with grey. Her marriage to the vicomte had been one of love rather than convenience and her grief at his death was deep. For the boy's sake, she found the courage to make an effort although life had now little meaning for her. This son, Gerard, was the only child left to her, her other three children having died of smallpox.

The vicomte's death affected the boy deeply, too. He changed from a laughing, mischievous, carefree lad to a serious, thoughtful youth with but one inflexible purpose in life—to vindicate his father's honor. But for his mother's need of him and his tender age, he would long since have set off in search of the Baron von Gottfried. When he found him, he vowed he intended to torture a confession from him before he killed him.

To this end the boy spent much of his time in preparation. He spent hours every day perfecting his fencing and swordsmanship. He was already remarkably accomplished with a pistol. But this was not all. He studied German until he could speak it as fluently as a native. And he studied the art of card-playing. For hour upon hour he practiced the handling of the cards; and whenever he could prevail upon his mother, Jules, or one of the other servants, he played faro, this game which had brought about his father's disgrace.

Inevitably, life changed for the de Valles. They were dropped from visiting lists. Where once they had been the most regular of guests at *le Palais de Compiègne*, attending the receptions given by Marie Antoinette in the beautiful ballroom, now they were no longer invited. Gerard had never, as had all his ancestors, hunted with the royal party in the surrounding forest. It was many years since the banquet hall in the Château de Boulancourt had been graced by the presence of the kings and queens of France. It was never used now, although in winter huge peat fires were kept burning in the hearths. The huge kitchens were no longer fully extended with the preparation of magnificent feasts for illustrious guests. Only four of the liveried footmen in their maroon coats and gold buttons and the butler remained to serve the vicomtesse and her son. They dined alone or with the abbot or one or two of the few loyal friends who remained.

While her son and Jules were happily engaged in shooting in the forest, the vicomtesse de Valle was receiving the abbot from nearby Corneille in her private salon. She was a tall, slim, beautiful woman, her Italian origin made evident by her olive-gold complexion. Her hair, powdered and curled over her ears, fell to her neck, around which was a black velvet band holding a locket containing a miniature of her son Gerard at the age of three.

Her dress, a pale blue silk taffeta with hooped skirt, was cut low over her bosom. Her face was unsmiling as she sat opposite her visitor, listening intently to his counsel, anticipating the nature of the news he was bringing her; she had encouraged her young son's hunting expedition, not wishing him to be present when the abbot called.

She stood now at one of the tall windows opening onto the wide balcony, her eyes on the dark forest beyond the marble nymphs in the center of the fountain basin below. Her hand rested on one of the purple velvet curtains lined with silver cloth. She loved this room and spent more and more time in it since Antoine's death and the subsequent curtailment of her social life. Above the fireplace was a treasured portrait of her husband as a child in petticoats with long curls and two King Charles spaniels at his feet. On either side were two small sacred paintings of the Madonna and Child by Raphael and on the mantleshelf a jeweled chiming clock. The ceiling was painted with rosy cherubs, flowers, and white clouds. Beside the window was a huge bowl of white magnolias.

The news the abbot brought her was even worse than she had anticipated. Paris was a blood bath. The future of the king and queen was in doubt. Moreover, the safety of any of the French nobility was questionable, let alone their wealth and estates. Fouillon and Berthier had been brutally lynched on the twenty-second of July. There were now volunteers, armed and organized in Compiègne itself, set up to safeguard food supplies and to maintain law and order. The people no longer had faith that the king would or could do anything to improve the conditions. Bread and food prices had risen appallingly after the failed harvest. The people believed the aristocracy was responsible. Farmers were arming themselves against roving bands of vagrants to protect their growing crops.

It was not only possible but likely, the abbot told the vicomtesse, that the Château de Boulancourt would be attacked. Not only were the peasants hungry but in those châteaux in France that had already been attacked, the manorial rolls had been the prime target. The vicomtesse and her son were no longer safe, he urged her. They must emigrate as soon as possible. The vicomtesse had friends in England. She could go there at once with the young vicomte.

The vicomtesse, having thanked the abbot and bade him farewell, looked up at the portrait of her late husband, her large dark eyes requesting advice he could not render.

On the one hand, she could not believe that the people of Compiègne, who had known and loved Antoine de Valle since boyhood, could bring themselves to attack his wife and child. In his earlier years Gerard had roamed freely about the farms, was fed and spoiled by the farmers' wives. Gerard knew everyone of the peasant families by name and if word reached him that one was ill or another in need, he would often go in person with assistance.

Yet on the other hand, she had received many letters not only from her own family in Italy but from friends of Antoine's in England, exhorting her to close the Château de Boulancourt and make her way to some haven before harm befell them. The abbot had made it clear that there was no more time left to make up her mind.

The vicomtesse sighed deeply. Of one thing she was quite certain. She would never close or leave her home unless she were physically forced to do so. But Gerard— ah, there lay the reason for her indecision! She could not endure the thought of separating from him—all she had left that was a living part of the husband she loved even after death. But Gerard was an only son. If their name

was to endure, Gerard must survive at all costs, so that
when law and order were restored, as it must surely be in
time, the estate would be intact. In her heart, she knew
this was what Antoine would have wished.

She stood up, crossed the room to her rosewood bureau,
and withdrew a letter. She walked over to the window
with it in her hand and stared out with unseeing eyes
across the lawns and parkland stretching to the bank of
the river Oise. She was waiting for Gerard.

The young vicomte de Valle approached his mother
with glowing eyes.

"See, Maman!" he cried. "I am returned safe and sound
despite your fears for me. And Maman, Jules and I have
had the most magnificent day's sport."

"I am so pleased, Cheri!" she replied, smoothing his
damp hair with her cool hand. Her French, though mark-
edly accented by her Italian origins, was otherwise faultless; her voice was soft with the intensity of her love for
the boy. "You are pleased, then, with your new gun?"

Gerard was nearly as tall as his mother. Affectionately,
he put his arm around her shoulders, drawing her close to
him.

"It is quite perfect!" he said. "I have never shot so
well. Jules said Papa would have been proud to see me."

The smile left the vicomtesse's eyes. With the mention
of his father, she knew the moment had come to speak of
the unhappy decision she had reached.

"Sit down, Gerard." she said quietly. "I have something
to tell you. Something . . ." she added warningly ". . . that
I am afraid you may not wish to hear."

Gerard seated himself obediently beside her. Of late,
they had had many serious talks as his mother had tried
to outline for him the political events of his country. Patiently, she explained to him that France had repudiated
once and for all royal absolutions. The commons were
asking for equality with and not superiority to the aristocrats. But such sentiments, humanitarian though they were
and in keeping with the sentiments of Gerard's father,
were far from acceptable in French society. The vicomtesse cautioned her son to be guarded about confiding
such ideas.

Gerard had seen with his own eyes the pitiable state of some of the poor of Compiègne. Once a week, on his way to school with the monks at the abbey he took with him in the carriage a collection of food which would later be distributed to the starving. He had seen children huddled in doorways in the snow, dying of cold, and returned to the huge fires of oak and beechlogs in the château with a deeply troubled conscience.

On one occasion, the servants had brought before the vicomtesse two men who had been caught stealing from the kitchens. One, in tears, had pleaded that his wife and children were starving and the other had not eaten for three days. Gerard had felt a warm rush of love for his mother when, instead of punishing them, she had ordered that both be given a hot meal and money and the promise of work on the estate if they returned the next day.

He looked at his mother's face anxiously, uneasy that she seemed to be avoiding meeting his eyes. To give her courage to impart the bad news she was obviously reluctant to pass on to him, he said boldly, "Whatever danger we are in, Maman, you need have no fear. I shall protect you. I am nearly a grown man now. Have you forgotten today is my birthday and I am thirteen?"

Tears sprang to the vicomtesse's eyes. Her son's chivalry and the youthfulness of his boastfulness touched her heart.

To hide her emotions, she spoke quickly and harshly.

"The abbot was here to see me this afternoon, Gerard. He confirmed what I already knew—the people are attacking the châteaux. Our home is no longer a safe place for you to live in." She held up her hand as he made move to interrupt her. "Not even with all the household servants to assist us could we withstand the attack of a mob gone wild," she said. "As a woman, it is unlikely that I should be molested but you—you are my only son, my only child, Gerard." She was pleading now, begging for his understanding. "You are all I have left of your father. It is imperative that I send you to a place of safety."

She ignored the protest that had burst from his lips. Holding out the letter in her hand, she commanded him to read it.

"It is from an old friend of your father's—an English

nobleman by the name of Sir John Danesfield. I wrote to him some months ago asking him, if the situation in France were to deteriorate, would he be willing to have you to live with him and continue your education in England." She looked briefly at her son. "It is understood, of course, that Sir John would be reimbursed for the expense of your living and schooling. This letter, Gerard, is his reply. You will see that he has very graciously invited you to be his guest for as long as we desire."

"I will not go!" Gerard defied his mother for the first time in his life. By the way she had phrased her words, he knew already that she had no intention of escaping to England with him. "I will never leave you." Shrewdly, he added, "You know Papa would never countenance that I should abandon you in times of danger, Maman."

To his dismay, his mother showed no signs of weakening.

"It is for your father's sake as much as for mine that I am sending you to England!" she said firmly. "Never forget, Gerard, that you are the vicomte de Valle and the head of the family. Moreover, there is no one but you to vindicate your father's honor. I am depending on you, as soon as you are old enough, to clear the name of de Valle. You cannot, therefore, put your life at risk for any lesser cause."

So the vicomtesse effectively silenced the boy's protests and won his albeit reluctant consent.

"When must I leave?" he asked, his voice suddenly very young and close to tears.

"As soon as possible!" the vicomtesse said. "Tomorrow, if we can arrange it. Jules shall drive with you in the carriage to Boulogne where you can embark upon a ship for Dover. It would be safer, I think, if you travelled during the night. You should be in Amiens by morning. . . ."

Gerard had ceased to listen. That so perfect a day should conclude in so terrible a manner was almost more than he could bear. He would not permit himself to cry, but at this moment, he longed to bury his head in his mother's lap and give way to the despair he felt at the imminent parting from her.

As if guessing his emotion, the vicomtesse said, "Do not

look so shocked, *mon petit!* It will not be for long. Moreover, it will be good for you to learn English. Your father
spent much of his youth in that country and Sir John
was his very good friend." Seeing that the boy looked no
more cheerful, she added gently, "The English are a very
sporting race, Gerard. You will doubtless enjoy some excellent shooting and must take with you your new gun
for that purpose. I shall hope to have a good account
of all the pheasants and partridge you kill."

At last she had succeeded in diverting him. His voice
nearer to normal, he said, "I have heard that there is no
sport so interesting as the shooting of *le coq de bruyère
d'Écosse.* Perhaps Sir John Danesfield will take me there
on one occasion."

The vicomtesse smiled.

"In that case, you should learn the English name!" she
said. "I think the bird is called a 'grouse', but you must
ask if that is correct when you reach England. Your father
spoke good English. I, too, learned the language."

But Gerard had once more stopped listening.

"What will you do here alone, Maman?" he asked her.

"Oh, many things, Gerard. I shall have to see to the
estate affairs, won't I? And see that the château is kept
clean and tidy for your return. As to the dangers—well,
the abbey is but a kilometer from here—and there, as
you know, I should find sanctuary if I needed it. You
need have no fear for me."

"Come to England with me, Maman!" he pleaded.

But he knew even before he phrased the question, that
she would not leave their home.

CHAPTER FOUR
1790

Sir John Danesfield regarded his wife's petulance with
ill-concealed impatience. Druscilla, he thought, was always

able to find some fault to complain of and when there was none, she invented one.

He glanced at his watch and saw it was too early to call upon his mistress. Clarissa had warned him yesterday that she would be visiting her milliner this afternoon and unable to receive him before five o'clock.

Bored and impatient, he stared round his drawing room. Typically of the tall, narrow houses in Piccadilly, the room was large with high windows overlooking Green Park.

It could have been a beautiful room, yet despite the vast sums of money that he had spent on it, it always struck him as colorless and dreary. The carpet was charcoal grey and the paintwork a shade lighter. The walls were covered with religious paintings in black frames and although they were recognized masterpieces of Raphael and Velasquez, the faces of the suffering saints and martyrs were hardly subjects for pleasurable viewing. The room contained tall plants with dark green leaves and funereal arum lilies made of white wax; his wife had an antipathy to the pollen of flowers. The mahogany furniture was heavy and dark. Over the mantlepiece was an oil painting of their two daughters, whom even the most tolerant critic would not find attractive. In his view, Druscilla had created a replica of a convent parlor.

"You said we need only take Gerard to live with us for a month or two. It is now nearly a year since the boy came," she complained.

Sir John sighed deeply. He felt she was stupid about most things but more so than usual when it came to politics. He looked at her pale, thin face and wondered, as he so often did, how he had ever come to bed her. Theirs had been an arranged marriage, of course, not a love match. The Danesfields fortunes had taken one or two severe knocks in his father's day and he, the eldest son, had been required to marry wealth. Even at seventeen, Druscilla Wilson had been no beauty but her father, a Lancashire landowner, had made himself a small fortune from the manufacturing of cloth following the invention of the fly-shuttle. Wilson had been astute enough to introduce it into his mills in the 1730's, appreciating the advantages in the pace of weaving and the increased width of cloth it made possible.

The old devil was still making money, Sir John thought, not without admiration, and this time it was from the introduction of spinning jennies and the frame. Moreover, he was rapidly replacing his old mills with steam mills and if he wasn't already a millionaire, it would be long before he would be. Druscilla was his sole heir.

Sir John wondered now, not for the first time, how such an astute old man could have produced such an offspring. Yet, he told himself ruefully, he, himself, had done little better!

"M'dear," he said now, his voice as always polite, but with an edge to it borne of his reflections. "When I informed you Gerard would be staying with us a few months only, I was under the impression that he would be able to return to his mother in France as soon as the dangers there were over. Now, even if it were safe for him, a viscount, to return to that unhappy country, which it is not, you know very well that the Château de Boulancourt has been burned out, his lands confiscated and that there has been no word whatever from his mother, the vicomtesse de Valle. Gerard is but fourteen years old. How can I, a friend of his late father, refuse the continued hospitality of my home?"

Druscilla Danesfield put down her embroidery and looked at her husband with dismay. At forty-seven, he was an extremely handsome man, still immensely virile. It was this virility, attractive to other women, that most repelled her. She had spent all her girlhood in a convent school where men did not exist. Her mother died when she was born and her father, whose only interests lay in the development of his business affairs, had neither wish nor inclination to take part in his daughter's upbringing.

Druscilla, therefore, had remained at the convent when other girls returned to their homes for the holidays and eventually came to look upon it as her real home. Perfectly content with the secluded life of the cloisters, she had more or less decided that she would become a nun; then her father declared his intention of marrying her into the nobility. Sir John Danesfield, one of the most eligible young men in society, was the perfect husband for her, he told her. Such a match would raise the comparatively lowborn family of Wilson to the echelons of the aristocracy. Druscilla was given no option to refuse. Her professed vocation for a religious life was swept to one side as of no importance.

Druscilla preferred not to remember her wedding night, nor the occasions, few though they were, when her healthy young husband claimed his marital rights. He was not a brutal or unkind man and his treatment had by no means been inconsiderate. But she had found his attentions revolting, and a horrifying invasion of her privacy; the resulting pregnancies mercifully came to an end after the birth of her youngest daughter, Selina.

It was at this stage that Sir John took a mistress, the first of many. With a sigh of relief, Druscilla Danesfield was able to put an end to this side of her wifely obligations and concentrate upon the domestic duties she infinitely preferred. By tacit agreement, she and her husband saw as little of one another as was required by society and they led their separate lives in comparative harmony.

She and her daughters had made for themselves a quiet life of seclusion not unlike that of the convent of her own childhood.

Prudence and Selina were now of an age where their father expected them to find husbands. He had begun to insist that they "come out" into society and complained more and more often that they were old-fashioned in their attire and were not making the best of their not very prepossessing appearances.

Privately, Druscilla hoped that the girls would not marry but she did not dispute her husband's wishes. When she learned that a young Frenchman of noble birth was coming to stay with them, she wondered if perhaps the boy might turn out to be a possible husband for the fifteen-year-old Prudence. But Gerard de Valle had been a bitter disappointment to them all. Silent, morose, he remained for long hours in his big bedroom, studying, writing endless letters or, a habit Druscilla strongly disapproved of, playing cards.

The girls, at first taken with the young viscount's extreme good looks, soon lost interest in him when he showed no sign of becoming a companion. Although they spoke each other's languages, they had no common interests and apart from the necessity of social contact at meals, they parted company as soon as was polite.

Gerard went to Eton. During the Christmas holiday he was invited to the home of a school friend, the Honorable James Pettigrew, and stayed with him in Buckinghamshire. At Easter he went salmon fishing in Devonshire with Sir John. It was not until now, the commencement of the long summer break, that Gerard spent much time at Wyfold House in Piccadilly.

Sir John had given him a horse for his birthday, a thoroughbred mare Gerard named Colombe because her pure white color reminded him of the doves at his home. He rode every morning in Hyde Park. Druscilla could not say the boy was a nuisance but his presence in the house did irritate her. Although the boy was always scrupulously polite Druscilla felt that he compared her very unfavorably with his beautiful, adored, and tragic mother. Perhaps it was as well her nature did not allow any display of affection, for it was unlikely the boy would have returned it.

"If you are going out later, perhaps Gerard could go with you?" she suggested to her husband. This would at least remove the boy from his bedroom where he was engaged in his interminable writing of letters to France.

Sir John, on the way to see his mistress, was on the point of refusal when the thought struck him that there was no reason why the boy should not go with him to Richmond. Gerard was old enough at fourteen to learn a little of the ways of the adult world and moreover, he would have a sight better time at Clarissa's than in this mausoleum. They would almost certainly play cards later in the evening and Gerard was obsessional about card playing. Sir John knew, of course, about the disgrace the boy's father had suffered, but being a lifelong friend of Antoine de Valle, he steadfastly refused to accept his guilt, no matter how strong the evidence against him. He understood Gerard's desire to re-establish his honor although he could not envisage how the boy could hope to achieve this.

Sir John took a last look around his drawing room. He felt a renewed pang of impatience to be in Clarissa's house. He thought eagerly of the comfort and welcome that would be waiting for him there. His mistress' salon was a room he had grown to love. It was always full of flowers and the ceiling was painted gaily with roses to match those in the dainty little firescreen.

He approved Clarrie's taste, and liked everything about the little bijou residence, built at the turn of the century. The house was surrounded by trees and the garden, full of flowers, led down to the river.

Clarissa Manton was a plump, good-natured woman to whom he was married in spirit. Widowed in her twenties, the wife of a physician, she had been living in very limited circumstances when he'd first met her fifteen years ago. She had been trying, unsuccessfully, to keep her head above water earning a pittance as a seamstress. With her well-rounded figure, large laughing blue eyes and an innate sensuousness which had not, then, fully developed, it was not long before Sir John had seduced her to their mutual satisfaction. So successful was their physical liaison that within a few months, Sir John decided to purchase the small house in Richmond and install her there as his mistress.

Delighted to be free of her fear of penury, Clarissa had quickly accommodated herself to her less respectable mode of living. Sir John was an ardent lover, jolly and kind, and she soon fell in love with him. What had started as an affair of convenience became something else. Sir John had had his fill of brief experiences with ladies who took his fancy for an hour or two, but he had not hitherto had occasion to experience the companionship of a woman. Clarrie, as he told Gerard in the carriage on the way to Orchid House, was jolly company. He often invited his friends to the house and she would join in the card games, or play the harpsichord while they drank and smoked.

If the boy was surprised to hear of Sir John's liaison, his face revealed no sign of it. He merely nodded his under-

standing of the situation. He had observed at first hand
the total lack of genuine affection between Sir John and
his wife. He missed the company of his beautiful mother
beyond everything else. He longed for the warmth of her
embraces and her deep personal involvement in everything
he did and thought. Their separation was intolerable, yet
he knew he must bear with it for her sake. The fear that
she might have perished in the fire which ravaged their
château was constantly with him. He wrote daily to the
abbot, to Jules, to the Compiègne official, to the marquis
de Guéridon, to all who might be able to send him news of
his mother's whereabouts. He longed for the reply that
never came as much as he dreaded to read of her death.
News filtered through from France of the deaths or ruina-
tion of members of the nobility, sometimes directly from
the emigrés daily arriving in London. Occasionally he
would hear word of a friend of the family, but none had
seen nor heard of his mother.

Gerard knew that only last month the Assembly in
Paris had accepted a new Civil Constitution of the Clergy.
Church lands were being appropriated and monastic vows
prohibited. The king had accepted the Civil Constitution
and was seeking the sanction of the Pope. Gerard could
not even be sure of the fate of his mother's friend, the
old abbot, and he feared that the lack of replies to his
urgent letters might well indicate the old man's death.

Occasionally, with youth's resilience, Gerard forgot his
worries and managed to enjoy life to the full. His sojourn
with his school friend in Buckinghamshire had been highly
entertaining, not only on account of the excellent shooting
but for the amusing company of James Pettigrew's delightful sister. A year younger than James, Anne, with her almost white blonde hair and violet eyes, reminded Gerard
of one of the china figurines in his mother's salon. Neither
girl nor woman yet, she nevertheless flirted with Gerard
with instinctive coquetry but was child enough to announce to anyone who cared to listen that she would one
day marry the young vicomte and that his wishes in the
matter were irrelevant since she had decided for both of
them.

Gerard had fallen just a little bit in love with Anne,

dancing the minuet with her, skating on the frozen lake of the lovely Pettigrew house. It was Gerard's first experience of an English Christmas and he had joined in the festivities with an enthusiasm the Danesfields would have found difficult to associate with their morose young guest. He had eaten huge quantities of Christmas turkey, goose, game, and pigeon pies, mince pies, and plum pudding. He had drunk wine and cognac, smuggled, so he was told, across the English Channel. He had even kissed the pretty little Anne beneath the traditional bough of mistletoe, in front of everyone and accompanied by much clapping and laughter.

Gerard had learned that not all English people were cold-hearted and without any frivolity in their lives. He taught James and Anne some of the card games he knew; piquet, triomph, primero, and was himself taught by them to play the shortened game of whist. He was much in demand by the houseguests to perform card tricks and he enjoyed his popularity, the more so for being something of a loner at school. His inability to speak the language and the swamping homesickness of his first term there had made him something of an outcast although James's friendship was slowly altering this state of affairs. He wished desperately that he could invite James to the Château de Boulancourt as it had once been. He had no inclination to ask Sir John if he might invite James to the somber Wyfold House in London.

Gerard had mixed feelings about Sir John. He respected him as a former friend of his father's and was, quite naturally, grateful for his hospitality. He knew that the money his mother had sent with him must have been exhausted a year after his arrival, and he was greatly indebted to his host. Sometimes Sir John rode with him in Hyde Park and the time they had spent together in Devon had passed pleasantly enough, but they were never completely at ease in each other's company.

Well-meaning, Sir John declined to talk French politics, fearing the subject might distress his young charge. Similarly he kept off all reference to finance lest Gerard should be made uncomfortably aware of his penury. Since the topic of sport invariably led to discussions of the

French way of life, Sir John kept from mentioning this, too. Consequently he was frequently embarrassed by his own enforcement of silence upon subjects that held interest for Gerard. He took the easiest way out by avoiding the young vicomte's company whenever possible. Not understanding the reason, Gerard felt unwelcome.

Now, however, Sir John had found a subject that could have no possible bearing on the boy's past and might well prove enlightening for his future—women! Becoming more and more loquacious, he relayed his views of females to an interested and amused Gerard.

"I will ask Mistress Manton to invite some young people one evening to entertain you, my boy!" Sir John said as the carriage turned into a side street and pulled up outside Orchid House. "At your age, your father and I had long since left the age of innocence behind us. I'll warrant you've not so much as kissed a girl yet, eh m'boy?"

Seeing the color flare in Gerard's cheeks, Sir John let out a bellow of laughter.

"So you're your father's son after all!" he shouted, slapping Gerard jovially across the shoulders. "Mind you, m'boy, your father's peccadillos took place before he met your mother. After that, he lost all interest in other females. . . ."

He broke off, aware that he was on tricky ground once again. Hurriedly, he climbed out of the carriage, sending the coachman home and telling Gerard they would get a hackney carriage back to Piccadilly in their own good time.

Gerard waited with considerable interest for his introduction to Sir John's mistress. When Clarissa Manton appeared in the hallway to greet them, she surprised him. Somehow he had expected a ravishingly beautiful woman, a former actress, perhaps, with the looks and attire and mannerism of her kind. Instead, he saw a plump matronly woman, not yet forty but already showing signs of considerable maturity. Her black hair was strongly peppered with grey and the neck and face above her ample bosom were already lightly wrinkled. Her mouth, large and smiling, took attention from the first signs of a double chin. She was, Gerard thought, like one of the huge full blown roses in the rose arbor at the château; luxuriant, heavily perfumed, drooping ever so slightly in the sunshine of the summer, petals like soft velvet.

Sir John, in high good humor, bussed his mistress playfully and turned to introduce Gerard.

Clarissa had managed to squeeze her ample curves into a striped silk gown with a full skirt falling to the ground behind her.

It was not, Gerard thought to himself, what Maman would have worn in society but somehow it seemed to suit Clarissa very well. There was both warmth and friendliness in her smile as she bade him welcome.

Gerard had heard that the English were inclined to be reserved and austere but neither Sir John and still less his mistress, deserved such adjectives.

Clarissa approached Gerard, holding him for a moment at arm's length, and regarded him from twinkling forget-me-not blue eyes. The next minute she folded him against her buxom breast and said in a warm, soft voice, "How kind of you to come and visit me, Gerard. Sir John has often spoken of you and I am delighted to meet you!" and she kissed him roundly on each cheek.

The boy felt tears prick his eyelids. Not since he left his mother's embrace so long ago, had he known the comfort of a woman's lips. He was immediately enslaved; his affection for Clarissa was to grow and last her lifetime. He did not know it then, far less did she, that by her simple welcoming gesture, she had set a pattern that Gerard was to look for in every woman he met with: this spontaneous warmth and ability to express it simply from the heart.

Clarissa had four servants—cook, housemaid, maid, and manservant. The latter now served them an excellent repast of cold beef and jellied pork with delicious stuffing and apple sauce. The meal was eaten in the dining room next to the salon. French windows opened out to a little garden with a large magnolia tree. When they had finished eating Clarissa took him to see it.

Seeing his pleasure in the white flowers, she questioned him with the genuine interest she showed everyone who came within her orbit, and hearing of the gardenias at the Château de Boulancourt and that they were his mother's favorite flower, she at once picked a bud and placed it in Gerard's buttonhole. Drawing the boy down beside her on the little white wrought-iron garden seat, she invited him to tell her more about his home.

Sir John remained at the dining table, contentedly smoking his cigar and sipping brandy. He eased the starched muslin cravat at his throat; it was a very warm evening. He could see Clarissa and the boy and hear their voices raised in animated conversation. It was the first time, strangely enough, that he had ever seen Clarissa in the company of a young person. He had little idea of her latent maternal instincts and was both amused and interested. It was obvious she had a way with the boy and was opening a flood gate of confidences. It pleased him. Moreover, it opened thought for speculation. He had been thinking a great deal about his strange little daughter in Sussex, how in a year or so, he must bestir himself to do something about her. She could not remain forever buried in the meadows of the Sussex Weald. An alternative would be to bring her to live with Clarissa.

Not a week later, he received a lengthy letter from Mr. Arthur Glover. This yearly report upon little Mavreen was more of an eulogy than an assessment of her progress. His daughter had a phenomenal intellect. She was already conversant with three languages, could play the pianola and the harpsichord, had a passing understanding of history, politics and the sciences, and ate her way through books like a mouse through a barley sack. Mr. Glover took pleasure in enclosing with his own, a letter written and composed by Mavreen which he hoped would please Sir John. He wished he might also enclose a portrait of the child which, unfortunately, he did not possess, for Sir John might be interested to hear that she was "as charming to look at as she was intelligent to teach." The formal little letter from his daughter did, in fact, please Sir John very much.

My dear, kind Benefactor,
   It is hard for me to find words with which to thank you adequately for the great pleasure and gratification you have given me by the furtherance of my educa-

*tion. I am seeking to prove worthy of your generosity
and trust that you will approve kind Mr. Glover's
report upon my progress.*

*I think often upon the happy and eventful day when
I had the good fortune to make your acquaintance
and whenever I am in Alfriston, I call upon the landlord of the Star and his good wife remembering the
delightful evening I spent there in your company.*

*Master and Mistress Sale and all the children ask me
to convey their good wishes for your continued health
and prosperity. I might add at this point, kind sir,
that Owlett's Farm is prospering also, thanks to your
goodness of heart.*

*I pray that I shall have the good fortune to renew
your acquaintance in the near future and so be able
to express my thankfulness to you in the person of,*

> *Your humble servant,*
> *Mavreen Ashworth.*

Sir John wondered how much prompting she got from
the old scholar. Clarissa, to whom he had shown the letter,
believed the document to be archetypal, as Mr. Glover
had professed. At all events, it aroused in the recipient a
desire to travel to Sussex to renew his acquaintance with
his daughter and see for himself how she was developing.

He poured himself another brandy and reflected that his
life had taken an odd turn of late. In the past two years he
had acquired two protégés. The thought made him feel a
trifle old. His soldiering days were over, as were his financial worries; his ambitions moderated to the enjoyment
of his day-to-day life. At forty-seven, he had reached a
turning point—his adventuresome spirit had given way to
a desire for peace and quiet. He wished very much that
he could retire to the country with Clarissa and enjoy the
life of a country gentleman.

But first he must find husbands for his daughters since
it seemed highly unlikely they would succeed in attracting
suitors for themselves. He could settle upon them very
substantial sums of money; honey with which to attract
the impecunious bees the way he had himself been attracted to marriage with the wretched Druscilla. His
wife's family lineage was little above that of Clarrie and

had he been a wealthy man, he might have had Clarrie for a wife, he thought regretfully.

He sighed. Young Gerard was shortly going to find himself in the same position—impelled to marry money. As far as Sir John could ascertain these damned French revolutionists had helped themselves to a great many family fortunes and estates, and the prospect of them ever being reclaimed seemed doubtful unless the duc d'Artois, Louis's banished younger brother, and the prince de Condé succeeded in overthrowing the new régime. For two years now, the prince de Condé had been forming an army of émigrés and it was rumored that he had assembled sizeable forces at Worms and Colmar and was preparing for an invasion of France from the Rhine, the duc d'Artois having established his headquarters at Coblenz, but everyone realized that the French king was as ineffectual as he was indecisive and was not giving the émigrés his full support.

Gerard's future looked far from prosperous and Sir John thought it might not be a bad thing if he were to implant in the young vicomte's mind, the idea of a wealthy marriage in a year or two's time. Fortunately, the boy was very handsome. Sir John had noticed, even though it seemed the boy did not, the furtive glances of adoration on the faces of the young servant girls about his house. Gerard looked every bit an aristocrat, fine-boned but manly enough. He dressed well but was no dandy. As Clarrie was later to remark, the brooding, haunted look occasionally crossing his face was romantic and intriguing to a woman. Gerard de Valle should not, Sir John thought, find it any more difficult to attract women than he had in his youth.

His mind returned to his other protégée. Marriage for Mavreen would be considerably more of a problem. Through the circumstances of her birth, he could not launch her in society. The Prince of Wales might "marry" a commoner, if indeed he had done so, but Sir John thought it unlikely a young man of good family would be permitted to marry his poor natural daughter.

He wondered, suddenly, if his impulsive decision to adopt the child was, in the long run, going to prove a mistake. Perhaps it would have been kinder to leave her in the environment he had found her where no doubt eventually she would marry a farmer or miller and produce a clutch of children.

This did not dwell long in Sir John's thoughts. Two years ago, when he'd caught his first glimpse of Mavreen, filthy, unkempt, bedraggled, she had shone like a flower amongst the weeds. Once seen, once known, she was not to be forgotten and, by all accounts, she was proving worthy of his interest in her.

He made up his mind that when Mavreen was old enough, he would bring her to London to live with Clarissa. Clarrie would be greatly taken with the idea, for she had never had a child of her own, yet it now seemed she was the most maternal of women. Her childlessness was the only regret he knew Clarrie to have in their life together, but Clarrie was quite incapable of tutoring the child and Sir John himself had no wish to install a governess into his ménage at Richmond, so he determined to leave Mavreen where she was until she had reached the age of maturity.

It was growing dark. Outside in the garden, the air had cooled and the magnolia blossoms folded their petals against the approaching night. Clarissa, her arm about the boy's shoulders, had risen from the garden seat and the two were walking toward the house. Despite the fact that she was a large woman, she moved gracefully, her innocence part of the appeal she had for Sir John. It was not a false modesty. She was and always had been genuinely unaware how the movements of her breasts or the sway of her hips could arouse in him such strong passions, undiminished by time or familiarity.

Sir John emptied his brandy glass. He would, he decided, send Gerard home in Clarrie's phaeton, permitting himself an hour or two alone with his mistress. Tomorrow, he would make arrangements to journey to Sussex. He would take Gerard with him for the companionship. He might even take the coach so that Clarrie could go with them. She and Gerard could then meet his little daughter and voice their opinion of her.

CHAPTER FIVE

1790

Sir John decided to break the sixty-mile journey to Alfriston with an overnight stop at the George Inn in the village of Crawley. He liked the old Tudor house and had stayed there on numerous occasions as a halfway stop to Brighthelmstone. He, Clarrie and Gerard spent a pleasant evening there, dining well on fried oysters, calf's head and bacon and plum pudding.

They retired early to bed and rose at dawn the next day. After several stops for visiting, eating, and drinking, they set off in mid-afternoon for the home of Mr. Glover. A stable boy had been sent on horseback from the inn to forewarn the old gentleman of their coming and at the sound of their approaching carriage wheels both he and Mavreen came to the doorway to welcome their guests.

Mavreen was speechless with excitement. She had questioned her tutor a great deal about her generous patron, Sir John. She remembered him as the most handsome and kindly of men she had ever met—except, she added shyly to Mr. Glover, himself, her much loved tutor. She wished desperately that she could have had forewarning of this visit from Sir John so that she might have worn her Sunday best dress, but with the aid of Mr. Glover's good natured cook, her own simple muslin dress was washed, quickly dried in the hot sunshine, starched and ironed freshly in time for Sir John's reception.

Between the ages of eight and ten, Mavreen had not altered a great deal. The roundness of babyhood had given way to the more delicate lines of approaching womanhood, but the bright, questioning hazel green eyes were as alive as ever with eagerness and curiosity. Her hands and body were seldom still and her thick, honey-gold hair, no matter how long she spent combing it, lay in curls

63

that were always unruly about her rosy cheeks. She glowed with good health.

Her hand, holding tightly to Mr. Glover's, trembled with excitement as Sir John stepped out of the carriage and handed down the visitor Mavreen assumed to be his wife. She quickly dropped into a curtsy and therefore failed to see Gerard as he in turn alighted from the carriage. His foot missed the step and he toppled forward and lay sprawled on the ground before them.

He stood before her, his dignity in shreds but with such a proud, furious look upon his face that Mavreen forgot her manners and broke into a peal of laughter. Nevertheless, it was she who stepped forward and gently dusted his green cutaway coat, saying kindly, "I trust you have not hurt yourself, sir?"

Gerard, breathing deeply, straightened himself to his full height, made a bow, and said in his accented English, "Not in the least, mademoiselle, I thank you. The Vicomte Gerard de Valle at your service!"

The formality of his reply silenced her as effectively as the enigmatic look in his large, black-brown eyes. Never in her life had Mavreen seen so beautiful a young man. But she had no time to stare at him, for Sir John lifted her up in his arms and holding her high above his head, teasingly inquired if she had fallen in any dung heaps of late. He kissed her soundly on both cheeks, set her back upon the ground and introduced her to his "very dear friend" Mistress Manton. Mavreen was once more warmly embraced and, all the introductions now made, Mr. Glover conducted the party into his house. China tea was served in the library together with slices of cherry and ginger cake. There had been no time to prepare victuals of a daintier kind for the London visitors.

Mavreen, sitting upright on the sofa, found herself face to face with the young vicomte. She was sorry that she had laughed at his earlier misfortune but thought him uncommonly lacking in humor that he could not laugh at himself. She wondered if this was normal behavior for foreigners. She found his stony-eyed, tight-lipped silence a challenge. Mischievously, she smiled at him, a smile that would most certainly have caused Dickon to recover *his* humor. But the young man remained haughtily unresponsive. Provoked, Mavreen was determined to break his resistance.

"You be unaccountable quiet, sir!" she said in broad Sussex dialect. "Don't 'e speak no English surelye?"

Startled out of his self-imposed withdrawal, Gerard lapsed into French as he replied with a puzzled frown, *"Pardon, mademoiselle?"*

Ignoring the question mark in his voice, Mavreen smiled prettily and excused him, *"Pas de quoi, monsieur!"*

The conversational tables had been neatly turned on him and Gerard, against every intention, found himself smiling at her quick-wittedness.

Despite the simplicity of her muslin dress, flat black slippers and cotton stockings, she looked charming and strangely, the color of her hair made him think of *le miel* which came from the hives of the bees at home. Sir John's protégée is not only pretty but spirited, too, he thought. She had in no way been intimidated by his uncivil behavior toward her.

Curious to learn more about her, he engaged her in conversation and was charmed as much by her total lack of artifice as by the boundless happy enthusiasm that emanated from her as she described to him her simple everyday life. He was further impressed by her knowledge. Though four years older than Mavreen, he found her better informed than he on some subjects.

While the older people discussed the subject of Prime Minister Pitt's failure to appreciate the seriousness of the revolution in France, Gerard followed Mavreen into the garden where they could continue their more personal discourse undisturbed. Lying in the long grass in the shade of a giant-copper beech tree, he propped himself up on one elbow beside her, while Mavreen told him about her life at Owlett's Farm and of the kind farmer and his wife who had cared for her since her mother's death.

He found himself not a little curious about the fellow, Dickon, to whom she referred with obvious affection. Dickon, so it seemed, was her great companion. With Dickon she enjoyed all the pursuits more commonly indulged in by boys. Dickon, she informed Gerard, was a veritable encyclopedia of knowledge about wild life, the district, and, she confided in a whisper, even knew the smugglers' routes and many of their caches, too.

Gerard was fascinated. By the sound of it, nearly every living soul in Sussex was in some way involved in outwitting the excise men. Mavreen explained that along all the land routes employed by the smugglers, there were cottages and farm houses where tubs might be hidden. In some houses, there were secret recesses and vast cellars where a ship's cargo could be safely concealed and stored until it could be taken to London.

"But if the law is against smuggling, why do so many people disobey it?" Gerard inquired, puzzled.

Mavreen laughed.

"Because the law is stupid. No one believes the king is justified in taxing good liquor. So in the name of justice, we turn a blind eye to the law and to the smugglers, too, if we should glimpse them on a dark night!"

"And is anything other than liquor smuggled into London?" Gerard asked.

Mavreen returned his gaze with a shrug.

"Dickon told me that sometimes your countrymen use the French smugglers' boats to escape from their enemies in the revolution," she said. "Only last month a fishing boat landed at Cuckmere Haven with some French aristocrats on board. They had been fired upon by one of His Majesty's revenue cutters and one of the noblemen was injured."

She saw the look of excitement cross Gerard's face. Innately curious, as always, she pressed him to tell her his thoughts.

He had just formulated an idea that might allow him to realize one of his vainest hopes. He hesitated to speak of it but knowing that he might need the girl's assistance if his brilliant new scheme were to prove possible, he decided to confide in her. It was her mention of emigrés that had put his idea in mind.

As briefly as he could, he related his own circumstances to her; the situation in France and his parting with his mother; his arrival in England to live with the Danesfield family; the news of the appropriation of the de Valle estate; the subsequent burning of the Château de Boulancourt, and his desperate fears for his mother's safety.

"I have thought of returning to France many times," he said, his dark eyes burning with the intensity of his emotions. "Sir John will not hear of it. He promised my mother he would be responsible for my safety and I understand his obligation to honor his word. But the circumstances have changed, Mademoiselle Mavreen, since he made that promise. *You* must see, even if he cannot, that I have to go back to France. Not even for my father's sake can I continue to remain in England, protecting my own life when my mother may be in mortal danger. Beside which," he added, "I know that Artois and Condé will soon launch the emigré armies into a counter-revolutionary battle. Indeed, they may already have done so, and I would like to fight for my birthright and for my king!"

Mavreen drew a deep breath. Her sympathies and sense of adventure were aroused, but her intelligence forced logic to keep her imagination in check, and she said doubtfully, "But are you old enough, yet, to fight in a war?"

Gerard looked back at her with scornful impatience.

"I am fourteen!" he told her, as if this answered her question completely.

"But what about the completion of your education?" Mavreen persisted.

"Pah! And fiddlesticks to that, Mademoiselle Mavreen!" Gerard retorted. "What is book-learning compared with the imprisonment or perhaps even the life of my mother!"

Mavreen sighed. She understood the young viscount's emotions but she thought, too, of his mother who, by sending him to England, obviously desired his safety above her own. This too, Mavreen understood. Gerard was an only son and no doubt the Vicomtesse de Valle loved him very dearly.

"Will you help me, mademoiselle?"

She turned her head to look at him as he appealed to her again, "Please, mademoiselle! *Aidez-moi!*"

She felt herself weaken. Suddenly, in that sunlit garden, with the bees buzzing around the lavender bushes, the

grasshoppers chattering and the soft swish of the beech
leaves above their heads, nothing seemed more important
than giving the beautiful young French boy his heart's
desire.

"What exactly is it you wish me to do?" she asked
quietly.

He grasped her hand, his eyes now full of warmth and
friendliness.

"I want you to ask this farm boy, Dickon, to show me
the way to a smuggler's hideout. I have a little money. I
could buy a passage on one of the fishing boats to France.
Don't you see, mademoiselle, I could be smuggled *in* instead of *out* of my country."

She grasped the plausibility of the scheme but she was
more far-seeing than her companion.

"How would you manage to survive once you reached
France?" she inquired. "Have you enough money, French
money, to make your way to Compiègne? You would
need a horse, food. . . ."

"I will dress myself as a French peasant. If I can land at
Boulogne, I shall not be much over eighty kilometers from
my home. There are many people who will help me, priests,
monks, for example."

Such a plan had been formulating in his mind for many
months but he had never, until half an hour ago, seen a
way to surmount the first and most important problem of
how to get back into France. Mavreen had supplied the
perfect answer.

His mind sobered suddenly. Sir John, his appointed
guardian, would quite rightly be angry with Gerard for
disobeying his command. He would be angry too, with
anyone who assisted in his departure. This young English
girl, whom he had involved in his affairs might reap very
serious consequences if she were discovered to have aided
and abetted him. He must at all costs protect her from
such a possibility.

"Was the farm boy to be trusted?"

"I'd trust Dickon with my life!" Mavreen said with
conviction so solid Gerard at once accepted the veracity
of her statement. "Dickon would do anything in the world

for me!" Mavreen went on, not boasting but stating a fact which Gerard found impressive. "If I ask Dickon to assist you to please *me,* he will do so!"

"And *will* you ask?" Gerard inquired softly, persuasively.

"If you say 'please'!" Mavreen said, smiling, the seriousness gone from her voice, as she teased him. "You may say it in French if you prefer—*S'il vous plâit, Mademoiselle Mavreen!*"

He knew she was mocking him, but now he laughed with her. In like tone, he replied, "Do you desire me to kneel at your feet in supplication, mademoiselle?"

Mavreen stood up, turning her head to one side as she considered the matter with matching gravity. Her eyes twinkled with suppressed laughter.

"Since you started our acquaintance falling at my feet," she told him, "I see no reason why you should not return there. It is not, after all, a daily occurrence for me to have French aristocrats falling over themselves to impress me!"

So saying, she ran off like a small hare toward the grove at the end of the rose garden. He jumped to his feet and pursued her across the lawn. Suddenly she disappeared from his view. He stood in the cool shade of the grove, listening for the rustle of her dress or the sound of her footfall. He was reminded suddenly of his hunting days with Jules in the Compiègne forests. At first, he could hear only his own quick breathing. Then, from above his head, he heard Mavreen's laughter.

Astonished to find her in so unladylike a hiding place, he stared up into the branches of the great oak tree, not quite believing he would see her there. But there she was, perched among the oak apples and acorns. He was once more transported to the forest in France, remembering with an aching heart the day of his thirteenth birthday when he had surprised Jules by not shooting the little grey squirrel.

"What is wrong, Monsieur Gerard?" she called down to him. "Why do you stare at me so strangely?"

Gerard sighed, shivering despite the heat of the day.

"It is nothing. I was thinking of a little *écureuil*."

"A squirrel!" Mavreen said happily. She came down from the tree as effortlessly as she had ascended it, landing near his feet.

"That is Dickon's special name for me!" she told him confidentially. "I am not quite sure if I approve of it. Some people say that squirrels are tree rats. But Dickon says I am like a squirrel because I store things in my mind."

The young vicomte looked at his small companion's face, streaked now across one cheek with lichen, and suddenly he was smiling again.

"I think you are like a squirrel, too. I hope you will store a happy memory of me, *petit écureuil?*"

Unaccountably, Mavreen blushed and for a moment the young man saw her not as a child but as the woman she would one day be.

"I will not forget *you!*" he said softly. "One day, when my affairs in France are settled, I will come back and visit you if you would like me to."

Mavreen was all child again, laughing merrily as she reminded him that he might never get to France, let alone return to visit her since he had not said *"please"*.

Her demands met, they returned to the house to find Sir John also in excellent spirits.

Glover had made use of Mavreen's absence to give her father a glowing account of her abilities. Clarissa, too, was quite charmed with the child's appearance and happy nature and Glover beamed proudly as he listened to the good lady's compliments. Like all men, he was very much at ease in Clarissa's company and privately found himself congratulating Sir John in choosing for himself such an agreeable mistress. Any moral scruples he may have had before meeting Mistress Manton were swept aside.

He fell in willingly with Sir John's suggestion for a dinner party at the Star in Alfriston. Not usually a gregarious man, Mr. Glover was nevertheless not yet too old to enjoy good company.

He was anxious, too, to show off his pupil. Such behavior played no part in her daily life at the Owlett's; luncheons between lessons at the grange were always conducted on a formal basis and Mavreen corrected for any lapse in protocol.

This evening, watching her at the dinner table, he had every reason to be satisfied with her. She forgot nothing he had taught her despite being busily engaged in conversation with the young vicomte on her right-hand side, or Sir John on her left. Glover could see that Sir John was well satisfied with the child, too, and his contentment was lessened only when Sir John made mention of removing Mavreen to London when she was thirteen years old. It meant he would have only a few years to expand the child's rapidly developing brain; he feared that once in London, her academic education might be put aside for the frivolous pursuits of a young girl of her age.

He was also worried about her position in society. Pleasant as Mistress Manton might be, morally she had placed herself outside society and the young Mavreen would be in serious moral danger. Sir John seemed not to care about this point. No thought had been given to this question nor to the way the girl might react when she discovered the limitations the circumstances of her birth imposed upon her. Her marriage prospects, if any, were very limited.

Clarissa, playing the part of hostess for Sir John, was handsomely clad in a cream and green-striped gown, the jacket laced across the bosom and worn with a little white fichu. On her dark curled head she wore a saucy black hat adorned with a yellow cockade. She kept them all much amused with her latest toy—a yoyo, which each tried in turn to manipulate but none with Clarissa's skill.

The hours slipped past. Sir John had made arrangements for himself, Gerard and Clarissa to stay the night at the inn, but the question of Mavreen's return to the farm and Mr. Glover's to the grange was not yet resolved. Gerard volunteered to escort them home in the carriage.

The journey to the grange was accomplished without mishap and Gerard and Mavreen set off in the carriage. Gerard, dropping the more formal tones he employed when addressing Mr. Glover, turned to Mavreen and said eagerly, "I trust your friend, Dickon, will not yet be abed? I am hoping, as no doubt you have guessed, to speak to him tonight. This journey is a heaven-sent opportunity I do not wish to miss for the furtherance of my plans."

Mavreen leaned back against the soft satin upholstery of the coach, enjoying to the full her first ride in such luxury. She thought the coachman looked like a highwayman— not that she had ever seen one, but as she imagined one to look. She, too, hoped that Dickon would not be abed for she wanted him to see her arrive home in such style.

Since it was past nine o'clock when the carriage drew into the yard, Mavreen was surprised to see a light glimmering from the kitchen window.

She lifted the heavy latch of the door to see Dickon lying half asleep across the kitchen table. Rubbing his eyes, he looked up, staring at them sleepily.

"We thought you'd be abed, Dickon!" Mavreen said, drawing Gerard into the room. Dickon stood up, looking from Mavreen to the richly-clad young gentleman by her side.

"Not afore I knowed you was safe and sound!" he said, eyeing uneasily the elegant companion following Mavreen into the kitchen.

The big wooden table was scrubbed white. A stub of candle spluttered in a brass candleholder, casting weird shadows on the white-washed walls. Two farm cats lay in front of the range, where a huge iron stockpot simmered. A ladle and other kitchen implements hung on the oak beam above. A keg of ale stood on the wooden sideboard and a delicious smell of proving bread came from the oven in a wall beside the range.

Mavreen walked round the table and took Dickon's big square hand, holding it simply and affectionately to her cheek.

"Stop your worritin'!" she said softly.

Dickon knew well that Mavreen's use of his own form of country speech was her way of teasing him. As a rule, he did not object and sometimes even mimicked her king's English, which always made her laugh, but tonight, he was silenced by the presence of a third party in the form of the young gentleman whose dress and bearing revealed his aristocratic background.

Mr. Glover had thoughtfully dispatched a lad from the grange earlier to advise them at Owlett's Farm that Mavreen would not be home for supper since she was to dine in Alfriston with himself and Sir John Danesfield. Nonetheless, Dickon had fretted. Though he was tired after the long day in the fields, he had been unable to take to his bed when the rest of the household retired. Ever since Mavreen was born, and Dickon had heard her first cry, he had not slept one night since without first assuring himself she was safely tucked up in her big feather bed beside his two sisters. And this night he never slept at all, wondering what had become of her after she failed to return from her journey to Alfriston with Sir John Danesfield.

"Dickon!" Mavreen said, tugging at his elbow. "I want to introduce you to the vicomte de Valle. Gerard has taken refuge in England from the revolution in his country and Sir John Danesfield is his guardian."

Gerard made his customary bow. Dickon, blushing, touched the fringe of red hair that hung over his forehead.

"Dickon, will you help him? It is very important."

Mavreen's voice took on a pleading note Dickon recognised.

"Mayhap! What be you wanting of me, M'vreen?" he asked quietly, his eyes uneasy.

Gerard stepped forward. It disquieted him to see Mavreen begging favors from this farm lad on his behalf. Somewhat uneasily he eyed the boy in his faded jerkin and short brown breeches patched at both knees. Yet as Dickon's eyes looked directly into his, he was aware of a certain dignity and was impressed. With growing confidence he said quietly, "I wish to return to France—secretly! Mademoiselle Mavreen advises me that you know where I might make contact with some smugglers. It is very important I return to my country. My mother's life may be at stake."

Dickon nodded, his face expressionless as if Gerard's request were commonplace. He looked down into Mavreen's eyes, and then back at the young Frenchman.

"Mayhap I can show you where the smugglers be. But I don't know as ever they could take ye to France."

Gerard's face fell but Mavreen tugged once more at Dickon's arm, saying, "The fishing boats might take him over the Channel, Dickon. You know, the boats that our boats go to. . . ."

"Hush!" Dickon broke in quickly. The least said about such things the better. He wished he could flatly refuse to assist. The foreigner might accept such a refusal but not Mavreen. She could be as stubborn as a little jackass when her mind was set on something. He knew he would help the French lad—to please Mavreen. But he did not want her involved in the matter.

"Tis purty nigh morning!" he told her. "You should be abed surelye."

Mavreen was on the point of argument when, tired as she was, her quick mind grasped Dickon's reasoning. Her face relaxed into a smile and she stood on tiptoe and planted a kiss on his cheek.

"Thank you, kind Dickon!" she said. "I knew I could count on you." And bobbing a curtsy to Gerard, she lit a candle for herself and disappeared up the narrow stairway, leaving the two boys alone in the kitchen to hatch their plots.

"Taint no use promising nothing afore harvest be done!" Dickon said.

Gerard nodded. He sensed the other lad's suspicion of him and tried to overcome the gulf between them.

"I understand. I was brought up myself amongst farms. In any event, I must have a few weeks to make my own preparations."

"Say three weeks hence?" Dickon suggested. "You be at Cross in Alfriston on Market Day at sunset." He looked at Gerard's cutaway coat, his linen breeches, white frilled shirt, colored waistcoat and top boots and for the first time his face relaxed. "I'd best be lending ye the loanst of some of my clothes!" he said wryly.

"It's kind of you, Dickon, but not necessary. I will arrive at our meeting place more suitably attired, I assure you. We will travel in darkness and t'would be best therefore if I wear dark clothing."

Both lads had seated themselves at the table and were

leaning forward upon their elbows, facing one another as they talked in conspiratorial whispers.

"There is the matter of my mare, Colombe!" Gerard told Dickon. "If it is possible, I would like to ride her down from London. She could prove a useful means of reaching the coast, I don't doubt. But I am deeply attached to her and would not wish her to fall into bad hands after I am gone. If I were to give you money to care for her, do you think. . . ."

"'Tis not necessary for you to pay me!" Dickon protested. "There be no lack of good fodder on a farm. The mare would be handy, too, for M'vreen to ride to and fro the grange. She be a natural born rider," he added, "lest you be thinking your mount too spirited for her."

Gerard nodded, well pleased with the way plans were shaping, but there remained one worry.

"I fear circumstances force me to deceive Sir John in this adventure," he said. "You see, Dickon, I cannot confess my intentions to him lest he come to France in search of me. I am sorry that you and Mademoiselle Mavreen must lie as to my whereabouts should you be asked. Do you think Sir John might discover my mare Colombe is with you? I will not risk leaving her if it could mean your incurring his wrath."

"I dunno as that be likely to happen," Dickon replied after a moment's thought. "Sir John don't have no occasion to come to Owlett's Farm. And if he did—" Dickon gave his slow, wide grin, "then Mavreen and me could hide your mare so he won't find her nohow. Sussex folk be good at hiding things—not only smuggler's bounty."

The matter of the horse's future settled, Gerard pressed Dickon to tell him more about the smugglers, but the English lad turned mute. Although he knew one or two of the local smugglers, not even to Mavreen would he reveal their names. Penalties were very severe.

Moreover, there were one or two occasions in the past year when Dickon himself had helped a cargo on its way to London, for which he had received payment of half a guinea. Not even Mavreen was aware of his activities and if his father and mother suspected, they knew better than to ask any questions. Dickon smiled to himself, remembering a Sunday not long past Easter, when the parson had feigned a sickness lasting all day, in order to keep his parishioners out of the church, to hide a cargo stashed there Saturday night. The revenue men had all but caught the culprits, forcing them to use the church for sanctuary. They'd not been caught and parson had been left a nice thank you for his pains.

Apart from the fact that most able-bodied young men in and around Alfriston were likewise engaged, Dickon's involvement with the smugglers meant something else to him. In a way he could not have explained, the danger compensated for the loss of Mavreen's companionship, gave him the feeling that his life, as well as hers, had opened up. Since her tutoring with Mr. Glover began, he realized Mavreen would never settle down again to the quiet backwater of farm life. He determined therefore, that he would not follow in his father's footsteps, as was expected of him as a matter of course. Deep though his love was for the farm house, the land, the beasts, his need to go into a wider world was stronger than his family ties or his roots. That need, unvoiced, was to be as near as he could to Mavreen. If she was going to London, then somehow he would go there, too. And for that, he knew he would need money. His smuggling activities were conveniently profitable.

"So it is all arranged!" Gerard broke in on Dickon's thoughts. "I have to thank you, Dickon. I wish there were some way I could show my appreciation."

"Taint no need for that," Dickon said.

He stood up and shook the French boy's outstretched hand.

"Best wait afore ye thank me!" he said dourly. " 'Tis never no good to count your chicks afore they's hatched."

But in Gerard's mind, he was already on his way to Compiègne.

CHAPTER SIX
1793

Clarissa Manton was mortally afraid that her darling John would, despite having reached his fiftieth birthday, somehow involve himself in the war with France. He had reacted violently when news of the beheading of the French king had shocked the world and seemed pleased when barely a week later, France declared war on England.

"Now we can do something about this damned state of affairs!" he told her gleefully. Clarissa feared that Sir John, always a man to welcome action, might volunteer his services as, indeed, he had in the war in America. But she realized he was no longer fit for active service. He had never fully recovered from the fever he had contracted in India, and he was no longer a young man, even if his looks belied his age.

It was Clarissa, therefore, who suggested it was high time to bring John's little daughter from the backwoods of Sussex to live with her in Richmond as he had promised three years before. Clarissa knew that Mavreen might well prove a diversion from a day-to-day life which, pleasant and agreeable, nonetheless lacked novelty.

Their affair had settled into a comfortable domestic existence, Sir John spending as much time with her as his duties to his family allowed. Sometimes, but rarely, Clarissa felt a niggle of resentment over her position as mistress in lieu of wife. But at such times, she reminded herself that the arrangement between them was absolutely stable; he had made her secure not only financially but by his proven faithfulness. If ever he did enjoy the favors of another woman—and Clarissa never pried or spied—he was discreet about it and kept his real love for Clarrie; it made up for the fact that she was barred from society and

had to limit her friends to other women, frequently ac-
tresses who were in the same position as herself with
protectors rather than husbands.

"I'll send for the little imp, if you are really sure you
wish to be troubled with her," Sir John said when she
pleaded with him to do so. They had not long before
left Clarissa's big four-poster bed and Sir John was at his
most indulgent. "You know, m'dear, that my greatest
pleasure is to give you your heart's desire!"

She smiled back at him.

"Your 'little imp', John, must be nigh on thirteen years
of age—a young woman, I'll warrant."

She drew Sir John over to the writing bureau and put
before him quill and paper.

"There now!" she said. "You may write to Mr. Glover
this very minute if you would please me. Never put off
till tomorrow what may be done today!"

Clarissa was always ready with an apt proverb and Sir
John, well used to them, came back with "Haste maketh
waste, m'dear!"

But he sat down obediently and wrote both to Mr.
Glover and to Master Thomas Sale, clearly expressing his
wishes.

Now, after three weeks of eager anticipation, Mavreen
arrived at Orchid House escorted by Mr. Glover.

The February afternoon was cold, but a fire blazed in
the beautiful Adam fireplace as Hannah showed the old
gentleman and the child into Clarissa's drawing room.

She went forward at once to embrace Mavreen, whose
small piquant face was swamped by an ugly-poke bonnet
sizes too large for her. But the eyes beneath were unchanged—larger, perhaps, a beautiful hazel green and
filled with inquisitiveness.

Hannah took the child's cloak and bonnet and Clarissa
gazed at the great sweep of shining gold hair that fell to
Mavreen's waist. It was beautiful, but far from modish,
as was her simple dress cut modestly high at the neck.
The fashion was now for low-cut bodices, showing as
much as was possible of the bosom, and already Mavreen
had curved out into womanliness in this direction.

"Sir John will be here directly!" Clarissa told both her

guests. "Meanwhile, please do sit down and make your-
selves comfortable. I trust you had a safe journey?"

At once Mavreen burst into a soft but excited chatter.
She had seen so many new things, it was hard to remember them all.

"But I shall recall all the details when I have time to
collect my thoughts," she said, eyes and cheeks glowing. "I
keep a diary, and I will write it all down so you may
know what an uncommonly exciting two days I have
had."

Clarissa met Mr. Glover's eyes and saw in them the relief that she herself was feeling that despite the long hours
of travel, Mavreen was on her feet, clearly delighted to be
in London.

"I have never seen so charming a house," Mavreen cried,
and added quickly that the grange was lovely, too, but
different.

Clarissa said tactfully, "Mr. Glover is a bachelor and a
scholar, my dear, and would not want trinkets cluttering
up his library. These are women's interests."

But Mavreen's attention had already passed from the
figurines to the flowering pot plants on their tall, mahogany stands.

"When you have time, madame, will you please to tell
me their names? Dickon has taught me the names of all
the wild flowers but I myself am unhappily ignorant of
such plants as these!"

"Mistress Mavreen will plague you to death with her
questions!" Mr. Glover told Clarissa. "There is no peace
when she is present."

Mavreen looked at him reproachfully.

"But, sir, you have told me many times that if I do not
know I must ask. . . ." she began. Then realizing her tutor
had been mocking her, she ran to him to plant a kiss upon
his bald head. "You are very wicked!" she said, her voice
vibrant and warm with affection. "But I love you dearly
and I shall miss you sorely!"

Now it was Clarissa's turn to receive a hug from the
child. She thought that, regrettably, she would have to
curb Mavreen's impulsive habit of kissing anyone who was
agreeable to her, now she was growing to womanhood.

But for the time being, she could not bring herself to rebuke her, and returned the embrace warmly.

Sir John was ushered into the salon and Mavreen dropped him a curtsy. Her father caught his breath at the sight of his daughter. He had forgotten his prediction that she would grow into an uncommonly pretty woman. Now, he was quite taken by the comeliness of the young girl before him.

"So you are safely arrived then!" he said, kissing first Clarrie's plump, white, beringed fingers and then Mavreen's small firm hand. The nails were shaped like filberts, unbuffed but perfectly clean. Her eyes were startling, not only for the strange green-brown color, the brighter for the blue whiteness of the iris, but for their size and brilliance. They dominated her face so that the rather long straight nose and large mouth added to the character of her face.

All resemblance to her mother had vanished. If the child reminded him of anyone, it was of his grandmother —a strong-willed woman whose portrait, painted when she was twenty, hung in the dining room of his house in Piccadilly. She had been one of the great beauties of her day and it was rumored that Sir Robert Walpole had been greatly enamored of her. Mavreen resembled her in some curious fashion he could not exactly define.

It peeved Sir John suddenly to realize that he could not take Mavreen back to Wyfold House to show her her great-grandmother's painting. Sensing his mood as always, Clarissa tucked her arm through his and whispered in his ear, "I think your daughter very charming, John. You have made me very happy, bringing her here. She is such a gay child."

Mr. Glover had a cousin in Chelsea with whom he had arranged to dine and pass the night. When he departed, Mavreen sat down to dine with Sir John and Clarissa. She was instructed to address them as Uncle John and Aunt Clarrie.

She was a little puzzled that Sir John did not return to his own home for dinner but Mr. Glover had stressed during the journey that she must never refer to Sir John's wife unless he or Mistress Manton first did so.

In the ensuing weeks, Clarissa found it difficult not to give way to the selfish wish to satisfy all Mavreen's desires and reap the tender hugs and loving words of gratitude with which they were received.

Mavreen was nearly always gay, sad only at moments when she recalled "her family," as she called the Sales. Time spent in Mavreen's company was time spent pleasurably. Sir John, upon Mr. Glover's advice, purchased for her one of the new pianofortes. Room was made for it in the little salon adjoining Clarissa's drawing room; originally intended as a gentleman's study, it became a perfect music room for Mavreen. To her speechless delight, a music teacher was engaged for her, an Austrian gentleman by the name of Herr Franz Mehler who was currently the rage with London society because of the excellence of his tutoring; himself a pupil of the famous Abbé Vogler in Strasbourg, he was very much impressed with Mavreen's musical ability. Although virtually untrained, she had a light touch upon the keys. Few of the society women who had engaged his services were concerned with technical aptitude. They wished merely to be able to perform charmingly at musical evenings. But upon first hearing Mavreen play, Herr Mehler had known that Mavreen had a natural talent which the Abbé Vogler himself might have wished to develop.

His interest in the young girl was not confined to her musical ability. He found her utterly enchanting. She lacked the guile, the coquetry, the artifice of most young ladies of her age. Her movements were fluid, graceful, her manner refreshingly natural and totally disarming. If she was pleased, interested, happy, she showed it. If she was puzzled or absorbed, a tiny frown would bring her eyebrows down, and she had a habit of biting her lower lip whenever she was concentrating.

Within days of meeting her, Herr Franz Mehler was wishing himself younger than his forty years. In three years time, Mavreen would be of marriageable age and although he knew very well that the circumstances of her birth could not be very savory since she resided with Sir John Danesfield's mistress, he continued to nurture romantic thoughts about her in his artistic mind.

There were no such thoughts in Mavreen's. Laughing mischievously, she told Clarissa that Herr Mehler reminded her of one of Dickon's silky bantams.

"His hair sprouts from his head in just the same way as the fowls' feathers spring from their backs!" she said; but because she was never willingly cruel, she added, "But he is very kind and patient with me!"

Clarissa told an amused Sir John that she thought his daughter, young though she was, had made a conquest.

"Be sure you chaperone her well then, m'dear!" he cautioned. "Mavreen tells me Herr Mehler wishes to teach her in future in his studio in King Street."

"It is because the acoustics there are so much better!" Clarissa explained. "Our little salon does not do justice to the music. You have no objection to Mavreen going there, my dearest?"

Sir John patted her hand, smiling.

"Not if you go with her. Are you certain you do not find this new role tedious, Clarrie?"

"Far from it!" she assured him. "Mavreen is such good company for me when you are absent. As to the music, you know I much enjoy listening and I, too, am receiving a musical education at second hand."

Sir John put an arm around her plump shoulders and drew her closer against him. His face softened to tenderness.

"You are a good woman!" he said simply. "And I love you very dearly, Clarrie. You believe that, don't you?"

"But of course I do!" Clarissa answered. "And I love you very dearly, too. You know, John, even if I could not love Mavreen for herself—which indeed I do—I would love her because she is your child. I like to think, and I hope you will not consider this presumptuous of me, that she is now *our* child. Does that displease you, dearest?"

"On the contrary, it pleases me very much!"

Sir John looked at her with a mischievous glint in his eyes that Clarissa had seen often in his daughter's.

"Where is the girl?" he asked. "I have not seen her this afternoon."

"She has gone with Hannah to the modiste!" Clarissa informed him. "She is having a cloak made, for that one she arrived in is wretchedly outmoded. I thought—" she added meaningfully "—that you might upon occasion, wish to be alone with me, and I let Hannah accompany her in my place!"

"You know, my dear, you are a very clever woman!" Sir John said as he stood up. He drew Clarissa to her feet and leading the way upstairs to their bedroom added, "Learned you may not be in bookish matters, but about men I'll wager you are the wisest woman in the world!"

It would have been impossible for anyone as sensitive as Mavreen not to be aware of the love between her Uncle John and Aunt Clarrie. Even in Sir John's absence it was all about the little house. Everything that was bought, prepared, arranged, was for his pleasure; and he, in turn, made known his affection for Aunt Clarrie by looks, gestures, numerous little gifts and most of all by the reluctance with which he rose to leave at the end of an evening. They were more formal toward one another than Mother and Father Sale, behaving always with great courtesy, as they did toward her, too. But Mavreen felt, rather than knew, that they loved one another deeply and puzzled a great deal why Sir John married some other lady instead of Aunt Clarrie.

Her life was filled with bewildering new experiences. Owlett's Farm seemed a continent away. Once every week, she sat down at the little bureau in her room and wrote a news-filled letter to Dickon to read to the family. She feared they would be missing her sadly, and Dickon especially. She had received but one letter from him, badly misspelled but which she eventually interpreted. He told her the old boar had died, that Anna had found some eggs in a deserted swallow's nest, that Colombe, the young mare, was likely foaling in the spring having been served by one of Mr. Glover's carriage horses, that Edward had had the whoops but otherwise they were all well and would Mavreen not forget to write for they missed her sorely.

For an hour or two Mavreen was filled with longing for her home. But then it was time for her first visit to Herr Mehler's studio, and once there, she was so excited she forgot all about Sussex. Herr Mehler had obtained a box in the Opera House and it would be his great pleasure, he said, to escort them to hear the composer, Weber, conduct his latest score. Mavreen was speechless with delight. When she had recovered her breath she turned to Clarissa.

"We may go, may we not, dearest Aunt Clarrie?"

Clarissa smiled, nodding her assent and thanking the Austrian. Silently she was agreeing with Mavreen's comparison of Herr Mehler to a bantam. With coattails falling either side of the pianoforte stool, his head nodding up and down just as a chicken pecks at food, he played for them one of Clementi's sonatas.

Clarissa, carefully observant, noticed that the Austrian tutor seldom drew his eyes away from Mavreen. Upon occasions, his hand rested on the girl's fingers, instructively, but lingering longer than was strictly necessary. She was relieved to see that Mavreen seemed quite unconscious of Herr Mehler's ill-concealed attentions. Indeed, the child was innocently unaware of any of the admiring glances that were cast her way when they drove out together in the phaeton. From the young errand boy to the old bookseller, all male heads turned when Mavreen passed by and she met with nothing but smiles.

"How very pleasant-natured the folk are in London!" she remarked to Clarissa. "Everyone is always smiling!"

With her well-dressed hair and modish gown, Mavreen looked older than her age. Clarissa frowned unhappily. The child was not yet fourteen. Were she and Sir John, for their own amusement, dragging her too quickly into womanhood? It was not a criticism Sir John would accept kindly.

But despite Clarissa's intentions to keep Mavreen in the safe environs of childhood a little longer, an unfortunate plan to accommodate a friend in an *affaire* merely precipitated Mavreen's developing maturity.

Lisa von Eburhard was Clarissa's oldest and dearest friend from their childhood years when they shared a tutor. Lisa, unlike Clarissa, had married well but her husband, a baron, was many years older and incapable of satisfying Lisa's passionate and volatile nature. As was the fashion, Lisa contented herself with various lovers, the most recent of which was a young hussar of much personal beauty but little intelligence.

Mavreen's visits to Herr Mehler on Tuesday afternoons were sacrosanct and Clarissa had felt no misgivings when she offered Lisa the privacy of Orchid House as a safe meeting place with her young lover. What she had not foreseen was that poor Herr Mehler would become suddenly indisposed shortly after she had deposited Mavreen at his establishment; he was clearly quite unfit to proceed with the lesson and in great distress, informed Mavreen that regretfully he must send her home in a carriage.

"The sun is so warm and I would so much prefer to walk than to ride in a stuffy old carriage. Please, Herr Mehler!"

But although he turned pink and stammered with embarrassment he could not be dissuaded from calling the carriage. His housekeeper would accompany her, he insisted.

Mavreen was still smiling at the absurdity of London conventions as she pulled the bell rope of Orchid House.

She was more than a little surprised when the door was opened by a strange servant—a young footman who stared at her in equal surprise.

"Who are you?" she inquired as she pushed past him into the hall. "What are you doing here? Where is Hannah? Is Mistress Manton not at home?"

She was already halfway to the stairs as the scarlet-faced young man hurried forward and laid a restraining hand upon her arm.

"There is no one in. That is, you cannot go upstairs. I mean, you should not be here at all. I was told you were attending your music lesson!"

It was not in Mavreen's nature to be haughty yet now she reacted with instinctive authority.

"What I do is my business and it is not yours to tell me where I can go in my own house!" she said firmly as she pulled her arm away from his grip. Turning her back on him, she ran upstairs to her bedroom.

As she dropped her cloak and music case upon the bed, she frowned at the oddity of the footman's presence here in Aunt Clarrie's house. She decided to seek out her aunt at first hand for an explanation.

The door of Clarissa's room was ajar. Mavreen would

normally have called out and knocked before entering but it crossed her mind that Aunt Clarrie might be taking an afternoon nap. Not wishing to disturb her, she tiptoed into the room.

It was empty but as Mavreen paused, she heard the faintest of voices from the adjoining guest rooms. Perhaps Aunt Clarrie was there with Hannah or Rose. Only a day or two ago she had spoken of refurbishing the rooms.

Eagerly she ran next door and entered the antechamber. The room was filled with a strange perfume—certainly not that of roses—Aunt Clarrie's preference in scents.

Mavreen knew this room well for she had often come here to admire some of Clarissa's treasures such as the Mecklenburg china clock upon the mantleshelf and the painting of the nymph hanging upon the wall. The girl in the picture lay nude, ivory-white, upon her side, her hair flowing over her shoulders as golden as Mavreen's own and only half concealing her pink-tipped breasts. In the background, half hidden behind the heavy green foliage of the trees, the bearded face of a satyr peered down upon the reclining nymph. This painting fascinated Mavreen. The face of the satyr reminded her of the Bird Man and to see him so portrayed, somehow lessened her remembered fear of him. She could now relegate him to the myths of olden times so that he had no more substance than the half-man, half-goat painted upon the canvas.

As she turned the handle of the door, she realized where the voices had come from. There were two people in the double bed. They lay entwined in each other's arms, so engrossed in one another that they neither heard nor saw the girl standing there. They were naked, their bodies as ivory-white as the girl's in the painting. The man in the bed was speaking softly.

"You are more beautiful than the fairest flower in the Royal Gardens, my lovely Lisa!"

"And you, my sweetest of boys, are my own beloved Adonis!"

Mavreen gave the tiniest of gasps, as silently she stepped backward into the antechamber. She was about to cross to the door and depart from the room when the man spoke again, "Hush, my love! I heard something. Someone is about! Did you not hear a noise?"

Appalled at the prospect of discovery, Mavreen shrank back toward the window, hoping to conceal herself behind the drapes, lest the lovers glance through the bedroom door and imagine her to be spying upon them.

Her fears were not unfounded. The lady laughed softly and said, "Since you are already distracted, go and see for yourself, my darling, though I do assure you no one but ourselves and my servant are in the house. Clarissa quite clearly said she would be absent until late afternoon and the child is not due home for a further hour and a half. Nonetheless, see for yourself."

Pulling the curtain across her body, Mavreen held her breath. There was a stirring of bedsprings as one of the occupants rose from the covers. A young man appeared in the bedroom doorway. His eyes turned at once to the open door of the anteroom and with a look of consternation, he crossed to the door and quickly closed it, turning the key in the lock. Then, retaining his hold upon the key, he again passed by Mavreen and entered the bedroom.

It was the first time Mavreen had glimpsed a grown man's nakedness. Thoughts of the Bird Man were far from her mind for this young Adonis was strong and beautiful. Her mind and body were besieged with strange thoughts and reactions. While concealment was still of paramount importance, she found herself wishing that she could emerge from her hiding place and plead with the young man to halt his departure so that she could drink in his beauty a little longer. His skin was so white and only lightly sprinkled with golden hairs. The muscles of his body rippled smoothly as he moved, and she felt a strange desire to place her hand upon his arm, his thigh. His maleness did not surprise her for she had been born and raised on a farm. It was the delicate whiteness and satin smoothness that fascinated her. It seemed the lady, too, was fascinated. Her voice was softly beguiling as she bade her lover hurry back to her.

"I am impatient, am I not, my sweeting!" she said.

"No more so than I!" replied the young man. Mavreen

heard the bedsprings move once more as he returned, no doubt, to his comfortable position beside his mistress.

Mavreen swallowed and tried to calm her breathing. There was no escape for her now unless she were, at this moment, to announce her presence and she lacked the courage for it.

Mavreen listened with curiosity as the lady spoke again.

"Do not cover yourself so with your hands!" she said, her voice teasing but tender. "You have no need for shyness, my Adonis. Let me touch you as I please and I promise that it will please you, too. Now, is that not delightful?"

The young man's voice, roughened with desire, was urgent as he begged his lover not to cease her attentions.

"Your touch is both heaven and torment. Kiss me, I beg you. Kiss me, my lovely desirable lady of delight."

Unaware of her actions, Mavreen's hand rose to her lips as with eyes closed, she imagined that it was she who obeyed the command. Her eyes remained closed as the voices from the adjoining room became murmurs and then cries of pleasure, leaving her in no doubt that they were joining together as she had so often observed the birds and beasts mating. Yet this was different, for there was no brutal possession of the female by the male, but a willing surrender enacted with words of love.

Trembling, Mavreen sank to the floor, her senses bombarded with emotions she barely comprehended and yet which left her with a feeling of loneliness and exclusion. Within sound, if not within sight, had been enacted a scene such as had never before crossed her mind. Such loving seemed so natural, so desirable that she could not understand how she had been hitherto unaware of so vital and passionate a part of life.

Suddenly, she became aware once more of her predicament. The lovers, satiated, were talking again as they rose from the bed and began dressing.

The lady was laughing softly and gaily.

"I would not give you a week's wage as a ladies' maid!" she reproved the young man. "Have you never buttoned a dress before, my darling?"

"Would you have me say 'yes'?" her lover replied, "for

that would be to admit that I have had many mistresses before you."

"Then I would have you say 'no', for it pleases me to think that I am your first love. I should know better, should I not, than to take a mere boy for my lover?"

"Do not say such things! You know full well how desperately I have longed for this moment. 'Twould break my heart if you were to tell me that my youth and inexperience have proved me inadequate."

"Far from it, I swear! It has been an afternoon of delight and we shall repeat it often, with dear Clarrie's compliance. I must send her flowers tomorrow as a small token of thanks. You, too, my love. She is a good friend —and quite dependable. You need have no fear on that score."

So engrossed were they in each other, they passed through the anteroom and onto the landing without noticing the girl crouching behind the purple drapes. But Mavreen knew it was only a matter of time before the lady's footman informed his mistress of her presence in the house. She waited only long enough for the lovers to descend the stairs before running along the passage to her own room.

She threw herself onto her bed and buried her face in the cool pillow. Her heart was thudding furiously with a myriad emotions—shame, fear of discovery, but above all, excitement. The thought that one day she might find a handsome young man who would want to caress her so tenderly and possess her so sweetly roused all the dawning sensuousness that was latent within her.

Now she understood at least some small part of what life might hold for her. She eagerly awaited Clarissa's return so that she might discuss with her this new discovery, but on reflection she decided that it might be wiser to keep her own council. Clarissa might be angry with her. Mavreen was intelligent enough to realize that she was not intended to know anything of the secret assignment; that the lovers' meeting was to have taken place while she was safely out of the house; that for some reason Clarissa wished her to remain ignorant.

Believing that by a stroke of good fortune, her friend

Lisa von Eburhard and her lover had remained undiscovered by the child, Clarissa confidently persued her resolve to safeguard Mavreen's youth a little longer. With this in mind, Clarissa laid down the edict that at the forthcoming card party for Sir John and his friends, Mavreen could be present at the dinner but must retire before the gambling began.

Inevitably, Mavreen wanted to know about card games, faro in particular since this was Sir John's favorite. Much of one afternoon was spent in the little salon while Clarrie taught Mavreen the rudiments of the game. Although she seldom played herself, Clarrie had presided over a sufficient number of gaming evenings to know the rules as well as Sir John. By the time he arrived in the late afternoon, Mavreen had mastered the essentials. Sir John was much amused when Clarrie informed him that Mavreen had an instinct for cards. He played a pack with them, Mavreen winning often, and laughed aloud.

"You shall be my lucky mascot next week!" he told her. "I'll wager Gilbert will not be a little astonished if a moppet of thirteen takes a guinea or two off him!" He chuckled at the thought of tricking his lifelong friend.

"But, John, dearest!" Clarrie protested. "You do not intend that Mavreen, a young girl, should gamble at cards with Lord Barre!"

Sir John shrugged his shoulders and grinned mischievously.

"And why not? This is our house and we can do as we choose in it, m'dear. As for Gilbert, well, let him criticize if he wishes. Now pay heed, ladies. I want no word spoken of Mavreen's knowledge of the game. It is to come as a complete surprise. At the dinner table, we shall talk of anything else but cards! It will be a jolly evening. I shall enjoy Gilbert's discomfiture hugely."

After Hannah had served them their evening meal, Sir John decided to give Mavreen some further practice. Within an hour, she had won five sovereigns from him. He was delighted, assuring her that it was not just a matter of luck but that she had, as Clarrie told him, an innate card sense.

"An instinct for cards!" he said. "I've had it all my life!"

Mavreen, happy to please him, although not fully understanding the reason it should do so, practiced her card
playing with the same energy and enthusiasm as she practiced the piano and studied fashion. Her mind and hours
fully engaged, she had no time for boredom.

Each night she slept deeply and soundly—so soundly
that it was some time before she became aware one night
that someone was throwing stones against her bedroom
window.

Sleepily, she climbed from between the warm sheets
into the chill of the room. Moonlight flooded across the
rose-patterned carpet so that she had no need for a candle as she went to the casement to pull back the curtains.
Still half in slumber, she wondered if she were dreaming.

Down below, in the street, she could discern a dark
figure in riding cloak and boots; the hood was thrown
back so that the moonlight clearly illuminated the face
beneath the dark crown of hair. More curious than frightened, Mavreen drew up the window and leaned out. She
could see now that it was a young man who stood there,
his face puzzlingly familiar.

He, too, stared up at her.

"Mademoiselle Mavreen?" he asked cautiously.

Instantly, she knew him. It was the young vicomte
de Valle.

"What brings you here at this time of the night, sir?
How did you find me? Have you seen Dickon? Has Colombe had her foal? . . ."

"Mademoiselle, pray could you assist me first and question me later?"

There was a hint of amusement behind the impatience
of the request. Gerard decided that his *écureuil* had not
ceased her endless quest for information to store in her
pretty head.

"How shall I help you?" Mavreen called down. "What
time is it? Mistress Manton is abed and. . . ."

"Mistress Manton is here beside you and to whom,
pray, are you talking?"

Mavreen swung round to find Clarissa at her elbow,
candle in hand, nightcap on her head and a thick shawl
about her plump shoulders.

"Oh, Ma'am!" she cried excitedly. " 'Tis Gerard, the vicomte de Valle. He is in need of our help. May we allow him to come in?"

Clarissa, still befuddled with sleep, shook herself more fully awake and decided anything was preferable to standing in the freezing air in her nightgown.

"Put your horse in the stable, sir!" she called down to Gerard. "We will open the door for you as soon as we are dressed."

Mavreen, wide awake now, was already putting on her clothes, her eyes alive with excitement.

"Perhaps he has come from France, Aunt Clarrie!" she said breathlessly. "Who knows but there may be cutthroats and spies pursuing him. Hurry, do, I pray you!"

Within minutes, Mavreen was racing downstairs to the front door. She was unaware that she was not only throwing it open for Gerard de Valle, but to let into her life a love that would never cease until she died.

CHAPTER SEVEN
1793-1795

Not until the embers of the drawing room fire had been fanned to flame, and Hannah had served Gerard with a cold repast and mulled wine, was he allowed to explain his presence. Mavreen sat curled by the fireplace at Clarissa's feet, silently regarding the seventeen-year-old youth who had replaced the boy she'd last seen three years ago in Sussex.

He had aged beyond the mere growth to manhood. Now well above six feet in height, broad of shoulder, narrow of hip, he looked a deal older than his years. There were small lines around the mouth, dark shadows beneath his eyes. His movements were quick, nervous, restless, as if he were permanently listening for some danger signal. They were the movements of a buck deer hunted in the woods by enemies; both proud and fearful.

Mavreen thought him beautiful; exciting and somehow dangerous. But as the warmth of the room and the solid meal restored his energies, he changed again, became more relaxed and smiled at Mavreen and Clarissa with such gratitude and satisfaction that both were conscious of his charm.

"I arrived in England the night before last!" he told them, taking from his mud-bespattered coat pocket a tiny snuff box, and to Mavreen's delight, applying snuff delicately to both nostrils. She noticed his hands, slender and beautifully shaped but no longer the delicate white hands of the aristocrat unused to labor. "I came from France as I went—in a fishing boat, landing at Cuckmere Haven where a kind man, who shall remain nameless, lent me a horse to carry me to Alfriston."

Mavreen's eyes lightened at the mention of Alfriston.

"You have seen Owlett's Farm? You have seen Dickon? And the family? How are they? Did you see Colombe? Has she foaled?"

Gerard laughed, his eyes alight with amusement as he looked at the flushed face.

"Mon Dieu, you have not altered one whit, Mademoiselle Mavreen! I'll wager you have not ceased asking questions since I left three years ago!" he teased.

"And you would not be far wrong!" Clarissa put in.

Despite his remark, Gerard noticed that Mavreen had changed physically and he approved of what he saw. The flower bud was opening into blossom. The childish figure had rounded to womanhood. The olive-green suiting of her full skirt and tight jacket became her well. Her low-heeled black slippers were modish, her hair fashionably coiffed in soft ringlets. He remembered the last time he had seen her and had envisaged the woman she would grow to. That moment had not yet come but was not long away. Mavreen, he thought, was more than pretty. He had difficulty in concentrating upon his story.

He had indeed seen the Sale family. Colombe had foaled and he believed the mare had recognized him. It was Dickon who had given him Clarissa's London address, which he had lost. As he had come from his own country

totally without financial resources, he added ruefully, and
was uncertain of his reception from Sir John Danesfield
whose hospitality he had so abruptly abused, he had but
one other close acquaintance in England who might receive him, his friend James Pettigrew. He had called at
their house in Chelsea only to be informed that the family
was in Buckinghamshire. He was, therefore, forced at a
late hour either to sleep in the street or beg hospitality
from Mistress Manton, presuming upon their slight acquaintance and her own friendship with Sir John.

"Indeed, madam," he ended, "I hoped also that you
might be able to enlighten me as to Sir John's feelings
toward me."

Clarissa refilled the young man's goblet, patting his
shoulder maternally as she handed it back to him.

"I do not think you need worry Sir John will close his
door to you, Gerard," she said, to Mavreen's relief. "He
was, of course, not a little disturbed by your departure,
and without even the courtesy of an explanation!" she
added with a hint of reproach in her voice. But she went
on, "I know he suspected that you had returned to France,
although by what means you found your way there, he
knew not. But when he was over his initial anger, he told
me he would have done no different at your age and were
he in your position. He believed you went in search of your
dear Mother?"

Gerard's face took on an expression of intense bitterness.

"My search proved fruitless!" he said in a low, intense
voice. "My home was in ruins, part of the château so
burned that I doubt it can ever be repaired. Jules, all the
servants, were gone. I could find no one who knew of
my mother's whereabouts. At very best, I can still hope
that she is alive for no one was able to tell me of her
death. It is my hope and prayer that Jules may have
taken her to Italy to my grandparents, but there has been
no letter in answer to mine and I fear my communications
have been destroyed before leaving the country. As you
know, my poor country has been in turmoil and continues
so to be."

"You must have had the unhappiest of experiences!"

Clarissa said sympathetically. The hunted look was back in Gerard's eyes and both she and Mavreen longed to put their arms about him and comfort him.

"At least I have done some fighting!" Gerard told them proudly. "I was one of the defenders against the attack upon the Tuileries last summer. . . ." he broke off remembering the bloodshed and terrible massacre that had followed the defeat of King Louis's men. He had been lucky to escape and flee across the frontier to safety. He had fought again in Brunswick's army under the duc de Provence in the battle at Valmy. But this attack had ended in defeat and Gerard had become ill with dysentery so severe that he had come close to death, but for the tender care of some nuns who took him to their convent and nursed him back to health.

The execution of the king and the declaration of war on England had reinforced Gerard's wish to return to the country which had once before given him sanctuary. He needed time to regain his health, and, if necessary, use what influence he could to enlist aid for the émigré army to which he hoped to return.

"It is not only for my mother, the Château de Boulancourt, my estates and my birthright that I must continue fighting," he said finally. "It is for France itself. My country is now in the hands of butchers, as no doubt you have heard."

Mavreen would have plied Gerard with further questions but Clarissa noted the pallor of the young man's cheeks and the intense fatigue in the attitude of his head and body. Within minutes, Hannah was instructed to make up a bed for the vicomte in the spare bed chamber. She herself filled a warming pan with embers from the fire. A night shirt of Sir John's was found and Gerard despatched to bed.

"We will have plenty of time to talk on the morrow!" she said, seeing the disappointment on Mavreen's face. "Now off to bed with you, too, my dear. I dare not think what time it may be but I think it cannot be far from dawn."

Obediently, Mavreen went back to her bedchamber. But not to sleep. Even so brief an account as Gerard had given of his adventures since last she had seen him had stirred her imagination—and her envy. How unimportant her own life seemed in comparison! She wished there were a happier ending to Gerard's tale. His fighting had brought no victories and most disappointing of all, he had no news of the mother she knew he loved.

"I will pray for her myself!" Mavreen thought dutifully, but somehow she did not have the impression that God paid much attention to her prayers. She had prayed several times God would somehow find a way to bring Dickon to London, but He had so far done nothing to grant this relatively simple request.

Her mind returned to the young vicomte, no doubt sleeping soundly in the next room. She hoped he would be able to remain with them in London for a long time. Until now, she had not realized how much she had missed companionship of her own age.

She was still planning their joint entertainment in her dreams when Clarissa despatched an errand boy with a note to Sir John, telling him that the young vicomte was with them.

When she woke at ten o'clock, Sir John himself had arrived at Orchid House to escort Gerard back to Piccadilly.

"He cannot stay here with you, my dear!" he told Clarissa apologetically. "It would cause far too much gossip. I know you will understand that it could be important for the boy to guard his reputation and here with you. . . ."

"Say no more, John!" Clarissa broke in. She knew only too well the rules of society, but she showed no bitterness. Instead she complimented him. "It is uncommonly good of you to receive Gerard after the way he behaved in deserting you. Will your wife receive him as kindly?"

Sir John scowled. He very much doubted it, but, as he said to Clarissa, "I shall not ask her approval, Clarrie!" thereby silencing any further discussion on the subject.

When Mavreen came downstairs, wearing her prettiest white dress, cut low and draped over her small firm breasts, a wide blue-satin ribbon tied beneath, it was to discover Gerard on the point of departure. She stood upon the last step of the wide stairway, her eyes puzzled above the delicate fan she held to her lips.

"You are leaving us so soon?" she inquired, undisguised disappointment clear.

"Sir John has kindly invited me to return home with him," Gerard told her, coming toward her with a friendly smile. "I am much indebted to you and Mistress Manton for your kindness to me last night. I shall not forget it."

"But there are so many things I wish to discuss with you! I wish to hear more about Dickon and the farm and Colombe and the smugglers and. . . ."

"I shall have the pleasure of answering all your questions very soon, I hope!" Gerard broke in, taking her hand and kissing it lightly. "I am to remain in London for some weeks. Sir John thinks it likely he might get word to Italy concerning my mother and naturally, I shall remain a while lest there should be a reply. So I hope I may have the pleasure of calling upon you?"

"You may certainly call upon Mavreen and Mistress Manton if you so wish, Gerard," Sir John said to the young man in the carriage on the way back to Piccadilly. "But you must, of necessity, do so discreetly. I am sure you are aware of Mistress Manton's position in society and, regrettably, little Mavreen's likewise. Lest there be any misunderstanding in the matter, I will confide in you, and I rely upon your honor that this shall go no further. Mavreen is my natural daughter."

Gerard managed with difficulty to conceal his surprise. He felt a rush of pity for Mavreen. He knew only too well the distinctions of birth and breeding.

"Does she know that which you've just told me?" Gerard asked.

Sir John shook his head.

"Mavreen is but a child, entirely innocent of such matters. I intend to leave her in ignorance a while longer."

Gerard thought of the young girl's eager, happy face and something deep inside him rebelled at the blow she must one day receive. He did not doubt her innocence although it might seem strange to others that anyone as perceptive and intelligent as Mavreen living in the house of Sir John's mistress, should be unaware of their relationship, even if she were unaware of her own kinship to Sir John.

But this was none of his affair and he had more serious matters on his mind. Not the least of these, as Sir John was in the process of telling him, was the need for money.

"I shall see you are not without adequate means for your daily requirements, m'boy!" he said generously. "Nevertheless, now we know you cannot hope to regain your former wealth and position in France, I must strongly advise you to start thinking in terms of a good marriage."

"Marriage?" Gerard echoed. "But, sir, I am but seventeen years of age. I have no desire for a wife. . . ." But Sir John would not permit him to continue his protest.

"Your desires and your needs are separate issues, m'boy! A wealthy wife, English to boot, would be a great asset. You have no other means of support and it would be quite improper for a young man of your title to find employment. You have not lost sight of your vow to your mother to restore the name of de Valle to its former honorable status, I trust?"

"Indeed, I have not, sir!" Gerard said indignantly.

"To achieve anything in this life, boy, you need two things—money and influence. A rich wife can bring you these with a deal less worry than you can obtain them for yourself. I'll do what I can for you. My own two daughters will be on the shelf soon if I don't find them husbands but I doubt either would suit you, despite the money they will bring with them to a marriage. You need a woman who can make her mark in society, put the right word in the right ear, get you to court if you need it. That's the kind of female we have to find for you; someone with a bit of fire and liveliness about her—someone who'll look like a vicomtesse, the way your dear mother did, eh?"

Gerard remained silent. He did not think such a woman existed. The few rich ones he had met so far were, like Sir John's daughters, excessively plain. Those with fire were usually without means or, he thought suddenly, without the right breeding like little Mavreen. In a year or two, doubtless, she would be all that Sir John intended and he, himself, would like for a wife, if have one he must. It was a sad reflection that the only one he could imagine wanting was one he had just been informed was forever barred to him.

Mavreen's disappointment at Gerard's rushing off again was forgotten in the preparation for the following evening's dinner party. There were ten gentlemen invited, all friends of Sir John's; all were in their late forties, or, like Sir John, their early fifties. They were all gentlemen of wealth and position; two of them were associates of the Prince of Wales. Mavreen was greatly excited to be present at a table abounding with important gentlemen.

The usual spate of questions poured from her. Were they actually friends of the Prince of Wales? Was Clarissa not flattered that such important people came to her small house?

Clarissa laughed. It was not her they came to visit. They came to enjoy the good food and drink and cards. They all gambled heavily—Lord Barre in particular.

"Why so?" Mavreen asked. "Is he so very rich?"

Clarissa nodded.

"Rich, yes. And he has no wife and children to support. There is only a distant cousin to inherit from him when he dies and I have oft heard him remark that he positively dislikes the man. Since he cannot prevent his cousin inheriting the title, he swears he will endeavor to see he doesn't inherit his fortune as well—hence the high stakes he plays for."

Mavreen laughed, certain she would like this particular friend of Sir John's.

But she had no opportunity to meet any of them, or indeed see Gerard de Valle again. That very evening, she complained of the cold and shivered violently despite the fire Clarissa had built up to increase the heat in the already-warm room. She became flushed, thirsty, feverish, and later that night, complained of a sore throat. By morning, a bright scarlet rash had appeared on her neck and breast which by mid-day had begun to spread to other parts of her body.

Clarissa called in the physician, although as a physician's widow she had already seen similar skin eruptions before; she was not therefore surprised to learn that Mavreen had scarlatina. There was nothing to give her as medicine although the physician left behind some chlorate of potash lozenges to ease the throat and instructed Clarissa to apply poultices to the skin to soothe the rash.

For two weeks, Mavreen was severely ill. Her pulse rate quickened and her temperature climbed so high she became delirious. Clarissa nursed her devotedly until at long last, both the rash and the fever began to abate.

Sir John called daily to inquire after her health.

"She is so thin and pale, John, I am beginning to fear for her complete recovery. I have been thinking. Perhaps London is not the best climate for her. She is country-born and bred and a change to country air might be vastly beneficial to her. I asked the physician this morning and he agreed it might be so."

"Then you must take her at once to Brighthelmstone!" Sir John began, but Clarrie put up a restraining hand.

"No, my dear, I think it is to Alfriston we should send her. In her delirium, her talk was ever of the farm and her family. The weather is perfect and she could be perfectly well cared for by Mistress Sale. I think Mavreen would be happiest there with nothing new to tax her mind."

Sir John looked at Clarissa. He had, for a few days, believed with her that Mavreen might die of her illness. He had been unexpectedly distressed and railed against his inability to do anything helpful other than to have fruit and flowers sent to the house daily. He knew that Clarissa had had little sleep herself, devoting herself to the child's care day and night. She, too, needed a rest. To return Mavreen to the farm for a while might be beneficial to them all. He could meanwhile take Clarissa for a little holiday to Brighthelmstone.

So it was arranged, although it was a further two weeks before Mavreen was pronounced fit enough to make the journey by carriage to Sussex.

Her welcome there was never in doubt. Mistress Sale clucked over her like a mother hen; Dickon arranged an invalid bed under the apple trees in the orchard where she could lie in the sun or shade and drowse the days away.

Young and healthy as she was, within weeks her strength began to return. Soon she was able to undertake such small tasks as throwing corn to the chickens, collecting eggs and packing fruit which Dickon handed down to her from the trees.

Mavreen and Dickon's relationship had subtly changed. Mavreen was as sweet and friendly and loving toward him as ever but even in so short a while as she had been in London, she had become more remote from him than ever. Her speech, mannerisms, appearance, were now that of a young lady of society. Although she might run barefoot in the fields, her beautiful hair let loose from its confines, her laughter spontaneous and unaffected, still that mark of distinction remained and he could not overlook it.

He was seventeen years old; old enough to have a man's feelings and longings. He had caught many a girl's glance in his direction on market day for he was a strong, rugged, not unattractive youth. The kitchen maid at the Star Inn never failed to smile at him if he went past the window. There was, too, the dairymaid at their neighbor's farm who blushed when he addressed her. But he had no room in his heart for any girl but Mavreen. He loved her and being a simple fellow, never thought beyond loving her until the end of his days.

Through those summer months, he was able to adjust to the idea that this love would never be requited; that in a strange way, he would not even wish it himself for he felt too much respect in his adoration of her. He was content simply to be near her, to have the right to serve her, guard her, be within call of her sweet, clear voice. In his limited way, he was happy.

Mavreen, too, was happy. London was exciting and she would, in due course, be pleased to return there. But meanwhile the countryside was ablaze with columbines and dog roses and soon there would be blackberries and crab apples to gather.

Mistress Sale would be making bramble and crab apple jelly. This was home. Only occasionally did she regret her return to Sussex and that was when she saw Colombe and her foal grazing in the meadow. Then she remembered the young vicomte.

Mr. Glover wanted to know if her mind had made as complete a recovery as her body. Mavreen assured him that it had, whereupon he demanded to know why then was she not employing it? Had she forgotten how much there was to learn? Was she not aware of the great moves history was making while she dreamt away the summer days? Was she aware of the momentous developments in the war? Did she know of the treaty England had concluded with the king of Sardinia? Of the plight of the Roman Catholics in Scotland? Of Sir John Sinclair's Board of Agriculture and what this might mean to her foster family and other farmers?

Successfully, he stirred her mind as the sun had stirred her body and without any spoken agreement, there was a tacit understanding between them that Mavreen would renew her studies with him.

Summer passed to autumn. Sir John paid Mavreen a visit, diverting a journey back from Brighthelmstone via Lewes. Clarissa, he told Mavreen, was having the entire house painted and redecorated and the very moment the work was complete, wished to have Mavreen return if her health permitted. There was little doubt that she was well enough but Mr. Glover pleaded with Mavreen's father to leave her where she was for the time being.

"She is a child here with us!" he said. "Let her remain so a little longer, Sir John. I will give my assurance that she continues with her pianoforte practice. Beyond her music, there is little that could be said to be beneficial to her in the London life she described to me, greatly though she enjoyed the experience."

Sir John was of two minds. He knew that Clarrie sadly missed the child. At the same time, there was much wisdom behind Glover's suggestion. He, himself, was involved in trying to marry off his two daughters. Now eighteen and twenty, Selina and Prudence had no suitors and their mother was making little effort to find them husbands. It was his duty, he believed, to be at home more often to entertain for them and, when necessary, escort them to functions.

This would inevitably give him little time to be involved with Mavreen's life were she in London. Moreover, the child did unknowingly curtail his private life with Clarrie.

He let Glover persuade him to leave Mavreen in Sussex until she was fifteen. By then, she would have reached womanhood. It was soon enough.

Mavreen did not demur. She missed the privacy of her own bedroom and all the beautiful objects and furnishings of the little house in Richmond. Beyond that, she felt no urgent longing to return to the city. Unknown to her, the alterations taking place in her body as she changed from child to woman demanded that she have leisure for the transition. She was going through a chrysalis stage when nature ensured that the lethargy of adolescence overtake the wild restlessness of her physical and mental make-up. Her lessons with Mr. Glover were never too exacting, and her activities around the farm were watched carefully by Dickon.

By the time her fifteenth birthday arrived in 1795, Mavreen the child had vanished except for glimpses in the clear bright innocence of her gaze and the trust she placed on all around her. Physically, she was much taller, too slender to be called statuesque but nearly so. Her breasts had filled to a voluptuous roundness; her high cheekbones had become more marked, the lips fuller and innocently sensuous. Her movements, always graceful, were slower, her voice mellifluous. She sparkled with vitality, health and self-confidence.

The day she bade Mr. Glover farewell before setting out for London, he held her at arm's length and said, "You have grown to become a beautiful woman, my dear. Many men will love you for that beauty. It will not always be easy for you to know when you are loved for yourself alone. I tell you this so that you can be aware of the dangers that may assail you. Beauty is an asset for a woman but the adulation and adoration it will ensure can never content you. I know you better even than you know yourself. You are a person, Mavreen—a human being who demands more from life than pretty compliments. You seek always for the truth, for honesty, for fairness, and these cannot be easily come by for a female. You will meet with opposition wherever you demand equality. A husband who understands this core of your nature could help you to realize yourself. A husband who wants only a pretty decoration may pander to what he thinks are your whims in order to please you, but he will not know how to satisfy you."

Such a sermon was unusual coming from the academic old scholar. Mavreen listened with her customary intentness, but this time, she failed to understand him.

"What is it you wish of me, sir?" she asked.

He sighed, realizing she was too young and inexperienced to see the pitfalls that awaited her. He said, "I ask only that you should remain true to yourself, my dear. Never accept second best or second rate or second hand. Most of all, in matters of the heart. Now, be off with you, girl, and remember you have given me your promise to write."

Her farewell from Dickon was harder. Mavreen could read the terrible sadness of parting in his eyes. She was aware of his love for her but since it had existed ever since she could remember, she accepted it as normal though she knew that in some indefinable way it had changed. Dickon no longer held out his arms for her to run to with kisses and no matter how much she had teased him this past year, he behaved toward her with formality which kept her at arm's length. She supposed he wished it this way and moderated her own natural impulse to treat him with the intimacy due to a favorite brother. But now, she longed to set aside his sadness and she hugged him childishly, promising, "It will not be for long, dearest Dickon. I shall send for you. All the noblemen there have grooms and you could soon find work. It is my intention to speak for you with both Sir John and Mistress Manton. Maybe they will agree, one or other, to give you employment. Then we can see each other often."

This promise, which Mavreen intended to fulfill, seemed to satisfy Dickon, and when the carriage Sir John had sent pulled out of the farm yard, Dickon was smiling as he waved his hand. Between her own, she clasped a posy of cowslips and forget-me-nots, his parting gift to her.

CHAPTER EIGHT
1795

"Dear, dear Aunt Clarrie," Mavreen cried, embracing Clarissa with warmth in her voice. "It is truly wonderful to see you again. You are exactly as I remember you."

Clarissa laughed, helping Mavreen to remove her cloak and bonnet and drawing her closer to the fire.

"I am two years older!" she reminded her. "And so are you, my dear child. You have changed almost beyond recognition!"

"Oh, surely not, ma'am!" Mavreen replied, curling herself at Clarissa's feet and leaning her head against the soft satin of her skirt. "I am no different, I promise!"

Clarissa put a hand on the shining honey-gold hair and stroked it lovingly.

"I believe not. You are my same sweet unspoiled little girl who left here covered in scarlet spots!"

"That I did not, Aunt Clarrie. My spots had long gone when I went away!"

They laughed together, instantly firm friends, as if there had been no years since their last conversation.

"I have so much to inquire about!" Mavreen said, with an eagerness Clarrie had half forgotten. "How is dear Uncle John? And Hannah? And poor Herr Mehler? And what, pray, happened to the Vicomte de Valle? Is he still in London? Is . . . ."

"Halt one minute, my dear, or I shall never remember which questions I have to answer. Sir John is well, but tediously busy with his affairs. Hannah, too, is well and missed you sorely. She told me so often that I became quite cross with her and implored her not to keep reminding me of your absence."

"I'm happy she is still with you, ma'am. I had feared

she might be gone when another servant opened the door to me."

"That is Rose, the maid. Had you forgotten her? And as to Herr Mehler, poor man, he has been like a lovesick goldfish forever circling around me when we meet for news of his *'Schoene kleine Fräulein!'* "

They shared another moment of laughter and then Clarissa said, "As to the handsome young viscount—you wish for news of him, but there is little, I'm afraid, to tell you. He called upon me not long after you had left for Sussex, to thank me once again for my hospitality but also to bid me farewell as he was off once more to France. News had arrived from Italy to say that his mother had not returned to her family there and was presumed to be still in France. Gerard was afraid she might be imprisoned."

Clarissa watched the color come and go in Mavreen's smooth cheeks and was not surprised when she said wistfully, "Did he not ask for me?"

"Why, yes, I think he did!" Clarissa teased. "In fact, I have to confess he first asked for you and I think the bouquet of flowers he handed me was really intended for you since it was tied with the selfsame color of ribbon that adorned the dress you wore that morning Sir John took him away."

"Oh, Aunt Clarrie!" Mavreen said happily. "I'm so happy to know it. I have thought a great deal about him and reached a conclusion that were we to know one another better, we could become the very best of friends!"

Clarissa was glad that Mavreen could not see the shadow that passed quickly over her face. It would not do for Mavreen to develop romantic notions about the young vicomte. Sir John had only a short while ago spoken of a titled young woman of considerable wealth whose father he had approached with preliminary inquiries on behalf of Gerard de Valle. It seemed the two young people had met one another at a musical evening at Sir John's house and Mercedes de Faenza, daughter of a Spanish nobleman, had been greatly enamored of the boy and made little secret of it. Her father had not rejected Sir John's suggestion of a possible marriage between the two. Mercedes did not need to marry money for she was rich enough to support three husbands! But an only daughter, she had been much spoiled throughout her childhood and now her father was finding it difficult to select a husband to suit her. At twenty-three, she was voluptuous and passionate and he feared if he did not soon arrange a legal union for her, she would disgrace him by engaging in an illegal affair of her own accord. Gerard de Valle was the first young man she had fancied who might be considered eligible. Moreover, he was a Roman Catholic as many Englishmen were not.

Gerard, of course, was not in England to be consulted upon the matter, but Sir John felt confident, he had told Clarissa, that the boy would see the advantages of such a match. There was no likelihood, therefore, of Mavreen and Gerard becoming friends, and for them to fall in love could only be disaster.

To distract Mavreen's thoughts away from the boy, Clarissa talked for a while of the forthcoming marriage of the prince of Wales to his cousin, Caroline, daughter of the duke of Brunswick-Wolfenbüttel. The prince was really being blackmailed into the marriage by Parliament who had agreed to pay off his vast debts, Sir John had told her. Clarissa informed Mavreen that these were believed to be in excess of £650,000. There was much sympathy for the prince's morganatic wife, Maria Fitzherbert, her marriage with the prince having been invalidated.

Mavreen already knew much of this information from talks with Mr. Glover. Both had concluded that the Prince of Wales was not of the same caliber as his father and that it was as well King George had apparently recovered from his illness and that the prince was not made regent.

So Mavreen slipped back into her London life with as much ease as she had returned to Sussex. Clarissa, warmhearted and loving, was like a kindly mother and friend to her. Sir John, when he visited, spoiled and flattered her and made her feel most welcome. Herr Mehler, when she began her music lessons once again, was pink with emotion as he stood listening to her playing which, he told her generously, had improved even without the continuance of his teaching.

Her bedroom was entirely redecorated and Clarissa had continued for her her collection of books, which now included a magnificent copy of Samuel Johnson's Dictionary—something Mr. Glover had often spoken of but did not possess. It was, Clarissa said, a gift from Sir John. Mavreen was speechless with pleasure but had little time, in the feverish preparations for the evening's card party, to browse among the new words whose meanings she wished to discover.

She had a new dress for the party, copied from a picture in the *Gallery of Fashions* published in London by the Swiss artist Nicolaus von Heideloff, and in the height of the current mode. Mavreen was more excited than nervous, but when the moment came for her to descend the stairs to join Clarissa and Sir John in the drawing room where they awaited their guests, the sophistication of her new dress gave her added confidence.

Sir John, watching her approach, felt a surge of paternal pride. The bodice of the gown she wore was of pink silk, the straight skirt of white silk edged with lace. A tiny black lace sleeveless cape covered her bare shoulders; pink, white, and black feathers adorned her Grecian hair style. Beside Mavreen, his beloved Clarrie was but a star dimmed by morning. Mavreen was the sun itself, dazzling the eye, blinding in her radiance.

"My dearest Mavreen," he said kissing her hand with a formality which made her smile impishly at him, turning her once more into a child. "I shall have the greatest pride and pleasure in introducing you to my friends this evening. You look most engaging!"

"And the dress suits you to perfection," Clarissa added generously. She lacked the envy or jealousy another, lesser woman might have felt on finding herself so eclipsed. "And there, I think, are our first guests arriving."

"Gilbert, I'll wager!" laughed Sir John. "He is ever first to come and last to go, that fellow. Believes in enjoying himself to the full."

Lord Barre was exactly as Mavreen expected him to

be; she felt she already knew the short, fat, red-faced and heavy-jowled man. He radiated jollity. Obviously given to self indulgence, he was equally generous to others and his natural kindness and good nature were apparent in his whole demeanor.

He kissed Clarissa familiarly upon both cheeks, reminding Sir John that he was the "devil of a fortunate fellow to have such a lovely woman to entertain for him"; then he held Mavreen at arm's length, though they did not reach far beyond his rotund waistcoated middle, and told her she was pretty enough to eat for his dinner.

"Indeed, I shall not eat my food with any pleasure, dear Clarrie, if I do not have this beautiful young lady beside me. Rearrange the seating places, I insist, for I will have no other neighbor but Mistress Mavreen."

Mavreen caught Sir John's eye and smiled, enjoying the flattery.

Dinner was a sumptuous affair. The large oval Georgian mahogany table was brilliant with shining silver and sparkling crystal glass. Mavreen had arranged two flower bowls with snowdrops and mauve croci and tied them with white and mauve ribbons. Hannah and Rose served the food which the cook had been preparing in the kitchen for days—scalloped oysters, buttered lobster followed by a raised giblet pie, or for those who preferred it, a fricandeau of veal. Cheesecake, jellies, trifles and Mavreen's favorite syllabub rounded off the dinner.

Wines and political talk flowed freely. Mavreen sat quietly listening. It was Lord Barre who finally turned to Mavreen and patting her hand, said, "My apologies, m'dear, I am afraid this conversation must be uncommonly tedious for you."

"On the contrary, sir!" Mavreen replied sincerely. "I am very much interested. I feel most strongly upon some of the subjects you have been discussing."

He looked at her flushed face with amusement.

"And what would a pretty young lady like you know of such matters!" he teased.

"Not nearly enough, sir!" Mavreen replied, taking his question quite seriously, as it had not been intended. "I think, for example, that it would have been a great injustice for our ally, Austria, to have been denied assistance merely because the king of Prussia used our money for his own ends."

Lord Barre stared at the young girl in total surprise. Sir John Danesfield smothered a smile and the other gentlemen stopped their conversation to listen as Lord Barre asked, "And can you enlighten me as to your sentiments regarding the slave trade?"

Mavreen returned his gaze unblinking.

"Indeed, sir, I feel strongly about this also. I cannot believe it is right to sell human beings as if they were animals in the market. I am sincerely praying each night that since the question of abolishing such trade has only been postponed for six months, that when there is a further vote, those seventeen who cast their lot against abolition will have reached a less selfish and more human frame of mind. After all, sir, Denmark abolished slave trading three years ago."

To her surprise, the gentlemen at the table clapped their hands. Lord Barre raised his glass to her.

"An uncommonly well-informed young lady, by my faith. Were all the females in England as knowledgeable as Mistress Mavreen, I do believe we might consider taking them into government."

"Heaven forbid, sir!" said one of the politicians amid much laughter. "We have troubles enough with the ladies without adding politics to their differences with us!"

Mavreen's cheeks flushed.

"I do not agree that we would differ in every particular had we the right to express our views freely," she said with quiet determination. "It is our misfortune that because we are born female, our opinions are ridiculed, yet I believe it is a fact that we are born with brains proportionately as sizeable as your own, sirs!"

"Then 'tis a pity more of the ladies don't use them!" remarked one of the barristers, whereupon all the gentlemen laughed once more.

Seeing the flash of fire in Mavreen's eyes as she drew breath to take up the challenge, Clarissa stood up.

"We will leave you, gentlemen, to your port wine and masculine ribaldry!"

Mavreen followed her out of the room. The men, who had risen to their feet, now reseated themselves. Lord Barre leaned across the table to Sir John.

"I must congratulate you, John. I have not been so vastly entertained in years. Tell me more about the child. How old is she? Where did she come by her learning?"

"I will tell you on some other occasion, Gilbert!" Sir John said, highly delighted with the impact his daughter had made. "And to whet your appetite, I will inform you that you have only glimpsed the tip of the iceberg. The child is better instructed even than I, or you, I'll wager!"

Unaware of the compliments being paid to her, Mavreen watched with interest while two of the servants brought in a large baize-covered table in preparation for the card game that was to follow the dinner. Sir John's guests, eager to begin the night's play, rejoined the ladies and seated themselves at the table.

Mavreen watched each player and mentally noted their personal form of placing bets. Some proved impulsive gamblers, another compulsive, for he placed a bet even when there seemed little likelihood of his winning. Sir John and Lord Barre bet less often but for larger stakes. As the third pack of cards was placed in the box, Sir John called Mavreen to his side.

"Stand here and call the tune for me, my dear, that is if you gentlemen don't object?"

None did, although Lord Barre remonstrated that it was not fair to hold so young and inexperienced a young lady responsible if Sir John lost the winnings he had so far accrued. Mavreen thought it very kind of him to seek to protect her and smiled warmly back at him.

She did not find the play of the cards and the placing of the bets in the least difficult. For a round or two, she did have difficulty in making herself place large sums, remembering the long columns of figures in Master Sale's ledger. His whole year's earnings were less than half the amount she was placing in jeopardy upon the turn of a card.

By the time the last three cards remained in the box,

she no longer hesitated. She had no doubt in her mind that among them was a pair. Her small hand reached for a hundred sovereigns. Lord Barre, who was playing for the house, raised his eyebrows and glanced at Sir John.

"You have my permission to withdraw the amount!" he said.

Sir John shook his head.

"On the contrary, if Mistress Mavreen believes she can win, I will not stop her attempt."

All at the table gasped as a pair of threes was turned. Mavreen gave a little cry of pleasure and jumping to her feet, embraced Sir John, crying, "Thank you for allowing me to try my luck. I am so happy to have won for you."

Lord Barre, too, stood up. His round, heavy-jowled face showed surprise, disbelief, humor and interest.

"And if that 200 guineas were yours, my dear, to spend as you wish, may I ask what you would do with it? Some pretty new clothes, perhaps? A piece of jewelry?"

Mavreen shook her head, hazel-green eyes wide and serious.

"Oh, no, sir, I'd have better use for such a fortune!" she said. "I would send it to Master and Mistress Sale and Dickon and the children."

"Farmers who cared for her and her mother in the past!" Sir John explained. "Now be off with you, child. You should have been abed long since."

Obediently, Mavreen curtsied to each of the guests, kissed Sir John lovingly on both cheeks, hugged Clarissa, and went happily up the staircase. Downstairs, the game was resumed.

At the end of the evening, carriages were sent for and one by one, the guests departed until only Lord Barre remained. Tactfully, Clarissa retired to bed, leaving the two friends alone.

Although he had drunk much, Lord Barre was fully in possession of his faculties when he turned to Sir John, saying, "That child of yours, John—she is quite remarkable. A pity she is not your legitimate daughter, if you don't mind my making such personal comment."

Sir John leaned back in his chair sighing.

"You and I are too-old friends to take exception to in-

sults, let alone compliments. In any event, I heartily endorse your views. It is my lasting regret, too, that I cannot
openly acknowledge little Mavreen. I dare not do so."

Lord Barre grunted. "I realize that. But what can become of the girl now, John? There's not much future for
her the way things are."

Sir John drew another long sigh. "I know it. At best I
can hope for some mediocre marriage for her. Clarrie
tells me that the Austrian music master has his eye on the
girl, but I think she might do better than that."

"I'm not surprised to hear some man has his eye on
her, John!" Lord Barre said, throwing his cheroot stub
into the fireplace. "If she were a year or two older and I a
year or two younger, I'd ask for her hand meself and be
damned to the gossips!"

Sir John laughed.

"They wouldn't be much trouble to you, Gilbert. You're
high enough placed—and rich enough, to marry whom
you please."

"I hope you'll let me use what influence I can on the
child's behalf. I am much taken with her," Lord Barre
said, lighting a new cheroot.

"That is more than obliging of you, Gilbert. I'll think on
it and advise you if I see any way you can assist."

When Lord Barre finally departed, Sir John went upstairs to bid Clarissa goodnight. His last words left her
with many misgivings.

"It has only just occurred to me!" he said as he began
the task of re-dressing himself, having no servant to help
him. "In a year or so Mavreen will be seventeen and
marriageable. Gilbert will not yet be fifty-five. He's probably the most eligible bachelor in England and if he chose
to marry the girl, no one could prevent it. If Mavreen plays
her cards right, she could become Lady Barre. How about
that, m'dear?"

"I think it is a shocking idea, John!" Clarrie said with
unexpected vehemence. "You have quite forgotten the
most important thing to any woman in marriage—love."

"Fiddlesticks!" was Sir John's short comment. "She can
do the same as I've done and find love outside marriage.
And now, my dear, it's high time I was off."

He had no inclination to hear Clarissa's views. He bade her an affectionate goodnight and left her, determined that he had found the perfect solution for his daughter's future.

CHAPTER NINE
1795

Back in the little house in Richmond, Mavreen found herself thinking more and more frequently of the fleeting nocturnal visit of the young Vicomte Gerard de Valle. Whenever she raised his name in conversation, Clarissa proved strangely evasive, so Mavreen waited for an opportunity when she was riding alone with Sir John in Hyde Park to question him.

Sir John hedged also, but when Mavreen pressed him for news, he admitted he had received word of Gerard not long ago to say that he had been fighting for the Royalists under Charette throughout the winter, but that it seemed as if his leader was going to take the advice of his secret agents and conclude a peace treaty with the French Government.

"Gerard had still no news of his mother but in the absence of ill tidings had not given up all hope," he concluded.

Mavreen looked about her at the early signs of spring and sighed.

"Is the Royalist cause doomed, then?" she asked. "Can they never regain power now?"

Sir John shook his head.

"It appears unlikely," he said.

"So Gerard is not likely to come back to England soon?"

Sir John heard the wistfulness in his daughter's voice and was made as uneasy as Clarissa. He was glad that

Gerard was not in London where his little Mavreen's heart could be further moved.

"Uncle John, look there. Three ladies are waving to you!"

Mavreen's voice brought him abruptly from his reflections on royal affairs.

"Damn!" Sir John exclaimed, his face darkening to a deep red. "Come, let us turn down this ride, and quickly!"

"But they are trying to attract your attention," Mavreen protested innocently. "Do you know them? Certainly they seem to recognize you!"

Sir John was well aware of it. The three ladies were his wife and daughters. He disliked the thought that he had to run away from them, disliked the feeling of guilt, not so much toward them but because he must hide the innocent child beside him, whose bastardy was in no way a fault of her doing. She was as much his daughter as Prudence or Selina and he loved her a great deal more. It irked him that he must turn aside as if he were ashamed of her.

Mavreen was sensitive to his mood without understanding its cause. She remained silent as they retraced their road homeward. Sir John sat deep in thought beside her. The time had come, he thought, when he must reveal her parentage. He would consult Clarissa about it. If nothing else, Mavreen had a right to know why he could not publicly acknowledge her. Yet he dreaded the risk the truth might entail. Suppose Mavreen were to love him less? Trust him less? She was a proud, independent, little madam. She might take her mother's part and turn against him. It was strange how much her regard had come to mean to him.

Clarissa agreed that it was time Mavreen learned the truth, but Sir John was cowardly in presenting his confession. Matters were very nearly brought to a head and his hand forced when he called one afternoon to find Mavreen in tears and Clarissa nearly so.

"Tush!" he exclaimed. "My two pretty ladies a-weeping?"

Mavreen rushed from Clarissa's arms and threw herself

into his. Her cheeks were flushed and her eyes filled with distress.

"Oh, Uncle John, it is the Mozart concert next week at Almack's Assembly Rooms. Aunt Clarrie and I hoped so much to go but we have been refused admission. No one will tell me why for we had ample enough money to pay for our tickets. It is most disappointing!"

Sir John wiped her wet cheeks with a lace handkerchief and gave Clarissa one of the few angry looks she had ever received from him.

"You should never have taken her there!" he said harshly. "You must have known you would be refused! Why raise the child's hopes unduly?"

Clarissa's eyes filled with tears.

"I did know. I tried to warn Mavreen but she would agree to nothing else but that we at least make the attempt."

Sir John, a fair man at all times, at once left Mavreen and went to comfort Clarissa. He should not have reproached her. He knew poor Clarrie could never have convinced Mavreen a thing was impossible without logical proof. And that she could not give since Mavreen knew nothing of the circumstances of her birth or of Clarrie's place in society. The Assembly Rooms were run by a committee of ladies of high rank and without a voucher from a patroness of standing, no ticket would be offered.

But still he refrained from telling Mavreen the truth, convincing himself that she had had enough upsets for one day. He would wait, he decided weakly, for the morrow.

That same evening, however, his close friend, Lord Barre paid his third call since the card evening at the little house in Richmond. On this occasion, as on the others, he brought flowers and sweetmeats for Mavreen and Clarissa. He also brought a book, bound most beautifully in soft calfskin, for Mavreen's collection.

"That is uncommonly good of you, Gilbert!" Sir John said as Mavreen disappeared upstairs with her newest treasure, her cheeks pink with pleasure. "You spoil the child!"

Usually jovial and light hearted, Lord Barre's face took on a look of embarrassment.

"I hope you've no objections, John?"

Sir John raised his eyebrows in surprise.

"But of course not! As a matter of fact, your gesture was more than timely. The girl had a disappointment to-day and had been weeping!"

Briefly, he told his friend about Almack's.

"Tush! Those damned females!" Lord Barre said disgustedly as he listened to the story. "Small wonder I steered clear all my life of marriage to one of 'em, eh? Begging your pardon, Clarissa, my dear, for I don't place you in the same category," he added truthfully.

"Yet you should have married, Gilbert, if for no other reason than to acquire an heir," she reminded him gently.

Lord Barre took the glass of wine the footman handed him. His face still unusually serious, he said, "As a matter of fact, John, Clarissa has hit upon the very matter I wish to discuss with you."

"Then I will go upstairs to Mavreen and leave you in peace!" Clarissa said. "You'll stay to dinner, Gilbert?"

"Thank'ee, ma'am, but I much regret I have another engagement."

When Clarissa had gone, Sir John turned to his friend with a smile.

"Don't tell me you've been up to my tricks and found an heir tucked away in the country?"

Lord Barre took a pinch of snuff, returned the little jeweled box to his pocket and drew a deep sigh.

"Unfortunately, no! As you are aware, John, when I die, my entire fortune, not to mention the title—goes to that damned cousin of mine—that tedious parson fellow who lives in Cumberland. Never did like the fellow. Don't think he approves of me, either. But there it is—unless. . . ."

Sir John took a pinch of snuff at each nostril and looked at his friend curiously.

"You're thinking of getting married, then?" he asked.

Lord Barre's silent nod supplied the answer.

"Damn, Gilbert, you're a dark horse if ever there was one. Who's the fortunate lady, may I inquire?"

Lord Barre's ensuing silence confirmed Sir John's suspicions. It was the first time he'd ever seen his friend at a loss for a word and a laugh.

"Well, out with it, man. I shan't comment adversely, if that's what is worrying you!"

"Then I'll tell you, John, although before I do, I want you to understand it is only an idea I have in mind, nothing more. But I am serious about it."

"I can see that!" Sir John said, laughing. "Marriage, especially at your age, is a very serious matter!"

"Then hear me out, John. The wife I have in mind is your daughter, little Mavreen. And don't speak, I pray you, until I have finished all I wish to say. I'm well aware there is an age difference of thirty-seven years, that I'm the same age as yourself, her father. But John, this is the disadvantageous aspect of the matter. I could raise your daughter to a position in society she could never hope otherwise to achieve. As my wife no one would dare raise an eyebrow as to her origins. Moreover, I'm rich enough to give her anything in the world her heart desires. Furthermore, I don't expect to live beyond my three-score years and ten, if as long, the way I indulge myself eating and drinking. So Mistress Mavreen, bless her heart, would be a widow in her early thirties. Time enough for her then to remarry and enjoy the pleasures a younger fellow could give her. Think on it, John, and I'm sure you'll agree the scheme has merit."

Sir John, not a devious man, said immediately, "I'm not against the proposition, Gilbert. To be truthful I was talking the other day to Clarrie about Mavreen's marriage prospects and I have to admit they look far from promising. You do her a great honor. But, of course, the girl is still but a child. At fifteen years of age. . . ."

"I'll wait a year or two. It's sufficient to know you don't object to my proposal, John. I feared you would consider me too old. I can't tell you how happy your approval has made me!"

Lord Barre raised his rotund form from the sofa and shook Sir John's hand with a complete return to his customary joviality. "I wouldn't have held it against you if you'd said the age difference was too much for your liking, yet the little minx has quite captivated me. I swear I'll be good to the girl, John, if she'll have me. You'll plead my cause, I trust? 'Tis more than likely she'll favor a younger man."

Sir John nodded thoughtfully.

"Perhaps it would be best not to rush the matter too hurriedly, Gilbert. Mavreen is but newly returned to London and is not yet aware of the restrictions her birth has imposed on her. Today's rebuff from Almack's was the first, and I have no doubt the first of many," he said.

Lord Barre looked indignant.

"Damned shame. But I can put that right, John. Every door in the country will be opened for Lady Barre, as you well know."

"You do the child an honor, Gilbert!" Sir John said again. "Her mother, you know, was only a parson's daughter, though I will say a girl with intelligence and refinement."

"I've no interest in Mavreen's past," his friend said, shrugging indifferently. "She's your daughter and a damned sight prettier than you, John!"

They laughed together, each well satisfied with the other's opinion.

"I'll speak of your proposal as soon as I can find an apt occasion," Sir John promised, as Lord Barre rose to take his leave. "First, I must apprise her of the truth about her breeding. It will come as a shock, I'll wager. The truth will doubtless help her to realize that your idea is not only kindly on your part but immensely advantageous to her."

"The child obviously loves you very dearly, John. I wish she had the same affection for me. I don't doubt she'll be proud to learn you are her father!"

Sir John sighed.

"I wish I had the same confidence, Gilbert. I don't lack for sensibility, but instinct tells me she might not take it too well. She is so damnably honest and straight herself in all her dealings. And she's totally innocent of the ways of the world. Clarrie tells me the girl has no inkling of our particular relationship, but then, how would she? Mavreen has lived most of her life in the simplest of country backgrounds; such forms of immorality would be unknown to her and adultery a very serious sin."

Lord Barre nodded sympathetically.

"Nevertheless, John, her natural affection for you and Clarrie, not to mention her keen intelligence, will assist her understanding. Besides, old fellow, you have no choice but to tell her the truth. Sooner or later someone will advise her of it and t'would be a deal better coming from you."

They parted on this agreement. When Mavreen came downstairs to rhapsodize to the visitor about his gift to her, she found him departed and Sir John alone.

She went across the room and in one of the most charming of her many pretty ways, gently touched his cheek with her cool fingertips.

"Why so serious, sir? Is something amiss?"

"I hope not, child. A lot depends upon the way one interprets a problem as to how serious or otherwise it is."

She bent and kissed his cheek affectionately.

"Aunt Clarrie would say that a problem shared is a problem halved!" she told him, twinkling. "So tell me what is worrying you, dear Uncle John, that I may remove that troublesome frown from your forehead."

He was much moved by her concern, and only with difficulty did he reach the decision to use this opening to confess the truth to her.

"My worry concerns yourself, Mavreen!" he said. "So sit yourself here beside me and hear me out. I need your understanding and your forbearance. May I have your word you will try to give me both?"

Surprised, and not a little alarmed by his serious tone of voice, Mavreen nodded and curled herself on the floor against his knees. His hand rested lightly on her head.

"I married many years ago a woman I did not love!" he said. "It was an arranged marriage; her father desirous of finding her a titled husband and I of restoring the family fortunes which, unfortunately, my own father had dissipated. Such marriages are common amongst royalty and the nobility. You understand me so far?"

Mavreen nodded.

"My wife after the birth of our second daughter was too ill to provide me with a further child. I had wanted an heir. However, that was not to be and my wife engaged a governess to assist her with the two girls. That governess, my dear, was your mother. She was an uncommonly pretty young woman, intelligent and kindly by nature. It was impossible for me not to be aware of the great charm and sweetness of her presence about my house. Your mother was a very well brought up young woman with the strictest of moral codes. I must confess that I did nothing to hide my personal regard from her, nor assisted her in her fight against temptation; indeed, I encouraged it for I found her quite irresistable."

He paused, uneasy because of Mavreen's unbroken silence. On any other occasion, she would have interrupted him continuously with questions.

"I am to blame for what finally happened!" he said. "I was much older than your mother, experienced in the ways of the world as she was not. Moreover, she was under my roof and I was therefore responsible for her. Nevertheless, I allowed my feelings for her to overrule my obligations. Unhappily, your mother did not tell me of your impending arrival. She left my house without stating her condition. In due course, my dear, you were born. I knew nothing of your existence until I received a letter from her written shortly before she died. In short, I am your father."

Imperceptibly, Mavreen had moved away from him as he spoke. Now she turned to face him, her eyes very large in a face become chalk white.

"My father was a naval officer!" she said coldly. "He died at sea. My mother told me so."

Sir John coughed.

"Your mother had to protect her unmarried state. It was necessary for her to invent a father for you."

"But why, when I already had a father living? Why could she not tell me your name, if indeed you are my father!"

The clear, accusing voice troubled the man as deeply as the look in the child's eyes. She demanded answers, explanations he would have preferred not to give her.

"I was already married, Mavreen. I could not give you or your mother my name."

She paused and then said coldly and quietly, "She protected you but you did not protect her!"

"I did not know she was with child!" Sir John pleaded for his daughter's understanding. "I did not even know where she was. She left my house without giving word where she had gone. If she had written to me, perhaps I could have helped her."

Mavreen made no reply. The momentous revelations that had been made to her were only just beginning to penetrate. She was that most unfortunate of all beings, a bastard. She had heard the farm laborers speak disparagingly or pityingly of a youth they called "that poor bastard." He had no standing in the community and his mother had been able to get only the most menial of kitchen work to support herself and her son.

"But for Mother and Father Sale, my mother and I might have starved!" she said aloud.

"Mavreen, I did not know your mother's plight. It was not my fault."

"Was it not, sir?" Mavreen replied, her voice filled with scorn and condemnation. "Who begat me if you did not?"

He was silent, wishing desperately that Clarissa would return and somehow ease his discomfiture.

"I fear this has been a shock to you, child. But when you become accustomed to the knowledge, I trust it will not seem so objectionable. If it comfort you to know, I hold you dearer than my other two daughters for whom I have little affection."

"That, too, is reprehensible!" Mavreen retorted with a child's cruel logic. "They are your flesh and blood, as I am, so it seems."

Sir John scratched his head, uncertain how to reach her. Her hostility was becoming more marked each minute that passed.

"Mavreen, I pray you not to judge me so harshly. I had a very great affection for your mother, as did she for me."

"You mean she loved you enough to give herself to you and you repaid her with a child that could only bring her disgrace. Does Aunt Clarrie know? But of course she does!" she went on bitterly. "I suspicion I am the only one who did not know the truth. I wish . . . I really do wish you had never told me!"

She sounded near to tears and Sir John said quickly, "Dear child, you would have had to be told the truth sooner or later. You will soon be of marriageable age. Any husband would require such knowledge, and. . . ."

"Did Gerard know?" Mavreen broke in, her cheeks now stained a dark red.

He was tempted to lie but decided against it. She accepted his silence as assent and said, "Then he must despise me! Yet he seemed so anxious to be friends that night he came here and Aunt Clarrie and I took care of him."

"My dear, Gerard was much taken with you and spoke of you often before he left London. He would not be uncharitable about such matters. In fact, the boy has a deep affection for your Aunt Clarrie despite. . . ."

He broke off, realizing he was once again in deep waters. But Mavreen's quick mind had completed his unfinished sentence.

"Despite the fact that poor Aunt Clarrie is your mistress. She has no place in society either. We are both disgraced."

"Come now!" Sir John said, more sternly than he had spoken so far to her. "That is not the case. Mistress Manton is much honored by my friends. I love her very dearly and would marry her were that possible. My friends have a deep respect for her, as, indeed, they will have for you, my daughter."

"I see, sir. Being the natural daughter of a peer still leaves room for pride, is that it?"

"Tush, child. You must not speak with such bitterness. You will not suffer, I promise you. Before long, you will be married and have the status your husband gives you."

For a moment, Mavreen stayed lost in thought. Then she said, "Then that state cannot come soon enough. I have already selected whom I will carry. If he will have me, the Vicomte Gerard de Valle shall be my husband."

Sir John stared down at her in dismay.

"But that cannot be! Gerard's family name is already

dishonored. The boy must marry someone of consequence, someone with wealth. And you, Mavreen, must do likewise. I did not mean to speak of this so soon, but now it would seem the proper moment to advise you. This afternoon, Gilbert, Lord Barre, asked my leave to pay court to you. That is a very great honor, and one I hope you will consider most seriously."

"Lord Barre—wants to marry me?" Mavreen gasped. "But he's old. Ugly! He's older even than you!"

"Nevertheless, Lord Barre has much to offer you, Mavreen. As his wife you would be one of the foremost ladies in the land. Your rank would be unassailable and your riches immense. Moreover, as Gilbert himself said, the thoughtful fellow, you will still be young enough for a second marriage when he departs this life. Such a union has many advantages for you, m'dear. Think on it."

"But I don't love him," Mavreen said flatly. "I like him well enough but I could never be a wife to him. Never! Never! Never!"

She gave him a long, hard stare and added, "Nor, if I may presume to say so, sir, should you suggest a loveless marriage to me seeing what became of your own—two mistresses and a natural child. I would prefer to raise my children in wedlock!"

She rose swiftly to her feet and without a backward glance at him, ran from the room, narrowly missing a collision with Clarissa who appeared with Hannah behind her, bringing refreshments.

When Hannah was gone Sir John looked at his mistress with such dismay that she at once asked what had happened to disturb him. Had he quarrelled with Mavreen? Nothing less could upset him so much.

Wretchedly he recounted his conversation with his daughter.

"I fear she may never wish to see me or speak to me again," he ended unhappily.

Clarissa hid her alarm. Instinct told her that she might have handled the confession, if such it was, in a less abrupt and more acceptable manner. It was typical of dear John's impetuosity to blurt out the truth so suddenly. Naturally, it had come as a shock. Mavreen would need time to adjust to it, she told him. The arrival of Princess Caroline would shortly be upon them and this would help to distract the child for she was wildly excited by the royal occasion. "She will not be able to avoid conversation with you, John. You will have much to tell us of what happens at court since Lord Malmesbury is a good friend of yours!" she said consolingly.

The king had chosen the tactful and wily Lord Malmesbury to act as his envoy and he had successfully negotiated for the hand of Princess Caroline of Brunswick on behalf of the Prince of Wales. He was now engaged in escorting her to England for the wedding.

"Mavreen will want to hear all you can relate to us," Clarissa continued. "I know she has promised to write to Dickon and the children with a full account of every detail. She will speak to you then, if not before. Her curiosity will overcome her injured pride!"

She put her arm round Sir John's shoulders and hugged him maternally. "Do not look so woe begone, dear John. The child will get over it, I promise you. At the moment she is reacting just as you might were you in her position. You are both hot headed and impetuous and you cannot complain if she so resembles you."

"Where would I be without you, m'dear!" he said fondly, kissing her plump hand. "I will leave the matter in your hands."

But Clarissa was not as convinced as she sounded. She was made further uneasy by Mavreen's refusal to discuss the matter with her. Loving though she remained toward Clarissa—perhaps even more so than before—Mavreen made no mention of Sir John's name and no reply when Clarissa spoke of him. It was as if for her, he no longer existed.

CHAPTER TEN
1795

Mavreen lay on her bed staring at the patch of blue sky to be seen through her casement window. She was fifteen years old and it was her first experience of unhappiness.

Her mother's death, following upon several months of ill health, had been a shock and she had suffered a terrible sense of loss. But at the tender age of seven, she had very quickly recovered her natural joie de vivre.

Mavreen had loved her mother very dearly. Letitia's memory was a private treasure in the girl's heart; her dearest possession, a small gold locket containing her mother's miniature.

She held it now, regarding the pale, serene face smiling gently back at her.

"Oh, Mama!" she thought bitterly. "How could you have allowed yourself to be so terribly wronged!"

Sir John—and she would never again call him "Uncle John"—had spoken of their deep affection for one another but Mavreen could not envisage her quiet, self-effacing mother setting aside her moral convictions for any purpose whatever, least of all for a man already married and who could never, therefore, make her his wife.

With the harsh judgment of the young, Mavreen condemned her mother's seducer, for so she now saw Sir John. His generosity and kindness to her seemed now, in retrospect, the reparations of a guilty man. It was obvious to her that her father, if such were the unsavory truth, was a man without scruples. Notwithstanding the assault upon her own mother's person, he was even now enjoying an immoral liaison with poor darling Aunt Clarrie! And worst of all, Aunt Clarrie defended him when she must know how terribly she, too, was being wronged.

As for her own part in all this, Mavreen was slowly

facing the fact that she was born out of wedlock, a bastard, with less standing even than the servant girl, Rose, who waited upon them at table. Those who knew the truth could only have pity for her. For that humiliation alone, she would never forgive Sir John Danesfield.

Her first instinct was to leave London at once and return to the loving bosom of her "family" in Sussex. The Sales knew the truth about her but still loved her. To Dickon, she was a princess no matter what the circumstances of her birth! But two factors stayed her restless feet—the first being the distress she would bring to poor Aunt Clarrie were she to go away; the second, barely admitted even to herself, the thought that if she left London, she had even less hope of seeing Gerard again.

Color stained Mavreen's pale cheeks as the memory of the young vicomte possessed her imagination. She seemed never able to remove him from her thoughts for long. Until now, when suddenly she seemed to have grown up and left childhood behind her, Mavreen had not seriously considered love in her life. The boy who five years ago had fallen out of the carriage at her feet was now the young man dominating her heart and thoughts. She knew that she loved Gerard de Valle.

During these first reactions to the shock her father had dealt her, was the bitter knowledge that Gerard, a viscount in his own right, could never ask for her in marriage. She could neither expect nor desire him to return her affection.

That dear, kind Lord Barre had actually tried to remedy her situation by offering to marry her, was one solitary ray of warmth. The absurdity of wedding a man three times her age would have been laughable but for the goodness of heart she was sure prompted his proposal. He had felt sorry for her.

"But I will have no man's pity!" Mavreen said aloud. "He who marries me shall first beg my hand and prove his love is foremost, else I shall never marry."

Her pride was small comfort for her lost happiness and there was even less comfort in the knowledge that she could do naught to remedy the position. Poor Aunt Clarrie, though, was attempting to console her.

She knocked on the door and herself brought in a tray of hot chocolate to Mavreen.

The steel around Mavreen's heart melted. She dissolved into childish tears, and Clarissa gathered her into her arms.

"There, there, my precious! Just you enjoy a good cry!" She sighed deeply. "I'll have Sir John transported to the American Colonies for choosing so untimely a fashion to enlighten you. Although, my dear, I am certain he had no desire to distress you. In truth, he is much upset himself."

Mavreen sat up, angrily brushing away her tears.

"How can you defend him, dear Aunt Clarrie? Even now he wrongs you just as he once wronged my mother. I hate him and shall ever do so!"

"Tush, tush! Hate is an ugly word, dear, and best used only for one's enemies. Sir John is never that. He loves you and has your well-being much at heart."

"You mean he wants to marry me to a gentleman older even than himself? Is that for my well-being, Aunt Clarrie?" Mavreen said indignantly.

Clarissa caught her lower lip anxiously between her teeth. She did not approve of John's plan to marry Mavreen to Lord Barre, however much it might raise the girl's social status.

"Let us not talk of such serious matters as marriage, my dear!" she said pacifically, for it was not in her nature to countermand any wish Sir John might have in such regard. "I have something a deal more exciting to tell you of. You are to be invited to a soirée!"

"A soirée?" Mavreen echoed, eyes widening in surprise. "Where? When is it to be? Who has asked me, Aunt Clarrie? What gown should I wear? Will there be dancing?"

"It is an evening dinner party to be given next week by my friend, the Baroness von Eburhard," Clarissa explained. "We have intrigued together so that you may attend her house as a distant connection from Yorkshire, since we cannot admit to your true identity. It is unlikely that anyone will inquire too deeply into the matter. You are unlikely to meet any of her guests again, so you should be quite safe!"

Clarissa saw the tightening of Mavreen's mouth and the proud tilting of her head. Tactfully she chose to ignore them.

"A soirée at the Eburhards' will be a great experience for you, my dear. We have not much time but I shall arrange for you to have a special gown made and I will instruct you fully in the correct protocol. It falls upon the day of the royal wedding which is in itself a day for celebration. The evening's guest of honor is a Spanish marquis who will be accompanied by his daughter. That means there will be young gentlemen present, too, so you will not find the company tedious.

"Your chocolate is cooling, my dear!" she said. "When you have drunk it, perhaps we might take a walk together. It is a beautiful afternoon and we should make the most of this spring sunshine. I will attend you downstairs."

When she was gone, Mavreen jumped off the bed and ran to the window. It was, indeed, a beautifully sunny day. She had spent far too long lying on her bed sorrowing. Life was still beautiful and interesting. Now she had not only the arrival of the new Princess of Wales to look forward to, but her first grown-up party.

She sang softly to herself as she changed her dress and brushed her hair. She was still humming as she reached the top of the staircase, but just in time, she saw Clarissa looking up at her and she quickly ceased her singing and slowed her pace to one more befitting a girl whose life was recently ruined beyond repair.

Mavreen was elated as she and Clarissa made their way by carriage from Richmond to St. James's Park. It was a fine spring morning with the sun shining and no hint of a rain shower to mar the pleasant drive.

Sir John had told them that the princess was expected to leave Greenwich in time to arrive at St. James's Palace for luncheon and had warned them to take up their place early. Clarissa began to worry as their carriage approached London through streets gaily decorated with flags and draperies. The crowds were so thick she feared it would be impossible to get anywhere near the Palace by midday.

Their destination was the park and they arrived in good time to join the large gathering of people with the same intention as they. On Clarissa's instructions, the coachman went to seek information on the royal procession and came back with the news that Princess Caroline had been delayed at Greenwich, although no one was certain of the reason for the delay. Rumor had it that she was not "quite up to expectations."

Clarissa looked at the man crossly and ordered him back to his driving seat. She turned to Mavreen and smiled a little doubtfully.

"These *on dits* are not to be taken seriously, my dear. I would sooner believe the report in the London *Chronicle* which describes Her Highness as having 'teeth as white as ivory, a good complexion, a beautiful hand and arm' and that 'certainly she may be deemed a very pretty woman.' I cannot think the prince will be disappointed with such a bride."

They would, of course, have a better picture of the princess before the wedding. There was to be a dinner in her honor at the palace this evening and Sir John would learn all the details from his friend, Lord Malmesbury, who would be one of the guests. Sir John had told Clarissa that Malmesbury was much involved in this historic occasion, having been to Brunswick to make arrangements for the princess's journey to England, a highly dangerous undertaking since they had had to pass through France, dodging the revolutionary armies.

It was fortunate that Clarissa had had the foresight to provide a meal since time crawled on to two o'clock before distant cheers, growing ever louder, heralded the approach of the royal entourage. In her eagerness to miss nothing, Mavreen stood up to stare at the seven carriages, manned by grooms and coachmen in scarlet and blue liveries and silver wigs. They were escorted by a detachment of the Prince of Wales's own regiment, the Tenth Hussars, with their fur busbies and swinging jackets. Eagerly she strained her neck to catch a glimpse of the princess in the most grand of all the carriages, a glass coach drawn by the famous Windsor Greys.

At first Mavreen did not recognize the rather plump,

fair-haired, over-rouged woman sitting with her back to the horses. She wore a white satin dress that did nothing to enhance her appearance and it was difficult to reconcile this figure with the description of the princess Clarissa had quoted from the *Chronicle*.

Seated opposite the princess was the far more imposing figure of Lady Jersey, reputed to be the prince's mistress, though Clarissa had not deemed it necessary to pass this information to Mavreen. Lady Jersey had recently been appointed one of the princess's ladies of the bedchamber, together with Mrs. Harcourt, the lady who had been sent to Brunswick as the princess's official chaperone. It was the sophisticated, haughty, beautifully groomed Lady Jersey who best fitted Mavreen's idea of royalty.

Then the procession moved out of sight and Mavreen was left with an odd feeling of sadness, promoted by the overheard remark of an old woman standing nearby, "Poor young creature! I pities her, I does. Fancy having to stand up and marry a man you never clapped eyes on—even if he is a handsome young prince!"

Certainly his portraits showed him as slim and strong, but Sir John had said that though but thirty-two years of age, the prince weighed seventeen stone. She had been shocked to hear this. She disliked very fat people, with the exception of the rotund Lord Barre who seemed more portly than obese, and was always so charming to her that somehow he made her feel like a princess herself.

Her curiosity about the royal family was curbed until the following day when Sir John arrived in the late afternoon as promised. She had resolved not to speak one word to him, so as he came into the drawing room, Mavreen remained seated, and listened in fascinated silence as he gave an account of the happenings at the Palace.

"I fear the Princess Caroline is not to the Prince of Wales's taste," he informed them. "Malmesbury tells me that she cannot, with the best good will, be described as a fastidious woman. Nor is she endowed with tact. Owing to the machinations of Lady Jersey who clearly hoped to insult her, there was no one to meet her at Greenwich, save the staff and inmates of the hospital who had turned out to cheer her. The princess made a silly, flippant joke typical of her, Malmesbury says. She looked at the crippled pensioners standing outside the chapel and said, 'What, is every Englishman without an arm or a leg?' "

Clarissa's face revealed her disapproval. Mavreen was longing to ask for further details but contained herself with difficulty. So far she had said no further words to Sir John than a cold "Good evening, sir!" which politeness demanded.

" 'Twas impolite of the king and queen to have had Lady Jersey made a lady of the princess's bedchamber!" Sir John went on. "She is forever making a great nuisance of herself. Malmesbury tells me she was impertinent enough at Greenwich to express herself dissatisfied with the princess's mode of dress. She actually persuaded the unfortunate lady to change from a not unattractive muslin gown and blue satin petticoat to a far less becoming one all in white."

"Indeed, we saw it!" Clarissa said. "Poor soul! It cannot be pleasant for her arriving in a strange country to such a welcome!"

Sir John shrugged.

"From all accounts, the princess is not in the least discomforted. She spent most of the journey from Greenwich relating in her far from melodious accent, an account of her love affair with a man unequal to her station in life and from whom she had perforce to part. Nevertheless, Malmesbury says she is a good humored lady and friendly to everyone. It is a vast pity that her personal cleanliness is not attended to and that she is so coarse and vulgar about her speech. The Prince of Wales must dislike this even more than most."

"But surely fastidiousness is not lacking in a princess?" Clarissa protested. "She is, after all, the daughter of the duke of Brunswick!"

"That is as may be!" replied Sir John. "I regret that the prince's instant dislike of his future wife can be matched only by hers for him. Malmesbury informs me the prince was drinking heavily before and at the dinner and deeply offended the princess by drinking punch from Lady Jersey's glass. You will never believe, dear Clarrie, the princess's reaction to this insult. She snatched a neighbor's pipe and puffed out smoke at him."

Involuntarily, Mavreen clapped her hands in approval. She longed to say, "Well done, Princess Caroline!" for she, herself, would not have allowed such insulting behavior from the man she was about to wed. But she remembered her vow of silence toward Sir John and let her applause speak for her.

"It is all very distressing!" Clarissa commented. "I hope, since the Prince of Wales did not afford his bride great welcome, that the other members of the royal family played their part?"

Sir John nodded.

"The king greeted her most affectionately, but the queen was clearly not happy with her son's bride. Nor yet his sisters, the princesses. I am afraid she was well aware of their feelings and it bred in her a defensive manner which manifested itself in vulgar chatter quite unseemly in a future queen. Malmesbury felt pity for her, as, indeed, do I."

Mavreen, too, felt sorry for the newly arrived princess. She remembered her own disappointment on discovering how gross was the Prince of Wales and understood how reluctant any woman might feel to be wedding such a man. Involuntarily, her thoughts went to Gerard, slim, strong, perfectly proportioned, as a man should be. She longed to ask Sir John if there was still no news of him. But pride forbade the eager question.

"So you managed to be in place in St. James's for the royal cortège yesterday!" Sir John addressed them both. "I hope it made a pleasant outing for you."

Mavreen affected to be repositioning some daffodils in a cut glass vase and not to have caught her father's glance in her direction. Clarissa replied for them both, assuring Sir John they had greatly enjoyed their day. When Clarissa told Sir John about the soirée for which she had engineered Mavreen an invitation, his reaction was far from favorable. In a constrained voice he said, "That is perhaps a little unfortunate. Clarrie, my dear. You were not, of course, to know it but—" he hesitated and then went on even more awkwardly, "—there are

certain reasons why I would have preferred Mavreen did
not go to the Eburhards'."

He broke off, uncomfortably aware of the accusing look
in his daughter's direct gaze. He felt unhappy and disappointed. He had hoped that by now Mavreen would
have recovered from the shock Clarissa seemed to think
he had inflicted on her.

The fact was, Gerard de Valle was back in England
and although Clarissa could not know of it, the baroness
had arranged this soirée somewhat hurriedly at the request of the marquis de Faenza who was anxious to
further his daughter's acquaintance with the young
vicomte.

Gerard was only to be in England for a few weeks. He
was now an aide to the comte d'Artois and engaged upon
some secret assignment concerning the enlistment of men
and money for the continued struggle against the French
regime. It was the marquis's hope that within this short
period of time available, a betrothal could be affected between Gerard and his daughter, Mercedes.

Sir John had promised to assist in the matter with encouragement to Gerard to pursue the young woman, and
although the boy had not as yet shown an active enthusiasm for the idea, he had not spoken against it. However, Mavreen's vulnerability to the indubitably handsome
Gerard was of concern to Sir John, the more so since
Clarissa had added her own suspicions that his daughter
was much taken with the young vicomte and might
easily, at her impressionable age, fall in love with him.
They had agreed it would be best for all concerned to
keep the two apart.

He could see no way out of the situation. Clarissa had
taken so much trouble to arrange the soirée to please the
child, and now only illness could excuse Mavreen's absence at such a late hour. He decided to chance throwing Mavreen into Gerard's company rather than risk
further invoking her antagonism. Her continued coldness
and silence distressed him.

Mavreen was not the only one to suffer from an excess
of pride. He, too, was disconcerted that his daughter
should so dislike the discovery that he was her father.

He was, after all, a peer of the realm and one who enjoyed great popularity amongst his friends. That a fifteen-year-old by-blow should turn up her nose at such a parent was an affront. If he had not been so uncommonly fond of the little baggage, he would, he vowed, send her posthaste back to Sussex to recover her temper amongst the chickens and cows!

Secretly, he admired her. He liked pride in a woman. He resolved, in his turn, to remain as silent with her as she was with him.

But by the end of the evening, made uncomfortable for all three of them by this state of armed neutrality, Sir John began to weaken in his resolve. After one such long period of silence, he said suddenly, "I have been thinking of buying a horse!"

Both females looked up from their tapestry work in surprise.

"A horse?" Clarissa echoed. "But, John, you never ride any horse but old Raven and. . . ."

"Not for myself, my dear, for Mavreen. She has few opportunities to ride here in London and the thought struck me that there is plenty of room in your stables for another beast."

He saw the sudden excitement in Mavreen's eyes and continued as if he were addressing Clarissa alone, "As you do not ride, m'dear, it would be necessary to employ a groom to escort Mavreen when she wished to take exercise. It crossed my mind that the Sales' eldest boy—Dickon, I think his name is—might be enticed to London to assist your man, Harry, and act as groom when Mavreen needed him. What say you, my dear?"

Clarissa understood the bribe very well. But she was uncertain if the child would rise to the bait.

"I think it is a perfect idea, John. And I know Mavreen would wish it, too, would you not, dear?"

Sir John looked pointedly at Mavreen. He was determined to force her to speak.

"And you, my dear? You haven't told me your opinions?"

Mavreen stood up, drew in her breath and straightened her back.

"If Dickon can be persuaded to come to London, I'm sure he would serve Aunt Clarrie very well!" she said, and dropping Sir John a curtsy, she kissed Clarissa goodnight, professed herself too sleepy to remain awake another moment, and retired, head high, to bed.

"Damn! The little minx!" Sir John exploded when she was beyond hearing him. "She would not be bribed to talk to me. And I thought I'd won her over."

Despite herself, Clarissa laughed.

"Surely you did not really think so?" she said and went to him to put her arms round him. "You are ever forgetting she is your daughter, John. It is her spirit you most admire in her, and did from the first time you set eyes on her, for I well remember you telling me so. Would you really want her on bended knee?"

She felt the tenseness ease from his shoulders and his face broke into a smile.

He sighed. "She should have been a boy, Clarrie. A woman has to submit and it's going to come hard for her if she will not do so."

"It isn't hard for a woman to surrender if she loves well enough," Clarissa said, caressing his cheek as was her wont.

He caught her hand and kissed it with passion.

"Ah, for you, my sweeting, perhaps it is not!"

"Nor for any woman who loves as I love you!" she replied softly. "Hearken to me, John, for I am wiser than you in these matters. Do not force Mavreen to marry Gilbert. I doubt not he will be kind to her, but she can have no love in her heart for a man of his age. Let the future take care of itself, my dearest. She is still but a child."

Sir John drew a deep sigh. He wanted to please Clarrie who, as he approached old age, was yearly becoming more and more dear to him. It was rarely, if ever, that she requested anything of him, for herself or anyone else. It behoove him, therefore, to accede when she did make her desires known. But he could not act against his convictions and he was far from convinced that such a marriage would not be beneficial to Mavreen. There would be time enough for love when old Gilbert was laid to rest, and by then, as Lady Barre, Mavreen could take her choice of husbands. Clarrie, he told himself, was sentimental like all women and far too romantic.

"Enough of talk for tonight!" he said. "I have not seen you for close on a week, my dear, and the girl is long since abed. Let us go likewise. Or——?" he asked with a twinkle "——are you yet another female in this household who is not inclined to submit?"

For answer, she took his hand and holding the candle, led him upstairs to the privacy of her bed.

CHAPTER ELEVEN

1795

Gerard waited in the drawing room at Wyfold House. Lady Danesfield and her daughters had not yet completed their preparations for the evening soirée. Sir John stood beside him, an imposing figure in royal blue velvet coat and breeches, white lace ruffle, frilled shirt and white silk stockings, his short white wig freshly curled and powdered. Gerard himself was without wig for they were fast going out of fashion among the younger generation.

"A word with you, m'boy, while I have the opportunity," Sir John said quietly when the footman had left the room and they were alone. "About the guests at the party tonight. . . ."

Gerard already knew that the beautiful Mercedes de Faenza was to be present; moreover that the entire party had been arranged so that he and the Spanish marquis's daughter could further their acquaintance. Sir John had several times stressed his view that Gerard should consider the good lady as his future wife.

Not unnaturally Gerard was flattered to be told that a woman of her wealth and breeding was sufficiently enamored of his good looks and charm to disregard his impecunious state and profess herself willing to receive his attention. It seemed that neither she nor the marquis were discouraged by the slur upon Gerard's father's name.

"There will be a young lady at the party with whom you are acquainted," Sir John broke in on Gerard's musings. "To be precise, my daughter Mavreen. The baroness will introduce her as a distant relative of her own who has come down from Yorkshire to London on a sojourn. None of the other guests know Mavreen's real identity and I have to ask you to pretend that you do not recognize her. Indeed, it would be best if you speak as little as possible to one another, lest an ill-chosen remark reveal the truth to some bystander and confound us all."

Gerard, who had not forgotten the young girl, was intrigued and amused. He gladly gave his agreement to the ruse. Now that Sir John had brought Mavreen to mind, he began to recall her fascinating, beautiful eyes, the freshness of her shining hair and creamy whiteness of her skin. Her radiance and intelligence had enlivened everything and everyone around her. He remembered, too, her endless, eager questions and the variety of expressions that flowed continuously across her face.

Gerard had known many women in the years since he had last met Mavreen. He had discovered not only their variety of physical forms, but their infinite wiles and whims. He had loved several women of differing ages, classes and background, but without really losing his heart to any. He had come nearest to doing so when he had spent a week in near-solitary confinement with an Austrian countess in her thirties. This woman had taught him many lessons in the art of loving; and his gratitude to her for the experience was heightened by a close affection for her. Young as he was, he realized that he had been the most fortunate of youths to have such a kindly and competent teacher in the art of love. They had parted with sadness when Gerard was recalled to the service of the count d'Artois.

Mavreen did not know the evening would bring a reunion with Gerard, but she felt happy and self-confident in the beautiful gown Aunt Clarrie had chosen for her. It was made of rose-colored taffeta, with frill after frill falling from her small waist to the tip of her satin shoes. The hairdresser from Bond Street had come to the house and curled her hair high at the back of her head, leaving a small fringe at her forehead and curls over her ears, with two pink moiré ribbons tied one behind the other across the top of her head.

The somewhat Grecian style of hair and dress made her look several years older and more sophisticated, which pleased her greatly. Clarissa and the servants had openly expressed their admiration and thereby added to her confidence.

Since she was supposed to be a houseguest of the von Eburhards she arrived early at Arlington Street and was greeted warmly and with many compliments by Aunt Clarrie's friend, Lisa. The baroness was short, dumpy and flaxen-haired. She was wearing a puce-colored gown, the skirt opened in front to show a cream satin petticoat, the bodice cut low, barely concealing the cleft between her ample breasts.

Mavreen was enveloped in a firm embrace.

"My dear, you are even prettier than Clarrie described you," Lisa said. "Give me your cloak but keep your mittens on. Your dress is quite lovely, child! Now come, I want to introduce you to my husband."

Mavreen was puzzled. The baroness's voice was vaguely familiar, reminiscent of that of the unknown lady she had surprised with a lover in Aunt Clarrie's guest room. But that was impossible! The baroness was married and. . . . The memory vanished as Lisa took her arm and led her through the double doors into the salon.

Mavreen's quick, curious glances took in the size of the room, at least three times that of Aunt Clarrie's drawing room at Richmond. The furniture was dark and heavy and highly polished. On the walls, in place of pictures, were beautiful tapestries showing forest hunting scenes. Huge bronze branched candelabra lit the room with hundreds of spears of flame. She noticed also an enormous cabinet full of delicate Dresden china. Fat cherubs and plump maidens festooned by chiffon clouds were painted on the ceiling. The air was heavily perfumed.

By the fireplace stood the imposing figure of Baron von Eburhard wearing full military uniform and three impressive rows of decorations. He had a fierce face, white whiskers and a white wig, and Mavreen observed delightedly that he was a live version of the portrait beneath which he was standing.

The severity of his face relaxed as he caught sight of the pretty girl on his wife's arm. Lisa had mentioned something about a distant relative but had omitted to tell him the child was so charming.

Mavreen could have listened to the baron and his tales of the royal family all evening but the room was rapidly filling with people announced each in turn in the stentorian voice of the butler. To her regret the baron left her to greet his guests. Growing a little nervous at the sight of so many beautifully-gowned ladies and imposing-looking gentlemen, Mavreen welcomed the sight of the portly Lord Barre as he hurried across the room to her side. His compliments were as reassuring as his company.

It was not, therefore, until a pause in their conversation when Lord Barre's attention was distracted by the arrival of her father, that Mavreen turned once more to survey the glittering room—and saw Gerard.

He was talking to a young woman of astonishing beauty, golden-skinned, with great dark almond-shaped eyes and Titian hair piled high on her head. She was an arresting figure, with jeweled combs and huge violet-colored flowers adorning her hair. Her violet satin dress was heavily embroidered with silver and a silver lace mantilla was draped delicately about her bare shoulders.

Mavreen's instinctive reaction to the intense pleasure of seeing Gerard was to impel her forward to greet him, but her father anticipated her intention and laid a quick restraining hand on her arm.

"Remember you do not know each other, my dear, and besides—" he added in a low tone "—Gerard is engaged in conversation with Donna de Faenza. It would not be proper for you to approach him."

He watched the bleak look creep into his daughter's eyes and was much discomforted.

Mavreen's emotions were in turmoil. She was at one and the same time happy to see Gerard again and yet humiliated by the reminder that she was here in this house on false pretenses and must hide her true feelings as well as her identity. With quick intelligence, she realized that Gerard must already have been told of her presence here and given good reasons why he, in turn, should not greet her as an old friend. The knowledge was an even deeper humiliation.

She spoke no word of her thoughts to Sir John, but in order to discomfort him, asked him in a loud voice if he would be good enough to present her to his wife and daughters, who, she said, she had not yet had the pleasure of meeting. Her father, she was well aware, had been trying to avoid the encounter.

He had no alternative now but to take her over to the fireplace where Mavreen saw a tall, thin, grey-gowned lady of none too personable a mien, seated between two equally colorless daughters. None of the three looked as if she was enjoying herself and when Sir John made his introductions, no one attempted to return Mavreen's smile; their greetings were a mere formality. No gentleman in the room seemed inclined to talk to them and Mavreen was not surprised, although her pity was momentarily stirred.

She stared unobtrusively at Lady Danesfield, unable to engender any liking for Sir John's wife—the woman whose presence had barred her father from marrying her mother. As for her half-sisters, Mavreen was bitterly disappointed in them. She could see little advantage in trying to establish a mutual relationship with them, not even to provoke Sir John.

She did not, however, have time to search for further ways to irritate her father for the butler was announcing that dinner was about to be served. Her spirits, already low, dropped to zero as she noticed the proprietary way in which the gorgeous Spanish lady leaned on Gerard's arm as he escorted her from the room. But the kindly baroness, knowing nothing of Mavreen's friendship with Gerard or Sir John's desire to keep them apart, had thoughtfully seated them beside one another at the table, imagining that her two youngest guests would enjoy one another's company. Mercedes de Faenza she had placed opposite Gerard where, if she wished, she could continue her coquetry across the centerpiece decorations.

When Mavreen, escorted to the dining room by the ever attentive Lord Barre, saw Gerard's place name beside her own, her pleasure and excitement were boundless. With difficulty, she managed to keep her eyes on her lap until Gerard seated himself beside her. Then she heard his voice with the familiar French accent, saying, "Good evening, *petit écureuil!*"

She looked up, her eyes eagerly searching his face for changes that might have occurred since she had last seen him two years ago. But although he was taller and man instead of boy, he had not otherwise altered. But Gerard noticed an amazing difference in Mavreen. When he had last seen her, she had been pretty with a promise of beauty to come. Now she was a fascinatingly lovely young woman—different in so many particulars yet with a familiar glint of amusement in her eyes as she saw the admiration in his.

"Will you not bid me good evening?" he asked.

She laughed happily, then composed her face into an expression of mock seriousness.

"Pray do not address me, sir!" she said severely, "for we have not been properly introduced."

"Indeed! Then may I present myself to you, mademoiselle? The Vicomte Gerard de Valle, at your service!"

The serving by the liveried footmen of the first dishes momentarily prevented their further conversation. Gerard had time to think and found himself intrigued. The young girl beside him was so different from the woman who had occupied his thoughts before dinner. Mercedes, with her huge dark slumberous eyes and fully developed rounded figure was entirely a creature of the senses. She was sophisticated without being particularly intelligent, letting her ample charms attract men to her as bees to a honey pot. Her coquetry was composed of deep languorous looks, unaccompanied by smiles or laughter but suggestive of deeper passions to stir a man's blood. Gerard had been more than a little interested.

But now, the young girl beside him occupied his full

attention. Mavreen's curious hazel green eyes sparkled with laughter and fun. Her vitality shone in every part of her, from her bright golden hair to the quick graceful movements of her hands. Her mouth, rosy and full-lipped, was constantly changing with her mood; her face mobile and charming be she serious and thoughtful or laughingly mischievous.

She was not, he thought, one woman, but all women. And this was the daughter Sir John had wished a boy!

"When last I heard news of you, you were in Sussex," he said when he was once more able to address her. "Have you word of my Colombe, Mademoiselle Mavreen?"

"Oh, yes, indeed! Dickon has broken in the foal and Gerard, I have wonderful news to tell you. Dickon is almost surely coming to live in London. He is to become Aunt Clarrie's new groom and I am to have a horse of my own and can ride every day if I wish."

Her pleasure in so simple an arrangement captivated Gerard. Not an hour earlier, Mercedes had professed herself filled with gloom because her father had bought her the most costly emerald necklace and ear pendants, and green, she told him, was a color she disliked.

Across the table Mercedes de Faenza toyed with her food. Mavreen, like Gerard, ate heartily. Between mouthfuls she questioned him. How long would he remain in London? Had he had news of his poor mother? What had he been doing these last two years in France? Was the fighting very unpleasant? Had he been wounded? Had he witnessed the terrible Madame Guillotine? Had he ever met Nelson? What view did he hold about Napoleon Bonaparte?

Gerard called a halt, professing himself unable to remember the first question.

"Still storing information, *écureuil?*" he teased her gently.

A soft flush colored Mavreen's cheeks.

"I am aware I talk too much. Aunt Clarrie tells me I must learn to curb my tongue, and she is quite right. But, Gerard, there is so much I want to know."

"And I, too!" Gerard said warmly. "I want to know about you. Are you still studying your books? Do you enjoy London life? When did you return from Sussex? And are you fully recovered from your scarlatina? How is Mr. Glover and. . . ?"

"You are teasing me, Gerard!" she broke in laughing. "I will not ask you one further question. I shall remain silent until the meal is finished. Would that be to your liking?"

"I knew you could not keep your word, for there already is yet another question!" Gerard rebuked her. "Moreover, it would not be to my liking for I should find it a dead bore! You may talk as much as you wish and never heed Mistress Manton's dictums."

Mavreen was filled with an intense happiness. It was complete and perfectly satisfying until she looked up and caught Sir John's warning glance. Only then did she remember that she was not permitted to "know" Gerard, or he to "know" her.

Defiantly, she turned back to Gerard but he was looking at the marquis's daughter seated opposite him. Mavreen could not see Gerard's face but there was no mistaking the expression in the woman's eyes. Inexperienced as Mavreen was in the ways of flirtation, she knew instinctively that the Spanish noblewoman was trying her utmost to attract Gerard's attention. And Gerard must be responding for he was being rewarded with a tender smile.

Jealousy, deep and painful, lodged in Mavreen's throat so that she could not swallow her food. Nervously, she sipped at the wine before her. The blood seemed to be racing in her veins and her hands encircling the goblet were shaking. Mercedes de Faenza was very beautiful. If her jewelry was an example of her wealth, she was very, very rich. She looked at home in this luxurious, aristocratic setting. Mavreen felt gauche and inferior and that it would be unreasonable to blame Gerard if he were at this moment wishing himself seated beside Mercedes de Faenza rather than beside her.

But Gerard had no such desire. He, too, had recognised the invitation in Mercedes' burning gaze and knew that the conquest was his if he so wished it. But he had more urgent matters on his mind. Mercedes could wait. He wanted to know more of the girl next to him.

He had never met one quite like her, her innocence combining with a spontaneous warmth which he believed was intended for him alone. Yet he could not be sure since she showed the same happy interest in her conversation with the elderly gentleman on her left. Despite his advancing years, the old gentleman seemed greatly interested in her. Gerard disliked the way his eyes turned so frequently to the tender white curves of Mavreen's bosom. Although merely a glance, and quite within the bounds of propriety, Gerard found himself resenting it as if it were a direct affront. Surprised by the intensity of his thoughts, Gerard realized his resentment was irrational. He was not guardian of Mavreen's virtue.

Nevertheless, he turned to the baroness at his left and asked her the name of the gentleman to whom Mavreen was speaking.

"Do you not know him, vicomte? He is Lord Barre, one of Sir John's closest friends." She added in a conspiratorial whisper, "I have heard rumors, though I will not vouch for it, that there could be a betrothal before long."

"A betrothal?" Gerard echoed stupidly. "Between whom?"

The baroness winked at him knowingly.

"Why, between winter and spring!" she said archly. "Can you not see for yourself how Lord Barre hangs upon the child's every word? I don't doubt he will wed her if she will have him. 'Twould be an excellent match for her, poor child."

She broke off, aware that she was being indiscreet. She did not wish the young viscount to question her as to Mavreen's background, since she had given Clarissa her word not to talk of it to anyone.

Gerard made play with his food. He was no longer in the least hungry. In fact, he felt ill. No matter what the advantages, marriage between that fat old man and his little Mavreen was unthinkable. The baroness must be mistaken. It would be an offense against nature, a profanity. Mavreen would surely never consent to such an arrangement. Yet the two seemed on excellent terms, a fact confirmed by Mavreen herself when she turned back to Gerard, saying, "My head is positively swollen with compliments. Lord Barre, I fear, is as blind to my faults as you are aware of them!"

"I am not aware of any fault in you, Mademoiselle Mavreen!" Gerard replied, his voice no longer teasing but in earnest. "If I should have given you cause for thinking so, then please allow me to correct such misinterpretation."

"So I do not ask too many questions and talk excessively much?" Mavreen asked.

"It was you, not I, who said so," he reminded her. "I remarked only that I could not keep abreast of your questions with answers since there were so many!"

Mavreen's face broke into a smile.

"That is true. Nonetheless, sir, I sense your disapproval!"

"Then your senses mislead you!" Gerard said in a low voice. "For I am much fascinated by everything about you."

Mavreen caught her breath. The raillery between them had suddenly ceased and in its place was a current of emotion stronger than either had imagined or intended.

As always when she felt most deeply, words deserted Mavreen. She clasped her hands together beneath the white table covering, trying to still their trembling. But at once she felt the firm warm touch of Gerard's hand covering her own. Their emotions communicated through their touch. Gerard, too, began to tremble. Neither spoke, for their hands were speaking for them.

Unseen by either, so lost were they in their myriad emotions, two pairs of eyes were observing them with anger and hostility—Sir John's a steely blue, and Mercedes de Faenza's a burning black fire. Sir John could barely contain his irritation. Gerard had assured him earlier in the evening that he would avoid Mavreen; not that the boy could be blamed for sitting next to her, but he could have confined himself to a passing remark and concentrated his attentions upon Lisa von Eburhard. From the looks of things, the foolish boy had eyes and ears for no one but the girl and judging by the high color in her cheeks, Gerard had clearly succeeded in exciting her attentions. The fury in the face of Mercedes de Faenza confirmed Sir John's opinions. She was staring at the couple with a very ill-concealed jealousy. If Gerard were not careful, he would lose the opportunity so painstakingly prepared for him. The marquis's daughter was not one to be slighted with impunity.

Gerard neither knew nor cared what his intended fiancée was feeling. He, himself, was too overcome by the desire to take the beautiful young girl beside him in his arms, carry her far away from the crowded room and kiss her until she pleaded with him to stop. She made no attempt to conceal how she, herself, was feeling. This itself excited him further for he was more used to the artifices and pretenses of females who sought to entice his interest.

"Mavreen!" he whispered her name. "Mavreen! How came you by such a name? It is as strange and unusual as you are. Yet you are no stranger to me. I feel as if I have known you all my life. Does this surprise you?"

She shook her head, the ringlets falling across her cheek so that he longed to brush them aside that he might look anew into her eyes.

"I feel as you do, Gerard. Yet though I have known you since childhood, this feeling I have now is somehow different. It is as if I have rediscovered a long lost friend. We know so little about one another, and yet I believe we understand each other's thoughts.

"We will always be friends now, will we not?" Mavreen asked him, needing no more than the acknowledgment to be happy.

It was not exactly what he had meant but he nodded nevertheless.

"Yes, we will always be friends now, little Mavreen!" he said softly.

Her head rose with a return of her old pride and spirit.

"I am no longer a child!" she informed him with a haughtiness he found amusing. "I shall soon be sixteen and at that age, quite old enough to be wife and mother if I choose."

Her words sobered him, reminding him of the baroness's remarks about her possible betrothal.

"It is not true, is it, that you are considering marriage with Lord Barre?" he asked bluntly.

Mavreen's eyes widened in amazement.

"Who can have told you such a thing?" She frowned, deep in thought, and then enlightenment came. "My father, Sir John. He told you this?"

"First tell me if there is any truth in it!" Gerard persisted impatiently.

Mavreen sighed.

"I believe Lord Barre wishes it. My father, too. He has counseled me to think seriously on it, but. . . ."

"But that is scandalous!" Gerard protested. He lowered his voice. "Lord Barre is old enough to be your father. You cannot marry him. No reason could justify such folly."

"I did not say that I would do so!" Mavreen answered quietly. "As to my father's reasons—you, of all people, must know of them, Gerard. He is desirous of raising my social status."

He was silent. He had forgotten Mavreen was Sir John Danesfield's natural child. He had forgotten everything but her charm and beauty and the fascination she held for him. He felt sick with dismay—and disappointment. Her need to contract an advantageous marriage was as great as his own. Sir John was right on both their accounts. If he himself cared anything for the de Valle name, he must marry wealth and influence. And for Mavreen, the need was even greater. Her presence here tonight in the midst of London society had only been achieved by subterfuge. Lord Barre offered her his name and protection and if she married him, she would become one of the highest ranking ladies in the country.

But logic was lost when, deep within him, his whole being revolted. Mavreen was so very young—innocent, untouched. He could not bear to think of her young girl's body lying in the old man's embrace. She was fashioned for love—the love of a young man who could awaken her dormant passion, rouse it to flame and kindle it with the sweet rewards of satisfaction. How could she know, he asked himself, what marriage entailed once the bed curtains were drawn? She had no experience to guide her, to enlighten her as to the intimacies of love between man and woman. He knew how enraptured such nights of joyful union could be; how tender, how gratifying. All such would be lost to her forever without her knowing what she had forsworn.

"You cannot. You cannot!" he said aloud.

Unaware of his thinking, Mavreen sought only to bring back the gentleness to his face, for he looked hard and angry.

"Then I will not!" she said smiling in her teasing way. "Now tell me what it is I cannot do?"

"Oh, Mavreen!" Gerard gasped. "Do not make light of what I am saying."

The tiny frown of incomprehension drew her brows together.

"But I do not understand what it is you are asking of me!" she said, and added seriously, "No matter what, I will grant your wish if it will make you happy!" Her sweetness unnerved him still further. Choosing his words with difficulty, he said, "I ask only that you do not marry without love. That is all!"

Mavreen was spared a reply for at this moment, the meal reached its conclusion and the baroness rose to lead the ladies from the room.

Partly from a natural kindness, but also because she was fond of Clarissa, Lisa von Eburhard linked her arm in Mavreen's and as they withdrew to the powder room, said, "He is a charming boy, the young vicomte. I think, my dear, you have made a conquest, for he barely addressed a word to me!"

Mavreen's cheeks burned.

"Oh, ma'am, I fear you must blame me. I talk too much. I did not give Gerard a chance to speak with you although I am sure he wished to do so!"

Lisa von Eburhard's small blue eyes twinkled gaily at the girl.

"So it is already 'Gerard', is it? Then my nose has not failed to guide me. I am like a field dog, my dear—I never fail to scent the blossoming of a romance." She addressed a few words to one of the other ladies and then turned back to Mavreen.

"I suppose you know that your young vicomte is soon to become betrothed to Mercedes de Faenza?" she asked.

Seeing the look of dismay on Mavreen's transparent face, she sighed.

"So no one has told you. My little soirée was arranged to further the match. I doubt if your Gerard has much heart for it, but Mercedes—well, be warned, child, she has set her heart upon your young admirer and from all accounts, that spoiled young woman does not often fail to get her own way. Take my advice and do not let your heart run away with you. Amuse yourself, but only for this one evening!"

Mavreen nodded. Her throat felt choked and she could not speak. The baroness no doubt meant well but her words were as deadly to Mavreen as the guillotine itself. Gerard betrothed! Or at least on the point of betrothal: and he had said nothing to her. He had spoken to her as if . . . as if. . . .

Angrily, she brushed away the tear that had escaped down her cheek. The ladies had all departed to the salon where a musical interlude was to fill the next hour. Alone, she summoned all her inner strength to combat the tears that threatened to overwhelm her. What a stupid, foolish romantic jacksnipe she had been to think for one second that Gerard felt anything more than liking for her! Aunt Clarrie had spoken much to her on the subject of flirtation and the entertainment to be had from this harmless game between men and women. It was not only permissible, Aunt Clarrie told her, but meaningless and a pursuit enjoyed as much by men as by women. Mavreen could see now that for the past hour, Gerard had been playing this game while she, oh, insensible fool that she was, had let his words and looks plunge like arrows into her heart.

"Do not marry except for love!" he had said, and since he intended marriage to the voluptuous Mercedes de Faenza, it followed that he must, indeed, love her.

Her tears gave way to anger. She felt herself betrayed; not so much by Gerard as by her own weakness in caring what he did or thought or said. If his loving could allow for sweet words and the holding of hands with another woman, then she wanted none of it. Mercedes de Faenza was welcome to him. And he to her!

Proudly, she descended the stairs, head held high, two bright spots burning in her cheeks.

The musical evening was about to begin. Most of the chairs arranged around the room in a semi-circle, were already occupied by ladies and gentlemen. Lord Barre, seeing Mavreen standing uncertainly in the doorway, beckoned her to come to the vacant seat beside him, kept especially for her. She was grateful to him for offering this haven, for her eye had caught sight of Gerard, seated in one of the foremost chairs near to the pianoforte. In front of it, staring down at him, stood Mercedes, a sheet of music in her hands. She was about to sing.

Some of Mavreen's careful armor of pride gave way to a renewal of intense pain. Her heart felt as if there were a steel band about it—a vise that tightened as the Spanish voice soared into a Haydn lied. The rich contralto filled the room with perfect sound. Her voice was as beautiful as her person, the violet satin gown enhancing the golden texture of her skin, her bosom rising and falling with each deep breath, her dark, almond-shaped eyes luminous as she sang with uninhibited Spanish emotion. She sang unashamedly for Gerard, her eyes never leaving his face.

Mavreen turned her head away, glad that she could see no more than the back of Gerard's dark head, but the pain threatened to engulf her totally when Mercedes sang a second song, this time a hauntingly sweet love song. Mavreen could understand Spanish; the words seemed almost torn from her own heart.

The hot sun warms me like your love,
The cold wind chills me like your anger,
The music sings to me of your desire,
The rain falls on my face like your kisses,
The branches of the almond tree are like your arms,
The returning swallows speak to me of your
    faithfulness,
All living things bring joy—but only you bring love.

And as the last words filled the big room, Gerard turned his head, his eyes searching the sea of faces until at last they came to rest upon Mavreen. The baroness's caution and her own doubts were swept away as she saw the words forming on Gerard's lips.

". . . only you bring love!"

It mattered not how the remainder of the evening progressed. A gentleman played the piano, a lady performed on the harp, Mercedes sang again. Mavreen heard them only as in a dream. Gerard did not glance at her a second time but there was no need for it. She knew with a deep conviction, so strong that she could not doubt it, that Gerard had intended those words for her. He did not love Mercedes de Faenza. Somehow, at some time, she knew he would find his way to her side.

There was little opportunity for him to do so until the music ended. Some of the older people, including Sir John and Lady Danesfield, began to take leave of the host and hostess. A footman came across the room discreetly to inform Mavreen that her carriage was awaiting her. She felt a stab of humiliation that it was expected of her to slip away unobserved. She cordially bade Lord Barre goodnight. He had been most kindly and solicitous throughout the evening and she was grateful to him for his attentions. She thanked the baroness with equal gratitude for inviting her and felt no pain when the good lady patted her arm and said, "We must make the hay whilst the sun shines, no?'

She went upstairs to collect her pelisse and muff and as she descended the stairs once more, she saw Gerard waiting for her on the bottom step.

At first Mavreen trod slowly but her feet would not obey her command and she ran down the second half of the stairway, her face glowing beneath the escaping tendrils of hair. She looked to Gerard like the child in the garden of Mr. Glover's house in Sussex.

"Mavreen!" he said urgently. "I must speak with you. Alone. Is it possible for you to absent yourself from the house in Richmond unattended? I could meet you by the bridge any time of day."

The departing guests milled around them, but Mavreen saw no one but Gerard. Her heart was singing with joy.

"I am not permitted to go walking unchaperoned. But perhaps I could arrange to take Rose with me. She is devoted to me and will not betray my confidence. I can trust her."

"I will be by the right bank," Gerard said urgently. "After luncheon, Mavreen? No matter how long you be, I will wait until you come."

He turned quickly away as the marquis de Faenza approached him across the hallway. "I am searching for my daughter," the marquis said. "It is time we departed."

"Is she not with you, sir?" Gerard asked. "I will try to find her for you. It is my earnest hope you will permit me to escort you both home."

The marquis looked at Gerard wearily. He had found the evening tedious and was suffering from gout. He longed to be home in bed. He knew Mercedes would wish him to invite the young Frenchman into their house if he accompanied them home and this would further prolong his exhaustion.

Nevertheless, he knew better than to thwart his daughter's wishes. She had left him in no doubt that she intended to add this impecunious young man to her many other possessions.

At least this drain upon his purse would have some positive purpose, he consoled himself, for the sooner Mercedes was married and living in a home of her own, the sooner he could begin to devote himself to his own pastimes. His indulgence with his only child had been stretched to the limit and her stubborn rejection of all the Spanish noblemen who had asked for her hand had brought him to despair.

The marquis bowed to the young English girl standing a little apart from them, apparently on the point of leaving. He had not noticed her among the many guests but now he looked at Mavreen with interest. There was something hauntingly beautiful in that clear, shining gaze, in the graceful tilt of her head, the sweet expression of her mouth. He sighed, wondering why at his age he had never learned what made one woman beautiful and another not. This child, for she was little more, had a radiance about her that caught at the heart. He could not account for it and accepted that all beauty was an enigma.

CHAPTER TWELVE
1795

It was not as simple as Mavreen had anticipated to escape from the little house at Richmond. Aunt Clarrie, understandably, wanted every detail of the soirée she herself had been unable to attend. And after luncheon, when Mavreen professed to have a headache which only a breath of fresh air could remedy, Clarissa offered to accompany her upon her walk.

"Dearest Aunt Clarrie!" Mavreen protested, hating the necessity for the lie, "I would dearly love your company but you know that you do not really care for lengthy walks. After my country rearing, I am well accustomed to go five miles without tiring and it is this kind of exercise that I need."

"Then Rose is the person to go with you," Clarissa agreed.

Mavreen hugged her, her heart nearly overruling her head in a longing to tell the dear lady the truth. More than anything in the world, other than to see Gerard again, she wanted to be able to say to Clarissa, "I fell in love last night with Gerard and I believe he loves me. I am so happy I could die of it!"

But she stayed silent, adding extra kisses by way of contrition, then hurried to her room to change into her walking dress. The phaeton was waiting at the front door, old Harry holding the horse's head; Rose, the little maid, looked almost as excited as Mavreen.

Rose would have died for Mavreen. To be the one to assist her in a secret assignment of love was a romantic adventure to her, spiced with the danger of possible discovery.

Within minutes of leaving the house, the phaeton was approaching the new Richmond bridge. It was nearly three o'clock, and Mavreen was on tenterhooks, fearing Gerard had arrived an hour before and ceased to wait for her, or worse still, had not come at all.

But as she drove the phaeton the hundred yards over the shining river Thames, she saw a horseman standing beside his mount and knew at once by the stature that it was he. Man and horse seemed to have been fashioned for each other. They were both beautiful, Gerard, his dark hair unpowdered, his coat, cut away at the waist, as black as the horse's mane, the gilt buttons glistening in the sunshine, as were the spurs on his high black riding boots.

"He's here, Rose!" Mavreen breathed.

Rose giggled with excitement. She had never seen a French viscount before and from Mavreen's descriptions, the young man now approaching their carriage seemed by far the most handsome gentleman in the whole world.

The April sun was shining warmly upon Gerard's bare head as he came toward Mavreen. His face was unsmiling until he realized that it really was she in the phaeton.

"So you have come!" he said, bowing as he helped her down from the carriage. "I was in torment all night and day fearing you would not do so."

Mavreen took a deep breath in an effort to steady the violent beating of her heart.

"But I promised I would be here, Gerard. Nothing could stop me."

Wordlessly, he took her hand. Rose, bobbing a curtsy, pronounced herself quite equal to holding both horses' reins if required to do so, but Gerard called over an urchin playing by the riverbank and instructed him to mind the horses while he was gone and left Rose in charge of supervising him.

With Mavreen's hand still held tightly in his own, he walked with her away from the winding river down to the woodlands. The bluebells carpeted the floor of the woods in a sea of violet. Primroses and wood violets lined the paths. Mavreen drew in a deep breath of sweet scented air and looked at Gerard radiantly.

"It is like Sussex!" she said. "I had almost forgot how beautiful the countryside is in April."

"And I had almost forgot since last night how beautiful you are!" Gerard said, drawing her closer to him. There were no people in sight, nor likely to be, for this was the time of day for working, not walking.

As if it were the most natural thing in the world, Mavreen reached up and touched his face.

"And you seem beautiful to me!" she said softly.

"Ah, Mavreen!" he cried, taking her fiercely into his arms. "I have dreamed all night long of kissing you."

She made no protest that she wished it otherwise and raised her mouth to his with the simple eagerness of a child. But it was not as a child that her body responded as his mouth came down upon hers. A terrifying sweetness swept through her veins, sending her pulse and her blood racing. Her legs felt as though they must give way beneath her and but for the tightness of Gerard's embrace, she might indeed have fallen.

He, too, was trembling. When he finally took his lips from hers, his voice shook as he said, "I love you. I did not think it would be this way, but I want you, Mavreen, my dearest *petit écureuil! Je t'aime. Je t'aime.*"

Joy flooded Mavreen's whole being. Eyes shining, lips parted, she gave him a smile filled with radiance.

"I love you, too. *Moi aussi. Je t'aime*, Gerard!"

He was entranced by her use of his native tongue and laughing now with happiness, he kissed her again. This time his lips moved from her mouth to her small white neck, to her shoulders and the snowy upper curves of her breasts. He felt her quick passionate response and knew that he had not been mistaken in her. There was a fire beneath her innocence like a glowing ember that needed but the breath of love to stir it into flame.

The thought sobered him. All night he had wrestled with his troubled emotions. The hour he had spent at the de Faenzas' house had left him in no doubt that the marquis would willingly hand his daughter over to him, and with a very handsome dowry to boot. Mercedes herself, had left him convinced that she would more than welcome his proposal; in fact, she had shown some ill-concealed irritation with him that he had not made any advances to her though she had seen they were alone for a few minutes before her father rejoined them.

But Gerard's thoughts had been filled with the girl who had totally captivated his mind and emotions and he had had no heart for furthering his proposal to another woman. Now that he actually held Mavreen in his arms, he knew that he did not want Mercedes, that were he to marry her he would be unfaithful. He wanted this girl and no other. He wanted to be the one to show her the infinite variety of love. He would love her as no other could. And she—she was irresistably fascinating, looking now like the young Sussex maiden of several summers ago, her hair in disarray about her flushed cheeks, her eyes laughing up at him with trusting candor and love.

"Oh, Mavreen, my very dearest!"

He would have taken her in his arms again but she protested, her face serious as she said solemnly, "Gerard, I too, was in torment all night long on account of something Baroness von Eburhard told me. I cannot bear the thought it might be true. She told me that you are shortly to be betrothed to Mercedes de Faenza. Tell me it is not so."

She waited for what seemed an eternity for Gerard's reply. It came almost upon the instant.

"It has been spoken about and indeed, I promised to consider the matter!" he said with complete candor. "But that was before I met you again, my dearest. Now I want only you!"

Mavreen gave a little cry of joy. Reaching up, for he was nearly a head taller than she, she kissed him fully on the mouth. It was now Gerard's turn to hold back.

"And you, Mavreen?" he said urgently. "Tell me it is not true that you are to marry that stupid old buffoon, Lord Barre?"

Mavreen caught her lip, stifling a laugh.

"He is neither a buffoon nor stupid!" she said. "He is, in fact, an exceedingly kind and pleasant person and I have the deepest regard for him."

Fiercely, Gerard caught her arm. Strangely, she found herself enjoying the sight and sound and feel of his jealous anger. It only proved to her how deeply he cared.

"And you mean to marry him?" Gerard cried through clenched teeth.

Mavreen's eyes twinkled back at him.

"Was it not you who told me at the dinner last night that I must marry only for love?"

His face relaxed and he pulled her back into the circle of his arms.

"So it is not true! And I was right, my darling. You are created for love and loving. To live otherwise would be an offense against Nature, nay, against God." He kissed her until she could scarce breathe. His voice was filled with the urgency of a young man's passion as he said, "If you but knew how greatly I desire to teach you the ways of love!"

Mavreen's eyes widened.

"I, too, desire it!" she said seriously. Then her mood changed again to intense happiness and as always when she was happy, she laughed. "I have learned much already!" she said. "How to kiss and be kissed, for example. I had not thought it could so pleasure me."

He was enchanted by her frankness and innocence.

"It is but a beginning!" he told her.

"Then you shall tutor me!" Mavreen replied. "You will find me an eager pupil, Gerard, I promise, for I declare no lesson I enjoyed with Mr. Glover did give me one small part of the joy of your kisses!"

"Ah, Mavreen," Gerard cried, trying hard to keep control of his senses. "You do not know of what you speak. To share love to its fullest is—is the closest of all unions between man and woman. It cannot be undertaken without full understanding."

Mavreen was listening intently to every word. Believing she understood his meaning, she said simply, "Have no fear, Gerard, for I was reared on a farm and I know of such matters. Each spring I watched the male beasts and

birds and butterflies and fowls select their mates and find
peace in their union. It is beautiful to see. I was taught
from infancy that this was God's intention and when the
time was right, all females must submit to it."

"Mon Dieu!" Gerard said, such was his sense of shock
at the way this young girl expressed herself. Her innocence
he had taken quite for granted and yet now she spoke as
if total love were known to her and acceptable to her.
Was it possible she had already experienced some country
lad's attentions? The thought both angered and excited
him. Beyond every other desire, the need to protect her
was still uppermost. "Mavreen, have you thought deeply
enough upon this matter? If you and I—it would mean
you could never marry Lord Barre, nor any other gentleman. 'Twould mean. . . ."

Mavreen broke in, her face shining.

" 'Twould mean no less than I desire!" she said. "How
can you believe, dearest Gerard, that I could wish for
marriage with Lord Barre or with another? My heart lies
with you and always will so do. I know it here . . ." she
said solemnly placing a hand upon her breast, "and here!"
Her hand went to her forehead. "So loving you, how
could I love another?"

Nevertheless, he was still uncertain. He knew it was
wrong that a young girl, not yet sixteen years of age,
should decide so speedily and irrevocably her whole future. It was not as if he could marry her. At best he
could offer her his protection, and little money with
which to accomplish it. Moreover, he was soon to return
to his country and could not even protect her with his
person.

Deeply disturbed, his emotions in terrible conflict with
his desires, Gerard turned and walked a few paces away
from the temptation she presented. Puzzled, Mavreen
watched him and her joy gave way to anguish. Did Gerard, after all, not love her deeply enough to wish to
make her his own? Had she by her unguarded words,
offered him more of herself than he really wished to
have?

"Gerard, I pray you speak with me. What is distressing
you?"

He turned and hastening to her, gathered her once more into his arms, holding her fiercely and possessively.

"I fear it is that I love you too much!" he said with truth. "I find your happiness is more important to me than my own!"

Mavreen let out her breath, her uncertainty vanished.

"Then there is no cause for sorrow!" she said. "For so do I feel, Gerard."

Gerard let his hands fall to his sides.

"We have been absent too long a time!" he said. "Your maid and the boy may have trouble with the horses. They will be restless after so long. And your dear Aunt Clarrie will be wondering what has become of you!"

"I fear you are right!" Mavreen agreed, sighing. "But we will see one another again soon, will we not? I could not bear too long a separation." Her mouth widened into a mischievous smile. "Besides, dear Gerard, you have promised me further lessons in love and I am most eager for you to commence my tutoring!"

All Gerard's uncertainty returned. With great self control, he refrained from kissing her again but took her hand and guided her back along the path toward the river. Mavreen said suddenly, "Tomorrow evening, Sir John is escorting Aunt Clarrie to the opera. It is to compensate her for being unable to attend the baroness's soirée, for she would dearly have loved to go. Sir John has also invited me; if it should please you, Gerard, I could pretend an indisposition. Then, if Rose can help me, we could secrete you into the house without Hannah knowing. What think you, Gerard?"

"I think it would be vastly improper but quite wonderful!" Gerard said. "I will hide myself beneath your window, my love. Then you shall signal to me when it is safe for me to approach the door."

Mavreen's feet quickened to a little dance of happiness. She was pleased to see her own excitement at the proposed adventure reflected in Gerard's face.

"I am so happy," she told him. She tilted her head to one side reflectively in a manner he found captivating. "Do you not think love is a wondrous thing, Gerard? I really had no thought it could bring such joy. I feel like a

swallow sailing through the blue sky on the south wind!
Never have I been so happy. And you, Gerard, have you
felt so before this day?"

He hesitated, but only briefly. He could tell her in truth
that he had never loved in such a way before. No woman
in his life had stirred him to such depths. Mavreen had
found her way not only to his senses but to his heart.
For the first time, he contemplated the thought that he
might marry her. It mattered not that her lineage was
marred. He felt quite certain that he could be endlessly
content in her company and instinct told him they would
find themselves perfectly matched. But there remained the
insoluble matter of money. Neither had any and it was
imperative for him if he were not to forget entirely that
he was his father's son, the vicomte de Valle, and honor-
bound to his dear mother to restore the family name and
fortunes.

He resolved to think the matter over in the privacy of
his apartment in Sir John's house. There was much to
consider. Sir John would never approve a match between
himself and Mavreen. His mother, were she still living,
might surely feel affection for Mavreen but likewise could
not approve her as the future vicomtesse de Valle. Married they would never again be welcomed in high social
circles, for he had neither power nor influence in England
or in France.

As for money, were he to join the Army to ensure their
financial support, Mavreen would be ostracized by the
officers' ladies as soon as they discovered the truth of her
birth and most probably, he would be asked to resign his
commission.

The problems were endless and he was no nearer solving
them when the following night he called upon Mavreen at
Orchid House. True to her word, she had pleaded an indisposition and secured Rose's help in leaving a garden
door unfastened so that he could slip into the house.

Mavreen greeted him in the darkness of the salon with
a whispered caution.

"Hannah is not yet abed! We must go to my bedchamber. Rose will wait by the door for the sound of
Aunt Clarrie's carriage and give us good warning."

On tiptoe, they climbed the stairs, unheard and unseen by the housekeeper, only Rose aware of their movements. Within minutes, they were in Mavreen's bedchamber. By the light of the fire burning softly in the grate, Gerard saw her face, laughing and happy like a child truant from Sunday sermons.

Hungry with his need of her, he crossed the space between them and took her in his arms. Before even he could kiss her, her mouth was against his own.

"I have missed you so terribly!" she whispered. "No day ever seemed so long waiting for your coming, and all night long, I dreamed of you!"

The warmth and sweetness of her welcome brought about his decision. No other consideration mattered at this moment than that he and she should love one another now and for evermore.

With great tenderness, curbing his own impatience, he drew her to the soft virginal white of her couch. Her perfume was all about him as they fell together upon the coverlet. Her hair covered his face and he had to smoothe it gently backward so that he could look into her eyes.

She showed no fear as his hand reached up to loosen the bodice of her dress. When his fingers first touched her naked breast, she drew in her breath with a little cry of pleasure and reaching out her own hands, pressed his more firmly upon her.

"My love, my heart!" he whispered, kissing her again and yet again. As his hands disrobed her further, he broke into his own language. *"Mon amour! Ma chère petite. Comme je t'aime!"*

Despite the new sensations which threatened to engulf all thought, Mavreen's mind remained in some part quite clear. Though having no experience of love, she was as she had told him, familiar with the matings of nature and longing for what was about to happen to her. If she had fear at all, it was that Gerard himself might not find pleasure in her. There had been no talk of marriage but she never doubted his words of love and assumed therefrom that as soon as it could be arranged, they would be made man and wife in the eyes of the world, just as they were about to become man and wife in the eyes of God.

Vaguely, she was aware of the difficulties of such a marriage; knowing that socially she had nothing of worth to bring Gerard. Yet she answered such misgivings with her heart for she knew without doubt that she could love him as no other woman could. She would willingly, if required, die for him. Her love would be her dowry. And Gerard, her lover, must think it sufficient else he would not now be claiming her for his own.

She returned every caress with answering passion. There was no reticence born of false modesty. She reacted as nature had fashioned her so to do, and Gerard's delight in her was beyond anything in his experience. He dreaded the moment when he must hurt her yet when that came and his sweet love drew him but closer into her being, he felt both glorified and humbled by the magnificence of her giving.

As they lay side by side in each other's arms, all passion spent, Gerard knew perfect peace and happiness. He knew, also, that no other woman, past or future, could again mean to him what this girl now meant. He had made her part of himself and he was a part of her. There could be no return.

As a log fell in a shower of sparks, he saw his own reflection in Mavreen's eyes. She was staring at him, dreamily memorizing every line of his face, her finger tip running from his forehead down the bridge of his nose, over his high cheekbones, down once more to his lips. He kissed them as they passed down further to his strong, muscular shoulders, his narrowing waist and firm hips. To know that he pleased her, for her delight showed in her eyes, was a further joy. He felt young and powerful—a king among men; he would dare the world for her, cherish her, protect her.

"I will love you always!" he said, the dark chestnut brown of his eyes seeming to deepen with the intensity of his vow.

Mavreen sighed.

"I fear we cannot tarry too much longer!" she said.

"Oh, Gerard, it will be so hard to part from you. I wish we could remain like this forever. Can we not escape to some hidden place where we can be alone? And how shall I hide from my face the change in me, for change there must surely be. I am a woman now, am I not?"

He smiled tenderly at her many questions.

"Mon écureuil!" he said, kissing her gently but not without a hint of sadness. "I, too, will find it hard to part from you. Soon I shall have to return to France. D'Artois is preparing another attack upon the régime. I cannot say how long I shall be gone."

Mavreen caught her breath. She had not, till now, given thought to the future, still less that Gerard's visit to England might be of temporary duration. Yet she had known the situation in France and his commitment to restoring the royalists.

"Oh, no" she breathed. "You might be killed, Gerard, or wounded. I cannot bear the thought!"

"My dearest, you would not have me fail in my duty? Nor can you doubt that I would leave you for aught less."

She shook her head slowly, miserably.

"When will you go?" she asked with difficulty.

"In a week or so. I am awaiting orders. But do not look so sad, my love. We will see each other many times before I leave. We have much to talk about, to plan. But you must give me your word now you will not let your father, nor anyone else, persuade you into marriage. Promise me that you will wait for me."

"Oh, Gerard, there is no need for my promise. You must know I am yours alone. Yet I give my word gladly if it will make you happy."

But he was still not fully confident of his possession of her.

"Loving is a very sweet pastime!" he said. "If it should happen I am gone for a year or more, and many men will desire you, it could happen that you will favor the looks of one, the character of another, and will forget me."

Mavreen smiled her denial.

"I want no other but you, Gerard, nor ever will. Loving is truly sweet but only because you made it so."

He was overcome with his love for her.

"You understand now, my darling, why I said you must not marry Lord Barre. Can you imagine. . . ."

She put a hand over his lips, her eyes dancing with laughter.

"Do not speak of it. I had not thought of marriage in such a manner."

"Yet as your husband, he would have a right to your bedchamber!"

"Then I not only *shall* not but *cannot* marry him," said Mavreen logically, "for I desire no other lover but you." She sat up, her hair in disarray, her body exposed to him without thought of shyness. "Gerard, I have been thinking. If what you have taught me this evening is the first lesson in loving, what then will be the second? Most certainly a disappointment, I fear, since naught could be sweeter."

He pulled her down on top of him, laughing happily.

"Not so, my sweeting. There are a thousand ways to love and we will invent another thousand. As for your second lesson, it shall begin now, thus."

Ten minutes later, Rose knocked urgently upon the door. Mavreen pulled on her bedrobe and hurried to open it.

"Oh, ma'am, hurry, I pray you. I heard a carriage but two minutes since turn down the street. It is Mistress Manton for sure!"

Gerard was already half dressed. Not troubling to pull on his hose, he pushed them into the pockets of his coat, thrust his feet into his shoes and kissing Mavreen quickly upon the lips, hurried after Rose down the stairs.

Mavreen straightened the bed covers, took off her robe and put on her nightrobe. Then she climbed between the sheets, pulling the covers to her chin. In the room below, she heard a door open, followed by Sir John Danesfield's voice and the higher pitched tones of Aunt Clarrie and Hannah. A minute later, Rose crept into the room.

"The vicomte was away betimes!" she whispered. "Have no fear, Mistress Mavreen."

"Thank you, kind Rose!" Mavreen whispered back. "We are both most grateful!"

"And both so comely!" Rose breathed excitedly. "I do not doubt you love him excessively, ma'am. He is so handsome, I durst swear no lady can resist him!"

After the little maid had gone, Mavreen lay thinking, her head in the indentation where Gerard's head had lain. Rose had spoken the truth. Gerard was handsome—and irresistible. She had given him her maidenhood without thought, or indeed on reflection, without regret. But it was also true that other women might feel as she did, the beautiful Mercedes de Faenza for one. Gerard had extracted a promise of faithfulness from her, but she had extracted no such promise from him. Suppose he had gone to the bedchamber of the marquis's daughter.

"I would kill her, and Gerard, if such were true!" Mavreen thought. Jealousy was an emotion as new to her as the others she had experienced tonight. Quickly she pushed it from her mind. It was unworthy of her lover. Gerard's words still rang in her ears. "I will love you always!" he had said, and so had made his vow. She knew he would no more break it than she would break her promise to him.

She closed her eyes, and with a child's suddenness, was asleep.

CHAPTER THIRTEEN

1795-1796

Mavreen heard no word from Gerard on the morrow. Nor on the day following. Her face lost its rosy coloring and her eyes were shadowed with the urgency of her longing.

Clarissa, believing the feigned indisposition to be the cause of Mavreen's listlessness, confined her to her bedchamber, fearing an outbreak of illness. Rose came in and out of her room with sympathy and reassurance, none of which consoled Mavreen for she knew the girl had no knowledge of Gerard's whereabouts.

When Rose burst into the room late on the third afternoon, Mavreen did not bother to raise her head from the pillow.

"Ma'am, ma'am, I have news for you. Oh, Mistress Mavreen, sit up, I pray you take notice. I have a letter—from him!"

Now Mavreen sat up, all but snatching the thick parchment paper from the girl's hands.

"How came you by this?" she asked, her heart thudding, her cheeks now flushed with happiness.

" 'Twas a messenger boy, ma'am. He had been given instructions by his lordship, the vicomte, that is, to wait in the street till I came out and not to hand the letter to none else nohow!"

Mavreen's face broke into laughter.

"Thank you, Rose. Now leave me, for I would read this alone. But thank you again."

As soon as the door closed behind Rose, Mavreen tore at the seal. Her hands trembled and she closed her eyes, trying to steady herself since her excitement was making it impossible for her eyes to read Gerard's beautiful lettering.

My dearest, my darling, my love, I have no heart for writing this, my first letter to you. I would to God that I had different words to speak yet I have no choice. Believe me, mon amour, they cannot give you more pain than they give me, the author. . . .

Mavreen sat down on the edge of the bed. She did not wish to read further for fear of what she would discover, but she knew she must.

At long last I have had word of my dearest mother and know you will rejoice with me in my happiness at this. Moreover, unbelievable of miracles, I have had word from her—in her own writing. As you can imagine, my love, I was overcome.

Mavreen felt a little of the tension ease from her body. The disaster was no worse than that Gerard was on his way to France to see his mother and could not therefore keep his promise to meet her once more before he rejoined his army. But he would be returning when the battle was fought. He loved her. He had said so and now he had written "my love", "my dearest".

I do not know if you are aware that my mother is of Italian birth. Her family have, like myself, been trying for many years to trace what had become of her. One of her cousins was married to a Corsican nobleman. This gentleman, Don Emanuel de Corte, was friendly with the mother of Napoleon Bonaparte. He, too, had been making endless inquiries since our château and estates in Compiègne were burned and looted.

I will not inflict upon you the ways and means by which influence made possible the discovery of my dear mother's whereabouts in a prison in France. Her release was secured and though ill and frail, she is alive! Napoleon has used his influence to have restored to her our ruined home, the Château de Boulancourt, although the land is partitioned and cannot as yet be reclaimed.

My mother was, of course, overjoyed to hear that I, too, had survived the revolution. She longs to see me and I must, of course, go immediately to her. She is living alone in the château with two old servants, but in the direst of straits for there is no money even to buy the necessities of life.

She does not complain but I know her pride will keep her from telling me how bad things are. She asks nothing from me but that I remember my promise to her to vindicate my father's honor and if it is within my power, restore his estates to their former greatness.

Mavreen, you are but fifteen years of age and I doubt if that be old enough to understand the torment this gives me. When I took you for my own, I hoped and believed that no matter what difficulties beset our future, I could make you my wife; that somehow we would, by our love, overcome all obstacles to our marriage. I beg you to believe this for I swear it upon

*my life. Since the moment when I sat beside you at
the baroness's soirée, I have thought of naught else
but you and in so doing, forgot my dearest mother
and all that I had sworn to do for her. I think, in my
heart, I believed her dead.*

Mavreen's eyes were so full of tears, she could read no
further. She put down the letter and went to her bureau
to find a small lace cambric kerchief with which she
wiped her eyes. Then slowly, she returned to her bed and
once again, took up the letter.

*I am come now to that which is hardest of all to write.
I cannot marry you. I am my father's only son, responsible to him for my mother and for my heritage.
I must put my honor and duty before my own happiness.*

*I love you and will always love you, but when Sir
John next calls upon you, he will announce my betrothal to Mercedes de Faenza. I know how much this
will hurt you and prefer that you should hear it from
me rather than from another.*

*I pray you, think kindly on me if you can. I do not
expect you to go on loving me but do most earnestly
beg you not to forget what has passed between us, and
to remind you, because of it, of your promise not to
wed Lord Barre, even though we never meet again.*

*You will remain ever in my thoughts as the most
beautiful, generous and loving of women.*

Je t'aime!

> *Gerard, vicomte de Valle.*

"Even though we never meet again!" The words leapt
from the page and she said them over and over again until they lost all meaning. She could not, would not believe
it. Gerard was her love, her very life. He could not leave
her so. Bitterly, she blamed vicomtesse de Valle. No
mother had a right to take her son against his will from
the girl he loved.

But it was not against his will, Mavreen reminded herself, the tears drying on her cheeks. Gerard, alone, had
made the choice. He had talked urgently of honor, as if

honor demanded that he should betrothe himself to a rich
nobleman's daughter. This did not seem to Mavreen to
be so honorable as politic. It was merely a means of restoring his family's wealth and through that, no doubt, his
estates. He had sold himself to gain his own ends more
swiftly.

"Ah, Gerard!" she whispered the words aloud. "That is
not love."

She did not in her youth and suffering leave room for
question when she condemned him. For her, love was absolute and did not take account of Gerard's love for his
mother, nor yet for his heritage. Love had come upon her
swiftly, unexpectedly, totally overwhelming all other consideration. She had held the greatest of all prizes in her
hands a single afternoon and evening and knew nothing
more than that it was lost to her forever.

She did not weep. With slow deliberation, she read the
letter through a second time and then burnt it in the unlit
grate. When the big bell on the front door rang in the
servants' quarter, she did not lift her head for she knew it
would not be Gerard. Nor did she allow herself the folly
of hope for Gerard had offered her none.

Rose knocked upon her door.

"More flowers have come for you, ma'am!" she said,
holding out the beautifully arranged and beribboned basket. "There were tulips for Mistress Manton but none so
beautiful as these tiny white rosebuds come for you. Will
you not look at them, ma'am? They are sent by Lord
Barre."

Mavreen looked long and deeply at the delicate petals,
white as snow, as yet uncurled.

Each one was like her love, she thought, beautiful, perfect, a miracle from God. Yet unlike these flowers, her
love would never unfold and bloom in its full glory. Perhaps, in time, it, like the rose she touched, would finally
lose its petals and die.

"Let it be soon!" she thought. "Dear God, let it be
soon."

The front door bell rang again and Rose scuttled away.
This time it was to announce the arrival of Sir John
Danesfield.

"His Lordship said to tell you that he would be very happy if you would favor him with your company," Rose repeated the message carefully.

It was on the tip of Mavreen's tongue to send back a polite refusal, but as she saw Rose's glance upon the ashes in the firegrate, she suddenly drew her head up and straightened her back.

"Tell Sir John I will be down shortly!" she said.

Carefully, she changed her dress, brushed her hair, rubbed at her cheeks to put color back into them. With deliberation, she broke a rosebud from the basket of flowers and fastened it in her hair, pinning another to the drapery around her bosom. Critically she studied her reflection in the mirror, as if she were observing someone else. The girl facing her was slim and graceful, the lilac-colored Grecian gown accentuating the smallness of her waist which was encircled with a deep blue velvet ribbon. She was gratified to note that no child but a fashionable young woman gazed back at her.

Satisfied, she left the room and went downstairs.

"My dearest Mavreen!" Aunt Clarrie greeted her. "Are you well enough? You are looking better. The roses are back in your cheeks and . . ." she added smiling . . . "in your dress and coiffure, too. How charming you look, my dear."

Mavreen curtsied to her father and for the first time since his admission that she was his daughter, she spoke to him of her own will.

"Good afternoon, Papa!"

His astonishment was ill-concealed, as was the look of pleasure on his face. She had not until now called him father.

He wished he had not brought news that would distress her. He very much feared that young Gerard's betrothal to the Faenza girl would come as something of a shock to Mavreen following upon the young man's attentions to her at the soirée.

"Do you see, Papa, how pretty the roses are?" Mavreen broke in upon his reflections. "Lord Barre sent them. He is always most kind to me."

"He's a nice fellow!" Sir John said, agreeably surprised. "You'd do well to think on my remarks to you t'other day regarding Gilbert."

"Indeed, I have given them much thought!" Mavreen said calmly. "At first I did consider Lord Barre was . . . well, a trifle old to wed. But after Baroness von Eburhard's party, I thought how nice 'twould be to be a lady of great consequence, with a beautiful house and clothes and jewels. I believe Lord Barre is very rich, is he not?"

Clarissa could not have been more surprised, nor more dismayed. She had never thought her little Mavreen to be avaricious or grasping; yet she was now sounding both. Moreover, Clarissa could not happily see her marry a man so old, no matter how practicable and desirable dear John considered it. He, however, was positively delighted.

"My dear child, I cannot tell you how much this pleases me," he said, beaming. "As for Gilbert, he will be beside himself. He will, of course, make a formal proposal as soon as I tell him it would not come amiss. You do not have to accept him on the first occasion. In fact, it might be more politic to await his second attempt. Then, my dear, we will see what can be done about a wedding and a trousseau for you. You must have the very best I can afford for I'll not have you going to Gilbert like a beggar maid."

Clarissa could no longer stay silent.

"Mavreen is but fifteen years of age, John. 'Twould not be right to marry her so young."

"Pah!" Sir John retorted, but not unkindly. "Me own mother was married at fourteen. Nevertheless, I don't object to a year's engagement; that would be quite proper. There is no great hurry in the matter and we wouldn't want anyone to think otherwise. What say you, Mavreen?"

"Whatever you think best, sir!" Mavreen replied with a meekness that slightly discomforted him and made Clarissa distinctly uneasy. "Meanwhile, Papa, you said I might have a horse of my own to ride and Dickon as my groom. This, with my music, will help the year to pass most pleasantly."

"And so be it!" Sir John said, patting her hand, ready to please her in any matter. "I will write to the Sales this very day; I will also make inquiries about a suitable mount for you. Nothing too sedate, eh?" he added, for he knew Mavreen to be an excellent and fearless horse-woman.

Only as he was rising to take his leave did he remember the reason for his visit.

"I almost forgot to advise you both," he said. "Young Gerard is betrothed to de Faenza's girl. A good match, don't you agree? It may interest you to know, Clarrie, that the vicomtesse's whereabouts have finally been discovered. The poor soul had been imprisoned these last years but her family used influence with Bonaparte and secured her release. Gerard, of course, has returned at once to France where his mother is now living in the ruins of their château. The marquis de Faenza is giving his daughter a huge dowry. It will be much needed by the de Valles."

Mavreen clenched her hands. In all other respects, she maintained complete composure. But Clarissa, who knew her so well, was aware of her tension.

When Sir John was gone, she drew Mavreen down on the sofa beside her and said gently, "I think I am only just now understanding why you have agreed to wed Lord Barre. Mavreen, I know it is your father's wish and such a marriage has many advantages, but I pray you, think carefully on it before you make a formal agreement. No word has been spoken beyond these walls and it is not too late to retract should you wish it."

With a last desperate attempt to control the threatening tears, Mavreen replied, "Why should I wish to do that, Aunt Clarrie? Lord Barre is a delightful man and has much to offer me. . . ." But her voice trembled before she could complete her sentence and Clarissa drew the shaking girl into her arms.

"My dear, you don't love him in the least, do you? It is the young vicomte who has your heart and methinks your decision to wed Lord Barre is but to show the world you care not a jot for Gerard de Valle!"

Tears ran down Mavreen's cheeks. Her desire to confide her unhappiness was overwhelming. She sobbed broken heartedly against Clarissa's soft bosom.

"There, there, my sweeting!" Clarissa crooned. "I understand your suffering and have no intention of making light of it. But my dear, you are very young and in time, you will cease to think so much about the young man. There will be others, just as handsome and charming, who will steal your heart. You have no need to close the door on love simply because on this occasion you are disappointed. May your father forgive me for so advising you, but do not marry Lord Barre. Wait until love comes a second time."

Mavreen raised a tear-streaked face and looked at Clarissa solemnly.

"There can be no second time for me, Aunt Clarrie. I shall never love anyone but Gerard; I will love him until I die. Nor do I wish to lose my heart a second time. I think love is uncommonly cruel. I believed Gerard loved me for he had so declared himself, but I am not good enough for him by birth nor rich enough for his needs. Such things matter more to him than his love for me and if this, indeed, be love, I want none of it!"

Clarissa sighed. Her instinct had not been wrong. The very thing had happened at the baroness's party between the two young people that she had feared; Mavreen had always felt tenderly toward Gerard, and he, poor young man, must have found her quite irresistable for she had looked truly lovely that evening.

At least, Clarissa thought with relief, their love had had no time to blossom and the unhappy girl would soon recover from her first love.

"You will feel quite differently in a while, I promise you!" Clarissa said confidently. Mavreen listened to this counsel and had no faith in it.

"I have decided that I shall fare a deal better in this world as Lady Barre!" she said. "Do you think, Aunt Clarrie, that I welcomed the knowledge I could only be present at the baroness's house through the perpetration of a deceit? Had I been Sir John's true daughter in the eyes of the law, I would not be forced to such indignity. Moreover, Gerard's marriage to me would have been perfectly acceptable, would it not? I have not forgot . . ." she added bitterly ". . . that you and I were refused entrance to the Almack Rooms. We were not good enough for the society ladies, were we, Aunt Clarrie? You a man's mistress and I a bastard!"

"Oh, Mavreen, do not speak so!" Clarrie cried, near to tears herself. "It cannot be helped. We cannot change our destinies or our pasts so it is better not to fight against them."

Mavreen stood up, drawing herself up to her full height.

"I cannot agree with you, Aunt Clarrie. I shall fight to the end rather than go through my life accepting that I am 'not good enough'. I understand exactly what it is I have to do. I am taking a leaf from Gerard's book and shall accept a marriage that will raise my circumstances. And as my father so aptly informed me not a week since, as Lady Barre, no one will dare speak a word against me and I shall be on every invitation list. Is that not so?"

Clarissa nodded unhappily.

"Then speak no more against my betrothal!" Mavreen said quietly. "Since I cannot have love, Aunt Clarrie, I shall have wealth and power instead for I most certainly do not intend to go through life without either!"

Dickon was happy, almost perfectly so. It was a beautiful spring morning in 1796, and he was riding beside his young mistress on the Surrey hills. Mavreen's slim upright form in smart royal blue velvet riding habit, was a little ahead of him, her thoroughbred mare, Celeste, more spirited than his own mount. She had removed her hat with its bright blue feather and her hair blew in the passing wind like ripe corn in the field.

They were galloping hard, as was her wont as soon as they left the roads behind them and came to the countryside. He never questioned her wishes but sensed that this wild chase across the hills was somehow necessary to her to free her from the restrictions of her London life. Dickon loved to see her so. Mostly, when he drove her to London town to the big shops to select materials and trimmings for her trousseau, she looked pale and sad and lost in thoughts of which he knew nothing. He longed to comfort her but knew no way to do so.

Once, upon one such ride, Mavreen waited for him to draw level with her as was her custom, and they talked not as mistress and servant but intimately as had been their wont in childhood. Mavreen spoke of her pending marriage to Lord Barre.

"I shall be so rich I shall have anything in the world I want, Dickon!" she told him. "I will have money of my own and Lord Barre has said he will not object if I wish to send some of my allowance to Mother and Father Sale. And, Dickon, he has agreed you shall come with me to my new house as my groom and he has promised me that when his head groom departs, you shall have his place. You are to have your own apartment over the stable and, if you so wish, we may bring Colombe's foal to London too. He never says me nay. Am I not fortunate?"

Dickon had oft met Lord Barre who was a frequent visitor to the Richmond house, as was Mavreen at Lord Barre's imposing residence in Piccadilly. He considered him a very pleasant gentleman who, despite the fact that he was a peer of the realm, was always civil to Dickon and his own servants. There was no doubting his adoration of Mavreen, nor the honor he would bestow upon her making her his wife. Nevertheless, Dickon could not reconcile himself to the vast difference in their ages and wondered why, when young Mavreen had grown to be so beautiful and accomplished, she had not selected a younger and more handsome husband. But it was not his place to question her and although she treated him still more as a friend than a groom, Dickon had imposed the gap in their stations of his own volition. He asked nothing more than to serve her.

His arrival in London a half-year ago, had been a great comfort to her. Since the afternoon when she had talked so openly to Aunt Clarrie, there had been a rift between them which left Mavreen often lonely, and Dickon was the companion she needed. There was something simple and honest and dependable about him. He belonged to the kind of life that had continuity, was dependent not upon the whims and quirks of society but upon the seasons, the sun, the rain. She could continue to believe in the goodness of man and nature when Dickon was by her side.

So long as she could keep her thoughts from Gerard,

she was not actively unhappy. Since the announcement of her betrothal to Lord Barre, she had lived in a whirlwind of activity. The planning and acquisition of her trousseau with Aunt Clarrie took the best part of every day. The hours were filled with visits to and from the milliners, the bootmakers, the drapers, the lace merchants, the hatters, the furriers. The spare bedchamber became filled with dresses and cloaks, stockings, ribbons, tippets, boxes of handkerchiefs, even a bathing suit in case she should go to Brighthelmstone to dip in the sea.

When there was any time to spare, Mavreen was invited to Lord Barre's house, so, he had said kindly, she could familiarize herself with his residence and his large staff.

Large, indeed it was. Although he lived alone, his household consisted of a housekeeper, a groom of the bedchamber, a wardrobe keeper, a chef, a butler, four pages, five maids, a kitchen boy, a kitchen maid, a porter and four footmen, all identically decked out in green and silver liveries, so that Mavreen could never tell one from another. There were further outdoor staff she had no time to meet, with the exception of the head groom, George, to whom she introduced Dickon.

As for the house, Mavreen doubted she would ever find her way about it. There were endless bedchambers which she had not yet counted. Downstairs there was a splendid hall, with Ionic columns of brown Siena marble, from which rose two graceful staircases to the floor above. Portraits of Barre ancestors, going far back in history were hung in the vast dining room.

Below stairs were endless dark passages in which she would most certainly have lost herself but for the guidance of the housekeeper. The steward's room, where the butler, housekeeper, head valet and head coachman had their meals apart from the other members of the staff, was warm and comfortable. These upper servants even had a maid to wait on them. The rest of the household staff ate in the hall adjoining the kitchen and Mavreen was introduced to what seemed to her an unending number of chambermaids, footmen, valets, and boys in working overalls.

At the time of Mavreen's visit luncheon was being prepared. Chickens were roasting in the oven and a cauldron of soup simmered beside saucepans of vegetables and sauces. Servants hurried in and out. Each one seemed well aware of his allotted task and those who were not otherwise engaged were soon sent about their business by the butler.

The prospect of this new life did not frighten her, despite her lack of experience. It presented a challenge she was determined to meet. If Gilbert Barre, Sir John, and Clarissa believed she was capable of running a great household like this one, then she could surely do so. She resolved to make lists of all the servants' names and their individual tasks; to memorize the layout of each room in Barre House and how it was situated and decorated.

Lord Barre left her in no doubt that he had but one objective, which was to please her. One of the anterooms was to be made into a musical salon for her and he had promised that, should she desire it, Herr Mehler could attend regularly to give her music lessons. He was also, he told her, having the bridal chamber completely refurbished and restyled as a little surprise. His "little surprises" were endless. Upon one occasion, a carriage arrived loaded to the roof with boxes from the perfumers.

Mavreen tried to persuade Clarissa to take up residence in Barre House after the wedding. But Clarissa had steadfastly refused. Orchid House was her home, hers and Sir John's, she said. And although she would miss Mavreen's presence beyond telling, she hoped the child would visit her often.

The matter of the wedding had raised some problems. Plainly Mavreen could not be married from her father's house, still less from the little establishment in Richmond. In the end the warm-hearted Baroness von Eburhard solved the difficulty by offering to act as hostess at a vast reception in Barre House after the marriage ceremony, which was to take place privately in the chapel of a friend of Lord Barre's not far out in the country on the edge of the great heath at Hampstead. Immediately following the ceremony, carriages would take the bride and groom and their few favored guests back into London. No one would know that the bride had no retinue of friends and relations, since the von Eburhards' friends were many and varied and could as well be Mavreen's family acquaintances as Lord Barre's.

The fact that she must even be married "in hiding" did not distress Mavreen unduly. This side of her marriage held no interest for her; indeed, she would gladly have hibernated for a year and woken to find herself already established as Lady Barre. Yet she was both young and feminine enough to find herself enjoying the excitement of new dresses more costly and beautiful than she had ever dreamed of possessing. She tried not to think that she would be wearing such lovely gowns for Lord Barre's approval. When she permitted herself to think of the future at all, it was a recurring dream that she would one day meet Gerard with the lovely Mercedes upon his arm, herself so magnificently begowned and bejeweled that she would far outshine the wife Gerard had chosen in her preference.

But it was not to happen so.

Two days before the wedding, Mavreen told Clarissa that no matter how many last-minute details required her attention, she must go for a ride in the fresh air, hoping as always to work from her system her fears, doubts, regrets with the most violent of exercise. Tiredness, she had discovered, helped to dissipate the torment of longing that so often plagued her mind and body.

She and Dickon had turned their horses' heads toward home when they spied a horseman, galloping fast in their direction. Expertly, to Dickon's admiration and approval, the man succeeded in controlling his horse so that he stopped directly in front of them. Disregarding Dickon's presence, the stranger said, "Mavreen! Thank heaven I have found you!"

Dickon looked anxiously at his young mistress. She was first pale as death and then color flooded her face. The man's appearance was vaguely familiar to him and became fully recognizable only when Mavreen spoke his name.

"Gerard!" she said weakly. "What brings you here?"

Gerard dismounted and stood by her saddle.

"Send your groom aside!" he said urgently. "I must speak with you alone."

Dickon, who heard the command, looked at Mavreen questioningly. She nodded to him, dismounting with the help of the vicomte who handed both horses' reins to Dickon. Then he took Mavreen's arm and walked her swiftly away from Dickon's uneasy eyes, back along the path.

Mavreen's thoughts were in turmoil. Only with the utmost effort could she control the incredulous joy that was pervading her whole being. Gerard was here. He had come to find her. Was it possible at this eleventh hour that he had realized that nothing mattered but love?

"What brings you here?" she asked for the second time.

For answer, he put his arms around her and kissed her fiercely upon the mouth, bruising her lips though she did not mind the pain.

"You cannot marry!" he said, when at last he released her. "I have today heard of the wedding. Mavreen, my love, you promised me upon your oath you would not do this. Yet it is all arranged—for the day after tomorrow."

Mavreen almost laughed at the comic indignation on Gerard's face. It mattered not what words passed between them; the marriage would never take place. Gerard loved her and had come for her. She thanked God that he had not come a few days later.

"I rode forthwith to see your Aunt Clarrie," he said. "She at first refused to tell me your whereabouts until I convinced her that it was for your sake as well as my own that I must see you. When she told me you were riding in the woods beyond the river, I guessed you had come to 'our' place. Or so I prayed. When I passed the point of our tryst, I near died of anxiety in not seeing you. Mavreen, Mavreen. . . ."

She was laughing and crying together as he took her again into his arms, showering her face and hands with kisses.

"And you," she asked, when finally he left her lips free to form the words, "what is become of your marriage?"

Gerard grimaced.

"I have not yet seen the de Faenzas. I was, upon my arrival, advised by Sir John of his preoccupation with your wedding the day after tomorrow. I cannot tell you, my dearest, what pain his words gave me. But within minutes, I knew that it must not happen. You had given me your promise. Tell me now that you love me and only me. Speak the words, Mavreen, I beg you."

Quietly, she did his bidding.

"I love you and only you, Gerard. When I heard that you were to marry Mercedes de Faenza, I knew that all was over between us and I wished to die. I had no desire for life without you. But then my sorrow gave way to anger. I saw my marriage to Lord Barre as a way to protect myself against rejection, by you or by society. As Lady Barre, I would have entry to the highest circles in the land, nay even to court if I so chose. I would be rich beyond my dreams. But Gerard, none of this is of any account now that you have come back to me. I care not one jot for title, wealth, position, if to forgo it means I will never lose you again. You are all that matters to me."

"Oh, my darling!" Gerard whispered humbly. "I fear I do not deserve such devotion. But you will never regret it, I swear upon my honor. I will love you truly and constantly to my dying day."

He put his arms about her and looked deep into her eyes, his own shining with relief and joy. He had not thought she would submit so easily, if indeed at all.

"I could not endure life without you!" he said, kissing her yet again. "We shall be happy together, my dearest, more even than Mistress Clarissa and Sir John. We will pattern our lives upon theirs for it seems most satisfactory. If you would like it, my darling, I will buy a little house for you near to your Aunt Clarrie so that you may enjoy her society when I am not there. I have told Maman about you and she quite understands why I should love you so much and will understand our situation. You and I, Mavreen. . . ."

"No!"

Her voice, cold, hard, resolute, stopped him short.

"What is wrong, my love?" he asked. "You cannot doubt that I love you. Is that it? You think I do not love you enough?"

"No, Gerard!" Her gaze never wavered from his face. She spoke quietly and with great pride and dignity. "I do not doubt you love me. I doubt only your interpretation of the word 'love'. It is not the same as mine. I do not wish, nor ever shall desire it, to be your mistress. Or any man's. No, do not interrupt me. I do not condemn you for what you ask of me, but nor must you condemn me for my sentiments. I will never accept as a lover a man who does not consider me worthy to be his wife. Lord Barre, therefore, has more importance to me than you do, since he intends to defy society and wed me. I consider you have released me from my promise by your words and actions. The day after tomorrow, I shall be wed."

Gerard tried to embrace her but she pushed his arms angrily away from her, her eyes and voice so steely, he made no further effort to touch her.

"Don't ever seek to demonstrate your love to me again, Gerard," she said coldly. "I have discovered that lesson one is quite sufficient for me to know that I desire no further tutelage from you in the subject. Now I bid you good-day, for it is time Dickon and I were going home."

In silence, he followed her along the path to the spot where Dickon stood holding the horses. He was in torment, yet knew not what to do about it. He loved her. He could not bear the thought of her marriage to another man. He believed he could prevent it, yet now she had made him feel as if his proposition were an insult. Angrily, he reminded himself that she had forgot her breeding.

But when she and Dickon galloped out of sight without a backward glance from Mavreen, he knew that he should have offered her no less than marriage. But he could not marry her. His experiences in Compiègne had only confirmed and strengthened his decision to marry wealth.

He had found his mother, the vicomtesse, aged beyond belief. Frail, ill, she had been unable to prevent breaking into tears upon sight of him. He had not seen her weep since his father's death.

Day by day, with love and care, she began to recover from her ordeal. He learned of the indignities and privations she had endured during her life in prison. Degraded, impoverished, ill and alone, she retained her pride and would not tolerate sympathy, even from her beloved son.

Her ordeal, terrible as it was, had strengthened not only her religious belief, but her desire to restore the erstwhile grandeur of the de Valles. It had become an obsession with her. When Gerard told her of his proposed marriage to Mercedes de Faenza, she showed the first dawning signs of happiness and recovery. She spoke with enthusiasm about the match between the two families. She knew the de Faenzas were aristocrats of the old days, the family line as long and unbroken as the de Valles'. Had Gerard realized, she asked, how much could be done with the dowry Mercedes would bring with her? The château could be restored, maybe even some of the land bought back. Money was everything, these days, she said. Enough of it placed in the right quarters could effect miracles.

As her health and mind improved, she began to notice Gerard's quietness whenever she mentioned his betrothal. Her instinct guided her to the source of his sadness. Was there some woman he loved more than he loved his future wife, she asked him?

Gerard broke down and confessed in fullest detail his attachment to Mavreen.

"She is the only one I shall ever love!" he said. "How can I endure marriage to another woman when I desire only the girl of my heart?"

"Such sentiments will pass with time!" the vicomtesse counseled him, as Clarissa had counseled Mavreen. "Since you love her, *mon petit,* I do not doubt she is as sweet and lovely as you describe her. But you know you cannot marry her. You are the only de Valle left. Your duty must come before love."

Although Gerard did not wish to leave his mother alone again, the vicomtesse pressed him more and more frequently to return to London. She was afraid that despite the many loving letters Mercedes wrote to her son, the girl might find another suitor in the tedium of awaiting him.

Gerard was finally persuaded to go, although he had no heart for it. He was afraid of the pain he would feel were he to see or hear Mavreen on his return to London; Sir John would most certainly speak of her.

But when the moment came, and Sir John informed him of Mavreen's impending wedding, all his resolves de-

serted Gerard. He determined that he would not allow
Mavreen to marry Lord Barre; that if he, himself, must
marry Mercedes de Faenza for his mother's sake, he must
convince Mavreen that he could best ensure her happiness
by making her his mistress, giving her not only his protection but his love.

He did not stop to think that Mavreen might not be
willing to accept his offer. Now, too late, he knew he had
truly lost her and his grief was beyond bearing.

He sat upon his horse, tears blinding his vision, and let
the beast wander with him where it willed.

CHAPTER FOURTEEN
1796

Clarissa sat on the end of Mavreen's bed. It was the night
before the wedding. Mavreen's hair hung in tendrils loose
about her face; it would be newly washed and coiffed first
thing in the morning. Her white cambric nightgown was
tied demurely at the neck with pale blue ribbons. She
looked young—far too young to be the bride of an old
man. Clarissa's heart was heavy.

"You have no mother living, my dear, so it behooves
me to talk to you of tomorrow. But it is not of the ceremony I wish to talk. Or perhaps I do," she added, seeing a
way to the subject. "You see, Mavreen, there is more to
marriage than the wedding service itself, or the reception
that is to follow. There is the matter of your wedding
night."

Clarissa saw the color flare in Mavreen's cheeks and
knew that they understood each other on the matter for
conversation.

"I would prefer not to think about it now," Mavreen
said quietly. "It will come soon enough tomorrow!"

"I know, dear, and I am anxious that you should not be

afraid of what will happen. I thought if I were to tell you. . . ."

"Dearest Aunt Clarrie!" Mavreen broke in. "You forget I was reared on a farm. I know what will happen."

Clarissa sighed with relief.

"Then there is little more I need speak of," she said. "It is, of course, your duty to submit to your husband's wishes and desires in bed as in all things. You may quite possibly feel some discomfort upon the first occasion. Do not fear it will always be so for it happens that way only upon the surrender of your virginity."

Mavreen caught her breath. Although she had told Clarissa she did not wish to think about it, it was fear made her so reluctant. Now that the matter was in the open, she made up her mind to tell the truth, for she was sorely worried about her wedding night.

"I am not a virgin!" she said, so quietly Clarissa only just caught the words. "I allowed Gerard to love me."

Clarissa's eyes widened in dismay.

"You let Gerard *seduce* you?" she asked, horrified. "Oh, child, what folly is this!"

Mavreen, despite the gravity of the situation, smiled.

"He did not take advantage of me in the way you think, Aunt Clarrie. I wanted to give myself to him as much as he wanted to possess me. I do not regret it. I believe it is the only time I shall love truly, despite all the years of my life to come. I beg you not to look so distressed. At least I have known what it means to love with all my heart."

Clarissa clasped and unclasped her hands in apprehension.

"We cannot undo what is done!" she wailed, "so there is no point to my telling you it should not have been allowed to happen. I blame the boy, whatever you say. He has ruined you!"

Mavreen's eyes narrowed in anxiety.

"How so, ruined me?" she asked. "You mean, Lord Barre—Gilbert—will no longer want me for his wife?"

Clarissa groaned.

"I cannot answer that. But I do know he will most surely expect you to be a virgin."

"Then I must go to him and confess the truth. Then he may choose if he wishes to marry me or not!" Mavreen said calmly, making a move as if she were about to rise from her bed and dress.

"No, no, child!" Clarissa cried, becoming agitated. "Such a thing is unheard of. Get back into bed, child, and let me think!"

"I should have considered this before. I cannot marry Lord Barre under false pretenses!" Mavreen spoke nonetheless. "He is a good man and it would not be fair!"

Clarissa gave a deep sigh. Mavreen's honesty was as alarming as it was admirable. It hurt her to think that she must nevertheless encourage the child to deception. As she learned of Mavreen's passionate and heartbreaking encounter with the young vicomte two days ago, she reversed all her objections to the marriage to Lord Barre. She now felt that it was eminently desirable. She knew only too well the weaknesses of a woman in love. Were Mavreen to remain unmarried, Clarissa feared the girl might weaken and drift into the inferior relationship Gerard had suggested to her. The quicker she were married the better. Gerard would, of course, have to keep his distance from Gilbert Barre's wife!

"You must never speak of this again!" Clarissa said. "If Sir Gilbert asks you if you have ever had a lover, you must deny it absolutely. Perhaps he will believe you, and this way he will remain content. Were you to confess to him your love for Gerard, it would only make him unhappy. You do see that for yourself, do you not, child?"

Mavreen had no wish to upset her future husband. Lord Barre had been unfailing in his kindness and generosity to her. Only this evening, a beautiful leather box had been delivered by his coachman, containing a magnificent triple strand of pearls.

"These were my mother's," he had written on the note within the box. "It will make me proud and happy to see you wear them on the occasion of our marriage."

Lord Barre had guessed her humiliation over the matter of her birth and found this way to make her feel worthy to be his wife; though she and Aunt Clarrie had confessed their doubts to one another as to whether his mother would have been as pleased or proud to see Mavreen in the family jewels.

"I do not wish to hurt Lord Barre!" Mavreen said. "I cannot love him as I loved Gerard, but I am deeply fond of him, Aunt Clarrie. I suppose that, too, is a way of loving. There are many ways, are there not? I love you like a mother and I love Dickon, too, in yet another fashion."

Clarissa leaned forward and embraced the girl.

"You have a big heart, dearest, and room in it for many. I am sorry dear Mr. Glover is not well enough to travel but I am sure your sweet letter to him was ample consolation. That was indeed a beautiful book he sent you as a wedding gift." She sighed. "You have had so many, I'll wager there will be no room for them in Barre House. Lord Barre has many friends, of course. I believe he told me there would be three hundred guests at the reception."

Mavreen returned her embrace.

"I am so happy you are to come, Aunt Clarrie. It is another reason I love Gilbert, for had he refused you hospitality in his house, I would not have wished to live there!"

Clarissa smiled.

"He can refuse you nothing, my dear. I believe from all accounts your bridal chamber is quite beautiful." The room was to be a surprise to Mavreen who had not been allowed to see it while work was in progress. "You will live like a princess—nay, a deal more cherished than poor Princess Caroline from all accounts. 'Tis a fact that not even the birth of a little daughter has brought the prince to more affectionate disposition' toward his wife. Lord Malmesbury was saying to Sir John the other evening that the princess's lively spirits which she brought to England with her are all gone, and they say the melancholy and anxiety in her countenance are quite affecting."

"I would not let myself be so treated!" Mavreen declared. "She has less rights even than a servant in that she may not even leave her husband's service."

Clarissa sighed.

"Fortunate is the woman whose husband seeks to please her! For it is true she has no rights of her own. You will find it more easy than most to have your way, my dear, since Lord Barre loves you. But if, by your behavior, you should displease him. . . ."

She broke off, remembering, as did Mavreen, the earlier part of their conversation.

"Let us hope he will never learn the truth!" she said. "It might prove hard for you, child, were he to do so. Use what artifice you can in the matter and let him believe he pleases you, no matter that he does not. To a man of his age, your admiration will be important to him and could deflect him from other concerns!"

Now, twenty-four hours later, the ceremony and reception over, Mavreen waited alone in the huge four-poster bed in the bridal chamber at Barre House. Her new lady's maid, Dorcas, had removed her beautiful creamy satin wedding gown, bathed and perfumed her in the big bronze bath tub, filled to the brim with steaming hot water brought up from the kitchens. The girl, employed especially for the new Lady Barre, was almost as nervous as Mavreen, for although she had been previously in the service of the baroness and obtained her new job expressly because she knew in every detail what was correct for Her Ladyship to wear upon all occasions, she had never before prepared a lady for her wedding night.

Mavreen's nervousness increased as soon as she was abed. She dismissed the girl, preferring to await her bridegroom unattended.

Beneath the folds of her nightgown, her body trembled, shaking first from the cold of the satin sheets, next from a feverish heat brought on by her anxiety. Only now, when it was too late to prevent what was to happen, did she realize why Gerard had begged her not to marry without love. She had felt no fear with Gerard. Her body had ached with the desire to be ever closer to his.

But now she awaited the coming of her husband, whose body she did not desire and whose hands upon her person she dreaded.

Dear Gilbert had made himself as handsome as possible for the wedding. He wore a bottle-green silk coat with claret-colored stripes and breeches, his waistcoat silver, richly embroidered as were his cuffs. He looked imposing.

No doubt in order to make himself seem more youthful and fashionable, he had discarded his wig and wore his own grey hair powdered and dressed in the mode of the Prince of Wales. Mavreen had been suitably impressed. But now, he, like herself, would be disrobed and he would come to her as nature had fashioned him, paunched with age and indulgence.

She shivered again. There was no escape from her ordeal. If only Gerard, like a prince in a fairy tale, would come to her window and fly away with her! If only he would materialize like the angel Gabriel, sword drawn, and standing between her and the bedroom door, declare: "No one but I shall ever share her bed!"

Mavreen fought back her tears. In an effort to distract her mind, she gazed about the room. It was indeed magnificent. Sir Gilbert had had the huge bed chamber entirely redecorated and refurbished for her. The vast four-poster on which she sat was hung with heavy palest-green silk curtains, the walls covered with a floral French paper. Deep crimson Aubusson rugs covered the polished oak floor. The same deep red was repeated in the damask curtains drawn across the triple casements.

But taking a detailed itinerary could not keep her mind engaged forever. Her eyes went once more to the door. Gilbert was a long time a-coming. The last guests had departed two hours before.

Her hopes soared. Perhaps he would not come at all. Perhaps, having eaten and partaken of so much liquor, he had fallen ill and was too indisposed to attend his bride. But even as she prayed this might be so, she knew in her heart that it would not happen. Gilbert had put his arm around her shoulders earlier and said, "Hurry, my dearest, for I am filled with impatience to have you to myself!"

Ladies and gentlemen had filled the great house until even it seemed about to overflow. Mavreen now mused on the people she did not know who came up to her, curtsied, wished her happiness, complimented her upon her beauty, and were replaced by others. Her husband's beautiful collections of silver and glass were all in use. There were white flowers everywhere; white for virginity! Mavreen

thought now. What would become of her if Gilbert were
to leave her bed this night in anger? What kind of happiness could come from a marriage begun in such deceit
and disillusion? Yet still she could not wish herself the
virgin her husband expected to find. Although she hated
Gerard now with all the intensity which is the other side
of the coin of love, she held in her heart like a prize, the
glory of their loving. Her fear was for herself, her regret
only for her husband.

She heard his step outside on the landing and then his
knock on her door. She pulled the sheet further upward
to her chin, and bade him enter.

Such was her tension she nearly laughed when she saw
him, so comical a figure did he present in voluminous white
nightgown and tassled cap, a candelabrum held aloft in
his hand. But the laughter faded from her eyes as he
approached the bed, his expression not jovial but forbidding in its grimness. Fear came once more upon her
and she trembled.

Making no move to touch or kiss her, Gilbert sat on the
edge of the bed. The room was warm. A huge fire burned
in the grate and as the draft from the door fanned the
flames, a log fell in a shower of sparks, startling both
bride and groom.

"I have something I wish to discuss with you, Mavreen!"
he said, his tone ominous. "I should, mayhap, have spoken
of the matter before our wedding and in this judgment,
'tis likely I have done you an injustice."

Mavreen held her breath. She had little doubt that somehow he had received word of her affair with Gerard.
Could little Rose have been bribed to reveal the truth?
Yet this was hard to believe. Her husband was about to
question her and she did not think herself capable of the
lie Aunt Clarrie had instructed her to tell.

"Love!" pronounced Lord Barre stentoriously, "is a serious facet of human nature. It can bring great joy—and
great pain. 'Twixt man and wife, it can make or mar a
marriage. Do you understand what I am saying to you,
child?"

Unable to find her voice, Mavreen nodded. Her husband

did not recommence his speech and her nerve deserted her, so that she could bear the waiting no longer.

"Do not fear to address me, I beg you!" she cried. "I am willing to accept your judgment for I know you to be a fair and kind man. Speak, I pray you!"

Lord Barre gave her a quick glance and then turned his head aside as if he could not bear to see her.

"It is not easy for me, Mavreen. The matter most deeply concerns you, your future, your position as my wife. . . ."

"Have no fear, sir!" she said proudly. "If it is your wish that we should be unmarried. . . ."

Gilbert looked directly at her for the first time. He seemed more surprised than angry now.

"Not that, child. Most certainly not that!" he said.

Had he, then, already made up his mind to forgive her, Mavreen wondered, but could not yet overcome his distaste for a wife who was not pure? Since he seemed quite unable to broach the subject, she did so for him.

"Is it your wish not to bed with me?" she asked bluntly.

Gilbert's face took on a look of astonishment. He had not expected his child-bride to be so plain spoken.

"Dear child!" he said earnestly. "It is most certainly not my wish, for I can imagine no greater delight. Mavreen, my dearest little girl, my sweet wife, I have done you most grievous wrong. I should have confessed long since that I am impotent and cannot bed anyone."

His eyes searched her face for anger, disillusionment, disappointment—disdain. To his utter astonishment, she threw back the covers and, kneeling upon the bedside, touched his cheek tenderly with her hand.

"Oh, Gilbert!" she said. "Dearest Gilbert. Now I am free to love you!"

She was laughing and crying at one and the same time.

PART TWO
1797-1799

CHAPTER FIFTEEN

1797

"Oh, milady, you've never looked more beautiful!"

Mavreen surveyed her reflection in the dressing table mirror and smiled back at Rose, who had paid her the compliment. Dorcas was now in charge of her wardrobe and since it was a full-time occupation, Rose left Clarrie's to become Mavreen's personal maid.

"I think the style and color of the dress become me!" she replied. Reaching up her hands, she touched the necklace of emeralds Rose clasped around her neck. "How clever of Lord Barre to select emeralds for they match exactly the color of my gown!"

Seeing Rose's pink cheeks, she added, "Why, Rose, you told him! He knew what color the dress was to be all along."

Rose giggled.

"Yes, milady. It was a secret. He made me promise on my word not to let on. They're ever so beautiful, milady!"

Dear, kind, Gilbert! Mavreen thought as she fastened the two matching emerald pendants into her earlobes. What a wedding anniversary present—on top of all the hundred and one gifts with which he showered her upon every occasion. His greatest delight lay in surprising and pleasing her, and she was touched by the thoughtfulness that had prompted him to discover the color of her new dinner gown for tonight's big celebration. Presently she would go and thank him but he would turn aside her gratitude, as he always did, saying her pleasure and his pride in her were thanks enough.

"I am fortunate to be married to such a good man, am I not, Rose?" she said, sighing. "I had never thought it was possible to be as content!"

The hidden meaning in Mavreen's words did not escape

Rose, who had met the young vicomte de Valle, made possible their secret appointment, and knew their relationship. Although Mavreen did not confide in Rose, the young girl understood very well the agonies of losing a first love. But she, like her young mistress, had grown to like and respect the elderly Lord Barre and to appreciate that Mavreen had much to be thankful for even if her marriage did lack passion and romance.

It did not lack for love. In one short year, a very real and lasting affection had blossomed between what Baroness von Eburhard called winter and spring. Gilbert, Mavreen thought now, was if anything overindulgent. She lacked for nothing that money could buy. Moreover, her husband gave her complete independence—something very rare in the marriages Mavreen had seen around her in which men dominated and women obeyed. Gilbert asked nothing of her but to at all times uphold and respect his family name.

"I do not wish to know if you desire to take a lover, my dear!" he had said on that strangest of wedding nights. "That is for you to decide for yourself. I ask only that you be discreet should you have such an affair. I want you to consider yourself free to do whatever you wish so long as it is consistent with your role as Lady Barre."

Confession of her love for Gerard was on her lips, but instinct forbade its utterance. That affair was ended forever. Gerard had forfeited all right to her love by his humiliation of her, and even were he free as she to take a lover, she would never give herself to him again. Not that Gerard *was* free, for his betrothal to Mercedes de Faenza had been announced not long after her wedding, before his return to France.

Mavreen did not permit herself the weakness of thoughts about Gerard. To do so was to court desires and longings which brought only bitterness and pain. She was, as she had told Rose, content. Her life was filled to overflowing, leaving no time for regret. Such moments of sadness came upon her only in the dark hours of the night when sleep eluded her and memories forced their way into her exhausted mind.

Fortunately, the hours of the day were not long enough

for her to fulfill every engagement that came pouring into the Barre household. Lord Barre and his wife were on every visiting list; invitations to their twice-weekly dinner parties were greatly coveted, and would be even more so after tonight when the Prince of Wales, himself, was guest of honor.

"My dear, you've scored a very big hit with his Royal Highness!" Gilbert had told her proudly after a day at the races when Mavreen had first been introduced to the Prince of Wales. "But I'm sure I don't need to tell you so. He scarce took his eyes off you all afternoon!"

Naturally enough, Mavreen had been interested to meet him, but he did not appeal to her as a man, for he was gross and dissipated even at thirty-five. She had heard too many items of gossip to his discredit, not the least important in her eyes, his treatment of his wife.

Mavreen found it hard to believe that within the short space of one year she had come to know so many important and interesting people. Equally to her surprise, it appeared that she, herself, was becoming quite notable. Ladies who a year before would not have opened their doors to her, now followed the fashion in clothes set by Mavreen. She loved the feel of rich fabrics and the beautiful combinations of colors and trimmings and frequently designed her own gowns, adapting the current trend to suit her perfect figure. That other women copied her styles, she considered a compliment and she was childishly pleased and amused, though not proud, as was Gilbert himself, at her social success.

Lord Barre's friends and contemporaries loved his young wife, finding her not only attractive in looks but fascinating in conversation. Her opinions were always her own, logically arrived at, intelligent, well-informed. Her husband's guests accepted her even though she was a female. They were amused by her individuality. When it was the custom to wear a hat, Mavreen would be seen bare-headed; upon occasion she was even seen to be riding level with her groom and talking to him as if he were Mr. Pitt himself. She spoke openly of her concern for the poor, farmers in particular. Living as she now did, where money was so abundant that it need not be considered, it was

natural that she should compare her present circumstances
with the hardships and privations of her childhood and
find the two extremes impossible to reconcile.

Mavreen was known to have little time for idle gossip
or the frivolities of court ladies. She seemed, therefore,
never quite one of them and they accepted her only because she was Lord Barre's wife. There was a wealth of
speculation as to her lineage and it was commonly supposed that she was the natural daughter of Sir John Danesfield and Mistress Manton though none spoke openly of
their suspicions and gossiped only in the privacy of their
homes. No one doubted that she was an aristocrat for her
manner and bearing were always perfectly correct. She
was a law unto herself yet always within the bounds of
convention.

There were to be one hundred and fifty guests at tonight's dinner party, nearly three times as many as were
normally invited. All the most prominent members of
society would be there—with the exception of the ladies
who had barred Mavreen from Almack's Assembly Rooms
in the days when she was considered a nobody. She had
not and could not forget the snub meted out to her and
Aunt Clarrie and she remained adamant on this point
despite Gilbert's gentle remonstrations.

Among the guests were many who had become her
personal friends—Lisa von Eburhard for one, and the
Honorable James Pettigrew and his sister Anne of whom
Mavreen was particularly fond. Sir John was to be present, for despite her intentions, Mavreen was now on good
terms with him once more. At first she had accepted recon-
ciliation to please Gilbert, her father's closest friend, but
as the first months of her marriage passed by and her new
status eased the scars to her pride, she began to learn
tolerance and to understand how easy it must have been
for Sir John to succumb to temptation. Honesty forced
her to admit that she, too, had succumbed when she fell
in love with Gerard. But for a kindly Fate, she too might
have produced a child out of wedlock.

Mavreen tried not to think too much about children.
When some lady of her acquaintance declined an invitation because she was *enceinte,* Mavreen had felt a stirring

of envy. But her longing for a baby did not last and was soon put from her mind when she realized that it was not Gilbert's but Gerard's child she longed to hold to her breast. She told herself that since she now hated even the memory of Gerard de Valle, she could not possibly desire to bear him a child.

Nevertheless, she was very conscious that among her guests tonight was an old friend of the de Valle family, and of her father—a certain marquis de Guéridon. Now an émigré living in London, it was not so long ago the marquis had lived in Paris and frequented the Château de Boulancourt, Gerard's home.

Mavreen could not help wondering, as she completed her toilette, if he had news of the family. She told herself that idle curiosity propelled her to the marquis's side as soon as his arrival was announced. He was among the first arrivals in company with her father. Sir John greeted her warmly and presented the marquis de Guéridon to her. The distinguished-looking gentleman quizzed his young hostess with a Frenchman's appreciation for a pretty woman.

The marquis was curious on other counts, too. All London was talking of the new Lady Barre and in every drawing room, her name was spoken sooner or later, often with open admiration by the gentlemen, with envy and more grudging compliments from the ladies. He could understand why. The young woman, little more than a girl, had a vitality about her. It emanated from her in a way that was instantly exciting to a man—even to one of his advancing years. Old Gilbert was to be envied his young bride, he thought.

But not least of his curiosity was on account of a letter he had received from his dear friend, the Vicomtesse Marianne de Valle. She was deeply concerned about her son, Gerard, she told him. His betrothal to Mercedes de Faenza seemed to bring him no joy, despite its advantages and that, according to her miniature, she was a handsome woman who would do him credit. Marianne feared Gerard was unable to forget the young English girl with whom he had foolishly fallen in love on his last visit to England. Would the marquis be good enough to confirm that the girl was now safely married and beyond her son's reach? For only if he knew this did she feel the boy would cease to pine for her and smile once more.

The marquis gave an inward sigh. If this young girl was haunting Gerard's memory, he could not offer poor Marianne de Valle much in the way of consolation. Mavreen would not be easy to forget.

"I must not monopolize your time, madame," he said. "Nevertheless, I can see no other lady present who could entice me from your side!"

Mavreen laughed at his extravagant compliment and replied to his faultless English in equally perfect French, "Then you flatter me, sir, for there are many lovely ladies present!"

"You have lived in France?" the marquis asked. "Your accent is quite pure!"

"I was instructed by a very charming old scholar by the name of Mr. Glover. I shall be happy to write and tell him you approve his tutelage!"

Suddenly the announcement of the arrival of the Prince of Wales brought all conversation to a halt. Mavreen hurriedly joined Lord Barre as he went forward to receive their royal guest.

The Prince of Wales was, as always, immediately surrounded by a crowd of ladies seeking his notice and gentlemen to whom his patronage was important, but this evening he was interested only in the young woman Barre had married. He kept Mavreen by his side. He was at present very unsettled in his love life. He was, therefore, delighted to find someone new to occupy his thoughts, if only for the evening. His association with Mavreen could be but a flirtation and no more, for Barre had lent him very considerable sums of money and the prince felt it would not be politic to give offense by making a cuckold of him. At least, not publicly.

It was a credit to the girl's personality, he thought as he escorted her into the dining room, that he found her so attractive despite the fact that she could scarcely be called voluptuous in stature—his usual preference in women. Her conversation during the long drawn-out lavish repast amused and interested him. She seemed to understand the intricacies of finance and to approve the new idea of using bank notes in preference to gold coins. She was well informed as to the state of the war and discussed with him the newly signed French treaty with Austria, forced upon them by Napoleon's victories. Moreover, Mavreen was sympathetic toward his own complaints that he, the Prince of Wales, had not been given higher rank in the army and was excessively humiliated by being outranked by his younger brothers.

"When you are king of England!" she remarked, "you will have the opportunity to put right many such injustices, the bad pay and conditions of our sailors, for example. My husband told me this very morning that the fleet is on the point of mutiny. And have you heard, sir, what news there is of the French invasion in Wales?"

"Pah! 'Tis nothing, I'm told, but a band of vagabonds and criminals pushed into uniforms. I have no doubt Lord Cawdor's army will repel them within the week." the prince dismissed the affair scornfully.

But conversation waned as the prince drank more and more of his host's good wines, which, although they made him even more loquacious, took the edge of intelligence from his words. Mavreen was glad when the dinner finally came to an end and she could excuse herself from his company.

Gilbert had engaged a popular quartet, and later, there would be faro in the card room. But before the music began, Mavreen found time to seek out the marquis de Guéridon and on the pretext of showing him the decor of the Chinese room, managed at last to ask him the question she was too proud to ask her father— Was there recent news of the de Valles?

Concealing his interest in his young companion's inquiries, the marquis admitted to having but recently received a letter from the vicomtesse.

"Seeing our countries are at war, this letter was most unexpected," he remarked. "But by whatever devious route the letter travelled, it was no more than a month since it was penned. I can, therefore, assure you that both the vicomtesse and her son are well, despite the impoverished state of their living."

He watched tiny spots color Mavreen's cheeks, noticed the way her eyelashes closed over her eyes to conceal their expression, and correctly surmised that the young viscount's interest in her was reciprocated. He felt a surge of pity for the girl. There could not be much pleasure in marriage to a man older even than her father. What could be more natural than that the two young people had met and fallen hopelessly in love. Hopeless the situation must be. Gerard de Valle was on the point of marriage to the wealthy Mercedes de Faenza and the young Lady Barré lived this side of the Channel, her country at war with Gerard's, and was unlikely to see him. From Marianne's letter, it was clear that the young man was now devoting his energies to restoring, as best he could, the ruins of the Château de Boulancourt. Most of the valuable treasures, tapestries, ornaments, and furniture had been looted when the château was burned. The de Valles were using but two rooms which they had made habitable and with only the old manservant, Jules, to wait upon them.

The marquis recounted these facts to Mavreen. She listened in silence, comparing her own luxurious life with Gerard's and finding herself filled with pity for him. This emotion entirely replaced the bitterness that had so far kept her heart in check.

"Fortunately, there is still enough money to live on!" the marquis was saying. "Marianne, the vicomtesse, was prudent enough to bury some of her smaller treasures, jewelry and the like, in the gardens of the château. They were not discovered by the looters and when the vicomtesse returned to her home, she found everything intact. From time to time, Jules, the old retainer, sells a piece of jewelry or an objet d'art and this keeps the family from starvation. I wish very much that I could assist them. Antoine de Valle was one of my closest friends. But unfortunately, as an émigré, I had to leave most of my own fortune behind me in France, and even were I in a position to offer assistance, the vicomtesse would be too proud to accept it. So that is their story. Circumstances will change for them, of course, as soon as Gerard's marriage takes place."

"And will that be soon?" Mavreen asked quietly.

The marquis shrugged his shoulders.

"The war makes things difficult, as you will appreciate. Gerard cannot come to England as he pleases, and I understand Mercedes de Faenza has no wish to travel to France to be married. She is insisting upon a fashionable wedding in London. Between you and me, I cannot see that spoiled young woman ever desirous of living in the Château de Boulancourt under the present régime in France. Nor do I deem it likely that Gerard will be parted from his mother to live in England. She is far from well and needs his support."

Mavreen was shaken out of her self-imposed disinterest in Gerard's affairs to say, "But what will become of such a marriage? Surely, if Mercedes loves Gerard, she will want to be near him!"

The marquis sighed. He no longer doubted that this young girl felt as deeply for Gerard as from his mother's account, the boy felt for her.

Mavreen regretted that her duties as hostess forbade a more lengthy conversation with the marquis. It was sad, he reflected, that Marianne de Valle could not meet and judge the young Lady Barre for herself. Marianne would like the girl, of that he was certain.

As he watched Mavreen's progress across the floor of the Chinese salon, graceful, very much alive with the quick movements of youth, the marquis shook his head regretfully. The instigators of the revolution in France had much to answer for; and though insignificant measured alongside the rivers of blood that had flowed in the battle, the tragedy of Mavreen's and Gerard's young lives was nevertheless real to the two of them. Had the de Valles retained possession of their former great wealth, Gerard might have met and married the girl despite her background, defying convention just as Gilbert Barre had done.

But it was Mavreen's heart rather than her head in control of her emotions as she rejoined her husband and their guests in the room where the music was about to begin. Despite her love of music, she could think of nothing but Gerard; his pending marriage; his devotion to his

mother; and not least, of the brief moments of love they
had shared. All feeling of bitterness had left her, and she
was vulnerable once more to the pain of lost love. It was
so much easier to live without him when she could hate
him. Now that was no longer possible. The kindly marquis
himself had confirmed the necessity for Gerard to marry
into wealth. He had had no real choice and she knew it
was childish and illogical of her to have imagined that he
could propose marriage to her in his circumstances.

Such thoughts made her realize yet again her own good
fortune in becoming the wife of such a good, kindly man
as Lord Barre. He treated her at all times with the utmost
courtesy and respect and in no way infringed on her
privacy. He had become in many respects both friend
and indulgent father and her devotion to him was very
real. It pleased her that he should feel so proud of her and
it made her the more determined to be a good wife to him.
Although several men had made their interest in her
known in various subtle, and sometimes not so subtle ways,
Mavreen had not taken a lover, nor contemplated doing
so, despite Gilbert's generous agreement. She felt no inclination for the casual flirtations that seemed to abound
amongst their rich friends. As a married woman, her eyes
had been opened to many such affairs, those of Lisa von
Eburhard being as changeable as the fashions. With the
Prince of Wales himself setting the pattern, it was fashionable to have a lover. No one would have thought the
worse of her for it. But apart from her own disinclination
for such a relationship, she wished to protect Gilbert from
the inevitable gossip that went with such behavior.

As the sound of music filled the salon, Mavreen, lost in
her own thoughts, sighed deeply. A year ago this very day,
she had ceased to be Mavreen Ashworth in name, but only her title and her surroundings had changed with her
marriage. She knew herself to be the same girl who had
run barefoot through the Sussex meadows.

Inside her woman's body lay the same heart, singing
with joy and happiness when Gerard had chased her into
the grove and called her his *petit écureuil*.

The musical performance over, Mavreen found herself

talking to young Anne Pettigrew. The same age as herself, Anne had but recently come to London to be presented at court and to find a husband. Anne was a gay, pretty girl with flaxen ringlets and eyes as blue as cornflowers. Her mouth was wide and her nose had a definitely saucy tilt to it. She was popular enough to be invited everywhere, especially as she had a charming older brother, James, to escort her to her friends' parties.

James was Mavreen's openly confessed admirer. He made no attempt to hide the fact that he was "madly in love with her" and would have no other.

"James has been searching everywhere for you!" Anne told Mavreen. "You must spare him a few words, Mavreen, else he will be inconsolable for days and I shall suffer for his ill temper!"

Mavreen linked her arm with Anne's and smiled.

"You know very well that your brother is never ill-tempered!" she said. "I know of no other so continually good-natured, unless it be my own dear Gilbert."

The young girl surveyed Mavreen from two round curious eyes.

"You are really very happily married, are you not, Mavreen!" she remarked. "Do not think me impertinent but James and I have talked of you often—he will talk of little else!—and we have sometimes wondered on account of the big disparity in ages, whether. . . ."

"It makes little difference!" Mavreen broke in. "I have so very much to be grateful for in my husband."

Anne sighed, her eyes still puzzled.

"I do not believe I could love a man so much older than myself, although I can fully understand how fond of dear Lord Barre you must be. I fear I am a romantic. I am like my brother James. I cannot be satisfied with second best!"

"And who is first best?" Mavreen inquired laughing. "For from all accounts, you have so many suitors even you have lost count."

"But only one who I would care to marry!" Anne argued. "And he cares not one jot for me. In truth, he is shortly to marry another!"

"And will you confess his name to me?" Mavreen asked fondly, for she was much attached to the sweet, friendly girl beside her.

"I do not think you know him!" Anne said, her blue eyes dreamy. "He was at school with James, a French viscount by the name of Gerard de Valle." She did not notice Mavreen's quick intake of breath but went on innocently, "On two occasions, Gerard was a guest in our house in Buckinghamshire and I made up my mind then that I would like to marry him, although I was but ten or eleven years old. Alas, I must have seemed but a silly child to him although I think he enjoyed my society almost as much as that of James's." She smiled mischievously. "He did once kiss me, albeit under the mistletoe. If I could only find another like him, I would gladly be wed!"

Mavreen was silent. Too many eager questions trembled on her lips. She had had no inkling that Gerard and the Pettigrew family were known to one another. Her meeting with Anne and James, arranged by her father, was recent and mainly a kindness to Anne's parents who wished to introduce her to London society in the highest circles. Both James and Anne had been frequent guests at the Barres' dinner parties and James's adoration of Mavreen was admitted even to Lord Barre.

"Had you not snatched her from my grasp when you did, sir, I would have proposed to your beautiful wife upon my first meeting with her!" James had declared.

Delighted as always to hear Mavreen praised, Gilbert had taken a fancy to the boy and shown no jealousy when the three young people went riding together or played cards or went shopping in each other's company. Nor had he needed to be jealous, Mavreen assured him. Fond as she was of Anne's tousle-headed, freckle-faced brother, her heart was in no way stirred by him. James was, indeed, like a brother to her too.

"You are as James forever tells me, good-hearted as well as beautiful. Have you no vices, Mavreen?"

Mavreen laughed.

"Indeed, I have many!" she said.

"Then confess but one fault!" Anne demanded.

"Well, for one, I have an unpleasant nature. If a person does me an injustice, I cannot easily forgive it and will go out of my way to inflict a greater hurt upon them than they wrought upon me. I am, in short, vindictive, and that is not a nice trait."

"I find it hard to believe!" Anne said truthfully. "For who would wish to do you a wrong in the first place, Mavreen? Everyone I know adores you; even the servants seem to love you and serve you because it pleases them. As for my groom, William—I do believe he would as readily lay down his life for you as your Dickon!"

Anne Pettigrew was referring to the man who had once been in the service of a certain Lady Sinclair. Not long ago, her ladyship had been kept waiting for her carriage through no fault of the groom's but had nonetheless dismissed him on the spot—this being upon the doorstep of the Barre house. Dickon had reported the incident to Mavreen and next day, she had sent him to find William and offered to secure employment for him, albeit he had been dismissed without a reference. Fortunately for all concerned, the Pettigrews were looking for a man and Mavreen had been able to arrange for William's re-employment.

"It was no more than a matter of justice!" she said now. "He did not deserve his dismissal!"

"Yet there are many others who would not have troubled themselves about a mere servant!" Anne insisted. "I do not think I would have done so, myself, although I know now that you were right in what you did. Servants are, after all, still people, are they not?"

At that moment, James was approaching them with a beaming smile of recognition.

"So Anne has found you!" he said, kissing Mavreen's hand and looking with exaggerated love-sickness into her eyes. "Though I fear I shall not long be able to engage your attention. His Royal Highness was asking for you but a few moments ago and Lord Barre sent me in search of you!"

Mavreen would have preferred to remain talking with the Pettigrews but she went at once to Gilbert's side. The prince was ready to begin the evening's gambling and having heard that Lady Barre played an excellent game of faro, was insisting she play at his table.

"Be cautious, my dear!" Gilbert warned her. "He is quite reckless with money and his debts legion. Moreover, it would not be politic to win too heavily from him!"

The prince's behavior toward his young hostess was alternately amorous and boastful, depending upon the current run of his luck. Having won a pair of threes, he was in the best of humor—pushing a hundred gold sovereigns to Mavreen's place to "recompense her for her losses," and following up the generous gift with an invitation to go down to Brighthelmstone to enjoy the delights of his pavilion. But a subsequent run of bad luck had the effect of increasing his alcoholic intake and his speech became less and less meaningful. When Mavreen excused herself from the table, he was quite incoherent and seemed unaware that he had twice spilt brandy down his beautiful cinnamon-colored waistcoat.

It was now past three o'clock, and the Prince of Wales and nearly all but the card-playing guests had departed. Mavreen found her husband quietly entertaining Sir William Fawkener in the library. Sir William rose, smiling at Mavreen. "I am too old for these late hours, lacking both your youth and beauty, Lady Barre!"

Gilbert, too, stood up, putting his arm about Mavreen's shoulders.

"I am a fortunate man, am I not, William?" he said rhetorically. "I think even the future king of England envies me my bride!"

But it was Mavreen who had the last word when she said with complete truth, "Yet I would not exchange you, dearest Gilbert, even for England's future king."

CHAPTER SIXTEEN

1797

Clarissa sat beside Mavreen in the warm May sunshine, the glass of the little summer house reflecting the golden rays in their eyes. The magnolia tree was in full bud and everywhere the birds sang as they flew to and from their nestfuls of fledglings.

"Take off your cape, my dear!" Clarissa said, as Hannah came toward them with a tray of tea. "The weather is like midsummer."

Mavreen smiled.

"Dearest Aunt Clarrie!" she said. "You have no idea what happiness it gives me to see you so well and happy. I do wish you would call upon me at Barre House. Gilbert has assured me many times that he would be as pleased as I to see you there!"

But Clarissa shook her head.

" 'Twould not be in your interest, child. From what your dear father tells me, there is quite enough speculation about you as it is. All London is endeavoring to learn the identity of your mother and some are already supposing that I am she!"

"Then I am proud if they so think!" Mavreen declared, leaning over and hugging Clarissa. "I remember my real mother only with difficulty and although I loved her dearly, I love you also, dearest Aunt Clarrie!"

Clarissa was sufficiently moved by this tribute that for a moment or two she was unable to speak. Then she withdrew a parchment from her reticule and showed it to Mavreen, saying, "This was delivered to Orchid House yesterday, my dear. Obviously, I have not opened it but there was a covering letter from a lady in Switzerland which left me in no doubt that your missive is from young Gerard de Valle. Before I hand it to you, will you give me your assurance that you will not permit it to upset you? You are looking well and happy, and I would fain not be the one to cause any reversal. In fact, I have been of two minds whether I should pass it to you or not."

"Oh, Aunt Clarrie, give it to me I pray you. Do not keep me in torment. Is it really from Gerard? Pray let me have it."

As Clarissa obeyed, she broke the seal, her heart pounding.

The letter was dated over a month previously. It had clearly been penned on impulse and the words chosen with difficulty.

Dearest Petit Écureuil,

I make no excuse for writing to you. There is none. I know that you are now Lord Barre's wife and that I have forfeited all rights to your thoughts, let alone your affection.

Yet I cannot permit another month to pass without telling you how deeply ashamed I am of the way I have behaved toward you. I can but beg your understanding and forgiveness, bearing in mind your fairness of heart, that I was so much disturbed by my mother's plight and by the necessity to help her that I lacked all consideration for your feelings. Though you may find it difficult to believe, I loved you so dearly I could think of naught else but preventing your marriage to another man; and in the proposal I put to you, I acted entirely selfishly.

If any man paid for his mistakes, then I have done so, Mavreen. I am tormented by the thought of how deeply you must despise me. I do not blame you for so doing. Nevertheless, I ask you to believe that despite all appearances to the contrary, I did and still do love you with all my heart.

Doubtless, you will know that I am engaged to marry Mercedes de Faenza. I do not love her and despite my mother's promptings to hasten the wedding, I continue to make every excuse for the avoidance of a relationship that is abhorrent to me, the more so because I believe, if you think of me at all, you will consider my marriage yet another form of betrayal of

*the love we shared. I know that for my mother's sake,
I must marry soon. I think I could endure the prospect more readily if I were to receive word from you
that you will not think too badly of me. My mind
would be further eased were I to know you are happy
in your marriage and did not regret in any way a
decision made, I fear, in anger directed against me
rather than for the advantages such a marriage offered you.*

*My dearest love, for I cannot call you less—since
it is the truth before God—I think of you every day
and every night of my life and with sadness and regret. Mayhap I would find peace were I to hear from
you that you think of me sometimes and not in
anger.*

> *Tóujours!*
> *Gerard.*

"My dear, you must not weep!" Aunt Clarrie begged
as the tears rolled down Mavreen's cheeks. "You will
force me to regret my decision to give you that letter.
Come now, dry your eyes and prove me right to have
placed it in your hands!"

"Oh, indeed, yes!" Mavreen said, choking a little on her
words. "I am not really sad, Aunt Clarrie. A little, yes,
but happy, too. Gerard loves me. He has always loved me.
For that I am truly joyful!"

Clarissa sighed. She had made no mention of the letter
to Sir John, fearing that he might forbid her to pass it on
to Mavreen. Sir John knew nothing of the young lovers'
secret trysts and certainly would not sympathize or approve of them. But Clarissa had confidence in Mavreen's
good sense, as she told her now. Her marriage was of
over a year's standing and a happy one. It would be
wrong to let anything interfere with its success.

"I know that, Aunt Clarrie!" Mavreen agreed. "Nor is
there anything I could do to place my marriage in jeopardy, even if I would. Gerard is many miles away in
Compiègne, although his letter passed through Switzerland to reach me here. But don't you see, Aunt Clarrie,
I can at least now write to reassure him. We parted in
anger and that has caused Gerard much pain. I can tell

him in my reply that I have not only forgiven him but that I understand far better than I did last year the obligations that were then and still are upon him in relation to his family. I feel no bitterness toward him. I want him to know it. If I could only be sure a reply would reach him!"

"That is simple enough!" Clarissa said, glad to have the matter so easily settled. "Gerard's letter came enclosed within another from a Countess von Heissen. She stated that she is an old friend of Gerard's and requested me to guard his letter most carefully and to deliver it to no one but yourself. I have her address on her notepaper in my bureau. You have but to write your reply to her and doubtless she will find means of getting it safely to Gerard. Switzerland is, after all, a neutral country."

She had barely finished the sentence before Mavreen was hugging her with all the impetuous enthusiasm of her childhood days.

"I will write at once, with your permission!" she cried, cheeks aglow. "Oh, Aunt Clarrie, if you but knew how happy I am. I know that it is madness to feel so since I cannot hope to see Gerard, hear him, touch him. Yet it is enough to know he loves me and that I love him. Oh, how I wish this terrible war would end and there was free passage between our countries! It isn't easy to be happy without love, is it, Aunt Clarrie?"

"And doubtless as difficult for your young vicomte, too. Be guarded how you address him, child. To show too much dependence upon him may distress him even further, since there is naught he can offer you without endangering your marriage."

Mavreen remembered this counsel as she sat in the quiet flower-filled salon and composed her reply. Through the French windows, she could see Clarissa dozing peacefully in the sunshine. There was no sound in the room but the calls of garden birds and the humming of the bees in the lavender bushes.

Her heart ached with longing for Gerard as she penned his name. Only with great self-control did she refrain from re-living in her memory those hours of sweetness in the bedchamber above her head.

"Dearest Gerard!" she wrote, and paused until her
fingers had ceased to tremble.

> *Beg my forgiveness no more for I have long since
> given it, nay, of my own accord reached full under-
> standing of all that passed between us. We were vic-
> tims of our birth, you no less than I. It is I who should
> demand your tolerance for my selfishness, for I of-
> fered you none, seeing only my own suffering.*
>
> *I pray most earnestly that your marriage to
> Mercedes de Faenza will prove as happy as my own to
> Lord Barre. He is ever kind and good to me and
> though no other living soul knows of this, we are hus-
> band and wife in name only. It was by my husband's
> choice that we so live and I am therefore able to afford
> him all the affection he asks of me without the necessi-
> ty to withhold that part of me which belongs to you,
> dearest Gerard, and to no other. I am content; the
> more so now that I know there is no bitterness and no
> misunderstanding between us.*
>
> *True happiness cannot be mine if I am not assured
> of yours. Therefore, for my sake, if not for your own,
> I pray you to remember me with gladness and not with
> regret; to approach without remorse your coming
> marriage to another woman. No one can take from us
> nor mar what is in our innermost hearts and it is there
> you lie, forever safe and secure, deep within my soul.*
>
> > *For always, Gerard,*
> > *Your Mavreen.*

She went back into the garden and showed the sealed
letter to Clarissa.

"How shall we despatch it?" she asked.

Clarissa stood up.

"I will put your letter within a covering one of my own
and Dickon shall deliver the two together to Lisa von
Eburhard. She will set them upon their way to Switzerland. Lisa has friends everywhere, in the diplomatic world
and the navy, even in those countries with whom we are at
war. Never fear, child. It will reach Gerard in due course!"

The matter disposed of, they settled down once more in
the quiet garden.

"I have had a yearning to go to Sussex!" Mavreen confessed. "When Dickon and I are riding in the park, we talk of home and now that the weather is so much improved, I intend to ask Gilbert if I may go there for a short sojourn. Little Edward and Patty and Anna will be so grown I shall not know them. And I would dearly love to visit dear Mr. Glover. I have not heard from him for some weeks and fear he may be unwell!"

Some strange premonition must have found its way to Mavreen's heart for but one day following her visit to Clarissa, she received word from Mr. Glover's lawyer that he had collapsed and died that same afternoon. Mavreen, the letter stated, was his sole heir and not only was the modest sum of £5,000 hers but the four acres of garden and three grazing pastures. The most magnificent bequest of all was his wonderful library of books.

The death of her tutor was a great sadness for her, the more because she had not seen him since her marriage. She had wanted so much to tell him that she was happy. His last letter to her, written shortly before her wedding, cautioned her against marriage to a man so far her senior in years. He reminded her then of words he had spoken to her before she left Sussex to start a new life in London —"a husband who wants only a pretty decoration may pander to your whims in order to please you, but he will not know how to satisfy you," he had said. She would so much have liked to tell him he was wrong—that she was happy with Gilbert and satisfied with the life she had chosen for herself.

Nevertheless, as she traveled down to Sussex with Dickon in order to attend Mr. Glover's funeral, she was haunted by a memory of the look that would cross his face whenever she made a rash statement she could not justify. It was as if the old man were at her elbow, asking, "What is happiness, child? Frittering your life away adorning yourself in pretty clothes and jewels; drinking chocolate with idle young women with nothing to talk about but finding a husband; saying the right thing to the right person as hostess at your husband's dinner parties; listening to the inebriated ramblings of the profligate prince. Is this what you meant to do with your life, Mavreen?"

"Oh, Dickon!" Mavreen said aloud as he slowed the horses to a trot—they were but ten miles short of Alfriston. "Tell me truthfully, upon your word, do you think I am wasting my life?"

Dickon frowned, as was his wont when he was thinking. He knew Mavreen would not have asked the question frivolously; that she really wanted his opinion. But how could he judge such a serious matter for her?

"You are a great lady now!" he said, his speech slow and considered. "There's many as 'ud give a half of their lives to change places with thee!"

Mavreen sighed.

"I know that, Dickon. And I'm not ungrateful for all the wonderful things I have. But I fear my life has no real purpose. I might live forty more years and at the end of it, what will I have achieved?"

"Why, you beant meant to achieve nothing!" Dickon said flatly. "You being a female!"

"It ought not to make any difference!" Mavreen protested.

Dickon grinned.

"I never did hear of no lady prime ministers, nor no lady generals nor admirals nor the like."

"I know it sounds silly when you say it, but, Dickon, why not? We may not be as physically strong as men but we can use our brains. I find myself quite fascinated by some of the so-called eminent gentlemen I meet. When I discourse with them, I often find them quite stupid in their reasoning—or lack of it. Many have achieved their importance by influence of birth or wealth or by clever opportunism and not because they are more able than another."

"I don't know about such things!" Dickon replied, aware that Mavreen was now talking of matters beyond his understanding. "All I do know is poor people in Lunnon is surelye worse than poor folk in country. 'Tis pitiful to see so many starving chillun in the streets."

"There are people who are striving to better this state of affairs," Mavreen said. "We are living in a period of great change, Dickon. Lord Barre was but recently explaining to me that we are fast becoming an industrial nation. Our new factories in the Midlands and the North will bring our country great prosperity. We are benefitting, too, from the monopoly we have of the carrying trade. Under no other flag but the British can goods be safely transported to and from Europe, and the numbers of our exports these last few years has increased vastly. We are on the brink of great wealth, Dickon."

For a moment, Dickon did not reply. Then he said quietly, "Country may be getting rich, but farmers isn't. Small farmers is having to sell to the rich and be no better than laborers on the land they once owned. I dunnamany young lads is leaving land for to get work in factories or building these here new canals."

"At least your family is secure!" Mavreen reminded him. "Tell me truthfully, Dickon, do you ever wish yourself back at Owlett's Farm? You know I would release you at once if you wanted to leave London and go home."

Dickon's mouth tightened.

"I go where you goes!" he said simply. "Edward has my place on farm and that's all there is about it."

Mavreen smiled. She recognized the stubborn set of Dickon's features and knew he would brook no argument.

Their brief sojourn at the grange was a melancholy one. Mavreen's grief at the loss of her dear friend and tutor was very real and despite the admonition of Mr. Glover's lawyer to sell the estate, she resolved firmly to do no such thing. She would, she informed him, retain the house exactly as it was, for her own use. There might be occasions in her life when she would be glad to have a home of her own in Sussex to which she could retreat in quietness and privacy. In the cool of Mr. Glover's library, she might, if she wished, lose herself for a while in the world of books and recharge her intellectual energies.

The lawyer drew her attention to the cost of keeping up an establishment for which she had no immediate requirements but Mavreen explained that since she had everything she needed in her life already, she would use Mr. Glover's legacy for the upkeep of the grange. The elderly cook and gardener would remain as caretakers.

This decision required, of course, Lord Barre's agreement, but Mavreen had no doubt at all that he would comply with her wishes, even if he did not fully understand her reasons for keeping the house. They were prompted not solely from a feeling of sentiment in regard to Mr. Glover himself, but from an inexplicable need to have a place that belonged to her and only to her; a refuge, though she knew not what from.

Dickon returned home to sleep the following two nights with his family at Owlett's Farm but Mavreen remained at the grange, carefully tidying Mr. Glover's personal belongings. During the evening, she rode over to Owlett's to join the family, keeping her attire simple and unpretentious so that the children were not overawed by her grandeur. Nevertheless, neither she nor the Sales were able to regain the former easy family atmosphere. No matter how hard Mavreen tried to impress on them that she was unchanged, they all knew that she was now Lady Barre and took their cue from Dickon who treated her as a friend but one deserving always of the utmost respect. Patty and Anna bobbed curtsies to her whenever she spoke to them; Edward and little Henry—now grown to a big boy of ten—were too shy to address her of their own accord. The gulf was there even between her and her foster parents, although they at least called her Mavreen and were warmly pleased to see her.

The farm was prospering. True to his promise, Sir John had made sure that there was sufficient capital to enlarge the number of outbuildings and in the last few years, two neighboring farms had been added to their own fields and Farmer Sale employed a dozen laborers. These men were well treated, their pay and housing for their families well above the usual standard and Patty, now fifteen years old, schooled the young children in the three R's. It was not education of a high standard since Patty herself could do little more than read, write and count. But Mr. Glover had provided the makeshift school, held in the old haybarn, with reading books and slates and at least the children would not be illiterate, as were their parents.

Mavreen took a great deal of interest in the school. She made arrangements for the barn to be repaired, the inner walls plastered and whitewashed and a new oak boarded floor laid. A huge chimney with inglenook fireplace was to be built at one end, to provide warmth and a means of drying the children's wet clothes and shoes in winter. Then, with Dickon and Patty accompanying her, she rode into Alfriston and bought more books, colored chalks and a supply of paper. Finally, she took from Mr. Glover's library the big revolving globe of the world and instructed Patty on the geographical positioning of the countries.

Mavreen was happy during the hours she spent at Owlett's Farm despite the indefinable estrangement from her "family." But she was happier still during the hours she spent alone at the grange. The weather remained warm and sunny and she spent much of her time in the garden beneath the great tree where she had sat years ago alone with Gerard. She permitted herself the simple luxury of remembering every moment she had spent with him. Her longing for him was both pain and pleasure and the thought of his impending marriage to Mercedes de Faenza a torment which no amount of reasoning could quell. She discovered a book in Mr. Glover's library about northern France and read every word that related to Gerard's home, Compiègne.

The following day, Mavreen and Dickon returned to London, each in their separate ways sad at having to leave the quiet peace of springtime in the Sussex countryside and in no way excited by the prospect of the sophisticated life which awaited them.

CHAPTER SEVENTEEN
1797-1798

The summer passed quickly enough. Mavreen and her husband were now frequent guests at court and on several occasions were invited by the Prince of Wales to join him and his friends at Brighthelmstone, where there was much to enjoy by way of entertainment—concerts, balls, masquerades, theatres and the races. And, of course, the Steyne. Here all manner of curious contests took place. Officers and gentlemen, ridden by other officers and gentlemen, competed in races with octogenarians. Strapping young women were induced to run against each other for the prize of a new smock or hat. Such absurdities were harmless enough amusement but Mavreen did not care for the cock fighting and bull baiting. She was glad, too, when Gilbert failed to join in the night-long games of faro and hazard, played by the prince and his friends. So much brandy was consumed on these occasions that it was a wonder they could make their way back to their beds.

But Mavreen enjoyed the theatre and the picnics on the Downs, where the prince often held a review. The Hussars looked magnificent as they charged up to the saluting base, plumes flying, sabers waving and people cheering. The ladies displayed themselves like peacocks in their finest gowns.

Sea bathing was much enjoyed by many. Mavreen herself descended from the wooden bathing hut on wheels down the ladder and plunged into the water, watched over by the guides employed to assist swimmers and keep the bathing machines within reach.

Cricket was a pastime infinitely preferred by Lord Barre, and Mavreen liked to see the two teams in their white flannel coats and knee breeches, top hats and silk stockings, competing against one another in friendly rivalry.

But her longing for Gerard had never been more acute; nor her mind so filled with thoughts of him that she would not have been surprised if he had materialized beside her like some strange spirit.

"I can never be truly happy without him!" she thought. "All that I am doing, each day, is to fill my hours so full of activity that I have no time to be aware of my loneliness. I have everything in the world to make me content but the company of the one person who can bring me contentment."

Late one evening at the end of the month of March in 1798, there was a knock upon the door of Mistress Manton's house. Gerard de Valle had returned to England. He had but one question upon his lips.

Travel-weary though he was, he would have remounted his horse and set out for Barre House at once upon hearing that Mavreen was there, but Clarissa forbade it.

She insisted that he eat and drink for he had not stopped in the ten hour ride from Newhaven where he had landed in the early hours of the morning. Next, she provided him with a plentiful supply of hot water so that he could bathe the dust from his person. While the manservant was carrying water to and from the kitchen to the tub, Hannah brushed and ironed Gerard's coat and breeches and Clarissa found a clean shirt of Sir John's for him to put on. He had brought no luggage with him.

Refreshed and relaxed, Gerard allowed himself to be led into the salon. Curbing his impatience to be on his way, he explained his mission to his kindly hostess.

"I can speak freely to you, dear madame!" he said. "For you alone know that I love Mavreen with all my heart. And that she loves me!"

Clarissa nodded. She was uneasy. The behavior of the young could be very rash and she must not allow anything to compromise Mavreen. But her womanly sympathies were drawn to the tired young man seated beside her. She had always sustained a soft spot for Gerard and she could understand only too easily why Mavreen loved him. Not even in his youth had her own dear John been as handsome; nor, she had to admit, so ardent and headstrong in his manner of loving.

"Mavreen's letter reached me at Compiègne about a week ago," Gerard continued. "I cannot describe to you the relief it gave me to learn that she still loved me. I had feared that she would never forgive me for my past behavior toward her. I had to come to England to see her. You understand my sentiments, do you not, Mistress Manton?"

Clarissa sighed.

"I understand, Gerard, but you do not need me to remind you how hopeless your love for each other must be.

Mavreen is married—to a good, kind man who is devoted to her. She will do nothing to hurt Lord Barre. And you, Gerard. Are not yourself betrothed?"

Gerard's face took on a look of anguish.

"It is true I have asked Donna Mercedes to marry me. I had to deceive my mother as to the reason for my hurried departure for England. Her heart is set upon my marriage and in her anxiety for me to arrange a wedding date, she was as enthusiastic as I to expedite my way to London." He looked at Clarissa, pleading for her understanding. "I do not love Mercedes but cannot disappoint my mother. It is not easy for me to describe how old and frail she has become. She depends entirely upon me and lives only for my marriage and the hope of a future heir for the de Valles. She has even spoken of naming my first son after my father, Antoine. It is her hopes for the future which keep her alive. The present offers her nothing. There is no one but old Jules, the manservant, a stone mason from Compiègne and myself at work upon the restoration of our château. Progress is slow and we lack the necessary money. It is hard for her to live in such a manner."

He held out his hands and Clarissa was shocked to see that they were as roughened and sunburned as a farm laborer's.

Seeing her expression, Gerard smiled.

"Do not pity me!" he said, "for to tell you the truth, I much enjoy my physical exertions. It is man's work, Mistress Manton, and I am the better for it. I shall be able to tell my grandchildren that I have helped to build our home. That is good, is it not?"

Clarissa smiled back at him.

"Yes, it is good, Gerard. But you are too thin. You have been working too hard!"

"But no, it is not the work that is responsible," Gerard said quietly. "It is that I have pined day and night for the sight and sound of my *petit écureuil*. Ah, Mistress Manton, love may bring great joy but it can bring great suffering too. You are not going to forbid my seeing Mavreen now that we are on the point of being reunited?"

For a moment, Clarissa did not reply. She sensed that

at this moment, she might be able to persuade Gerard to refrain from reopening a wound that was surely not yet healed in Mavreen's heart. Yet she did not feel justified in taking the responsibility for so influencing him. Mavreen was eighteen years of age—old enough to decide for herself what road her life was to take.

Clarissa knew that Lord Barre had given his young wife freedom to take a lover if she should choose to do so. Unable himself to play a husband's full role, he had generously put his own feelings aside in order that Mavreen should not feel she had been unfairly coerced into a marriage that could never be complete. But so far Mavreen had remained entirely faithful to her husband. For Gilbert's sake? Clarissa asked herself. Or had Mavreen been faithful to Gerard?

"I think you should write a note and have it delivered to Barre House," she said thoughtfully. "Tell her that you are in London; that you are staying at Orchid House as my guest and that it is entirely up to her if she wishes to see you or not. If she does so, then she can come here without attracting attention to her movements, it being her custom to visit with me here at least once in a week."

With difficulty, Gerard forced himself to accept this plan.

"But suppose she should not wish to see me!" he cried out.

Clarissa was moved to put her hand over his. "I have little doubt that she loves you as deeply as you love her," she said. "I believe she will arrive the very instant she can arrange her absence without upsetting her husband. You must be wise in this, Gerard. Do not make her choose between what her conscience and sense of fair play require of her and her desire to be with you. She will not be willing to hurt Lord Barre. He is a good husband to her."

"Would that he were not!" Gerard burst out. "Then I might in all fairness take her from him. Fate is cruel, is it not? Were my mother not to have survived the revolution, I would willingly abandon my heritage and marry Mavreen. Moreover, I am far from happy about my forthcoming marriage. The letters I have received from Mercedes have convinced me that she will never be content to settle down in Compiègne. Or at least, not until the château is fully restored and we can entertain there as she wishes. But Mistress Manton, I seem unable to make her understand that there is no social life for her to enjoy. It is in Paris that General Napoleon and his wife, Josephine, hold court. My mother seems to think that given a little time and a child or two to occupy her, Donna Mercedes will settle down to life on a country estate. Alas, she does not know Mercedes!"

Clarissa sighed, a frown creasing her forehead. Sir John had but recently spoken of Gerard's betrothed and in none too salutary terms. It seemed Mercedes was becoming impatient with her fiancé's continued absence and bored with London life. Dear John had professed the opinion that if Gerard did not soon return to marry the girl, she might turn her thoughts elsewhere.

"Sir John is away in Buckinghamshire with Lady Danesfield and his daughters," she informed Gerard. "They are sojourning with the Pettigrews whom I believe you know. I think Sir John is making one last vain attempt to marry one of the girls to young James Pettigrew, but I fear the boy is not to be persuaded."

"And little Anne?" Gerard inquired, remembering his school friend's amusing young sister. "Is she married?"

"Betrothed, but not married," Clarissa said. "She and Mavreen and James are the closest of good friends. They ride or meet nearly every day when the Pettigrews are in their London residence."

Gerard's eyes narrowed as he read more into her remark than she had intended.

"Are you trying to tell me tactfully that James and Mavreen. . . ."

"No, no, indeed I am not!" Clarissa broke in smiling. "Or if you wish the exact truth, I think James *is* a little in love with Mavreen . . . but then most men are, Gerard . . . but she remains faithful to your memory."

Gratefully, Gerard raised Clarissa's hand and kissed it fervently.

"You have always been kind to me, Mistress Manton, and those words from you make me happier perhaps even than you realize. I do not blame James, nor any man who loves my Mavreen. I only pity them, for to love her is to be imprisoned for life. She is unforgettable and irreplaceable."

Clarissa stood up and went to the bureau where, not so very long ago, Mavreen had penned her letter to Gerard. Here, Clarissa told him, he could write his message to her and she would have the groom deliver it to Barre House without further delay.

"Meanwhile, you shall stay the night here with me!" she informed him. "I am not expecting visitors and no one will be the wiser. It is fortunate that Sir John is away for I do not think he would applaud my part in this affair."

"While I shall never cease to be grateful to you," Gerard said, as he too stood up, "there is little I can do for you now, Mistress Manton, but if ever the day should come when you need my assistance, I will come from whatever part of the world I am in to repay my debt to you."

As Gerard seated himself at the bureau, Clarissa felt impelled to renew her words of caution. Mavreen might be unwilling to see him; or circumstances might prevent her doing so. He must not set too much store by the message. It was even possible she and Lord Barre might be out of town for she, Clarissa, did not know all of Mavreen's social engagements.

Within ten minutes, Clarissa's groom was on his way in his mulberry-colored livery to deliver Gerard's note to Lady Barre herself or to the maid, Rose. He had explicit instructions that on no account was he to deliver it to any other person. He was to await a reply unless Lady Barre was away from London.

Somehow, Gerard managed to contain his impatience as the hours ticked by. Clarissa engaged him in a game of cards to keep his mind occupied but he played badly, his thoughts continually upon the clock on the mantlepiece, listening, as indeed was Clarissa, for the clatter of horse's hooves upon the cobbles.

When the groom finally returned, it was after eleven o'clock. He had been gone four hours and Gerard's nerves were stretched to the breaking point. Clarissa was almost as nervous as he and as relieved as Gerard when the groom held out a letter, not his own returned to him unanswered or undelivered, but penned in Mavreen's script.

Even before the man had left the room, Gerard tore open the seal, his eyes eagerly scanning the words that danced before them. They were few and guarded, saying nothing more but that Mavreen would be at Orchid House before midday on the morrow. They gave but one clue to her sentiments and that was by the signature—*Petit Écureuil.*

Transported with hope and happiness, dark eyes aglow, Gerard showed the letter to Clarissa.

"See, Mistress Manton, she signs with my special name for her. She would not do this if she wished to end our association, do you not agree? Ah, if she but loves me still, I shall be the happiest man in the world. I ask nothing more. Tell me, Mistress Manton, that you do not believe I hope in vain?"

Clarissa reassured him as best she could. But she was far from easy in her mind. Mavreen was still an impetuous, impulsive child beneath the cloak of urbanity and sophistication her marriage and new way of life had given her. With Gerard in such a state of wild abandon and Mavreen in like state, who could tell what fires might be lit! And they would have been ignited with her help and connivance. Sir John might be everlastingly angry with her if he were to discover the part she had played. But this was the least of her worries. What of Gerard? What of Mavreen? There could be no future for them.

Mavreen, on receiving Gerard's letter, was beside herself with joy. None but Aunt Clarrie knew of his whereabouts or intentions, and she felt that God himself was offering her a last brief glimpse of happiness. The hours to be endured before she could go to him could be well spent, she thought, in planning the scheme she was busily forming in her mind. If she could engineer some reason requiring her presence at the grange in Sussex, Gerard might conceivably go there with her, albeit for but one night or two. They could be quite alone there but for Mr. Glover's old servants. She could despatch Dickon ahead to send them off on a brief holiday to Bognor or Brighthelmstone, expenses paid. They might wonder what had precipitated such generosity but they would be away from the grange before she and Gerard arrived and would know nothing of what took place there. For Gilbert's sake, there must be no risk of gossip.

Mavreen tentatively spoke to Gilbert of her possible visit to Sussex. It distressed her that Gilbert did not once question the lie she was forced to tell him, giving a letter from Mr. Glover's lawyer as reason for her required presence there. "It does seem a long journey for you to make at this time of year!" Gilbert replied solicitously. "Can these legalities not wait until later in the spring? Perhaps I should accompany you and deal with the lawyer's problems myself?"

"I am sure that it is not necessary," Mavreen replied, "and I shall quite enjoy the journey. Dickon, as you know, will take good care of me. But it is not yet certain I must go. I will let you know tomorrow."

Lord Barre asked no further questions. This last year had been the happiest of his life. But by virtue of Mavreen's youth and energy and the number of invitations that poured in from all quarters because of his young wife's popularity, his social life had increased tenfold and he sometimes found the continuous round of entertaining a little exhausting. Mavreen always asked him before she accepted an invitation or herself gave a party. Such was the kindness of her nature that he knew she would in an instant forego any amusement if she were to believe him over-tired or unwell. It was, therefore, only during one of her rare absences away from him that he felt free to relax and give way to his advancing years.

Mavreen herself could think of nothing else but Gerard's letter, safely concealed in her reticule. Her excitement was so intense it was difficult to keep her hands and body in repose. The thought he was this moment at Orchid House was almost beyond belief. He was no doubt asleep at this moment, perhaps even in her own bed chamber where they had lain together as Rose stood guard on the landing.

It seemed as if tomorrow would never come and she did not know how she could live through the remaining hours of the night.

CHAPTER EIGHTEEN

1798

Gerard had stood at the window of Clarissa's salon since early morning. One hand upon the satin drape, he stared out upon the street, his nerve ends quickening at the sound or sight of a horse or carriage, his eyes constantly scanning the passing traffic for his first longed-for glimpse of Mavreen. He only knew that she had promised to come before midday.

It was not long after eleven when she arrived on horseback wearing a velvet riding habit of emerald green, a cockaded hat with two waving ostrich plumes dancing in the breeze. Dickon helped her to dismount. Within seconds, Gerard was out the door and before Mavreen could reach for the big brass door knocker, he was there beside her, taking up her gauntleted hand and pressing it to his lips.

"At last, at last you have come!" he said.

Mavreen's face, whipped to a glowing pink by the wind and the ride, regarded him with an intense concentration. But as he stared at her, her eyes suddenly crinkled at the corners and her lips parted into a smile of purest happiness.

"Did you think I would not come, Gerard?" she asked teasingly. Now, he, too, laughed in relief and joy at seeing her. He linked his arm through hers and drew her into the house. The maid took Mavreen's hat and riding crop, showed them into the salon, and closed the door behind her as she left the room. Clarissa was conspicuous by her absence.

Once more, Gerard took Mavreen's hand, now ungloved, and pressed it to his lips.

"You are lovelier than ever!" he murmured truthfully. "Mistress Manton did not warn me that you now had the grace and comeliness of a princess. You have grown up, my beautiful Mavreen!"

"I think I have!" Mavreen agreed. "And you, too, Gerard. You, too, have changed. You look . . . older! Thinner! Are you well?" she added seriously.

He held her at arm's length, rejoicing in her concern for him.

"I have not changed in the way I feel toward you!" he said pointedly, his eyes serious, his voice intense with emotion. "I love you, Mavreen. I have always loved you. There is no happiness in this world for me without you."

He saw her eyes close as he drew her against him. Before the heavy fringe of her lashes hid her expression from him, he read an acceptance, a longing equal to his own.

Fiercely, he brought his mouth down upon hers. Her lips were warm and moist and her response to his kisses as fervent as his were eager. Impatiently, he drew his mouth away and quickly unfastened the buttons of her velvet riding coat. Beneath the soft silky fabric of her blouse, he could see the outline of her shoulders and arms and the contours of her breasts, fuller than he remembered and even more thrilling to his senses.

Mavreen, in her turn, was running her hands across his back, resting a moment as they discovered the new strong muscles he had developed by his physical labors, seeing the golden tan of his skin beneath the white shirt. He was, indeed, thinner, but immensely stronger and she sighed in satisfaction at this change in him.

Briefly, his hands cupped her breasts and her hands rose to cover his and press them even closer. But she knew she must fight against the weakness that was beginning to pervade her body. Aunt Clarrie's salon was no place for such love making. Their true reunion must wait a while longer.

Gerard looked so crestfallen when she pulled his hands away and drew back from him, that she laughed delightedly.

"Look not so woebegone!" she chided him tenderly. "For I have a proposition to put to you, dearest Gerard! One I am certain you will approve."

He would have taken her in his arms again at the sound

of the endearment on her lips, but she kept him at arm's length.

"You must pay close attention to what I am about to tell you," she said, her eyes dancing in a way he found irresistable. But he kept his distance in order to feast his eyes upon her.

"Gerard, I beg you, stop regarding me in such fashion and hear what I have to tell you, for it will make you happy, I promise you."

"I am happy now!" he told her. "I have never been so happy in my whole life!"

"But you will be more so, I promise!" Mavreen said, her face serious once more as she began to outline her plan. They could, she told him, travel together that very afternoon to Sussex. They would have to stop along the way for it would be too far to travel in one afternoon. Nevertheless, they would be at the grange the following afternoon.

"There will be no one there, Gerard. It is my house now since poor dear Mr. Glover died and left it to me. We can be there alone and in complete safety. That is—" she added, suddenly shy "—if you should wish it so."

Gerard's expression was at first astonished. But as the meaning of her words penetrated his consciousness, he gave a shout of pure joy and his dark eyes glowed with such happiness that Mavreen caught her breath. It was as well Clarissa chose this moment to make her appearance or Mavreen might herself have returned to the tempting haven of Gerard's arms.

"Aunt Clarrie!" she cried, warmly embracing Clarissa. "I cannot begin to tell you how grateful I am; how happy I am. And Gerard, too. We are going to Sussex together! I have already secured Gilbert's permission to go there. Is it not wonderful? Say you are happy for me!"

Clarissa bit her lip anxiously. Mavreen could not mean she had actually told Lord Barre she intended to take the young vicomte as a lover? Seeing her expression, Mavreen laughed and hugged her anew.

"Do not look so perturbed, dearest Aunt Clarrie!" she cried. "We will be perfectly safe there. No one in the world but yourself will know that Gerard is with me and **I know you will keep our secret.**"

Clarissa breathed a sigh of relief. At least Mavreen had her wits about her and was considering the consequences of her actions. She spent the next hour issuing warnings to the young couple. Dickon was to be trusted and Rose, too, for Mavreen would need at least one servant to attend to the domestic side of life.

"But I can cook!" Mavreen argued, her face radiant, her hand clasped tightly in Gerard's. "Have you forgot, Aunt Clarrie, that I was raised on a farm?"

Reluctantly, Mavreen tore herself away for she had much to prepare before she would be ready to leave London. And Dickon was despatched to make sure the servants were gone before their arrival. He would have to ride all night to precede them to Sussex.

It was arranged for Gerard to take the stagecoach to the far side of Westminster Bridge, where he would join Mavreen in her carriage at three in the afternoon. All being well, they would travel as far as East Grinstead before nightfall, at which town they would find an inn in which to pass the night. It was agreed they would have a week's sojourn together. It did not seem to be too much out of a whole lifetime to be spent apart.

When Mavreen left for Barre House and her preparations, Gerard went upon a shopping expedition. He could ill-afford the kind of jewelry he would like to give her but chose a small circlet ring of tiny pearls set in gold, partly for its charm but partly on account of its history. The jeweler informed him that the ring was reputed to have been given by Charles II to his beloved Nell Gwynne, passed on by her to her daughter, and given by her to a lady of quality in gratitude for her assistance in some political intrigue. The ring, therefore, was certainly over a hundred years old and, symbolically, had been made for a king for his loved one.

"It is a delightful and romantic idea, Gerard!" Clarissa commented when he showed it to her. "I have little doubt that Mavreen will be enchanted by it. How clever of you to find it!

"Take care of her!" Clarissa said, tears in her eyes. "Mavreen loves you very dearly, Gerard, and when the week is over and you must part, it will be as hard for her as for you. Make your farewell as easy for her as you can."

The drive was uneventful but for an encounter with a party of grenadiers, commanded by a Lieutenant Hyde, who overtook them on the road and brought the carriage to a halt. They were, the lieutenant informed them, in pursuit of a band of smugglers who had but a few miles back, fired upon them with pistols and then ridden off in a southerly direction. Mavreen and Gerard were warned to beware of the outlaws, for they were known to be desperate men and murderers.

Gerard smiled at Mavreen as the soldiers rode past them. He owed too much to the smugglers to betray any one of them, he said, had he known their whereabouts. He told Mavreen how, when Dickon had first put him in touch with the Alfriston smugglers, he had been taken in a large sailing vessel carrying an illegal cargo of wool on its way to Dunkirk. The men had treated him with rough kindness and seen him into good hands once he landed in France. The smugglers had their own resident agents who saw to it that they returned to England well loaded with spirits, tobacco and tea. Those same agents had given Gerard money and French clothing and seen him upon his way to Compiègne with no more reward than his promise to pay them for their trouble when his fortunes were restored.

"Smuggling will never be stopped in Sussex!" Mavreen agreed. "There are too many involved in every town and village. Why, Father Sale told me only last summer that it was at times hard to find a good laborer as so many men are now employed in the smuggling trade. It's said in Alfriston that the lawful traders are hard put to compete!"

Gerard shrugged his shoulders. "The law will not be respected whilst the duty is so high, upon tea especially," he said.

The horses were tired when they arrived at East Grinstead and stopped at the Cat Inn. The inn, which had been built in the sixteenth century, was warm and comfortable. By prior agreement, Gerard and Mavreen pre-

sented themselves as "le comte et comtesse de Vallence",
Mavreen's command of French being more than adequate
for the deception. The landlord was not unused to French
aristocratic émigrés, and seeing Mavreen's clothes, was de-
cidedly of the opinion that his guests were not without
adequate means, and went out of his way to make them
welcome.

Before dinner was completed, he had little doubt that
the young couple were but newly married. They held
hands unashamedly and could scarcely see what they ate
so busily were they looking into one another's eyes. The
beautiful young comtesse glanced continually at the ring
on her finger.

At Gerard's request, a log fire was lit in the bedchamber, for the night was cold despite the springlike weather
of the day. The couple retired as soon as the meal was
over, so intent upon each other they barely glanced at the
landlord as they bade him goodnight.

Gerard had no intention of letting his ever-growing desires for Mavreen hasten to their conclusion. He had waited
an eternity for this moment and now that it was come, he
wanted to make every minute of every hour of the night
as beautiful for his love as he knew it must be for him.

Gently, with trembling hands, he played the part of
milady's maid, unfastening the tiny buttons down the back
of her dress, slipping the soft grey silk over her shoulders
so that she stood naked from the waist, so perfectly fashioned that he held his breath, half fearing to put his hands
upon her lest he mark the satin smoothness of her skin. As
he pressed his lips against the hollow of her neck, she
turned and revealed her beautiful body to him, her stance
both proud and shy at the same time.

"Mon amour!" he cried. *"Comme tu es belle!"*

She stood quietly as his lips moved downwards to her
breasts. The nipples stood hard and erect, betrayers of the
desires of her body, which must, she thought, be equal to
his own.

"I love you, I love you!" she whispered, pressing her
hands against his dark curly head, rocking gently to and
fro.

Both stood naked in the firelight, their young bodies

golden, pulsating, trembling as they gazed at one another. Together, they fell backwards upon the soft feather bed as if by unspoken agreement, constraint was abandoned as they gave way to the desperate urgency of their need, one for the other. When the moment of consummation came, they were as two healthy young animals intent upon their mating, the world forgotten as their bodies merged.

Gerard was first to speak. Tenderly brushing a damp tendril of hair from Mavreen's face, he leaned on his elbow and kissed her with great tenderness.

"If you could only know what indescribable delight you give me!" he said softly. "If you could but share with me the beauty and pleasure . . ."

Mavreen smiled.

"But I do, Gerard. No one can have surpassed the intensity of my excitement, the satisfaction and now the peace I feel." She saw the tiniest of frowns on his forehead and touched it with her forefinger.

"Was something wrong, my dearest?"

Gerard hesitated. He could not help himself but he was besieged with miserable forebodings of jealousy.

"It is unusual for females to derive much physical pleasure when men love them. . . ." he murmured guardedly.

Now it was Mavreen's turn to feel jealous.

"And was it a female who so informed you?" she asked. Receiving no answer, she added, "So it was! Yet I have been faithful to you, Gerard. No man has laid hand upon me since last I lay with you!"

Gerard, who had been holding his breath, released it in a long sigh.

"Forgive me, my love. I was afraid some man had taught you the art of loving so freely and with such pleasure. I beg you, forgive me my doubts. I, too, have been perfectly faithful to you. I swear it upon my oath!"

They were back in each other's arms, kissing with relief and a renewed closeness. But Mavreen's mind was not yet at rest.

"I know there have been other women in your life, Gerard. You would not be a man else! I do not mind what is past, but I would like to know if there has been any woman you have loved as you love me."

"None! Ever!" Gerard replied. "I love you even more now, this minute, since passion has been spent. All that you are as a woman, as a person—that is what I love. Without you I am incomplete as a man. There now, I have confessed my weakness!"

Mavreen covered his mouth, his eyes, his whole face with kisses. She suddenly sat upright, in the impulsive manner of a young girl.

"I have this moment remembered some lines from a book I read not one week past. It was written by the playwright William Congreve, and this passage remained in my mind because it so well described my own feelings when I did not know if I should ever see you again."

Gerard lay on his back watching the swiftly changing expressions of Mavreen's face with loving attention. He felt he could never tire of looking at her, or listening to her, for he was forever discovering some new fascination.

"Mr. Congreve wrote, 'Life without love is load'; and 'time stands still; what we refuse to him, to death we give; and then, then only, when we love, we live.' "

Gerard reached out and drew her quickly back into his arms. Her words had struck a cold chill of fear in his heart for they were unbearably true. This past twelve months without his love had been an eternity and now, time would cheat them and race away with their all-too-few precious hours of life.

Mavreen's body lay above him, covering him, enveloping him in its soft, sweet warmth. With urgency, he pressed her even closer against him as if he would merge their two bodies into one.

"You are life itself!" he murmured as his mouth sought for her breast like a child for the comfort of its mother.

Yet as he possessed her for a second time, Mavreen felt as if it was Gerard who was giving her life, quenching the thirst of her need for him, his very spirit passing from his body into hers. She cried out, not in pain but in joy. This time, they remained united, their breathing as unified as their bodies, until they slept.

They were awakened by what seemed like a thousand wild birds outside their window. Sleepily, Mavreen opened her eyes and saw a shaft of brilliant spring sunlight shining through the parted drapes onto Gerard's face. She lay, her head turned upon the pillow, staring at him.

In sleep, he looked but a boy again, dark curly hair tumbled about his face, thick curtains of dark lashes lying on the golden tan of his cheeks. She longed to put out a finger and trace the line of his cheekbone, down the strong muscular column of his neck, but she remained motionless, unwilling to wake him when she could so secretly imprint his image upon her mind.

Her eyes crinkled into a smile as she saw the dark shadow of his beard and moustache and for a minute or so, she forced herself to imagine him as moustached and bearded, as an old man, perhaps, and wondered if in thirty years' time, her body would still melt with this same overwhelming tenderness and love. She thought that it would and closed her eyes, praying with sudden desperation to God to make it possible for them to be together again before they died. If Gerard were to die, she thought, she would wish to die, too.

As she turned and found him awake, she smiled and threw herself into his arms as he reached out for her.

"I love you!" she said radiantly, at the same moment as he said, *"Je t'aime, je t'aime!"* Laughing with sheer happiness, she tweaked his nose, mocking him.

"I said it first!"

"We said it together!" Gerard argued, gently pulling a strand of hair.

"Then I thought it first. I was awake before you!"

"But I thought it in my sleep, all the night long!" Gerard countered, smiling at Mavreen's pout as she conceded the victory to him. "Besides," he added slyly, "I love you more than you love me!"

"And I have loved you far longer than you have loved me!" Mavreen declared triumphantly. "I loved you ever since you fell down the carriage steps and landed at my feet. You were so cross!"

"And you were so cruel, you laughed at me!"

"But I was the one who helped you to your feet!" Mavreen declared.

"And for that, you earn a kiss which I shall give you now!" Gerard promised and proceeded to give her several.

Mavreen lay in his arms sighing.

"I am so happy, Gerard!" she said. "I did not know it was possible to be so perfectly happy. And even God is doing his best for us. It is the most beautiful of days. If this weather continues, we shall have such lovely ways to spend our time at the grange."

"I care not what I do so long as I am with you," Gerard said truthfully. "We will do whatever pleases you."

"There are so many things I'd like to share with you!" she said breathlessly. "We will fish for trout in the river, and ride upon the Downs and see the windmills and hear the larks; and we can watch the new lambs in the meadows and pick bluebells in the woods and search for birds' eggs. Sussex is my real home, Gerard. I am really a country maiden and find most joy in nature itself. Does that displease you?"

"On the contrary, my darling, it pleases me beyond belief. For I, too, was born and raised in the country and could never live a city life for long." Mavreen would have had him tell her more about his home but Gerard wanted to be up and on their way. Before rising, he kissed her again and the kiss led to another and another until both forgot their intention to make an early start, and wasted a precious half hour of time delighting in the infinite joys and pleasures of their love.

CHAPTER NINETEEN

1798

The young lovers saw no one but Dickon and Rose. Occasionally, they would pass a shepherd on the Downs, or a farm laborer herding his cows down a country lane back to his farm for milking. But they avoided contact with people, afraid someone would recognize Mavreen.

Not that she would have been recognized by any of her

London friends. She had discarded all pretenses of grandeur and wore a country girl's cotton dress, frequently
running barefoot, her head uncovered to the sun. Gerard,
too, discarded cravat and boots, wore only breeches and a
shirt, chest and feet bared.

Each day, the sun shone from a blue sky spattered only
by a few wispy streamers of cloud. Mavreen knew that
the farmers wanted rain to germinate their crops but as
she told Gerard, they would have to wait until the week
was over for God had answered her prayers and was
giving them summer in springtime.

Gerard tried not to show his unhappiness whenever it
was mentioned that eventually this idyll must come to an
end. He dared not think how it would be possible to return
to London and resume his courtship. Indeed, he did not
think it was possible. But not wishing to distress Mavreen
with talk of the future, he hid his misgivings from her.

Mavreen, too, hid her own fears. As each day, each
night, each hour, brought them closer to the very essence
of love, the thought of renewing her London life as Lady
Barre appalled her. She understood very well now why
Clarissa had been unenthusiastic when she had planned
this week with Gerard. Clarissa had known, as she had
not, how frighteningly dependent a woman could grow
when love became a way of life. It seemed as if she had
lived with Gerard always. Sometimes they would both
begin to speak at once, the same thought in their minds,
the same words on their lips. If they were not laughing
together, they were serious only because they were loving
one another. Their bodies, like their minds, were in perfect unison. In the space of a few days, she had come to
know Gerard's mind and heart with an intimacy that she
had been unable to achieve with her husband after more
than a year of marriage. She loved Gilbert no less when
she thought about him. Pity added to her affection for him
for she realized that he could never know the extra dimen-
sion a perfect love gave to life.

She feared that on her return to London, Gilbert would
notice the change in her and wonder at its cause. She felt
like a different person, as if she had been living in blindness
and could suddenly see, as if her body itself had been

transformed into light, fire, song. The words of Congreve seemed more true than ever—"then only, when we love, we live."

In the atmosphere the young lovers created around them, romance spread its wings and blossomed elsewhere. Dickon and Rose were thrown much upon each other's company. At first, it was their mutual love for Mavreen that served to bring them together. Dickon disapproved the whole venture, not simply on moral grounds but because he feared the consequences for Mavreen should she be discovered to have a lover. But as the days passed and he came to know the young vicomte better, his liking for him increased. There was no doubting that Gerard loved Mavreen as deeply and sincerely as she loved him. Dickon no longer feared that he was merely taking his pleasure as so many young gentlemen were wont to do if the ladies were willing. Now he feared for the future. He understood at once what Rose meant when she confessed to him that she could see no happy ending to this fairy-tale romance.

"I do reckon there'll be more than one tear shed for every smile upon their lips!" she said.

Despite the gravity of the subject, Dickon grinned.

"That were purtily said, albeit you be a furriner!"

Rose, pink-cheeked beneath her mob cap, flicked her apron in his face and said indignantly, "Furriner, indeed! 'Tis you Sussex lads as speak furrin, not us Lunduners!" Seeing the blush spreading across his face, the girl was sensitive enough to make allowances for his shyness. She added gently, "Though I'll admit, to be sure, you are a well-mannered boy and milady says there isn't no one as can better you in the care of horses! And you be stronger than city lads!" she added as Dickon deposited his load of logs for the kitchen range at her feet as if they were a feather pillow.

In London, Rose had given little attention to the young groom. Plump, good-natured, always singing cheerfully, Rose was not without her admirers at Barre House. The head footman, for one, was always trying to waylay her as she went about her business and he was not a bad looking fellow, especially when he was dressed in his livery

with his hair powdered and pomaded. His Lordship's
valet, for another, had tried to steal a kiss, but he was
German and Rose did not fancy a German for a husband.
Dickon, with his ginger hair and freckled skin did not
attract her attention, but now she found herself beginning
to like and respect him. She was discovering that still
waters run deep. Beneath the quiet exterior, a lot went on,
and Rose began to take notice.

Had she given him no encouragement, it is doubtful
Dickon would have overcome his shyness sufficiently to
begin courting her. But when she found him staring at her
as she was bent over the flat iron or serving food, she held
his glance and smiled at him, not boldly, but sweetly.
Soon, he was bringing her big bunches of cowslips from
the fields, or wood violets, and once a speckled thrush's
egg which he had pricked and blown so that she could
keep it.

Mavreen and Gerard were too engrossed in each other
to notice the love growing between Dickon and Rose. She
and Gerard welcomed the additional privacy of the empty
house and asked no questions. Mavreen played songs upon
Mr. Glover's pianoforte and Gerard sat behind her on the
piano stool, his arms around her waist, his cheek resting
lightly against her hair as he sang operatic arias in a soft
tone. He could not bear for her to be far away from him
and his eyes and hands sought her ceaselessly.

Sometimes Mavreen pretended not to notice when his
hand touched her arm or her breast, then suddenly, she
would turn to him and clasp him fiercely to her and the
ever-smoldering embers of their need for each other would
burst into flame. Impatiently, they would undress one another, kissing, murmuring words of love and desire until
the force of their own passions silenced them.

Upon occasions, they could not wait for the privacy of
their bedchamber but loved wherever they happened to
be—in the tall green grass of the meadows; on the soft
dark emerald moss in the woods, crushing the thick petals
of Star of Bethlehem flowers to a white carpet. If Dickon
and Rose were out of the house, they would pull the satin
and brocade cushions onto the floor rugs and forget that
the servants might return to the house and discover them.

With mock sadness, Gerard confessed that Mavreen had ruined his future pleasure in any other woman. He was destined to remain unfulfilled for the remainder of his life, and he had hoped to experience the love of so many different women!

"Would that I had never lain with you!" he said, biting softly on her shoulder. "Now I want no one but you!"

There was but one more night remaining before they must bring an end to the idyll and Mavreen was too aware of it to share Gerard's humor as she would otherwise have done.

"Do not speak of lying with other women!" she begged him. "I cannot bear to think on it! Yet I know it must happen. You will marry Mercedes de Faenza and it will be your duty to give her children. . . ."

Her voice trembled as she broke off in mid-sentence. Shocked and now as unhappy as she, Gerard hugged her fiercely to him.

"I will not marry!" he cried. "I cannot! My mother could not ask it of me if she but knew how it was between you and me, Mavreen. I love you. *Je t'aime.* You alone. No other!" Frantically, he sought to reassure both of them. He had meant what he had said. There could be no other women in his life.

Mavreen's silence was torture to him.

"I swear upon my mother's life that I will stay faithful . . ."

But Mavreen covered his lips with her hand.

"You must not, Gerard. I love you more than life itself but I do not want you to make such a vow. You *must* marry. I know it just as you do. Aunt Clarrie made me see that it would be wrong for us to contemplate any other way. I am already married. I am not free to come to you. And you, Gerard—you are a Catholic and even if I were to obtain a divorce from poor Gilbert, we could not marry."

"But we could be together!" Gerard cried desperately. "Is it not enough for you?"

She longed to say yes. If it were only a matter of what she wanted for herself, how easily she could give her assent. But, for one thing, she could not hurt Gilbert—and her disgrace would be his humiliation. For another, there was Gerard's own future. She would never agree to anything that might bring dishonor upon him. Moreover, when his passions had cooled and common sense and an awareness of his obligations returned, he would begin to hate himself, if not her too, for the distress he would bring to his mother.

"I love you too much!" she said. "Gerard, we must help each other to be strong. God has given us this week and we have no right to ask for more. Consider how many poor mortals there are in the world who in their whole lifetime have not known one tiny part of the happiness we have shared. We have lived a lifetime in seven days, not one single hour, nay, minute wasted. Do not let us waste these last hours in vain longing for what cannot be."

Her logic silenced him although his acceptance brought him no happiness. He marvelled at her strength for he had no doubt she loved him as greatly as he loved her and that parting would come no more easily for her. At least he could draw comfort from the knowledge that although she was returning to her husband, it was not to his bed. Yet even this saddened him for he could foresee how lonely and unfulfilled her life would be, the more so now that she was so fully awakened to love. It was not even as if she had the comfort of children around her.

As so often of late, their thoughts were in harmony and Mavreen said softly, "If I but had your child, Gerard, I could bear the parting with you more easily. I would so deeply love to bear a son with your likeness."

"But I would wish for a daughter!" Gerard told her. "A little girl with golden hair and green eyes and love in her smile like her mother's."

"Both girl and boy!" Mavreen said dreamily. "What should we call them, Gerard? Marianne for your mother? Antoine for your son?"

"Marianne, perhaps. But for a boy, I wished always that I had been called by my second name, Darius. That is the name I would give my son."

Mavreen turned her face to the pillow, afraid her lips might betray her into voicing the request that trembled upon them, "Give me your child, Gerard. Give me your son and I will call him Darius if it pleases you. If leave me you must, then leave me with part of yourself that I can hold to my heart, a living proof of your love."

But she knew the request must never be made. It was not possible for her to bear Gerard's child while she was Gilbert's wife. And Gerard's children must, for the sake of his heritage, belong to another woman.

"*You* are my child!" she said as she pulled his head down to her breast. "My child, my lover, my friend, my heart. You are all I want, all I need!"

She did not know then that she was already with child.

Hard though they endeavored to make it so, the last day could not be carefree. Rose and Dickon were busy setting the house to rights before Mr. Glover's old housekeeper and her husband returned. Mavreen's London clothes must be got ready and her portmanteau packed. Preparations for their departure could not be ignored.

As if in keeping with the sadness that prevailed in all four young hearts, the weather took a turn for the worse and the light rain which fell at the start of the day became a heavy downpour by luncheon.

Gerard paced restlessly up and down the salon as Mavreen tried to concentrate on a letter to a distant relative of Mr. Glover's. She had put off doing so until the last minute, unwilling to spare the time for any pursuit that did not include Gerard. But now her thoughts, like his, were fixed upon their impending departure and the separation to follow.

"I could almost wish 'twere over!" Gerard said suddenly, his voice constricted with his emotions. "Yet even as I think it, I know that every last minute is infinitely precious."

Mavreen turned from the bureau where she sat and looked at his unhappy face with a heavy heart.

"We have both tried so hard not to think of the future. Perhaps 'twould be easier for both of us if we talked of it now, faced the truth together," she suggested. "What will you do, Gerard, when you reach London? I think I would be happier knowing where you are than if you simply disappear and I hear of your movements only through the lips of others."

Gerard sighed deeply.

"I opine that I shall go to your father and announce my arrival in England," he said. "Mistress Manton told me Sir John would be returning to Wyfold House during the first week of April." He turned suddenly and covered the distance between them with quick strides. His face was now alive with excitement.

"Mavreen, my love," he said urgently, "it has only just occurred to me that we could at least see one another at Orchid House. I shall call upon Mistress Manton as a matter of courtesy in any event, and you will go to visit her. We. . . ."

Gently, her eyes filled with tears, Mavreen silenced him.

"I have thought in like manner but it cannot be so, my love. Such restrictions as there would be upon us would be harder to bear even than total separation. And Gerard, you have come to England to arrange your marriage. And though your heart may not be in it, you will have to pay court to your future wife. There is no other way than that you try to put me from your mind, as I must try to put you from mine. We cannot—indeed, we dare not meet again."

Gerard's face betrayed his sense of shock. "It is not possible!" he said when he could find his voice.

"We must make it so; both of us!" Mavreen said with a firmness of conviction that she certainly did not inwardly possess. "Do you not see, Gerard, that we love each other too much for half a measure ever to be tolerable for us? Were we to meet again, we would end up in each other's arms regardless of whom we hurt or dishonored. I am not strong enough to be sure I could greet you merely as a friend. Even if you were so, I would betray us both."

"Then it is your wish that we never see one another again?"

His voice and eyes were so tortured that tears sprang to Mavreen's eyes.

"If you think on it, Gerard, you will know in your heart that it is best."

"It cannot be so!" Gerard said violently, but Mavreen could see in the way he hid his eyes from her that he knew she was right. But in his pain, he felt the need to strike out at someone against the cruelty of Fate and since only Mavreen was present, he said bitterly, "From the sound of it, you will not find it very difficult to make the parting!"

"I do not know how I shall bear it!" Mavreen said softly.

Instantly, Gerard was on his knees before her, his head buried in her lap. Her heart aching, Mavreen stroked his dark head, her tears falling now unheeded. But her weakness evoked Gerard's strength. His own unhappiness seemed suddenly unimportant measured against Mavreen's and he could not bear to hear her weep.

"Come now, my love!" he said, "this is no way to pass these last precious hours left to us. The future may seem all darkness for us today but who knows but fate has already decided that some day in the years to come, we shall be reunited."

"If I could only believe that, I could bear anything!" Mavreen said as she clung to him despairingly.

"God created us for one another!" Gerard said fervently. "Of that I have no doubt at all. Merely consider, my dearest, how improbable it was that we should ever have met. So you see, *mon amour,* we were destined to meet against all odds!" And now he smiled. "See there, my love, the rain was only one of your English April showers. The sun is shining and that must be a good omen for us!"

So the threatened breakdown of their mutual resolve was averted and somehow they managed to pass the remainder of the day in comparative happiness.

Dickon came to report that one of the carriage horses, Bess, had gone lame. He was concerned as to its fitness to be on the road the next day. Was it possible, he asked, for their return to London to be delayed for twenty-four hours?

Mavreen shook her head.

"I have promised his Lordship I would return tomorrow at the latest!" she said. "We have a dinner party arranged for the following day and it cannot now be canceled so late."

"Then there is naught as can be done noways but to hire a horse in Alfriston," Dickon said.

Mavreen nodded.

"You could remain here for a day or two, Dickon, until Bess is fit to be ridden back to London. We can return by stagecoach. But how will you get to Alfriston now, Dickon?"

"I'll ride t'other horse and bring the hired one back on a leading rein," Dickon said sensibly. But Mavreen was worried their carefully-laid plans to stay at the grange unobserved were undone, for Dickon would certainly be recognized in Alfriston and word would soon spread that he had gone to hire a carriage horse, an unlikely enough requirement for Dickon were he alone in Sussex.

"That presents no problem," Gerard said. "I will go in Dickon's place. No one in Alfriston knows me and provided I can pay for the horse, no questions will be asked. I will leave at once as soon as Dickon has told me where a horse can be obtained."

It was dusk when Gerard rode off down the lane. There were dark clouds racing across the night sky and another rain storm was threatening. Mavreen and Rose lit candles and Dickon put a light to the log fire. Mavreen had barely spoken to him all week and when Rose left the room to prepare the evening meal for Gerard's return, she said to Dickon, "I know you will never speak of this week to a living soul and that I can trust you absolutely. Dickon, the consequences would be quite disastrous, not just for me but for the vicomte de Valle too, were our affairs ever to become known. Do you think I can rely upon Rose, also?"

"I do, surelye!" Dickon replied instantly, his cheeks coloring. "I reckon as young Rose be as trustworthy as I am!"

Mavreen looked up at him, smiling.

"You speak with such certainty, I'll have no further doubts!" she said. "You like Rose, then? She has clearly won your approval."

The color in Dickon's cheeks deepened.

"I don't know as I ever knowed a finer girl. I do reckon as how she'd make a man a larmentable good wife."

"Why, Dickon!" Mavreen said. "I do believe my Rose has stolen your heart. Does she favor you, too? How wonderful that would be if you two were to wed!"

Dickon scowled.

" 'Tis early days for talk of weddings. I'd no ought to have said as much as I did."

Mavreen laughed.

"All right, we'll say no more about it. I did not intend to pry, Dickon. Nevertheless, I am delighted and unless you bid me otherwise, I shall make it my business to speak well of you to Rose upon every suitable occasion."

Now Dickon, too, smiled.

"I'd take it as a kindness!" he said simply. "Rose is a right knowledgeable girl, and purty too. I reckon I'm not the only man as thinks she'd mek a good wife."

"But Rose has a deal of good sense in her pretty head!" Mavreen said comfortingly, "and if she thinks about it, she won't find a better man than you to wed, Dickon, and I shall tell her so, if she is not already aware of it."

Mavreen put her hand on his arm, her face suddenly serious.

"Don't let anything come between you and Rose, not if you really do love her," she said. "Where true love lies, lies happiness also!"

Her eyes were so filled with sadness, Dickon could not fail to notice. Clumsily, he offered what comfort he could.

"I do be sorry!" he said. "For ye both."

Tears threatened again and Mavreen looked quickly out of the window to distract her thoughts.

"It's raining unaccountable hard!" she essayed a joke by way of using the Sussex dialect. Dickon grinned.

"I did loanst the viscount my own cloak. 'Twill keep him dry enough."

But Gerard, at that same moment they spoke of him, was never wetter in his life. He lay sprawled on the bank of the river Ouse, his body three parts submerged in the muddy water, only Dickon's cloak, caught upon a splintered spar of the wooden bridge above him, keeping his head above the reeds and preventing him from drowning.

CHAPTER TWENTY
1798

There was no better horseman than Gerard, who had ridden since his earliest childhood. But his horse had stumbled in the darkness as they crossed the bridge, rearing when an owl hooted eerily, and Gerard was thrown sideways into the water. As he somersaulted over the timbers, his head struck the spar on which the cloak was now hooked, and instantly he lost consciousness.

The cold water rushing past his body in no way helped to revive him. Darkness had now fallen and the sky was moonless and black as pitch. There was no sound but the eddying of the water and the steady downpour of rain on the rushes.

The horse, now recovered from his fright, cropped the spring grass on top of the river bank, reins hanging over his head, curtailing the movement of his legs. He waited patiently for his rider to remount. Suddenly, he lifted his head, pricking his ears. He whinnied softly and there was an answering whinny followed by the sound of men's voices.

"Whist! There's someone about!"

There was a jangle of harness as the approaching horses were reined to a standstill. Then silence. Gerard's horse whinnied again. Minutes later, a man's dark figure edged through the long wet grass toward the bridge, pistol cocked. Pleased to find himself once more in the company of human beings, the horse hobbled forward until his soft muzzle was within reach of the man's hand.

The silence was broken by a rough laugh and then a call to the waiting horsemen, " 'Tis a riderless horse!"

"Take heed. His owner may be lying in wait!"

"He'd have hitched his horse, then, not left the reins dangling to break the poor beast's legs!"

There were now six men gathered around Gerard's horse. A lantern was lit and the animal carefully examined.

" 'Tis a magnificent animal!" one man said. "No poor man's mount, that's for sure!"

" 'Tis a fine saddle and bridle, too!" agreed one of his companions.

"Leave it be. We're late as it is!"

"Why don't we take it with us? 'Twill fetch a sovereign or two!"

"And maybe be recognized and we'll be hung for horse thieving."

A chorus of laughter greeted this sally for the men were smugglers, on their way to Pevensey to join the privateer that was sailing under cover of darkness with the morning tide.

"I'll look around afore we go!" the first man, Thomas Spray, said. "Give us the lantern, Will Bennett!"

But it was the third man, George Pring, who spotted the edge of Dickon's dark red cloak, and taking the lantern from Will, discovered Gerard's unconscious body in the river.

All six men assisting, they hauled him up the bank and held the lantern over him. George Pring searched and quickly found the bag of sovereigns Gerard had about him for payment of the horse he was to have bought. The men looked at one another conspiratorially.

"He b'aint dead!" said one.

"Not yet!" said Will Bennett meaningfully, pulling out a knife from his belt.

"No need for that. Weather'll finish him off soon enough."

"He's no poor man!" Thomas Spray said thoughtfully. "I reckon as how he's a gentleman of some consequence. If he's found dead it could bring the law down these parts asking questions."

" 'Taint nothing to do with us!" Will Bennett protested.

The older man struck him roughly across the face.

"Wouldn't be if you hadn't shown your face in the Fox and Partridge this e'en."

"How was I to know there'd be an excise man a-drinking there!"

There was a burst of laughter, not untinged by fear.

"Trust you to find one as recognized you, jackass!" said a burly fellow by the name of Spencer Collison.

"We'll tek him alongside!" said Thomas authoritatively. He was a shrewd man with more intelligence than his companions. "Happen when he comes to and finds himself at sea, he'll pay us a tidy sum to land him alive at some port or other. Rich men's lives is worth saving."

The men considered this piece of logic and were in agreement, all but Will Bennett.

"What'll Captain say if we tek an extra man aboard?"

There was another burst of laughter for it was a large sailing vessel they were joining and the crew was often shorthanded when it came to a running battle with a man-o'-war.

Thomas took out a flask of brandy and forced some of the spirit down Gerard's throat. Within a few minutes, he stirred and moaned but remained unconscious. The man named George Pring took a bundle from his horse's back and unrolling it, produced a pair of seaman's breeches, coarsely woven woolen jacket, and a red and white striped woolen cap. He peeled off Gerard's wet clothing and pocketing anything of value, proceeded to attire him in seaman's outfit. Dickon's cloak, still dry but for the wetting by the rain, was wrapped around him and he was lifted across the saddle of his own horse.

"By the time we get to t'other side of the Downs," said Thomas, "happen he may have recovered well enough to ride prop'ly!"

They remounted, putting out the lantern and allowing their eyes to become reaccustomed to the darkness before they set off across the meadows toward the dark hills outlined indistinctly against the sky. The rain had ceased and a pale moon glimmered feebly through the scurrying clouds. The smugglers, with Gerard's horse in tow, guided their mounts with practiced stealth through the shadows, making what use they could of the woods and hollows for concealment.

The party halted once and took shelter from the wind in the lee of one of the windmills on the Downs. The men ate and Gerard was given another measure of brandy. There was further discussion about the advisability of taking him with them but Thomas, the self-proclaimed leader by virtue of his stronger will, determined to do so. He had no doubt that Gerard was of noble birth and that his family could be expected to pay a ransom that would bring in a deal more than his smuggling might in a year of risking his life more often than not.

By daybreak, they were approaching Pevensey. Here they stopped at an inn where the landlord could be trusted and their horses safely stabled. Gerard's horse had been left tethered at the windmill where no doubt it would be discovered by the miller in due course with nothing to relate it to the smugglers.

Gerard's condition seemed no better and the landlord suggested the men might leave him ashore, but it was soon agreed that this would be too dangerous. If Gerard were to die, the landlord would be in danger. At sea, they could simply tip the body overboard.

"We'll take him with us!" Thomas said stubbornly. "I'll look after him. Two of us can shoulder him up the gangplank. He'll not be the only 'drunken sailor' going aboard!"

The tide was on the turn as Gerard was "walked" aboard the cutter, the *Four Winds*. No one took notice of Thomas or his "drunken companion" for the privateers were busy preparing to sail.

It was not until they were well out to sea in rough water beyond Pevensey Bay that Gerard's inert figure was tumbled out of the hammock in which Thomas had put him and it became known that they had a sick man aboard.

"I reckon he had a blow to the head when his horse threw him," Thomas explained to the captain. "A few days at sea and he'll be as right as rain."

"But *who* is he?" the captain insisted. "Don't you even know his name?"

Thomas grinned cheekily.

"Don't reckon as how it matters. He's young and strong and when he gets his mind back, he can be put to work. And if he doan't get his mind back, he can still haul a rope or scrub pans in the galley."

The captain was busy and disinterested. Thomas himself was a good sailor and trustworthy. He was content to leave the "prisoner" in his guardianship.

So Gerard, vicomte de Valle, was signed on as a crew member of *Four Winds,* and given the first name Thomas could think of, George King. His mates enjoyed the joke for poor old King George had been as mad as a hatter and Thomas's prisoner was clearly out of his mind, too. They gave mock salutes as they passed Gerard's hammock and egging one another on, began to treat him as if he were, indeed, royalty. They gave him the warmest blanket, the softest pillow. They took it in turns to force spoonfuls of gruel down his throat. On sunny days they took him up on deck and laid him in the sunshine. They danced attendance upon him with mock civility, whenever they were not about their own duties. And gradually, day by day, Gerard began to recover.

With the greatest difficulty, Dickon and Rose persuaded Mavreen to return to London. There was a serious problem in relation to the shortage of horses, for not only was Bess still lame, but Gem, the horse Gerard had taken, was gone, too. Riding two double on his own horse, Dickon took Mavreen into Lewes whence she caught the stagecoach to London.

None of the three had slept that night. Mavreen was beside herself with worry. Dickon's theories that Gerard might have decided to take shelter from the rain in Alfriston, that he might have had to ride further afield to obtain a horse, that he had mislaid his route and would be back in daylight did nothing to distract Mavreen from the certainty that some harm had befallen him.

"He would have returned no matter what obstacles beset him!" she said over and over again. "If he lost the horse he would walk. I know him, Dickon. Nothing would have kept him from me this last night!"

Rose was inclined to agree with her mistress but seeing the warning look in Dickon's eyes, upheld his various arguments until dawn broke and it became certain to all of them that Gerard was not coming back. While Dickon boiled a kettle of water to make tea, Rose tried to comfort Mavreen.

"Mayhap he wanted just to disappear!" she said, staring at Mavreen's chalk-white face. "Mayhap he was thinking it would be easier for you, leastways with no good-byes."

"Oh, Rose!" Mavreen cried, shaking her head. "I wish I could believe that were true. Hard though it is, at least I could be sure Gerard was alive and well. But he cannot have thought it better just to vanish. He must have realized how I'd worry—how we would all worry!"

"But, milady, Gem has not returned!" Rose said sagely. "If the viscount had been thrown from his horse, Gem would have come back here by hisself. Dickon told me so last night. I durst say he is safely in Sir John Danesfield's stables by now and that's where Dickon will find him."

"In Sir John's stables?" Mavreen echoed, too distraught and fatigued to think clearly anymore. "But why there, Rose?"

"Leastways, 'cos that's where the viscount was going when you left for London, or so he said, milady."

"That's quite right!" Mavreen agreed. Gerard had planned to stay with her father. It was on this possibility that she permitted herself to be persuaded to return to London.

But it was agreed that Dickon should remain at the grange in case Gerard had indeed met with some accident and returned there later in the day. Should this happen, Dickon was to ride at once to London to Mavreen. If Gerard were not back before nightfall, then Dickon was to set out in search of him. Mavreen, on her return home, would meanwhile send one of the pages round to Wyfold House to discover discreetly whether Gerard had arrived there or not. If he was there, she would despatch a messenger instantly to Sussex to inform Dickon.

"I will not be at peace until I know he is safe!" she told Dickon. "Swear to me you will not give up searching until he is found, Dickon," she added. "Even if—" her voice faltered but she managed to speak her mind, "—even if he is dead, I must know it."

"He's alive somewhere and I'll find him, surelye!"

Mavreen returned to Barre House where she made what explanation she could to Lord Barre as to why she was without Rose and not in the carriage, blaming the lame mare. Dickon, in the meantime, began to doubt the veracity of his own words. True enough, Gerard's horse, mud-bespattered and with reins broken, found his way back from the windmill from which he had broken free not long after the men had departed. It was, therefore, obvious that the young viscount had not been making for London and Wyfold House.

Because the smugglers had chosen a route across the Downs from Alfriston well away from human habitation, the horse had not been observed as it retraced its steps, the memory of a warm stable and a warm bran mash guiding him back to the grange.

Rose burst into tears at the sight of him and Dickon did not know whether to comfort her or see to Gem's needs first.

"Milady was right. Some harm has befallen the viscount!" Rose wailed.

Dickon put an arm about her shoulders and Rose promptly threw her arms around his neck and clung to him.

"What are we going to do?" she asked.

"Shush, now!" Dickon said. "I'll think on something. But first I'd best attend to the horse."

Rose suggested she catch a stagecoach back to London.

"Milady will be needing me, Dickon, and I can tell her Gem is home and you'll be setting off to look for the viscount as soon as you be back from Lewes."

Dickon nodded. As he rubbed down the horse, whistling softly through his teeth as was his custom when he was grooming, he thought happily of the way Rose had flung herself into his arms, and how, like Mavreen, she seemed to think that if he were the one to go in search of Gerard, then the viscount must surely be found. Their trust in him made him feel good even though his heart felt sore for Mavreen.

Dickon hoped that if he let Gem have his head upon the road to Alfriston, he might follow the path Gerard had taken and lead him to some clue, however slight, from which he could make a beginning.

It was by good fortune alone that when Dickon crossed the wooden bridge outside Alfriston late in the afternoon Gem stumbled a second time on the same raised plank of wood that had tripped him two nights before. But for the fact that it was daylight, with no owls to startle the horse, Dickon, too, might have been unseated. In considering this possibility, Dickon glanced about him and spied a torn piece of dark red cloth hanging over the water from one of the spars.

His heart thumping with excitement, he dismounted and retrieved the piece of cloth. He had little doubt that it was from his own cloak. Apprehensively, his eyes scoured the river bank. There were muddy tracks scored in the reeds but his countryman's eyes quickly noted that the reeds were flattened upwards. What body had made the marks had traveled upwards rather than downwards into the river. So the viscount had not met a watery grave, he thought with relief.

Above the bank, the meadow grass had been severely trampled and horses' hooves had left their prints in the wet ground. Dickon went down on his knees and studied them carefully. Before long, he was able to calculate from the size, pattern and shape of the prints that at least five men had stood there and as many horses.

Dickon looked up at the sky and noted the position of the sun. There were two hours of daylight left. His eyes narrowed thoughtfully. These marks on the bank might have no connection with Gerard's fall, and Dickon was now certain in his mind that he had fallen. Common sense suggested that a party of travelers would hardly be likely to halt their horses by the bridge since there was no possible reason for so doing. That they had stopped here added to his certainty that there was a connection between the party and Gerard's disappearance.

Carefully, Dickon went back to his study of the ground above and below the river bank. His meticulous search was rewarded, his quick eye noticing a tiny piece of charred cotton. He was now certain that this tinder had been used to light a lamp and that the horsemen had without doubt been night visitors.

A slow smile spread across Dickon's face. If they were smugglers who had gone to the Viscount's assistance, he could soon discover Gerard's whereabouts. It might take time, but he knew it could be done. He, himself, was well known to the gangs which operated in this part of Sussex. Whilst the men would kill before informing to the law men or the soldiers, they would surely tell Dickon what he wished to know, regarding him as one of themselves.

His only fear was that they had killed Gerard, perhaps mistaking him for a law man or to rob him, and then buried him.

Dickon did not dare dwell on the likelihood. He consoled himself that Gerard could have talked to the men, and discovering they were smugglers, related his own earlier associations with the Alfriston men who had helped him in to France and out again. The men had no reason to kill him since he was the unlikeliest of informers.

Thoughtfully, Dickon returned to his horse and remounted. There was nothing he could do now until dark. Then he would make his way to Lullington on the hillside to the southeast of Alfriston. Small it might be but it was a favored meeting place of the local smugglers.

He stopped at an inn there and over a tankard of ale, considered the extraordinary events. The day was coming to an end, but not his adventure, he thought. That was only beginning.

He wished very much, as he sat on the settle in the big inglenook fireplace, staring up the great chimney to the stars, that there were some way he could get a message to Mavreen so that she would know he was keeping his promise to her and would not rest until he had found the man she so dearly loved.

CHAPTER TWENTY-ONE

1798

Gerard spent close to two months on *Four Winds*. The severe concussion caused by his fall had resulted in a curious state of amnesia. He answered readily now to the name of George King although well-aware that this was not his real name, of which he had no memory. Neither did he know his age, which his shipmates gauged to be in the early twenties, nor his nationality. He spoke English as this was the language spoken to him, but with a slight accent which none could correctly interpret. He recalled nothing of his home, his childhood, nor had he the slightest idea of how he had spent the years of his life.

The privateers, including the captain, a huge burly sailor with a merchant seaman's background, spent a large part of their time trying to place the man Bennett and his friends had kidnapped. Captain Wells had little doubt that Gerard was an aristocrat and his guess that he might be a French émigré was close enough to the truth, but it suited him not to give voice to these suspicions; if Gerard was assumed to be no better or worse than the remainder of the crew, he could be treated as one of them and put to work.

It was some weeks before he was fit for work of any kind aboard the privateer. But as his physical health improved, he was given light duties to perform. It was clear he was no seaman but he seemed to have a particular interest in the gunnery and was never loath to clean the men's pistols nor oil and polish the ship's guns. He was also an adept swordsman and the captain believed he could be counted on to fight should they be set upon.

Four Winds had carried a cargo of cotton twist to Gibraltar and was now bound for Italy to pick up its illegal lading of silk. Not only were they in danger from enemy ships—and the Mediterranean seemed unusually full of moving fleets—but from any English man-o'-war which, if it could catch up with them, had the right to board them and pressgang as many of the privateer's best men as could be removed without endangering the vessel.

So far, they had successfully evaded any such encounters and George King, or King George, as the crew liked to call their strange prisoner, was now believed by the men to be a lucky mascot. Gerard was not treated as a prisoner; in fact his four captors had been overruled by the majority when they had spoke of putting him on shore for ransom at Gibraltar. Pring, Spray, Bennett and Collison did not contest the matter too hard for they realized that it would be difficult to ransom a man of whose identity they were ignorant and, moreover, who showed not the slightest inclination to regain his freedom. "His Majesty," they agreed, could stay aboard.

The crew was a strange medley of men, seamen, riverwatermen, landsmen, regular privateers. There was one young farmer called Ted Burrows from 'Friston who had joined *Four Winds* when his smuggling activities had brought the revenue men a little too close for his safety. He spoke the broadest of Sussex dialects and with his round, ruddy face and blue laughing eyes, struck some faint chord of memory in Gerard's confused brain and compelled him to seek out the companionship of the lad. There was always plenty of work to be done and not much time for talking; but Gerard felt that if he could spend long enough engaged in listening to Ted's reminiscences, he might solve the tantalizing enigma of his past.

There were moments when he felt an overwhelming sadness but could not reason why; at other times, he was filled with a sense of joy and again, knew not the reason for his happiness. But these occasions happened only in Ted's company and Gerard was convinced that somehow, the young farmer held the key that would unlock his memory.

"You kip up your sperits, George!" Ted said. " 'Taint no use worritin, leastways I don't reckon so!"

Which seemed sound enough advice although there were days when Gerard could not prevent himself from feelings of total disembodiment, as if he were watching a real George King go about his duties and that this sailor had no relationship to himself whatever. There were times when the men spoke of their womenfolk and he would wonder whether he had married or loved a woman. Sometimes he dreamed of a beautiful fair-haired girl with green eyes and lips as red as a sunset on the sea's horizon. But even these dreams were confused. The girl would be in the strangest of places—high up in a tree top and might turn suddenly into a little squirrel at which he was aiming a gun. He would wake, drenched in sweat, wondering why he could possibly want to have killed so beautiful a woman even in a dream. Or she might be lying naked, her body white as alabaster against the crimson rug on which she reclined, arms and breasts reaching up to him, filled with promise and desire; he would bend over her only to feel himself falling, falling, until the icy cold of the water's depths closed over his body.

He knew that he often cried out as he woke from such nightmares and Ted, lying in the hammock close by his own, would call softly to him.

Physically, Gerard was now as strong as he had been before his accident. The salt air and the hot Mediterranean sun had turned his skin a brown as dark as his shipmates. Now, when someone asked Gerard a question for which his memory failed to provide an answer, Ted developed a habit of answering for him while Gerard floundered in his confusion.

"He disremembers!" Ted would say flatly, eyes narrowed warningly for he was a huge lad, with great muscular arms and after some fisticuffs, was respected by the other men as someone not to be taunted. "You shouldn't ought to ask him!" And with that, Gerard's tormentor would slouch away.

It was not surprising, therefore, that when *Four Winds* was finally caught up by one of His Majesty's seventy-four-gun battleships and a pressgang took off eight of the crew, including Gerard, he was considerably less disturbed by the event than he would have been had Ted not also been taken with him. The naval officer selecting the sailors rightly took Ted for an able-bodied seaman but was misled by Gerard's physical appearance into supposing that he, too, was a good seaman. As soon as they were put to work, Gerard's deficiencies became apparent.

Since he was incapable of giving any account of himself, he was referred to one officer after another, until finally Gerard stood before the ship's surgeon, who viewed him with some interest. Sickness of the mind was rare enough to him to arouse the surgeon's curiosity. It was obvious, from the remarks passed by his fellow officers, that the young man before him was no doltish half-wit. He talked, so they suggested, in an educated and intelligent manner which put him in a class way above that of the ordinary seaman he supposed himself to be—if, indeed, he was really in ignorance of his origins and not merely professing a loss of memory for multifarious purposes of his own. The possibility that he might be a French spy was in the forefront of everyone's thoughts, but the captain, being fair-minded and not wanting to shoot an innocent man, requested the surgeon's opinion before a final decision was reached.

Gerard himself was unperturbed by this confrontation despite the dire warnings of the officers that the ship's surgeon was unlikely to be taken in by his story if it were not genuine. He answered the physician's questions truthfully and openly. The third question was spoken in French and without hesitation, Gerard replied as quickly in the same language. His interrogator's eyes narrowed. That Gerard might be a spy after all now seemed probable and yet the very frankness with which he replied to all questions and with which he willingly revealed his knowledge of not only the French but the Italian and German languages also, began to have its effect upon his questioner.

Before long, it was established that Gerard was not only a linguist, and that he could read and write with the ease of an educated man, but furthermore that he was adept with sword, pistol, but not with cannon; that when asked to describe a horse, a pianoforte, a carriage, a banquet, he could do so in detail but was unable to recall why or how he came by the knowledge. No matter how quickly questions were fired at him, he answered directly and openly and could not be tricked into revealing glimpses of the memory he claimed not to possess.

The surgeon was finally convinced that Gerard was suffering from a sickness of the brain of which he had known one previous example. This man, he informed his patient, had fully recovered his wits within six months of receiving the blow to his skull which had brought about his illness. Doubtless, Gerard too, would get well in time. In the meanwhile, he felt it would be improper for Gerard to be returned to the seamen's quarters since it was no longer in doubt that Gerard was of good family and should be treated as a gentleman until his true identity was established.

"Meanwhile, Mr. King!" the surgeon said, his face warming to a smile, "I'll give orders for you to be moved to the officers' quarters and given suitable clothing."

He was given a uniform and moved to officers' quarters. Being untrained for naval duties, he was given the task of assisting the ship's clerk.

It was thus that Gerard came to the attention of Rear Admiral Horatio Nelson.

The admiral, seeing a strange face among his officers in the wardroom, became curious to meet him. Gerard had quickly made himself popular with his fellow officers and the genuineness of his illness was now accepted, even though the question of his true nationality was still in doubt.

Nelson asked Gerard how he felt about wearing the British naval uniform.

Gerard's reply was straightforward.

"Since I am in ignorance not only of my nationality but also of my political beliefs, I am without convictions or animosity toward any country!" he said. "Therefore what loyalties I possess I must direct toward those who are at present time my hosts and I am therefore content to serve under your flag to the best of my ability, sir!"

"And no man could say fairer than that!" the rear admiral approved. "I am told you are something of a scholar.

Come to my cabin tomorrow morning. I can make use of a good secretary if it be true you have a neat hand."

So began a relationship that Gerard found exciting and stimulating, for the commander, he soon discovered, had an intellect and a sharpness of mind far superior to that of most men.

With no memories to clutter his brain, he was finding it remarkably easy to absorb new information and detail. The war and the various naval and military engagements carried out on the vast map of Europe which the rear admiral showed to him, seemed like some giant game, made the more colorful by the danger, and by the courage, the tactics and personalities of the various players. Gerard was quick to grasp Nelson's explanations of events and recognizing this, the rear admiral's liking for Gerard's company increased. They now spent many an hour together with the highly intellectual forty-year-old man enjoying instructing of the young stranger whose mind was so impressionable and alert.

It was, therefore, from Nelson himself that Gerard heard the stories of his most recent exploits and opinions. Last March, under the commander-in-chief, the Earl of St. Vincent, Nelson had been detailed to blockade Cadiz. Practically every night, he went off in his barge personally to inspect the boats of the inshore squadron which, whenever the weather served, rowed a close guard on the entrance to the harbor to prevent ingress and egress.

During this time, mutiny broke out among the British fleets, first at Spithead and then at Nore.

"I am much in sympathy with the need for the reforms demanded by the mutineers," Nelson admitted confidentially to Gerard. "Nevertheless, mutiny cannot be tolerated since there could be no discipline if it were ever to be condoned. I do not condemn St. Vincent, as some have done, for hanging any man under his command court-martialed and found guilty of the offense of mutiny. The admiralty was sending out to us its worst-disciplined ships and had St. Vincent not taken such stern measures to stamp it out, mutiny could have spread quickly in our own fleet."

"I doubt your own men would ever mutiny, sir!" Gerard

replied. "I have heard that obedience to you is most willingly given and that you are by nature little inclined for repressive measures!"

Nelson seemed pleased with the compliment. He went to his bureau and selected a piece of paper from among the letters and documents piled there. He handed it to Gerard, explaining that it had been found upon the quarterdeck of *Theseus,* a thoroughly bad ship to which St. Vincent had transferred him on its arrival from England.

> *Success attend Admiral Nelson. We are happy and comfortable, and will shed every drop of blood in our veins, and the name of* Theseus *shall be immortalized as high as the Captain's.*

It was signed Ship's Company.

Discipline had been successfully restored.

Nelson went on to tell Gerard that in order to relieve the men's boredom, inevitable during the long weeks of the blockade, it was decided by the commander-in-chief to divert them by goading the Spanish into activity. Bombardments of the harbor took place and there were periodic skirmishes between the boats and the small craft on both sides. Nelson himself had been involved in some hand-to-hand fighting.

By July, Nelson was engaged in a combined naval and military attack upon the port of Santa Cruz. After one unsuccessful attempt to land, a second was made on July 24th. The landing parties, a thousand strong, planned a massed attack on the town harbor. Scaling-ladders, tomahawks, grappling irons and other such paraphernalia were piled into the boats and when darkness fell, the boats shoved off in pitch darkness and pouring rain, Nelson in one of them.

It was during the ensuing battle that Nelson received a grapeshot hit in his right elbow, smashing it badly and rendering his arm useless. He was taken off by boat to *Theseus* where the surgeon amputated his arm.

Although the British troops were successfully repelled

by the Spanish defenders, those who survived the night were given a safe conduct back to their boats. Nelson had returned to the fleet at Cadiz, deeply depressed by his defeat and suffering from shock from his amputation. In September, he returned to England on sick leave.

"Now after the tedious months of recuperation, I am at sea again," he said with obvious satisfaction.

"I see you are now quite fully recovered!" Gerard said. "And I have been told that you are determined to do battle once more, this time with the French fleet."

Nelson smiled.

"I'll find them!" he said, "God willing!"

On 8th May, they were in position outside the port of Toulon where they could keep a watch upon the French, but a heavy gale sprang up. First *Vanguard*'s topmast went over the side, then the mizzenmast and finally the whole of the foremast.

Officers and men were everywhere. *Vanguard* was in danger of being destroyed by the heavy wreckage trailing in the water and beating against the hull. Where he could be of any physical assistance, Gerard helped the men as the officers shouted their orders. They were now in further danger of drifting.

Somehow, the night passed. The gale continued throughout the following day, until finally it abated sufficiently for *Alexander* to take them in tow. They were dragged to an anchorage in Sardinia.

Now, at last, Gerard could do something constructive. All spare hands from *Vanguard* and *Alexander* and the third of Nelson's battleships, *Orion*, were called upon to fit *Vanguard* with a jury rig in the quickest possible time. Gerard worked tirelessly helping to care for the wounded below deck. He was glad to be able to prove himself useful. In the amazingly short space of three to four days, they were at sea again.

By now, Gerard was stronger physically. Life at sea suited him and the disturbing nightmares had given way to snatches of daydreams he believed, but was not certain, were memories. He was convinced that in some way, the Italian language was associated with the beautiful white-haired lady in the French château. Nelson, on hearing this, suggested that Gerard might have once lived in this château and the lady in his dreams was his mother. During another conversation, this time with Ted, the name of his shipmate's home village of 'Friston sounded so familiar that Gerard was convinced he had either been there or somewhere similar. Ted named the neighboring villages of East Dean and West Dean, but these struck no chord in Gerard's memory, whereas Ted's description of the South Downs with their windmills and flocks of sheep and cornfields convinced him they were part of his own past.

Most strongly of all, Gerard found himself thinking more and more often of the fair, laughing girl with the green eyes and outstretched arms. He was convinced that he had loved this woman and was tormented with a longing at least to recall her name. Ted obligingly thought of every female name he knew but none seemed to fit Gerard's dream girl. Nevertheless, fragments of past sights and sounds were becoming recognizable. One day when he was looking at some white gulls perched on the mast he remembered quite clearly a flock of doves on a roof, and he knew that he had once owned a white mare called Colombe after the doves. On another occasion the sound of the wind in the rigging brought back the clearest of memories of crossing a rough sea in a small fishing boat; of the call to muffle oars as the shore came in sight; of men lashing together tubs of smuggled goods and sinking them as they signaled their position to the smugglers on land. A second boat came out to meet them and Gerard recalled transferring to it while the men in the first boat muttered anxious curses at the delay in getting themselves at a distance as soon as possible. The remembered emotions of tension and danger were too real to be imagined.

He recounted these memories to Nelson, but the rear admiral laughed at Gerard's fears that he might have been a smuggler by profession.

"A man who talks, writes, plays cards with your proficiency and intelligence comes from a very different background!" he said reassuringly.

"It seems that it is people and events where my memory fails!" he said, sighing. "I seem well able to perform most activities I must have engaged in in the past without any effort."

"Patience!" said Nelson. "Piece by piece, your memory is returning. When it does, you may regret it. Who knows but that you'll find yourself married with half a dozen youngsters and a load of responsibilities weighing you down; then you'll be wishing you had remained in happy ignorance."

Laughing, Gerard agreed that he would not care to discover himself so encumbered. But he refrained from commenting to the rear admiral that he would not in the least object to finding himself married—if it were to the beautiful girl of his dreams.

CHAPTER TWENTY-TWO
1798

A week passed before Dickon returned to London. During those seven days, Mavreen became ill with loss of sleep and worry. Only to Clarissa did she reveal the full torment she suffered.

"I alternate between despair that Gerard is dead!" she told Clarissa in the privacy of the little garden at Orchid House, "and the torment of believing him alive."

Clarissa looked anxiously at Mavreen's white, strained face and deeply shadowed eyes.

"The torment of believing him alive!" she echoed, bewildered.

Mavreen's face sharpened.

"I've no doubt you will think badly of me but I shall speak the truth to you, Aunt Clarrie!" she said, in a small hard voice. "I have to confess that I do not possess the same forgiving nature as yourself. Do you remember how, that spring three years ago, Gerard deserted me without warning when our love was at its first blooming?"

Clarissa patted Mavreen's hand. She was now worried

not only on account of Mavreen's physical health, but for her mental condition. Her quiet voice bordered on hysteria and trembled alarmingly.

"Suppose, Aunt Clarrie, that Gerard has run away a second time?" Mavreen went on harshly. "That he was too cowardly to face a final parting that night at the grange. If this be the truth, then I believe I do indeed prefer that he should be dead."

"Mavreen, child, you must not say such things!" Clarissa cried. "You cannot both love him and wish him dead. It is Gerard's well-being and happiness you should have at heart, not your own."

Mavreen sighed.

"I knew you would disapprove, Aunt Clarrie, but that is the way I am made. I fear I have a vindictive streak that I, myself, deplore yet cannot surmount."

"You are condemning Gerard before you know what has transpired!" Clarrie rebuked her. "That is wrong for a beginning. As for his having engaged your affections without true love—that, too, is a falsehood. But no one, my dear, can be certain how they will feel in the future. It would not be to Gerard's blame if, after a week in your company, he discovered that his affections had lessened."

Color flared into Mavreen's pale cheeks.

"It was not thus!" she said violently. "Each day we became closer in thought, word, deed. I *know* he loved me more, not less!"

"Then, my dear, how can you demean both him and yourself by so mistrusting him?" Clarissa said with unusual sharpness. "I have every sympathy with your fears for his life, child, but none at all for your fear that he has deserted you."

But Clarissa's manner softened quickly when Mavreen broke into a storm of tears. Until now, for Gilbert's sake, Mavreen had had to keep an iron control upon herself whenever unhappiness beset her at Barre House. Moreover, as if she had not enough worries about Gerard, she was also deeply concerned about her condition. Not even to Clarissa did she confide her fears that she might be with child. Until this uncertainty was fact, she attempted to put such thoughts from her mind. But they obtruded whenever she relaxed her self-control.

There was some relaxation of tension when Dickon returned to London with the news that Gerard had almost certainly fallen from his horse at the bridge, been picked up by smugglers and taken aboard a privateer by the name of *Four Winds*. At least Gerard was alive! Mavreen thought exultantly. Dickon had actually spoken to the landlord of the inn at Pevensey and been told that four smugglers with a sick prisoner had stopped there for breakfast the morning following Gerard's disappearance. The man had assured Dickon that the prisoner, though unconscious, was not dead. From the smugglers' conversation, the landlord gleaned that the fellow had been thrown from his horse and that the beast had been left tethered to a windmill up on the Downs.

There seemed little doubt that Gerard had not disappeared of his own volition but was most probably aboard *Four Winds* bound for the Mediterranean. Mavreen could but pray and try to go on with her life in the hope that he was still alive and would one day return. She despatched Dickon back to Pevensey at monthly intervals to inquire among his smuggling contacts whether there was fresh news of the privateer, but nothing more was heard of *Four Winds*.

April gave way to May, and May to June. Mavreen was no longer in doubt that she was carrying Gerard's child. She vacillated between confession to Gilbert and withholding her knowledge a while longer. Deception was foreign to her nature. She hated the idea of living a day-by-day existence with her ever-kindly husband while he remained happily ignorant of the fact that she would soon disgrace him. Only Rose suspected the truth for she alone knew the reason for Mavreen's occasional morning "indispositions". Gilbert believed her sickness was due to the aftereffects of too many late nights and overindulgence in rich foods. When, finally, Mavreen decided she would delay no longer and steeled herself to speak with Gilbert, he, himself, became indisposed and the confession was once more postponed.

June gave way to July. Fortuitously for Mavreen, who although well enough, was beginning to find herself more easily fatigued, Gilbert's continued ill-health necessitated that she decline as many social engagements as possible. He was suffering from what the king's physician, Dr. John Willis, believed to be a severe digestive disturbance giving rise to the pains he complained of beneath his rib cage. He had also lost the partial use of his left arm, due, Mavreen was informed, to bad circulation. Gilbert was bled, but felt little better. He felt that Mavreen should not curtail her own pleasures, and her conscience troubled her sorely when he supposed that her own retirement was for his benefit. They spent the hot summer days in lethargic inactivity. July was nearing its end when upon one particularly hot afternoon they took a gentle stroll around the garden and paused for a rest in one of the grottoes. Gilbert suddenly took Mavreen's hand in his.

"I have never lacked in love for you, my dear!" he said, "but when I asked you to be my wife, I did not hope—or even expect—that my deep affection for you would be reciprocated. I want you to know how very happy you have made me at all times; moreover, I would add that I doubt I have ever felt more content than at this moment. You have made me the perfect wife, my dear."

Tears in her eyes, Mavreen leaned over and gently kissed his cheek. She did not wish to spoil his happiness but her conscience would not allow her to accept the illusion of perfection.

"Dearest Gilbert, I cannot permit you to say such things. They are not true. I am very far from perfect. I . . ." she began. But Gilbert raised his hand and put one finger across her lips.

"I don't know what it is you may wish to tell me," he said, "but whatever the transgression may be, and I mean this, my dear, *it is of no importance to me*. Even if you have committed some unforgiveable crime . . ." and he smiled at the absurdity of his thought, ". . . it is still of no consequence. I, alone, can gauge my state of mind and heart and I am a contented man. Is that not enough?"

Speechless, and near to tears, Mavreen nodded her

head. If only it were true that there was nothing of consequence. But Gerard's child was moving within her.

"You are a good man and a wonderful husband, dearest Gilbert," she said huskily. "I do love you, you know, whatever others may say." This much, at least, was the truth.

"I think I know your feelings for me. If I did not believe it, how else could I be so content?" he argued logically. "You know, my dear, I have done a deal of thinking lately and I have reached the conclusion that the Lord has given me a good life and kept the best for the end. What more could a man ask of his Maker?"

As he spoke those last words, Gilbert gasped and clutched his hand to his chest. Before Mavreen had time to realize he was ill, Gilbert's heart stopped beating and to her indescribable fear and dismay, his body fell forward across her lap.

It was, of course, Clarissa who came to comfort Mavreen, setting out for Barre House the moment Dickon rode up with the sad news. Sir John saw to the distressing affairs relating to Gilbert's funeral. It was Clarissa, ever-wise, who upon listening to Mavreen's account of her last conversation with Gilbert, eased Mavreen's distraught mind.

"Can you not see, my dear, how glad poor Gilbert would be to depart this world at such a moment of awareness of joy? He suffered no long, distressing illness, only a second's pain; and he went to his Maker the happiest of men."

"But imagine how he would have hated me had he lived!" Mavreen wept. "You do not understand, Aunt Clarrie. In five months time I shall be birthing Gerard's child. If Gilbert had known. . . ."

"But he did not know; and now he will never have to know. Think on it deeper, child. The world will believe it is Gilbert's son or daughter you are bearing. Think how it would please him that his friends believed him capable of producing an heir at his age! He would delight in their congratulations."

Mavreen stared back at Clarissa from eyes reddened with weeping.

"How can you believe that, Aunt Clarrie? He would

have known I had taken a lover and that my child was not his!"

"My dear, you yourself told me that Gilbert had condoned any future liaison before ever the thought had crossed your mind of being untrue to him. As to the child—well, I think he would have accepted it simply because it was yours. You must try to think of it now as your last tribute to Gilbert. If it is a son, it will bear his name and title and that horrid cousin he so disliked will not inherit. I can imagine dear Gilbert chuckling with delight at the thought."

Clarissa extracted a promise from Mavreen that no one, not even Sir John, was to know the truth. The one exception, she agreed, was Gerard. But only after he, himself, had sworn upon his oath never to reveal the child's true identity. This would be the price they must both pay and willingly, for the safe keeping of Gilbert's honor.

A week had passed after Gilbert's funeral, and Mavreen was still engaged in replying to the hundreds of letters of sympathy she had received, all paying tribute to him in one way or another, when she received further news of Gerard.

Dickon, his fair-skinned face red with excitement, informed her that *Four Winds* had returned to England. He had spoken with one of the privateer's crew, he told Mavreen, a man called Thomas Spray. From the smuggler Dickon had learned that Gerard, among eight men, had been pressganged into a British naval man-o'-war—none other than Rear Admiral Nelson's own ship, *Vanguard*.

"The viscount was alive and well but suffering a lamentable loss of memory!" Dickon said. " 'Tis a fact he disremembered even his own name and the men did call un George King, for they reckoned he be an Englishman, and the name good as any."

She was now confident that she could trace Gerard's whereabouts. Someone in the navy would know where Nelson was and Mavreen intended to find out and get word to Gerard by some means.

Without revealing her reasons, she questioned her father about the influential men he knew in the admiralty and their accessability. Paying careful attention to everything he said, she learned the admiralty dealt with policy and operations of war but the navy board built and repaired ships, provided stores, victuals and ammunition and kept accounts. Therefore, the head of the navy board was in a position of great power. Nelson's uncle, the late Sir Maurice Suckling, had been comptroller and head of the navy board and during his administration, had become friendly with Admiral Sir Peter Parker. Sir Peter and his wife had become friendly with Nelson and Sir Peter had made him commander of the brig *Badger*. Sir John knew Sir Peter well and was only too pleased to give Mavreen a letter of introduction to him, though he failed to see why she required it. She let him believe it was on behalf of a friend with a young son who needed an influential patron.

Without going into any great detail, Mavreen explained to Anne Pettigrew that she needed to get in touch with Gerard de Valle; that she believed Sir Peter could assist her but for obvious reasons, did not wish Sir Peter to think that she herself, so recently widowed, was interested in the young viscount's whereabouts.

"I know it is asking a great deal of you, Anne," Mavreen said as the two girls sat talking in the garden in the rose arbor. "I would not do so were it not of importance to me. Will you assist me in this small deception?"

Anne Pettigrew was intrigued. She had an openly confessed soft spot in her heart for Gerard de Valle, despite the fact that she had not seen him since her childhood. Now she surmised that Mavreen, too, might have fallen a little in love with the young viscount. It did seem strange that with Lord Barre not one week buried, Mavreen should show her interest in another man, but Anne was not unkindly by nature and she needed no convincing of Mavreen's genuine distress at her husband's death; she did not condemn her as unfeeling and readily agreed to help.

Mavreen handled the interview skilfully; first showing a personal interest in Rear Admiral Nelson's exploits and then turning the conversation to Anne's desire to discover the whereabouts of a Mister George King, a friend of her brother, James. Mr. King was believed to be aboard the

Vanguard, and Mavreen explained Anne wished to send a letter to him; or failing that, to be advised as to his state of health and well-being.

The admiral smiled agreeably, in no doubt that the young lady was engaged in an affair of the heart. He was willing to assist, he told them, but regretted that there was no news from Rear Admiral Nelson. No one could understand how, when the French fleet had long since left Toulon, Nelson had failed to locate it, although the fleet was now known to have appeared at Malta in early June.

He promised, however, to forward Miss Pettigrew's letter.

This had been previously drafted by Mavreen, copied by Anne, and was, of necessity, guarded. It was addressed to Mr. George King and read,

> *Dear George,*
> *It is such a long time since we last met, I am afraid you may have forgotten me. However, I hope that it may refresh your memory to hear that my dear brother, James, speaks often of you and of your school days.*
> *Other of your friends inquire about you, including my own dear friend, Lady Barre. She asked me to recall to you your enjoyable visit to her tutor, Mr. Glover, at his delightful house, the grange, in Sussex.*
> *I should be delighted to receive news of you and trust you will write to me at the above address.*
> *Your obedient servant,*
> *Anne Pettigrew.*
>
> *Postscript. I have omitted to inform you that dear Lord Barre passed away recently. Should you desire to write your condolences to Lady Barre, she is at present in residence at Barre House, although she plans shortly to retire to Sussex whilst she is in mourning.*

Anne had placed her own seal upon the wax but should this break during passage, the wording of the letter's contents was harmless enough to bear outside scrutiny. And, hopefully, it would serve to refresh Gerard's memory.

Now that Mavreen was once more, however indirectly,

in contact with Gerard and the letter, so she believed, shortly upon its way, she completed the legalities arising from Gilbert's death with the aid of her father; ordered the servants to close up Barre House, packed her personal belongings and retired to Sussex to the grange.

It was assumed by everyone that Mavreen was in mourning. Her pregnancy had not been revealed except to the lawyers, since the birth of a son would affect the inheritance. Only Clarissa knew that Mavreen did not intend to return to London until after the birth of her child, which they assumed would be toward the end of December. Fortuitously, perhaps, Sir John was suddenly involved in the Irish rebellion and his proposed absence from London left Clarissa free to accompany Mavreen to Sussex for an indefinite period.

Anne Pettigrew wrote at regular intervals saying there was no reply to her letter to Mr. King. Anne did, however, receive one letter from Admiral Parker informing her Admiral Nelson was now known to have reprovisioned in Syracuse in mid-July, and that Miss Pettigrew's letter had meantime been despatched to the commander-in-chief, Lord St. Vincent, who, Admiral Parker believed, was in the best position to ascertain *Vanguard*'s movements. Unfortunately, the letter was despatched too late for its onward transmission to Syracuse to reach *Vanguard* during her four days in harbor there.

There being nothing she could do, Mavreen settled down to a further long wait. It became her practice to sit in the hot August sunshine beneath the great copper beech tree where once she had sat with Gerard, and think about him and their coming child as if, by sheer concentration, she could will her thoughts across the ocean to him. She felt a strange certainty that not only was he very much alive, but thinking equally intensely of her. She allowed herself to relax into a state of placidity and concentrate upon the approaching birth of their child.

CHAPTER TWENTY-THREE
1798

Gerard could see that the rear admiral was worried. Two months had passed since they learned that Malta had surrendered to General Bonaparte and the huge French armada had sailed away to some unknown destination. Nelson believed the French were on their way to Egypt, the stepping stone to the Indian Ocean and India. He set sail for Alexandria, but it was to find the harbor void of either the French fleet or rumor of its whereabouts. He was still without his frigates and was in a constant state of mental agitation as he tried to anticipate the movements of his quarry.

Lord Nelson decided to drop anchor off Syracuse in Sicily and was there re-provisioned by the governor. Although he received all the fresh food and water he required, he did not receive what he most wanted—news of the French fleet.

He outlined his plans to his commanders. He would first look for the enemy in the Aegean, then Cyprus, then Palestine, and finally in Egypt again. It looked as if they were never going to catch up with them, and Gerard was no less discouraged than Nelson himself or his officers and men.

Finally they learned from Turkish officials that the French were attacking Egypt. Elated, they set sail, but although they made excellent passage, when they finally arrived once more at Alexandria, it was to discover but a few minor French war vessels remaining. They were too late. The rear admiral confessed dejectedly to Gerard that no doubt the French army was safely ashore by now and the warships equally safely on their way back to France. Failure in their mission now looked inevitable. But as they sailed half-heartedly eastward along the coast, Gerard was sitting down to dinner with the dispirited Nelson and his officers, when suddenly there was an unusual commotion on the deck. Protocol was thrown to the winds as Ted Burrows himself burst into the wardroom, crying excitedly, "*Zealous* has seen 'em! The French Frenchys! De signal flags wuss surelye a-saying so. Dey's at anchor in Aboukir Bay!"

Now Gerard felt a thrill of excitement that he might have a hand in arresting the onslaught of the Corsican giant. As the squadron approached Aboukir Bay, Gerard counted thirteen of the French line at anchor. The British also should have been thirteen in number but *Alexander*, *Swiftsure* and *Culloden* were still miles astern. Moreover, they lacked any but a few old French charts of the bay. But Nelson did not hesitate in his decision to attack. He hoisted signals which revealed his battle plan to his captains, his intention being to mass all his ships against a portion only of the enemy's.

By nightfall, the first five French ships had eight British ships engaging them on both sides. As he paused to watch the battle in progress, Gerard knew he would never forget the weird and lurid spectacle before him. Vivid gun flashes flared in the darkness up and down the western end of the bay, illuminating the hulls and masts of the ships and lighting up the huge clouds of cannon smoke. Across the murky waters rolled the thunder of four to five hundred guns punctuated by the occasional crash of a falling mast, human shouts and the rumbling of gun carriages. The French flagship, *Orient*, caught fire, flames running up masts and rigging until the whole ship was a huge bonfire throwing a ghastly orange light over the two battling fleets.

Suddenly, *Orient* blew up, the roar of the explosion stilling the fighting so that for some minutes there was a dead silence but for the falling debris.

Gerard felt as if the explosion had occurred inside his own head. His ears hummed and his thoughts whirled in confusion. It was at that moment he remembered who he was.

He stood on the deck, aware that the gunfire had re-

commenced but unable to think of anything but the
memories that were flooding one upon the other into his
mind. His thoughts travelled backwards from his crossing
of the bridge outside Alfriston when his horse had stumbled, to Mavreen at the grange. Mavreen! Her image was
so real in his imagination he could almost believe it possible to reach out and touch her. Dickon, Rose, Mistress
Manton, and backwards through time to his mother and
his home.

How long he stood there lost in the total isolation of
his revived memory, Gerard did not know. But he became
once more aware of his present surroundings when Ted
ran up and informed him that the northern half of the
French fleet had surrendered. It was midnight and the men
were exhausted. Hands were falling asleep at their posts.
Gerard gathered his wits about him.

As *Vanguard* set sail for Naples, Gerard wondered how
long it would be before the news of the battle reached
London. Nelson told him it would most probably take at
least a month or more.

It occured to Gerard that he must, at the very earliest
of opportunities, despatch letters home, both to his mother
and to Mavreen. He could scarcely bear to envisage their
separate concern for him; Mavreen's the more so since his
mother did not know how long he had intended to remain
in England. It was now five months since his departure.
Mavreen must have suffered every conceivable agony of
mind. He could but hope that somehow she had learned
the truth of what had happened to him and derived a
measure of comfort from the knowledge that he was at
least alive when he boarded the privateer.

Gerard would have liked to discuss his private affairs
with Nelson but the rear admiral was unwell, partly from
his head wound, partly from the nervous exhaustion of
the long chase. All the responsibilities had been his and
the strain greatest upon him at all times.

Gerard did, however, reveal to Ted that he now knew
his real identity, having first extracted a promise from him
that he would not allow anything he told him to spoil
their friendship.

"Dont reckon ders much as could!" Ted said laconically. "Not now us have bin shipmates and fought along-side each other way we did!"

But at first, despite his promise, Ted was overawed by Gerard's title. He was further confused to find that Gerard was a Frenchy. However, Gerard reminded him that many of the French aristocrats had fought against the new regime and they were not looked upon by the British as enemies. Indeed, many had joined the fighting forces.

Ted soon recovered his composure and grinned broadly when Gerard confessed there was a girl he loved who came from Sussex.

"Der ain't no girls purtier than Sussex girls!" he said. "Be you goin' to marry her?"

Seeing the strange expression on Gerard's face, he added quickly, "I'd no ought to have asked ye that."

"It's all right, Ted!" Gerard said sincerely. Ted's question gave him the opening he needed to talk about Mavreen, not by name, of course, but of his intense and hopeless love for her. He did not for one moment believe that the simple farm lad could offer any advice on his insoluble problem. Nonetheless, he knew better than most the straightforward honesty and directness with which Ted dealt with life. He knew he could trust Ted's loyalty to the same degree that Mavreen trusted Dickon's. They were two of a kind. Any confidence given to one of Gerard's fellow officers might endanger Mavreen's reputation.

Gerard was prepared for Ted to approach the problem on simple moral grounds. There were "girls you wedded and girls you bedded." Yet having listened quietly to Gerard's account of the impasse in his relationship with Mavreen, Ted's solution was as unexpected as his condemnation. It was his opinion that Gerard should have stayed away from his beloved once he had made up his mind that his duty required him to marry another. Doubtless she now believed him dead, and she must somehow have come to terms with her loss. Were Gerard to renew their association yet again, what happiness could it bring her, a married woman and he betrothed elsewhere? At best Gerard could offer her happiness for a brief while and then leave her once more.

"Best let sleeping dogs lie," Ted advised. " 'Tis hard on you, surelye, larmentable hard. But I guess it be a deal easier on her as loves you."

This long, slow, carefully delivered speech left Gerard in confusion. Since the restoration of his memory, he had had no other thought but of his reunion with Mavreen at the earliest possible moment. In his roundabout way, Ted advised him, just as Clarissa had advised Mavreen, that real love required the loved one's happiness first with no regard for self.

Bitterly, Gerard reflected that it might have been better had he never recovered his memory but spent the rest of his life as George King, knowing nothing of Mavreen nor the torments of loving the unattainable. Torturing himself, Gerard revived every memory of her, each word spoken, each gesture made; each kiss, each moment of tenderness, of passion, of desire. He faced the knowledge that no matter what happened in his life, he would never love a woman more than he loved Mavreen, nor receive from any woman so total a gift as hers. She had given with her heart, her very soul. It had seemed to him then, as it did now, that she had offered him life itself. As the ship sailed slowly toward Naples, Gerard realized that Nelson's victorious battle at Aboukir Bay had brought his own personal defeat.

CHAPTER TWENTY-FOUR
1798-1799

On Christmas Eve, 1798, Dickon drove the horses through torrential rain to collect his mother from Owlett's Farm. Mavreen's baby was due and her occasional pains during the day suddenly became regular and acute soon after darkness fell.

Mavreen, herself, would have waited until morning before sending for Mother Sale, but Clarissa insisted Dickon should go without delay. Although a first labor was often of many hours duration, she said she was not prepared for the baby to make its arrival without adequate help at hand.

Both Clarissa and Sir John had done their utmost to persuade Mavreen to return to London for the birth of her child. At Barre House, she could have had the very finest of medical attention, and the ever-present dangers that always accompanied childbirth would have the best chance of being averted.

But Mavreen never waivered in her refusal to have her child elsewhere than at the grange, and under the surveillance of Mother Sale. She argued reasonably that not only had the farmer's wife had five children of her own but she had delivered countless neighbors' babies, not to mention livestock.

Clarissa was shocked by this allusion to animals.

"Nature has determined no difference between animals and other females when it comes to the matter of birthing and suckling," Mavreen pointed out. "Moreover", she added, "I intend to feed my child myself, and not, as so many ladies of quality choose to do, hire a wet-nurse for the purpose."

Clarissa was far more afraid than Mavreen. As the hours dragged by and Mavreen clung to Mother Sale's hands in what was proving no easy birthing, Clarissa began to fear for the outcome. Mistress Sale told her that the baby was choosing to make its appearance feet first, and would have explained the attending complications had Clarissa been willing to listen. Clarissa told the woman that should it be necessary, the child must be sacrificed if it would help to ensure Mavreen's life.

In the big bedroom where a huge log fire warmed the damp cold of the night, Mavreen hung on to the bed-sheet, sweat pouring down her drawn face, and begged Mistress Sale to save the baby's life even at the cost of her own.

Mistress Sale was afraid Mavreen was giving up the difficult struggle: "I never *heerd* such nonsensical talk!" She wiped Mavreen's forehead with a wet flannel and set to work again.

Early on Christmas morning, Mavreen's child was born —a seven and a half pound girl with a mass of dark hair and sky blue eyes. When Mistress Sale put her into Mavreen's exhausted arms, there was no doubting that this was Gerard's daughter, the infant features a perfect tiny replica of his own.

Mavreen had thought only of bearing a son. She was convinced their child would be a boy and desperately hoped, during the long months of waiting, that her wish would be realized. But now, as she gazed into the minute crumpled face so resembling Gerard's when he scowled in anger, she smiled in total contentment before she fell asleep.

The difficult birth left Mavreen very weak for over a month. The baby thrived but she herself was very slow to recover her health and strength. For long hours, she lay motionless. Clarissa fretted, thankful that at least Mavreen showed interest when she nursed the baby. Day by day she became stronger, but her apathy remained.

Sir John was fretting for Clarissa to return to London. He had twice visited them at the grange, shown a polite interest in who he believed to be Gilbert's offspring—but would have shown more had she been a boy—and spent most of his sojourn explaining to Mavreen that she was now an extremely wealthy young woman. Being a girl, the child would not inherit either the title or family entrustments, he informed her. She would, however, bear the title of Lady, and it was high time Mavreen chose a suitable name for the infant.

Only Clarissa knew why a name had not yet been decided upon. Mavreen wanted the baby to be christened Geraldine but knew that this was, if not impossible, very inadvisable, yet despite all Clarissa's suggestions, she wanted no other. Eventually it was decided, against Sir John's wishes, to christen his first granddaughter Tamarisk. Clarissa agreed to the naming of the little girl after a wild rose but Sir John would have preferred something simple, such as Charlotte or Augusta, like the Prince of Wales's only daughter, or perhaps Elizabeth, Sophia or Amelia after one of the Royal princesses.

But Mavreen remained stubbornly determined that her

daughter, a child of nature despite the circumstances that made her birth legitimate, would bear the name of one of nature's wild flowers.

"Besides, Father," she said with the faintest of smiles, "does she not look like a wild rose with those pink cheeks?"

Not even for Clarissa's sake would Mavreen agree to go back to London, although Orchid House had rooms enough to include Mavreen and the child as well as Rose, who had now become the baby's nurse. If there was anyone who loved the tiny Tamarisk more than Mavreen and Clarissa, it was Rose. She confessed shyly to Dickon that she now longed for a child of her own. She agreed that as soon as her mistress was settled down, she would wed Dickon as she had promised him on the day of his return from Sussex after his search for Gerard.

Dickon, too, was attached to the dark-haired, golden-skinned child. He took care not to reveal his feelings, but Rose saw through his pretended indifference and loved him the more.

As Mavreen watched Rose pack Clarissa's belongings in preparation for her return to London, she was aware how much she was going to miss her. No mother could have been more sympathetic and understanding. "We will come and visit you often!" Mavreen promised. "As soon as Tamarisk is old enough to travel, we will come and stay with you."

Clarissa sighed, near to tears. Although she had missed Sir John often during their long separation, time had passed swiftly at the grange. The parting with Mavreen and the baby would leave a gap in her life not even dear John could fill. Moreover, she was deeply troubled about Mavreen's state of mind.

Sir John brought news of Lord Nelson. After the brilliant and victorious battle with the French fleet, the admiral, now a baron, had repaired to Naples where he was a guest of the British minister, Sir William Hamilton. Mavreen knew, therefore, that if "George King" were with Lord Nelson, Sir Peter Parker could well receive a belated reply to his inquiries. Anne Pettigrew had written to Mavreen to congratulate her on the birth of her daughter, adding a postscript to the effect that she had had no communication from Sir Peter. Now, at last, news could be expected. Clarissa had discussed the possibilities as to what had in truth happened to Gerard endlessly with Mavreen during the long dark evenings before the child was born.

He might be dead. He might not have been the "George King" supposedly put aboard *Four Winds* suffering from loss of memory. He might have been killed and buried by the smugglers. He might have feigned his loss of memory in order to mislead anyone trying to trace his disappearance. He might have died at sea. He might have been taken aboard *Vanguard* and subsequently put ashore at some port of call in the Mediterranean. He might have been killed in the naval engagement in Egypt. He might have recovered his memory and returned to his mother in France.

The suppositions were limitless and Clarissa knew that they never ceased to torment Mavreen. Of them all, Mavreen clung to the hope that Gerard had returned to France. They were certain of only two facts—that Gerard had not returned to London and that Donna Mercedes de Faenza had announced her intention to marry an English lord.

"At least this news must bring you some joy!" Clarissa said. But Mavreen shook her head.

"Don't you see, Aunt Clarrie, that in a way Gerard's freedom only makes everything harder to bear? I, too, am now free. I am also a very rich woman. If Gerard but knew this, there is nothing to stand in the way of my marriage to him. Yet I cannot tell him so. I do not know even if he is alive, or if he still loves me."

Mavreen wrote to Gerard sending her letter in care of Helga von Heissen, the Austrian countess living in Switzerland, asking her to forward the letter to him at the Château de Boulancourt in France. But Napoleon had displaced the ruling families in Switzerland. The country had been made a republic, and neither she nor Clarissa believed the baroness still to be living there. Doubtless she had sought sanctuary elsewhere, Mavreen said, but nevertheless clung to the faint hope that she might one day receive a reply.

It was fortunate Mavreen had the baby to occupy her thoughts and emotions. She was otherwise apathetic with little enthusiasm for a life that seemed pointless without the man she loved. The child gave her reason for her continued existence and since it was Gerard's child, too, she loved it obsessively.

Left alone at the grange without the stimulus of Clarissa's conversation, Mavreen began to delve into Mr. Glover's vast library of books. But they could not hold her interest for long. When her father sent her copies of the latest newspapers, she took but a cursory glance at the contents. She read that the plague had broken out among Napoleon's army fighting the Turks in Syria; that Britain, Russia, Austria and Turkey had formed a second coalition during the autumn. She read an account of a massacre of the French by the people of Cairo which had taken place last September; and of a further massacre when the Moslems called for vengeance.

The news relating to Rear Admiral Nelson did, however, hold her interest. Following upon his victory, he was raised to the peerage and was now referred to as Baron Nelson of the Nile. Rewards were pouring in from all over the world, from the East India Company, the Turkey Company, the king of Naples, the king of Sardinia, the czar of Russia and the sultan of Turkey. The latter had sent Nelson a magnificent diamond aigrette, known as the Chelengk. Parliament voted him a pension of £2,000. She read every scrap she could find, to see if Gerard had indeed sailed with Britain's hero and shared in some way in his exploits.

With Clarissa gone and the weather still too cold for outdoor sorties, her spirits fell lower. Dickon, prompted by Rose, told her that she was doing neither the baby nor herself any good by brooding. His mother and father and the children were repeatedly asking to see the baby. Would Mavreen not change her mind and allow him to drive them both over to Owlett's Farm one day? Moreover, he added, it would give him the opportunity to introduce Rose to his family.

At once Mavreen was full of contrition.

"You should have told me *you* wanted to go with Rose,"

she said. "Each time you suggested the visit, Dickon, I thought it was for my entertainment. Of course you must go."

"Beant you a-coming then?" Dickon asked. "Mam's not seen de liddle 'un leastways since day arter she were born. She's been quite in a quirk over it."

"I'm sorry, Dickon!" Mavreen said repentantly. "Of course we'll all go together." With a sudden flash of her old mischievousness she added, "When you see Mother Sale next Sunday, tell her not to get in a pucker over my visit!"

The following week, they drove in the carriage to Owlett's and spent the most pleasurable of days at the farm. Mistress Sale took charge of the baby, putting her into the same carved oak cradle used in turn by all the children including Mavreen. She crooned to her while she mixed dough with her everbusy hands and rocked the cradle with her foot.

Dickon took Rose to the meadows to show her the new lambs. Mavreen went with Patty and the children to approve the many changes and improvements made to the school in the barn. Patty now taught, as best she could, twenty-five children of varying ages, which, she told Mavreen, she found quite a task.

Patty, now a pretty red-haired freckled-faced seventeen, was herself betrothed. But she would not be marrying until her young man had completed his apprenticeship as a thatcher. Next year, she told Mavreen, her father was building them a small cottage on the ten-acre field known, because of its shape, as the Punch Bowl. He was giving them the land as a wedding gift. Young Edward was this very day plowing it with his father's new cast-iron plow.

Master Sale was more excited by his new plow than by the baby Tamarisk.

" 'Twas invented but two years since by an excellent gentleman, name of Charles Newbold!" he informed Mavreen proudly. "A valiant plow if ever I did see one."

Life had not really changed a great deal on the farm since Mavreen had lived there as a child, she thought. It was true the Sale family had prospered. Neighboring farms had been bought and added to the land. Master Sale now employed laborers and used more modern equipment. But all the family from Father and Mother Sale down to the youngest worked as hard as ever at the self-same tasks. The cycle was continuous every season and could not be ignored for illness, bad weather, old age, or any other reason. Its relentless continuity was somehow comforting, reassuring. Mavreen returned that night to the grange with the stirrings of her old spirit.

This revival of hope was soon followed by a return of the determination that was so strong a facet of her nature. To give up—be it a game, an argument, a plan, a problem, had been hitherto unacceptable to her. Mr. Glover had encouraged this side of her.

Mavreen found herself remembering his advice now and reapplied her mind to the problem of her own life. This time she did not waste her mental energy on self-pity or bitterness at the cruelty of fate. She faced up to the certain positive facts that were all she had to work on. She loved Gerard as much as she ever had; she would love him always. There was no proof that he was dead, and if he were alive, the most likely place she would find him would be at Compiègne. Letters did not reach him. *But she could.*

As the idea of going herself in search of him formed in her mind, Mavreen's spirits spiraled upwards. Apathy was replaced with a glowing vitality and excitement. Ideas poured through her mind in a steady stream. Rose could take Tamarisk to London to live with Aunt Clarrie, or to Owlett's Farm. Either place, the baby would thrive. She, herself, would go to France, taking Dickon with her. If Gerard had been able to pass between the two countries in war time, then so could she. If necessary, Dickon could enlist the help of his smuggling friends. She had plenty of money, and the mere thought of the adventure stimulated her. There was no one now to say no to her. As the widowed Lady Barre, despite the fact that she was not yet twenty years old, her father could not forbid her, even were he to discover her intentions.

Mavreen summoned Dickon to her and outlined her plan.

"I have to do this, Dickon!" she said finally. "You will come with me, won't you?"

Dickon looked at Mavreen uneasily, lower lip caught between his teeth, one hand scratching his red thatch of hair.

"You beant strong enough!" he said doubtfully.

"But I am!" Mavreen protested. "I'm perfectly well, Dickon, and you know it. You're only making excuses. You don't want me to go because I'm a woman. That's it, isn't it? If I were a man. . . ."

She broke off, her eyes dancing with excitement.

"Dickon, I'll dress in boy's attire. Henry can lend me some of his clothes. I'll cut my hair shorter and dirty my face and hands. And, I can talk Sussex dialect if need be. I ride astride a horse, shoot a pistol, use a sword. Come now, Dickon—" she added with smiling persuasiveness "—if *I'm* not frightened, leastways *you* shouldn't be!"

As always, she succeeded in bringing a smile of compliance to Dickon's face. She had overruled his scruples with the logic of her reasoning. The journey *could* be made. And if it would bring the young viscount and Mavreen back together again, then he would be glad to help.

"I'd no ought to say it," he muttered, "but if it's what you want, then I goos wid you."

Exactly one week later, Dickon and his young, fair-haired boy companion set out upon their way to France.

CHAPTER TWENTY-FIVE

1798

Gerard lost all enthusiasm for life. He was concerned only about his mother. Now that his mind was made up not to see Mavreen again, he did not care what became of him personally, but his strong sense of duty and his love for his mother whom he knew must be tormented with worry about him, troubled his conscience.

Soon after his arrival in Naples, therefore, he decided to return as quickly as possible to France. Lord Nelson, however, suggested that a letter to the vicomtesse would set her mind at rest while Gerard remained ashore a few more weeks to fully recover his health and spirits. Nelson used his influence to have a letter from Gerard to his mother dispatched at once. With the urgency for his departure removed, Gerard, far from recovering his energies, allowed the lethargy that had hitherto threatened, to get the better of him.

The whole of Naples and everyone at court, were en fête over the British victory. With Napoleon's army successfully cut off in Egypt and the Turkish army advancing into Syria to attack Napoleon, hopes were high that the French army as well as her navy was on the brink of defeat. Lord Nelson and his men were treated like the conquering heroes they indeed were.

King Ferdinand and the queen were passionately grateful that someone had finally, after five long years, struck a blow against the murderers of the queen's sister, poor Marie Antoinette. Gerard was invited to the palace. He was also invited by the British minister, Sir William Hamilton, to live at the legation, where the rear admiral was also an honored guest.

Before long, it became obvious to Gerard that Lord Nelson was greatly attracted to Sir William's strikingly beautiful wife, Emma. Although Gerard himself was not attracted by her looks, there was no denying her beauty or her seductive charm. She had once been Sir William's mistress. Gerard thought the endless flattery she showered upon Lord Nelson fulsome and obvious, but the admiral appeared to enjoy it.

Gerard also felt antipathy toward Lady Hamilton's florid vulgarities, but he could not fault her as a hostess. She was forever arranging lavish entertainments and he as well as Lord Nelson were both soon heavily involved in Neapolitan society life.

It was through Lady Hamilton that Gerard met Donna

Faustina Monte-Gincinto. Their first encounter took place one hot afternoon, as Gerard was driving in his carriage, loaned by the Hamiltons, through the dusty streets of Naples toward an assembly in honor of Queen Maria Caroline's birthday. The church bells were ringing and there was to be a special display of fireworks and a gala ball that night.

A magnificent carriage with coat of arms emblazoned on the sides, swept past him, pulled by four matching greys, obviously en route to the palace. Gerard had a glimpse of the middle-aged couple who were seated side by side facing the horses, but he had a far longer glimpse of the pale, golden-haired girl seated opposite them and who stared shyly at him as Gerard's coachman slowed to allow the faster and more imposing equipage to pass.

"The Prince and Princess Monte-Gincinto!" his coachman answered Gerard's question as to who they were. "With their daughter, Donna Faustina. The princess is lady-in-waiting to the queen!"

Gerard recognized the family instantly upon seeing them again later that night at the ball. They were walking down from the throne room, the Prince Monte-Gincinto a regal figure in tight gold trousers and long crimson velvet cut-away coat which was surmounted by a rolled collar of ermine. Around his neck hung the royal insignia of state. The princess, still youthful at the age of forty, was dressed in a magnificent white diaphanous ball gown embroidered with silver roses. On her head was a diadem of diamonds, sparkling in the light of the hundreds of candles lighting the throne room.

Between them walked their daughter, the Donna Faustina. She was undeniably pretty and charming, but Gerard would not have troubled to ask for an introduction. However, when Lady Hamilton suggested she be presented to them, he was not averse to the idea. There was no woman in the galaxy of beautiful Neapolitan ladies and girls such as the Donna Faustina but only Mavreen, his one true love, had the power to stir him to excitement, he thought sadly.

Nevertheless he behaved courteously and pretended an interest when the introductions were made. Upon hearing that Gerard was actually on board Lord Nelson's *Vanguard* during the recent victorious battle, Prince Monte-Gincinto at once invited him to his own palazzo.

Three days later, he drove along a magnificent avenue bordered by palm trees, waving in the breeze from the sparkling waters of the Bay of Naples where Lord Nelson's fleet lay at anchor. At the end of the tree-lined avenue were the great gates of the Prince Monte-Gincinto's palazzo, nearly as vast and imposing as the Royal Palace itself.

Gerard's host and hostess made him welcome. Tea was served informally in a small but beautifully furnished library filled with flowers. The little Donna Faustina sat silent but smiling shyly at Gerard from time to time, her duenna sitting equally silent in the background.

Eventually, the prince and princess departed leaving the two young people together, chaperoned, of course, by the ever-watchful duenna. Gerard and the young girl sat opposite one another. He guessed that this was probably the first occasion upon which she had entertained a young man without her parents present, for she was both nervous and shy, so he talked easily and fluently hoping in such kind manner to put her at her ease.

The girl looked even more like a Dresden figurine than she had at the ball. She was in a transparent white muslin gown falling in delicate tiers of little frills to her tiny feet. Small drop pearls hung from her ears. Around her neck there hung only a gold chain and cross. Her face was heart-shaped, her skin a pale olive-gold, eyes a surprising dark brown in contrast to the light ash-gold hair. Her eyes were enormous and fawn-like. The face was not, in the strictest sense, beautiful, but delicate and feminine.

The young girl evoked in Gerard the strongly protective masculinity that was so dominant a part of his nature, encouraged perhaps from the necessity of having to care for his mother from such a tender age.

He questioned her about herself. What did she do with her time each day?

A delicate pink colored her cheeks as it did each time she looked up and met his eyes.

"I am engaged on a very special tapestry of a sacred

subject. When it is finished, I shall present it to the Reverend Mother in gratitude for her care of me during my years at her convent!" she explained, her command of the French language nearly perfect.

"I would like to see the tapestry!" Gerard said kindly.

"I have it upstairs in my salon. Perhaps—if you would like—" she suggested tentatively, "—and my duenna, Donna Torrina will permit—I could take you to see it?"

"I would like that very much!" Gerard agreed kindly.

Faustina approached the little old woman hunched in a big armchair like a small, dark toad in her bulging black dress, her two fat chins sunk in a crisp white lace ruffle.

Donna Torrina was fond of her charge for the child was always quiet and obedient and little trouble to her. Moreover, she herself, approved of the handsome Frenchman who had smiled at her so charmingly. She therefore nodded her agreement and followed them up the wide marble staircase into Donna Faustina's private suite. Everything in her salon was white and gold—the walls, furniture, curtains, even the pianoforte. The room was as virginal as the girl, herself.

The duenna seated herself in a far corner of the room where a beautiful doll's house and a doll's bassinette stood, childhood treasures, Gerard supposed, which Faustina was not yet ready to part with.

The girl led him toward a beautiful piece of needlework stretched on a walnut frame. The hot Neapolitan sunshine filtered fitfully through the shutters of the three tall windows, sufficient to light up the tapestry, yet leaving the room shaded and cool in the afternoon heat.

Faustina was watching his face as he regarded her handiwork.

"Do you like it?" she asked shyly. "I fear the blue of Our Lady's mantle is not quite right in tone."

"I think it is perfect!" Gerard replied, for the work was most beautifully done. The subject of the tapestry was the Annunciation. It was obvious that religion played a big part in the young girl's life.

"You have other pastimes?" he inquired.

"I have my pets to care for!" she told him. "You shall see!"

She led him to the far end of the room where a magnificent scarlet-plumed cockatoo with a gold crested head, clattered the chain securing one of its legs to the silver stand on which it perched.

It propped its head on one side and peered suspiciously at Gerard from an evil black eye. But Faustina approached it fearlessly and kissed its beak.

"This is Macaro! My father brought him back for me from the south of America. Is he not truly handsome?"

She led Gerard next to an alcove where in regal splendor on grey satin cushions two Italian greyhounds dozed peacefully. Upon seeing the girl, one of them rose gracefully to its feet, stretched out its silky body and waved its long tail in welcome.

Faustina lifted the hem of her muslin dress and knelt down to stroke the dogs.

"They are brother and sister!" she said. "I call them Mario and Marianne!"

Gerard's heart lurched. He had not heard his mother's Christian name spoken in so long! Now her image sprang into his mind and he vowed that he would return home soon. His mother would be as hungry to see him as he was to see her.

But Faustina was pulling gently at his sleeve.

She held out a canvas to him showing a sepia-tinted painting she had recently completed of the interior of a chapel.

"It is the Capella del Tesore, here in Naples!" she informed him. "Do you recognize the tabernacle behind the high altar? One of those gold cups on the altar is filled with the blood of our patron saint who died two hundred years ago."

She now led him to the white painted pianoforte and, prompted from the shadows by her duenna, offered to play for him. Ungallant as it seemed, Gerard had to refuse the offer. His heart was aching with the memory of Mavreen playing upon Mr. Glover's pianoforte in the room at the grange where they had known so much happiness.

Did Mavreen remember him or had she forgotten him after so long, he wondered wretchedly. She could not have forgotten! Their shared love had been of too passionate a nature for it to be put out of mind.

The tears stinging his eyes, Gerard looked up to see the young girl regarding him curiously. With a surprising sensitivity she said quietly so that the duenna would not overhear,

"So tell me, *per favore,* what object in this room has brought you sadness of heart and I will have it removed at once."

Despite his thoughts, Gerard smiled. It would be no simple matter removing the pianoforte, he told her. Shyness momentarily forgotten, Faustina laughed with him, then added seriously, "I will not ask why music should have sad memories for you—only that you should forget them and be happy."

"I will try!" Gerard said. It was a promise he knew he must make every effort to keep; if only happiness could be commanded at will!

"Are you not pleased to have left your convent school?" he asked. "I imagine that most young girls, especially such pretty ones as you, look forward to taking part in the adult world."

Faustina's face glowed.

"I was happy at the convent but I am more happy still to be home," she said. "Perhaps I am fortunate in that I seem to find happiness everywhere. Each day has some new joy, and today especially . . ." she broke off, her cheeks deepening now to a confusion of blushes. She had no intention of revealing to Gerard how exciting his visit was for her. Her parents had talked a great deal of the handsome, romantic young French vicomte. Their approval of him added to her own interest. The days could not pass quickly enough before she saw him again. Now, at last, he was here in the room with her.

Faustina had known for some time that now she had left the convent, a suitable husband must be found for her. Girls in her society were frequently required by their parents to marry older men, ugly men, far from their own choosing. Love was considered of secondary importance to wealth and social background.

Faustina's heart beat more swiftly at her thoughts. From the manner in which her parents had been speaking, her father and mother both looked upon the Vicomte Gerard de Valle as eligible despite the fact that his family had no wealth. Money was of little importance to them since the Prince Monte-Gincinto was himself rich enough to give his only daughter a huge dowry.

"I hope you will permit me to call upon you again soon, Donna Faustina, and share a happy day in your company!" Her blushing assent charmed and flattered him.

In the ensuing weeks he found himself more and more frequently in her company. He suspected that Princess Isabella, who was a friend of Lady Hamilton, was involved behind the scenes in engineering that he be invited to all the events where Faustina, too, was present. Faustina was never in any danger. She was not permitted to put one step in front of the other without her duenna hovering in the background. Nevertheless, the more passionate and ardent Neapolitan gentlemen might, but for Gerard's attendance, have put unwelcome thoughts in Faustina's head, merely by their conversation. Such thoughts were certainly not there as yet. She was childlike in her total purity and innocence.

It was this quality more than any other which kept Gerard by her side. He became her self-appointed protector, as if he were an elder brother. The passionate side of his own nature was in no way involved.

He thought often of Mavreen. At night, with the sound of the love songs of the fishermen down by the bay drifting through his casement window and a brilliant moon hovering over the great mountain of Vesuvius, he lay awake fighting with the unbearable need of her in his arms. In his fevered imagination, he envisaged their reunion, Mavreen's golden body held once more against his own, their hearts beating in tumultuous unison, their limbs entwined in the urgent desire to be closer and ever closer until their bodies finally became one.

But when daylight came, such ideas seemed the fantasies of a love-sick fool whose injured pride and scarred heart would not permit him to face the fact that his mistress had forgotten him. Or worse, found another lover. He dared not dwell on such thoughts for they were likely to drive him to frenzy or total despair. His fear that he might not be strong enough to stay away from her should he return to England or even France, kept him a willing prisoner in Naples.

Perhaps fortunately for Gerard, circumstances became such that Lord Nelson had need of him. The admiral was recovering his spirits. Wishing to exploit his victory over the French, he persuaded the king of Naples to form an alliance with Austria. Under the admiral's forceful persuasion, King Ferdinand declared war and despatched 30,000 men to march against French-occupied Rome.

The Neapolitan army was no match for the French and was forced to retreat. It became obvious that before long, the enemy would march into Naples. Lord Nelson, having provoked the crisis, was therefore under a moral obligation to save the lives of those he had endangered. The evacuation of the city was inevitable.

It was essential that the king, queen, their children and their retinue must at all costs be saved from the approaching French, together with as many as possible of the leading Neapolitan families, British residents and, of course, Sir William Hamilton and his wife. Lord Nelson's plan was to take them all by sea to Palermo in Sicily.

Gerard was approached by Faustina's father. The prince had been offered a chance to escape but, so he informed Gerard, he would not leave his home to the mercy of the invaders. His wife had elected to remain with him. But Faustina, clearly, could not stay in Naples.

Was Gerard, the prince asked in a roundabout way, in any position to offer Faustina the protection of his own home in France? In plainer terms, he intimated that there need be no concern in matters of finance.

"Once the war has been resolved," the prince said, "I could come to France myself to fetch my little daughter home. Meanwhile, mon cher vicomte, would you consider my problems for a day or two while there is still time for reflection. I would be eternally grateful for any help you can offer that will be for Faustina's safekeeping."

Gerard understood very well what was being asked of him. He had been invited to ask for Donna Faustina's hand.

Gerard knew he must marry to restore the family fortunes. Several months earlier he'd heard that, tired of waiting, Mercedes de Faenza had married an Englishman. There was no hope of having Mavreen and he was fond of little Faustina. He lay awake that night, tormented. Circumstances beyond his control brought the decision upon him.

News arrived which filled the city with alarm—the Neapolitan army had disintegrated and the French were already on the outskirts of the city. Fear abounded and the mood of the once-gala city was as grey as the December skies. Lord Nelson ordered the embarkation to begin without delay. Time had run out for Gerard. He could no longer sit and ponder Faustina's future.

He called upon the Monte-Gincintos to find little Faustina in tears. She had only just been informed that she must leave her parents and home.

Her tears struck at Gerard's heart. Without thinking, he took her small trembling hand and carried it to his lips.

"You must not be afraid!" he said softly. "I will be at hand to look after you. So dry your tears, little Faustina. You will be perfectly safe with me!"

She raised her face, her dark eyes shining with tears. As she took in his words, the fear vanished and was replaced by a smile of purest joy.

"If I am to be with you, then I shall not mind leaving everything else behind me!" she said simply.

It was a declaration of love about which there could be no mistake. Gerard intended only to offer his protection. But his words had been misinterpreted. Perhaps he might have extricated himself from an embarrassing and distressing situation if he had instantly made it clear that marriage was not his intention. But he did not do so. He felt suddenly as if his mind had been made up for him.

"With your parents' permission, I want to ask you to marry me!" he said, setting the seal upon it before he could change his mind again. He smiled at the happiness so clearly visible in her eyes, and added gently, "And I don't think they will refuse me, if you will not, Faustina?"

But for the presence of her duenna, Faustina would have flung herself into his arms.

They were married by Edward Berry, the captain of the flagship *Vanguard*, in the midst of a heavy gale that pursued them as they fought their way toward Palermo. Faustina was too frightened by the violence of the storm to feel any real happiness, and Gerard, not usually a superstitious man, was made uneasy by the fury of the elements. But for the strictest control he kept upon himself, he might have believed that Mavreen, if not Heaven itself, was invoking the anger and force of the wind in protest against the betrayal of his true love.

But there was little time for such fantasies. Faustina clung to him in such terror that he was afraid if he left her for one moment, she would die of fright. As he cradled her gently in his arms, rocking her to and fro as he would a child—and his wife was little more, being only fifteen years of age—he felt a return of that protectiveness which had first endeared her to him. She loved him and needed him, he reminded himself, and he vowed to make her a good husband. Determinedly, he refused to permit his thoughts to fly out across the raging sea to Mavreen.

It was not until they were safely disembarked at Palermo and Gerard was settled with Faustina in Sir William's house that news arrived from England. There were no letters for Gerard, but Lady Hamilton had word from a close friend of hers. It was a long, typically feminine letter, filled with inconsequential gossip and snippets of news.

Among the items Lady Hamilton repeated that night at the dinner table was the announcement that Gilbert Barre was dead.

"A heart attack, I believe!" she said in her bright gay voice. "Just imagine, that new young wife of his is now a widow."

Without warning, the wineglass Gerard was holding slipped from his grasp and fell at his feet. He watched the dark red liquid spread slowly over the carpet. It seemed to him as if it were his life's blood slowly draining away while he sat perfectly still, powerless to prevent it.

Opposite him, Faustina sat staring at him, her dark eyes fastened upon him with her innocent adoring smile.

CHAPTER TWENTY-SIX
1799

Despite the fact that Sir John was in a state of fury bordering upon apoplexy, Clarissa nearly smiled as he flung Mavreen's letter across the room, shouting, "The girl is quite insane! Has she no intelligent appreciation of the dangers of such an adventure! Pah! We are at war with France and she proposes a visit there as if it were no more than a sojourn to Brighthelmstone! I will not permit it. I disown her. She is no child of mine!"

Clarissa laid a restraining hand upon his arm and urged him into his favorite armchair.

"My dearest John!" she said gently, stroking his now iron-grey hair as she stood behind him, one hand still upon his shoulder. "Calm yourself, I pray you! In the first place, it is clear from Mavreen's letter that she is already on her way to France and however much you might dislike the fact, the reason that she did not first ask your permission to go must be as obvious to you as to me. As to her 'insanity', whilst I agree with you that your daughter may be foolhardy, her actions are those of a woman deeply in love. It is surely to her credit that she is prepared to face any danger in order to be reunited with Gerard?"

Clarissa's soft voice and movements were having the desired effect. The angry red of Sir John's cheeks diffused to a milder pink and his tone of voice was more moderate as he said irritably, "It is quite improper for a young lady to go chasing across the world to her lover. The young man should come in search of her!" he said. "From the way

Mavreen behaves, one would think she believes herself a man forsooth!"

Clarissa's lips trembled as she fought against the threatening smile.

"It was you, my dear John, who had her raised as if she were, indeed, a son, who insisted she should believe herself equal to any man. Now you threaten to disown her. Perhaps it would not be wrong of me to remind you that, in point of fact, you have never publicly declared your relationship to her."

Sir John frowned, scratched his chin and sighed.

"You know very well why I could not do so, Clarrie. In any event, it would have made little difference to her life."

"You cannot be sure of that, John!" Clarissa argued. "It was a great shock to Mavreen to discover that the circumstances of her birth made her unacceptable to society in general and to Gerard in particular. Her pride suffered and I think you will fairly admit that it was largely on this account that she agreed to the marriage with Gilbert!"

"And an excellent arrangement that turned out to be!" Sir John said adamantly. "The girl is now titled, widowed, and wealthy, and but nineteen years of age. She can marry whom she pleases."

It was Clarissa's turn to sigh.

"That may not be so, John, as well you know. We have no idea if Gerard is still alive, and he is the only man Mavreen will marry. Like it or not, my dear, those two young people are genuinely in love."

"Love!" Sir John echoed. "And what, pray, is the importance of love in the world we live in!"

"You ask me that?" Clarissa said quietly. "Then I will try to answer you, John. To a woman, it is everything. You are my whole life, John, and until now, I believed that I, in turn, played an important part in your own."

Sir John's face took on a new expression as he stood up and drew Clarissa into his arms.

"Forgive me, Clarrie!" he said. "I spoke without real thought behind my words. You are quite right, of course. All those months in Ireland, I longed for you constantly. I had no idea until we were parted how important you

were to me. You have given me some of the happiest
times of my life, and I love you very much, my dear!"

Tears sprang to Clarissa's eyes. She closed them swiftly
so that he should not see them as he kissed her. He could
not know that it was moments such as these, few as they
were, that were the real rewards for her unending devotion
and the sacrifice of her life for him.

"I fear I might not have had Mavreen's courage—even
at her age—to cross the Channel in search of you, John,"
she said shakily. "But I would have wished to go and I
cannot find it in my heart to condemn Mavreen. I admire
her, and so should you, John. She is very truly your daughter!"

"At least she had the good sense to take young Dickon
with her!" Sir John said, mollified. "I was much impressed
on my visits to the grange by the boy's devotion to her.
He'd die before he let harm come to her." He paused and
then added, "Clarrie, I am nonetheless extremely worried.
There are so many terrible things that could happen to the
girl! It is but three months since her child was born and
she is far from strong. It was madness for her to undertake such a hazardous journey! I shall not have a moment's peace until she is safely home."

"I know! I feel as you do, John!" Clarissa agreed.
"But there is nothing we can do. The baby will be safe
enough at Owlett's Farm with Rose and Mistress Sale.
Mavreen has arranged that young Patty Sale will write to
me once a week with an account of the child's health. I
fear there is nothing either of us can do to assist Mavreen."

"There is the matter of Barre House and the winding
up of Gilbert's affairs!" Sir John said. "I can, of course,
see to such legalities for Mavreen. The cousin poor Gilbert so disliked is taking possession, you know that
worthless fellow, Clarence Barre. 'Tis a shame, to say the
least, that Gilbert's child was not a boy!"

Clarissa remained silent. She, knowing the truth, felt
justice was more fairly done in the passing of the Barre
name and inheritance to Gilbert's cousin. It would not
have seemed right if Gerard de Valle's son inherited what
was not rightfully his. As it was, Mavreen and little Tam-

arisk were well provided for and would never lack for any
of life's luxuries, let alone necessities. As to the passing of
Barre House into Clarence Barre's hands, she, Clarissa,
did not think Mavreen would grieve for the house that
was never so much a home to her as the grange. And if,
by some miracle, Gerard were indeed alive and at Compiègne, no doubt Mavreen would live henceforth at the
Château de Boulancourt.

It was this hope which was sustaining Mavreen as she
and Dickon faced the perilous journey to Compiègne.

There had been little difficulty in obtaining the assistance of the smugglers in Sussex. Mavreen's disguise
passed unnoticed and she was accepted by the seamen as
Dickon's younger brother, Edward. There were moments
of difficulty. At the Inn where they awaited the sailing of
the privateer that was to take them over the water, Mavreen was unable to consume the huge mugs of ale pushed
across the wooden tables to her. Dickon cleverly passed
the difficulty over by giving her a scornful look.

"He was ever a lean, miserable skinny chap. I'd not
have taken him with me 'cepting he's sing'lar clever at
reckoning and he be a knowledgeable lad for all he ain't
much primer-looking than a sparrer!"

Dickon and Mavreen were at Bexhill. It was from here
that daily newspapers and correspondence were regularly
carried to France by the owners who, despite the war,
were openly in communication with the French sloops
which came to the coast. Dickon had no difficulty in
arranging passage to Dunkirk on payment of a large
sum of money Mavreen gave him for the purpose.

It was, therefore, less than a week before they disembarked on the French coast. They stopped at the first
coach inn they found.

Dickon had purchased French clothing for himself and
Mavreen. For this part of the journey, Mavreen was to
play the part of a young clerk from Belgium and he her
servant, his knowledge of the French language being too
poor for him to pass himself off as a local peasant. At the
auberge, the landlord accepted them without curiosity and
Dickon only needed to purchase two suitable horses before
they could be on their way. It was while he was away on

this mission that a party of French soldiers arrived at the auberge and demanded to see Mavreen's papers.

"I cannot show them to you at this instant!" she replied calmly to the officer in charge who was questioning her. "My servant has them upon his person. He will be returning presently and I shall be happy to identify both him and myself to you when he does so!"

The soldier met Mavreen's cool gaze with a look of suspicion. The "clerk" seemed to him a deal too young to be travelling on his firm's business. There was not yet sign of a beard on his smooth skin. Indeed, to the soldier's eyes, the young man looked positively girlish. The voice, too, was strange—high pitched and foppish. But the steadiness of his gaze and cool self-assurance disconcerted the officer. The young man did not look guilty of anything —an unlikely enemy of the people, too young to be engaged in spying activities. Nevertheless, instinct made him uneasy.

"You'll take a glass of wine with me while we await my man?" Mavreen asked with composure. "The landlord here keeps a good cellar, I'm told."

But the soldier had other business to attend to and declined Mavreen's offer.

"I'll be back before sundown!" he said. "Then you can show me your papers and I'll gladly drink a bottle of wine with you!"

Mavreen breathed a sigh of relief as the men rode off down the lane. She hoped that Dickon would not be long in returning and that he had found adequate mounts for them. The sooner they put distance between themselves and the soldiers the better.

Upon hearing of this encounter, Dickon resolved not to leave Mavreen's side again. He was shocked to think that the soldiers might have arrested her on some pretext and taken her away to some unknown destination where he would have been unable to defend her. She would not in such circumstances be able to conceal her true sex for long and who could tell what terrible fate might have befallen her had the soldiers discovered they had a young unprotected female in their midst.

Mavreen, however, was in the best of spirits. She was

happy to be riding astride the chestnut mare Dickon had found for her, happy to know that every hour they rode brought them nearer to Compiègne and Gerard's home. She convinced herself that she would find him there so great was her longing to do so. Her spirits rose ever higher and she sang gaily, reminding Dickon that they were at long last upon a real adventure together such as they had never dreamed of in their childhood.

Gradually, Dickon's spirits lifted, too. They rode fast, taking routes off the main highways. By evening, they were on the outskirts of Arras where they stopped at a wayside auberge for the night. Here they were served a delicious meal of trout freshly caught that day in the river and cooked in butter, garlic and almonds. There was freshly baked bread and goat's milk cheese made by the innkeeper's wife, which they washed down with two bottles of *vin du pays*.

There was but one other guest—a man dressed in velvet breeches with leather facings at the pockets, such as those worn by locksmiths or blacksmiths. His grey stockings and shoes with copper buckles were as neat as his forest of grey hair was unruly. The eyes beneath were large, open and intelligent. He was sitting alone drinking burgundy, on the excellence of which he complimented the innkeeper.

"His face is familiar to me!" Mavreen whispered to Dickon. "I do not believe he is a workman any more than I am a clerk. I mean to speak to him!"

Dickon tried to dissuade her, but Mavreen's curiosity got the better of Dickon's pleas for caution. He watched in dismay as she approached the stranger. But in this instance, her instinct was proved sound. One close glance into his aristocratic face confirmed Mavreen's certainty that she knew the man. It was the marquis de Guéridon.

"I believe I have already made your acquaintance, sir!" she addressed him quietly. "May I sit down at your table and introduce myself? I think we last met at the house of the Baron and Baroness von Eburhard!"

The stranger's first guarded stare gave way to surprise and then to dawning recognition. He would have jumped to his feet but Mavreen laid a cautious hand upon his arm.

"I am no lady, sir!" she said, smiling. "You have no cause to rise for a poor clerk from Bruges. And you, Monsieur le marquis? May I inquire your present identity?"

Her bright, laughing eyes and teasing smile quelled the last remaining fears of the marquis although he could still not recall the name of the young man he had last seen as a ravishingly beautiful girl at Lisa von Eburhard's assembly.

"I am Sir John Danesfield's protégée!" Mavreen said. "You may recall that I married Lord Barre just over a year ago? I do not think we met after my marriage."

"My dear Lady Barre!" the marquis murmured, as recollection flooded his mind. "Of course I remember you very well now. Indeed, how can I have forgotten you? It is only that at present you bear little resemblance to. . . ."

"I know!" Mavreen broke in laughing. "Nor you, sir, to your real self!"

The marquis gave a quick glance about him. Seeing that the landlord was well out of earshot, he said, "I have been in France this last year in the cause of the Royalists. The Directoire is fast losing its popularity. They have sent for Napoleon to return to France so badly are they in need of support. But who knows if he will succeed in evading the English ships patrolling the Mediterranean. If he does not, we may yet bring back a Bourbon to the throne of France!

"And you, Lady Barre? Are you in France in the cause of the Royalists?" the marquis now asked her.

She shook her head.

"On a less philanthropic cause, I fear!" she replied. "I am on my way to Compiègne to visit the vicomtesse de Valle. She is a friend of yours, I believe!"

The marquis was too well-mannered to show his surprise. Many strange things had happened during and since the revolution but it was nevertheless still highly unusual for a titled Englishwoman to be travelling across France in wartime disguised as a young man on what he assumed was purely a social visit. Or could it be that she was engaged in espionage for the British? If so, it was not for him to question her.

"Indeed, I have known Marianne de Valle for many years!" he said. "I do not know how long it is since you, yourself, last saw her, but you should be advised that she is now a broken woman. The years she spent in prison destroyed her health and the disappearance of her only son, the young vicomte de Valle, has broken her spirit, poor lady. I saw her not three months since."

Mavreen's heart fell tumbling to her feet.

"Then Gerard—her son—he has not returned home?" she enquired, forcing her voice to sound no more than casually interested.

The marquis shook his head.

"The vicomtesse had had no word from him since he left to go to England. She wrote to Sir John to ask about her son's movements but Sir John wrote back to report that Gerard had never arrived in London. I am afraid the prospects of the boy being alive are very remote. It appears as if he may have lost his life attempting to cross to England, perhaps drowned at sea, or shot before ever he reached the coast. In these days, an aristocrat apprehended in suspicious circumstances might be suspected of royalist sympathies and, if he were thought to be an enemy of the people, shot without too many questions asked. Poor Marianne has lost all will to live. It is very tragic!"

"Then the news I bring her will revive her hopes!" Mavreen said quietly. "For Gerard de Valle was in England. I will not go into details now, but I know also that Gerard suffered an accident falling from his horse and lost his memory. During this time, he was taken aboard a privateer by some smugglers and subsequently, as far as I know, pressganged by a British frigate. I have reason to believe he was with Lord Nelson's fleet in Egypt!"

The marquis stared at Mavreen in astonishment.

"If this is true, then your news will, indeed, restore her will to live. Since her husband died, the boy has meant everything in the world to her. But I pray that you should not impart such hopes unless you believe them well-founded, Lady Barre. I do not think Marianne's health would withstand a further disappointment."

They spent the remainder of the evening exchanging conversation on more general topics. Mavreen told the marquis of her husband's sudden death and the subsequent birth of her little daughter. He wanted news of the Danesfields and she was able to tell him that neither of Sir John's daughters were married.

"Indeed, I think he has given up expectations of marrying them!" Mavreen said. "Neither, so he says, is in the least anxious to find a husband and they seem content to remain in quiet seclusion with Lady Danesfield!"

The marquis sighed.

"I fear poor John gained little beyond material assets from that marriage!" he said. "He would have done better to remain a bachelor like myself!"

Mavreen looked at her companion with curiosity. He was still a handsome man beneath his workman's disguise. And he had great charm. Many women must have found him attractive in his youth for he was still, in his sixties, very personable.

He guessed her unspoken question and smiled.

"I did not always want my freedom!" he said, his eyes growing suddenly serious, even sad. "I will let you into a little secret, chère madame, since we are already in possession of each other's secret assignments. I was once very deeply in love with Marianne de Valle. She was, alas, interested only in Antoine, my closest friend. When they married, I gave up all thought of marriage for myself. If I could not have the woman I loved, I wanted no other."

Mavreen sighed.

"Then you did most truly love her!" she said. "But now, Monsieur le marquis? The vicomtesse is a widow. Is it too late?"

The man beside her nodded.

"Marianne's marriage to Antoine was one of perfect happiness!" he said. "When he died, leaving her with a young son, I at once believed I could be of assistance to her both as a husband and father to the boy. But she remained steadfastly faithful to Antoine's memory and the boy became her whole raison d'être—he and her determination that one day, Antoine's good name would be restored. You heard, I dare say, of the circumstances of his death?"

Mavreen nodded.

"There is no doubt in my mind as to Antoine's innocence. I had known him all my life and he could no more have cheated at cards than shot his own son. But we shall never be able to prove it—not unless someday, somehow, one of those of us who has not forgotten, comes across a Baron von Gottfried. But for the advent of the revolution, it was young Gerard's intention to search the world for the rogue and it was to this end his mother raised him."

Listening to the marquis's account of the past, Mavreen began to understand more fully the enormous pressures that had been put upon Gerard and were resting so heavily upon his young shoulders when they first met and fell in love. Perhaps not altogether fairly, the vicomtesse had, upon the untimely death of her beloved husband, laid an emotional burden upon her young son that must ever restrict his life. He might have been freer to follow his own destiny had his mother not confined him so rigorously to the destiny she had chosen for him, had she accepted the kindly marquis's proposal of marriage and ceased to live in the past.

The marquis had to be on his way as soon as darkness fell. He was making for Lille and preferred to travel by night. They wished one another a safe journey and the marquis penned a quick letter to Marianne before departing, for Mavreen to deliver. He neither signed nor sealed it lest it should come into strangers' hands, for he did not wish to implicate the vicomtesse in his political activities.

Mavreen lay awake for several hours, despite the extremes of physical and mental fatigue. Her mind kept turning to the painful thought that she would not, after all, find Gerard at the Château de Boulancourt—not unless by some miracle he had arrived home since the marquis' last visit three months earlier. It was to this faint hope she clung and for this hope alone that she continued her journey next day, saying nothing to Dickon of the likelihood of the fruitlessness of the mission.

They were on the road three more days. Dickon insisted that they ride easily and stop frequently to conserve Mavreen's strength. They made wide detours around Abbeville and Amiens keeping wherever possible to the forests or quiet country lanes. At night, they stopped at the remotest of auberges, saying that they had mislaid their route and were too tired to retrace their steps that night. They met no one of consequence and reached the outskirts of Compiègne unmolested.

Mavreen was tired, near to exhaustion. But her spirits rose when from the top of a hill, she looked down to the winding river Oise and saw the spires of the three old churches of St. Germain, St. Antoine and St. Jacques; and beyond the vast forest of Compiègne with its oak trees in full foliage.

"Gerard talked of his homeland so often!" she said to Dickon. "Now I understand why he thought it so beautiful. Oh, Dickon, if only he is here!"

Dickon looked up at the sky and saw the dark clouds rolling up from the west.

" 'Tis time we were on our way!" he cautioned. "Leastways if we want to reach the château afore the storm breaks!"

They had been fortunate so far, in that the weather although often windy, had remained fine. Now a change was coming and Dickon's country nose smelt the rain in the air.

They rode over the bridge and into the town, stopping once or twice to ask the way, choosing a child as informant in order not to invoke too much suspicion as to their presence.

The quickest way, one of the lads told them, was through the forest, but they must beware of wolves. They might take the longer road around the forest for safety, but it would mean an extra three hours' ride.

" 'Tis unlikely wolves would harm us!" she said confidently, for she knew the beasts fed on wild creatures of the forest and sometimes marauded the farms when times were lean for domestic animals, but it was rare they attacked human beings.

The small boy shook his head. Some of the wolves, it seemed, had formed themselves into a large pack. Only last month they had attacked and savaged a woodcutter. Once so emboldened there was no knowing whether they might attack a man again. The winter had been severe, food scarce and many people had supplemented their meager diet with animals hunted, trapped, snared, or shot in the forest. Perhaps the wolves, too, were short of food, and near starvation, were prepared to kill and eat men.

"We'll go through the forest!" Mavreen said to Dickon. "If the storm breaks, the trees will afford us some shelter. And you have the pistols. I am not convinced the wolves will try to harm us."

Dickon was uneasy. He knew from Mavreen that the woods covered some thirty thousand acres. They did not know their way and had no means of telling in which direction they were travelling now that the sun had disappeared. Moreover, the horses were tired. But Mavreen refused to listen to his objections.

Soon, they were riding slowly through the dark shadowy trees, the rising wind rustling the leaves above their heads, the darkness growing ever more intense as they headed toward the center of the forest. The horses pricked their ears nervously, hearing the sudden sounds of animals in the undergrowth and once, the eerie howl of a wolf not far away.

Dickon took the pistols from the saddlebag and handed one to Mavreen. She, too, was nervous now. For an hour they rode in silence, trying to keep their horses' heads straight so that they would not, as Dickon feared, travel in circles—an easy thing to do amongst trees. The path was overgrown and indistinct, used only by the occasional hunter or forester. It began to rain. Before long, icy streams of water penetrated the thick foliage above them and began to seep through their cloaks.

Dickon urged the horses to a trot but the light was bad and he feared losing his way. He thought he saw grey

shadows following them behind the tree trunks and
cocked his pistol anxiously. Suddenly, his horse reared and
the pistol went off with a violent explosion that frightened
Mavreen's mount into a gallop. It took all her strength to
pull the animal in from its terrified bolt and her taut
nerves caused her to cry out as Dickon's horse appeared
along the path behind her.

Dickon grinned, as much to cheer himself as Mavreen.

"Don't ee be froughtened!" he said, " 'tis only me!"

Mavreen let out her breath.

Suddenly they became aware that the trees were beginning to thin out and permit more light to filter onto the
path before them.

"We are coming out of the forest!" Mavreen cried.
"Look, Dickon—see yonder? Those turrets and towers?
The avenue of trees? It has to be the Château de Boulan-
court!"

It was at this unguarded moment that three of the pack
of wolves which had been silently following emerged from
the shadows behind them and sprang at Dickon's horse.
The animal gave one shrill neigh of terror, reared on its
hind legs, and Dickon fell to the ground. Stupidly he had
not recharged his pistol since it had accidentally gone off
and now he had nothing with which to defend himself as
the snarling, slavering beasts set upon him. Mavreen's
horse, terrified, broke into a gallop. As quickly as she
could she pulled him up, turned his head and forced the
reluctant horse to retrace his steps. She heard the wolves
before she saw them. She kicked her mount forward and
for an instant, was too horrified to do more than stare.
Dickon had disappeared beneath the snapping jaws of the
shaggy, starving wolves. Then she recovered her senses
and cocked her pistol, aiming at the animals now on top of
Dickon and obscuring him from the gun shot. Coolly, she
took aim, knowing that she risked Dickon's very life if
she erred, and pulled the trigger.

The explosion frightened her already terrified horse into
a wild plunge forward. Only with the greatest of efforts
did she manage to retain her seat and force the horse's
head round. To her unutterable relief, the pistol had, from

such close range, found its target. The uppermost of the
wolves, its head bloodied and shattered, lay spreadeagled
across Dickon's chest. Its companions had fled.

Swiftly, Mavreen dismounted and tied her horse to a
tree. Keeping an iron control over her horrified senses, she
ran to Dickon's side. It took all her remaining strength to
drag the mangy great animal off him. Dickon groaned. He
was covered in blood, some of it from the dead beast,
some of it his own pouring profusely from a dozen or
more severe bites. Mavreen stood staring down at him, her
mind whirling. She had nothing with which to bind his
wounds nor cleanse them. Although the château was close
at hand, where help might be obtained, she could not
leave Dickon lying here lest the remainder of the pack of
wolves should return. She bent over him.

"Dickon! You must try to get on your feet. If we can
get you onto my horse, we are not far from assistance.
Dickon, answer me, I pray you!"

He groaned, opened his eyes and struggled to lift his
head. Mavreen put her arm round him and eased him into
a sitting position. He seemed to have no strength left and
her own was quite inadequate for the purpose. She
glanced round fearfully. It seemed to her that there were
shadows moving among the trees. Dickon's horse had
bolted. Her own was shifting its weight restlessly from foot
to foot, ears pricked, eyes rolling nervously. She was
certain the wolves were not far away.

"Dickon, do you have the tinder box?" she asked, and
repeated her question more fervently as he looked vaguely
at her, only half-conscious as a result of pain, shock, and
loss of blood from his wounds.

"Saddle bag!" he muttered after her third time of asking.

Hurriedly, she gathered together some dry wood and
finding the tinder box, managed to strike a flame. At first
attempt, the wood smouldered and went out. But as, with
trembling hands she tried again, the sparks caught at some
dry twigs. A flame flared and the bigger sticks ignited.
With a sigh of relief, Mavreen saw the smoke begin to rise
and within minutes, the whole pile was burning. Hurriedly, she gathered more wood, fortunately plentiful beneath

the trees. She pulled Dickon closer to the flames. At least, she thought, the fire would keep the wolves at bay until Dickon recovered his senses sufficiently to be able to remount. She placed her own cloak over his legs, shuddering at the sight of the great gashes that were, by some miracle, bleeding less profusely now.

Gradually, the warmth of the fire increased and Mavreen, shivering almost as much as Dickon from shock and cold, began to regain some of her own ebbing courage. It occurred to her that if she were to build a circle of fires around Dickon, with wood to keep them burning and the two pistols loaded beside him, he could safely be left where he was while she rode for assistance. It might, in the end, be quicker than waiting for Dickon to recover. It was doubtful that with his legs so badly mauled, he would have strength to stand on them and she knew she was powerless to lift him unaided.

Dickon was recovering his senses. When Mavreen outlined her suggestion to him, he nodded approvingly. Without him, she could gallop at full speed to the château which was not more than three kilometers away.

Somehow, Dickon kept himself from groaning, although the pain from his wounds was increasing all the time. He could feel the warm sticky blood running down the inside of his thigh and knew that he was still bleeding badly. If help did not reach him soon, he would lose all consciousness and become an even greater burden to Mavreen.

He tried to talk confidently and cheerfully as she went about her task of collecting further armfuls of wood and lighting fresh fires. It was no simple task for they were burning fiercely and needed constant replenishing. He told her to find thicker branches that would take longer to burn and lay in agony as she struggled to carry weights far too heavy for her. Wryly, he thought that he had come upon this journey to protect her and yet here she was, having saved his life, risking her own in the cause of his safety.

She would not leave him until she was satisfied that he had a sufficient stack of wood within arm's length to last him in her absence. Somewhere not far off, they could hear the howling of the wolves. The same thought was in both their minds—the animals were calling to each other, excited by the smell of blood and the prospect of a kill.

"Take one of the pistols—I don't need both!" Dickon told her. But Mavreen refused, just as she refused to take her cloak.

"Keep the fires burning!" she cautioned him before she left. "I will need the smoke to guide me back to you. Courage, Dickon! I will not be long, I swear it!"

Fortunately, Mavreen's horse needed no urging to be as far away from the forest as quickly as its legs would carry it. She rode at full gallop, oblivious to the dangers of low-hanging branches.

She had been riding not more than five minutes before the sight of a horseman coming toward her across the meadows caused her to rein in her horse. It was the old manservant, Jules, come to see why columns of smoke were rising from the forest at this late hour of the evening. It was now late summer—a time of year when forest fires occasionally started—and now Jules was uneasy at the proximity of people to the château at such a late hour. He was afraid of some new political uprising which could threaten the vicomtesse's safety and that of the château. It was not so many years since he had watched it burned to the ground.

At first he was relieved to learn that the fires had been lit by the young man, then shocked to learn the reason. He at once offered to go to Dickon's assistance.

If Mavreen was disappointed to find the approaching horseman so old as to have little more strength than herself, she need not have been. Jules, despite his sixty-eight years, was still far stronger than his city-bred contemporaries. Years of hard physical work had toughened his muscles and sinews and he could, he assured her, lift her companion without difficulty and place him upon his horse. She was content to know that he intended to take Dickon straight to the château.

By the time she and Jules reached Dickon's side, he had lost consciousness and the fires were no more than glowing embers—insufficient to keep the encircling wolves at bay for more than a few minutes longer.

True to his word, Jules lifted Dickon with comparative ease and laid him across the saddle of his own horse. Mavreen remounted. They set out at a slow pace for the château. Only then did Jules introduce himself and ask who his companions were.

"Not the young man you take me for!" Mavreen said, smiling faintly. "I am Mavreen, Lady Barre, and a life-long friend of your master, Monsieur le vicomte. The man whose life you have helped to save is my manservant, Dickon."

Not even his many years of training could prevent Jules from expressing his amazement.

"Mon Dieu!" he said, staring at Mavreen's pale face doubtfully. "You have come from England—alone—in time of war?"

Mavreen smiled again.

"It was not so difficult!" she said. "Nor dangerous until we were set upon by the wolves." For one moment longer, she hesitated before asking the question which had been foremost in her mind ever since she realized that Jules was from the Château de Boulancourt itself.

"Monsieur le vicomte—" she said in a low desperate voice. "Is he at home, Jules? At the château?"

Even before he replied, Mavreen knew what his answer would be by the sadness on the old man's face.

"Je regrette—but no, milady!" he said. "He has been gone a very long time, we know not where. We do not even know if he is alive!"

Mavreen's last hopes were in that moment dashed. Her long journey had been in vain.

CHAPTER TWENTY-SEVEN
1799

Mavreen had felt in the past both anger against and pity for the Vicomtesse Marianne de Valle. She did not expect to feel love for the woman whose desires Gerard had put before his own or hers. Yet within a week of Mavreen's arrival at the Château de Boulancourt, she and Gerard's mother were united, not just by their mutual love for Gerard himself, but by a mutual respect and affection for each other.

The frail old lady who had greeted them at the great wrought-iron gates of the château, was dressed in faded, threadbare silks of the now bygone fashions of Marie Antoinette's times. She impressed Mavreen instantly with the cool, unruffled and efficient way she coped with the injured Dickon. A boy was despatched to Compiègne to fetch a physician, a young maidservant was sent scurrying to prepare a bedchamber; the cook was put to boiling water in the kitchen and the vicomtesse herself set about washing and bathing Dickon's wounds as soon as Mavreen and Jules had laid him on the sofa of her private salon. She seemed quite unconcerned by the sight of so much blood and went about her tasks single-mindedly, giving orders in a cool, calm voice of authority.

Mavreen was immensely glad to be able to hand over the reins of responsibility. Only now did she appreciate the tremendous toil the journey with its fearful ending had taken upon her slender reserves of strength. When the physician had sewn up the worst of Dickon's wounds and treated the other lacerations, the vicomtesse commanded him to give his attentions to Mavreen. She ignored Mavreen's protests and lost her composure only for a brief instant when it became clear to her and the astonished physician that her young visitor was a female disguised in man's clothing.

Mavreen was put to bed and given so strong a dosage of laudanum she slept as if dead. She did not awake until late morning when the vicomtesse brought her a Sevrès bowl of steaming hot chocolate.

The talk between them that began at this juncture, continued for several days. Gerard, of course, was the main topic of their conversation. Mavreen kept nothing back except the fact that it was Gerard's daughter to whom she had given birth. The two women walked together through the overgrown ruined gardens of the château, Mavreen now dressed in simple country peasant's dress Jules had purchased for her in Compiègne, the vicomtesse in her faded, threadbare silken gown. Her only concession to the changing fashions was that she had discarded her wigs and wore her grey hair cut short beneath a lace cap.

In the evenings, a log fire burning in the grate, they continued their talk, the vicomtesse now finding consolation in the relating of every small detail of Gerard's childhood. She had, in Mavreen, an avid, tireless audience. Together, they fed one another's hopes for Gerard's survival and because of their growing belief, each took on a new lease of life.

Dickon, meanwhile, made a slow recovery but a determined one. Within ten days, the physician removed his stitches and he was permitted to take his first faltering steps with the aid of a crutch. Marianne de Valle, hearing from him the full story of their journey from England, marveled at Mavreen's courage.

Mavreen's bastardy bothered the older woman not at all. She could see with her own eyes that Mavreen had aristocratic breeding as well as courage, intelligence as well as passion. Moreover, she had come to love Mavreen for her devotion to Dickon, her kindness to those around her without regard to self, her sensitivity and refinement. Most of all, she loved her for her selfless adoration for Gerard. That Mavreen had come to no serious harm had been merely a stroke of good fortune. She suspected that

Mavreen's child might well be her son's and now asked many questions about the baby, believing it to be her first grandchild. Naturally enough, Mavreen was ever-eager to talk about Tamarisk whom she sadly missed and would dearly have loved to hold in her arms again.

For the most part the vicomtesse led the life of a recluse since her return home from prison. Her once fabulous collection of jewelery had been sold to buy food, as were many of the great paintings that had adorned every room of the château. Now there were only faded patches of wallpaper to prove their former existence. Many were destroyed in the fire; others had been stolen. All that were left after the Revolution were those which had been safely hidden by the loyal staff beneath the flagstones of the wine cellars and vaults before they escaped to their own freedom. The cellars had been ransacked of wines; those items of furniture and rugs that were left by the revolutionaries were those too large and heavy for the rabble to carry away.

"Perhaps it was wrong for some of us to have so much when so many others were starving!" the vicomtesse said once to Mavreen. "I have had much time for reflection these past few years and I am less bitter now than once I was about the desecration of my beloved Antoine's home. Yet I cannot see what this Revolution has achieved for the ordinary people of France. The poor are still starving and conditions for them seem little better than they used to be. They are taxed so heavily and robbed of much they have worked to produce. Has it all been for nothing, *ma chère enfant?*"

"Money has to be raised somehow for the costly wars in which France is so heavily engaged!" Mavreen said sighing. "As to the spoils of war, they seem to find their way to the new elite. They, in their turn, exploit the poor, do they not? I do not believe there can ever be true égalité for which the Revolution was fought."

"It is to General Bonaparte I owe my return here!" the vicomtesse said, "so it does not behoove me to speak ill of him. Yet I know Antoine would never have accepted France's new regime. Had he lived, he would have fought to the death with the émigrés."

Mavreen, seeing the late vicomte's portrait, well understood why Marianne de Valle had fallen in love with him. Although Gerard mostly resembled his Italian mother, there were certain likenesses to the handsome Frenchman of the portrait. Marianne's dedication to her husband's memory was as total as her devotion to her son; she admitted openly to Mavreen that even were Gerard to be declared dead, she would never leave Antoine's home, no matter how poor her circumstances.

These were, indeed, poor. The majority of the rooms were bare, the casements closed, the once beautiful paper peeling in strips from the walls and discolored by the damp of winter. The once shining wood floors were unpolished and covered in layers of dust.

Only the vicomtesse's private salon, the small garden room where they now ate, the anteroom and the bedchambers, were still furnished and kept clean by the few remaining servants. The library was the most pitiful room of all, the rows of shelves empty, the books having been burned in a horrifying conflagration on the terrace. The vicomtesse commented upon the meaninglessness of such desecration.

Every day, Mavreen was learning better to understand Gerard's obsessive desire. She, too, felt the urge to do something to restore the once beautiful château to its former state. She set about repairing one of the Gobelin tapestries that had been partially damaged by fire. The task, which might once have seemed irksome since she had never cared for needlework, she now found soothing and rewarding.

There was no question of her returning as yet to England. Even if she had wished to go, Dickon was far from fit to travel and the physician whom she had consulted when he came to remove the stitches from Dickon's wounds forecast that he would be unable to ride a horse any distance for at least two further weeks. He had lost a great deal of blood and although his natural good health was promoting a remarkable recovery, he was still very weak and tired easily.

So it was that Mavreen settled down contentedly enough at the château, happy in the company of Gerard's mother, enjoying the beautiful weather and regaining her own strength and health. Except for the uncertainty about Gerard himself, she could have been entirely happy.

In June Dickon began riding every day for an hour or so to strengthen his leg muscles. Often, Mavreen accompanied him. They went hunting with Jules and brought back rabbits and pheasants to help fill the larder. It was on their return from one such expedition that Jules reined in his horse as they were emerging from the woods and held up a cautionary hand.

"There is someone at the château!" he said to Mavreen.

It was their habit to keep well clear of Compiègne and the surrounding farms for fear that someone might see them and report the presence of strangers in the area. The vicomtesse's servants could be relied upon for their loyalty but the fact of the matter was that Mavreen and Dickon were English and might easily, were they discovered, be suspected of espionage and arrested. So Jules, ever on the lookout, refused to permit Mavreen and Dickon to leave the shelter of the forest until he had ascertained who the unusual callers at the château might be.

He rode home at an unsuspicious, leisurely pace. The carriage standing in the front drive was attended by the coachman. He informed Jules that he had been hired to bring a young Neapolitan gentleman and his wife to Compiègne. His passengers were refugees from the recent war in Naples which, the coachman said proudly, the great General Bonaparte had had little trouble in winning. The young couple were wealthy, which no doubt had helped them to secure the necessary passes and papers to enable them to travel safely to France.

"I am being well paid for my services—*very* well paid —so I would be foolish to disagree with my bread and butter, eh? Not for any principle of égalité, especially when the butter is so thickly laid."

He winked at Jules and nodded his head in the direction of the château.

"Reckon you agree with me, eh?" he said.

Mystified, Jules made some noncommittal reply and hurried into the château. As he approached the vicomtesse's salon, he heard voices. He stopped instantly, his mouth open in amazement and fearful incredulity.

"Bon Dieu!" he said hoarsely. *"Est-ce que c'est possible?"*

It was, indeed possible—the miracle had happened. Young Monsieur Gerard had come home!

The vicomtesse, Gerard's arms around her shoulders, was in tears of delight as Jules entered the salon. Gerard left his mother's side and went across the room to embrace the faithful old man. He, too, was upon the point of tears so great was his joy.

"I'm no ghost, Jules," Gerard said, laughing. "Reassure *ma mère,* I pray you, for I'll swear she cannot believe her own eyes!"

Jules wiped his cheeks with his sleeve and returned Gerard's smile.

"You've grown to manhood, Monsieur Gerard!" he said looking at the broad muscular shoulders and seeing the new lines about the young man's mouth and eyes.

"I'd like you to meet my wife!" Gerard said, taking Jules's arm and turning him around so that he faced the young woman standing by the windows. "The Vicomtesse Faustina de Valle. *Chérie!* This is Jules, my faithful friend of whom you have heard me speak so often!"

Jules took a quick glance at the petite figure of the fair-haired girl smiling at him before her glance returned once more with intense adoration in Gerard's direction. The old man murmured his congratulations but this sudden appearance of a young wife was as much a shock to him as five minutes earlier it had been to the vicomtesse.

Jules, who asked no questions but shrewdly guessed the answers, knew that milady from England was in some way involved in Gerard's past. Mavreen had made no attempt to hide from Jules her intense curiosity about every aspect of Gerard's childhood and old as Jules was, he knew the young English girl loved his master.

Milady! Remembering he had left her with Dickon in the forest, he looked anxiously at the vicomtesse, unsure of himself.

"Your guests, vicomtesse!" he said. "I told them to await me under cover of the trees whilst I ascertained that it was safe for them to return home," he said. "I must go at once to reassure them!"

"Wait!" The vicomtesse's voice startled them all. She now had control of her emotions and spoke with her old authority. "Jules, will you first find Louise and ask her to conduct the vicomtesse to the blue bedchamber." She turned to Faustina and said, "I'm sure you must be very tired after your long ride from Paris and would like to rest and refresh yourself. Louise will bring you hot water and anything else you may require. Gerard . . ."

"Oui, Maman?" He looked at her inquiringly.

"I have need of a few words with you before you, too, go upstairs!" She saw the anxious glance Faustina gave Gerard, as if the girl were afraid to allow him out of her sight, and added, "You will be quite safe with Louise, my dear. Gerard will join you presently!"

Her commands brooked no argument but in any event, Faustina would have obeyed her new mother-in-law as submissively as she had always obeyed her own parents. She stood on tiptoe to kiss Gerard's cheek. He returned the embrace absent mindedly, his eyes on his mother's face.

As soon as they were alone, he went across to her chair and said, "What is it, Maman? Some secret neither Jules nor my wife must know of?" He smiled. "You have the look of a conspirator!"

"Gerard, do not joke, I pray you!" Her voice was as serious as her expression. "I do have news to impart but I felt it best I should not do so in your wife's presence. I do not know how you will receive such news but I think you will agree, you would prefer to hear it in private!"

Gerard frowned, bewildered by these remarks of which he could make neither head nor tail.

"Whatever it may be, Maman, pray tell me!" he said. "And lest it be bad news you so hesitate to tell me of, may I first inform you that Faustina is well aware of our financial circumstances. She is prepared to find my home the epitome of poverty and asks nothing more than that she remain by my side."

The vicomtesse hesitated a moment longer.

"It is not a matter of finance, Gerard. It is a matter of —of the heart!"

Gerard's eyes narrowed.

"Of the heart?" he echoed. "What can you mean, Maman? Do you not approve of Faustina? I can assure you that she comes from—"

"No, no, Gerard!" his mother cried. "It has nothing to do with your little Faustina—or at least, only in part. If only I had known you were married!"

"But, Maman, did you not get my letter?" Gerard asked. "I wrote, in all, three letters to you—the first telling you that I was safe in Naples, then that I was in Palermo and married, and a final letter to inform you that we were sailing back to France via Gibraltar!"

"I received none of them!" the vicomtesse said. "It is not surprising, Gerard. The marquis de Guéridon was here visiting me not many months ago and informed me that letters were frequently intercepted on the high seas by the British as well as by political agents in Paris. I had no news of or from you. We were unaware if you were alive or dead, if you had recovered your memory or were still roaming the high seas as George King!"

Gerard took her hand and pressed his lips to her fingers.

"I am so sorry to think of your worry and distress!" he said. "I was certain my letters would reach you. But Maman—how did you know I had lost my memory? That I believed for a while I was another man?"

The vicomtesse looked directly at him.

"Mavreen informed me!" she said. As Gerard gasped she added hurriedly, "She is here—in Compiègne. Gerard, she is even now in the forest awaiting Jules's report that it is safe for her to come back to the château. Her manservant, Dickon, is with her."

Gerard's face, which had flushed a deep red, now drained of all color. He swayed on his feet, his eyes never leaving his mother's face.

"*Mavreen, here!*" he breathed the words. "I must go to her at once. And you called it *bad* news? Maman, if you could but know how happy this makes me! I cannot even now believe in such a miracle. Mavreen here, in

Compiègne! Forgive me, Maman. I must leave you. I cannot wait another instant to see her."

He would have rushed from the room but for his mother's restraining hand upon his arm and her voice, equally forceful, begging him to reflect upon matters first. Quietly, she told him of Mavreen's love for him, strong enough to have brought her here to France in search of him; she knew from Gerard's face that he returned that love in full. But she had to remind him of what had momentarily escaped his mind—he was married. The little Faustina, innocent and unsuspecting, awaited him upstairs. No matter how intense his love for Mavreen or hers for him, he must not hurt his young wife.

Gerard covered his tormented face with his hands. He knew that his mother was right and yet every instinct urged him to go now without delay in search of the only woman in the world he could ever love.

"What am I going to do!" he said piteously. "I love her. I have always loved her. When I married Faustina, I believed Mavreen to be the wife of Lord Barre. I knew nothing of his death until after my marriage. Now Mavreen has come to me and I . . . ." his voice broke.

"It is hard, I know!" Marianne de Valle said gently, her heart torn by her son's agony of mind. "But you must consider Mavreen, too, Gerard. The news of your marriage will be a great shock for her. It might be kinder to let Jules break the news to her. It is possible she will not feel able to face you in the company of your wife. I think it possible that neither of you could hide your feelings in the presence of little Faustina."

"Then what do you suggest, Maman?" Gerard asked harshly. "*I must see* Mavreen even at the cost of hurting Faustina. I'm sorry if that shocks you but she is more important to me than anyone in the world. I love her, Maman. *I have always loved her.* And now she is here. . . ."

"She must return to England!" the vicomtesse broke in. "There is no alternative, Gerard. She is too fine a person and loves you too much for you to debase her by asking her to remain in the environs as your mistress even were this possible. This is not Paris where you could set her up

in a home of her own in which you could visit her. I
know such things happen, but not here in Compiègne.
Your little Faustina would soon discover the truth and
would be unbearably hurt. But you would be hurting Mavreen even more. Oh, Gerard, *mon petit!* You should
have waited. Did you not realize that a man as old as
Lord Barre could not live so many years more—even
had he not had a bad heart!"

Gerard looked at his mother reproachfully.

"It is easy to be wise now, Maman. Not so very long
ago, you were pressing me to make a good marriage and
provide you with grandchildren! Besides, I was certain
Mavreen believed me dead and would be happier believing me so. Because of my duty to you and my father's
memory we had agreed that we could not share our lives
and must part. We were on the point of separation when
my riding accident occurred. I thought it better for her if
she continued to believe me dead. Maman, you yourself
stressed so often that it was my duty to marry. . . ."

Marianne de Valle sighed. Her affection for Mavreen
and her son's distress had put such practical thoughts
from her mind. In reproving him for marrying Faustina,
she had considered only the plight of the two young lovers.

Mother and son stared at one another despairingly.

"Go to her then!" Marianne de Valle said, unable to
bear the tortured look in his eyes. "Let Mavreen decide
what she wishes to do. I am certain only of one thing—
that she will not wish to remain here in the château beneath the same roof as your wife. I believe she will wish
to return at once to England."

Dickon was uneasy. Jules had been absent a long time
—far longer than was necessary to reach the château and
return. He sensed danger to Mavreen. When he saw the
lone horseman galloping toward them and realized it was
a far younger man than Jules, he loaded his pistol and
took aim, telling Mavreen to take cover behind the trees.

But Mavreen made no move to obey. She stood perfectly
still, holding the horses' heads, her eyes staring at the
approaching rider. Her heart was hammering in her throat
and her legs were trembling—but not from fear.

"Dickon, 'tis Gerard!" she whispered. *"Gerard!"*

Slowly, Dickon lowered the gun as he too recognized the man approaching them. He looked at Mavreen's white face and held out an arm as she swayed on her feet. But she cast his arm aside and began to run forward. Gerard reined in his horse and vaulted from its saddle, running forward in his turn until he and Mavreen were clasped in one another's arms.

Dickon caught Gerard's mount and looked away, his throat constricted with emotion. Through his mind shot a picture of a similar meeting in the woods behind Richmond. It seemed a hundred years ago! And now, at long last, the lovers were reunited.

It was some minutes before Mavreen or Gerard could find their voices. They clung to one another in speechless joy, cheek pressed to cheek, heart pressed against heart, hands, fingers entwined. Then Gerard pushed her away to arm's length so that he could look into her face, her eyes.

"You are more beautiful than ever, my beloved!" he cried. "Ah, Mavreen—if only you knew how many times I have dreamt of this moment. I had given up all hope. . . ."

"And, I, too!" Mavreen broke in. "Oh, Gerard, can it really be true? Yet I know it is. I felt in my heart that you would come back here to France, that I should find you here in Compiègne. I never believed you were dead—even when all the evidence pointed to it. My heart told me you were somewhere on this earth. I never gave up hope!"

Gerard kissed her—violently, passionately, despairingly. When he released her, it was to say, "I stopped hoping, Mavreen. I did not believe we could ever be together again. Forgive me! Forgive me!"

Mavreen reached up her hands to cup his face, her eyes shining with happiness.

"But it doesn't matter now, Gerard. You have found me. I have found you. We are together. Nothing shall ever part us again. I am free now to marry you. Poor Gilbert is dead. I am free at last, Gerard, and I love you with all my heart!"

His face agonized, Gerard gripped her arms.

"I love you, too, Mavreen—more than you will ever

believe. I know that you are free and there is nothing in the whole world I would like more than to have you for my wife. But—Mavreen, *I am now married!*" So great was his horror of the words he had to speak, he shouted them angrily at her. Her eyes regarded him in total disbelief.

"That is not true, is it, Gerard? Tell me it is not true! You are joking with me, are you not? Gerard, I beg you, do not tease me about such a matter. Tell me it is not true!"

She, too, was shouting now—more in fear than in anger. The look in his eyes frightened her beyond measure. She tore at his shirt front, pleading with him, shaking him in her despairing efforts to make him deny the truth of his statement.

Tears filling his eyes, Gerard took her hands and held them imprisoned in his own. They were both trembling uncontrollably.

"It is true!" he said, almost inaudibly. "I was married on board ship six months ago to a young Neapolitan girl called Faustina, Donna Faustina de Monte-Gincinto. I did not hear of your husband's death until it was too late. I did not believe I would ever see you again. Mavreen, you must not doubt me. I love you—I never stopped loving you. I tried to put your happiness before my own. I was certain you believed me dead and would be happier if I remained no more than a memory. Faustina was— God forgive me for saying so, but I no longer cared what became of me. I married her without love. Oh, Mavreen. . . ."

She tried to draw her hands away but he would not let her go. He had to make her understand somehow. That she should believe he had betrayed her was beyond bearing and explanations poured from his lips. There was no expression on her stunned face as he spoke. He could not be sure she took in the meaning of his words. Again and again, he implored her to try to understand. When at last he ceased speaking, she seemed calmer. Her words, however, distracted him to a new distress.

"When you disappeared from the grange," she said in a small quiet voice, "I was with child—your child, Gerard.

Our daughter was born nearly six months ago—the child of our love!"

Suddenly, she was sobbing uncontrollably, the convulsions of her body so violent that Gerard needed all his strength to support her. He rocked her in his arms, murmuring endearments, his own tears falling on her head as they clung to one another.

Suddenly, Gerard's body stiffened. He drew back and his mouth had a new firmer look as he thrust his chin forward with determination.

"Mavreen, stop crying. I have decided what is to be done. I will not be parted from you again. I care not how badly others will think of me for what I intend to do but my mind is made up. I will never leave you. I will confess the truth to Faustina and ask her to release me from my marriage vows. Our religion will not permit of divorce but perhaps His Holiness the pope would agree to a dispensation—to annul the marriage. Mavreen, are you listening to me, my very dearest love? Dry your eyes! All will be well, I swear it. I love you."

Gradually, Mavreen regained control of herself. Faustina was but a name to her. She could not envisage that this girl Gerard had married could possibly love or need him as she, herself, loved and needed him. As to the possibility of an annulment of the marriage, there lay the first glimmer of hope. And even if such a thing were impossible, she, herself, would not care. Nothing mattered but Gerard. His mother must surely understand, for no one else except perhaps dear Aunt Clarrie, knew better than Marianne de Valle how deeply and sincerely she loved Gerard.

Hope revived her spirits. She pushed her doubts firmly from the forefront of her mind. Gerard was through with prevarication. His mind was made up to cast in his lot with her and suffer the consequences. Together, everything was possible. They did not need the approval of the world—only of each other.

"Come, *petit écureuil!*" Gerard said. "We will return now to the château and talk to my mother. She cannot refuse to give us her blessing since it was a love similar to ours that she enjoyed with my father. Perhaps she will have some idea how I should confess my purpose to poor little Faustina! Mavreen, let us not waste further time."

He turned and called to Dickon who was standing off at a discreet distance. He stepped forward, extending his hand and grinning.

"Welcome home, sir!" he said. "I be right pleased to see you safe and sound."

"And I to see you, Dickon!" Gerard said warmly. "I must have caused you a deal of worry when I disappeared that summer's eve in Sussex. When there is time, I'll recount my adventures to you."

"And I've a thing or two to tell ye of!" Dickon replied.

He glanced at Mavreen to reassure himself that all was well with her, but still holding tightly to Gerard's hand, she was staring up into Gerard's face with such a naked expression of love and longing that Dickon looked away. No man but Gerard had the right to see into her heart.

"Be you a-coming back to England with us?" he asked.

Gerard's smile faded and was replaced by a look of intense anxiety.

"I don't know, Dickon. That is what we must now do —ride back to the château to discuss affairs with my mother. Then we shall decide!"

Mavreen turned her head and stared at Gerard with a puzzled expression. She remained silent but her head was ringing with questions. "Then we shall decide!" Gerard had said to Dickon. And she had thought the decision already made.

CHAPTER TWENTY-EIGHT

1799

Faustina was in tears by the time Gerard returned to the château and went up to their bedroom. As soon as she saw him come through the door, she threw herself into his arms and clung to him.

"I thought some harm had come to you, Gerard!" she

cried. "I was so afraid. Louise told me there were wolves in the forest and that some young man called Dickon had been attacked and savaged by the beasts. I was frightened lest you. . . ."

She broke off, crying anew.

Gerard bit his lip and tried to disengage himself from her clinging arms. Faustina was frightened of everything, beginning with the storm at sea and even more distressingly, by his physical advances to her on their wedding night. She had been so carefully nurtured and protected by her parents and the nuns at her convent, that she knew as little about life outside the protective walls of her childhood as if she were six years old, not sixteen. He had, at first, delighted in his role of protector, but gradually her ever-increasing demands upon him became irksome and tiring. She was forever asking him what she should do and how she should do it, and not satisfied with this, further asked if she had performed the task to his liking.

Her adoration of him was as heavy a burden as her dependence upon him. He found himself avoiding her; if he heard her voice softly calling him in the passages, the garden, from a window, he would step back into the nearest shadow hoping to pass her unnoticed. Such behavior always made him feel guilty.

It had been the same in the bedchamber, where it was her custom to embrace him and urge him shyly to fulfill his duties as a husband.

"I know that it pleases you, Gerard!" she said. "And it makes me so happy to know that I can succeed in this. I am no longer afraid. I am happy that you need me."

Gerard was not at all happy that he needed her. She seemed not to have any violent passions of her own and was clearly content to lie in the safe circle of his arms, receiving no more than gentle kisses and caresses. That the proximity of her young body frequently stirred his blood to require more of her was, in some unaccountable way, humiliating to him. The transaction was too one-sided and when it was over, he would turn aside from her, sickened by his weakness, hating himself and the pathetic young girl beside him, and longing for Mavreen.

However hard he tried, he was never able to make love to Faustina without feeling he betrayed her, himself and his real love, Mavreen. He did not know if Faustina thought him lacking in passion for a young man of his age; probably she knew nothing of the hungers of the body be they her own or anyone else's. He could do no wrong in her eyes so he had to believe that she felt his infrequent visits to her bed were normal for a newly married man and that his devotion was as intense as it should be. Her total innocence made him feel even more guilty. He knew he should never have married her and yet not a day passed that she did not tell him how happy she was to be married to him. She begged him constantly to tell her if there were any special way in which she could please him. Keeping her happy was no problem for he had only to compliment her on a new dress or hair style for her expression to become radiant. Keeping himself happy was another matter, despite the fact that he had nothing whatever to complain of. While in Palermo they were invited everywhere since everyone loved his sweet young wife, the men for her femininity and shy charm; the women because she had a kind word and a smile for everyone. She alone of all the ladies spoke no ill of Lady Hamilton who was now conducting her affair with Lord Nelson quite openly.

Gerard would have wasted no time in Palermo but for two facts. Lord Nelson was now not only controlling the complicated naval operations in the Mediterranean, but the administration as well. Having no commander-in-chief's staff to ease his secretarial burden, he therefore made many calls upon Gerard's time. Gerard did not feel able to refuse the demands, being so indebted to Lord Nelson for the months at sea as his uninvited guest. Secondly, word was received that partisan operations had been taking place in the city of Naples waging war against the occupying French forces and the republican régime that had been set up there. Nelson sent his friend Troubridge with a few ships to blockade the Bay of Naples and by March, the French armies in Italy were in retreat. It looked as if the Neapolitan territories might soon be

delivered. Were this to happen, it was only natural that
Faustina would want to return to her home to reassure
herself as to her parents' safety before leaving with Gerard for France. So partly for her sake he waited.

By the end of April, the French evacuated Naples but
King Ferdinand and his queen seemed in no hurry to return. The court in Palermo was as active as ever it had
been in Naples. It was while Gerard was still deliberating
that Lord Nelson learned a French fleet had been seen
off Brest and he was warned by St. Vincent of a possible
attack upon Malta and Alexandria. He therefore set sail
at once with his available ships for Maritimo, hoping to
intercept the French fleet there.

Gerard would have dearly liked to go with him but
Faustina became hysterical at the first suggestion. She
was not only terrified for his safety but refused to be left
alone at Palermo without him. Disgruntled, Gerard had
decided that the time had come for him to return to
France and try, somehow, to pick up the threads of his
former life and ambitions. It was, after all, to this end that
he had sacrificed everything. For his mother's sake as
well as that of Faustina, he must delay his return no
longer.

Now he wondered what stroke of fate had brought
him home at the self-same time Mavreen had chosen to
come in search of him. A month later and she might
already have returned to England! If it were not for
Faustina. . . .

He broke his train of thought and pulled his wife's arms
gently away from him saying firmly, "There is nothing to
fear, my dear. Neither you nor I are in any physical danger.
You are over-tired and over-wrought. I have many things
I wish to discuss with my mother and I feel it would be a
good plan for both our sakes if you were to retire to bed
and enjoy a good rest. The journey has exhausted you."

Faustina's tears were already drying. She smiled at Gerard lovingly.

"If you think so, my darling. I will do whatever you
wish. It is true I am fatigued. If it pleases you, I will
ring for Louise and tell her to undress me and put me to

bed. But you will not be too busy with your Maman to come and talk to me later, Gerard? You know I am always lonely when you are not with me!"

Gerard curbed his impatience to be gone and stayed until Louise came hurrying into the room. Then he, in turn, hurried away to his mother's salon where she awaited him. She was alone. He wasted no time but went to her side and taking her hand in his, raised it to his lips.

"Maman!" he said, "I know this will distress you and I had desired above everything that my homecoming would make you happy, but now everything is so difficult. Maman, I cannot give her up. *I cannot!*"

Marianne de Valle surveyed her son's bowed head with eyes filled with pain.

"I will not dictate to you what you should do with your life, Gerard. You are a man now and must decide as your conscience directs," she said quietly. "I can repeat only what I said to you earlier. You are not free to marry Mavreen and for you to make her your mistress is to belittle the love you have for her!"

Gerard drew in his breath sharply.

"Mavreen does not feel as you do. She asks nothing more than that we shall be together."

The vicomtesse shook her head.

"It is natural she should feel so now, Gerard. But what of the future? What future is there for either of you. What have you to offer her, other than your love? Not even a name for your children! And your wife, Gerard? What would become of little Faustina? You are aware, I suppose, that she is with child?"

The look on Gerard's face was answer enough. He had been ignorant of the fact which Louise had noticed within minutes and reported with delight to the vicomtesse whilst Gerard had been in the forest with Mavreen.

"It cannot be!" he said hoarsely. But even as he spoke, he knew that it was only to be expected; moreover it explained Faustina's many recent indispositions.

"Does she know she is with child?" he asked hoarsely. "She said nothing to me about it."

"I don't know, Gerard. She is very young and innocent.

It is possible she only suspects the truth. One of us must tell her. Louise is in no doubt."

"Mon Dieu!" Gerard cried. "If I had only left Naples without her. But I felt so sorry for her. Maman, I cannot renounce my wife if she bears my child, but I cannot live without Mavreen. Only half an hour ago, I gave her my word that all would be well. I love her. I need her!"

"As I love and need you, Gerard!" Mavreen said, coming quietly unseen into the room in time to hear Gerard's last words. Her face was very pale beneath the golden tan of the sun, her eyes large and luminous with tears. "And it is because I love you so dearly, I know I must go away— far away—and that we must never see each other again."

Gerard left his mother's side and hurried to Mavreen's, taking her in his arms as if the vicomtesse were not present.

"No, I won't let you go!" he cried. "I cannot, Mavreen. Do not ask it of me!"

"Gerard, we have no choice. In your heart you know it is true, just as I do. You would grow to hate yourself if you deserted your wife and child and in time, you would grow to hate me, too. Nor could we live a life of deception. We could never hide how we feel about each other; and you would be forever torn between your duty to your wife and your wish to be with me."

"Mavreen is right!" the vicomtesse said quietly, "and by her decision has convinced me how deeply she loves you, *mon fils.* You must be worthy of her!"

Gerard looked from one to the other but although both women had tears in their eyes, there was no weakening of their hearts. The pain in his own was unbearable. Quietly, the vicomtesse rose to her feet. She walked across to the door and stood looking at them in deepest distress.

"I do not know if parting would be easier for you were Mavreen to leave at once, but if you feel strong enough to keep such a vow, Gerard, then promise me that you will take no more than four days to escort Mavreen to the coast, and I will see that your absence goes unremarked. I will inform Faustina that you have been called away to Paris on urgent business. This will at least give you both a little time together, as well as the opportunity to see Mavreen safely aboard a ship for England. I see no reason to hurt Faustina by telling her the truth! She need never know of Mavreen's existence."

Mavreen and Gerard stared at one another and at the vicomtesse. Her suggestion seemed like a reprieve from a sentence of death.

The vicomtesse smiled.

"Even I am capable of a lie, Gerard, if it is in the interests of all concerned." She was certain that if Mavreen were to leave alone and immediately, Gerard would never succeed in concealing his grief from Faustina. If he were to break down and confess the truth to the girl, all hopes of the marriage ever succeeding were doomed.

"Give me your promise—both of you—that Gerard will return here within four days—alone!"

Mavreen ran to the vicomtesse's side and fell to her knees, raising the delicate white hand and kissing it fervently.

"You have my word, madame!"

"And mine, Maman!" Gerard said.

"Then God go with you both!" she said. "It is best you should leave at once. I will inform Dickon and he and Jules can prepare the horses. Mavreen, I do not have the heart for good-byes. I think we understand each other and there is no need for words. I will take care of Gerard as best I can for you! I will go now and warn Faustina of your impending departure, Gerard. It will then only be necessary for you to make a hurried farewell."

She was gone before either could voice their thanks.

Gerard drew Mavreen into his arms and silently, kissed away her tears.

"Once before, God gave us a week of life together!" Mavreen whispered. "Now He, through your mother, is giving us four days. It is only a fraction of our lifetime, Gerard, but we will live every minute of it."

"I will not leave your side, day or night!" Gerard vowed. "Oh, Mavreen, my love. If only. . . ."

But she put her hand quickly over his lips.

"Let us not think of all we cannot have!" she said.

"Think instead of all the people in the world who will never know the joy we share, not even once in their lifetime. At least we have known real love, Gerard, and no matter how many miles separate us, I shall never cease to love you."

"Nor I you!" Gerard cried. He was suddenly impatient to be far away from the house where he must henceforth be an unwilling prisoner. He wanted desperately to be alone with Mavreen, hold her in his arms and love her as he had loved her in his imagination for so long. Words seemed inadequate to express the intensity of his feelings and now that the decision was made and they had four days of life to live, he could not bear to waste one minute of them.

He marveled at his mother's understanding. But for this reprieve, he would never have found the strength to make the decision to honor his marriage vows. If only he had never married Faustina! At the time, the decision to do so had seemed of so little importance to him, his life meaningless since he believed Mavreen beyond his reach. He knew men of eighty and even ninety still surviving. Mavreen might have remained Lord Barre's wife for thirty years! But now, in retrospect, the voluntary loss of his own freedom seemed a kind of madness he could not explain, any more than his conviction that Mavreen had long since forgotten him and made a complete life for herself without him.

His face grim, he turned away lest she should see the torment in his eyes.

"There is much to prepare for our journey!" he said. "Let us not waste time, my love."

Time! Mavreen thought as she carefully folded her few clothes and possessions. It had little consistency. How unendurably slowly the hours ticked by when she had not known if Gerard lived or died! How cruelly they raced round the clock face when she was with him! The week they had shared at the grange belonged to another life, another world. And yet, with Gerard's arms around her, they were as yesterday.

She thought of Gerard in his wife's bedchamber bidding her adieu. She, Mavreen, had no place there. She did not

wish to see the young Neapolitan girl Gerard had married.
Louise had already described her to Mavreen in far too
great detail, a flow of gossip Mavreen had not been
strong enough to curtail. Faustina, she knew, was very
young, no more than a child! She was pretty, helpless,
dependent, had been reared like some delicate hothouse
plant and protected from life's hardships and cruelties.
Her adoration of Gerard was total and charming, so the
French maid recounted, her love for the young vicomte
simple and unconcealed.

But Mavreen could bear no more. She sent Louise
about her duties and hurriedly washed her flushed face
and combed the unruly tangles from her hair. Now, as she
prepared to leave the Château de Boulancourt forever, the
first taste of bitterness narrowed her eyes and twisted the
corners of her mouth. Momentarily, she hated Gerard for
his infidelity. He had not waited to see her again before he
hastened into marriage. It was true they had made no
vows for lasting fidelity and she had always known that
Gerard must marry, but somehow the thought of Donna
Mercedes as his wife had never tormented her as did this
present betrayal. "I never stopped loving you!" Gerard
had sworn to her. Yet he had married the sixteen-year-
old Faustina. Without love, he told Mavreen. He had not
known until it was too late that she, Mavreen, was a widow, but he must have known that his marriage would put
him beyond reach forever.

Tears filled her eyes. She walked to the window and
stood staring out into the overgrown garden where the
wild roses now vied with the scarlet camelias and the
columbine, twisting delicately but ruthlessly up the stems
of the white and gold standards. They, like the delicate
Faustina, did not need strength to grasp hold of the stem
that gave them life. The young girl's very helplessness
forged the iron bonds that enchained Gerard. Mavreen,
herself, was strong. If she wished, she might yet persuade
Gerard to abandon his young wife and unborn child and
even his mother. She alone held the key to Gerard's
heart. Through love and passion she might win where the
frail tentacles of Faustina's dependence would fail, but
there could be no victory for her were she to win the

battle. Gerard was too deeply enmeshed in the past, his
sense of duty and obligation never far from the surface of
his mind. Passion might momentarily sway him but when
his ardor cooled and common sense prevailed, his conscience would reawaken to torment him, and his torment,
she knew in this moment of truth, would be her cross, the
destroyer of any happiness they found together. Gerard's
mother had known this as instinctively as she knew it.

Mavreen pushed her last belongings into her portmanteau and ran down the corridor to the vicomtesse's salon.

Gerard's mother was sitting by the window. She turned
as Mavreen entered the room and with an informality quite
unfamiliar in Mavreen's experience, held out her arms.
She ran to them and felt herself enveloped in a cool,
fragrant embrace.

"My heart is aching for you, child!" said Marianne de
Valle. "I know you love Gerard; you have proved to me
many times how great that love is. Now you are having
to prove it once more and I know better even than you
may realize what it is costing you. You are stronger than
he—and wiser!"

"I do not feel strong!" Mavreen said shakily. "I did not
realize that to give up was so much harder than to give!"

"Ah, but that is one of life's truths!" the vicomtesse
said, smoothing Mavreen's hair with tender fingers. "And
I, too, must make a sacrifice. I will confess that I have
come to love you dearly, my child, in these few weeks
you have lived here with me. At first, I admired your
courage and tenacity, but as I came to know you better,
my affection for you increased until I, also, prayed that
Gerard would return safely to make you his wife. I can
think of no daughter-in-law who would have pleased me
better. It is my sorrow, too, that this cannot be! I understand full well why my son loves you."

"If I could only be sure he will be happy!" Mavreen
cried. "You have met his wife, Madame la vicomtesse.
Tell me if you believe she can keep him contented!"

The older woman kept her face rigidly impassive. It
could do no good to pass on her fears to Mavreen that the
little Faustina was too insipid and timid a creature ever to

make an impact on a man's heart or passions. But doubtless she would be obedient, ready to fall in with her husband's wishes—and as such, could fulfill her role as Gerard's wife as well as another. Moreover, the Monte-Gincintos' great wealth would stand them in good stead and safeguard their children's future and the dynasty of the de Valles.

"It is too soon for me to pass judgment upon the girl," she said. "I found her both pretty and charming and her adoration of Gerard is not in doubt. I am sure he will ultimately find happiness, if not love, from this marriage."

But Gerard denied the future held any hope for him when finally, that night, he was alone with Mavreen in the seclusion of the bedchamber of a small whitewashed inn on the outskirts of Montdidier.

They had ridden, with Dickon close behind them, for four hours until darkness fell and they decided to call a halt for the night. The auberge looked clean and Dickon, who was not yet fully fit, and Gerard too, were showing signs of fatigue. It was not tiredness but the onset of the deepest depression that assailed Mavreen. Listlessly, she stood quietly as Gerard made arrangements for their overnight stop and inspected the bedchamber, which, he reported, was without luxuries but clean and comfortable.

When they were alone, he took her in his arms and kissed her hungrily. He seemed to have forgotten everything but the present and Mavreen's despairing cry as she clung to him saying, "We have so little time left, Gerard!"

She knew that it was madness to waste their last precious hours together bemoaning the future that could never be; in vain regrets about the past; and yet her heart remained heavy as she stood passively allowing Gerard to remove her clothing. His need for possession of her body was urgent and intense and she understood it and tried to hide her own heaviness of spirit. The sight of his strong, naked body, so well-remembered and so deeply desired, brought only a heightening of her despair. She found herself near to hating him because he had the power to arouse her senses when she desired so acutely not to love him, not to care so heartbreakingly.

As his hands encircled her breasts, lingered sensuously on her nipples, he murmured with delight at the change in her since the birth of their child.

"You are more beautiful than ever, my love!" he cried, and let his hands run down her sides, encircle her waist, outline her hips and finally draw her fiercely against him. Involuntarily, her own hands reached out to grip his back, feel the tenseness of his muscles and the fierce heat of his skin. She bit her lip to keep herself from crying out as he bent his head and bit into the soft white flesh of her shoulder. He seemed to take her physical response for granted and she resented his assumption, even knowing that it was more than justified. She could never deny Gerard; her body had no will of its own. It belonged to him and answered to his and not to her bidding. Hate and love mingled in violent combat.

They fell to the floor, locked in one another's arms. Mavreen's mind seemed detached from her body. She was remembering that this past agonizing year, she had remained faithful to Gerard. No man had laid hand upon her body since last he had loved her, yet *he* had taken another woman to bed. Young! Pretty! Charming! His mother had said. Made her his wife. He had lain with her, possessed her perhaps with the same passion as he now sought to possess her.

"No!" she cried out. "No, Gerard. I don't want to— please—no—no!"

But he was oblivious of everything but the furious need her beautiful body evoked in him. Not in his wildest dreams had he touched on the fascination she held for him. No other woman had this power to waken senses he scarcely knew he possessed. She was more than his love; she was desire itself.

"You are mine!" he cried out as he forced himself into her, feeling her first resistance melting in the sweetness and fire of union and becoming fierce and demanding as his own. Then they were as one, plunging together into a golden vortex of such rapture they came close to sublimity. Then followed peace and feelings of yearning tenderness that brought tears to Mavreen's eyes.

"I love you so much!" she whispered. "If I could only be sure you will be happy!"

But Gerard, as deeply moved as she, could but answer truthfully, "There can be no true happiness for me without you, *mon amour*. You are my life. You are all I need or want. I love you more than anything or anyone in the whole world!"

His words were both balm and inflammation. She reached out a hand and smoothed the dark, damp hair from his eyes.

"Gerard, I am afraid! We promised your mother we would part at the end of four days, yet I do not think I shall have the strength for it. I cannot be parted from you again. I cannot!"

The room was now in complete darkness. Gerard stood up and without a word, lifted Mavreen in his arms and carried her to the bed. He covered her with the soft down-filled quilt and then lay down beside her. His cheek, touching hers, found it wet with tears. The sadness that had held her in its grip now pervaded him. He longed not to think of tomorrow and yet there was no denying it. Like a ghost it haunted the room and held tranquility at bay.

He sensed Mavreen's weakness and because of it, forced himself to try to regain his own moral strength. There was only one way for them to stay together—if Mavreen became his mistress. And he would not so demean her. Once —how long ago it seemed—when he had been but a callow youth with no knowledge of life or love, he had suggested such a relationship to Mavreen.

Mavreen, he surmised, might, in this moment of weakness, express her willingness to be no more to him than poor Aunt Clarrie was to Sir John Danesfield, but Gerard knew his beloved better than she knew herself. She would never long be satisfied with part of him, never willingly share him with another woman, see her child—his, too— take second place to Faustina's child. It was possible he and Mavreen would beget more children and he, Gerard, could not be father to two families. He already had far too many responsibilities. What little there was left of him was all he would have to offer Mavreen and it was not enough. He wanted to give her his love; every moment of every day; his children; his life.

He longed to explain such thoughts to her, but Mavreen, guessing what lay behind his silence, laid her finger on his lips.

"I know it isn't possible for us to live together," she said softly. "I am sorry I was weak. It will not happen again, I promise you."

"Do not lay blame at your door!" Gerard cried despairingly. "I am the one who has brought ruin to our lives. I should never have married Faustina. I should have waited. If only . . ."

But Mavreen would not allow him to continue. No amount of regret would undo the marriage and now that Faustina was with child, there could be no annulment even if all parties desired it.

"You must not worry about me!" she said, seeking to comfort him. "I am very rich and will lack for nothing that I need. And I do have a part of you, Gerard, that will always be mine. I have Tamarisk. They say that girls favor their fathers so mayhap, she will grow like you. I will find happiness in her, I know it."

They talked briefly of the child and Gerard expressed a longing to see his firstborn, the little daughter conceived of their love. It was this wish which prompted his next remark.

"We vowed to my mother that you would return to England and I to my home at the end of four days!" he said. "But we made no promise about the future, Mavreen. We could make another vow to each other—to meet once every year in England and spend one week together there, at the grange. I could see our daughter, watch her grow up. And you and I—we would have that week to look forward to no matter how great the privations of the rest of the year. My love, tell me what you think of such a plan. Is it not possible? Does the mere thought not make everything more bearable?"

Mavreen felt the tension ease from her body as Gerard's suggestion reached her full consciousness. It *was* possible—even easy for her to keep such a tryst. There was the grange—a house they could go to as before with only Rose and Dickon accompanying them. If Gerard could leave his family and escape to England for a week, no one would ever know he was with her! It would indeed be a glimpse of heaven to look forward to, whatever the vicissitudes of her daily life.

"Oh, Gerard, my love!" she whispered. "Would it be possible? For me, yes. I have no ties. But for you?"

"There is nothing and no one can stop us!" he said. "Let us arrange a date on the calendar—in March, I think, because we were so happy there last year in the spring. What say you, *mon petit écureuil?* The final week of the month of March? Every year, from now until we die!"

"Every year!" Mavreen echoed, her eyes closing as his mouth came down upon hers. "Every year, my only love, until we die!"

The feeling of reprieve so affected Mavreen that Gerard was now to discover in her a passion far more abandoned than he had ever suspected. They both believed they had reached the summits of loving during that week of spring in Sussex. But now they found new ways to express themselves, each seeking to give the other the ultimate delight, their bodies fired with the deepest sensual pleasure, their hearts aflame with love and tenderness. Exhausted, they lay in one another's arms, seeking sleep neither really desired and rousing once more to fresh discovery and adventure as they passed the night in love.

Face white with fatigue, eyes deeply shadowed but smilingly at peace in body and spirit, Mavreen lay with her head on Gerard's shoulder watching the first grey lights of dawn filter through the casement window.

"How shall we find the strength to ride through the day!" she murmured, feeling Gerard's fingers entwine with her own. "We must try to sleep, my love."

He kissed her cheek softly and sighed.

"Were it not likely to over-tire our mounts, I would have you ride behind me so that I might continue through the day to feel your arms about me and your soft lovely body against my back!"

Mavreen pressed a kiss against his shoulder.

"No man and woman can ever have shared a love as great as ours, Gerard. If people but knew how it could be between those who feel so deeply."

He smiled in the half light, loving her more in this moment than ever.

"Ah, Mavreen, *comme je t'aime!*" Gerard cried. "Mavreen, I cannot live without you. I know that I must, but it will not be living. I shall pass each day seeing your face in every flower, hearing your voice in every bird call, searching for you in every shadow. I shall long for the night when I can close my eyes and meet you in my dreams. Such will be the sustenance of my existence until I can be with you again."

His words brought tears to her eyes.

"You must try to be happy, for my sake!" she said fiercely. "Your suffering is mine, Gerard, and 'twould be torment to me to think of you passing each day in sadness and regret. Land and ocean may prevent us holding one another's hands but we will be together in our thoughts, Gerard—in our memories. We must learn to make that enough."

Desperately, he drew her against him.

"It cannot be enough!" he cried. "I need you close to me, my most beautiful of women. Your strength frightens me for I cannot match it. My duty to my family seems as nothing compared with my need to be with you day and night. If 'twere possible, I would rescind my vow to my mother. I would travel to England with you, fight for you, work for you, steal for you if such was the only way of survival. I would kill for you, Mavreen. Yet all I may do is leave you. It is beyond bearing!"

"Gerard, no!" Mavreen whispered, holding back her tears only because his were now coursing down his cheeks. She struggled for words that would comfort him. "I am yours from now until eternity," she said. "I swear to you that I shall never love another man, that no matter what my circumstances, you have only to send for me and I will come to your side. Gerard, tonight you have made me yours more certainly than if you had placed a marriage ring upon my finger. No marriage bond could tie me more surely than I am tied now by my love for you. Even were

I never to see you again, I could not cease loving you. But we will see each other again, Gerard—every year, as we have vowed. Nothing can prevent me keeping that appointment so only you have the power to hinder our tryst. Do not doubt me for I swear now, before God, that nothing short of death will keep me from my meeting with you next March and every year of my life."

He buried his face in the soft warmth of her body, his tears drying slowly on her breasts. The need for sleep became overpowering.

"I swear it too, before God!" he said, as he drifted into slumber.

But Mavreen could not sleep. As she rocked him gently in her arms, the way she had once rocked his little daughter, she pondered the days to come. Though she might have convinced Gerard of her strength, she knew that in truth it was all too precarious. As the moment of parting approached, Gerard's agony, and her own, would be intensified. Somehow she must find reserves to continue in her resolve to leave Gerard.

Marianne de Valle, who loved him almost as deeply as herself, had shown Mavreen what her own conscience knew already—there could be no happiness for Gerard were he to abandon his wife and child. Duty was too deeply embedded in his soul, implanted in infancy and nurtured through the years. She herself might abandon all things for Gerard and glory in the sacrifice, but he would feel only shame.

This belief and the knowledge that their separation was not total or infinite, sustained Mavreen even to the moment of adieu. It was the smallest grain of comfort to have Dickon beside her as she stood on the scrubbed deck of the fishing boat as the *Jeanne-Marie* set sail for England. Gerard's figure on the quayside had long since disappeared from sight yet she would not go below. She could still feel his last kiss of farewell warm upon her lips. On the finger of her left hand was his signet ring, engraved with the crest of the de Valles.

"You are my true wife before God!" His last words to her still sounded in her ears against the sighing of the wind in the rigging.

Dickon urged Mavreen again and again to go below where the men were drinking hot tea laced with rum, for the night was cold and dark and only the stars were to be seen. But Mavreen would not move. So Dickon remained beside her, suffering a small part of her agony, feeling her loss as if it were his own.

So it was that when the first cannon ball from the British sloop of war fired across the bow, Dickon and Mavreen were instantly thrown into the icy Channel waters. Eight more guns were fired, each finding its target until the privateer was ablaze, debris littering the sea, the bodies of mutilated, dead, or dying sailors drifting among the remnants of their smuggled cargo.

The blast rendered Mavreen unconscious. Somehow, Dickon, though deeply shocked, found the strength to keep Mavreen afloat. As he realized their danger of drowning, he reached hold of one of the sections of splintered mast drifting past them. The remnants of the *Jeanne-Marie* were ablaze and she was sinking fast. There would be no help from that quarter. Painfully, he grabbed at a length of rope and tied Mavreen to the mast so that her head remained above water. Then he gathered further pieces of wood, several barrels, and somehow, despite the cold and his exhaustion, managed to construct a rough kind of raft. He was calling upon his last reserves of strength as he pulled Mavreen onto it. Then he collapsed beside her, no longer aware of their miraculous escape or their imminent danger.

Now it was Mavreen, recovering consciousness, who took their safety into her hands. Using her imagination, she constructed a makeshift sail from some remnants floating nearby. She steeled herself not to look at the dismembered bodies, torn limbs, dead faces that floated past her. She grabbed with frozen fingers at a passing cask and forcing it open, discovered its contents to be brandy. Using one hand as a scoop, she succeeded in transferring some of the spirit between Dickon's blue lips. He coughed and slowly came round. Now Mavreen drank and felt a little warmth stirring her blood. She was shivering uncontrollably. She saw with relief that Dickon's eyes were open.

"What next, Dickon?" she asked as calmly as she could, though her voice trembled.

"The tide is against our return to the French coast!" he said quietly. "We cannot hope to sail this bundle of wood against it. There is naught else we can do but set sail for England—and pray that we shall be picked up by a passing vessel."

Shivering in her salt-wet clothes, without any real hope of survival, Mavreen consoled herself that at least Gerard was in no danger. He had promised the moment her ship set sail to mount his horse and ride to the nearest inn for a good night's slumber. They had agreed that he must not linger on the quayside once the ship was out of harbor. Happily, he would know nothing of the sinking of their vessel. Dickon had vouchsafed the opinion that it was almost certainly a British sloop which had attacked the *Jeanne-Marie*, and she knew the British would not report its victory. By the time word reached the French port that the vessel was missing, Gerard would be back in Compiègne and know nothing of their plight.

But Mavreen's assumptions were painfully wrong. Gerard, unable to bear the sight of Mavreen sailing into the blackness, had repaired to the nearest drinking house. His agony of mind was such that he felt he could only continue to exist if he were oblivious to the fact that Mavreen had finally departed. He ordered cognac and drank slowly and steadily. Yet he had still not succeeded in dulling all his senses when a seaman burst into the drinking house in the early hours of the morning, shouting to all around him that the *Jeanne-Marie* had been blasted to smithereens by a British sloop.

Unsteadily, he rose to his feet and grabbed the man by his jersey.

"How know you this?" he shouted. "From whence came such lies?"

The seaman pulled away, angry, but instinctively respectful of the obvious note of authority in Gerard's voice.

" 'Tis no lie, sir. We was but a half-dozen furlongs distant when we saw it happen. I saw both ships with my own eyes. Might have been us those bastards aimed for but for the *Jeanne-Marie* being nearer. We'd no means to defend ourselves so we sailed for harbor quick as we could. With the wind behind us, we made good time despite the tide agin us."

"But the survivors!" Gerard cried hoarsely. "Did you not stop to pick up survivors?"

"Steady, sir!" the man said as Gerard swayed on his feet. "We'd have been blown sky high same as the *Jeanne-Marie* if we'd stayed about. Besides, 'tweren't no rhyme nor reason for it. Boat took full blast from all eight guns and was blazing like hell itself. Weren't no survivors, I'll swear to it."

Slowly, Gerard sank to the floor, his legs collapsing beneath him as the full force of the man's words penetrated his dulled mind. The *Jeanne-Marie* had sunk—all hands lost. Mavreen—his beautiful Mavreen was dead.

PART THREE
1803-1812

CHAPTER TWENTY-NINE

1803-1804

"My dearest Mavreen, will you not stop and consider? You reached the age of twenty-three years last week. Does that not frighten you a little?"

Anne Lade, formerly Anne Pettigrew, sat on a footstool at Mavreen's feet. Her dress of pale blue poplin did little to hide the fact that she was with child. Her small pretty face, rounder and fuller now, lacked none of the innocent sweetness that was so much a part of her nature. She held Mavreen's hand in hers.

Mavreen's mouth twitched.

Anne sighed. There seemed no way she could force Mavreen to realize the reputation she was rapidly acquiring. Three years ago, when Lord Barre's cousin had decided to leave London and offered Mavreen the use of Barre House, everyone had believed that Mavreen, recovered from her long period of mourning for Gilbert, would return to her former way of life. But Mavreen, absent from London society for two whole years, had returned to make her own rules, create her own society and totally disregard any convention which stood between her and her ceaseless quest for excitement, novelty—and men.

Anne's frown deepened. Even the clothes Mavreen chose to wear seemed to underline her unsavory reputation; though her cherry red gown was certainly fashionable, the short spencer jacket with its long tight sleeves and braid trimming that gave it a military air did not, in Anne's opinion, become her.

Anne, herself was now happily married to Percy Lade. As a couple, both were justly popular. But her staunch defense of Mavreen could not halt the many wagging tongues, nor soften the hearts of those who considered her behavior outrageous and an inexcusable flaunting of convention. Anne, alone, knew she had no such intention; that her behavior was the outcome of a desire to avenge herself upon the opposite sex.

When Mavreen was rescued with Dickon from their terrible ordeal at sea, she had chosen to recuperate at the grange in Sussex. Anne had visited her there and seen with her own eyes Mavreen's excitement mount every day that Gerard's expected arrival neared. She remained with Mavreen as the days of March ran out and with them Mavreen's happiness. She was witness to the agony of mind her friend suffered when Gerard failed to keep their tryst. She was powerless to do more than offer silent sympathy as Mavreen paced the floor for hour upon hour, tramped the fields and lanes, her eyes always turned eagerly to the south from which direction she tried to convince herself that Gerard might yet appear.

Mavreen refused to believe that Gerard had forsaken her. On the first day of April when clearly she could bear the waiting no longer, she announced that she would go to France to discover for herself why Gerard had not come. Unlike Anne, Dickon knew the folly of trying to dissuade her. She was grimly determined, even though such a journey entailed braving the sea which had so nearly cost her and Dickon their lives.

But the journey was never to take place. Before preparations were completed, Mavreen received a letter from Clarissa to say that the marquis de Guéridon had but recently visited Sir John and she, herself, had made a point of asking for news of the de Valle family. Gerard's wife had given birth to a son. Gerard, himself, was with Moreau in Germany preparing to do battle with the Austrians. He had joined Napoleon's army after much soul-searching. He believed it would be the most likely way in which he could restore the family estates and possibly bring him nearer to the Austrian baron whom, Clarissa added, Mavreen would recall was the rogue responsible for his father's death and downfall. Gerard, according to the marquis, was now single-mindedly dedicated to his son's future.

"I grieve for you, dearest child!" Clarissa ended her letter,

but you will at least have the compensation of know-
ing that his life has acquired both purpose and mean-
ing albeit without you. You must now try to forget
him.

For three days, Mavreen lay on her bed, refusing food,
tearless but so mortally stricken with grief Anne feared for
her life. With complete unpredictability, Mavreen rose on
the fourth day, dressed herself, announced that she had
decided to return to London that very morning. Rose
must pack at once. Dickon must prepare the horses.

"We have endured far too many dull and dreary days
down here!" she told Anne in a dangerously bright voice.
"We will go to the big city and make up for these wasted
weeks."

Anne's brother, James, who had loved Mavreen faith-
fully for years, agreed that Mavreen had now embarked
on the only remedy she could think of for her grief—the
artificial happiness that came from a pleasure-seeking
frivolous existence in which there was never a dull or
quiet moment for reflection; for memories. She was rich
enough to indulge in any extravagance. Champagne flowed
ceaselessly on every occasion. Her closets were filled with
new dresses, hats, slippers. She created her own daring
vivid fashions. She bought a huge stallion on which she
galloped wildly through the parks at all hours of the day
or night. With macabre humor, she named the great beast
Death, and indeed, Anne did not doubt that Mavreen
many times courted death on his back.

But this was not all. Mavreen had taken a lover—a
young golden-haired youth who was attached to the
Prince of Wales's regiment, the 10th Hussars. No sooner
had the tongues quietened their wagging, than she took
another lover, and another. She toyed with them cruelly,
inducing them to fall in love with her. When, finally,
they were at her feet, she laughed at them scornfully
and bade them cease boring her with their attentions. It
was not unfairly that she had been given the name The
Barre Diamond. As James remarked caustically, the diamond was the most valuable of all gems, the hardest of all
substances, and had two obtuse and two acute angles.

"Does that not fit my ice-hearted lady?" he asked sorrowfully.

James had proposed many times to Mavreen. Not unkindly, she laughed off the seriousness of his offer of marriage, reminding him that she was perfectly content to remain a widow and that he must find himself someone a deal more worthy of him for a wife. Anne puzzled privately why Mavreen did not add the ardent James to her long list of lovers. She was comforted by the thought that Mavreen, bitter though she was, still had heart enough not to hurt so good a friend and faithful a suitor. She had promised James that this very afternoon when she finally succeeded in securing an hour alone with Mavreen, she would press his suit.

She looked at her friend and sighed. Mavreen in her twenties was far lovelier than she had been as a young girl. Love, suffering, and motherhood had all contributed to her haunting beauty. Because it was fashionable to wear the chignon halfway up the back of the head, Mavreen placed hers, a smaller, neater version, nearly on top of her head, her own dark gold curls hanging over her forehead. The effect was at the same time regal and abandoned. Her figure remained perfect, full-breasted but with tiny waist and softly rounded hips. Only occasionally her expression seemed to deny the bright vivacious sparkle of her green eyes and the provocativeness of her speech, making her look vulnerable, hurt, sad, to those who cared to glance more deeply.

"Mavreen, please be serious for a little while, I pray you," Anne begged her now. "It is not only for your sake I speak but for little Tamarisk's, too. She is almost five years old and it will not be long before she is old enough to be hurt by gossip."

Just for an instant, Mavreen's face took on an expression of concern. Then she laughed gaily and tossing her head, said, "My dear Anne, did you not know that Tamarisk is the Princess Charlotte's very best friend? What better company could she keep than that of the king's granddaughter? Perhaps Charlotte will be queen of England one day."

Anne shook her head.

"One cannot depend upon the friendship of royalty," she said thoughtfully, "more particularly when the members of the family are so at odds with one another.

"Oh, Mavreen!" Anne cried. "Let us not talk now of the rights and wrongs of the royal family. It is of your future I wish to talk. Despite all you say, I know that you are not happy although you try to convince the world otherwise. I know, as does James, that you still grieve for Gerard and suffer for his desertion. But you must see that you can never find happiness, however slight, in your present mode of life. Why will you not marry James? You know that he loves you dearly, that he is willing to overlook all your scandalous behavior and help you back to a place of respect in society. He is deeply attached to Tamarisk and would make her an excellent father. Why do you refuse him?"

"Because I don't love him—nor ever will!" Mavreen replied quietly. With sudden tenderness, she put out a hand and stroked Anne's hair.

"You must know how fond I am of James, Anne," she said. "And I know full well that he loves me and I'm honored and grateful that he does. But I have nothing to give him. I *am* nothing!" Her face suddenly contorted with pain, she struck her breast and cried out, "There is nothing in here, Anne—no heart, no feeling, no love. I am empty—a crustacean without its shell. I walk, eat, talk, think, but I do not feel except with my mind. In there I can still receive pain and pleasure. I hear an accent that reminds me of Gerard and I suffer. I give some worthless lover his congé and I know pleasure because this time it is a man and not I who suffers. They call me The Barre Diamond but I am not hardhearted, Anne. It is simply that I have no heart!"

Anne jumped to her feet and embraced her friend.

"It is not true, Mavreen. If 'twere true, you would not feel the need to protect James from yourself, as you have just described. You do feel—enough to care about him. And that is enough for him. He has sworn it. Dear Aunt Clarrie agrees with me in this. You should marry James, Mavreen, and settle down. Perhaps, in time, you will be blessed with a brother or sister for Tamarisk. There are so many advantages. Nothing will convince me that you prefer to continue as you are!"

Gently, Mavreen detached herself from Anne's arms. She walked across the room and looked out of the windows into the garden where she had once walked with Gilbert. Suddenly, her eyes filled with tears. She was glad that he had not lived to see her future. He had loved her deeply and unselfishly and she could not have concealed from him her total commitment to Gerard. But total commitment had not been enough. In the end, Gerard had denied her in the name of duty, family, honor. His wife and son, his mother, his estates, were more important to him than love.

For a few weeks, when Gerard failed to keep their tryst that first March, she convinced herself that his reasons for not keeping his vow though still unknown to her, must yet be valid. It was possible he believed her dead, possible he himself was ill, possible his mother, wife, child, were on the point of death. Unable to accept the truth, she found a hundred such excuses. But Clarissa's letter had destroyed those last illusions.

"I never want to hear his name mentioned again!" she had told Clarissa on her return to London. "This is not the first time Gerard has run away. I despise him. I despise all men. They do not understand the meaning of love."

Nevertheless, James's steadfast devotion despite all she had done to discourage and deter him forced her to realize that all men were not as Gerard. James was gentle, like his sister; kind, tolerant, adoring. He was far from unattractive, ash blond like his sister and with the same violet blue eyes. Anne declared he hid a passionate nature beneath his bonhomie. Tamarisk was fond of him and many times she demanded of Mavreen to know why she could not have a father to pet and spoil her as did other little girls.

"I will talk the matter over with James!" Mavreen said. "I am still not convinced that it would be right—for him or for me. But I will discuss it with him. Will that satisfy you, my sweet Anne?"

In the autumn of 1804, Mavreen, Lady Barre, became

Mrs. James Pettigrew. To accommodate James's parents, who were too old and frail to undertake the journey to London, she and James were married in the church of the village in Buckinghamshire where the Pettigrews had their family seat. Anne, now the mother of a second son, Thomas, was out of the enforced retirement of pregnancy and was matron of honor. Little Tamarisk and Anne's three-year-old daughter, Emma, both dressed in violet-sprigged muslin, were bridesmaids; Harry, Anne's five-year-old son, was the only page. The Prince of Wales had generously offered his daughter as a bridesmaid, but the king who now had guardianship of his granddaughter would not allow it. Word of the notorious Lady Barre's escapades had found his ear and he was not inclined to do her any favor.

The wedding was relatively quiet, attended by Sir John, the Pettigrews and their neighbors, and, because Mavreen had made it a condition of her marriage, Aunt Clarrie, who was passed off as an old family friend.

Sir John watched the bride and groom walk down the aisle of the little stone church. Mavreen, looking lovely, was dressed as befitted the occasion. Her pale blue satin gown, ruched and lace-trimmed, was covered by a darker blue pelisse against the chill of the day. Sir John gave Clarissa, who looked upon the point of tears, an encouraging smile.

"Tush, now, my sweeting!" he whispered. "The boy will see to it she has a clutch of chicks before long and that'll keep her out of mischief. Mark my words, Clarrie, this is going to be a good marriage."

He could not understand why his beloved Clarissa should choose that moment to break into a storm of tears.

CHAPTER THIRTY
1804-1805

James agreed that they should not spend the first four weeks of married life travelling, as was the custom. He fell in readily with Mavreen's suggestion that their honeymoon should be spent settling into their Queen Anne house, Finchcocks, near the village of Kingston. He had allowed her complete freedom to refurbish the house as she wished, to arrange the staffing and the accommodation as she desired. He, himself, would remain away from Finchcocks until all the work was completed and be happy not to see it again until he took her to live there after their wedding. Such matters as staff and décor were unimportant to him, he assured her. Nothing mattered but that she was to become his wife.

Leaving only a married footman and his wife to caretake at Barre House, Mavreen closed up her London home and removed all the servants to Finchcocks. Most of them were the same staff as had been originally in Gilbert's service and apart from a footman and maid, Mavreen engaged no one new with the exception of the six gardeners employed by the previous owners.

Fires had been lit in all the rooms, for the September evenings were cool. The last rays of the sun poured through the windows setting the high ceilinged drawing-room aglow with golden light. Great vases of white, yellow and bronze chrysanthemums gave bright splashes of color to the delicate egg-shell blue of the walls and white, Chinese-patterned carpet. The furniture, imported a half century before, was made by Gilles Joubert, cabinetmaker to Louis XV.

Mavreen turned to look at James's face.

"Do you like my arrangements?" she asked, smiling.

James nodded, although his glance around the newly decorated room was but cursory and his eyes were upon his bride as he replied,

"Quite beautiful! But I never expected otherwise!"

"You must not flatter me too often, James!" Mavreen said, moving imperceptibly away from his side. "I fear I shall become of high conceit if you find no fault with me! Come, let me take you upstairs. Our evening meal will be prepared in half an hour and we have yet to change our clothes!"

James followed Mavreen up the wide, curving staircase. Intuitively, she knew that he was watching her movements and tried to overcome her increasing apprehension. It was, she told herself, the most ridiculous of sentiments to dread her wedding night—and she no virgin bride but a woman of experience. Man's desire was known to her in all its variations. But now that the hour was fast approaching when she must allow James to her bed and submit to his long-awaited possession of her body, she had begun to realize how greatly she dreaded the occasion.

Not for her, this time, the amused detachment with which she had permitted her lovers to seduce her, no cruel pretence that they were irresistible followed by the even crueler yawn of boredom when, at the moment of triumph, they looked in vain for her admiration and approval. She must not hurt James, who so adored her. Somehow she must submit. But she knew that she might all too easily fail. Her heart, like her body, craved only the touch of Gerard's lips, Gerard's hands, Gerard's love.

James, already hurt to discover that Mavreen had arranged separate bedchambers for them, albeit communicating, knocked upon the dividing door. Rose was helping her into the underfrock of the new tunic dress she had selected to wear for dinner. She bade him enter. Rose slipped the loosely hanging lace-frilled tunic over her shoulders.

"I am almost ready!" Mavreen said, smiling at him as she sat down at her dressing table so that Rose could more easily fasten the jeweled bandeau in her hair. "How elegant you look, James!"

His face, fair skinned, flushed with pleasure at her compliment. He wore a claret-colored coat with a high standing velvet collar and bright gilt buttons, beneath which was a quilted waistcoat. Claret-colored slippers with gilt buckles completed his outfit. His fair hair, curly and disheveled as was the fashion, gave him a youthful appearance that accentuated the vulnerable appeal in his eyes.

Strangely moved, Mavreen stood up and gently kissed James's cheek.

"There now, I am ready to go downstairs!" she said, linking her arm in his.

As the many courses of the meal were served and with each one, a different wine, James's cheeks flushed a dark red and he frequently laughed as his excitement steadily increased. His shyness vanished as he surveyed his beautiful new wife across the candle-lit table. He had loved her with a hopeless passion for many years, but never really believed that she would one day become his wife. He would, he told himself, be forever grateful to his sister, Anne, for helping to persuade Mavreen that her happiness would be well-guarded in his hands. It mattered little that she did not love him in return. He felt confident that once she became his wife, she would learn to love him. He convinced himself that the many lovers she had had were men of questionable character who had taken advantage of her position as a lone and wealthy widow and of her unhappy frame of mind following the desertion of that blackguard, Gerard de Valle. He forgot his former affection for the vicomte and told himself that he, like Mavreen, must have been mad to trust a Frenchie. Mavreen's declaration that she, alone, was responsible for her immoral way of life did not convince him. All that would be changed now that she was his wife. He would arouse her love by the very strength of his own. He had no doubt of it.

But the combination of excitement and the wine he had consumed made James's approach hurried and insensitive. No sooner had Rose left Mavreen's bedchamber when he strode into the room. Hurriedly he divested himself of his nightgown and slippers and climbed eagerly into the big four-poster bed beside her. In silence he pulled her gown over her head and stretched himself full-length upon her naked body.

"At last, at last!" he muttered. "I thought that girl would never go!"

Had he shown his usual gentle consideration for her he might have touched the maternal core in Mavreen's heart within their marital bed as surely as he could outside it.

"Oh, James, will you not at least extinguish the candles!" Mavreen begged, for the sight of his flushed face and moist lips was suddenly abhorrent to her, as was the touch of his hot hands upon her flesh.

"A pox upon the candles!" James expostulated with a quite uncharacteristic disregard for her feelings. "You have no need to pretend modesty with me, my sweeting."

The allusion to her past sent a chill through Mavreen's already-reluctant body. She knew exactly what was in James's mind—that far from being delicately innocent, she should know enough to make their wedding night a memorable one for him.

"James—" she pleaded. "James—let us not hurry. Can we not talk a while first?" She craved the opportunity to collect herself, to reestablish in her mind the wish to please him, to overcome her resistance to his advances.

"Talk?" he cried. "What need is there for talk? I wish no words except to hear you say you love me, for in truth, I love you, my beautiful bride. I desire you as I have desired no other woman. Now, at last, you are mine!"

And without further preamble, he forced himself into her, his cry of pleasure drowning her quiet gasp of dismay. Closing her eyes, she gritted her teeth as he rode her triumphantly to his victory. Tears stung her eyes, and rolled down her cheeks. She tasted their salt on her bruised lips. When he shifted his weight from her body and rolled onto his side, she was free to brush the tears away. But she did not do so quickly enough. Beside her, James said, "Weeping? How can it be so? Did I not pleasure you? Tell me why you cry?"

"I am not weeping, James!" she lied, but her voice

trembled. Released from the all-consuming urgency of desire, James was once more the lover. He reached out a hand and touched a last tear on her cheek.

"You are unhappy!" he cried, propping himself upon one elbow the better to see her face. "Whilst I believed myself the happiest man in the world!" His voice unknowingly held a note of accusation. "Did I disappoint you as a lover?"

"No, James, I swear you did not!" Mavreen forced the untruth through her lips. "Say no more, I pray you. All women are emotional on their wedding night. It is nothing, I promise you."

"You lie!" he said quietly. "Women are happy to be bedded by the men they love. You weep because you do not love me!"

Desperately, Mavreen sought words to convince him.

"I would not have wed you, James, had I not loved you!" she said. "It is only that the day has been long and eventful and I am much fatigued." She leaned over and kissed his cheek. James gripped her arms in a sudden fierce grasp.

"That was no lover's kiss!" he said. "I am your husband now, Mavreen—not your brother. Kiss me once more—as once you kissed your French lover, Gerard!"

Every nerve in Mavreen's body froze at the sound of his name. Helplessly, she stared into James's accusing eyes, knowing that he asked the impossible.

Her voice so quiet as to be almost inaudible, she said, "You gave me your word, James, that the past would be forgotten, that you wanted no more from me than that I should become your wife!"

He stared back at her, his face distorted.

"I did not know that my husbandly attentions would be met with tears of regret for your lost lover!" he said bitterly. "It is you, not I, who fail to put the past behind us!"

"Oh, James!" Mavreen protested, "you must surely know that love is never the slave of one's will. I do not deny that I cannot entirely erase Gerard's memory. You knew this truth when we exchanged our vows today, but with your help, that memory will diminish in time. I meant each one of the promises I made to you in church. I will be a good and loving wife to you, but you must not ask more of me than I can give. I beg you, James, that you should not entertain such jealousies now, on our wedding night. Let us try and be happy together!"

James's eyes narrowed.

"I was happy enough!" he said reproachfully. "I most certainly have no wish to be reminded of that blackguard's name, nor that his memory is more important to you than our loving. Was he so good a lover, then, that you cannot forget him?"

Mavreen put her hand quickly over James's mouth.

"I will not allow you to feed your jealousy with such thoughts," she said determinedly. "I am your wife now, James. If you love me as you have so often sworn, then cease this conversation now!"

James, blazing with jealous anger a moment before, now was perplexed. He knew that his outburst had been contrary to the promise he had made her not to demand love. In fairness to her, he was prepared to accept the blame, if such there was, for the rift in their relationship. His confusion was the greater for the realization that it was not Mavreen he failed to understand, but himself. In the very moment of his ultimate possession of her, he had discovered that though her body had accepted his without restraint, there had been no answering passion, that he had not really possessed her, the woman, at all.

His jealousy and the violence of it frightened him. Her softly spoken unemotional replies, far from quietening him, made him perversely eager to arouse anger in her, preferring that to the coldness of her logic. He was no longer master of himself, far less of her.

Yet he loved her! Her very strength of character wellknown to him over the years since he had first met her, was a challenge and commanded his respect. He longed to dominate her yet feared that he might not be able to do so.

He had convinced himself that once they were married, he, as husband, would naturally assume the dominant role. He had the right now to command her obedience, but he knew only too well that he could not command her love.

"Tell me!" he said, his eyes now soft and appealing. "Tell me how to make you love me, my Mavreen!"

"Oh, James, I do love you, I do!" Mavreen cried, the stiffness of her body now melting with desire to comfort him. He looked so young and vulnerable. "Only be patient and you will see how happy a life we will make together. It is the future that matters, James!"

She kissed him as she knew he wanted to be kissed. At once, his body hardened and he drew her against him in a second surge of desire. Mavreen fought against her own body's instinctive resistance. Now it was James, anxious to please her, who blew out the candles. In the darkness, it was easier for her to simulate a passion she did not feel. This time, James seemed content with her responses. But later, when he had at last left her to go to his own bedchamber, she lay alone in the crumpled bed, feeling relief at the privacy at last regained, but terrified that James might not be so easily be convinced next time.

Before their marriage she had told him clearly she did not love him. He had shrugged off her declaration.

"It matters not!" he had sworn. "You shall draw up the marriage contract yourself, Mavreen. So long as you will agree to become my wife, nothing else is of importance to me."

But nonetheless it had mattered a great deal.

Now, lying in the darkness of her new bedchamber, she was appalled by her stupidity. Never with the lovers she had allowed to her bed for an hour or two's distraction, had she felt such a sense of wrongdoing as now pervaded her whole being. The men to whom she had given her favors were men she had despised—for the most part court fops, of good breeding but minimal intelligence; vain, egotistical, but occasionally amusing and well able to protect themselves in the game of love. They courted her because she was beautiful and famous. It was, indeed, a sport among them to see who would succeed in melting the heart of The Barre Diamond. She had always been in complete control of them. The humiliations she enforced upon them seemed to spur them to greater efforts.

Her very last intention was to humiliate James. But she was deeply disturbed to discover that the man she had married was capable of violent passions and jealousy. In this he had deceived her. Gerard's name had not been mentioned between them for several years. Mavreen supposed that Anne had told him the facts and that James accepted Gerard had no place in her life. Yet somehow, her love for Gerard must have remained in James' mind as steadfastly as in her own. His reference to her "French lover" revived all the memories of Gerard she had tried so hard to subdue. Eyes closed, his image returned to her mind in the smallest detail. She felt a terrible sense of loss and pain as the hardness of the shell around her heart crumbled.

Unable now to weep, Mavreen accepted the fact forced upon her consciousness, that she still loved Gerard, would always love him, no matter how cruelly he treated her. These last years had been pointless; hurting other men had never lessened the hurt of losing Gerard. At long last, she was able to face the truth.

This, her wedding night, had revealed all too clearly how heavy a cross she had fashioned for herself to bear. She must never again think of Gerard, remember him, allow herself the bittersweet luxury of loving him. With James' help, the past must be forgotten and her affection for her husband fostered until it grew to a different kind of loving. She had only to acquire his understanding for their marriage to succeed.

She had yet to discover that James's heart ruled his head.

The following morning, she quietly discussed the matter with him. He, seemingly once more his quiet, reasonable self, agreed that no reference would ever again be made to Gerard; the past was to be forgotten, but he was not able to keep his promise in the privacy of their bedchamber. There, he took on the guise of another man, passion ousting all reason as he attempted again and again by his physical domination of Mavreen, to force her to surrender her heart. As often as he tried, Mavreen sought in calmer moments to explain that she gave him all that she could; that if it was in her power, she would give him her heart, too.

"How can you go on loving a man who has deserted you so cruelly?" James stormed, his blue eyes blazing, his face distorted with jealousy. "Are you not humiliated? Do you place no value on the man who really loves you?"

"Dearest James, you know that I value you most truly, that I have the deepest affection for you. Is that not enough? If I can put Gerard from my thoughts, does that not prove my devotion to you and my desire to make you happy?"

But it did not, and as the months passed, James became increasingly silent and taciturn whenever another man spoke to Mavreen. If only Mavreen loved him as he loved her, how happy he might be with his new family. Not for the first time, he wondered if she would become more submissive if she were to bear him a son or daughter. They had now been married nearly a year and there was no sign that she was with child. Mavreen had explained to him that all had not been straightforward at Tamarisk's birth, that Mother Sale, who attended her at the time, had warned her that she might have difficulty conceiving another child. Nevertheless, James longed for one, not because he was in any real sense paternal, nor even strongly wished for a son and heir, but because he felt such an event would surely bind Mavreen closer to him.

His envy of Gerard de Valle was in direct proportion to his now-obsessive love for his beautiful wife. He did not appreciate that it was he, rather than Mavreen, who made Gerard so frequently a topic of their conversation and such a bone of contention between them.

He was delighted when the uneasy Treaty of Amiens collapsed and war against France was renewed. He frequently toyed with the idea of joining the army so that he could go and do battle with the enemy. Since Gerard was fighting in Napoleon's army, James daydreamed of coming face to face with him in combat and putting a sword through his heart.

But overriding his desire to kill Gerard was his reluctance to leave Mavreen's side. Since their marriage, he found no peace of mind unless his wife were within sight or sound.

James was not entirely lacking in patriotism. After the kidnapping and murder of the duc d'Enghien in March last year, he was as convinced as any other Englishman that Napoleon, the Jacobin, was not a gentleman and in all probability was mad. He read the *Times* and agreed with Sir Robert Wilson's description of the French general as "a man of Machiavellian principles exulting in bloodshed."

The renewal of hostilities by the English seemed to James to be more than amply justified. It was common knowledge that the French general intended his country's aggrandisement in India, a threat to England which could not be discounted. Moreover, England deeply resented the exclusion by Napoleon of English ships and goods from French ports and the establishment of a French garrison in Holland. She had every reason to fear Napoleon's designs in the Western hemisphere as much as his growing popularity in the East.

Nor was James lacking in sympathy for the comte d'Artois, Auguste Polignac and for their friends who had plotted to kill Napoleon.

He continued to lead the leisurely life of a country gentleman, passing the time at cards or billiards, at dinner parties or in pursuit of some outdoor sport. He particularly enjoyed the Scottish game of golf and frequently played at Blackheath. But he was never far away from Mavreen. His possessiveness, silent but potent for remaining unvoiced, began to tell on Mavreen's nerves. Her first doubt as to the outcome of her marriage to James had grown into a reluctant certainty that she would never be able to make him happy or find happiness herself in their union. She could say nothing to Anne, whose first loyalty was to her brother, but to Clarissa she confessed her desperate misgivings and her feeling of imprisonment.

"It is not that James places any curtailment of a physical kind upon my movements!" she said on one cold afternoon in January of 1805 when they were closeted together in the warm, cosy salon in Orchid House. "James made no demur when I told him I would be calling upon

you today. But I shall pay the price of my freedom later,
Aunt Clarrie. Tonight, when I return, he will question me
endlessly—oh, not directly but deviously. He will ask me
this and that, pretending he really does have an interest
in our pursuits, his face innocent and smiling. But all the
while, he will be seeking to trap me."

Clarissa frowned uncomprehendingly. She was now
fifty-three years old; some of the bright blue of her eyes
had faded and there were new folds of flesh about her
face and chin and lines about her mouth. Always plump,
Clarissa had filled out to rotund, matronly proportions
and her dark hair had become quite grey. Nevertheless,
she had lost none of her gentle, kindly disposition nor
sweetness of nature. She was deeply distressed by this
revelation of Mavreen's unhappiness, for she loved her as
much as if she were really her mother.

"In what manner do you speak, child?" she asked. "Why
should James seek to trap you? I do not take your meaning."

"Because he does not trust me!" Mavreen said sadly.
"He is jealous to the point of insanity. He will be wondering even now if I have gone to meet some unknown
admirer. When I return home, he will fire questions at me
one upon the other with such rapidity that were I giving
false answers, I would most certainly be caught. Or else he
will await a moment when he imagines me to be unguarded and then ask a question of me so unexpectedly
that were I not innocent, I would be unable to avoid an
admission of the truth. It is as if I am in the dock and
James the prosecutor is attempting to extract a confession.
Yet all is done quietly as if he were but making casual
conversation and showing no more than a husbandly interest in my activities."

Mavreen sighed.

"What is so tragic, Aunt Clarrie, is that whilst he seeks
to catch me unaware, no one would suffer more than
James were he to hear me falter. He would, if 'twere
possible, drag a confession from me and then endure untold agony of mind for the hearing of it."

Clarissa stared at Mavreen in disbelief.

"What you tell me sounds so unlike James I can scarce

believe my ears!" she said. "You have given him no cause
for mistrust?"

Mavreen gave a slow, sad smile.

"Since I married him, none whatever!" she replied.
"But James knows my past and he can live with Gerard's
memory even less easily than I."

Not even to Clarissa could she describe the dread she
now felt when James knocked upon the door of her bedchamber and she knew she must try once more to make
him welcome. Despite his protestations, she insisted upon
maintaining the privacy of her own bedchamber in place
of the nuptial room he desired, pleading insomnia brought
about by James's snores. But her conscience would not
permit her to deny him ready access to her room and
her body. When he approached her, she would find her
hands clenching into fists and her teeth clamping so tightly together that her jaw ached with tension. His demands
were little short of an assault upon her. She endured them
silently dreading even more his remorse which inevitably
followed the assuagement of his desires.

"Forgive me, forgive me!" he would cry, near to tears.
"I love you so much, Mavreen. Say that you love me.
Swear it! Swear you will never leave me!" He would continue in such a vein until to end his self-torture she would
feign sleep, and then only would he leave her bed and,
sighing heavily, return to his own room.

She felt culpable, responsible. Yet there was little she
could do. Determinedly, she guarded both her tongue and
her temper and tried never to raise her voice in anger, no
matter how greatly his inquisitions irritated her. There
were times, she now told Clarissa, when she felt tempted
to give James reason for his suspicion, not because she
had any desire herself to be unfaithful to him but so that
his accusations would at least seem more fairly leveled
against her.

" 'Twould be better for him had he more to occupy his
mind!" Clarissa said wisely.

Mavreen nodded, looking suddenly happier.

"I must have given some such indication to Mr. Pitt
because a week ago Lord Harrowby, the foreign secretary,
offered James the post of chargé d'affaires in Vienna,"

she said. "I have been begging him to accept, and have promised him that Tamarisk and I will accompany him there. Unfortunately, with the threat of invasion still hanging over our heads James is fearful of the dangers attending such a journey at the present time. He may yet refuse the post on this account."

"Could he not go to Vienna and wait for you and the child to follow when it is safe to do so?" Clarissa inquired.

Mavreen sighed.

"You do not take account of James's possessiveness. It is such that he will not easily be persuaded to leave my side. Indeed, I fear he will positively refuse to go if I cannot accompany him."

Clarissa heard the note of despair in Mavreen's voice and patted her arm soothingly.

"Leave this with me, my sweeting!" she said. "I will speak with your father on the matter. He has much influence with James and mayhap he will have a word or two with him. That is, of course, if you assure me that you, yourself, would like to go to Vienna."

Mavreen's face flushed with excitement.

"Indeed I would! Herr Mehler tells me it is the center of great artistic activity. And the people are gay, charming and friendly."

Clarissa smiled.

"How is the poor dear man?" she enquired. "The last time I saw him at the opera he looked more like a plucked turkey than ever!"

Mavreen, too, laughed, though not unkindly.

"He still blushes when I speak to him and nearly was overcome with pleasure when I said I would engage him to teach Tamarisk to play the pianoforte if we should return to London to live. He was very excited to learn that I might be going to Vienna, most especially because Ludwig von Beethoven lives there now and so does Franz Joseph Haydn."

Mavreen's eyes sparkled.

"I have had to promise Herr Mehler that I will go to visit St. Mark's church yard. His favorite composer, Mozart, is buried there. It seems he died fourteen years ago in great poverty. None of his friends attended his funeral and when his widow tried to find out where he was buried, all she could discover from a grave digger was that he had been put in a common grave with a number of others.

"You will have much to distract you, then," Clarissa said. "We must see what your father can do to ensure that you get to Vienna. Now, tell me, child, does Mr. Pitt consider there is still likelihood of our island being invaded by that horrible Bonaparte?"

Mavreen shook her head.

"Far from it, Aunt Clarrie. 'Tis true Napoleon still has an army of two hundred and ten thousand men gathered in great camps along the North Sea and the Channel coast. But they have been there these past two years and, as you well know, it is we who are master of the seas. Mr. Pitt says Napoleon cannot concentrate in the Channel a fleet sufficiently strong to protect the transport and disembarkation of even a small part of his troops. It seems unlikely we shall have to set light to the warning beacons on the Downs."

"Your father tells me our English sailors are enduring all manner of hardship keeping vigil in the Channel," Clarissa commented. "I understand that they live on moldy biscuit or salt pork and must remain at sea in all weathers, fair or foul!"

" 'Tis true!" Mavreen agreed. "But have no fear, Aunt Clarrie. The great Napoleon Bonaparte is not always so clever. He is actually said to believe that our people are so downtrodden that they would welcome his armies were they to land on our shores to liberate them from the 'tyrannous yoke' of our poor King George! 'Tis hard to credit, is it not, that so brilliant a general who has subdued and conquered so much of Europe, could be so misinformed about our country."

Clarissa smiled.

"Mayhap we should invite him to visit our downlands and the hopfields of Kent so that he can see for himself the welcome he can expect if ever he manages to cross the seas!" she commented. "I, for one, would not care to encounter dear Farmer Sale brandishing his pitchfork were I a Frenchman!"

Mavreen, too, laughed.

"I must admit to feeling some sympathy with the poor Prince of Wales. You know how anxious he was to prove himself worthy of the promotion in the army that the king still denies him. For his regiment, the 10th Dragoons, to be withdrawn from the Sussex coast and sent to Guildford when invasion seemed imminent was indeed a humiliation from which he has yet not recovered. It was, of course, the intention of the king himself to command the defending army. But I sympathize with the prince when he said, 'It little becomes me, who am the first and who stand at the very footstool of the throne to remain a tame, an idle, a lifeless spectator of the mischief which threatens us. . . .' Do you not also feel a little sympathy for him, Aunt Clarrie?"

Clarissa sighed.

"I am not inclined to feel sympathy for any of the royal family!" she said. " 'Twould seem to me that they are quite incapable of living at peace with one another. I have tried to make allowances for the king because of his illness but if one is to believe but half the rumors, he is behaving in the most shocking manner—making improper suggestions to respectable ladies at his court; buying fish at the market and talking in loud, lewd manner to the fishwives; frightening the poor queen and the princesses. And now he has become so friendly with the Princess Caroline, yet his behavior at Blackheath is indiscreet to say the very least. Your father says she is a coarse and vulgar creature without morals or sensitivity."

"But what is the news of my father? I have not seen him these past three weeks. Is he well?"

Clarissa's face softened as it always did when she spoke of Sir John. Watching her, Mavreen found herself hoping, not for the first time, that the sickly Lady Danesfield might one day die, leaving her father free to marry Aunt Clarrie. Druscilla Danesfield was now retired altogether from society and was living in Yorkshire in her late father's house. Her constant ill-health afforded her the excuse she needed to withdraw from her place at Sir John's side and he had readily agreed to her proposal to live in quiet retirement in the north. He had also given his consent for his elder daughter, Prudence, to enter the convent nearby where Druscilla had once lived so contentedly, and take her vows as a novice. He expressed the opinion to Clarissa that when her mother died Selina would follow her sister there, but meanwhile she remained beside her mother to give her company.

The absence of his family left Sir John with the freedom he enjoyed; and most of it was spent with Clarissa. Her lasting contentment was marred only by her concern for Mavreen whom she loved, indeed, as a child of her own. She was grievously distressed when Mavreen embarked upon a way of life that could bring her no real happiness; deriving the bittersweet rewards of hurting others as she herself was hurt. With relief, she watched the end of this phase when Mavreen married James. Clarissa's hopes were high when the young couple made a start in the lovely Queen Anne house in Kingston. But that, it now appeared, had brought Mavreen little joy and a very different cross to bear. She felt herself responsible in having encouraged Mavreen to wed James. She had betrayed her own principles in persuading Mavreen into the marriage, although at the time, it had seemed the only way of restoring Mavreen to a happier way of life. Love was not generally regarded as a prerequisite for a successful marriage. Her friend, Lisa von Eburhard felt that the notorious Lady Barre had done very well for herself in securing the young Pettigrew heir for a second husband. Sir John agreed with the baroness. But Clarissa was not convinced before the marriage, and less so than ever now that Mavreen had described her unhappy state.

"Will you not stay to see your father, my dear?" she asked Mavreen, as she rose to her feet.

"I regret that I cannot on this occasion," Mavreen replied. "I promised James I would be home no later than five of the clock and Dickon will be hard-pressed now to drive me back by then. Would you pull the bell rope, dearest Aunt Clarrie? I must truly make haste."

Her visit to Clarissa had a soothing effect upon Mavreen's nerves. Later that evening, she was able to reply quietly and without too much irritation to James's many questions; and later still, to receive him to her bed with reasonably well-simulated pleasure.

As always, the moment James departed to his own bedchamber and she was alone, Mavreen's thoughts winged their way back through the years to the man she loved.

CHAPTER THIRTY-ONE
1805

Sir John Danesfield was successful in persuading James to accept the position of chargé d'affaires in Vienna. He had pointed out to James that since he was not rendering his country assistance in a military capacity, he could contribute his services very ably as a diplomatic agent, albeit of minor importance.

The fact that invasion by Napoleon's coastal army now seemed most improbable, tipped the scales of James's indecision. His mind made up, he had become quite enthusiastic about the prospect of traveling to a new country.

Had Mavreen been traveling with him, he would have embarked for the continent even more eagerly. As it was, he needed endless promises from her—even to the point of making her vow upon the Sacred Book—that she would follow him as soon as it was considered safe to do so. She was prepared to go now, but without Tamarisk, if James would agree.

But much as he desired her with him, James would not permit her to put her life at risk. Until they could be sure of Napoleon's intentions, James ordered Mavreen to remain at home. By home, James meant Finchcocks. But to Mavreen it meant Sussex. She had not visited there since the spring of 1800, afraid that her torn heart could not withstand the memories. Now she found herself longing to go there, taking Tamarisk with her.

But such a visit was not to be. Barely a week after James's departure, she received a letter from the vicomtesse de Valle. Such were its contents that Mavreen's personal plans were at once put aside. She summoned Dickon and informed him that they would be leaving for France and Compiègne within two days. He knew, without being told, that this venture must concern the vicomte, but it was not, alas, good news Mavreen gave him.

"The vicomtesse is gravely ill!" she said. "Her physician does not think it likely she can live beyond the end of the year. Gerard is still away from home fighting somewhere and she has been unable to get word to him. She makes no mention of his wife but says she is quite alone and longs to see me and little Tamarisk. . . ."

Mavreen broke off as tears welled into her eyes. Until now, she had not realized that the vicomtesse had guessed Gerard was Tamarisk's father. Her faithful Dickon knew the truth, so unable to trust her voice, she handed him the last page of the letter.

I wish before I die to hold my only grandchild in my arms. It would be a great consolation to me to see Gerard's daughter since he, himself, cannot be with me. Therefore, I pray you, chère Mavreen, to bring her and yourself to Compiègne as speedily as is possible.

I have obtained through the kindly offices of General Bonaparte, safe conduct passes for you and your child. You may travel across France without fear of danger provided you keep with you at all times the documents I enclose with this letter.

I shall pray hourly that circumstances will not keep you from observing the dying wish of
> *Your most affectionate Friend,*
> *Marianne, vicomtesse de Valle.*

When, a week later, Mavreen entered the vicomtesse's bedchamber and saw the ravaged face of the once-beautiful woman lying in the big four-poster, she could see at once that Gerard's mother was dying. So thin was she that she resembled a skeleton with skin stretched over it. Only the eyes remained unchanged—huge, dark, penetrating, but luminous with happiness as Mavreen went forward to embrace her.

"My dear child!" she whispered, "I had no doubt that you would come." She looked at Mavreen lovingly as she added, "You who once travelled in the midst of war alone with your Dickon, would have no fear of travelling with the permission of Napoleon!"

Mavreen drew up a chair and sat beside the bed, holding the Vicomtesse's thin hand between her own strong warm ones as if trying to pass some of her own life and vigor into the sick woman's body.

"I would have come long ago if you had invited me," she said simply. "And now that I am here, I shall stay as long as you wish!"

The vicomtesse smiled.

"You have not changed, Mavreen, although I do detect that you have not passed these last years since we met quite unscathed, my child."

"A child no longer!" Mavreen remarked. "I am twenty-five years of age, madame, with a daughter who approaches her seventh birthday!"

A look of deep satisfaction crossed the vicomtesse's face.

"You shall present her to me shortly!" she said. "But first I wish to talk with you, my dear. The last time I saw you, you were in boy's habit. It is hard to believe the elegant and very beautiful woman sitting beside me is my little Mavreen!"

"I have a present for you, madame, a shawl made in Norwich of silk and wool with Kashmir pattern. It should keep you warm whilst you are abed!"

"That was kind of you, my dear!" the vicomtesse said, as Mavreen wrapped the delicate shawl around her frail shoulders.

From the shadows of the far corner of the room, a nun stepped forward to settle her patient more comfortably against the pillows.

"This is Sister Marie Thérèse," the vicomtesse said. "She is one of my two most devoted nurses!"

The tiny rotund figure in voluminous white habit, smiled at Mavreen.

"Madame la vicomtesse has been most impatient for your arrival!" she murmured. "I am so very happy for her that you could come."

"And I that madame has you to care for her!" Mavreen replied.

The little nun wiped her patient's forehead with a cloth dipped in lavender water, after which ministrations the vicomtesse dismissed her.

"Now we can talk in privacy," she said to Mavreen. "Sit here beside me, my dear, and reassure me that these past few years have not been too unhappy for you."

While Tamarisk played happily with Dickon and Rose in the garden of the Château de Boulancourt, Mavreen and the vicomtesse slipped without difficulty into their former close relationship. Mavreen spoke freely of her undying love for Gerard, although for the vicomtesse's peace of mind she minimized the pain she had suffered at his hands. She gave only the vaguest outline of her years spent in the vain attempt to lessen that pain, and of her mistaken marriage.

The vicomtesse listened in silence, her eyes sad and filled with dismay.

"Then you do not know that Gerard remained as faithful to your memory as you have been to his?" she said. "He believed you dead, Mavreen, drowned, as were the remainder of the crew of the *Jeanne-Marie*. He was so informed by a sailor who witnessed the ship's sinking and saw no sign of your escape. Indeed, I, myself, knew nothing of your survival until a year later when the marquis de Guéridon called upon me and told me of your miraculous escape. By then Gerard had already taken up a commission in the army."

Mavreen jumped to her feet, her hands covering her flushed cheeks as the full import of the vicomtesse's words penetrated her mind.

"Then even now Gerard does not know I am alive?" she asked breathlessly.

The vicomtesse nodded.

A smile of purest joy crossed Mavreen's face. She flung herself down on her knees beside the sick woman's bed and pressed her lips to the frail hands on the coverlet.

"You have made me the happiest woman in the world!" she cried. "I believed Gerard had decided to put me entirely out of his life. If I had only known. . . ."

"You should have kept your faith in him," the vicomtesse broke in gently. "Your heart should have told you that Gerard would never have left you without word of explanation!"

"But he had become a father! I supposed him fully reconciled to his marriage."

The dying woman's face took on an expression of deep sadness.

"The baby—a boy—died a few weeks after his birth. He was born prematurely and there was never any real hope of his survival. I am afraid poor little Faustina was not strong enough for the ordeal of childbirth. She, in time, made a recovery, but the experience left her mentally affected. She cried ceaselessly for her mother and father and would not permit Gerard to come near her. You can imagine how deeply this wounded him. To his grief at your loss was added the loss of his baby son. Moreover, poor little Faustina blamed him for the suffering she had undergone and this distressed him deeply.

"It was cruel to blame Gerard!" Mavreen protested. "She must have known when she married him that children would result!"

The vicomtesse sighed.

"I am afraid Faustina was quite unprepared for the realities of marriage. Such matters had been kept from her throughout her tender years. Gerard did what he could to enlighten her. We both believed she would bear her pregnancy the better if she were not afraid of the coming birth. We assured her many times that such pain as she might suffer would not be unbearable; that a month or two after the baby was born she would feel perfectly well again. But we took no account of the fact that Faustina had never suffered pain of any kind. Her parents nurtured her too carefully and left her quite unprepared for life beyond the sheltered walls of her convent and her home. Her fear even more than her pain shattered her mind."

"And now—" Mavreen asked in a quiet voice. "What is become of her?"

"She is in the care of the nuns of the convent of St. Germain in Compiègne. There she is relatively happy. For a while I used to visit her every Sunday when I attended Mass. But her mind had become that of a child and although she was not afraid of me, I think she feared that I might bring Gerard with me, that between us, we would force her to return to her life here with us at the château. So I ceased my visits."

She regarded Mavreen with deepest seriousness.

"I am going to die!" she said softly, but her tone was resolute, brooking no denial from her listener. "I do not know how long I have left to live but I shall not rise from this bed again. I have therefore written to the Prince and Princess Monte-Gincinto to inform them that in Gerard's absence, Faustina will shortly have no guardian and that I feel it might be better for them to take their daughter home. We cannot be certain when Gerard will return— even if he still lives."

She pressed Mavreen's hand as if trying to instill in her a confidence she did not really have.

"I do not believe he is dead!" she said. "I believe that I shall see him again before I die. I pray for this constantly. You see, Mavreen, I need to ask his forgiveness—and yours, too."

"Forgiveness?" she echoed. "I do not understand!"

"Oh, Mavreen, when he came home last year on leave, I knew that you were alive. And I did not tell him! He believed you dead and it seemed to me that he was becoming reconciled to the fact that he must make his life without you. I had learned of your marriage to an English gentleman and supposed that you, too, had begun a new life without Gerard. I concluded that in the best interests of you both, I should stay silent. I know that if I had told Gerard you were in England, he would have gone at once to find you with who can say what heartbreaking consequences. I have thought so much about the matter and I now realize that Gerard was entitled to the truth and that the decision was his, not mine. Forgive me if I did wrong!"

Mavreen's hesitation was only momentary. The joy of knowing that Gerard still loved her, still wanted her, was followed by resentment that he had been prevented from coming at once to England, but deep in her heart, she knew that the vicomtesse had been right in her decision. Her marriage to James was difficult enough with only Gerard's memory as a bone of contention between them. If Gerard had been there in person, there was no knowing what might have resulted. James might possibly have provoked a duel and one or the other lost his life as a result.

"You acted wisely, madame!" she said, bending to kiss the parchment cheek. "Perhaps Gerard and I are destined never to find happiness together again."

The vicomtesse closed her eyes.

"Who can tell the ways of God?" she said. "At least you shared a few weeks of joy. And you have your child. How is your little daughter? Does she favor you?"

Mavreen's face relaxed into a smile.

"You shall see for yourself. Tamarisk is eagerly awaiting the opportunity to pay her respects to you." She drew in her breath and let it out again on a long sigh. "At birth, she greatly resembled Gerard. I hoped so much that she would continue so to do, but alas, each year she has become more and more my replica. Dickon, my manservant, who knew me at the same age, tells me Tamarisk and I, at her age, are as two peas in a pod. I regret it but perhaps for her sake and for that of others, it is as well she has lost all likeness to Gerard."

The vicomtesse smiled.

"Gerard himself would wish the child to resemble you!" she said. "As for me, your little Tamarisk is my granddaughter and for that alone I love her. After I have rested, you shall bring her to me." But when the child made her curtsy and kissed the frail old lady's hand, she looked joyfully at Mavreen and said too softly for Tamarisk to overhear, "You cannot believe how happy you have made me, my dear. Can you not see for yourself the resemblance to my darling husband? I see Antoine in every contour of her face, the coloring of her hair, the movements of her hands. Ah, Mavreen, I can die at peace with my God for He has truly sent me the greatest of blessings to ease my suffering."

It was the first time the vicomtesse had admitted to being in pain from the tumor that was slowly consuming her. Her physician came at regular intervals to give her fresh supplies of laudanum but nevertheless, there were hours in every day when nothing helped.

Understanding nothing of the illness from which the frail old lady suffered, the child ran about the room, playing with the many *objets d'art*, chattering happily and without shyness. Upon request, she would sing her little songs, dance to tunes in her head, arrange posies of flowers which she would lay upon the bed.

As the days became weeks, Mavreen found it increasingly difficult to ignore her nagging concern for James. She had left England without sending word to him of the alteration in her plan to sojourn in Sussex with Tamarisk. She had no deliberate intention to deceive him but at the same time, she realized that he would bitterly oppose her desire to be with Gerard's mother; that he might convince himself she had encouraged him to go to Austria in order to be free to go to France in search of Gerard. She knew him capable of such irrationalities and how easily he might be deterred from devoting himself to his duties as chargé d'affaires, but with no letters arriving at the château from England, she could not be certain if, after so long, James had written to instruct her to join him in Vienna and was even now awaiting her arrival.

She was loath to leave the vicomtesse without good reason. Moreover, there was always the possibility that Gerard might yet come home. Word had been sent to the officer commanding the army of the Rhine as it marched southeast toward Ulm, requesting that Gerard be given compassionate leave and sent home without delay, but despite the influential official contacts the de Valles had made when Gerard aligned himself beside Bonaparte, communications were difficult and no reply had been forthcoming.

Sometimes Tamarisk asked Mavreen about James and when they would go to join him in Austria, but the child seemed in no hurry to leave for she was by nature happy and contented, and had rapidly acquired an unexpected affection for the vicomtesse.

"I would like her to be well again, Mama," she announced one day. "But madame tells me that is not God's intention for He wishes her to go and live with Him. Mama, I don't think I like God very much." Tears filled her eyes and Mavreen quickly hugged the child to her.

"I think madame will be quite happy to go to live with God!" she said. "After all, you and I will be leaving soon to go to Papa and then she will be all alone."

Tamarisk's tears dried as quickly as they had been shed.

"Does madame not have a little girl of her own to keep her company?" she asked. "Nor even a little boy?"

Mavreen's heart lurched. She had never spoken Gerard's name to his daughter and now she hesitated before saying, "The vicomtesse had a little boy called Gerard, but he is grown up now and has gone to fight in the war."

"Tell me about him!" Tamarisk begged. "Did he live here? Is the rocking horse in the nursery his? Is that his portrait in the salon? When will he come home?"

"I don't know!" Mavreen whispered. "Soon, I hope!"

But her voice trembled and she could not trust herself to talk further about Gerard. Tamarisk was an intelligent and sensitive child. It would not be unlikely that she should sense a change of tone in Mavreen's voice and guess that Gerard had some special importance for her. And Tamarisk being the chatterbox she was, Mavreen dared not risk what she might recount to James.

Not that Mavreen intended to keep secret their visit to France once she was reunited with James in Vienna. By then, it would be in the past and she felt certain that she could convince James that it had been on humanitarian grounds and in no way impugned her marriage or her affection for him. In the last resort, she was prepared to put up with his displeasure. She was committing no crime and none could condemn her for a visit to an aristocratic old lady who lay dying and wished to see her.

Mavreen was convinced that it was only Marianne de

Valle's determination to survive long enough to see Gerard again which now kept her from passing through the
door of death.

August gave way to September and Jules brought news
that the French armies on the coast were being sent elsewhere. Mavreen received the information with mixed
feelings—pleasure for her countrymen for whom the
threat of invasion was now over, and dismay for herself.
There was now no further reason for her to delay her
departure for Vienna. Mavreen's unease communicated
itself to the vicomtesse. Where Mavreen once sat quietly
in the sick room, her face relaxed and soft with dreams,
she now paced to and fro, and there were shadows beneath her eyes betraying sleepless nights.

"My dear child," the vicomtesse said one afternoon
when Mavreen seemed more restless than usual, "I know
that you are unhappy and I cannot offer help or advice
unless I know the cause of it. Will you not confide in me?"

Mavreen ran to the bedside and knelt beside it, her
cheek pressed against the thin, perfumed hand, aware
anew of its bird-like frailty.

"There is no solution to my problem, madame!" she
said. "I want so much to stay here with you yet every day
that I delay my departure, my conscience troubles me
more sorely. I vowed upon the Holy Book that I would go
to my husband in Vienna the moment it was safe to travel
—indeed, without this promise he would not have accepted the post. Yet I cannot bring myself to leave you
and Compiègne."

The vicomtesse placed her other hand on Mavreen's
head and stroked the shining gold hair tenderly.

"You have no need for my advice," she said. "By your
words, I know that you have already decided where your
duty lies. You must not be saddened by our parting. You
and little Tamarisk have brought me the greatest joy. She
is a beautiful, charming child. Now, whenever I choose to
remember, I shall see her in my mind just as if she were
here in the room with me, as I shall remember you, too,
Mavreen. I love you as if you were my real *belle fille*. I
admire and respect you for your courage. I love you also
for the love you bear my son. It is a great comfort to me

to know that even after I, his mother, have left this world, there exists another woman who would not hesitate to give her life for him. But that must not include the sacrifice of your honor, Mavreen." She glanced across the room at the candle-lit statue of Our Lady above her prie-dieu. "You are not a Catholic as I am, my dear, but I am sure that you, too, believe a vow made before God is sacrosanct. Do you understand me, Mavreen? You must never allow Gerard to persuade you to abandon your husband or permit him to divorce poor little Faustina. Gerard is not so strong a character as you and the time may come when the honor of the de Valles will lie in your hands."

"I understand!" Mavreen said, close to tears. "I will do anything you ask of me. Only, I cannot cease to love him."

"Nor would I wish it!" the Vicomtesse said softly.

The tiny beads of sweat on the vicomtesse's brow gave certain indication of an oncoming bout of pain and Mavreen went quickly in search of Sister Marie-Thérèse.

Although the château had been only partially restored, there was now more money to pay for the two nursing nuns and for servants to clean the château. The large dowry that Faustina had brought to her marriage had greatly improved the circumstances of the de Valles. The vicomtesse lacked for nothing that money could buy but was, alas, unable to enjoy the good food that was brought to her room nor any of the improvements beyond the confines of her room. She insisted that she had ample funds to ensure the medical care and attention she needed, but before leaving Compiègne, Mavreen gave a sum of money to Jules to cover any unforeseen eventuality.

With tears in his eyes, the old servant assured Mavreen that he would guard the vicomtesse and her possessions with his life. If the young vicomte did not return in time, he promised he would use Mavreen's money for a funeral which would not dishonor the family name.

When Dickon finally turned the carriage away from the great doors and urged the horses down the long drive and through the wrought-iron gates, Tamarisk was in tears, but Mavreen remained dry-eyed, the pain and sorrow in her heart too great for weeping. She knew she would never see Marianne de Valle again.

CHAPTER THIRTY-TWO
1805

Upon her return from France, Mavreen found a letter awaiting her from her husband. It contained the disturbing information that he feared the Austrians might be at war with the French before the end of the year. He wished her to join him as soon as possible but strongly advised against her taking Tamarisk to Vienna.

I have no doubt that I can ensure your safety, but I consider it inadvisable for us to have the child with us. I know you will dislike being separated from her but it is in her interest. I long for you to join me. Vienna is a beautiful city. I, though fully occupied with my work, miss your dear company sorely and find it difficult to wait patiently for your arrival. Come quickly, my dear wife.

He ended the letter with a request for her to take with her his shotgun as there was much sport to be had in the woods on the far side of the Danube.

Coincidentally, another letter awaited Mavreen containing an alternative suggestion for Tamarisk's immediate future. It was an invitation to stay for an indefinite period with Princess Charlotte at Warwick House. It seemed that the little princess had been urging the king for some time to consent to her wish to enjoy Tamarisk's companionship.

Mavreen knew that she need have no worries as to Tamarisk's health and happiness since the royal child was most carefully supervised. And Rose, who was to go with Tamarisk to Warwick House as her personal maid, would keep watch over her.

Although Rose and Dickon fully intended to be married

one day, the right moment seemed not yet to have come. Dickon would never permit his own requirements to come before Mavreen's and that he would accompany her to Vienna, leaving Rose behind, was never in question. Even had she expressly ordered him to stay in England, she knew he would have disobeyed her. Dickon's loyalty was absolute.

"I am a-going your road!" Dickon said simply, "howsonever far it be. I dont reckon Austrian Frenchies be no better nor worse than the French Frenchies."

Tamarisk, overhearing this remark, clapped her hands and laughed.

"Why, Dickon!" she remonstrated. "You talk as if you had no affection for the French and yet you told me yourself you had taken a great liking to Jules! As to your going to Vienna with Mama, you know very well that Rose and I would not have a moment's peace of mind were you not there to take care of her!"

Tamarisk was not the only one to appreciate Dickon's guardianship. When the long journey was finally accomplished without mishap, James's welcome contained a special word of praise for Dickon.

"I had but the most trifling of concerns for my wife's safety knowing that you were accompanying her," he said to the grinning Dickon, but as he followed Mavreen into her bedchamber, he confessed that he had several times regretted his letter advising her to come at once to Vienna.

"I have heard rumors that the French armies are on the move," he said frowning. "The Prussians have finally been persuaded to abandon their neutrality and send an army to defend her territory now that the French have trespassed upon it to the southeast. The Austrian army, under the command of General Mack, is defending Ulm. Let us hope that the Prussians reach them in time, for 'tis rumored that Napoleon's army is moving at an unprecedented speed. If Mack were to suffer a defeat. . . ."

But the sight of Mavreen, looking pale and tired, but as beautiful as ever in her fur-trimmed caracul cloak, put all thought of war from his mind.

He dismissed the Austrian maid, Gretchen, and himself assisted Mavreen in the removal of her cloak and bonnet.

This done, he took her in his arms and kissed her passionately.

"You cannot have missed me as much as I have missed you!" he said, his voice breaking with emotion. "There were many times, my love, when I considered myself quite mad ever to have left England and your side."

Mavreen returned his kiss, determined that in no way would she dampen the enthusiasm of James's welcome.

"I have much to tell you," she said, as she sat down at her dressing table to comb her hair. "But my news can await a while. First, I wish to take stock of this beautiful house you have found for me."

James had rented an imposing residence, called the Rosenkoegel, in the quiet, tree-shaded Lienzerstrasse and was anxious that Mavreen should approve his choice. The Gothic style of architecture with its high pointed arches and clustered columns appealed to her only a little more than did the heavy, dark, ornately-carved furniture, but she gave no inkling of this unfavorable first impression of her new home and praised James unstintingly for finding them such a suitable house.

"I anticipate that we shall have much entertaining to do on your behalf," she said. "It is as well we have plenty of room to accommodate our guests. Tell me about your work, James! Are you finding it of interest? Have you made many new friends?"

But James was unwilling to discuss such matters. He intended to be the sole usurper of Mavreen's time and attention for at least a week, he informed her. They had been apart too long. He wanted her exclusively to himself.

"Then you shall show me Vienna!" Mavreen agreed. "Before my time becomes taken up with social duties."

Such was James's good humor that Mavreen felt this evening of her arrival might, after all, be a suitable occasion for her to mention, in the most casual of manners, her visit to France. James listened quietly, without interruption, as she spoke of the seriousness of the vicomtesse's illness and her letter begging Mavreen to visit her before she died.

"I was not aware she held you in such affection as to demand you travel in such dangerous times!" he commented, his eyes narrowed as he stared at his wife across the dining table.

"The vicomtesse made no demands!" Mavreen replied, curbing her irritation at James's tone of voice. "She is dying, James, and people on the point of death are known to develop strange obsessions. She did not *demand*, but her request was so worded that I felt obliged to go. Moreover, she had acquired safe conduct passes for us."

James, who was toying with his food, laid down his knife and fork.

"Us? You mean that Tamarisk went with you?"

Mavreen's heart sank. While appreciating her husband's right to question her, she nevertheless resented having to account for her movements. Before her marriage, she had been answerable to no one but herself. Nevertheless, she continued to speak calmly, explaining that the vicomtesse had a special fondness for children and that she, herself, had thought it might be a useful experience for Tamarisk to travel to a foreign country and speak the language.

James, looking partly mollified, resumed his eating. He said no more until the servants had cleared away the last dishes. He dismissed the waiting footmen.

"I do not believe they speak our tongue!" he said to Mavreen, "but lest one or two should understand the English language, 'twould be better not to speak of private matters in their hearing. Now tell me, Mavreen, why did you not think fit to write to me of your intention to go to France before you departed thence? All this while, I have been imagining you in Sussex!"

"Oh, James!" Mavreen protested, suddenly weary of the accusation in his tone of voice. "I was aware that you might think my visit to Compiègne must concern Gerard de Valle. I felt it best to wait until I saw you so that I could explain matters more fully. I was anxious not to cause you distress when there was no need of it."

Mention of her consideration of his feelings pleased James. He stood up and went round the table. Standing behind her chair, he bent and kissed the top of her head, his hands upon her shoulders.

"You were quite right!" he said huskily. "I might have felt the twinges of jealousy. Let us not talk of it further.

Have I told you how beautiful you look? The green of your dress is the self-same color as your eyes! My sweet and incomparable Mavreen! What strange power you have upon my senses!"

Docilely, she allowed him to lead her upstairs. In his eagerness for their physical reunion, he would have undressed her himself but Gretchen, pink-cheeked and smiling, appeared not to understand his gestures of dismissal and remained to disrobe her new mistress.

James had, therefore, to retire to his own bedchamber to await such time as his wife's toilette was completed.

Exhausted as she was by the weeks of travel, Mavreen wanted only to sleep. Her lack of desire for James's attentions was in proportion to the intensity of his. But she knew that the rest she craved could be accomplished only by the surrender of her body to her husband.

As if it were not she, herself, but someone quite else, Mavreen lay in total uninvolvement as James's need of her, accentuated by their separation, was quickly sated. Fortunately, he was too engrossed in his own desires to require more from her than a willingness to satisfy them. She had only to murmur endearments, caress his hot face afterward and assure him of her enjoyment for him to sigh contentedly and turn to lie upon his back. She did not think of Gerard while James possessed her, aware only of relief when his passion reached its climax and she could reclaim the privacy of her separateness. Uppermost of her sentiments toward her husband was pity since she knew, far better than he, how much of her true self she withheld from him.

James, for the time being, was perfectly content. He was immensely proud of Mavreen's beauty and having already established himself at court, was anxious to present his wife as soon as possible.

For the moment, there seemed little concern for the approach of war amongst the citizens of Vienna. Mozart's opera, *The Magic Flute*, was being shown for the second time at the Freihaus Theatre. People promenaded in the many beautiful parks and gardens, drank wine in the company of friends at the White Swann inn, or coffee at one of the many cafés. There were always crowds waiting to be admitted to the impressive baroque hall of the Winter Riding School to gaze open-mouthed at the famous white Lipizzaner horses being put through their paces.

Mavreen spent as little time as was seemly in the confines of her home. Having first assured herself that James had acquired a competent staff to run the house without supervision, she set out with Dickon as escort to explore Herr Mehler's Vienna. Remembering his wistful envy, she thought often of her old music teacher and took the trouble to write a long description to him of the numerous concerts she attended.

Despite James's intention to take a leave of absence from his work, the pressure of his duties forced him to attend to his affairs. Mavreen was therefore free to indulge her interest in churches. She spent one whole day in St. Stephen's Cathedral in the Stephansplatz, impressed by its vast size and lofty tower.

On another day, she visited Peterskirche, where she was fortunate enough to hear the beautiful singing of the Benedictus by the choir and wished that not only Herr Mehler but Clarissa, too, was there to share her pleasure.

Without knowing what prompted her, she knelt before the candle-lit statue of the Madonna and child and offered up a whispered prayer for the vicomtesse, and another silent one, for Gerard's safety.

Despite the cold winter weather, Dickon drove Mavreen along the old town walls and fortifications which curved protectively around the city like a great horseshoe. He waited patiently as she feasted her eyes on the Royal Palace of Schonbrunn.

"Just imagine, Dickon!" she exclaimed, "not sixty years ago that impressive building was an ordinary manor house until the Empress Maria-Theresia decided to enlarge it and make it her home. Gretchen told me yesterday that it requires twenty servants just to light the candles!"

Mavreen and Dickon made other visits—to churches, houses, and parks, including the Prater with its small deer park where duels were fought and skittles played. The days passed swiftly and enjoyably.

CHAPTER THIRTY-THREE
1805

Mavreen had been in Vienna a little more than a fortnight when James arrived home with an invitation for them to attend a dinner party at the house of Baron Stern.

"You will recall I introduced him to you after the levee last week, and he is anxious to further your acquaintance!" James told Mavreen, in part with jealousy and in part with pride. "He could be a useful contact for me as he has considerable influence with the emperor, so unless you have other plans, my dear, I would be pleased if you would accept."

Upon hearing that the baron was an enthusiastic card player and that therefore she would almost certainly have the opportunity to play faro, Mavreen was delighted by the invitation. James played only piquet and cribbage so Mavreen had not enjoyed her favorite game since she had last played faro at Clarissa's house over a year ago.

She recalled the Baron Stern, an aristocratic, grey-haired Austrian with twinkling brown eyes in a thin, somewhat austere face; a charming, courtly man with a plump, plain, but equally charming wife. They were of a generation older than James and herself, close friends of the emperor and his wife. It was, James informed her, to be considered quite an honor to receive an invitation to their home. Mavreen, therefore, decided to do justice to the occasion.

When Mavreen presented herself to James in her new dress he said, "You look quite beautiful, my dear!" coming forward to hold her at arm's length. "I shall be the most envied of men this evening!"

Mavreen's dress, low-bosomed, high-waisted, was of white and silver gauze, decorated with silver thread and brilliants around and above the hem. Attached at the neck by an ornament of brilliants and diamonds set in silver, was a train of purple velvet which fell in graceful folds at her feet. Her slippers were of silver fabric.

Mavreen smiled.

"I am glad you approve, dear James!" she said, taking the elbow-length, white kid gloves from the waiting Gretchen. "You have noticed that I am wearing your present to me?" She touched the large silver hoop earrings, and held out the fan which was yet another of the many presents James was always bringing home for her. "See how perfectly it matches my dress?"

Gretchen handed her her reticule and James, noting how heavy it appeared, asked what was in it.

"Why *souverains d'or*, of course!" Mavreen replied laughing. "If I am to play cards this evening, James, I must needs be prepared to cover my losses!"

James looked momentarily disconcerted. An extremely wealthy man himself, he resented his wife's financial independence. When Gilbert Barre died, leaving Mavreen a fortune, she had quickly become accustomed to managing her financial resources under the guidance of her father, Sir John. By the time she married James, Mavreen needed no assistance and it irked him that she did not call upon him for advice. Pride forbade that he should assign her fortune to his own as was his right. He hoped that given time, she would invite him to take over the control of all her monetary affairs as was customary in any normal marriage, but as yet, there seemed no sign of weakening in her fierce streak of independence.

On this occasion, his irritation was only momentary. Mavreen's beauty was intoxicating and his sudden desire for her overwhelmed all other emotions. He felt immensely proud as he tucked his arm through hers and led her down the wide staircase to the waiting carriage.

The Baron and Baroness Stern lived in a large baroque house in Rotenturmstrasse near the Stephansdom on the far side of the city. Dickon lost his way by taking the wrong turn out of Albertplatz. All the other guests were there when James and Mavreen finally presented themselves. They had no opportunity therefore to meet their fellow guests until after the meal. It took several hours to consume the fish soup, roast venison, pheasant, partridge and young goose served with warm cabbage and white bread dumplings.

James came quickly to Mavreen's side once the repast was over. He had jealously noted the many admiring glances cast at his beautiful young wife and he intended to keep a watchful eye upon her. Mavreen, however, had little interest in indulging in harmless flirtations for she had noticed that the baron was assembling a number of his male guests to adjourn to the card room. He came across the room to James and asked if he would care to join the faro players.

"I rarely play cards!" James replied, and to Mavreen's pleasure, he added, "but my wife would greatly enjoy playing. She is quite skilled at the game!"

The Baron Stern bowed his head politely.

"It is entirely as madame wishes!" he said. He had not intended the card-playing, which he took with the utmost seriousness, to include any females, especially tonight when he had a certain Baron von Gottfried as one of his guests. Although he knew the gentleman but slightly, von Gottfried was said to be an extremely wealthy man with vast estates in the environs of Braunau. Stern had made his acquaintance but once at a gaming room where it had soon become established that like himself, von Gottfried was addicted to card games played for high stakes. He had, therefore, invited von Gottfried upon hearing that the gentleman was currently paying a visit to Vienna.

However, he was sufficiently *épris* with Mavreen's unusual beauty not to be able to refuse the English lady any wish she cared to name. Half of Vienna was talking about the newly arrived English couple and the ladies of society were vying with one another to be the first to add them to their guest list, so the baron and his wife counted themselves fortunate in having James and Mavreen attend their soirée this evening.

Mavreen entered the card room on the baron's arm feeling confident and excited. She knew that she was looking her best.

The gentlemen rose to their feet as Baron Stern introduced her to each in turn. The game had not yet begun.

When he presented her to Baron von Gottfried, Mavreen felt certain she had heard the name before. She searched her mind and recalled the occasion—only a few weeks before—when the vicomtesse had spoken so sadly of the unhappy death of Gerard's father. She looked searchingly at the heavy-jowled, balding, elderly man now clicking his heels and bowing to her. But for the ravages of age, he fit exactly the vicomtesse's description of the villainous Austrian card cheat who had brought about the death and ruin of Antoine de Valle.

The excited pink spots in her cheeks were misinterpreted by the baron as the blushes of a solitary woman finding herself in a card game obviously intended to be confined to gentlemen. Von Gottfried knew exactly who Mavreen was, for he had made careful inquiries about her at the dinner table. He was therefore fully aware that James was a wealthy English aristocrat and that his wife had been left a fortune by her first husband and was exceedingly wealthy in her own right. It had been the baron's intention to try to take a little of James's money at the card table. Now he smiled to himself in satisfaction. Females were not, in his experience, card-minded. He watched Mavreen closely. This elegantly dressed English milady was not lacking in intelligence, he thought. Nevertheless, she was behaving like a coquette, trying out her feminine wiles upon a young captain seated opposite her, dimpling and smiling and pouting at him, paying little regard to the setting out of the green baize cloth upon the table.

His eyes narrowed. Here, indeed, was a plum ripe for the picking! He hoped it would not be long before he could take over as dealer and banker, for only by the handling of the packs of cards could he effect the sleight-of-hand required to ensure his winning. He further hoped that Mavreen would not abandon the game if she found herself to be losing, as she most surely would! No doubt her obviously adoring young husband would replenish the pile of gold sovereigns flung so carelessly onto the table in front of her.

Baron von Gottfried had lived most of his life on his wits and his knowledge of human psychology. Left vast

estates but no money by his father, he had had little hesitation in setting out upon a life of roguery. He had no
desire to risk life and limb as a soldier and there were
few opportunities open to a gentleman to earn money and
none whatever to earn the huge sums he required to
maintain his lands. He therefore travelled about Europe,
and became more and more adept as a card cheat. Only
once had he been in danger of exposure, but cleverly
avoided it by accusing another man of cheating. The resulting duel brought about the death of a certain French
vicomte. On this occasion he left the country with all
speed, trusting that any curiosity about him would eventually die with time and distance.

Until recently, with increasing attacks of rheumatism,
he had never risked his reputation in his own country.
But now he was once more short of funds and he decided that there would be little danger in joining a few
card parties amongst the richer members of Viennese
society. He had not been to the city in many years and
with his respectability unchallenged by his compatriots,
he had no difficulty in acquiring invitations to the right
houses. Baron Stern was a new acquaintance and, von
Gottfried now decided, likely to prove a very profitable one.

Mavreen had no interest whatever in the blushing,
eager young captain facing her. With careful intention,
she was deliberately behaving in the manner of an empty-
headed coquette in order to give the baron a false impression of herself. She was now in little doubt that he
was the same man the vicomtesse had described to her,
"short, plump, with brilliant blue eyes and ginger hair,
about the same age as my poor Antoine."

Such would make the baron now in his sixties, and although the ginger hair had vanished, there were still
glimpses of it on his arms and the backs of his hands and
protruding from his thick fleshy neck. His eyes, sunken
now in folds of skin, were a brilliant blue.

Mavreen turned away from the captain and smiled
demurely at the baron.

"You have been to England, sir? How liked you my
country? And to France? How interesting! Was that before the Revolution?"

He supplied her with the date unhesitatingly—1786. He had not returned to Paris since.

Mavreen's heart began to pound. She felt exhiliarated as more and more facts fitted into place. Excitement brought a heightened color to her cheeks. Her look of recklessness was in keeping with her reckless play. She lost steadily and laughed prettily, saying on each occasion, "Oh, how silly of me! How can I have been so stupid!"

The gentlemen at the table, with the exception of Baron von Gottfried, were becoming embarrassed. James, who had come to stand behind her chair to watch her play, urged her to leave. Their host, Baron Stern, did likewise. He was for the present acting as banker and therefore the recipient of her winnings. But Mavreen pouted prettily, smiling over her fan at the circle of faces around the table.

"But I don't mind losing!" she cried. "Who knows but my luck will change! And if it should not, why, is it not true that those who are unlucky at cards are fortunate in love?"

Play was resumed. Mavreen won a turn or two. She patted her hands together childishly.

"Did I not say my luck would change?" she cried. "Now that I am winning I can afford to risk more, can I not, James?"

Nonplussed, James moved away from the table. He did not know Mavreen in this strange mood. She was never kittenish, never stupid. She was a skillful card player; her gambling always reasonable. Yet she now appeared no better than a novice at the game.

Baron von Gottfried awaited his opportunity and asked the host if he might relieve him of the task of dealing. His wish was granted.

Faro was a game which afforded very little opportunity to cheat. The betting was done by all the players against the house, or, since this was a private party, the man acting as banker. The thirteen cards of the spade suit, painted upon the green baize cloth, were unchangeable. On one or more of the cards, representing the ranks of all suits, the players placed their bets, either to win, or if they covered their money with a copper coin, to lose.

Only the banker handled the cards, shuffling and placing a full pack face-up in a box. It was, therefore, necessary for Baron von Gottfried to act as banker in order to shuffle the cards so that he knew their exact order of appearance.

Once the players had placed their bets, the uppermost card, called "soda", was removed unused. On the next card, money was paid to those who coppered their bets to lose; on the following card, to those on the correct number to win. The removal of one card and the exposure of the next constituted a "turn" on which bets were settled.

It was a simple matter, therefore, for the baron to assess at a glance the ranks of cards most heavily favored to win or lose. It was less simple, but possible with his acquired skill, to palm a card about to be exposed if that card would lose him a great deal of money. Later in the play, he could return it to the box—a necessity since a "case keeper" kept on display a running record of all cards played and those yet to come.

It required a remarkable feat of memory for the baron to be certain which rank followed upon the one exposed at the same time as assessing the amount of money at risk. But he was an expert. Only his fingers, stiffened with rheumatism, were less adept than before at rearranging the order of the cards within the box.

An evening spent when he could not hold the bank was an evening wasted for him. As a player he had to hazard his luck. On such occasions he kept his stakes low. As banker he placed no limit on the stakes, knowing that although he risked some losses, in the long run he could always ensure that he won.

"As you wish, madame," he said now with pretended reluctance in reply to Mavreen's request to raise the stakes. In mild, fatherly tones he added a caution not to risk too much upon a turn while luck was against her.

"Oh, tush!" Mavreen protested giggling. " 'Tis more fun if you risk more, is it not, sir? I am feeling brave. See, here are fifty sovereigns. I will chance them all on one turn!"

The baron coughed. There was no opportunity for him to palm the next card without risk. The silly female was watching him over her fan as if her very life depended upon his movements. The large pile of coins covering four numbers glinted up at him temptingly. At the same time, he was far from anxious to risk such a large sum of his own on the mere whim of chance.

Mavreen's apparent mood of gay abandon infected some of the other players. The young captain began to bet more heavily as did Baron Stern and a Spanish nobleman who until now had not felt it was proper etiquette to gamble highly in a private game.

The baron removed the surface card from the box and set it aside. His heart lurched as he saw the new card facing him—a seven of hearts. Only the captain lost to him. His host, the Spaniard and Mavreen were all staked on the winning number. He wiped his forehead. He was now sweating profusely with anxiety.

"Oh, poor you!" Mavreen cried sympathetically. "Never mind, dear baron. You will win it all back soon, I have no doubt!"

But the baron did not win. The pile of sovereigns in front of Mavreen grew steadily higher. Sweat now poured down his face. The mood of the table was now indefinably against him as the laughing gentlemen congratulated Mavreen and urged her to play for even higher stakes.

Within the half hour, the baron had lost all the money he had brought with him. He began paying out with promissory notes. Desperate, he decided to risk a sleight-of-hand, despite the fact that Mavreen's eyes seemed continuously riveted upon his movements. He palmed a card. Instantly, Mavreen called out with innocent sweetness, "Oh, baron, I fear the cards must be becoming very sticky for I think two passed together at the last turn, did they not?"

He had no alternative but to make use of the excuse she offered him for his "mistake" and make stumbling apologies to the players. Their mood was now definitely against him. When he haltingly suggested that he had played long enough, there was an outcry of "Shame!"

"But you cannot give up now, dear Baron!" Mavreen said gently as she placed his last note of credit with her other winnings. "I have won far too much money from

you and it would be most embarrassing for me were you
not to win some of it back. I have had all the luck, have I
not? But yours will certainly change presently just as mine
did at the start of the game!"

"Sportingly said!" cried the young captain. "Come now,
baron, another hand!"

The baron was losing control of his nerve and his temper. He had been drinking steadily in an effort to keep
calm. He was in no doubt now that the beautiful English
milady was an adept and clever card player despite her
pretended stupidity. For some reason unknown to him—
perhaps it was no more than a mere caprice—she had set
out to ruin him. He had a growing fear that she, herself,
was an accomplished cheat and therefore knew his chances
to change the order of the cards; that she was delighting
in watching him so closely that he could not employ his
usual methods of chicanery.

Incensed that a mere woman could make such a fool of
him, he was tempted to further follies. Instead of accepting his losses, he continued to play despite Mavreen's ever-
rising stakes. By the end of the second hour of play, he
knew that on the next turn he had pledged his entire
financial resources. There was a murmur of sympathy
from the other players when his trembling fingers exposed
the card. He had lost.

Mopping his brow, his face ashen, he rose unsteadily
from the table.

Mavreen rose also.

"You must not despair, Monsieur le baron!" she said,
placing a restraining hand upon his sleeve. "I do assure
you it was not my intention to ruin you. I have an idea—"
She turned to smile prettily at the gentlemen now leaning
back in their chairs staring at her with varying expressions of astonishment and admiration. "—I will give the
poor baron a chance to win everything back. That will be
fun, will it not?" She picked up a pack of cards and cut
them. "If the baron selects the higher card I shall return
to him everything he has lost."

The gentlemen clapped their hands. This was indeed
proving to be an evening's gaming they would long remember. They admired Mavreen's sporting spirit but saw

no reason why this beautiful woman should risk her winnings without hope of further gain.

"And what will the baron pledge if he loses?" one cried. "Double the stakes?"

"I do not have the money!" the baron said hoarsely. "I have nothing left but my castle and estates!"

But inwardly, he felt like a man reprieved. The Englishwoman was stupid after all. By choosing to cut the cards, she had handed him a foolproof opportunity to win this final gamble, for he knew he could palm any card he chose unless Mavreen were to cut the pack first and select the ace of spades—a chance he must take.

"Very well!" he said, controlling his inner excitement.

He picked up the cards Mavreen had a moment before held in her hands and shuffled them deftly. With a twisted smile he put the pack down in front of her.

"Ladies first, I think?" he said quietly.

Mavreen pouted.

"Oh, but I don't like the blue cards!" she cried. "I greatly prefer the pink ones with the pretty gold border. I am sure that is the pack that has brought me so much luck this evening!"

Without waiting for his acquiescence, she picked up the pink pack and shuffled it unhurriedly. With a charming smile at the baron, she cut the cards a third of the way down. It was the nine of diamonds.

The watching men gasped. The card by no means ensured victory. Mavreen pushed the pack before the baron.

"Now it is your turn!" she said. "Take courage, Monsieur!"

Hand trembling, the baron forced himself to cut the cards. Even before he dared glance at the face of the card he knew by the cheer the gentlemen broke into that he had lost. He had selected the six of spades.

"Oh, dear!" Mavreen said, looking helplessly around her. "I really am so sorry, Baron von Gottfried. Please don't go—" she added as he started to move away from the table. "If you will be so good as to give me a trifle more of your time, I would be very pleased if you would join me somewhere where we can talk privately?"

Baron Stern jumped to his feet. He was not a little

embarrassed by the ruin of one of his guests by another—
a lady at that. By tomorrow, the story would be all over
Vienna. Already some of his other guests were crowding
into the card room, James, who had long since absented
himself, among them.

"It is time we went home, my dear!" he said to Mavreen. Word had already filtered through to him of his
wife's phenomenal run of luck. He was now very much
afraid of what she would do next to further embarrass
him. Her behavior was quite incomprehensible to him.

"Of course, James," she said. "I had no idea it was so
late. We will leave just as soon as the baron and I have
had our little talk! Do come with us if you wish!"

James followed them into the library. He had no idea
of what was in her mind or what she could possibly wish
to say to the poor baron. He knew only that she was behaving totally out of character and that he dared not risk
trying to intervene, lest he force her into further indiscretions.

Baron Stern pulled back the chair behind his leather-
covered desk for his shaking compatriot. He wondered if
Mavreen intended to ensure that Baron von Gottfried put
his written word to the enormous debt he owed her. He
put quill, ink, and paper before his hapless guest.

Mavreen sat down on the opposite side of the desk and
James in a chair by the door. Baron Stern bowed and departed.

Baron von Gottfried held out his trembling hands toward Mavreen in a gesture of despair.

"I am ruined—totally ruined," he said. "Have you no
pity, madame?"

"No more nor less than you had when you ruined
Antoine de Valle!" she replied in a small hard voice. "For
it *was* you, Baron von Gottfried, was it not, who first
ruined and then killed him?"

His small blue eyes narrowed.

"Antoine de Valle?" he echoed uncomprehendingly.

"Yes, indeed, sir! Upon your own admission you were
in Paris in the year 1786. During that visit, you engaged
a young French vicomte in a game of cards and not content with ruining him, you twisted the truth so that it ap-

peared that he was the one who had been cheating. Upon this point of honor, he challenged you to a duel and you killed him. You showed no mercy!"

From behind her, James protested anxiously, "Do you have proof of this, Mavreen? If not. . . ."

"I do not need proof!" Mavreen said, "because the baron is going to confess to everything, are you not, baron? And the reason he will do so, James, is because I am now offering him the return of his castle and his lands in exchange for that confession. Do I make myself clear, baron?"

Von Gottfried's face was now so white James was afraid that the miserable man might be about to faint. His hands gripped the arms of his chair. He stared back at Mavreen as if mesmerised.

"If I were to give you such a confession—" he stammered, "—I could be sent to prison. I am old—and far from well. I could not endure imprisonment. The disgrace. . . ."

"I have not the slightest intention of using your confession for such a purpose!" Mavreen broke in. "Nor do I believe that such will be the intention of the vicomte's widow, nor of her son, Gerard de Valle. I do not imagine they would trouble themselves to bring disgrace upon you—unless, sir, it ever reached their ears or mine that you had once again embarked upon your wicked methods of extorting money unfairly."

"Then you are not entirely without mercy!" the baron cried. He stumbled to his feet and would have knelt at Mavreen's skirt had she not stood back in revulsion.

"Write!" she commanded. "And in French so that I may see with my own eyes that you are not cheating me!" The scorn in her voice caused the miserable baron to cringe.

Mavreen stood behind him as shakily, the baron began to write. The scratch of the quill on paper was the only sound in the room other than his gasping breath. Mavreen, looking over his shoulder, let out her breath as he signed his name.

"The money I have won from you will also go to the de Valles," she said as she took the paper from him and

herself sanded it. "You owe it to them as some small re-
dress for the suffering you have caused them all these
years. I hope you will now suffer as they have done,
baron. Goodnight—and pleasant dreams!"

Later that night, James accused Mavreen of being too
hard on the man. Furiously, Mavreen defended her right
to be vindictive.

"It is not a pleasing trait in my character!" she admitted, as she tossed her bulging reticule into her dressing-
table drawer. "But no one shall hurt me or my friends
and go unscathed, James. Such is my nature and I cannot change it!"

James sighed.

"The whole of Vienna will be talking of this on the
morrow!" he said. "I dare not contemplate what people
will say of you!"

Mavreen gave him a look of scorn.

"Do you care so much what strangers—foreigners at
that—say about me, James? I did no wrong. I think it is
even possible that they will take the same view as Baron
Stern, that I behaved very magnanimously towards 'poor
Baron von Gottfried.' After all, no one but ourselves
knows of the confession I forced from him. Yet all are
aware I relinquished my claims to his lands!"

"The less said about it from now on the better!" James
replied, cautioning Mavreen to lower her voice so the
servants would not hear her. "Pray what is your intention
now that you have the confession?"

"I shall have Dickon take it to France tomorrow!"
Mavreen replied quietly. "The vicomtesse has not long to
live, James—that is, if she is not already dead. This—"
she held up the parchment, "—this will allow her to die in
peace."

Reassured that his wife's concern seemed more for the
vicomtesse than for his rival, Gerard, James decided to let
the matter rest. He did not approve of the way Mavreen
had drawn so much attention to herself at Baron Stern's
party. Yet he secretly admired her courage. She had taken
a grave risk in assuming that Baron von Gottfried was one
and the same man as the rogue who had killed Antoine
de Valle. But her instinct had been proved right—albeit

not without moments of severe anxiety on his part. He dared not contemplate the consequences had the wretched von Gottfried proved unconnected with de Valle's murderer.

As he retired to bed, for the hour was now very late, James hoped that this would be the end of the matter.

But as he lay sleeping, the baron lay wakeful in his hotel room, sober now and beginning to recover from the shock of the evening's debacle. The sense of reprieve he had felt when it became clear that the English woman wanted nothing more from him than his confession and was not concerned with having him thrown into prison was wearing off. As the night progressed, his relief slowly gave way to an irrational anger, the greater for realizing that his humiliation had been brought about at the hands of a mere woman. Greedily, he imagined the frivolous little reticule Mavreen carried, bulging with *souverains d'or*, stuffed even fuller by his promissory notes. It was not, he thought, as if she had need of his money! And he was now penniless, with scarcely enough to pay for his hotel room and his journey home. He was a ruined man.

Dawn was breaking when he summoned his manservant, Georg, to him. This man was as great a rogue as himself and loyal to his master. Many years ago the baron was instrumental in preventing his imprisonment; there was nothing Georg would not now do for him—robbery, theft, murder if need be.

But the baron required no such extremes from him. He wished only for his servant to discover where the English couple were residing; and to ascertain every last detail of their movements, their servants, the layout of each room, the architecture of the house itself, and its approaches.

Georg, a dark ugly fellow with a sharp nose and even sharper eyes, grinned knowingly. The sympathetic retainer was fully aware of the events of the night and had been shocked by the unaccustomed sight of his master, abject and weeping as he recounted his experiences.

It was clear to him that the baron had now recovered not only his courage but his wits; a skillful thief himself, Georg begged to be allowed to commit the robbery his master was planning. But the baron decided upon a less dangerous way of entering Rosenkogel than by risking his servant burglarizing the house via the outer walls. James, he learned, had departed for Wiener Neustadt where he was visiting the military academy at Babenberg Castle. This information had been obtained from one of James's servants. A further *souverain* prompted the news that it was the Englishman's intention to stay the night in the ancient city and that he had taken a portmanteau containing night attire for that purpose. The baron, therefore, decided to go himself to Rosenkogel and confront Mavreen directly.

Mavreen welcomed James's absence. She dined alone, resolving to make use of this rare privacy to write a long letter to Tamarisk. She was so engaged when one of the servants announced that there was a gentleman at the front door wishing to see her on a matter of great urgency.

Mavreen glanced at the clock on the mantelshelf.

"At this time of the night! Who is this visitor?" she asked the footman. "Did he not give his name?"

The footman inclined his head.

"He refused to do so, milady. He would say only that it was a matter of life and death!"

Mavreen's heart missed a beat. But for the Austrian servants, she was alone in the house. Dickon had departed for France that morning. They had rejected the long and arduous route across-country as seething with French soldiers and being too full of risks for him. Instead, Dickon intended to travel down the Danube by boat until the river branched southward into Switzerland and overland into France. It was a longer but safer way of travel, although still fraught with danger for an Englishman who, if he were caught, could be shot as a spy by any Frenchman he encountered. Mavreen now deemed it unlikely that even if he had so soon met with disaster, word would not have found its way back to her in so short a period of time.

Nevertheless, it was Dickon's safety Mavreen had foremost in her mind when she agreed to see her unidentified nocturnal caller, for she could think of no other persons who might wish to see her alone so late at night.

When the footman ushered the Baron von Gottfried into the salon, Mavreen's curiosity gave way to apprehension. But the baron at once allayed her fears, kissing her hand with formal politeness and thanking her for her kindness in seeing him at so late an hour.

"Please state your business, sir!" Mavreen said coldly. She had no wish to renew acquaintance with this man and could think of no reason why he should desire to see her.

"It is of a private nature!" the baron replied, glancing meaningfully at the servant still standing by the doors. "I do assure you it is of the utmost importance, madame, to both of us!"

Mavreen hesitated. She did not trust the baron but at the same time she had no reason to fear him. Believing it to be the speediest way to be rid of her unwelcome guest, she dismissed the footman.

"Pray be brief, sir. This is hardly the conventional hour for me to receive guests!"

"I do apologize, dear lady!" the baron said, the faint smile that was close to a leer betraying his growing confidence as Mavreen fell neatly into his trap. "Nevertheless, as I said to your servant—it is a matter of life and death. Your life, madame, to be precise!"

Calmly, he put his hand beneath the cloak he was still wearing and produced a small pistol which he now pointed at her head.

"*I want you to return my confession!*" he said in a low threatening tone. "I also want you to return my promissory notes and my money. Do I make myself clear?"

Mavreen drew in her breath as the first thrill of fear set her nerves tingling. But she had not the slightest intention of letting this evil man realize how much he frightened her.

"You must be deranged, sir," she said coolly. "I have only to scream and my husband and servants will be here in an instant!"

The baron laughed.

"Your husband is a long way away—too far, I think, to hear your screams. As for your servants, I shall not hesitate to shoot them as well as you if you call for their

assistance. This is no charade, madame. I am in deadly
earnest."

Mavreen's fear increased. The baron's knowledge of
James's whereabouts proved this was no bluff.

"If you were to kill me or one of my servants it would
lead you to the guillotine. I do not think you will shoot
me!"

Again, the baron smiled. He was enjoying himself now,
sensing Mavreen's growing fear.

"There would be nothing whatever to associate *me*
with your untimely death, madame. Your servants did not
recognize me. Nobody in the street saw me enter your
house. And even if a description of me were given to the
police, I have plenty of people to witness that I left for
my home this afternoon. The hotel staff saw me depart
with my manservant; and he is even now upon the road
to Braunau in our carriage with a very lifelike effigy of
me inside attired in my clothing." Looking smugly satisfied
with himself, the baron continued. "My man will make
several stops upon the way, bringing a glass of brandy from
the inns to the carriage for his poor master, Baron von
Gottfried, who is not feeling too well. He will not be forgotten, I assure you, for he will tip most extravagantly at
one inn; demand a warming pan at another; pass on my
complaints about the quality of the brand at another. But
I have said enough I am sure, madame, to convince you
that it is exceedingly unlikely I should go to the guillotine
for your murder. It is a chance I am more than ready to
take. So let us waste no more time. Give me back what is
mine!"

Extravagant though it might be, Mavreen could see no
weakness in the baron's plan. She felt almost guilty in
having the one means to thwart him.

"I cannot comply with your demands, sir," she said
quietly. "My manservant is already upon his way to
France with your notes and your confession. How disappointing for you that your spies did not so enlighten
you! You have made your elaborate plans for naught,
Monsieur le baron."

The shocked expression on his face lasted only for a
minute. It was replaced by disbelief.

"I admire your quickness of mind, madame, but you lie. I will wait but one minute longer, then I shoot!"

"Then you will have to shoot me!" Mavreen said with a calm she was far from feeling. "For neither your money nor your confession are here, sir. You have my word on it."

His face became distorted with anger.

"Do not fool with me! If they are not here in this room, then they are in your bedchamber!"

Mavreen shrugged her shoulders.

"I assure you they are not! If it so pleases you, you may see for yourself!"

The baron had not anticipated this course of events. He suspected that Mavreen was merely employing delaying tactics—perhaps in the hope that a servant could be warned as they went upstairs.

Smiling once more, he tightened his grip on the pistol.

"You may lead the way to your bedchamber!" he said grimly. "And I shall be close behind you—with this. If we meet with any of your servants, you are to tell them you no longer require their services and that they may retire. Do you understand?"

"You would not dare to kill me!" Mavreen said, steadily. But even as she moved toward the closed doors, she knew that this man was desperate enough to carry out his threat. He was by nature a gambler and he was gambling now for the highest stakes. At the same time, there was no logical reason for him to kill her once she had proved to him that she was no longer in possession of the letter, notes or money. Therefore, the sensible and safest course of action for her was to permit him to search the house unhindered.

She did as he had commanded—dismissing the surprised servants who could barely believe their eyes when they saw the beautiful Englishwoman take such an old and unattractive gentleman upstairs. For an aristocratic lady to entertain a lover in her husband's absence was by no means unheard of, but such a lover . . . .

Mavreen stood quietly while the baron ransacked James's bedchamber and dressing room, his impatience growing with every minute. Ignoring his muttered curses and threats, she took him thence to her own room. Two pink spots of anger highlighting her cheekbones were the only indication of the resentment she felt at the sickening sight of the perspiring baron rifling through her most intimate belongings.

"Where have you hidden them?" he snarled at her as he failed again and again to discover what he wanted.

"You are losing control of your senses!" Mavreen replied. "Why *should* I have hidden them? I had no reason to suspect your coming. Had I done so, I assure you I would have hidden my jewelry, too!"

Her cold logic reached his fevered brain. He was now beginning to believe that her manservant really had departed for France. He grabbed at the scattered rings, necklaces, brooches, bracelets, and his murderous mood gave way to a sardonic humor. The jewelry must be worth a small fortune, he estimated.

"Rough justice, I think, madame! You took what was mine so I shall now take what is yours," he cried.

He began to stuff them into a pillowcase, made clumsy by the use of but one hand while he kept the pistol leveled at Mavreen with the other.

A sudden uproar reached them from the foot of the stairs. The baron paused, listening.

"Damn it, where is everyone? What is afoot?"

"It's *James!*" Mavreen gasped, recognizing his voice.

All color drained from the baron's face. He had made no allowance for the fact that Mavreen's husband might return unexpectedly. By the angry voices, it was easy to guess that he had aroused the servants and been told that his wife was "entertaining" a gentleman upstairs.

The baron dropped the pillowcase. Still holding the pistol, he blew out the lamps. As best he could, he concealed himself behind the heavy satin window drapes.

"Give your husband one indication that I am here and I will shoot you both!" he threatened in a hoarse whisper.

It was Mavreen's fear for the unsuspecting James rather than for herself which kept her silent as James burst into the room. She was shocked to see the unsheathed sword in his hand. On his face was a look of insane jealousy. Holding up the lamp, he saw in its circle of light the total disarray of Mavreen's bed where the baron had searched beneath the mattress.

"*Where is he?*" James shouted. "Do not think you can lie to me, you whore. *Where is your lover?*"

Mavreen stood perfectly still as James threw back the bedcovers, searching beneath the bed. He was growing wilder with each second that passed, and now he stabbed with his sword at the bedcurtains.

"He is here, I know it!" he shouted. Pushing Mavreen to one side, he began to cross the room toward the window.

Mavreen found her voice at last.

"No, James, no!" she shouted. "He has a pistol. He will shoot. James, *James* . . ."

But he was deaf to her cries. Although she tried to run past him and place herself between him and the danger that most certainly awaited him, he flung her to the floor and lunged at the curtains.

With shocking explosion, the pistol fired. James gave a terrible cry and as Mavreen lay staring in horror, he sank slowly to the floor. Blood began to pour from his leg.

The horror which had paralyzed Mavreen gave way to anger. She ran toward the window and pulled back the drapes.

Had there been need of it she would have attacked the baron with her bare hands. But James's sword had found its target. The Baron von Gottfried lay propped by the closed casement in an upright position, the sword blade piercing his chest and impaling him to the window frame. His eyes, wide open, stared at Mavreen in eternal surprise. He was quite dead.

By now, the room had filled with servants. One of the maids was hysterical. Her screams reverberated dully in Mavreen's head as she knelt at James's side. She, herself, was strangely calm. Deftly she ripped the bloodstained breeches from James' leg and paled at the terrible wound gaping in his tights. He was moaning. Quickly, she applied a tourniquet above the wound. Almost at once, the bleeding stopped.

"Get a surgeon!" she ordered one of the footmen. "The very best there is—at once. Explain that it is a matter of life and death. Hurry man—take the fastest horse, but hurry."

By the time the surgeon arrived, James had been carefully laid by the servants in Mavreen's bed. Warming pans had been put around him for he was cold from loss of blood and shock. Mavreen, by his side, sat wiping the sweat from his forehead. Servants stood waiting with steaming kettles of boiling water and there was an array of clean bandages made from torn linen sheets, clean cloths and basins on the bed table.

Professor Spiegel, a tall grey-haired man of imposing stature looked at Mavreen approvingly, and with a certain amount of curiosity. He was more accustomed to seeing ladies of quality having an attack of the vapors, or in a swoon, at the sight of blood.

"Your thoughtfulness may well have saved your husband's life!" he said as he proceeded to take off his coat and roll up his shirt sleeves. "But for your tourniquet he would most certainly have bled to death." He surveyed James's leg with a shake of his head. "It is very bad!" he muttered. "The shot has grazed and splintered the bone. We shall have to remove his leg else he will die."

James spoke for the first time. He had overheard the surgeon's comment. Eyes burning furiously in the greyness of his face, he stared up at the professor.

"Then let me die!" he said though clenched teeth. "I would rather die than live my life as a cripple. Do you understand, Mavreen? I will never consent to the amputation of my leg!"

CHAPTER THIRTY-FOUR

1805

As she hurried home along the snow-covered streets of Vienna from the *Apothekerkunst* with medicaments for

James, it seemed to Mavreen that she had seldom come closer to despair.

The year was drawing to a close. Tamarisk's seventh birthday had passed but a few days ago with no glimmer of hope that Mavreen might be reunited with her child in the near future. Austria had suffered the most serious of defeats at both Ulm and Austerlitz, and Napoleon's troops were already swaggering freely about Vienna, celebrating the ignominious Treaty of Pressburgh, signed on the day after Christmas by the reluctant Emperor Francis.

There had been no festivities in Austrian homes. Few could comprehend the speed with which Napoleon's armies, so short a while ago massed on the Channel coast, had marched in less than a month across France into Bavaria. It was rumored he had taken as many as fifty thousand prisoners in the fourteen-day campaign which ensued. Even before this news had filtered back to Vienna, the French armies had raced a further three hundred and fifty miles, occupied the city and defeated an Austro-Russian army seventy miles north of the city.

Despite the fact that the French forces were only half the size of their enemy's, victory was once more theirs. To crown this crushing defeat, Napoleon had proved himself the least magnanimous of victors.

The people were still too horrified by the French emperor's humiliation of them to feel, as yet, a desire for revenge. The mood of the city was of a people stunned. But Mavreen, herself, was more concerned by James's condition than by the French occupation of Vienna.

She was immensely grateful for the support of Baron Stern and his wife, Anna, who, despite the terrible defeat of their country, proved themselves of immeasurable assistance following James' accident a week before. The baron, to whom Mavreen had confessed the whole story behind her behavior at his soirée, insisted that he was partly responsible for the outcome since it was he who had invited the Baron von Gottfried to his house. Together with the British ambassador, he saw to the intricacies of Austrian law, ensured that neither James nor Mavreen were held culpable of von Gottfried's murder and arranged for the wretched man's body to be sent home to

Braunau for burial. Baron Stern's wife, Anna, a warm-hearted and kindly woman, insisted upon going each afternoon to sit at James's bedside when Mavreen took an airing, either in the carriage or on foot.

James, recovered somewhat from the shock of his wounding, was nevertheless in considerable pain. More-over, he suffered constantly from the fear that he might yet lose his leg.

Between them, he and Mavreen had persuaded the surgeon not to amputate his leg upon the first instant. Professor Spiegel explained to Mavreen that he believed the wound too serious for any other remedy, since the supply of blood to the lower leg was quite inadequate. Nevertheless, he had agreed to delay a final decision for a few days.

James was a difficult patient. He accepted that Mavreen was not to blame for the baron's presence in her bed-chamber; that he, himself, had been at fault in concluding that she was taking advantage of his absence to entertain a lover. Miserably, he admitted that he had returned home because he suspected that she might do so.

"But how could you imagine such a thing, James!" Mavreen had protested, too astonished to be angry. "You know very well that I am but barely acquainted with any-one in Vienna—let alone a possible lover. Besides which—" she added, "—I gave you my word when we married that I had put behind me my former way of life. How *could* you suspect me of such designs!"

"I know, I know!" James cried. "But you are so beauti-ful, Mavreen. Every man who meets you must desire you."

"That does not mean I desire them, even if what you say is true, and I assure you it is not!" she argued. "Let us be quite honest with one another, James, lest your un-happy suspicions should ever lead us to another such ter-rible consequence. There is only one man in the world who could tempt me to break my marriage vows. You know who that is and I do not seek to hurt you by men-tioning his name."

She walked over to the window and stared down at the snow-covered garden with unseeing eyes.

"James, you will do me justice and admit that I have never lied to you. You knew the day you married me that I could never be wholly yours. I wish most sincerely that 'twere possible. I would give all my wealth most eagerly to any magician who could wipe out the past for me and let me forget. There is no happiness for me in my memories. Do you not see that by your mistrust of me you help to keep those memories alive. Gerard is forever in the forefront of your mind, and so you keep him forever in mine, too."

But Mavreen knew that although James understood the logic of her remark, it would be no easy task, if a possibility at all, for him to destroy the worm of jealousy in his heart. This jealousy could destroy both of them—had perhaps already blighted their marriage beyond recovery. Her fondness for him had turned to pity, and it was pity rather than affection which kept her for long hours at his bedside.

The fear that he might lose his leg frayed James's nerves. His bouts of irritability and fretfulness alternating with demands for Mavreen's forgiveness, love and forebearance took a heavy toll upon her spirits. Nor could she ignore her own feelings of guilt that James's present predicament had come about through her personal vendetta against the Baron von Gottfried.

James was proving far from a man of courage in his adversity. His constant threat that he would shoot himself if his leg had eventually to be amputated tried her patience almost as greatly as his emotional dependence upon her.

The snow, increasing in volume, blew under her hat and settled on the collar of her coat. She shivered, increasing her pace. The winter days were short and it would not be long before it was dark. She had dismissed the servant who had accompanied her from the house when she set out for the *Apothekerkunst*. Her desire to be quite alone superseded the conventions that insisted upon a lady not walking by herself. She wished very much that Dickon were with her. He, alone, would have been acceptable company. But Dickon, to add to her depression, had not returned from France. She had no inkling as to whether he had even arrived safely at Compiègne. She longed for news, not only to ascertain Dickon's well being and that of the vicomtesse, but that he might bring back with him news of Gerard—even of having seen him at the Château de Boulancourt.

The street leading to her house was almost deserted. She passed a beggar crouching in a doorway and pitying the bundle of rags huddled in the biting wind, put a coin in his outstretched hand. Two women, their heads covered by shawls, hurried past her carrying loaves of bread. An Austrian soldier, still wearing the tattered remains of his uniform, crossed the road on crutches. She thought of James and her heart flooded with pity. She thought that if James were to lose his leg, it would become her foremost task to see that he suffered as little as possible from the tragedy. She would try to love him as he wanted. Perhaps, she told herself, she might learn to love him as a mother loves a handicapped child. . . .

So lost in thought was she that, head down against the wind, she was unaware of the man approaching her. As she swerved sideways to avoid a bundle of straw lying on the pavement, she collided heavily with the oncomer. The soldier, in the uniform of a French army officer, caught her in his arms to prevent her falling. Steadying herself, Mavreen stepped back with a word of apology on her lips. But it was never uttered. The man standing but inches away from her, staring at her in total disbelief, was Gerard de Valle.

"Gerard!" His name died on her lips. Mavreen knew that she must be dreaming. "It cannot be!" she murmured, swaying from this second shock.

But as Gerard's arms encircled her and she heard her own name cried out in joy, she knew that this was no dream but some miracle of reality.

Laughing and crying at once, she stared hungrily into his face.

"Oh, Gerard, *Gerard!*" she whispered. "I still cannot believe it is really you!"

"Or I that it is my dearest, dearest Mavreen!" Gerard said. His eyes were filled with tears of unutterable happiness. *"Mon amour! Mon petit écureuil!* How happy I am! How beautiful you are!"

Mavreen gave a sudden joyous laugh.

"Happiness makes all women beautiful!" she said. "Oh, Gerard, 'tis impossible and yet it is true—you are here, really here!"

"And feeling far too cold to be a ghost!" Gerard smiled delightedly. "Come, my love, let us find somewhere warmer than this street where we can talk. Is there no café nearby. A restaurant. A hotel?"

"But a few paces from here!" Mavreen said. "Around the next corner. Gerard. There is a coffeehouse in the Karlsplatz. We shall have warmth, if not privacy, there."

Within minutes, they were seated side by side, their cloaks removed, hands clasped. Their eyes eagerly searched each other's faces. They talked and talked, ignoring the cups of coffee put before them.

At first, Mavreen did not tell Gerard about her visit to Compiègne for she wished to learn from him if he already knew of his mother's illness. But as he recounted his extraordinary adventures as a French army captain, she realized that he knew nothing of events at his home. He had been sent to Bavaria in the summer of the previous year when Russia, backed by the English offer of £1 million for every 100,000 troops she put into the field, joined with Austria in an attack upon Napoleon's ally. It was Gerard's task to ascertain the strength of the enemy and report his findings to his commanding officer. Instead, he had encountered a Russian soldier, been slightly wounded in the arm, and taken prisoner. His wound had healed. As an officer, he had been well-fed and reasonably treated until the advancing French armies had secured his release a few months ago. He had decided to join forces with his rescuers and moved forward with them to take part in the battle at Ulm. He had then been given leave of absence and was paying a brief visit to the captured city of Vienna before returning home.

"And I find *you* here!" he ended his story. *"C'est incroyable!"*

He looked at Mavreen with tender, searching eyes.

"You are even more beautiful than I remembered!" he said.

She was wearing an open high-waisted coat of dark

green velvet with white facings on the standing collar and lapels. Her dark green velvet hat was decorated with pink plumes, its upturned brim revealing the small golden ringlets of hair falling forward over her forehead. Gently, he twisted one around his finger.

"Je t'aime! Je t'aime!" he whispered, overcome by her proximity and the joy of being able to touch her.

"I love you, too, dearest Gerard!" she whispered back, although none of the coffee drinkers at the adjoining tables were concerned with the lovers, so engrossed were they in their discussions about their defeat and the unhappy future of their country.

Mavreen could not find the courage as yet to tell Gerard about his mother. She knew that the truth would result in his instant departure for Compiègne.

"Tell me about yourself!" he said. "I want to know everything, my love. I still cannot believe that you are alive. What miracle happened that you survived the sinking of the *Jeanne-Marie?* And Dickon—tell me, my love, what transpired?"

Briefly, Mavreen covered the facts of that fateful year; of her failure to appreciate that Gerard might believe her drowned and her subsequent bitterness when he failed to keep their tryst in the ensuing March. She tried to gloss over her reactions to his supposed desertion but he forced the truth from her. He cried out bitterly against his mother for withholding the fact from him that Mavreen was alive.

"You must not blame her!" Mavreen defended the vicomtesse. "She did only what she believed to be for the best, Gerard. And she really made the right choice. You still have a wife, and I—I married James Pettigrew. Had you known I was alive, you might have been tempted to desert poor Faustina when her mind failed. And I. . . ."

"You might never have married the faithful James!" Gerard said. "Are you happy with him, Mavreen? He always loved you, I know. Is he kind to you? And to our child? How is our baby daughter?"

Mention of James had brought an expression of anxiety and unhappiness to Mavreen's face, but now it softened into a smile.

"Tamarisk is no longer a baby, Gerard. It was her seventh birthday but a few days ago."

Eagerly, lovingly, she described their child to him. Proudly, she produced a small gold locket from about her neck and opened it for him to see his daughter's face in miniature.

Gerard smiled.

"Mavreen, she is your image—so like the little girl I met for the first time in Sussex and was so smitten with love on beholding her that I fell at her feet!"

Suddenly, they were laughing together, the future, even the present, forgotten as they relived their past. But the moment could not last. Gerard was eager to hear what incredible fate had brought Mavreen to Vienna at the same time as himself.

Mavreen swallowed painfully, feeling her throat constrict as she realized she must no longer delay in imparting the news which would drain the happiness from her beloved's face.

As gently as she could, she related the details of the past few months. Never once did Gerard interrupt her except to catch his breath when she told him that his mother's illness was fatal. He smiled briefly when Mavreen gave him an account of the card game and how she had extracted the confession from the defeated Baron von Gottfried. But his face took on a look of horror when she told him of the terrible outcome.

"You were in danger on my account!" he cried at last. "I cannot endure the thought, Mavreen. Nor yet that poor James is suffering, too."

"If he had only trusted me a little better!" Mavreen said sadly. "If he had given me but one opportunity to explain—but he never doubted I had a lover concealed in my room."

Unhappily, she tried to explain a little of James's insane jealousy, seeking whenever she could to find excuses for him.

"James married me knowing that I had taken many lovers, and I believed it was of no import to him. But I was wrong," she said sadly. "Yet I have loved no one but you, Gerard. Can you understand that?"

"Oh, my love, what right have I to condemn since I was the cause of your behavior. I should have made more inquiries at the time I was told you were drowned at sea. I should never have accepted a sailor's word for it. I cannot tell you how greatly I, too, suffered—believing you lost to me forever. I shall never forget that spring six years ago. My world was a torment of memories of you. Then my baby son died and Faustina, poor child, turned against me in her delirium. I could bear my life at Compiègne no longer. I joined the army hoping, I think, that my life would come to an end. But for my poor mother's sake, I had lost all reason to live. I never doubted that you, my only love, were dead."

"And now we meet only to part again!" Mavreen cried. "Fate has been both kind and cruel to us, Gerard. I know you must go home at once to Compiègne and I will pray that you are not too late."

"And you must come with me!" Gerard said in a low urgent voice. "I will not leave you—not again, Mavreen. I care nothing now for conventions, nor for my honor, nor even for yours. *I will not be separated from you again!*"

Mavreen caught her breath. For one irrational moment she allowed herself to believe that she might match Gerard's mood and abandon everything for love, but the memory of James, his eyes doubtless at this very minute watching the hands of the clock for her return, brought her back to the bitter chill of reason.

"I cannot leave James!" she whispered. "I cannot, Gerard. It is almost certain that he will have to undergo an amputation of his leg and the very thought is driving him to despair. If I were to leave him to go with you now. . . ."

"If he loved you, he would give you your freedom," Gerard argued. "Does your happiness not mean more to him than his own?"

"I don't know, Gerard. I know only that I cannot ask him to let me go—not now, when he may be at death's door. In calmer moments, you yourself would not wish me to do so," Mavreen added quietly.

For a little while Gerard remained silent. Then he said, "And if James should die? You would come to Compiègne to me?"

"You know that I would, Gerard!"

"But if he lives?" His voice was barely audible.

"Then I must remain with him for as long as he needs me!" Mavreen replied steadily. "But though I might find the strength to remain at James's side, I am not strong enough to renounce you, Gerard—not again. Now that Austria has been defeated, I do not know when it will be possible for James and me to return to England, nor even when his health would permit such a journey. I think it is likely we shall remain here in Vienna for some months yet at the very least. Gerard—" her voice took on a new note of urgency. "If I cannot come to you in Compiègne, will you return here to Vienna to me?"

"I swear it upon my oath!" Gerard said at once. He saw Mavreen glance anxiously at the tiny watch fob at her waist and caught hold of her hands despairingly. "You are not going to leave me yet?" he cried.

Mavreen bit hard upon her lips. "I *have* to go, Gerard. I am already long overdue and James will be frantic with anxiety. But perhaps 'twould be possible for me to slip out of the house later tonight. Rose would assist me. Where are you staying, Gerard? Do you have rooms in a hotel?"

He nodded, his heart pounding at the promise in her words.

"I will bring a carriage to your house at ten!" he said. "I will wait there for you—all night if need be."

"It is James's habit to take a sleeping draft at night—to ease his discomfort and ensure a few hours rest. I always sit with him until he sleeps. When that happens, I will come to you, Gerard. Rose shall take my place beside James's bed." She broke off to look long and deeply into Gerard's face. "If James were well, I would not so deceive him!" she said softly. "I would confess to him that I had met you by chance and that it was my intention to forsake my marriage vows and go with you no matter how deeply he hated me for it, or what the consequences to my reputation. But I cannot afford the luxury of honesty while he lies so terribly injured on my account—on our account. Do you understand, Gerard?"

He looked at her with a mixture of love and despair.

"I understand that you are not only beautiful and brave, but kind too. If I had never loved you before today, I would love you now. Come, *mon amour,* I will escort you home!"

Later that night in Gerard's arms, lying against her lover's heart, she knew once more the perfect contentment of his embrace. Forgotten now was the unwelcome feeling of wrongdoing as she had crept out of the garden door and keeping to the shadows, run in the darkness to Gerard's waiting carriage like some miscreant servant girl. Gone was the memory of James's face, white with pain, demanding that she keep her hand upon his brow because it cooled the fever of his infection. Gone even was the memory of the little daughter she had left alone in England without her mama or papa, perhaps even now crying for them.

Her world held only Gerard—the man she loved with every fiber of her being, whose touch set her body alight as none other did. His body's scent, the contour of his limbs, the ripple of the muscles of his back and legs—all touched chords of memory as she explored anew and delighted in his masculine beauty.

She knew that Gerard found equal delight in her. His hands and lips were everywhere upon her. His kisses lay upon her thighs, even upon her toes. There was no part of her kept hidden from him as he reached for her in a hunger unappeased since he had last loved her. Theirs was no quiet giving and receiving of love but a fierce mutual passion which glowed, flamed to a tumultuous blaze and left them washed up on a shore of sweet contentment. Then their needs answered, they lay in one another's arms, exchanging the tenderest of kisses, whispering endearments, the world about them quite forgotten.

Outside the window of their hotel room, the great square of the Karlsplatz lay empty and deserted, the snow falling softly and silently covering the footmarks and carriage ruts of yesterday. On the opposite side of the square, the hands of the clock on the great tower of the Karlskirche moved inexorably forward. In the silence of the pre-dawn, the hour of five rang out relentlessly. Mavreen could no longer ignore the agony of separation.

It seemed to her, as she lay staring down at Gerard's flushed face and she gently stroked his cheek, that her life had been an endless torment of partings.

I cannot bear it yet again! she thought.

But deep in her heart she knew that she had no choice.

"Swear that you will come back to me!" she cried in sudden desperation. "I can bear whatever is to come if I can believe in your return. Give me your promise, Gerard —your sacred oath. Swear to me that nothing will prevent you from returning to me!"

He drew her fiercely against him.

"I will come to you!" he vowed. "Have no fears on that score, my love." He smoothed the hair from her forehead and kissed her eyes, her cheeks, her lips. "And I have little doubt what I must do. As soon as my mother is laid to rest," he said softly, "I shall take poor little Faustina back to Naples. She will be happier living once more with her parents and has no need of me. Then I shall return to you, my only love; and not even word of your death will prevent me from searching until I find you, for I would need to stand above your grave before I believed such rumor again!"

Tears of happiness filled Mavreen's eyes. But it was time for her to return to Rosenkogel. Since the only reason for their parting was to save James the pain of knowing the truth, it was folly to risk discovery by delaying.

"I must go!" she cried. "Help me, Gerard. Do not seek to detain me," she added through her tears as he put his arms around her. "I am really not as brave as you suppose! You must have courage now for both of us."

But Gerard was as near to tears as Mavreen when a half hour later they sat with hands clasped in the hired carriage bringing them every minute closer to parting. Gerard felt no hate or jealousy of James for being instrumental in keeping Mavreen from him. Mavreen had succeeded very well in arousing in him a pity akin to her own. James had been a good friend in their schooldays and could not be blamed for loving Mavreen. Nor even could he condemn James for his possessive jealousy of her. He himself could think of no greater agony than being married to the woman he loved knowing that her heart was in another's keeping. He had no such doubts. Mavreen was his love as he was hers. He knew they would continue to love one another to the end of their lives.

Such convictions brought Gerard a measure of calm; made it possible for him to place a last kiss upon Mavreen's cold lips.

For some minutes, Gerard kept the carriage waiting in the cold. He saw a lamp appear at the window of an upstairs room and knew that Mavreen was safely arrived in her bedchamber. There was nothing now to keep him outside her house and yet he waited a while longer until lights began to appear in the houses around him and smoke to spiral upward from the chimneys. A man went past, huddled beneath his rough-spun cloak, on his way to work. A woman opened a casement window and shook the dust from her broom into the street below. The coachman coughed and fidgeted on his seat, clapping his hands together for warmth.

Gerard leaned out of the carriage window and ordered him to be on their way. As the driver's whip crackled in the air and the horses sprang to life, Gerard did not look back. With aching heart, he tried to turn his thoughts to his forthcoming journey, but all the while dreading the distance that he must put between him and the woman who had imprinted her image forever upon his heart.

CHAPTER THIRTY-FIVE
1806

"Are you quite certain you wish to remain in the room, dear lady?" Herr Professor asked. "It is not a pretty sight even for those well used to it!"

The final decision to remove James's leg had been made and there could be no further delay. As if in keeping with

the somber occasion, the sky outside was black with snow-
clouds. In James's bedchamber, a huge fire burned in the
grate and the lamps were lit to give the surgeon better
vision.

"My husband wishes to have me near him!" Mavreen replied in an undertone. "Have no fears on my account, Professor Spiegel, I will not hinder you in any way."

The professor turned away, a glint of approval in his
eyes. It was said that there was none braver than an
Englishman on the battlefield. Perhaps he was now to
witness for himself the stalwart quality of their women.

Nothing that James needed was to be denied him. Money,
Mavreen made clear to the eminent surgeon, was of no
consequence. He had therefore engaged a capable colleague to assist him. It was not considered advisable
to administer laudanum before the operation, although
the patient would be allowed the pain killer afterwards if
he survived. Therefore, two servants stood by the head
of James's bed to hold him still at the critical moments
when the limb was severed. There was always a chance
that James might make a sudden unexpected move as a
result of the pain and be the unwitting cause of a fatal
hemorrhage. In the hospitals, of course, where Professor Spiegel dealt with men of a different background who
could not be relied upon to show the courage of a gentleman to sustain them in their ordeal, they were securely
strapped to the table. This greatly eased his work. But a
man such as James Pettigrew would consider such a suggestion an insult.

James's courage was at low ebb. He had meant it in
earnest when he said he would prefer to die rather than
live as a cripple. But Mavreen's insistence that he overcome
such wicked thoughts for her sake finally won his consent
to the operation, albeit half-hoping it would kill him.

Now that the moment had come, ashen-faced, he clung
to Mavreen's hand, drawing strength from her calmness.
He determined to keep his eyes fastened upon her face
throughout his ordeal, believing that he might find the
courage to endure the pain silently rather than see his own
suffering reflected in her eyes.

"If you will remain with me, I shall not disgrace you!" he had promised her earlier that morning. He did not give thought to what she might suffer by having to watch such a bloody and remorseless operation.

Professor Spiegel was known to be a brilliant man, greatly esteemed by his medical colleagues. He was reputed to have performed amputations in under a minute; an inept surgeon might take ten minutes for the same task.

The two surgeons removed their black tailcoats but not their waistcoats, and rolled up the sleeves of their shirts. They tied clean but heavily stained white cotton aprons around their waists. Mavreen turned her head aside as she saw the younger man begin his preparation, placing a bone saw, an eight-inch-long knife, needles, silk, cotton, swabs, upon the table beside the one on which James now lay. When he was satisfied nothing was missing, Professor Spiegel glanced at his watch.

"If everyone is ready, we will commence," he said.

Several more servants were now in the room; one stood at the foot of the table ready to receive the severed limb; another with cloths and a bucket, waited to mop up the blood that might spill on the floor and cause the surgeons to slip at a critical moment. Yet another was even now giving James a glass of cordial before his ordeal began.

Mavreen stood beside him, holding his hand. She hoped that the encouraging look on her face would instill some confidence in him. Remembering the pain she, herself, had suffered at Tamarisk's birth, her heart contracted in sympathy; for although James's suffering would not be so prolonged, it would be infinitely more severe.

"Attention! Ne bougez pas, monsieur!" The professor, whose French was considerably better than his English, gave his first command.

The servants tightened their grip upon James's body which shuddered convulsively as the knife bit swiftly and surely into the flesh of his shattered thigh. His fingers tightened in a fierce grip upon Mavreen's hands and she bit her lip as a groan tore its way through his clenched lips.

"It will be over soon!" she said. "Take heart, James—it will soon be over."

"Zwirn!" she heard Professor Spiegel say to his assistant who handed him the silken thread. Expertly, the surgeon tied the blood vessels, leaving long lengths of silk which could be pulled free once the wound had healed. Silently, Mavreen prayed that James might lose all consciousness as she heard the terrible noise of the saw rasping into the bone.

His moans echoed in her head. It was to be many months before she could forget them. With her free hand, she wiped continuously at the beads of sweat pouring down his face. His lips were grey with shock.

One of the men servants fainted and was dragged from the room by another.

At last, with blessed relief, Mavreen heard the surgeon's voice,

"C'est fini, madame! Je suis bien content!"

His colleague was bandaging all that remained of James's leg. The professor walked to the head of the table and looked at the ghastly pallor of James's face. He smiled reassuringly at Mavreen.

"All went well," he informed her. "Your husband is a very brave man—and you, too, madame, showed great courage. I think we may congratulate ourselves that the most imminent danger is over. I will, however, bleed your husband as a precaution against infection. Then it will be a matter for patience as we wait for the wound to heal!"

"Have you removed my leg?" James asked, his voice roughened by pain. "It still hurts me greatly!"

"It is gone!" the professor said gently. "It is customary for a patient to continue to feel pain in a limb even after its amputation. I will give you some laudanum and you will soon feel better."

By the time he had finished his minstrations, the servants had cleared and cleaned the room and James was asleep. Mavreen took the two surgeons downstairs to the salon where refreshments awaited them. She herself could stomach nothing but a cup of hot sweetened coffee. Her visitors, however, were in good heart.

When Mavreen returned to the sickroom, she found that James, a deathly white from the loss of so much blood and the shock of the operation, was semi-conscious. Recognizing Mavreen as she approached the bedside, he feebly held out his hand and grasped hers.

"Do not leave me!" he begged. "I need you here beside me."

"I will stay. Have no fear!" Mavreen promised. As James's eyes closed and he drifted into a semi-sleep, her thoughts uncontrollably set out in search of Gerard, even now, perhaps, in his own country though she knew that he could not as yet have completed the long journey to Compiègne. Gerard had chosen to go on horseback rather than in the comparative comfort of a carriage. He would therefore be exposed to the worst elements of winter. She could derive some consolation from the thought that Napoleon had control of all the territories through which Gerard must pass; that, unlike Dickon, Gerard would be in no danger from an enemy. Nevertheless, there were always hazards in travel—brigands, cutthroats, uprisings.

"If I were only riding beside him!" Mavreen thought, her memory taking her further back to the journey they had made together from Compiègne to the French coast, with Dickon ever-watchful for a surprise attack. Unhappily, Mavreen tried to find comfort in the memory of Gerard's vow to return to find her as soon as he could leave his mother at rest. But she could not realistically hope to see him for many months to come. "Perhaps it is as well!" she thought, seeing the pathetic stump of James's leg outlined beneath the coverlets. James was going to need all her attention and she could not deny it him. By his own admission, he had little enough will to live, and it must therefore be her duty to convince him that the future held many compensations for him, but her determination to serve him was sorely tested in the ensuing weeks.

Within four days of the amputation, James was fully conscious. Through the seemingly endless hours Mavreen sat beside him, he reiterated that he preferred death to mutilation; that he would not blame her if she could not bear to set eyes upon him since he himself could not stand the sight of his stump. He was, he insisted, but half a man and would understand if Mavreen chose to leave him for a whole one.

On the fifth day, Professor Spiegel pronounced that James might be allowed out of bed. At first, he was unwilling to make the effort, protesting that he was not yet strong enough. Insisting that the professor's commands must be obeyed, Mavreen threatened to shame James in front of the servants if he continued to desist and he was eventually lifted from his bed and permitted to sit for a few hours in a chair by the fireside. The following day, Mavreen brought James a pair of crutches and urged him to take a few faltering steps across the room. This movement, however brief and exhausting, had the desired effect of stimulating James to accept the premise that he would fully recover in time and to a limited extent, be mobile enough for a degree of independence. His spirits improved and when on the tenth day after the amputation, the professor pulled out the silken threads used to secure the blood vessels, he was both brave and cheerful. The professor pronounced that there was no further need for his attentions. James's complete recovery was now assured.

At long last there were letters from her father, from Clarissa and from Tamarisk. And James heard likewise from his sister, Anne.

Sir John's letter related political events and the death of Lord Nelson. It was Clarissa's letter, long and chatty, which gave Mavreen a detailed account of her daughter.

Tamarisk is growing prettier every day. She reminds me so often of you, Mavreen, when first I saw you. How long ago that seems! Your father and I were so happy to receive your letter telling us that you and James were settling down in Vienna and I trust that you are both well and finding much to enjoy in your new life. Tamarisk never ceases to ask when you and James will decide it is safe for her to join you. But your father thinks that that horrible Napoleon has rendered such a journey unsafe for some time to come.

I pray that you will be safe in Vienna and am much

comforted by the thought that you have dear James
as well as Dickon to protect you . . .

Mavreen refrained from passing this letter to James, reading only such extracts as concerned Tamarisk. She knew that Clarissa's reference to his ability to take care of his wife would foster his feelings of inadequacy, never far beneath the outward appearance of normalcy he now contrived.

As he slowly recovered his physical health, so did he recover his physical desires. Mavreen had prepared her mind for such to happen for there was no reason why James should not continue to live a normal married life. She believed herself strong enough to pretend an affectionate response, realizing that her acceptance of his attentions in bed would be of vital importance to him. He would, she knew, be only too ready to believe, if she refused him, that his crippling in some way revolted her.

When the night came, it was not Mavreen's failure to play her part that caused the painful scene which followed. It was James's inability to believe himself a whole man. Desperately, he tried again and again to prove his manhood. In the darkness, Mavreen whispered every assurance she could, swearing upon her oath that the professor had assured her James would in time recover all his capacities as a husband, that to lose a leg in no way touched upon his virility. But James's failure was total. He wept, unconvinced and uncomforted by her reassurances.

"Let us be patient and wait a while longer," Mavreen said at last, as exhausted and defeated as he by his impotence and resulting distress. "It is but a few months since your operation, James. You need more time to get well again. In a week or two you will feel stronger. Believe me, dearest James, there is no doubt on it!"

But although James continued his agonized attempts to prove himself upon many occasions in the months to come, he had already convinced himself of his incapacity and he was never able to possess Mavreen again.

CHAPTER THIRTY-SIX

1806-1807

Three days on the journey from Vienna, Gerard was surprised by a motley band of deserters from a squadron of the defeated Pavolgrad Hussars. Several of the soldiers were wounded. They were hiding in an abandoned farmhouse, not only from the victorious French invaders but from their allies. Many of the Austrians had had no love for the Russians even before their combined armies were routed by Napoleon.

The men were frightened, disillusioned and hungry. Without an officer to rally them when they first had run from the battlefield, they had neither the wits nor the knowledge to find their way back to their own retreating regiments. With a common plight they had banded together for companionship. Unknowingly, they had wandered farther and farther to the west, stealing food from the farms, terrorizing the peasants with their muskets; as often as not drunk, their uniforms, like themselves, filthy and uncared for.

Gerard, seeking shelter in the farmhouse from a particularly heavy snowstorm which had overtaken him between two inns, walked in on them. Instantly, there were a dozen bayonets at his throat. His gold watch, money, even his warm clothing, were torn from him as the soldiers shouted conflicting opinions as to whether or not to kill him.

One, named Nikolai Kuragin, more intelligent than his companions, argued fiercely in favor of keeping Gerard alive.

"There may be no truth in his statement that he is a vicomte," he admitted, "but there is no doubt he is of noble birth. As such, he can be a useful hostage!"

The life of an army officer and a gentleman had value,

Kuragin pointed out. They were in enemy-occupied territory. If they were caught by the French they could bargain their lives for Gerard's. If they reached the safety of their own country, the capture of a titled French officer might mitigate any punishment meted out by their Russian commanders for desertion on the battlefield. They could concoct a tale of having lost contact with their regiments accidentally while in pursuit of Gerard.

Finally they agreed that for the time being he might remain alive. Disarmed, he presented no danger to them and might, indeed, prove useful. There were more urgent matters requiring their attention—the basic need for food and warmth. It was still mid-winter and the severity of the elements was proving their greatest enemy. The map they had stolen from Gerard was now consulted at frequent intervals and a route northward toward Russia decided upon. They were all agreed that it was time to go home.

At first, Gerard remained passive, believing the slightest provocation from him might sway the more temperate of the soldiers to change their minds and agree with those already desirous of killing him. He was aware that, to some degree, they were still suffering from the fear and shock of the battle in which they had been routed. He knew it would not take much for one or other of them to run him through with his own sword. He hoped that somewhere on the long journey to Russia, he would almost certainly find an opportunity to escape. But for the time being, he was carefully guarded. Each in turn, his eight captors kept him under surveillance day and night. His hands were roughly tied in front of him and the rope attached to the belt of his escort. The men now had horses—stolen, emaciated, but at least affording them mounts. Gerard was permitted to ride his own stallion, a thoroughbred he had purchased in Vienna. The infantrymen who for the most part had never sat astride an animal before, considered the big chestnut too high-spirited for their own use.

Nikolai Kuragin had become their self-appointed leader. He, alone, had knowledge of the French language and took childish delight in showing off his ability to converse fluently in it. He rode many hours at Gerard's side, recounting the grim tale of the recent fighting at Austerlitz.

Nikolai was rough and more or less uneducated, but he was not by nature cruel. Gerard was kept tied day and night but only, Nikolai told him, because he refused to give his word as a gentleman that he would not try to escape. Otherwise, he was treated no better or worse than if he were one of them. He was not permitted to shave and only allowed to wash when they did, which was infrequently. From time to time, they would halt at some out-of-the-way farm and at pistol point, steal wine, food and clothing from the occupants. These spoils were shared equally among them.

Gerard had no opportunity to escape. He fretted continuously at this enforced delay in his journey to Compiègne, but not even the now friendly Nikolai could be persuaded to release him in order to return to his dying mother.

"If it was up to me alone, I'd let you go!" Nikolai said sympathetically. "But the others are afraid of what will happen to them when we get back home. You are the only proof we have that we aren't ordinary deserters—" He grinned sardonically, adding, "—which, of course, we are but dare not admit to it!"

It was mid-March when they finally crossed the border into Russia. Gerard was as unkempt as his captors. His face was roughened and weatherbeaten, his beard long, his hair as filthy as his hands and nails. So it was that his captors' hopes proved in vain when they were challenged by the border guards. Gerard's protests to the Russians that he was a French vicomte and an army officer and should be treated on such level as a prisoner of war were laughed at. His captors had long since disposed of his uniform and his papers and he had no means of identification. Not even Nikolai could convince the Russians that Gerard was no common prisoner. They determined that he was a French spy and decided to try to beat a confession out of him with their rifle butts. Nikolai, despite his own perilous position, rushed to Gerard's defense as the butt smashed into his face a second time.

Gerard could recall little of subsequent events. Later Nikolai told him that they had both been beaten into semiconsciousness. The other deserters were marched away by one of the border guards to a nearby military camp. He and Gerard were bound and taken by carriage and flung unceremoniously into a civilian prison to await trial as spies.

Despite a dislocated jaw and a face so swollen with bruises that any movement was agonizing, Gerard managed to speak.

"But why you, Nikolai?" he gasped.

"Because they are ignorant fools!" Nikolai replied.

"Because you came to my assistance!" Gerard argued.

Nikolai grinned sheepishly.

"I'll not stand by and see an innocent man beaten to a pulp by a bunch of savages!" he said. "Now cease talking and leave it to me to get you out of here. Won't be long, I promise!"

But even as he tried to cheer Gerard, he was intelligent enough to appreciate that without the means of identification for Gerard, there was little or no hope that they would ever leave the prison alive.

In Vienna, Mavreen continued to nurse James back to health throughout the spring. Professor Spiegel, delighted with his patient's progress, said they might return to England in June. With Baron Stern's assistance, Mavreen began to make inquiries as to the possibility of travelling home through France. The authorities were not unsympathetic to her request for papers guaranteeing James, herself, and their staff a safe passage across France.

The czar had bound himself in secret articles to join forces with Napoleon, to join in the continental blockade and force Denmark, Sweden, Portugal and Austria to make war upon English commerce. Napoleon, with Austria and Prussia at his feet, Russia now his ally, and Pitt dead, was convinced England would no longer dare to refuse him peace. The French authorities in Vienna saw no reason, therefore, to deny the Englishwoman a safe passage home. Mavreen, the former Lady Barre, was known by them to have many influential friends and connections. To assist her and her crippled husband at this juncture would cost them nothing and might prove useful in the future when their countries were at peace. The necessary papers were prepared and by the end of May, were signed.

It was now four months since Gerard had departed for Compiègne. Dickon had returned to Vienna with the news that the vicomtesse had died twenty-four hours after his arrival. Although Dickon remained in Compiègne a further month, having contracted a fever which rendered him too weak to travel, there was no sign of Gerard. Mavreen, upon hearing this news, grew daily more anxious. She knew that Gerard must have been waylaid, and worried for his safety. Now, even supposing he had finally arrived at the château, too late to see his mother alive, he would almost certainly have set out at once to return to her. But would he come to Vienna? Or would he assume that after so long a period of time, she would have gone back with James to England?

She vacillated between the two possibilities, alternately deciding to leave for England at the first possible moment James could travel without harm; and delaying their departure for Gerard's possible arrival in Vienna.

Finally, her own longing to see Tamarisk again as much as James' self-imposed resignation to the life of an invalid, prompted her. She hoped that in new surroundings, away from the country which had brought him such miserable misfortune, James might revive his spirits and take new heart. Once back at Finchcocks, the hoped-for change in James did not take place. Only Tamarisk, dancing in and out of the library where James now chose to confine himself, could bring the occasional smile to his face or a cheerful rejoinder. He was otherwise morose and withdrawn.

Sitting in the garden beneath the magnolia tree at Orchid House she was able to enjoy the simple pleasure of conversation far from James's hungry, brooding gaze. At home, his eyes followed her everywhere she went, demanding the love and attention she tried to give unstintingly but which was slowly becoming paralyzed by his possessiveness.

He had been fitted with a wooden leg but complained that it pained him too much to wear it. He had finally abandoned it and relied upon his crutches for a limited mobility. For the greater part of the day, he elected to remain in his armchair, occasionally reading a copy of the London *Times* but more often, without occupation, watching her as she went about her duties.

"It is not even as if he desires conversation with me!" Mavreen told Clarissa, her only confidant with regard to James. "He simply sits with his eyes fastened upon me, unsmiling. At times—and I know I should not be saying this—I feel he is my jailer and I his prisoner who might, if he turns his gaze away, escape to my freedom!"

Hearing the note of near hysteria in Mavreen's voice, Clarissa patted her arm soothingly.

"Illness does have strange effects upon folk!" she said. "Perhaps when James is fully recovered, he will behave less strangely. It is not, after all, much more than nine months since his dreadful operation."

Mavreen sighed, "It would seem as if the Fates never intended happiness for me," she said. "Gerard and I—we have had neither our youth nor, by the way of things, shall we have our later years beside one another. Oh, Aunt Clarrie, if I but knew where he was! If he reached Compiègne after Dickon had left, I am certain he would have lingered but a day or two to see to the vicomtesse's affairs. He would most surely be beside me now if harm had not befallen him. I have no doubt on it. Each night I pray for him. But there are days when I am filled with fear that he is dead and that I shall never set eyes upon him again."

Clarissa patted Mavreen's arm reassuringly.

"You would know, somewhere deep inside yourself, if Gerard had departed this earth," she said convincingly. "Since there are days when you believe him still alive, then I have no doubt he is so. There is some magic, witchcraft, call it what you will, that binds true lovers together as if they were but one person. You would be convinced of his death—nay, even the moment of it—if the worst had befallen."

As always, Clarissa was successful in calming Mavreen. She gave her fresh confidence which dissipated some of the tension in her body. But she suddenly remembered James, waiting for her return with anxious eyes. It was not yet five o'clock and with a sense of reprieve, Mavreen relaxed once more beside Clarissa.

"Tell me about Dickon!" Clarissa commanded. "Have he and Rose still not yet set a date for their wedding?"

"Perhaps they will wed next spring!" Mavreen replied. "I feel responsible that the date has so often been postponed on my account. But you know Dickon, Aunt Clarrie! If he is to undertake anything, it must be done to the utmost; and when I last spoke to him about Rose, he said he would not feel able to settle down to marriage until my life was more settled. Such devotion is admirable but leaves me with them both upon my conscience. Dickon is travelling to France twice every year on my behalf to inquire for news of Gerard. As you know, I cannot leave James, else I would go myself to Compiègne. It will be Dickon's third visit in December. I have told him that if Gerard has not returned home by then, we shall be forced to assume he is dead."

"Dickon has been a loyal servant!" Clarissa said. "I was pleased to see him looking so well when he brought you here today."

Mavreen smiled.

"Dickon is as strong as a bear!" she laughed. "Or so Tamarisk describes him. She adores him with a devotion not unlike mine own when I was her age."

It was on the tip of Clarissa's tongue to ask if Mavreen did not regret that she had no further children from her marriage to James, but tactfully, she remained silent. Mavreen had hinted that the marriage had been "incomplete" since the accident to James in Vienna; and, of course, Clarissa was already aware of the complications at Tamarisk's birth and Mother Sale's prediction that Mavreen might not easily conceive another child.

Reluctantly, Mavreen rose to her feet at last, gathering her parcels.

"I will have to leave you," she said, "but I will visit with you again next week! Meanwhile, will you tell father that James and I are hoping he will bring you to dinner with us very soon?"

But Clarissa's subsequent visit was not on any pleasurable account. James was ill.

At first, it was believed he had only a chill. Mavreen insisted he return to bed and nursed him herself until it became apparent that his fever was rising. Moreover, he had begun to spit blood.

She at once called in one of the king's physicians, Dr. Willis. At the start he refused to make a firm diagnosis, but two weeks after his first examination, Mavreen insisted that he inform her as to what ailed her husband. James, he told her bluntly, had contracted consumption. Mavreen at once called in his rival, Dr. Warren for a second opinion. They were in complete accord as to James's illness. They could offer Mavreen little hope of his recovery.

As the year neared its end, James's condition worsened. He was indifferent to advice or encouragement from anyone but Mavreen. It was she who handed him the drops of ipecacuanha wine when his cough was troublesome, who saw that he had his three daily drops of laudanum to relieve his pain; she who sponged his body twice daily with vinegar and tepid water; and supervised the administering of the doctor's orders within the sick room.

But although she assured James over and over again that a natural recovery from the disease was known to both his doctors, James seemed to accept that he had not long to live. Nor could Mavreen instill in him the will to do so.

She fought hard and relentlessly for his life but her greatest enemy, the doctor told her, was the depression that had never really left James since his operation.

With the added persuasion of his sister, Anne, who was once more residing at Finchcocks to give Mavreen the moral support she so badly needed, James was taken by Clarissa and Mavreen to Hastings, where the doctors believed the sea air would be beneficial to his wasting lungs.

But James's depression merely increased. By Christmas, they returned to Finchcocks.

Tamarisk, who had always been fond of James, was deeply distressed by his appearance. He had lost a great deal of weight.

Although Mavreen kept her as far as possible from the sick room, her small daughter was well aware from the servants' gossip that her stepfather was expected soon to die.

One night, a few days before her eighth birthday, Tamarisk clung to her mother as she bent over the child's bed to kiss her a fond goodnight.

"Oh, Mama, why do all my Papas die!" she wailed, tears welling into her blue eyes.

Exhausted and distressed as Mavreen was by the past weeks of fruitless effort at James's bedside, tears came also into her own eyes. First, poor Gilbert, who was Tamarisk's father by name, had died before his allotted span, leaving her alone and widowed. Now James was about to depart the world. And deep in her heart was the fear that Gerard, Tamarisk's real father, might already be dead, too. It seemed as if some evil fate awaited those closest to her.

"Perhaps Uncle James will get better soon!" she tried to comfort Tamarisk.

But he died in his sleep, following upon a catastrophic hemorrhage, on the morning of the first day of the New Year, eight years since Mavreen had brought Tamarisk into the world.

CHAPTER THIRTY-SEVEN

1807

Since Mavreen was in mourning, she remained in seclusion at Finchcocks, recuperating from the exhaustion that followed James's death.

She was genuinely distressed at the loss of her husband but, as Clarissa alone knew, James had made their last year together all but intolerable with his own undisguised unhappiness. Had he been able to rise above his misfortune, the recovery of his spirits as well as his health might have been possible. As it was, his physical incapacities became not only his burden but Mavreen's.

Anne assured her many times that no wife could have been more dutiful, more self-sacrificing, more loving. But Mavreen knew that to the last of these attributes, she could make no claim. She had never loved James.

It would, Mavreen knew, be a long time before she could put from her mind the memory of James's eyes following her about the room, demanding from her something she could not give him. She would never feel entirely guiltless about his death.

Tamarisk, with the resilience of the young, turned her affections to Sir John, her grandpapa, who, since James's death, made frequent calls at Finchcocks. Bouncing his pretty little granddaughter on his knee, he teased her affectionately.

"Why am I so cursed as to have none but silly females about me?" he would grumble fiercely into the many-folded muslin halter in which was buried the end of his chin.

Tamarisk would laugh, pull his side-whiskers and reply, "Because you love us, Grandpapa, else you would not come a-calling!"

He would tease her a little longer.

"I wanted your mother to give me a strong, brave grandson like young Master Lade. Now there's a lad who can sit his pony like a real horseman!"

Tamarisk beat her small fist against the dingy brown coat of his favorite morning suit.

"You know I can jump higher than Harry, Grandpapa. Come riding with me and I will show you that I am as brave as any boy!"

Still pretending disbelief, Sir John would change into his riding clothes and accompany Mavreen and the excited little girl down to the miniature race course made for the child under Dickon's direction.

"She is truly your daughter!" Sir John said to Mavreen as they watched the child fearlessly put her pony to the highest jump.

Nevertheless, Mavreen knew that she had disappointed him in not fathering sons during her brief marriage to James, although he never mentioned the subject. She, herself, was greatly relieved that no children had resulted from the marriage. She wished to forget as soon as possible the few but oppressive years of a marriage that should never have been agreed upon. She vowed that she would never again consider matrimony. The condition demanded more of her than she could give, she now realized. There was no love in her heart for any man but Gerard, and no matter how vehemently Gilbert and James had denied before marriage a need for her love, each in their own way had filled her with a sense of guilt for her failure to surrender her heart to them.

She did not, however, remain long without suitors. At twenty-seven she was far more beautiful than she had been at seventeen. Suffering showed in her face so that in repose, there was sadness there as well as courage and determination. There was still fire and spirit in the vivacity of her eyes, humor in the tiny lines about her mouth, but they were more rarely seen and the men who observed her felt challenged by the need to discover the depths beneath her outward composure; to unveil the imponderable facets of this fascinating woman who seemed to encompass all aspects of her sex. They felt a desire to dominate her proud spirit, to bring about her surrender to a will other than her own.

That summer of 1807, the reputation of the erstwhile "Barre Diamond" took on a new meaning. Where, before her marriage, she was known to take many men to her bed without loving one of them, now she was known to love many men without taking one to her bed.

The Baroness von Eburhard rented a house in Brighthelmstone and invited Mavreen, with Tamarisk, to sojourn there for the month of August. The elderly baron had now retired from all forms of social life and remained in their London house, so Lisa was delighted to have Mavreen for company. Sir John was taking Clarissa to Scotland, having received an invitation to go grouse shooting on the moors. Thus, Mavreen, Tamarisk and Lisa were free to enjoy themselves as they pleased.

Lisa, always a jolly and gregarious woman, had many friends at court, most of whom, like herself, were now in residence in Brighthelmstone in anticipation of the prince's birthday celebrations. It was not long, therefore, before Mavreen's presence became known and there was much gossip about her.

She had been absent from society for some years and now that she was back amongst them, there was much speculation as to the way of life she intended to choose. Would she remain faithful to the memory of her late husband? They supposed that James must have held powerful sway over her since he, alone, had been able to subdue her wild behavior before her marriage. Would Mavreen, they asked one another, retain her new respectability or would she revert to her old ways and scandalize them all with the importance and variety of her lovers? They deemed it unlikely that the chaperonage of the loving baroness would curtail Mavreen's escapades.

But although there were many male callers at the large house on the esplanade, there was no gossip from the servants' hall.

Among those who called at the house was John William Ward. He was three years younger than Mavreen but already a member of Parliament, and although shy and a little eccentric in his manner, he was clever and very well educated.

One of Lisa von Eburhard's many acquaintances, John Ward was but an hour in Mavreen's company before he found himself fascinated, as much by the quick intelligence of her mind as by her beauty. Within one week he was calling upon her every day. After ten days he declared himself in love with her.

Mavreen enjoyed his company as much as he enjoyed hers, but her interest in him was purely platonic. She therefore informed him kindly and gently that it was not yet a year since James's death; that she had no intention whatever of remarrying; thereby giving him the impression that she had loved James too deeply ever to desire to replace him.

Nevertheless, Ward continued to call upon her. Once his shyness had been overcome, he showed himself to be an amusing and sometimes malicious talker. His conversation was at times inclined to be gossip, especially about the royal family. He had told her that the prince was "sick with longing" for the unresponsive Lady Hertford, so it was with great interest that she found herself being introduced to this irresistable lady, she and Lord Hertford being the prince's guests at the Pavilion.

Later, Mavreen agreed with Lisa that Isabella Hertford was a beautiful woman. But she was nearing fifty and her expression, Mavreen commented, was haughty and forbidding. It was quite obvious to any observer that the good lady's continuing refusal of the prince's attentions was only serving to enflame further his extraordinary passion for her.

"Not really so extraordinary!" remarked the baroness later, "seeing that the prince has always been attracted to older women. Were you aware that Lady Hertford has been a grandmother these past twelve years or more!"

Much had been done to the Pavilion since Mavreen was last there. A Chinese gallery had been made in order to exhibit some lovely wallpapers that had been given to the prince.

The prince took Mavreen on a personally-conducted tour, proudly showing her the oriental porcelain and furniture, bamboo sofas and lacquered cabinet, weapons and curios, ivory junks and pagodas, lanterns and uniforms all of which he had had brought down to the Pavilion from Carlton House.

He took Mavreen outside to show her the immense Indian-style structure of the new stables and riding house. Under the huge central cupola, eighty-five feet wide, there was stabling for fifty-four horses as well as living accommodation for the hostlers and grooms.

The work, he explained to Mavreen, had been seriously curtailed by the inability to obtain sufficiently large timbers for the dome during the French blockade of continental ports.

"And further curtailed," he admitted ruefully, "because I am harassed with letters from the tradesmen in Brighthelmstone whom I can ill afford to pay. Nevertheless, we hope it will be completed next year."

Happy to have found in Mavreen an enthusiastic listener, the prince showed her Humphrey Repton's designs for an Indian Pavilion, which, he declared, he found quite perfect.

There were changes elsewhere in Brighthelmstone other than those at the Pavilion. With the baroness and Tamarisk, Mavreen went out in the carriage for an airing each afternoon and saw some of the many handsome new houses. Sometimes accompanying them on these outings was a nephew of the baron's. A handsome, amusing young man in his late thirties, Thomas Creevey was, like John Ward, a member of Parliament and a frequent guest at the Pavilion. Also, like Ward, he was greatly attracted to Mavreen. They both sent her flowers and paid compliments to the plump Lisa in an attempt to enlist her sympathies in their cause.

Lisa von Eburhard chuckled happily to Mavreen about her two suitors. An unashamed romantic, she enjoyed intrigues, whether they involved herself or her friends. She was greatly attached to Mavreen and not a little sorry for her that she had been twice widowed before she was thirty. Lisa was far too kindhearted to be jealous of her youth or of the attraction she held for men. She was disappointed that Mavreen would give neither suitor the slightest encouragement while remaining friendly and charming to both.

"Does not either one appeal to you, my dear?" she asked when yet another basket of flowers was delivered at the house.

"I like them both!" Mavreen replied smiling. "John is the more serious and I think possibly the more intelligent of the two and certainly the more intellectual. But Thomas is amusing. Do you not agree that we laugh more in his company than in John's?"

But Thomas was with the prince's party on the day of the royal birthday celebrations and it was therefore John Ward who escorted Mavreen, Tamarisk, and the baroness. Tamarisk was wild with excitement and had to shout to make her small voice heard above the combined noise of the church bells, the guns firing from ships offshore and the town band which played ceaselessly and with great gusto.

Lisa had arranged for her servants to bring a luncheon picnic to White Hawk Hill where long lines of carriages were drawn up in readiness to witness the review. The

Prince of Wales was very much in evidence, the frogged jacket of his Hussar uniform strained across his chest, his vast waist encircled with a belt of diamonds, his eyes twinkling merrily in his puffy face. A jauntily-set astrakhan cap crowned his head.

After the review, they went home. As a special favor Tamarisk was permitted to watch Rose remove Mavreen's straw bonnet and undo all the buttons on the back of her cambric frock. She sat in silence, gazing openmouthed as the dressing of her mother for the ball commenced. When the long process was at last finished she gasped with admiration. Mavreen stood before her, a fairy queen in white satin gown, the heavy gold embroidery glinting in the light of the candles on the dressing-table. Her long train was lined with emerald green velvet.

"It will be difficult to control when I have to make my curtsy to His Royal Highness," Mavreen said, smiling at Tamarisk as she pirouetted before her. "It has always been my dread that on an important occasion such as this, I shall trip and this beautiful tiara will fall from my head and roll to His Highness's feet!"

"Oh, Mama! How truly dreadful that would be!" Tamarisk breathed. "But it won't happen. Not to my beautiful and clever mama! You will be the loveliest lady at the ball, I know it!"

"Thank you, my sweeting. I would I could believe you to be right. Now run along and bid the baroness goodnight, then off to bed with you, my dear child. The hour is late and you will be too tired in the morning to listen to all I shall have to tell you."

It was an evening she would remember, Mavreen thought as she tried to memorize details with which to regale Tamarisk in the morning.

There were at least five hundred illustrious guests who sat down at the vast, flower bedecked table to partake of the lavish banquet. The Prince of Wales looked resplendent in bottle green and claret-colored striped-silk coat and breeches. His waistcoat was of silver tissue, richly embroidered with stones and colored silks in curious bouquets of flowers. The exiled French royal family were guests of honor. The lesser the importance of the personages, the further down toward the end of the table they sat; or else, like Mavreen and the baroness, were relegated to tables in the garden.

"I know 'tis wrong of me to dwell on such matters at such a time," Mavreen said quietly to her companion, "but I cannot prevent myself thinking of those born in so much less fortunate circumstances."

"Ah, the poor!" John Ward agreed, not unsympathetically. "Since the advent of the new Corn Laws, there are many thousands half-starving on poor relief."

" 'Tis the small holders with no great fields of wheat and the farm laborers who suffer," Mavreen said quietly, "whilst the landowners and the larger farmers benefit."

"Do not forget the vast numbers in the north and midlands," John Ward reminded her. "Even the wives and children work in the mines and foundries and the new factories for a pitiful wage and sometimes in appalling conditions."

"I shall call upon your sympathy for them one day in the future," Mavreen said softly.

"Any cause in which you have any interest will ensure mine own," he replied with utmost seriousness.

When the repast was finally over, the ladies withdrew to renew their toilettes before dancing began in the ball-room. The baroness smiled knowingly at Mavreen.

"Young John Ward is deeply in love!" she remarked. " 'Tis my opinion he may declare himself this very night, Mavreen. Do you think you might consider him?"

Mavreen shook her head.

"Never!" she said honestly. "I shall not marry again, dear baroness."

Lisa shrugged her plump shoulders.

"Mayhap in your case widowhood had its compensations. You can afford to be without a husband to support you and it is certain you will never lack for admirers!"

Thomas Creevey was not the only man to vie with John Ward to dance with Mavreen. Those who had not escorted relations or ladies of their choosing to the ball and hence were free to let their eyes roam, jostled one another in anxious enthusiasm to gain her promise to keep the next dance free for them. Mavreen took the floor with each in turn, favoring neither one nor the other.

The baroness, too, did not lack for partners. The heat from the many candles blazing all around the great ball-room made the atmosphere uncomfortably warm, and despite the frequent use of her ivory fan, the plump Lisa was perspiring copiously as she swept past Mavreen with a gay wave of recognition on the arms of a young hussar.

There was too great a pressure of people at all times around the birthday prince for Mavreen to catch more than a fleeting glimpse of him.

It was four in the morning before Mavreen, quite exhausted, climbed into her big four-poster and drew the curtains. But the room seemed airless and she drew back the bed curtains and opened the casement as wide as possible to let in the cool breeze blowing in from the sea.

A brilliant harvest moon hung in the sky. Standing alone at the window staring at the great golden orb, her thoughts turned inevitably to Gerard.

There was little hope now that he was alive. Dickon's last visit to Compiègne had proved as fruitless as the others. Jules, retired now and living in one of the farm cottages on the estate, had heard nothing of his young master. He, too, believed Gerard to be dead.

But as Mavreen climbed wearily back into bed, she comforted herself with the conviction that lay deep within her being, that despite all the evidence to the contrary, Gerard still lived; that even at this moment, he was regarding the same moon and thinking of her.

Suddenly, she heard the very slightest of footfalls on the landing outside her door. Slowly, as she watched, the handle turned and the door creaked open. Her thoughts flew to the tiny pistol she kept in the drawer of the table by her bed. Since the incident of Baron von Gottfried, she was never without it. But as her hand reached out for it, a small figure, white in the darkness, approached the bed, and she recognized her daughter, Tamarisk.

The child climbed stealthily onto the bedcover and reached out a small hot hand to touch Mavreen's eyelids.

"Mama, are you awake?" she whispered.

Mavreen smiled.

"I'm fast asleep and dreaming that Tamarisk has come to pay me a nocturnal visit!" she whispered back.

She heard Tamarisk's delighted chuckle and then the small warm body slid into bed beside her.

"I couldn't sleep!" she explained. "And I became lonely!"

"And how did you escape down here?" Mavreen enquired, knowing that Tamarisk's room in the nurseries on the top floor of the house led out of her governess's bedchamber.

"Mistress Payne was asleep!" Tamarisk replied, feeling for Mavreen's hand and twining her fingers around it. The small body suddenly shook with suppressed laughter. "She was snoring louder than a dragon, Mama. She never heard me, although I tiptoed right past her head!"

"Mistress Payne will be very angry if she finds out!" Mavreen told her daughter.

"But you won't tell, will you, Mama?" For a moment, the child was quiet, and then she said dreamily, "Mama, tell me a story!" she begged. "About you when you were a little girl like me."

"About Dickon and the farm?" Mavreen asked, for Tamarisk had never lost her affection for Owlett's farm and the Sale family.

Tamarisk shook her head.

"No, Mama, thank you. Tell me about the young Frenchman who rode a white pony called Colombe; the nobleman you loved when you were a little girl, but he rode away and never came back."

Mavreen's heartbeat quickened.

"There isn't a great deal more to say about him!" she replied with difficulty, for there was now a lump in her throat which forbade speech.

"Oh, Mama, there is!" Tamarisk protested. "Dickon said he had beautiful brown curls and brown eyes like chestnuts when you first take them out of their shells. Dickon said he rode a horse as well as himself—and you know how good that is! Rose said he was the most beautiful young man she had ever set eyes upon. I wish I had been born so that I could have seen him, too. Dickon said that you might have married him if he had come back to England, but when he didn't return from the war, you married Papa instead."

"All that is true!" Mavreen agreed. "That is how I became Lady Barre and why you are Tamarisk Barre!"

"Dickon said you went to France in the middle of the Revolution to try to find the nobleman. His name was Gerard. You were very brave, Mama, and saved Dickon's life when the wolves attacked him!"

"You and Dickon seem to have done a great deal of talking!" Mavreen commented, but now she was finding a strange happiness in hearing Gerard's daughter speaking his name.

"We talk when we go riding!" Tamarisk said. "Mama, shall I confide a secret to you?"

"If you tell a secret, it isn't one any more!"

"Yes, but telling *you* isn't really telling, is it?" Tamarisk argued illogically. "In any event, although I promised the vicomtesse I would never speak of her present to me, I don't think she really meant to exclude you because she loved you so very much."

"I loved her, too!" Mavreen said softly.

"She was Gerard's mama!" Tamarisk told Mavreen. "She told me lots and lots of stories of things he did when he was a little boy. And, Mama, she gave me this!"

She pressed something into Mavreen's hand. Mavreen sat up and lit the candle. In her child's hand lay a tiny gold locket in the shape of a heart. Even before she pressed the clasp, she knew that it contained a miniature of Gerard.

"Wasn't he a pretty baby?" Tamarisk said eagerly beside her. "I think he was even prettier than baby Thomas!"

"Oh, Tamarisk, how could you have had this all this time and I not known of it?" Mavreen murmured, but not reproachfully.

"I wanted to show it to you, but I wasn't quite sure if the vicomtesse would object!" Tamarisk explained. "I was lying awake in bed tonight thinking about it and I decided she wouldn't mind at all. Was I wrong, Mama?"

"No, darling," Mavreen said, blowing out the candle so that her child should not see the tears in her eyes. "You must always take great care of it because I think the vicomtesse has given you one of her most precious of treasures."

"Oh, I know, Mama—" Tamarisk said, her voice suddenly sleepy. "I know how carefully you guard the little miniature of me. . . ."

Tenderly, Mavreen smoothed the golden hair away from the now-sleeping child's forehead. Tears coursed silently down her cheeks as she remembered, with heartbreaking clarity, the brief glimpse of heaven that had been hers when she'd met Gerard in the snow-covered streets of Vienna and shown him the tiny portrait of their child.

CHAPTER THIRTY-EIGHT
1807-1808

Frederick William, king of Prussia, was a sad, vacillating man, who changed sides no less than six times in the three years preceding 1806. In the summer of that year, he finally allied himself with the coalition consisting of England, Saxony, Russia and Sweden, and issued an ultimatum to Napoleon to evacuate his troops from the Confederation of the Rhine else Prussia would go to war.

But in a six-day campaign, Napoleon annihilated the Prussian army at the battles of Jena and Auerstadt and followed up this victory by attacking the Russians and defeating them at Friedland. The czar, Alexander, had no alternative but to make peace and the Treaty of Tilsit was ratified in July of 1807.

It was this peace treaty which finally made possible Gerard's release from the prison where he had been for over a year. It was his former captor, Nikolai Kuragin, who saved him from certain death.

Raised as he had been in the direst poverty, Nikolai had learned at an early age how to fend for himself; and more important still, how to defend himself. The scum who shared their rat-infested prison would not have hesitated to kill Gerard for a crust of the moldy, filthy bread that was for the most part all they were given to eat.

Thieves, murderers, beggars—some innocent, like Gerard—most guilty, filled the jail. The prisoners received no trials were not permitted visitors or communication with the outside world. They were forgotten men. When the jail became too crowded, some of the worst offenders were taken out and executed in the prison yard for no better reason than to make room for the newcomers.

Gerard's health had stood up well enough to the rigors of their long journey to Russia through the bitter winter weather, but within two weeks of his imprisonment, he was sick with fever contracted from the stinking, stagnant drinking water. Nikolai, who had developed both a liking and respect for the young French vicomte, appointed himself Gerard's nurse and protector. Big, strong and self-reliant as he was, their fellow prisoners soon learned it did not pay to bully the newcomers. Nikolai was strong enough to break a man's neck with one hand and few doubted that he was not above doing so if pushed too far.

Before a few weeks had passed, Nikolai became the leader. His ragged, motley cellmates both feared him and respected his stronger character. Even the guards, who treated the prisoners no better than animals, had some respect for Nikolai and chose to keep on reasonable terms with him, never kicking him or taunting him as was their custom with other men if they so much as begged for food.

One guard, in particular, became susceptible to Nikolai's dominant personality. Less brutal and better educated than the rest of the prison staff, he alone believed Nikolai's story about Gerard. When the Frenchman lay near to death, Nikolai succeeded in frightening this man with threats as to what might happen to him and the others were Gerard to die.

"He is an aristocrat, idiot!" Nikolai shouted fearlessly at the man, with complete disregard for the respect due from a prisoner. "All aristocrats have relatives in other countries besides their own. This man has an uncle in Petrograd—

a prince, no less. He is married to the daughter of a prince of Naples. Do you think such people will shrug their shoulders and forget about those who allowed him to die? The vicomte needs medicine, a couple of warm blankets, hot soup. You can get all these things. Then, at least I'll be able to tell his relations that you, Leo Petrovsky, did your best to save him even if he dies in spite of all."

Gradually, by sheer force of will, Nikolai convinced the guard that it might be less of a risk to secrete into the cell a few extras than to do nothing and allow the Frenchman to die. Nikolai guaranteed there would be no fighting over the extra rations. He himself stood guard over Gerard's shivering body, spooned hot soup into his mouth, and sent any man who came within reach far across the freezing stone floor with one blow of his fist. Although close to starving himself, he never touched the food the guard brought in for Gerard, who often could not eat, but husbanded it until later when he would try once more to force it down the sick man's throat.

When Gerard finally showed signs of recovery, he was in no doubt that he owed his life to Nikolai.

"If I ever get out of here, I'll find some way to reward you!" he promised.

"We'll get out, never fear!" Nikolai grunted. "As for rewarding me, if you really think I have served you well, perhaps you could consider giving me employment as your servant? I'd be loyal to you. I'm sick to the teeth with army life. Private service would suit me very well if it was service to a man such as yourself!"

Gerard was surprised and grateful. He assured Nikolai that if they could but escape from the dungeon that was their prison, he would be more than willing to take Nikolai into his employ. Meanwhile, they must try to find a way to secure their release.

It was some months before Nikolai and Gerard between them could bribe their guard, Leo Petrovsky, with a mixture of threats and promises, to bring them pen and ink. Interested to see if Gerard really could write, since he himself could not, the guard finally produced the necessary materials. Since he could not read, he had to inquire of Gerard to whom he addressed his letter.

"To the French ambassador," Gerard informed him.

Leo Petrovsky spat on the floor and handed the letter back to Gerard.

"Don't you know we're at war with Napoleon? I'd be taken for a spy myself if I tried to pass on a letter to a Frenchman."

Eagerly, Gerard demanded news. They had now been imprisoned for three months and he thirsted for information about the outside world.

The man knew little of foreign affairs. He'd heard said that the defeated king of Prussia had sought refuge in Russia; that Napoleon had made one of his brothers, Joseph, king of Naples and Sicily.

He had also heard tell that Napoleon had his greedy eyes set upon Turkey and a large Russian army was concentrated in the Ukraine to guard the frontier.

"He may be on the doorstep but he won't ever put foot on Russian soil," he boasted. "As to that," he said, jerking his head scornfully in the direction of Gerard's carefully worded appeal for assistance, "might as well try sending that to the moon!"

The quill and ink were left in the cell, but since there was no paper, Gerard could write no further letters. Pleas to Leo Petrovsky were now to no avail.

The ink was used, thereafter, for the keeping of a calendar, scratched upon the wall. As the weeks dragged past, and Gerard regained his strength, his natural authority asserted itself. He was able, by degrees, to instill some sense of social behavior into his fellow prisoners. Although it was not possible to do much without water, the filth in the cell was reduced. Rats and other vermin were hunted daily and an extra cut from the loaf of bread or a larger helping of soup given to the man judged to have destroyed the largest number. Mealtimes ceased to be a mad and sometimes lethal scramble where the strongest took the largest portion. Between them, Gerard and Nikolai took control of all the food and any early resistance to this authority ceased as soon as each man saw that he was getting an equal share, larger portions going only to the sick or as daily rewards. Proper respect was paid to the men who died and although their meager possessions were removed for the benefit of the community, religious objects were left about the necks of the corpses.

To break the appalling monotony of their squalid existence, Gerard told the men stories. He had learned to speak Russian and now taught his fellow prisoners words in English and French. He tried without much success, to teach them to read and write but with no books or materials, they made little progress. The calendar was consulted every day. Religious days were observed by the saying of prayers by any man who knew them.

By now, everyone in the prison was talking of the French prisoner and the remarkable effect he was having upon his companions. Stories reached the governor's ears. The governor, who normally preferred to confine his duties to paper administration and to keep as far away as possible from the stench of the dungeons below ground, became curious. He ordered Gerard to be brought before him.

Nikolai was beside himself with excitement when Leo Petrovsky told Gerard to prepare himself for the interview.

"Now you will be able to tell him who you are!" he said. "By tonight, we shall be free!" Gerard, surveying his ragged clothes, long hair and matted beard, had no such certainty.

"It will not be easy to convince him I am a vicomte in this appalling state!" he said dismally.

As Gerard feared, the governor, a retired army colonel with much military knowledge but no imagination, regarded the gaunt-faced dirty prisoner with misgivings. He allowed him to tell his story, however, and noted that Gerard's French was of the highest class. He came to the conclusion that Gerard was no French soldier as he maintained, but a spy.

"You arrived at this prison in the attire of a peasant," he said accusingly. "Where is your uniform, if indeed you are a soldier?"

Patiently, Gerard recounted in detail his movements after he left Vienna. The mere mention of the Austrian city brought back memories of the Russian defeat there at which the colonel had lost a son. He looked at Gerard coldly.

"It is an unlikely story!" he said. "Any self-respecting Russian soldier, meeting with a Frenchman after the battle, would have killed you on the spot. Death to all Frenchmen I say!"

Gerard began to doubt the sagacity of this meeting. Far from regaining his freedom, it now appeared as if he might have laid himself open to a speedy execution.

"Sir, if your country were not at war with France, it would be a simple matter for you to confirm that I am, indeed, the vicomte de Valle and that I held the rank of captain in the French army," he said with dignity.

"Then you are in ignorance of current affairs!" the colonel said. "An armistice has been declared between our countries following upon our defeat at Friedland. The czar and the emperor of France are even now discussing a peace settlement at Tilsit."

Gerard's heart gave a lurch.

"Then, sir, can I most humbly ask you to make whatever inquiries you feel necessary to establish the truth as to my identity. To keep me imprisoned here for the rest of my life can bring you no benefit. But if, indeed, the war is over, I can assure you that I am not without influence in many quarters. I give you my word as a gentleman that any part you play in securing my release would not go unnoticed."

He could see that his carefully worded bribe was subtly changing the colonel's attitude to him.

"A question or two in the right quarter would take little of your time," he added, "and the rewards for my freedom would be considerable I assure you."

The colonel was impressed. He was not a rich man—in fact his very moderate wealth and estates had been his Prussian wife's and had been sadly deplenished by the recent wars. As Gerard had suggested, it would cost him little to make a few inquiries about his prisoner.

"I'll do what has to be done!" was the most he would promise. Gerard returned to his cell and the waiting Nikolai in reasonable good hope.

But it was another month and midsummer before word came from St. Petersburg. Gerard had almost given up hope of freedom when Leo Petrovsky announced that he was to be released

The colonel was now falling over himself with geniality when Gerard saw him for the second time. He took Gerard to his own apartments, allowed him to bathe and shave, and finally produced a suit of his own clothes for Gerard to wear.

He made no demur when Gerard insisted that Nikolai Kuragin be released so that Gerard could have the attentions suitable to his rank.

"But of course, my dear vicomte," the Colonel agreed, his voice as obsequious as his manners now that he knew his prisoner really was of noble birth. His apologies were endless. He handed Gerard a purse of gold sufficient to buy horses and meet all expenses for himself and Nikolai.

"You may return at once to France, if such is your wish, monsieur."

Gerard, smiling grimly, signed a promissory note in favor of the colonel.

"I gave you my word that you would be rewarded if I were set free," he said. "Meanwhile, I thank you for your hospitality, colonel, although I must confess that I cannot condone the disgraceful conditions in your prison. Criminals, even cutthroats and brigands, are nonetheless men, if I may be permitted to say so. At home in France we do not treat even our farm animals so badly!"

The colonel flushed an angry red.

"Nor do we Russians entertain the barbaric practice of guillotining our aristocrats!" he rejoined. "I regret your treatment in my prison but you suffered no worse than any other prisoner. Had you arrived with means of identifying yourself, you could have avoided such an unfortunate fate."

There seemed to Gerard little point in continuing the argument. Moreover, his host had been instrumental in securing his release and now that he was finally out of the dungeons, he was anxious to be as speedily as possible upon his way home.

Nikolai Kuragin took their release surprisingly calmly.

"I never doubted it!" he said, as he and Gerard went to the nearest hostler to buy horses. "As soon as I set eyes on you, I knew my future was going to be connected with you in some way. And though it didn't work out quite the way I'd planned—" he grinned affectionately at his self-appointed master "—I'm not sorry, for all it has cost me but near a year and a half in that stink-hole!"

"It cost me more than that!" Gerard replied quietly. "There is little hope now that my mother is still alive. My intention is to go back to France via Vienna. I have a very dear friend who may still reside there and whom I wish to see above everything else."

Nikolai glanced sideways at his new master.

"Happen that might be the lady whose name you called when you was near to dying?" he commented shrewdly. "But it's not my business to ask questions any more, although I'd like to believe you still look on me as a friend."

"How could I do otherwise?" Gerard replied simply. "You saved my life, Nikolai Kuragin."

Despite their long incarceration together in prison, Nikolai knew little about Gerard's private life. It came as a surprise to him to learn that Gerard's young wife was confined to a convent in Compiègne with a sickness of the brain following upon childbirth. Gerard did not yet know that the Prince and Princess Monte-Gincinto had long since gone to France and taken their daughter back to Naples with them.

He was doomed, therefore, to receive three disappointments: the first that Mavreen and James had returned to England over a year ago, the second that his mother had died the previous year, and that poor old Jules had not long survived her.

They found the Château de Boulancourt closed and shuttered, the servants dispersed. The gardener, who still resided at the lodge and acted as caretaker, was able to tell Gerard very little beyond the barest facts. Gerard did not know the man, and it was some time before he could make the rather simpleminded fellow understand who he was. Even then he knew nothing whatever about Gerard's wife, Faustina.

In the lowest of spirits, Gerard rode into Compiègne

and approached the Mother Superior of the convent of St. Germain. From her he learned what had become of his wife.

"Shortly before the death of your dear mother," the nun informed Gerard, "your wife's parents came to visit her. The vicomtesse had written to them to tell them little Faustina was living with us, and that since she herself did not expect to live long and you were missing, believed killed in battle, she felt obliged to ask them to make themselves responsible for little Faustina. The Prince and Princess Monte-Gincinto arrived last summer and took her home to Naples."

Gerard thanked the mother superior for taking care of his wife and departed after making a handsome donation to the convent.

He was deeply concerned. He now knew that Napoleon's brother, Joseph, had supplanted Ferdinand as king of Naples; that in August last year, while he himself had languished in prison, Joseph Bonaparte had abolished all baronial jurisdiction, all rights to personal services and had divided up all feudal estates among the small farmers who worked them. The former king, Gerard was informed by Baron Stern during his brief visit to Vienna, had taken refuge in Sicily under the protection of the English. It therefore seemed more than likely that the Prince and Princess Monte-Gincinto had lost their fortune and estates and in all probability had taken refuge in Sicily with poor Faustina.

More than anything in the world, Gerard wanted to go directly to England to see Mavreen. He wanted to explain to her why he had been unable to rejoin her as he had promised. His impatience to see her was a nagging torment which overshadowed any pleasure he might have felt in his newly regained freedom.

But his mother's last letter to him, delivered into his hands by the priest who had given her the last rites, directed his footsteps elsewhere.

. . . Your father-in-law was far from easy in his mind as to the future of his country. King Ferdinand ordered the books of Voltaire to be publicly

*burned as a demonstration of his enmity toward
Napoleon. The Prince Monte-Gincinto thinks it is
only a matter of time before the existing treaty
between France and Naples is violated, and that
Naples will almost certainly fall to the emperor.*

*The prince is an intelligent man, Gerard, and he
fears for the safety of his wife and Faustina in another war. When you return, as I pray to God you
will, then it must be your first duty to ascertain the
physical safety and well-being of your wife. The poor
child shows no sign of recovery and my physician
has been unable to offer hope for the future . . .*

The remainder of the vicomtesse's letter was given entirely to expressions of love for her son and reassurances
of her readiness to depart this life now that Mavreen had
secured the Baron von Gottfried's confession.

*Mavreen has shown great ingenuity and courage.
Her love for and loyalty to you, Gerard, is un-
swerving; greater even than her love for her sweet
child. I know that you will long to see her but
although you are past the age when I can dictate
to you, I must remind you that your duty to your
wife must always come before your desire to be
near the woman you love, as must Mavreen's happiness always come before your own. I trust you,
my beloved son, to do what is right and honorable,
as I know you will.*

"We must go next to Naples!" Gerard said, grim-faced
to the waiting Nikolai. "As soon as I have arranged my
family affairs we will discover the best and fastest means
of travel. My wife's life might be in danger."

The year 1807 had drawn to an end before Gerard and
Nikolai Kuragin, weary and exhausted, completed their
long journey, through Switzerland, the kingdom of Italy,
where Napoleon had established French government in
Florence and Rome, and southward through the Papal
States into the kingdom of Naples.

It was a very different country from the one in which

Gerard had lived nine years ago. Only three great abbeys, including Monte Cassino, were unsold, their secularized monks not pensioned off as were those in the remaining two hundred and thirteen monastic estates which Joseph Bonaparte had sold to secure enough money to pay off the national debt.

Copies of The Code Napoleon, destroyed by King Ferdinand, were being reintroduced.

Gerard told Nikolai that he had to admit that many of the changes were improvements, especially in the condition of the five million poorer inhabitants. Previously, a few thousand noblemen and clergy held all the country's riches and treated serfs very little better than cattle. Joseph Bonaparte's administration was therefore popular, and very efficient.

They found the Monte-Gincintos' Palace now occupied by government officials. Joseph, a lover of the arts, had insisted upon preserving the beautiful palazzo and although the furniture had been replaced by desks and bureaux and functional equipment, many of the priceless curtains, carpets, and furbishings remained.

Deeply depressed, Gerard learned that the former occupants had indeed fled to Sicily. No official to whom he spoke had met the Monte-Gincintos and although a thorough search of the records was carried out, no further details of the family's fate was forthcoming.

"Do we now go to Sicily?" Nikolai asked. "And how so, if it be in British hands?"

Gerard had no ready reply. In desperation, they acquired fresh horses and rode to the southern tip of Naples, where, two miles distance across the Straits of Messina, lay the island to which, as a Frenchman, he could not travel.

There were, however, as there had been in England, men who were prepared to take their boats across the sea provided the rewards were adequate. For the payment of a purseful of silver ducats, a young fisherman agreed to take a letter to Palermo, await a reply, and come back with it to Gerard.

For over a week there was no sign of the man's return. Nikolai vouchsafed the opinion that the Neopolitan had pocketed the money and would not be seen again. But Gerard knew the ways of fishermen and surmised that he would never abandon his home and family in the little fishing village of his birth.

Gerard's faith was justified, but the news the man brought back from one of the secretaries of the court in Palermo was distressingly factual. The Monte-Gincintos' carriage had been attacked by brigands while the prince and princess were conducting the young vicomtesse de Valle to a convent, where, they had hoped the quiet serenity of the mountains might be beneficial to her. All the occupants of the carriage had been robbed and then killed, as were the members of the *carabiniere* who were escorting them.

Gerard was aghast. His imagination gave him no peace. Again and again, he reiterated to Nikolai, "My wife was such a little, frightened creature! I cannot bear to think of her meeting such a terrible death. If only I could be certain that all died quickly and mercifully!"

Nikolai kept his thoughts to himself for it was his experience that all brigands were cutthroats and by the very nature of men, would likely have assaulted the women before killing them. He tried to comfort Gerard as best he could.

"They are at peace now, in Heaven, doubtless," he said, "where no further harm can befall them."

With shrewd intelligence, he reminded Gerard of his young wife's mental state and professed the opinion that likely she would have had no understanding of what was happening to her at the time of the attack.

"In the past two years, I have lost child, mother, wife, and the most faithful of family retainers, poor old Jules!" Gerard cried bitterly. "Is there no end to it?"

"What of the English milady we went to find in Vienna?" Nikolai reminded him. "The baron told us she was alive and well and had returned to England."

Mavreen! Gerard had forgotten her, so wrapped up had he been in horror and grief. Nikolai was right! The woman he loved most in the world, was, God willing, still alive; his little daughter, too.

"We will go to England and find her!" he said. "Make the horses ready, Nikolai. We will start our journey today."

Mavreen, alone, could help him forget the nightmares that now dogged his sleep; nightmares in which poor little Faustina lay covered in blood on the side of a dusty hill in Sicily; in which, no matter where he searched, he could never find her grave.

CHAPTER THIRTY-NINE
1808

By February of 1808, Gerard had crossed the border into France where Napoleon's troops were pouring across the Pyrenees on their way to Madrid.

It was by the merest stroke of chance that Gerard and Nikolai stopped to spend the night in an inn at the foot of the Pyrenees and came upon the colonel of his regiment. The man was eating a hearty meal at the inn while awaiting orders to move his men up in reserve of the troops already over the mountains.

Technically, Gerard was a deserter. His colonel, an ill-tempered man of none-too-savory a background, on recognizing him at once arrested him. It took Gerard some time and a deal of patience to explain to the colonel how he had been captured by Russian soldiers and subsequently imprisoned in a Russian jail, and that he was not a deserter.

Fortunately for Gerard the colonel had no immediate way of checking on the dates of Gerard's release. He ceased to talk about having him court-martialed and turned his mind to how Gerard might make himself useful in the ensuing campaign.

"I see you are fit to fight!" he commented. "And prepared, I trust, to do battle for the emperor? I shall be well-pleased to have another officer on my staff. I lost a captain who became ill upon our way here. Since a replacement has not yet arrived, your presence is most timely."

By such an inconsequential stroke of fate, Gerard became caught up in the Peninsular War. His request that he might be allowed a brief spell of leave before rejoining his regiment was rejected out of hand. It was obvious that the colonel considered such a wish a cowardly evasion of the coming campaign and its expected rigors. Gerard had, therefore, to abandon all hope of going to England. He had no option but to allow himself and Nikolai to be adequately equipped with uniforms and weapons and set out with his former regiment to do battle.

When Gerard had first volunteered to fight in Napoleon's Grand Army, it was the Austrians and the Prussians who were his enemies in the field. It had never been his intention to take up arms against the English or, as he was now compelled, against Charles, the Bourbon king of Spain, cousin to his own Louis XVI, the late king of France.

But Napoleon was determined to conquer Spain. Its people were violently opposed to his anti-papal philosophy and had been resisting French invasion of their land for many years. The French emperor had forced them to sign a treaty at Fontainebleau the year before, extracting a reluctant promise from them to join in his attack on Portugal. But although the subsequent conquest of Portugal had been relatively easy and the Portuguese regent had been driven to take refuge in Brazil, Napoleon was still determined to evict the Bourbon king and his strong-minded queen, Marie-Louise.

Gerard had no option but to advance with his regiment. They crossed the Pyrenees, seized the frontier fortresses against strong resistance. Before long they were in Madrid. King Charles abdicated to save the life of his prime minister, Godoy. The whole of the Spanish royal family was deployed to Bayonne and compelled to renounce all claim to the monarchy of Spain. The vacant throne was given to Napoleon's brother, Joseph, who had proved so able an administrator in Naples.

Gerard approached his commanding officer and asked

if, now the fighting was over, he might resign his commission and return home to see to his family affairs, but
although his request was forwarded with recommendation
to higher authorities, his release from the army was not
forthcoming. He was ordered to Portugal where, on the
twelfth of July, the English General Wellesley had landed
in Mondego with an army of 30,000 men.

Only to Nikolai did Gerard confess his extreme reluctance to fight against the English army now massed at
Vimeiro.

"I was educated in an English school and had an Englishman as my guardian for two years," he told his sympathetic servant. "Moreover, the woman I love is English
and I have many friends in that country!"

But he had no alternative other than that of desertion,
and not even his sympathies with his enemies could drive
him so to dishonor the name of de Valle.

So it was that on the twenty-first of August, under the
command of the French general Junot, Gerard and Nikolai
advanced with four columns of French soldiers against the
English now in position on Vimeiro Hill.

From previous battles, Gerard was familiar with Napoleon's practice of sending in a darting mass of *tirailleurs*
whose task it was—with guns to support them—to sting,
fluster, and confuse the enemy lines until they were sufficiently distraught to fall an easy prey to the solid wall
of infantry behind them.

Such tactics had succeeded admirably in the past but on
this occasion, the English general was prepared for the
skirmishers. He had posted a strong skirmish line of his
own at the foot of the hill.

As the French went in, they were met in rapid succession by obstinate rifle fire, a brief cannonade and then
by musket fire from infantry who had been concealed behind the crest of the hill and ordered to hold their fire
till the last minute.

Gerard, advancing with the right column under the
command of General Laborde, was appalled at the density
of the firing. The English were in lines only two deep so
that every weapon could fire. Musket-shot poured into
their lines from company after company down the whole

line until its deadly hail poured into the French flanks as well as the front.

Nikolai, close behind him, cried out as he was hit. Simultaneously, Gerard heard the shouts of command as his general tried to form his huge rectangular column, thirty men broad by forty-two deep, into line so that he might bring his rear rank muskets into play. Gerard tried to rally his own men but the British fire was too hot and the column began to disintegrate. Like a panic-stricken herd of sheep, his men started to run with the others toward the bottom of Vimeiro Hill.

" 'Tis the battle of Austerlitz all over again!" Nikolai gasped as he galloped alongside Gerard in the opposite direction to the brilliant flashes of the English bayonets pursuing their retreating enemy.

The medical orderlies were now fully occupied attending to the severely wounded who had not fallen on the hill but managed to reach safety. Gerard, himself, bound Nikolai's arm.

As Gerard and Nikolai watched, two more French columns moved into the attack. But they were driven back by the same murderous firing, as were the next two advancing columns.

From the ridge behind Vimeiro, three French brigades were driven down into the valley and away to the north of the ridge. Gerard was ordered with his company to reinforce the shattered brigades.

But although they were successful in halting the enemy for a brief while, the English general once more outflanked the French on the right and using the same tactics as before, sent the disordered mob of French infantry fleeing down the blood-stained slope.

There were now no reserves. Most of the French guns were captured and the will of the soldiers to fight was gone. The survivors began to retreat eastward, their defeat no longer in doubt. But Gerard could not go with them. Nikolai was missing. One of Gerard's fellow officers informed him he had seen Nikolai fall on the slope, either dead or wounded, during the last hopeless attack.

Gerard secreted himself in the hayloft of a barn on the

outskirts of Vimeiro village. Here, tortured by the heat and an intense thirst, he waited until nightfall.

As soon as it was dusk, he made his way back to the scene of the battle. He was in no doubt as to the correctness of the direction he had taken for the groans of the wounded and the stench of effluvia reached him some distance before he stumbled over the first corpse. Voices called for assistance in both French and English.

Softly, Gerard called Nikolai's name as he went from man to man, many of them dead, others groaning from their wounds. A pale moon had now risen, enabling him to see the vast numbers of the fallen, and in near despair at the magnitude of his task, Gerard bent to study the faces of the dead and wounded. He knew that there were far too many injured for there to be any point to his stopping to lend assistance. He forced himself to concentrate upon finding Nikolai while there was still darkness sufficient to enable them, should Nikolai be alive, to escape under cover of night.

He came upon the grim spectacle of two miserable victims, a French and an English soldier skewered together by the same bayonet in a deathly embrace. Shuddering, Gerard went quickly past them, continuously calling Nikolai's name.

He saw the ghostly outlines of men he took to be English stretcher-bearers carrying their wounded toward their own lines. He kept his distance and continued his search. He had lost all but the last vestiges of hope and energy when, by a clump of myrtle incongruously sweet-smelling amid the stench of death, Nikolai called back to him.

"Well, *mon vieux!*" Gerard said huskily as he bent over his wounded servant and surveyed his leg. "Your wound may pain you but I doubt 'twill kill you. So on your feet, man, and let us be away from this hell on earth!"

"I cannot!" Nikolai groaned, for he had sustained a severe bayonet thrust in his lower leg. "Leave me and find safety for yourself. There is nothing you can do for me! Leave me in peace to die!"

"So said I once to you!" Gerard reminded him as he put

an arm beneath Nikolai's shoulders and eased him to a sitting position. "But you had other plans for me and came near to choking me with that pig swill you forced down my throat. Remember?" He talked on cheerfully until he had succeeded in getting Nikolai to his feet.

"I'll not leave this hell-hole without you!" he said as Nikolai staggered on the point of collapse. "So lest you would have my death upon your conscience as well as your own, start walking else it will be daylight and we shall find ourselves prisoners of the English and mayhap languishing another year or two in a filthy jail!"

So, by an admixture of raillery and cajolery, Gerard managed to guide Nikolai safely back to their own lines.

By November, Nikolai was fully recovered with only an ugly scar and the slightest of limps to remind him of his experiences at Vimeiro. By December, he and Gerard were in Madrid. In February the following year, they were once more engaged in battle, this time victoriously after a long drawn-out siege at Saragossa. By November, the French had overrun the whole of Andalusia with the exception of Cadiz.

"Now, pray God," Gerard said to Nikolai, "we have done with fighting and may be permitted to return home!"

More than anything in the world, he wanted to be finished with bloodshed and battles. And to see Mavreen again.

Mavreen returned to Finchcocks after her sojourn in Brighthelmstone with the Baroness von Eburhard, and spent the remainder of 1807 and the spring of the following year devoting most of her time and attentions to her small daughter. Tamarisk was now nine years old and Mavreen found the child an agreeable companion. They rode together every day; and when Tamarisk's lessons with her tutor were ended, they often enjoyed a quiet evening together playing backgammon, a game for which Tamarisk had much enthusiasm as well as ability.

Mavreen found the days passing quickly enough. She visited Clarissa every week, attended concerts and operas either with Clarissa and her father, or with John Ward or Thomas Creevey, both of whom were still vying with one another for her favors.

Mavreen made it quite clear to both her suitors that she had no intention whatever of marrying either one. Nevertheless, each was persistent in calling upon her whenever their duties allowed and the gossips were convinced that she would eventually decide upon one or the other for her third husband.

The baroness, whose dinner parties Mavreen invariably attended, went out of her way to produce eligible men for Mavreen's approval. She was disappointed that Mavreen could not be persuaded to take a third husband, or at least, a lover.

"It is not good for a woman to live alone!" she said, refusing to believe that Mavreen was contented with her celibate existence.

In the summer of 1808, Anne Lade invited Tamarisk to sojourn with her and her own children at Worthing where she had rented a house by the sea. Believing that the company of other children might be as beneficial to her daughter as the sea air, Mavreen agreed that she might go.

"I, myself, shall take this opportunity to go to Sussex," she told Clarissa. "As you know, I have not been there for a very long time and I dare not think in what condition I shall find the grange. I shall take Dickon and Rose with me."

Clarissa had not been very well of late. Her feet and ankles had swelled, causing her a considerable amount of discomfort.

"Were I not so handicapped, I would come with you!" she said, fearing Mavreen might become depressed alone in the house containing so many memories of her lost love. Mavreen never spoke of Gerard de Valle and yet Clarissa was convinced she had not forgotten him. She had little doubt that the young man was dead and hoped that Mavreen would, in time, reach the same conclusion. Like her friend, Lisa, it was her hope that eventually Mavreen would remarry, albeit more happily than on the last occasion.

It was not of her own marriage but of Dickon's to Rose

that Mavreen was thinking as she and Dickon drove through East Grinstead on their way to Alfriston. She intended to arrange for the wedding to take place in Alfriston without further delay. Dickon was now thirty-two and Rose approaching thirty. If they were to have the family she knew Rose desired, the marriage must not be further delayed. They were much upon her conscience for she was well aware that they had put both loyalty and devotion to her before their own concerns. And Rose's affections for Tamarisk were equal only to Dickon's for her, Mavreen.

Rose was already at the grange, having travelled to Sussex three days earlier in order to prepare the house for Mavreen's arrival.

The hour was late as they left the beautiful tower of St. Swithin's Church behind them. Dickon tightened the reins upon the horses' heads as they bowled down Wall Hill toward the village of Forest Row. Here they intended to take supper at the Chequer's, the fifteenth-century posting inn, and rest the horses before completing the journey across the wilderness of Ashdown Forest, through Lewes to Alfriston.

"We have a tidy way yet to travel!" Dickon said with misgivings as they pulled into the yard outside the Chequer's Inn. " 'Twill be dark long afore we reach home!"

"Be you frightened, Dickon?" Mavreen asked with a mischievous smile.

"No more nor you," he replied, "but so we should be, nonetheless!"

But it was a balmy, moonlit July night, the fragrance of the countryside wafting in through the carriage window as they recommenced their journey and both delighted in the feeling of adventure as they set forth once more southward.

Mavreen was watching a roebuck, silhouetted against the skyline as it bounded away from them through the trees when with a shattering suddenness, Dickon reined in the horses and brought the carriage to a halt.

"What is amiss?" Mavreen called out as she regained her balance and leaned out of the window to see for herself the reason for the delay. Just as she glimpsed the dark, shadowy figure of a man on horseback, he called out, "Stand and deliver!"

She saw the glint of the pistols leveled at her through the window and simultaneously was aware of the steam rising from the great black stallion on which the highwayman was mounted.

"You've been riding him too hard!" she reproved him automatically, without prior thought of her situation. "See how the poor beast is sweating about his neck and withers! Shame upon you, sir."

For a moment, there was complete silence. Then the door of the carriage was swung open and Mavreen was ordered at pistol point to step down.

Mavreen saw at once that Dickon, holding the horses' heads in a vain attempt to calm them, could do little in her defense. She had heard many stories from people who had been accosted by highwaymen but had never yet suffered such indignity herself. She was in part scared, in part angry, and at the same time, strangely excited.

Suddenly, the man reached up his free hand and pushed back the hood of his cloak. His face was covered by a triangular silk kerchief. A mass of dark curls freed from the hood, fell over his forehead. He looked over Mavreen's shoulder, for he towered above her, and peered through the carriage window.

"There is no one else but me!" Mavreen said calmly.

He seemed disbelieving that a lady of her undoubted quality should be travelling unescorted. He laughed.

"Then that will make it all the easier! Waste no more of my time, milady, but deliver up your purse and your jewelry."

"And if I do not?"

"Hist!" Mavreen heard Dickon's warning gasp but she paid no heed to it. Now that the first shock was gone, anger far outweighed fear.

"Then you and your servant will be shot!" the highwayman said. Mavreen was more surprised by his voice than by his threat. It was undoubtedly an educated voice, cultured and with pleasing intonation.

"If so be you are a gentleman," she said, "then it does not behoove you to attack a lone woman. Yet I doubt you be of good breeding for only a coward conceals his face as you do, sir!"

Much later, Mavreen was to wonder what prompted her to challenge the highwayman to uncover. But the effect when he did so was shattering. For the first time in her life, Mavreen swooned. Instantly, Dickon let go the horses' heads to run to her side, whereupon aware that restraint was gone, the horses bolted.

The highwayman hesitated only momentarily. Then he dug his spurs into his own horse's flanks and galloped off in pursuit.

By the time he returned, leading the carriage horses behind him, Mavreen had recovered from her swoon and was standing on the roadside, leaning upon Dickon's arm. She looked very pale but she now had Dickon's assurance that the man she had thought to be Gerard de Valle was no more than his image.

As the highwayman approached, she forced herself to look deeply into his face. The likeness was extraordinary. The man had Gerard's dark hair and eyes. The nose had the same straight line; only the mouth and chin were different, stronger and more firm than Gerard's.

"I must apologize for my weakness!" she said quietly, as the highwayman handed over the reins to Dickon. "And also thank you for returning my carriage! Doubtless you have by now stolen all that you wanted!"

"As it so happens, milady, I have not! But since you now seem fully recovered, mayhap you will be good enough to oblige!"

With difficulty, Mavreen drew her eyes away from his face. She started toward the carriage but halted. The physical resemblance of this man to Gerard was uncanny. It was not he—and yet. . . .

"Be good enough, sir, to advise me of your name!" The request seemed to come from her of its own volition.

"I scarce see that it is of concern to you, but since it pleases you to know, Gideon Morris, at your service!" From horseback he made her a bow. "And may I know yours, ma'am?"

By now he was as curious about her as she was about him. Not only had he observed her remarkable handsomeness, but he was impressed at her courage. Most ladies he encountered dissolved into hysterics or else cowered in the recesses of their carriages crying and swooning alternately. Not least was he curious about the persistent intensity of her gaze.

"Why do you stare so, ma'am?" he enquired. "Dost think we have met upon another occasion?"

"No!" said Mavreen. "But you resemble someone I once knew."

She turned and climbed into the carriage, re-emerging with her reticule and her box of jewelery.

The highwayman dismounted. His horse cropped the grass quietly at the road-verge requiring no holding so that he was free to keep the pistol cocked as he reached out with his other hand to take the reticule from Mavreen. He stuffed it into his saddlebag without glancing at the contents.

"The jewel case!" he commanded, as Mavreen hesitated.

"There are within three items I will not part with—not even on pain of death!" she said quietly. "They have small value but are of great sentimental worth to me. Have I your permission to remove them or will you kill me first?"

The softness of her voice was more convincing than had she railed at him. The man, Gideon Morris, hesitated, not a little intrigued.

"Show them to me!" he ordered.

Mavreen opened the casket and extracted the signet ring Gerard had given her oh, so long ago, the gold locket containing the miniature of Tamarisk, and Tamarisk's gold locket containing the miniature of Gerard which she had handed into Mavreen's care for safe-keeping, afraid lest she might lose it playing on the seashore at Worthing.

Gideon Morris looked from them into Mavreen's face and his eyes narrowed.

"You said they were of no value—yet all are gold!" He saw the fire flash in her eyes and was suddenly vastly entertained by the challenge.

"If they are of such immense value to you," he said quietly, "what will you offer me in exchange?"

Mavreen's head lifted proudly.

"I am a woman of considerable wealth. I am also true to my word. Allow me to retain these trinkets and I will send you a hundred guineas as soon as I can obtain the money from London."

"A hundred guineas?" he echoed. "No great sum for a rich lady, I warrant."

"It is a great deal more than they are worth to you!" Mavreen replied. "But I value them, so name your price, sir, and if it be not too unreasonable, I will agree to it."

Disconcertingly, his face broke into a smile. Now, more even than before, his resemblance to Gerard was heart-breakingly marked.

"Suppose I were to name *you* as my price!"

The hint of seriousness behind his smile brought a swift rush of color to Mavreen's cheeks.

"Do not ridicule me, sir!" she said. "I will pay you two hundred and fifty guineas and not one penny more." She handed over the jewel case to him and her voice became scornful as she added, "A guinea or two here or there will not be of much import to you since you will find worth enough to satisfy your greed in these!"

He did not open the box but took it from her silently. Then he stood aside and reopened her carriage door.

"If you would care to ascend, ma'am?" he said. "I will escort you to your destination."

Mavreen's protest that she needed no escort merely elicited another smile.

"I desire to know whence I must come for my promised two hundred and fifty guineas!" he said. "I will give you two weeks in which to obtain the money."

He looked to be on the point of lowering his pistol but Dickon was brandishing his riding whip and although there was naught he could do but remount when ordered, his look was threatening enough to keep the highwayman alert.

True to his word, Gideon Morris escorted them as far as the driveway of the grange. Then he melted quietly into the shadows of the night.

CHAPTER FORTY
1808

Fourteen days elapsed without sight or sound of the highwayman.

" 'Tis my opinion he'll not return!" Dickon said to Mavreen as they took a last walk in the garden before retiring for the night. The heat of the August day had cooled somewhat, but despite the thinness of her muslin dress, Mavreen still felt her skin damp with torrid warmth. Dickon had forecast a thunderstorm before morning and there were, indeed, several black clouds gathering across the face of the brilliant moon.

Mavreen, feeling the cool breeze upon her bare arms and face, gave a tiny shiver.

"Mayhap you are right, Dickon!" she agreed. "For to risk his life by coming to the house would be madness, would it not? I might most assuredly have armed the grange with guards to await his coming and arrest him. 'Twould not be sense to risk his freedom for a few hundred guineas when he has already gained so much from his night's work."

Although Mavreen had lost money and jewelery worth a small fortune to the highwayman, it was not of this she had thought since last seeing him. Whenever her mind turned to the episode, it was to recall the man's extraordinary likeness to Gerard—a resemblance that even now, two weeks later, she found unhappily disturbing. Reason forbade that she should wish ever to set eyes upon the highwayman again and yet—yet she could not prevent a strange longing just to look once more upon his face as if it were to see but one more time the image of her lost love.

Dickon had been far more seriously affronted by the robbery than Mavreen. He deeply resented his own incapacity to fight off the highwayman or to prevent what had followed. He blamed himself for not having had his own pistol at the ready so that he could have shot the fellow upon the instant he appeared so suddenly from the bushes beside the road.

Mavreen had done all she could to distract Dickon from his self-reproach. She had insisted that Dickon go with Rose to see the parson and arrange for their banns to be called. She accompanied both of them to Owlett's Farm where the day was spent in celebration of the occasion of the engagement and in plans for the wedding itself. Since Rose's family could in no way provide her with a wedding of any consequence, it had been agreed that she should be married from the grange, her relations to be brought from London by coach and somehow accommodated in Alfriston for the night. The ceremony itself was planned to take place the first Saturday after harvest was done.

But although such matters occupied Mavreen's mind throughout the day, at night her thoughts went back to Gideon Morris. She both longed for and dreaded his return.

Dickon, Rose, and the servants who had once been Mr. Glover's and were now cook and gardener when they were not acting as caretakers, were all abed when Mavreen retired for the night. Unable to sleep, she decided restlessly upon selecting a book to read from Mr. Glover's library.

Taking a lamp, she went quietly down the stairs and was browsing among the shelves when a sudden flash of lightning lit up the room. It was followed almost at once by the rumble of thunder and then a knock upon the French windows leading into the garden.

Mavreen glanced at the darkened window but could see nothing. A second flash of lightning lit up the dark-colored figure of a man standing in the garden staring in at her. Involuntarily, she gasped. She recognized him instantly. It was Gideon Morris, the highwayman.

For a moment, Mavreen hesitated. She had no weapon at hand and she was in her nightrobe. It would be madness to unlock the windows! Yet her feet were already taking her across the room as if acting upon a will of their own.

The temper of the storm had risen. The flashes of lightning were following one upon the other in quick succession. The rumble of thunder had now become deafeningly sharp cracks as the storm moved overhead. As the highwayman stepped into the room, great drops of cold rain were spattering down and his uncovered head was bright with raindrops.

" 'Twould appear you are expecting me!" he said, glancing meaningfully at her dishabille. Mavreen recovered her composure. His sardonic smile was immediately familiar to her.

"On the contrary, sir! However, I have your money upstairs. If you will wait but a minute or two, I will fetch it for you!"

He took a step toward her.

"There is no need for it. I have not come for money!"

Mavreen could see now that he was concealing something beneath his cloak. Assuming this to be a pistol, she stepped back instinctively. Once more he smiled sardonically.

"I am unarmed," he said. "Does that surprise you, ma'am?"

"Very much!" Mavreen replied truthfully. "I have servants in the house. I have but to scream and. . . ."

"But you will not do so since I have come to return these to you!" he broke in, and produced from beneath his cloak her jewelery casket. "Everything is there," he added. "You may check on it!"

Mavreen stared at him incredulously.

"Then I do not understand! Is this all some stupid pleasantry?"

He shook his head, taking a further step toward her.

"It is no pleasantry. I have thought much upon the matter and I have made up my mind. It is you, ma'am, and not your money that I desire!"

Such was the determination of his tone of voice that Mavreen had little doubt that he intended his threat. She felt a shiver of fear yet was determined he should not see it.

"You would take me by force?" she asked scornfully.

"What irony when I had but newly reached the conclusion that you were a gentleman after all."

"Not by force!" the man argued as he now covered the few paces between them and caught her in his arms. "I am no stranger to women and will gamble my life—indeed, I am so doing—in the belief that you desire me as ardently as I desire you!"

Mavreen struggled with every vestige of strength within her. But his arms were like a vise around her body and his eyes—eyes so frighteningly like Gerard's—were but inches above her own.

"No!" she whispered. "No!"

But he paid no regard to her words and covered her mouth with his own. Like a wildcat, she bit into his lip and tasted blood. But he did not release her. With one arm still imprisoning her, his other moved to cover her breast. He tore the soft material in one swift movement, leaving her trembling body exposed to the waist.

"Let me go!" she gasped, scratching at his face as she managed to free her arm. But although she twisted and writhed in his embrace, he held her surely and savagely against him.

And all the while he was smiling down into her eyes.

Her senses reeled. It was ten years since she and Gerard had loved in this same room, abandoning themselves to their need for one another like two healthy young animals, glorying in their shared passion, oblivious to the world. Now it was as if those ten years had been swept away and she was back at last in Gerard's arms.

She fell to the floor, still entwined in the man's embrace.

"Gerard! Gerard!" she whispered.

As if in a dream, she watched him tear his white frilled shirt from his golden-brown body. His muscles rippled with his movements, the golden hairs of his chest and arms glistening in the lamplight. He never took his eyes from her, moving them only from her face to her body as he sank down beside her on the carpeted floor, ripping away the last shreds of her clothing until she lay naked before him.

Perhaps, were he to have spoken, she would have woken

from her half-dream; realized that he was no image conjured up from the past, but a stranger, a lawbreaker, perhaps even a murderer. But he spared no time for pretty speeches as he bore down upon her. Ignoring her muttered protests, sweeping aside her protesting hands, he subdued and finally conquered her. Her resistance ceased and her body began to move in answering rhythm to his own.

All else was forgotten as she let it follow its own designs. She was released from all restraints, knowing nothing but her own fierce desire to possess and be possessed.

As the storm crashed furiously overhead, so did the long pent-up storm of her passion flare to a crescendo and explode in a tumultuous conclusion.

For a short while, neither stirred. Then the man removed his weight from above her and lay beside her. Propped upon one elbow, he stared down into her face.

"You called me Gerard!" he said. "Is it he whom you love?"

Mavreen closed her eyes. The enormity of her actions was slowly making itself aware.

"Tell me," he commanded, his voice authoritative yet with a new gentleness behind it. "Do you love this Gerard?"

Her silence was answer in itself. He reached out for her nightrobe and pulled it over her body. His consideration, unexpected as it was, moved her to sudden tears.

He allowed her to weep for a moment or two and then said, "Come now, that is enough. It is no compliment to me that you should lie there crying for another!"

The audacity of his reproof revived Mavreen's spirit.

"You have no right to dictate to me what I shall do!" she cried. She jumped to her feet and stared accusingly down at him. "You took me by force and I could have you hung for rape!"

Now he, too, rose to his feet. The sardonic smile with which she was fast becoming familiar was back on his face as he stooped unhurriedly to pull on his breeches.

"If that was rape," he said, "then it would vastly interest me to take you again with your consent!"

Despite all that had transpired, a reluctant smile crept

over Mavreen's face. It was true that she had not been a totally unwilling participant. She went across to the window where stood a leather-topped table with a decanter of Madeira wine and several goblets. She poured the wine into two of the glasses and handed one to him, regarding him curiously.

"From your speech, it would appear you are of gentle birth!" she said. "Yet yours is hardly the profession of a gentleman?"

He sat down upon the sofa, crossing one leg over the other. He looked perfectly at ease.

"I have as much or little claim to good breeding as yourself!" he said, matter-of-factly. "And since I have made it my business to inquire as to your origins, then by my faith, you have every right to know of mine!"

Mavreen collapsed into the chair opposite him.

"You have made inquiries about me?" she echoed. "How so, sir?"

He shrugged.

"The how is of no importance. Suffice it to say that I know you are Sir John Danesfield's bastard; that your mother died when you were six years of age; that you were raised by farmers; tutored by a certain Mr. Glover; taken to London to abide with your father's mistress and eventually married the elderly Lord Barre!"

Mavreen's lower lip jutted forward.

"In all of which there is nothing to my discredit!" she remarked. "The same cannot be said of you, sir!"

He drained his glass of wine and without ceremony, handed it to her to refill. Mavreen did so.

"You shall be better able to judge of that when you hear the facts about me," he said calmly. "You already know that my name is Gideon Morris. I am thirty-one years of age. Like yourself, I was born a bastard. Unlike yourself, however, I was not raised during the early part of my life in poverty. My father, Sir Frederick Morris, took me into his charge not long after my birthing. I was given every luxury, the very best of scholastic educations. Although she showed me no affection, I believed his wife to be my mother. It was only upon my father's sudden and unexpected death that I learned the truth of my bastardy. My father had made no legal provision for my adoption and his wife lost no time in despatching me back to my real mother, an erstwhile dairy maid on one of my father's farms."

His expression had now become hardened, his voice harsh as he continued.

"I was thirteen years of age when I found myself cast overnight from the extremes of riches to those of direst poverty. Moreover, my mother had met with the severest of misfortunes with which I will not for the moment bore you. So my life as an outlaw began. I learned to fight— not only for my own survival but for my mother's, poor woman. I became a thief, then a pickpocket, a smuggler, and finally a highwayman. I am now rich beyond even the limits of my father's wealth. For the most part, I live in London under a false name. I have an excellent reputation and no one has thought to look too deeply into my obscure origins, suitably cited by me as the remote north of England."

Mavreen let out her breath. His story was indeed bizarre, if it was to be believed. Yet it had the ring of conviction.

"If you are now so rich," she said thoughtfully, "how so are you still a highwayman?"

The harshness of his expression gave way to laughter.

"For no other reason than for my amusement!" he vouchsafed. "Although I have forced society to accept me and nay, even at times to bow to my will, London life can become vastly tedious. I missed the excitement of danger to which, over the years, I had become very much accustomed. Moreover, it amuses me to rob the like of those who once robbed me of my youth and my mother, finally, of her life. There is a certain poetic justice in it, do you not agree?"

"Yet it is your practice always to return your spoils?" Mavreen commented on this ambiguity.

"Indeed it is not! That I returned *your* jewelery was for no better reason than that I found myself disinclined to rob another who had acquired wealth with the same difficulty as myself."

He stood up and crossed the room, coming to stand by

Mavreen's chair. He put a hand beneath her chin and raised her face.

"It seemed to me, when I thought on it these past few weeks, a cruel waste of nature for a beautiful, passionate woman such as yourself to be married at the tender age of sixteen to so old a man. Now that I have lain with you, I am certain on it!"

She pushed his hand aside, resenting his familiarity.

"Now that you have had your will of me, will you not do me the favor of leaving!" she said coldly. "I think we may consider ourselves to be on equal terms now?"

He gathered his cloak from the floor and flung it carelessly around his shoulders.

"I will take my leave, since you demand I do so," he said, "but I will be back, Mavreen!"

His use of her Christian name furthered her anger.

"Do not consider returning!" she said. "For if you should do so, the next time you will find my servant armed and with my instructions to shoot you upon sight. I hope I make myself clear!"

For answer, he caught hold of her robe and pulled her against him, his mouth bruising her lips in a kiss that seemed to Mavreen to have no ending.

"You will await my coming tomorrow night as eagerly as I!" he stated. And before she could raise her hand to strike him, he had slipped quietly out of the French windows and disappeared into the night.

Mavreen returned to her bedchamber convinced that sleep would be impossible. Yet no sooner had her head touched the pillows than slumber came as quickly as to a child. She did not awaken until Rose came in with her breakfast at nine o'clock, drawing back the curtains to reveal a brilliant blue, cloudless sky.

"Excepting for the puddles on the ground, you'd not know there'd been such a storm in the night, ma'am!" she said. " 'Tis a beautiful day!"

After she left, Mavreen lay on her pillow staring dreamily out at the sunlit treetops beyond her window. She felt carefree, relaxed, happy as she had not felt in years. For a little while, she successfully convinced herself that her meeting last night with Gideon Morris was but an extraordinary and vivid dream. As such, the encounter was not without its pleasant memories.

But such self-delusion could not last for long. Her torn nightrobe, the bruises on her shoulder, the soreness of her lips, all gave the lie to any dream.

She jumped out of bed, overturning the silver pot of hot chocolate Rose had brought to her, and ran to her dressing table. The casket of jewels lay where she had left them the night before, fortunately unobserved as yet by her maid.

She opened the lid, and saw Gilbert's wedding pearls, the diamond necklace and pendants that James had given to her in Vienna, her diamond and ruby brooch—he had stolen nothing.

Without quite understanding what prompted the need to do so, Mavreen hid the casket in a dark corner of her wardrobe where Rose would be unlikely to find it. She was not yet ready to confess that Gideon Morris had returned. To do so was to lay herself open to Dickon's questioning and she knew that she would be ashamed to tell him what had transpired; nor could she lie to him and accuse Gideon Morris of rape.

It was the first and only secret she had ever kept from Dickon.

Throughout the day, Mavreen vacillated between a furious determination never to let the highwayman set foot in her house again, and an ever-increasing longing to experience just once more the vicarious pleasure of imagining his were Gerard's kisses, Gerard's arms about her, Gerard's eyes smiling down at her with love. She felt alternately disgusted with herself and weak with longing. She knew that the sensible way out of her dilemma was to tell Dickon he had come to the house—there was no need to tell him *all* that had transpired—and that he had threatened to return. Dickon would upon the instant arm himself and watch over her so meticulously that Gideon Morris would not dare to approach her again.

But she did not do so. Instead, she invented some pretext that would take Dickon to Owlett's Farm and keep him there overnight.

No sooner had Dickon departed than she regretted her actions.

" 'Tis folly! I am truly out of my mind!" she told herself with a sense of shame at her weakness of will.

But such self remonstrations did not aid her. Her eyes turned continually to the face of the watch at her waist, watching the hands bring her nearer to a meeting she both feared and desired.

In an effort to find distraction, she took one of the horses and rode out to Firle Beacon, galloping the horse too hard and then, remorseful, allowing it to pick its own way slowly homeward at walking pace. All that this achieved was to bring the hour of darkness closer and with it, the approach of Gideon Morris.

As dusk fell, Mavreen's torment of indecision increased. Upon one instant, she loaded her own small pistol and hid it beneath a cushion in the library ready to send her visitor upon his way; the next, she was unlocking the French windows to facilitate his entry.

It was five minutes short of ten when finally Gideon Morris slipped through the open casements as silently as he had departed the night before. Mavreen, exhausted by the nervous tension of the day, was half asleep over a somewhat tedious book on astrology when, unobserved, he crossed the room to her chair. Her first awareness of his presence was when she felt a kiss upon the back of her head.

She swung round, her heart pounding, and saw him. It was Gerard! Yet it was not. Gideon Morris was taller, broader, stronger—and a deal more ruthless. As if she were a child, he lifted her out of the chair and held her against him. She could feel the fierce throbbing of his heart against her own. He did not speak but with swift, expert fingers, unfastened the buttons of her gown. Inconsequentially, the thought crossed her mind that he was well used to disrobing females. But then all rational thinking ceased as he began to caress her.

As if to prove to her that her surrender to him the night before was as much of her will as his own, he used no force with her this night. He gave no sign that he was aware of the tumult of feeling he aroused in her with his kisses and caresses, nor did he desist until she showed herself as desirous of him as he of her. Her undisguised responses to him seemed to delight and excite him still further. When she glimpsed his face, his eyes were filled with a wild laughter that was not cruel but triumphant as he rode above her. There were no tender words. Indeed, he never spoke. There was no sound in the room but for their breathing and Mavreen's gasp as he plunged into her pulsing body.

As the sweet aftermath of love passed through and beyond Mavreen and her body's fervor cooled, rational thought returned. With coherence came a strange, deep sense of shock at her behavior. She knew quite clearly that this man, lying now beside her in watchful silence, was not Gerard, but a total stranger, unscrupulous, without honor, lawless; a man she could neither respect nor love. Yet she was honest enough to admit to herself that her body had craved his with no lesser passion than she had once craved Gerard's. She knew that she should feel dishonored, debased. Yet she felt neither.

Her mind turned back to the many lovers she had taken when she was The Barre Diamond. Strangely, there had been no such sense of wrongdoing when she had lain with them—merely a cold, quiet satisfaction that she was debasing them with her total indifference. It was as if she had been standing apart, an onlooker, observing the discomfiture of her partners as they strove to possess her cold, unresponsive body.

Was it then her own participation that was now so troubling her in her relationship with Gideon Morris? Or the fact that she knew him to be an outlaw?

As he had done the night before, he handed her her robe so that she might cover herself. As before, Mavreen rose and poured wine for each of them while the man put on his own attire. But on this occasion, he did not allow her to sit on the opposite side of the room but drew her down on the sofa beside him.

He laughed as he felt her body stiffen in resistance.

"It is time you learned you cannot fight me!" he said, speaking for the first time since his arrival. "You and I —we belong together."

"You are not in your right mind!" Mavreen cried. "I belong to no man!"

But his look silenced her.

"Now that we have discovered one another, you can no more resist our loving than I!" It was no question but a statement. "I have been searching far too long for a woman such as you and now that I have found you, I have not the slightest intention of letting you go. Nor do you wish me to if you will be honest with yourself. Your need of me matches mine own for you!"

Mavreen stayed silent. She was the more deeply shocked because deep down in her heart, she was aware that he spoke the truth. Her need of him was not of the mind or heart but of the deep rich satisfaction of the body. She had been starved of such completion far too long. Her nature, fierce, passionate, primitive, had been too long subdued. Gideon Morris, highwayman and outlaw, had somehow succeeded in breaking the dam and now there was no stopping, no denying the cravings that he had set loose.

Yet still she struggled to desist.

"I shall be returning to London within a day or so," she said coldly. "There will be no occasion for us to meet again—indeed, I have no intention of ever seeing you again. Do you understand me, sir?"

He laughed and leaning forward, kissed her slowly and meaningfully. He felt her body tremble and laughed again.

"Lies do not become you, my fine lady!" he said softly. "You see, I know already that your maid and manservant are to be wed in two weeks' time—and from this house. I have every intention of being at the wedding!"

Mavreen stared at him.

"How come you by this information?" she gasped.

"Oh, I have ways and means!" he said airily. "I am everywhere about, you know, and people love to gossip—especially if there is a piece of silver to whet their tongues." His boasting tone became suddenly gentle. "I was in Alfriston yesterday inquiring about you. I think, mayhap, you are not aware of my feelings toward you."

"Nor wish to be!" Mavreen broke in quickly, but he only smiled and continued, "My interest in you was aroused that selfsame night I held up your coach! Since then I have discovered myself unable to put you from my mind.

You are a very beautiful woman, Mavreen. But that is not all. You are different from any other female I have known, infinitely more exciting. Moreover, you have no lover though I doubt but that this is from your own choosing and that you have many suitors. It was meant that you and I should meet. It was our destiny!"

His cool assurance rendered her momentarily silent, but slowly she was regaining her composure.

"You are mistaken, sir!" she said. "You have no importance for me and I care not whether I see you again or no. As for your feelings for me, I would recommend that you speedily subdue them. 'Tis true that I have no lover but that is because my heart is engaged elsewhere."

Gideon's dark brown eyes narrowed dangerously.

"Gerard!" he said briefly. Then he laughed. "So you love this man! What of it? Clearly he himself is engaged elsewhere else he would even now be at your side. But *I* am here, my beautiful Mavreen, with my youth, my vigor, my desire. And you will not say nay to me. This night I have made you mine."

He rose to his feet, pulled his cloak about his shoulders and bowed extravagantly as he took her hand and kissed it.

"You will see me soon!" he said, as he slipped out as silently into the garden as he had come.

Mavreen could not be sure if he had intended threat or promise. But she was certain that she would see him again.

CHAPTER FORTY-ONE
1808-1809

Mavreen's immediate reaction to his absence was one of relief. She convinced herself that sanity had now returned and that her strange wayward behavior with the highwayman was a temporary madness brought about by his resemblance to Gerard. She resolved that as soon as the wedding was over and Dickon and Rose departed for a brief honeymoon to Brighthelmstone, she would return to London. There she could quickly forget that she had ever permitted herself to succumb to Gideon's undoubted attraction. Meanwhile, she tried to concentrate all her attentions upon preparations for the wedding, but, despite all her resolves, she found her thoughts straying far too often to the ignominious highwayman and in the evenings, would listen for his soft footfall, half hoping, half dreading his arrival. As the days passed with no further sign of him, she was both relieved and, with the illogicality of all females, piqued that he had so soon forgotten her. At least, she told herself, his continued absence resolved the perplexing question of whether she desired to see him again or not.

Gideon's totally unexpected and uninvited presence in the little church at Alfriston shocked and excited her. He slipped quietly into the pew beside her just as Rose appeared in a white silk gown, on her father's arm. Mavreen, like Dickon, was watching the approaching bride, and neither observed Gideon Morris's arrival. He followed in the wake of Rose's bridesmaids, her two youngest sisters in satin dresses and bonnets, clutching posies.

As Mavreen had ordered, the little church was festooned with bright summer flowers. The parson wore a clean lawn surplice and white wig. The congregation was festively attired in Sunday best.

"I could not come sooner!" Gideon whispered in Mavreen's ear. "I was detained in London!" He glanced at her flushed cheeks beneath the pink straw bonnet tied with dark red ribbon. "I declare you look almost as pretty begowned as unattired!" he said, causing her to blush a deeper color. "Didst think I had forgotten you?"

"I gave you no thought at all!" Mavreen lied.

But the marriage service had begun and further conversation made impossible as the congregation knelt to pray.

Gideon was arrayed in the most fashionable attire. His tailcoat was a brilliant peacock blue, his waistcoat canary yellow, his trousers a brilliant white as was his high neckcloth. His dark hair was unpowdered and cut short in the Brutus style. He had laid upon the seat beside him a curving brimmed top hat of the same color as his coat. His yellow kid gloves matched his waistcoat. He looked the picture of elegance.

" 'Tis just as well!" Mavreen thought, for it soon became apparent that Gideon had every intention of returning with her after the wedding to the grange where a lavish table of refreshments had been laid out in the gardens. In such garb, she thought, it was unlikely that Gideon would be recognized by Dickon as the ruffian who had held up their coach.

Happily, the sky was cloudless and the early September sun shone brilliantly upon the gathering as the horse and bullock carts arrived at the grange for the reception. Not only were the entire Sale family and all Rose's vast number of relations present, but so too was every friend and neighbor of the Sales for several miles around. No one came empty-handed. Shyly, but without doubt radiantly happy, the bridal pair received their guests and their gifts.

" 'Twill never happen I'll be wed a second time!" Dickon grinned, as Mavreen approached him to offer her congratulations. "There's a deal too much to-ing and froing for my liking, surelye! I reckon as there be two hundred people a-scrouging about!"

"Hush you, Dickon!" Rose reproved him, blushing. "Complaining that-away when Milady has done us so proud!"

Mavreen laughed.

"We shall need to call him *Master* Dickon now he is become a married man!" she said.

Rose dimpled.

" 'Tis true enough the rosemary will ne'er bloom except when the mistus is master, so mayhap I'll take my orders from him now—if I've a mind to!" she added with a mischievous glance at Dickon.

Before the sun went down, the whole roasted bullock had been eaten along with all the other food. The kegs of ale were emptied as adults and children ate, drank and danced the afternoon away to the gay tunes of Rob, the fiddler. Slowly, the jolly shouts and singing died away as one by one the families packed themselves into their gaily-decked carts and began the journey back to their farms. Mavreen had insisted that Dickon should take the phaeton to drive Rose to Brighthelmstone and when their final farewells were spoken they, too, prepared to depart upon their way.

Rose bobbed a curtsy and kissed Mavreen's hand, her cheeks pink with happiness and excitement.

"I don't know as how I can find the words, ma'am, to thank you for giving Dickon and me such a fine wedding." She leaned forward and added in a whisper, "And we both want as how you'll tell the fine gentleman from London how thankful we are for his generosity. Dickon said there's enough sovereigns in the purse he gave us to buy the Pavilion if we'd a mind to!"

Mavreen stayed silent, once again confused by the ambiguities of the man who had never been far away from her side throughout the day. His wedding gift was a generous thought and the more admirable for having been given unobtrusively. Yet the purse without doubt contained money that was stolen. Dickon and Rose would be shocked to think the "fine gentleman" they clearly approved was no more than a common thief.

As soon as they departed, Mavreen turned her thoughts to practicalities but the bridal couple had organized the clearing up to be done so she would not be left with her home in disorder. By dusk, all was straightened and the last of the visitors departed. Mavreen was suddenly glad to find Gideon at her elbow.

"You have done well!" he said. "There are not many ladies of your station who would provide such a wedding for their servants!"

"Nor many who have servants as loyal and devoted as mine!" Mavreen replied. "Come, let us go inside and sit down, for I profess my feet will keep me upright no longer!"

Despite the heat and activities of the day, he still looked cool and elegant. Watching him covertly as they sat drinking wine together, she found it even harder to reconcile the Gideon Morris of today with the man who had come to her house in the night, like the thief he was, with no other thought than to have his will of her. Now he was quietly conversing as if he were any ordinary London gentleman calling upon a lady.

But his conversation was far from ordinary for he chose this quiet hour to relate to her something of his childhood.

His mother, he told her, was upon the point of starvation when, as a boy of thirteen, he had been unceremoniously dumped upon her doorstep. It had taken him some time to reconcile himself to the fact that he was her child. She had the ways of speech and habits of a country lass and he had, until then, known only the society of gentlemen. Despite this gulf, her affectionate welcome gradually won him to her.

It was some days before he fully appreciated the horrors to which she had been subjected not long after his birth. His mother, already an outcast from village society because of the illegitimate child she had borne, was accused by her neighbors of witchcraft. She had been allowed to retain her job as dairy maid, but one particularly hot summer the milk curdled three times in succession, and the gossip began. One evil old woman recalled that his mother had cured her rheumatism with herbs when she herself had tried the same remedy and failed; another, that the black farm cat followed at his mother's heels wherever she went and was most surely her familiar. The farmer himself, who had tried and failed to seduce the poor young woman, let it be known that if she were about, he could not persuade his horses to ride past her.

" 'Tis nigh on a hundred years since the last case of witchcraft was tried in an English court," Gideon said, his voice and eyes hard. "Yet those villagers tried and condemned my mother just as certainly as if they had legal power so to do. She lost her position as dairy maid. Her own family turned her out. By the time I went to live with her, she existed alone in a derelict wooden shack on the outskirts of the village. She became a recluse for if she was seen about, the children threw stones at her and the women shouted 'Witch' at her. Yet she was no more a witch than you or I!"

"She was unfortunate, poor soul, as indeed were you," Mavreen said. " 'Tis not everywhere witches are looked down upon. In this neighborhood, as in many others, the Wicca were invited to hold mass covens to generate the power to hold Napoleon back from crossing the Channel. And, it would seem, were successful! They may be feared, but are yet respected."

" 'Tis accepted, I think, that there are good and bad witches, but my poor mother was believed to be of evil influence. She was young, helpless, and alone. Yet no one tried to help her."

"Until you came!" Mavreen said softly, suddenly beginning to understand the enigma of this strange man.

"The village children threw stones at me when I went amongst them; called me 'Witch's Spawn'. At first I tried to fight with my fists. But such encounters only resulted in my battering by gangs of yokels bigger and stronger than I. That was when I resolved to use my head rather than my fists to improve our penury. I crept out of the house at night and stole—food, at first, since hunger was our prime concern. But then I stole money—everything I could lay my hands on that was not beneath lock and key. On several occasions, I was nearly caught, so I taught myself to move silently, like a cat; to wear dark clothing so that I could merge into the night; to see without being seen."

He stretched out his long legs and smiled at Mavreen as she stooped to light one of the oil lamps.

"It was not long," he told her, "before I came upon the smugglers, also bent upon illegal nocturnal pursuits. I joined one of the gangs. Our circumstances improved beyond measure and we had enough money to buy a small cottage in a village near East Grinstead. I was able to remove my mother there and we changed our name."

"It did not then occur to you to change your way of life also, to one more law abiding?" Mavreen inquired.

"What chance had I?" Gideon replied. "We were no longer poor but of a certainty we were not rich. Moreover, I had no place in society, being unable to claim my position as a gentleman's son nor willing to reduce myself to the life of a laborer."

"It cannot have been easy for you," Mavreen agreed.

"I was by now twenty-four years old," Gideon continued. "When I was not engaged upon my smuggling activities, I continued my own education from books which I now had money to buy. I became friendly with a certain William Beatson, the adopted son of a likable rogue called Joseph. They earned their living by robbing coaches. They took me with them upon several occasions and I discovered that theirs was a way of getting rich far more speedy than mine own."

He looked at Mavreen with a wry smile.

"Fate must have looked kindly on me at the time of my birth," he said, "for I have many times evaded death by seconds. But on this particular incident I will advise you of, I was never closer to a hanging upon the gallows. The Beatsons had decided to rob the mail coach as it passed through the village of Forest Row. It was agreed that I should go with them. But at the eleventh hour, my mother fell down the stairs and broke her leg so that I had need to go in search of a surgeon for her, and I was prevented from keeping the appointment."

Mavreen's eyes widened.

"I have heard tell of this robbery," she said. "Dickon heard about it in Alfriston. Did the Beatsons not conceal themselves in a meadow at the bottom of Wall Hill until the coach passed them?"

Gideon nodded.

"They did no harm to the driver but dragged the mail-bags across the meadows to nearby Hartfield, where they concealed themselves in a field of standing corn whilst they opened the bags and sorted the contents. The coach had been carrying the remarkable sum of £14,000. William and his father took away with them the Bank of England and country notes, leaving in the field the remainder of the contents amounting to £9,500. It was discovered a week later by two farm laborers who went in to reap the field."

Mavreen nodded, for she had heard much of this already from Dickon.

"There was a hue and cry raised all over the country

and the robbers were finally caught at Liverpool, were they not?" she asked.

Gideon nodded.

"They were taken to Horsham to await their trial," he said. "I went to see them there and William told me that he planned to escape. But although he nearly succeeded, he was recaptured in a nearby sewer. He and his father were tried the following March and, as you no doubt know, were hanged that April on a gallows erected on Wall Hill. It was a public hanging and I attended, not to gape as did so many others, but so that I could pay my last respects to them. They were not evil men and deserved death no more nor less than I, who might, but for my mother, have hanged there with them!"

Mavreen was silent. She could see that Gideon was still saddened by the memory of his friends' deaths. She felt strangely glad that he had not met with the same fate.

"Yet you continue to risk your life!" she said at last, "and for no better reason than your amusement. That is not easy to comprehend."

"Mayhap you would understand better were you to feel the excitement of knowing your life is in danger and survival depends upon your own speed and timing. I am never more alive than when I am holding up a coach, aware that I might be shot before I myself can fire my pistol!"

"You have killed many men?" Mavreen asked curiously.

"Fortunately, there has never been the need. I have no wish to take life. I am not even certain that I would do so were it to become necessary. But I have been fired upon many times as I rode away with my spoils!"

Mavreen sensed the excitement in his voice and could not altogether gainsay it. Danger always brought excitement with it.

"Were you a man, I would take you with me to discover the delights for yourself!" Gideon said, laughing. "But since you are a woman—and the most beautiful woman I know—then let us give ourselves to other delights, just as exciting but far more befitting. What say you?"

Mavreen's refusal died upon her lips. The house was empty, the old servants long since retired to their beds.

Although she was physically tired after the events of the day, her mind was wide awake. Moreover, Gideon's strange attraction for her was making itself felt as he came toward her with open arms.

This time, he did not merely lift her from her chair but carried her across the room and up the stairs to her bedchamber. There seemed no disloyalty to Gerard's memory as he laid her upon the bed where she had once lain and loved with him. The confusion of their two identities was back once more, stirring her senses, causing her blood to heat to a fever of desire, in no way lessened by the fact that Gideon had been absent these last ten days.

As was his habit, he loved her without speech, intent upon their mutual satisfaction and pleasure. Strangely, Mavreen found greater joy in their union than had been possible with Gerard since she had never lain with him without the agony of impending parting tearing at her heartstrings. With Gideon, there was no love; therefore no memories of yesterday nor fears for tomorrow's loneliness; only the vivid pleasures of the present as they gave themselves up to the delights of their bodies.

Gideon proved himself at all times a fastidious man and sensitive lover, but withal, he left her in no doubt that he was the master. To her surprise she discovered an inexplicable satisfaction in his domination.

Her life began to take on a new pattern.

She spent her days alone, putting her house in order, writing letters to Tamarisk, riding or walking or visiting the Sales. She was peaceful and happy. With the approach of darkness came the first stirring of excitement, for now it was become Gideon's custom to slip through the unlocked French windows in the library and find his way without lamp or candle to her bedchamber. And just as quietly, he would leave before the break of dawn.

But this extraordinary idyll could not, she knew, continue. If she did not take some drastic step to prevent it, she would cease altogether to consider the immorality and pointlessness of her existence. There was no future, no stability in such a relationship. Moreover, she sensed that Gideon was falling in love with her. She had no wish to hurt him unduly by awaiting such time as he declared himself and only then telling him that she could never love him—nor any man but Gerard. She knew that it was time for her to return to London—to sanity, and to forget as speedily as possible the madness of the summer.

"You will come back!" Gideon said quietly when she told him she had made up her mind to leave. "I have no doubt on it. I shall await your coming."

"I pray you do not look for me," Mavreen said. "You must know that I cannot continue with a liaison such as ours. I have a young daughter to consider as well as my reputation. I do not regret our association, Gideon, but I do not wish it to go on any longer. If you have any affection for me, then do not seek to detain me here in Sussex."

He let her go without demur. Perhaps, she thought wryly as she prepared for her departure, he knew her well enough to realize that woman-like, she would be piqued that he did not put up more fight to deter her. Nor was he mistaken if such was his intent.

In London, Clarissa who was much recovered, gave her the warmest of welcomes and congratulated her on her appearance.

"I have not seen you look so well in a long while!" she said, hugging Mavreen to her. "You have proved yourself quite right in taking a holiday in Sussex. The country air always does you good!"

Mavreen gave a little supper party to welcome Tamarisk home from Worthing, to which Clarissa and Sir John were invited. Much had happened in her absence from London, and he brought her up to date with current events.

Mavreen listened with interest as he lauded the exploits of the British army in Portugal under the leadership of Lieutenant General Wellesley.

"He has done brilliantly in the field," he said. "Forget the indecisive result of the battle at Rolica and consider the battle at Vimeiro. There Wellesley proved himself well worthy of his promotion last April. Though not yet forty and doubtless the youngest lieutenant general in the army, the Frenchies had to give him best."

"So Napoleon's army is not invincible!" Mavreen commented.

"Far from it. 'Tis said he lost 23,000 troops in Spain, at Baylen. Some say it is the first crack in his empire, but to my mind that is an over-optimistic opinion. Nevertheless, he has been able to proclaim his brother, Joseph, king of Spain and Spain itself a kingdom within the French empire. 'Twill not be easy to bring about the downfall of such a man. It would be a vast mistake to underestimate his power or his ability."

"What has become of King Charles and his queen?" Mavreen asked curiously.

" 'Tis said Napoleon offered them refuge in France—at the palace of Compiègne."

Sir John immediately regretted that he had not thought, before so enlightening his daughter, for at the mention of Compiègne the color rushed to her cheeks. He had momentarily forgot that it was young de Valle's home and that Mavreen had never lost her affection for the boy.

He was saved the necessity for further conversation upon the matter by the announcement that supper was served, and afterwards the subject of Compiègne was not mentioned again.

Dickon and Rose arrived back from Brighthelmstone and life at Finchcocks settled back to normal.

Thomas Creevey and John Ward renewed their calls upon Mavreen, each swearing that the weeks she had been absent in Sussex were "unendurably tedious." But although she was still able to enjoy their intellect and witty conversation, Mavreen felt dispassionate about both her suitors. She now found herself unable to enjoy the casual flirtations with which she had passed the time so lightheartedly in Brighthelmstone. It was only with a great deal of tact and patience that she was able to divert the amorous intentions of her two faithful admirers and establish a more platonic friendship with each of them.

In such manner her life proceeded uneventfully to the turn of the year. The Lades, with yet another addition to the family, came to Finchcocks for Tamarisk's birthday and the Christmas festivities. On New Year's Eve, Mavreen gave a ball, inviting those many friends to whom she owed hospitality, including Lisa von Eburhard.

The baroness, who had not seen Mavreen for many months, eyed her knowingly.

"You are looking so charming, my dear," she whispered, "that I suspicion you may have taken a lover, despite all your denials in Brighthelmstone of the likelihood."

To her private discomfiture, Mavreen blushed at the memory of Gideon Morris. She had almost succeeded in forgetting him although she had not been able to prevent herself at public functions from glancing about her lest she should glimpse him in the crowd.

It was not until March of the following year, 1809, that she most unexpectedly did see him. She was seated beside the baroness at the opera, when glancing around the glittering assembly, she was convinced that she recognized him in the box directly opposite to her.

With a beating heart but with an assumed casualness, she asked Lisa von Eburhard if she knew who the gentleman might be in attendance upon Lady Esther Ingram, a friend of Lisa's but only slightly known to Mavreen.

"Why, yes, I know the gentleman," Lisa said at once. "Although it would be more true to say that I know of him for I have never actually made his acquaintance. His name is Sir Peregrine Waite and he is a friend of Beau Brummell, I believe—another such dandy who spends his days adorning himself to look beautiful." She smiled wickedly at Mavreen. "Although I grant that his stature is most handsome and manly, I have heard that he is singularly foppish—not at all to *your* taste, Mavreen!" She lowered her voice to add from behind her fan, "He is quite rich, I believe, but unmarried. The ladies of his acquaintance contend that despite his appearance, he is most effeminate and would not know what to do with wife or mistress!"

Mavreen's mouth twitched with laughter which she kept carefully concealed. Gideon had told her that he lived a very different life in London, but he had not told her that he assumed the role of an effeminate. Remembering his excessive masculinity she was vastly amused and at the same time, terribly tempted to make her presence known to him. But she fought the temptation, hiding her face behind her fan. She was afraid of the weakness of her will if he were to come close to her; and even now, knowing that he was near at hand, she felt her pulses racing and her breathing quickened. It took all her strength of mind to shake her head in refusal when the baroness offered to effect an introduction to "Sir Peregrine" if she so desired.

"As you so rightly surmise, dear baroness, I have no interest in such a man!" she lied.

Upon her return home from the opera, she resolved that on no account would she go back to Sussex during the summer.

But fate was conspiring otherwise. The Lades invited Tamarisk to join them once more at the seaside and the child eagerly requested that she be allowed to go. At the same time, Rose's first baby was due to be born and Mavreen insisted that Dickon should accompany his wife to Owlett's Farm and remain there with her for a week or two until mother and child were strong enough to return to Finchcocks.

Clarissa announced that she would, once again, be travelling to Scotland with Sir John for the grouse shooting. Although he was now in his middle sixties, he was of robust good health and greatly enjoyed the sport. The baroness was already gone to Brighthelmstone. There was no one to detain Mavreen in London. Yet still she resisted the ever-growing desire to go down to the grange.

This resistance was finally undermined by the strangest of encounters with Gideon Morris outside the London home of her friend, Mistress Elizabeth Fry.

Mavreen arrived punctually at St. Mildred's Court where she had arranged to take tea with Elizabeth. When the butler admitted her into the house, she was informed that her friend was not yet back from an earlier appointment and Mavreen was conducted to the library to await her hostess.

It being a hot and airless afternoon, she went to stand at the window so that she might obtain what benefit there was of the cooler air filtering in through the open casements. A carriage drew up outside the house which Mavreen assumed to be Mistress Fry's. It was not, however, Elizabeth who emerged from the interior, but Gideon Morris. Mavreen recognized him instantly, despite the hat pulled down low over his face.

He did not look up or approach the house but walked some paces along the street until he happened upon a ragged urchin playing in the gutter. To Mavreen's astonishment, he put his hand in his pocket and drew out a silver coin which he gave the child, at the same time leading him back toward the carriage. Reaching inside, he pulled out a package which he handed to the urchin. Then clearly pointing his cane at Mistress Fry's front door, he urged the boy toward it. He waited only long enough to see his messenger tug upon the bell rope before he jumped back into his carriage and with a sharp command to the coachman, drove off at high speed down the road.

His movements seemed so extraordinary to Mavreen that as soon as Mistress Fry arrived and greetings and apologies were exchanged, Mavreen questioned her friend about the mysterious caller.

As she removed her bonnet, Elizabeth's face took on an expression that was part smile, part frown. She dismissed the footman and drew her chair closer to Mavreen's.

"I feel certain that my secret will be safe with you," she said, her voice lowered to confidential tone. "I will therefore acquaint you of this most strange of conspiracies, though no other living soul knows of it." She looked so anxious Mavreen hastened to assure her that her confidence could be totally relied upon.

"I had best begin at the beginning!" Elizabeth said. "And that was a long time ago, Mavreen, when I was but nine years of age. I lived then with my father and my brothers and sisters in Norwich. One day, a friend of my father's, by the name of Sir Frederick Morris, came to visit with us. He brought with him his son—a boy of twelve who, I learned several years later, was his natural son. My brothers and sisters and I found the boy most delightful company. He and his father remained with us for a week, or perhaps longer, and then returned to London. Not long after this visit, Sir Frederick Morris died. I did not hear what had become of his son until some six years later when I was brought to London for the occasion of the Prince of Wales's marriage. I was walking in St. James's Park with my governess when a footpad stole my reticule. My governess screamed and the thief was caught by a passer-by. Can you believe my astonishment and horror, Mavreen, when I saw that the young man who had robbed me was Gideon Morris. Despite his condition, for he was poorly dressed and looked half-starved, I had no doubt that it was he."

Mavreen, who knew the outline of Gideon's childhood, pretended the surprise expected of her.

"There was such a to-do!" Elizabeth said, sighing at the memory. "My governess and the gentleman who had come to our assistance insisted the poor boy be handed over to the law. But I began weeping and begged that he be allowed to go free. I think my governess was so afraid that I would have hysterics and that she herself would miss the spectacle we had come to see, that finally she supported me. Gideon Morris disappeared into the crowd and I did not see him again for a further few years. I did, however, ascertain from my father some facts about him —that he had met with misfortune after his father's death and shamefully, so I thought then and do now, returned to his mother who was of lowly birth and unfortunate situation. My father did not know what had eventually become of the boy and I said nothing of my recognition of him as the thief. I thought never to see him again."

"But you did so?" Mavreen prompted her informant as she paused in her tale.

"I did not see him in person, but he wrote to me. By this time, I was married to dear Joseph and was living here in London. By some means, Gideon Morris discovered my whereabouts and must also have learned of my work among the poor. He sent me by messenger a purse of gold telling me to use the money as I wished and thanking me for the mercy I had shown toward a poor young thief who had once stolen my purse from me!"

Mavreen let out her breath. She felt elated. Gideon's Robin Hood behavior lessened enormously the immorality of his chosen profession.

"I know that I should feel grateful," Elizabeth said,

shaking her head doubtfully. "But alas, I fear the poor young man has remained a thief and become more proficient as such every year. The parcels he sends me have grown ever larger; and their contents—" she lowered her voice, "—frequently there are watches, jewels, snuff boxes, personal property which I could not possibly keep—or sell!"

Despite the gravity of Elizabeth's expression, Mavreen smiled.

"Since I assume you have no address to which you can return them, am I to believe you have no alternative but to throw them away?" she asked.

"Do not joke, Mavreen, for I am most deeply concerned as to the problem of my own morality in this strange affair. Doubtless Gideon Morris anticipated the confusion of my conscience since he has never failed to include in his gifts the names of his victims. Naturally, I return them at once to their rightful owners. All have told me that they have not long before been robbed by a highwayman."

"So your ertswhile common thief has become a 'gentleman of the road,' " Mavreen remarked.

Elizabeth nodded.

"Of course, I require no reward for the lawful return of the valuables, but such is the gratitude of those who are receiving back what they believed forever lost to them, that I invariably have forced upon me a handsome donation to my charities. If Mr. Fry were to discover what I was about, he would be quite horrified; and, moreover, he would not rest until Gideon Morris were hunted down and exposed for the villain he is! The whole affair has, therefore, to be carried out in the utmost secrecy."

Mavreen stood up and crossing the room to her friend, warmly kissed her cheek.

"I do not think your Gideon is such a terrible villain," she said quietly. "Moreover, you yourself are doing no wrong, Elizabeth—indeed, the benefit to your charities must be very satisfying to you. Were I in your place, I would have no hesitation in following your example. I do congratulate you upon your common sense! As for Gideon Morris—I should leave his fate in the hands of God who will best know how to judge him!"

But in her own mind, judgement was already made— the more easily in Gideon's favor since he had told her nothing of the philanthropic side of his nature but only of his misdeeds.

"I cannot help but worry that I should be in conspiracy with a highwayman!" Elizabeth sighed. But Mavreen laughed.

Mavreen kissed her friend goodbye, warning her as she did so that she would not be calling in the near future since she had made up her mind to spend the rest of the summer in Sussex.

"The country air will be good for me!" she said.

But it was not for the country air that she was going.

CHAPTER FORTY-TWO
1809

"I had no doubt that you would return!"

Gideon Morris smiled down into Mavreen's eyes. She had been at the grange two days when he came silently through the French windows, no longer attired in his London finery but looking exactly as she had first seen him, in breeches and white-frilled shirt. As before, his likeness to Gerard took her breath away.

"I had determined not to do so!" she answered him, piqued by his self-assurance which, indeed, she had forgotten.

"You shall tell me all about it presently!" he said, his kisses leaving her in no doubt as to his more immediate intentions.

"No!" she commanded. "I do not wish. . . ."

But he stopped her protest with kisses and as before lifted her easily into his arms and carried her up the staircase to her bedchamber.

"I will not—I forbid—" she tried to protest.

But he paid no attention and held her flailing fists with

one hand as he disrobed her with the other. The resulting damage to her thin gown worried him not at all. Only when she was quite naked beneath his gaze did he let her go free, saying, "Now order me to leave you and I will do so!"

Accepting at last her own weakness, she held out her arms and he fell on top of her, their hunger for one another as unabashed as it was mutual.

When their loving was done, he drew her close into the circle of his arms. His brown eyes, soft and brilliant, stared down at her in tenderness.

"I have been watching for your arrival since your manservant and his pretty little wife arrived at Owlett's Farm," he said quickly. "I knew you would not be long behind them!"

"I had quite forgot your ability to spy out my movements!" Mavreen replied with an attempt at haughtiness, which dissolved instantly when he laughed.

"Do not pretend disapproval with me, my fine lady!" He kissed her bare shoulders, then doing so a second time, he said, "No faint-hearted lover for you, my lovely! It is my audacity that attracts you!"

"That is true enough!" Mavreen conceded, and added mischievously, "I do not think I could bed with the foppish dandy in gold breeches and rouged cheeks whom I last saw dancing attendance upon the Lady Esther Ingram!"

Gideon's dark eyes glinted with amusement.

"Then you, too, have been spying!" he accused her. "And since the only occasion upon which I escorted that tediously dull woman was to the opera, I must assume you saw me there. But I saw you not!"

"Such was my intention!" Mavreen smiled. "But I saw you a second time, Gideon."

She chose this moment to confess that she had been at Mistress Fry's the day he delivered a parcel to her. Now that his actions were known to her, Gideon further enlightened her.

She learned from him something of which Elizabeth herself was unaware—that upon the instant of robbing her in St. James's Park, he had, in fact, recognized her as one of the young Gurneys. He never forgot her. When, by chance, he heard of her marriage to Joseph Fry and that she had come from Norwich to live in London, he had made it his business to discover her address so that he might not only repay her merciful kindness to him but at the same time, assist her efforts for the poor, with whom, quite naturally, he had much sympathy. In such a manner he made retribution.

"Nevertheless, you continue to lead the life of a reprobate!" Mavreen reproved him, "and I dare not think what poor Elizabeth would say if she could see us now. I dare swear she would pass into a swoon from which she would not recover!"

But by now Mavreen admitted to herself that it was not merely Gideon's likeness to Gerard that she found so exciting. It was the very dare-devilry of his life which fascinated her. And the more he told her of his exploits, the greater that fascination became.

Gideon was aware of it.

"You would enjoy such adventure!" he said one night. " 'Tis most surely a pity that you are a female else you could have accompanied me tomorrow. 'Tis the day of the Lewes races and I don't doubt there will even now be many carriages bowling down the highway in readiness for the occasion."

"I could disguise myself and accompany you," Mavreen said, suddenly reminded of the youth's clothes she had worn when she accompanied Dickon to Compiègne. She had been but a girl then. "Nevertheless," she said breathlessly to Gideon, "a cloak would conceal my more womanly appearance. Let me come with you, Gideon! Please! I will not hinder you in any way."

Gideon seemed far from enthusiastic about her proposition.

"It was wrong of me to enlist your curiosity," he said, frowning. "However skilful a highwayman may be, however swift his horse, there is always danger. We could be shot at, or at worst, apprehended. And that, Mavreen, could mean hanging. I would not care to see you on the gallows at Tyburn!"

"Nor would you see my untimely death since they would

hang you first!" Mavreen replied recklessly. She sat up and looked at Gideon with a new seriousness. "I do not speak lightly when I say I do not fear death. Once, a long time ago, life was very sweet. But now—now the only man I have ever loved, or could ever love, is of a certainty dead. Without him, living is but an existence and at times, an excessively dull existence. I am prepared to risk my life."

Gideon's expression was now become as serious as her own.

"You should not speak so casually of death!" he reproved her. "As to this man you once loved—no man on earth is worth *your* life, and that is what you are wasting, Mavreen, each day that you mourn for him. *He cannot be worth it!* Moreover, he cannot have been willing so to sacrifice his life for you else you would long since have married him. No, I do not wish to hear of your past—" he went on hurriedly, as Mavreen sought to interrupt him, "—since that belongs to you alone. But I do condemn this man's hold upon your present. He has forfeited all right to it, if not by his death then by his leaving you alone. Were I the man you loved, I would never leave you."

"Even if you are right and Gerard did not love me as I loved him, I cannot forget him. There is no future happiness possible for me without him."

"Think not on the future!" Gideon said harshly. "It is today, tonight that is life. It is *now* that you live, not the next minute or the last, but now as I kiss you so, and touch you so, and hold you in my arms like this. Your body lives, my beautiful Mavreen, and so will your heart if you will only release it to discover its own resting place!"

There was wisdom in his words but still she could not agree with all he said. Her heart was not in her keeping, and this all-important factor she failed to make Gideon understand. But at least she prevailed upon him to agree that she might go with him the next day. He would himself find a mount for her, he said, since a tireless horse was of prime importance. He knew already that she was an accomplished rider, and that she could handle a pistol with skill.

Mavreen's excitement increased as they made further plans. She would find breeches, cloak and hat for herself. Since they would be departing from the grange at midday in broad daylight, she would conceal these clothes in a parcel telling the servants she was taking it to Owlett's Farm. A long walk, she would inform them, would be excellent exercise for her, and as she might well remain for supper, they must not concern themselves if she were not to return before nightfall.

Her absence thus satisfactorily accounted for, it would be a simple matter to meet with Gideon by the mill stream a mile from the grange, change her attire, mount the horse he brought for her and so be upon their way unobserved by any.

"You are quite certain that you wish to engage upon this enterprise?" Gideon asked before he left that night. "It is a risky adventure! I am far from easy about your part in it."

Mavreen's eyes sparkled.

"Was it not you who but recently instructed me to live for the day and pay no heed to yesterday or tomorrow?"

But he would not smile and his eyes were serious as he took her into his arms and kissed her for the last time before leaving.

"I would not forgive myself if harm came to you," he said, his voice soft and urgent. "I find myself uncommonly fond of you, Mavreen. . . ." he broke off, struggling to find the right words to express himself. "I have never yet told a woman that I loved her. Indeed, I have not before felt for any woman as I feel for you. I do not even know if it be love. When my mother died, I swore never to let myself care about another human being and yet—yet I cannot keep away from you. Even apart from you, I find myself thinking of you day and night."

Mavreen put a hand against his mouth but he twisted his head free and continued: "Do not prevent my speaking of my affection for you. I am aware that your heart lies elsewhere and that even if it did not, it would be presumptuous in the extreme for a lawless highwayman to expect that you might return his affections. Nevertheless, I sense that there is more between us than either of us expected when first I bedded you. We are different from others but similar to one another. You, like myself, would do or dare anything to have your way if it were of sufficient import to you. Is that not true, Mavreen?"

She nodded, her heart strangely uneasy.

"We belong!" Gideon said quietly. "I suspicion that it is only with me that you can be your true self—wild, headstrong, passionate, without need of restraint of that part of your nature you cannot subdue. Oh, you can play the grand lady of society just as I can play the dandy, and deceive everyone into believing your tame respectability. But beneath the façade you are as much a child of nature as I."

Mavreen understood his meaning, but the coldly logical part of her mind reasoned that similarity of nature in no way guaranteed the inclusion of that strangest of emotions—love. And while Gideon Morris appeared to have discovered a very great deal about the person that she was, she knew little enough about him. She recognized that he was stronger than she, a law unto himself; that no matter how attractive he found her or in what high esteem he held her, she would never be able to twist him around her little finger or even cajole him into giving her her own way if it did not suit him to do so. She was both intrigued by him and a little afraid of the fascination he had for her, it seeming quite beyond her control to disregard him. Yet she could not love him.

Gideon, the highwayman, was little different from Gideon the lover. He made it clear from the moment he met her at the appointed place of assignation that he would give orders which she must obey without question or delay.

He introduced her to a thoroughbred bay mare by the name of Amabel he had brought for her to ride. Mavreen ran her hand along the mare's back and sides. Her coat was dry and silky. She was small but well-proportioned.

"Don't let her size deceive you!" Gideon said, as Mavreen looked doubtfully from the delicate lines of the mare toward his own great black stallion. "She is as swift as an arrow. She's out of an Italian stallion and as sensitive to her rider as a violin string to the bow."

As soon as Mavreen had changed her attire, Gideon lifted her into the saddle. At once she realized why he had spoken so lovingly of the little mare. Amabel was prancing like a ballet dancer but was instantly responsive to the pressure of Mavreen's knees upon her flanks.

The sun shone from a brilliant sky as they set off toward Firle Beacon. They skirted the summit and let the horses have their heads as they galloped westward across the Downs. The air was sweet-smelling with sundrenched grass and wild thyme. They saw no one but an occasional shepherd tending his flock of sheep and heard no sound but their own breathing and the singing of the larks high above their heads.

" 'Tis a world so far apart from London and so wild and beautiful," Mavreen said as they slowed their horses to a walk, "that I wonder why any of us ever live in that crowded city."

> Too many folk in London city.
> 'Tis hardly a joke. 'Tis almost a pity!

Gideon quoted laughing.

She told him about the black stallion her father had once owned called Raven and remarked upon the likeness to Gideon's mount.

" 'Tis useful to have a black horse at night!" he said, grinning. "But the bay is a good enough color—too common to be remarkable when the victims report the hold-up to the law!"

They travelled at leisurely pace the ten or so miles to Falmer, outside which tiny village they tethered the horses to a rowan tree and concealed themselves behind the hedgerows of hawthorn and clumps of yellow gorse.

Gideon lay on his back and pulled Mavreen on top of him. His eyes smiled up at her as he said, "Mayhap when you don your cloak and hat you will look like my male accomplice, but at this moment, despite the breeches, you still appear the most desirable of females!"

He kissed her lingeringly.

"Are you not just a little afraid of what we are about to do?" he teased her. She shook her head vehemently.

"Not in the least! Only excited! There will be no bloodshed, will there?"

"You have my word on it that I shall not fire one shot —unless we ourselves are first fired upon!"

Somewhere in the distance, a different sound to that of country noises reached their ears. It was a carriage bowling toward Brighthelmstone from Lewes down the brown ribbon of the dusty road. As it came closer, they could see it swaying and lurching as it bounced over the hardened ruts made by the farm carts.

Mavreen looked at Gideon questioningly. But he stayed motionless as it passed by them, grey-white with dust, the creaking of harness and leathers audible above the breathing of the four horses, and the occasional shout from the coachman.

"It's not the first coach but the last I'm after!" he explained. "The races will be over and the carriages coming by one after the other now. We would run a risk of assistance reaching our victims before we'd completed our work if we apprehend the firstcomers."

He had scarcely finished speaking before, indeed, a second and then a third coach went by. There were horsemen, too, and phaetons, broughams, even farm carts, some travelling at speed while others passed at more leisurely pace.

"There was scarcely ever a soul to be seen on this road before the Prince of Wales made Brighthelmstone a fashionable place for the gentry," Gideon told her. " 'Tis high time the road menders improved the surface. The occupants of those carriages will be pitched about like driftwood!"

"And steamed like so many puddings in this heat!" Mavreen added, laughing.

Her excitement mounted as the number of coaches passing by them increased. When, at last, they began to thin out, Gideon stood up and helped Mavreen to her feet. He pulled on his hat and cloak and masked his face with his silk kerchief, motioning Mavreen to do likewise.

"Whatever happens, you durst not speak!" he cautioned her. "Let me do all the talking. And when I give the signal to depart, ride like the wind and stop for nothing. I'll not be far behind you."

He took his pistols from their saddle holsters and checked them carefully. He helped Mavreen to mount and then sprang easily into his saddle.

Atop the mare, Mavreen now had a perfect view of the wide ribbon of road and the single carriage approaching them. It was drawn by six horses and was escorted by an outrider. Gideon put his pistols back in his saddle holsters and nodded to Mavreen, grinning broadly.

"We'll take this one!" he said. "Doubtless 'tis someone of consequence and if he hasn't lost all his money at the races, we'll make a pretty haul!"

A minute or two before the coach drew level, Gideon dug his heels into the stallion's flanks and moved out into the road. Catching her breath, Mavreen did likewise. As the coachman caught sight of two highwaymen, there followed a great wrestling with the reins as he brought the horses to a fumbling stop and shouted out a warning to the postilion. He, too, drew to a halt and dismounting, stood holding the bridle of his horse as he stared white-faced into the barrels of Gideon's pistols.

The dust began to settle. The protective leather curtains drawn across the carriage windows were pulled back. A scarlet-faced, heavily jowled gentleman leaned out.

"Devil take it! What's a-foot?" he asked.

"Pray open the door and come out!" Gideon commanded in a low coarse voice. "And you, coachy, and you—" he nodded toward the postilion, "you'll not move from your place or I'll shoot!"

The gentleman's hat had fallen off, revealing a pink bald pate. His face was now purple with fury.

"You poxy rogue!" he shouted at Gideon. "I'll see you in hell before I hand you a penny piece!"

Gideon moved his horse forward.

"Your servants are already at pistol point," he said, "and you are at the point of mine. Out with you and no more delay!"

"Insolent rogue! Thief!" the man expostulated, but he opened the door and stepped down into the roadway.

A stout, bejeweled lady peered out after him and fell back screaming at the sight of Gideon's masked face and pistols.

"Your wallet, sir! Your money and your jewels!" Gideon commanded.

The portly gentleman began fumbling at his belt but his trembling fingers could not untie the knot. Gideon leaned from his horse's back and gave it a wrench whereupon the string broke and a fountain of newly-minted gold coins spread in the dust around them.

Gideon nodded to Mavreen who dismounted and started to gather up the coins as Gideon relieved his victim, now on the point of apoplexy, of his watch and jewelery, and that also of his now-hysterical wife. Of her own accord, she pulled the necklace of pearls from her neck and thrust it out of the window into Gideon's hands, crying, "Take it! 'Tis worth a fortune, but spare my life, sir."

Mavreen had now remounted and Gideon lowered his pistols.

"Drive on, rattler!" he ordered the coachman, grinning to see his portly victim scrambling back into his carriage like a scalded cat.

"Devil take you!" his victim shouted in a last miserable and belated attempt at defiance. But Gideon had already turned his horse's head and with Mavreen's mare a length in front of him, jumped the hedge in a flying leap and disappeared behind the clump of hawthorn trees.

They rode at full gallop until they had breasted the curve of the smooth green downland and were well out of sight of the road. As they slowed to a walk, Gideon pulled off his mask and laughed to see the bright color in Mavreen's cheeks.

"So you enjoyed your first adventure as an outlaw!" he said. He halted his mount and lifted Mavreen down from Amabel's back.

" 'Twas easy this time. 'Tis not always so. Upon one such adventure, I met with a very stubborn, very beautiful young woman who refused even at pistol point to deliver!"

She laughed breathlessly as he stared down at her.

"Will you not look at the spoils?" she asked. "I suspicion that we have untold riches in that bulging saddle bag of yours!"

"I have all the riches I want here!" was his reply as he put his hands beneath her chin and raised her face so that he might kiss her full upon the mouth.

They rode home in slow contentment. By the time they reached the mill stream, a mist was rising from the water and a pale sickle moon hung in the sky.

"I must take the horses back and see them into warm stables," he said, as Mavreen changed back into her ordinary clothes. "But I will come to you later, Mavreen!"

He did not ask her if that was her wish. He seemed to know already that it was so.

Mavreen was quite unprepared for the reception that awaited her at the grange.

During the day, Rose's baby, a boy, was born and Dickon rode over from Owlett's Farm to advise Mavreen of the good news. Upon being told by the elderly servants that Mavreen was gone to the farm, Dickon presumed to have missed her somewhere upon the road and at once rode home. When there was still no sign of Mavreen, nor word that she had been there, he became frantic with worry and was convinced that harm had come to her. Leaving his mother and sisters to take care of Rose, he gathered together his brothers and one or two farm laborers and formed a search party to look for her.

By some happy stroke of fate, Gideon and Mavreen were not observed by the searchers on their return to the mill stream. But Dickon, white with worry, saw Mavreen approach the grange in the gathering dusk. He was deeply alarmed. Her hair was dishevelled, her cambric dress crumpled, her shoes muddy and her face covered with dusty smears.

"Wheresomever have you been?" he asked as he ran forward to greet her, his relief and anxiety in comic admixture upon his face. "You shouldn't ought to've been out by your own self. I been near out of my mind with worritin'!"

"Oh, Dickon!" Mavreen cried, her cheeks flushed with guilt. "I'm so sorry you have been worried. There was no need. I am perfectly safe!"

" 'Tis gone nine of the clock!" Dickon cried, wringing his hands. "And you bin gone since midday, leastways so cook said!"

Mavreen decided that she had no alternative but to confess the whole story of her escapade to Dickon. It would not have sufficed for her to tell him only that she had been out riding with a gentleman since he would naturally have wanted to know why her escort had not brought her home; or, indeed, why she had not ridden her own horse or worn her riding habit. Moreover, she disliked having to tell lies to Dickon of all people.

Upon her command he accompanied her into the library and stood in silence as she began at the beginning and told him of her second encounter with Gideon Morris; how it led to a closer relationship despite her return to London and her efforts to forget him, and had been renewed this summer. His shocked expression told its own story.

"I know it sounds extraordinary—even wrong!" Mavreen cried, "but you will understand better if I tell you Gideon Morris is not a bad man, Dickon. Everything he takes from the rich he gives to Mistress Fry for the poor. Do not look so disapproving, I beg you!"

When he finally spoke, his voice was stiff and unyielding.

"I dunno but what it is none of my affair nohow what you have a mind to do!"

"Dickon, please!" Mavreen pleaded, hating to see the unhappy look in his eyes. Dickon had not only loved her all his life but respected her, too, and she hated the thought that she might have lost his respect. "Please try to understand. I am happy. I have not been so happy since—since I was with the vicomte in Vienna, and even then—well perfect contentment was denied me for I knew from the first that I would soon be separated from him again. Dickon, today I was alive—really alive in every part of my body. I cannot describe to you what exciting adventure it was and—and I was never in any danger, I promise you. Gideon—Mr. Morris—took care of that."

Dickon felt his resistance weakening. There was no denying the glow in Mavreen's eyes, the radiance of her expression. He had not seen her so happy in many a long year; and her happiness was more important to him than anything in the world other than her safety. If this highwayman was the gentleman she described and took care of her . . . .

"I reckon it t'aint no use my saying you'd no ought to be mixed up with no highwayman nohow!"

But he was grinning, albeit halfheartedly, and Mavreen gave a sigh of relief.

"Stop with your worritin'," she said, her eyes mischievously teasing. "My highwayman be an unaccountably valiant man and just about able to tek care of me as good as you, Master Dickon!"

Only now did it occur to her to ask what had brought Dickon to the grange this day. Upon hearing his news, she insisted upon opening a bottle of champagne to toast the baby's health.

"If your son grows up to be but half the man you are, Dickon, you will be a proud father!" she said.

Gideon, when he came to the house later that night, was unexpectedly pleased that Mavreen no longer wished to conduct her association with him in utmost secrecy.

"Now I can call upon you openly," he said. "I have no liking for creeping into this house in the darkness like some common thief!"

He did not fully understand Mavreen's concern for keeping the respect of one of her servants until she explained more fully her early life with Dickon on the farm.

"There are not many women in your position who would remain loyal to the friends of her childhood in such circumstances," he remarked, his eyes resting approvingly upon her. Suddenly, he laughed.

"If your Dickon will accept it, I think we might make his child a handsome christening present. Amongst today's haul there was a singularly handsome gold watch. What say you, Mavreen? 'Tis unlikely the little lad will ever meet the true owner and will have far greater appreciation of its worth."

Mavreen remained in Sussex a further month. She accompanied Gideon on three more forays. She would have stayed longer but for the fact that she could no longer ignore the deepening of Gideon's affections for her and her own growing dependance upon him. She believed, quite rightly, that he was on the point of proposing marriage to her and this, at all costs, she wished to avoid. For her, their present relationship was perfectly satisfactory. Gideon was the ideal companion and lover. They loved frequently and with the utmost pleasure, although by unspoken consent, the word love was never spoken between them. But Gideon could no longer conceal his growing affections and she was certain that he desired their relationship to be put on a more permanent basis. It was this she feared, for she knew full well that the affection he wanted from her was only possible for her to give Gerard de Valle.

"I am returning to London," she announced one day, without preamble.

Gideon's expression changed only fleetingly, then resumed its customary nonchalance.

"Why not?" he said. "The summer is nearly over. 'Tis an excellent decision. Tell me which day you prefer to travel and I will prepare myself to accompany you!"

Mavreen opened her mouth to argue with him. But she closed it again, wordless in the face of his presumption.

She ought, she told herself, to have known that she could not dispense with Gideon Morris so easily.

CHAPTER FORTY-THREE
1809-1812

"I cannot think why you should honor that nincompoop with an invitation to your soirée!" Thomas Creevey said, nodding in the direction of Gideon Morris. "Moreover, I think your father disapproves of him even more than I!"

Mavreen smiled as she glanced across her salon at Finchcocks at the outrageously dandified figure of her highwayman. He was now attired in an extravagantly cut olive-green waistcoat much adorned with gilt buttons; lemon-yellow coat; white velvet pantaloons with side embroidery and vents gaping to reveal natural-colored stockings. His feet were encased in black beribboned shoes and there were rings on the four fingers of each hand.

She nearly laughed aloud but controlled her amusement to say with some degree of seriousness: "I find Sir Peregrine Waite most entertaining, Thomas. And so, by the look of it, does my dear friend Lisa von Eburhard. He has quite a way with the ladies, has he not?"

"Popinjay!" Thomas muttered beneath his breath. Mavreen patted his arm, remarking mischievously, "You cannot surely be jealous of such a man, dear Thomas?"

Nevertheless, she knew he, like her other constant suitor, John Ward, deeply resented Gideon's presence so often at Finchcocks. Refusing to be left behind in Sussex, he had followed her to Kingston and was now a frequent visitor under his assumed name of Peregrine Waite. Her father disapproved of him almost as much as Thomas. But Clarissa, like Lisa, confessed that he made her laugh with his outrageous compliments, his colorful clothes and exaggerated courtesies to all the ladies.

As for Tamarisk, she rose hotly to Gideon's defense, declaring to her Grandpapa that Sir Peregrine was not at all what he seemed but a brave and fearless man who could sit a horse and take a jump "even better than Dickon!"

Fortunately, no one believed the child and put her fondness for Gideon down to the fact that he always brought with him a toy or sweetmeat for her. Gradually, Tamarisk ceased to recount stories of her "escapades" with Sir Peregrine, and Gideon, so long as no one else but Mavreen or Dickon were present, ceased to play the dandy and was always his true self in the company of the child.

Tonight, however, he was playing his part as usual, causing the baroness to squeal delightedly as he passed on to her the latest tit-bits of gossip. There was no lack of it in London.

She had begged him often to cease playing the dandy.

"Could my influence upon you not be such that I have prevailed upon you to become more of a man and less of a fop?" she asked him. "There is not one of my friends who can understand why I invite you to my house or allow you to escort me to social functions!"

"That wish I will grant the day you say you will marry me!" was Gideon's reply. Instinct kept him from talking seriously about the future, although he often mentioned marriage in a light-hearted way, as if not really serious in his intent. In such manner he remarked to Tamarisk,

"I have instructed your Mama that it is high time she provided you with a new Papa. Do you not agree that I would be most eligible for the part? Think how handsome a groom I should make in wedding attire! What say you, Tammy, that your Mama and I should be wed before the year is out?"

But when Tamarisk squealed with delight at the prospect, he shook his head and said, sighing, "I doubt your Mama will approve. I think she fears I would outshine her in company—beautiful though she is. She desires all the admiration to be focused upon her rather than upon me."

"You are just teasing!" Tamarisk accused him, shrewdly. "I know you don't really mind that Mama is prettier than a princess. Why, no one looks more proud than you with her upon your arm!"

"That is because she makes such a pretty accessory!" Gideon mocked. "I declare she adorns me better than a dozen jewels!"

Such banter made the continuation of their relationship possible. Mavreen guessed that Gideon had devised this means of pursuing his intent without seeming seriously to do so. Except when they were alone together in the privacy of her bedchamber, he was serious about nothing.

Sir John complained bitterly to Clarissa that Mavreen spent "a deal too much time in the company of that popinjay!"

"I do not think you need concern yourself on the matter!" Clarissa said consolingly. " 'Tis my opinion she can enjoy with Sir Peregrine a particular relationship that is of a platonic nature. A man such as he places no emotional strains upon her, John, whereas with Mister Ward and Mister Creevey she must ever be keeping them at arm's length. Besides, my dear, she has decided once again to spend the summer months in Sussex. There she will be far distant from the attentions of Sir Peregrine Waite."

Sir John sighed. He had not felt at ease about his independent daughter since the end of her marriage to James Pettigrew. It was not right, he believed, for a woman to bury herself in the remote countryside in social isolation. How could she hope to find a new husband, so far removed from events?

He would have been a deal more concerned had he known of Gideon's frequent visits to the grange and, far worse, Mavreen's sorties upon the highway as his accomplice.

Mavreen, however, was content with the strange admixture of the life she had adopted. The days of the year 1810 slipped by, unremarked but by events beyond her immediate sphere. Before she went to Sussex for the summer, she heard the news that Napoloen had married the eighteen-year-old Hapsburg archduchess, Marie Louise. Word that they had celebrated their marriage in the palace of Compiègne brought an ache to her heart. She accepted that if such details were forthcoming from France, Gerard, were he in Compiègne, could not have failed to get word to her. Reason dictated that he must surely be dead. Yet still she could not bring herself to believe she would never see him again.

She and Gideon were in Sussex when the king became seriously ill again in August, as likewise did his favorite daughter, the poor Princess Amelia. Undoubtedly, the king's state of mind was not improved by her death in October and by November, he was once again forced to suffer the indignities of a straitjacket. He was seventy-three years of age and almost totally blind.

No one was particularly surprised when in February of the following year, the Prince of Wales was declared regent.

Thomas and John Ward were both present at the ceremony of the swearing-in of the prince at Carlton House.

"A most stately and splendorous occasion!" John described it to a breathless Tamarisk, and her mother. "It took place in the grand salon. The prince is grown enormously large, and sat at the head of an immensely long table covered with crimson velvet.

"And Princess Charlotte?" Tamarisk enquired eagerly. "Was she there, too, to see her Papa made regent?"

John Ward laughed.

"She was riding her horse up and down in the garden whilst the band played in the courtyard; and every once in a while, she peered through the windows. So she could be said to have witnessed the big event, albeit at a distance!"

By July, the poor king was raving mad. Princess Charlotte was sent to Bognor for the sea bathing and Tamarisk was invited to accompany her. Mavreen and Gideon returned once more to Sussex, passing the warm summer weather in days of idle inactivity alternating with days of dangerous escapades upon the highway. By October, Mavreen was once more back at Finchcocks. Tamarisk received an invitation, undoubtedly instigated by Charlotte, now a spirited self-willed young lady of fifteen, to the party given by her aunt, the duchess of York. It took place in the duchess's Weybridge home, Oatlands—an extraordinary house adorned with stucco ornaments, battlements, turrets and Gothic arches.

Although not yet thirteen, Tamarisk looked unusually grown up in her new gown, made especially for the occasion—a dainty white muslin dress tied with a rose-colored sash. Her roman sandals were laced with the same ribbon and her hair, dressed in the very latest fashion, was tied at the back of her head with matching ribbons and hung in pretty ringlets. Around her small white throat was the gold neckchain from which hung the locket containing Gerard's miniature.

"If only her father could see her!" Mavreen thought, with a lump in her throat; but had to be content with the shy blushes of pleasure brought to Tamarisk's cheeks by Gideon's compliments.

That Christmas, Mavreen gave a party at Finchcocks for Tamarisk's thirteenth birthday. Like the duchess of York's, it was in part for children but with an equal measure of adults present.

To please the child, instructions were given to the musicians to include the new waltz among the dances. Some element of romanticism about the dance prompted all three of the men in Mavreen's life to choose the occasion for proposing marriage to her.

As kindly as she could, Mavreen once again let Thomas and John know that she had no intention of remarrying and that, fond of them although she was, she could not entertain any serious thoughts as to a change of heart in the future.

With Gideon she was less adamant. When the party was over and the guests departed, she lay with Gideon in her bedchamber and for the first time since she had met him, she heard him plead with her.

"We have been lovers these past three and a half years!" he said. The only outward sign of his emotion was the trembling of his body against her own. "I would venture to say we know each other very well indeed. Therefore, you must be aware that I have grown to love you very deeply, Mavreen. If it would please you, I am even prepared to renounce my lawless exploits and settle to quiet respectabilities if you will but consent to become my wife."

He put his hand gently over her lips to prevent her speaking.

"Allow me first to finish my speech!" he said with a wry smile. "For though it may surprise you, my dear, I am very much in earnest. I would have done with our clandestine encounters; with the lies and deceit. They belittle us both and belittle the love I have for you. I am in constant anxiety on your behalf lest your little daughter or your admirable father and sweet Aunt Clarissa should discover what we are about. Marry me, Mavreen. I know that you believe yourself still enamored of your past lover but you cannot mourn him forever. Will you not trust your future to me?"

Mavreen lay silent. She was filled with uncertainties. She understood exactly how Gideon felt. She herself had begun to resent the secret nature of their relationship. And Gideon offered sound enough counsel when he advised her that she could not live in the shadow of Gerard's memory.

"If I were convinced Gerard was really dead—" she murmured.

Gideon was suddenly angry.

"Then permit me to go in search of him!" he said. "I cannot continue to share you with a ghost! I love you, Mavreen—all that is good and all that is bad in you. And I cannot believe that you care nothing for me, not when we are so perfectly matched in so many ways!"

Mavreen knew that he was not simply referring to their equal enjoyment of their loving. In three years, their passionate enjoyment of one another was in no way diminished; rather was it increased. But Gideon was a rarity among men, approving her independence of thought and action as a woman. He only insisted upon his right to dominate her within the bedchamber. This she would not have had otherwise since she enjoyed his physical domination over her as much as her surrender to him. Beyond the bedchamber they were companions, friends and accomplices.

"Leave me a little while longer to consider the matter!" she pleaded. "I am not saying you nay, Gideon, but I cannot in truth say that I am ready to marry you yet."

Reluctantly, he agreed not to speak of it again until after their summer together in Sussex.

"You will be going to the grange as usual, will you not?" he inquired anxiously, for she had told him that the Lades had invited her to go with Tamarisk to Bognor.

But although Mavreen could fully understand her daughter's pleasure in the company of the five Lade children, she herself found Percy's Quaker ways much at variance with her own nature, and she had very little in common with Anne, now become matronly and matriarchal.

"I would not wish to be elsewhere!" Mavreen smiled as Gideon took her in his arms. "I am much addicted to the excitement of our activities there as I am to moments such as this!"

"When you so speak, you are irresistible!" Gideon cried. And now he ceased to be the supplicant but became the master once more.

But the summer of 1812 was chilly, showing only

occasional glimpses of the warm sunshine to which they had become accustomed. When the skies were grey with sweeping clouds of rain, Mavreen and Gideon were disinclined to venture upon the highways. Instead, they remained quietly within the house, playing backgammon or cards, or reading books.

Sometimes Gideon would read aloud from the newspapers sent down from London, recounting with pleasure the duke of Wellington's victories abroad, while Mavreen embroidered her tapestry. Sometimes, Mavreen would play the harpsichord and Gideon, who had a fine baritone, would sing as she played. When the rain ceased, they rode, sometimes over the Downs or else to Lewes to The White Horse for luncheon or supper. They presented, Mavreen said one afternoon, the most domestic of scenes and it was as well the servants could be relied upon not to tittle-tattle.

Dickon, Rose and the baby were now happily installed in the roomy apartment over the stables. If either disapproved of Gideon's presence, they gave no indication of such opinion. In fact, Dickon cared for little else but that the inclement weather had put a stop to Mavreen's dangerous escapades with her lover.

With two such volatile people, however, such inactivity could not continue indefinitely. Upon the dawning of the first sunny day in August they resolved instantly upon a hold-up. When their preparations were completed, they set out upon horseback for Chailey Common.

Some twelve miles or more away as the crow flies, the Common was considered by Gideon sufficiently far from Alfriston to make unlikely any recognition of them at the scene of the hold-up.

They reached their destination by two o'clock, riding at a leisurely pace so that the horses would not be over-tired should a hard gallop be required to ensure a quick departure. The land shimmered in the heat of the blazing sun. From horizon to horizon the road lay empty, baked as a flattened crust, not a soul upon it.

"And to think that only yesterday we were complaining of the chill!" Gideon remarked as he handed Mavreen a flask of wine to quench her thirst. "Mayhap we should lie down beneath that elm yonder and rest until it is cooler!"

But before Mavreen could voice her opinion upon the matter, they heard the faint rumble of wheels heralding the appearance of a coach. Instantly, both remounted and readied themselves for the attack, pulling their kerchiefs about their faces. Mavreen, now perfectly familiar with Gideon's plan of campaign, waited until the coach was almost level with them; then spurred her horse from behind the bushes which concealed them.

As was customary, the coachman offered no resistance when he caught sight of the two highwaymen and instantly brought the carriage to a halt. The gentleman within the coach, however, was in no mood for quick surrender. He burst out of the carriage scarlet-faced, brandishing a pistol, and waved it wildly in Gideon's direction.

Mavreen gave a gasp of horror mingled with disbelief. Their victim was her own father, Sir John Danesfield.

Gideon must also have recognized him for he said not a word but sat silently upon his horse, unmoving.

Close behind Sir John came Clarissa, fussing over him as was her wont regardless of any danger to herself, as she left the comparative safety of the coach.

"Take heed, John, I pray you!" she cautioned him. "Such men are desperate! They might kill you!"

Gideon found his voice. Disguising it by lowering his tone to the deepest note he could achieve, he told them to be on their way.

"We intend no harm to your good selves!" he growled. " 'Tis others we mistook you for we mean to rob!"

Sir John looked as if he had no intention whatever of returning peaceably to his carriage. But Clarissa pulled at his arm.

"Let us be on our way!" she begged, tugging at Sir John's sleeve. When still he would not move, she sank gracefully to the dusty road in a well-contrived swoon.

Instinctively, Mavreen moved forward to her aid but Gideon, seeing their chance of escape, grabbed at Amabel's reins, giving the mare at the same time a sharp whack upon her shining rump. The mare sprang to life and nearly throwing Mavreen from the saddle, galloped off not inches behind Gideon's stallion.

Gideon did not slow for several miles. Then only did he turn to Mavreen, a look of dismay on his face.

"What misfortune!" he gasped. "What ill stroke of fate brought them to the very part of England where we. . . ."

"Gideon, they must surely be on their way to visit me!" Mavreen broke in breathlessly. "We must return home at once—let everything seem perfectly as usual when they arrive. Aunt Clarrie stared at me so strangely I cannot be sure she did not recognize me!"

Gideon wasted no time in discussion. As anxious as Mavreen to be out of their predicament, he set a fast pace for Alfriston.

By the time Sir John's coach rolled up the driveway of the grange, Mavreen, in spotless white muslin dress and carefully coiffed hair was sitting in the garden drinking tea with a dandified Gideon. He had changed into sage green trowsers and white shirt with collar so high it reached almost to his cheeks, a waistcoat hardly above a finger's length and, to Mavreen's secret amusement, had put a patch upon his cheek.

The faithful Dickon, aware of their hurried return and guessing at the reason for it, vowed that if he were questioned, he would swear that neither Mavreen nor Sir Peregrine had left the grange all day.

"We were waylaid by a pair of ruffians," Sir John roared. "Rascals! Bandits! Thieves! Robbers! Brigands! Devils incarnate!"

But Clarissa seemed unwilling to discuss their hold-up and turned the conversation, relating one of the reasons for their unexpected visit. Lady Danesfield was dead.

Successfully diverted, Sir John took up the story. His wife, he said, had been a semi-recluse for many years, seldom venturing forth from her home in Yorkshire. But on hearing of the rising of the Luddites, she had believed it was her duty to see into the matter of safeguarding her father's mills, not trusting to the efficiency of her foreman who had run them most competently since her father's death.

"Her actions were uncalled for!" Sir John commented. "The fellow warned her of the dangers. As I am sure you are aware, the Luddites have been moving farther and farther north throughout the summer and become ever more violent in their fight against the textile industries!"

"Mills have been fired, and machinery smashed," Clarissa interposed. "In fact, so serious is the position that whole companies of regular soldiers are being sent north to help quell the revolution."

"But too late to be of assistance to my wife!" Sir John said sighing. "She had the misfortune to be at one of the mills when it came under attack and not even the armed watchmen were able to assist her when it was fired. She and several others were trapped and perished. The foreman himself was so badly burned he was scarce able to give me a coherent account of what had transpired."

"Mercifully, Selina was not with her mother," Clarissa said. "She is gone now to join her sister, Prudence, at the convent."

Naught was said upon this occasion about the future, although Mavreen thought instantly that the unfortunate Lady Danesfield's death now left the way open for her father's marriage to Clarissa. She supposed that the possibility of marriage might be the topic for discussion when Clarissa called Mavreen to accompany her for a little walk so that they might enjoy a moment or two of private conversation.

But Clarissa had other more urgent matters upon her mind.

"Doubtless you are aware that I recognized you, Mavreen, despite your disguise," she said quietly, as soon as they were beyond earshot of Sir John. "Nor am I in doubt as to the identity of the second highwayman, Gideon Morris." She looked pale and anxious. "Much that I had before failed to understand is now made clear to me. Oh, my dearest child, what can have possessed you to entertain such a terrible way of life! What would your father say if he knew! I can only suppose that you have fallen under the influence of this *wicked* man!"

Despite the seriousness of the situation, Mavreen smiled.

"Dear Aunt Clarrie!" she said. "You know that no man could influence me to any action that did not meet with my approval. It was I who persuaded Gideon to take me with him."

She halted beneath the shade of the big beech tree and turned to look Clarissa full in the face.

"Try to understand!" she begged. "Gideon is not at all as you suppose. If you will listen, I will tell you the whole story, his story and mine. Then perhaps you will understand how my life has become so closely linked with his!"

Clarissa sat down on the garden seat and folded her hands. She listened attentively, her face impassive. Only when Mavreen had recounted the truth to its final episode this very day did she speak. Taking Mavreen's hands in hers, she said urgently, "You have told me that you do not believe yourself to be influenced by this man, but, dearest child, can you not see that his likeness to poor Gerard has clouded your judgement to the point of insanity. You have convinced yourself you care for this man for himself as the years have passed by, but this is a confusion in your mind. It is not Gideon Morris you desire, respect, need. It is Gerard de Valle!"

Mavreen let out her breath in a long sigh.

"Even if you are right, Aunt Clarrie, and I am not yet ready to admit that my only affection for Gideon is because of Gerard, what happiness can come to me by such admission? Gerard is lost to me. I have despaired of ever seeing him again in this life!"

Now it was Clarissa's turn to take a deep breath. She searched in her reticule and withdrew a letter which she handed to Mavreen.

"It is from the marquis de Guéridon!" she said. "He has news of Gerard—indeed, *a message from Gerard to you!*"

All color drained from Mavreen's face.

She crumpled into a heap at Clarissa's feet as for the second time in her life, she swooned.

She was unconscious but a few minutes before she revived and at once sat up. Disregarding the bottle of smelling salts Clarissa was trying to press upon her, she took up the marquis's letter. The color had returned to her cheeks which now burned with excitement.

"Oh, Aunt Clarrie, he is *alive!*" she cried, forgetting that

Clarissa had already read the letter. "The marquis explains that Gerard has been all these years caught up in the fighting in Portugal and Spain. He was never free to come to me. And now, at last, he has met with the marquis. Aunt Clarrie, do you understand? *Gerard is alive!*"

She jumped to her feet and hugged Clarissa in a paroxysm of joy.

"He loves me still!" she cried, taking up the letter once more. "But for the war, he would be in England at my side! Oh, I am so happy I could die of it! Why did you not give me the letter before? Are you not happy for me?"

But Clarissa's face was unsmiling. Warningly, she advised Mavreen to calm her hopes before she read further. She knew what must come even before Mavreen's radiant face took on a look of intense anxiety.

"He is to go with Napoleon's Grand Army to fight against Russia!" she whispered. Swiftly, she turned back to the beginning of the letter, eagerly searching for the date.

"This was penned in June!" she gasped. "So Gerard is even now upon his way!"

Gently, Clarissa clasped Mavreen's hands in hers.

"I fear that is not all!" she said. "When this letter arrived, I made some inquiries on your behalf, concerning the French campaign in Russia. I have been reliably informed that the Grand Army is already on the outskirts of Moscow and that the Russians are expected to defend the city at all costs. I am afraid, Mavreen, there will be a deal of heavy fighting. You must prepare yourself for the possibility that Gerard might not return. We will pray for his safety but I would not have you too dependent upon seeing him again, and certainly not in the near future."

As she took in the import of Clarissa's warning, Mavreen's mind began feverishly to search for facts. Dragging the plump Clarissa behind her, she hurried back to the house and into the library where Mr. Glover's globe still sat upon its table by the window. Eagerly, she turned it until her finger lay upon Moscow. Her cheeks paled.

"Is it not unwise to penetrate so far into Russia when winter is not far off?" she asked, as much of herself as of Clarissa.

She searched her memory for snatches of information and recalled her tutor's descriptions of the rigors of winter in Siberia.

"Napoleon *cannot* intend to engage in a winter campaign!" she said. "He will surely order his army's return!"

But even as she spoke, she felt the deepest of misgivings. The emperor, so many said, believed himself invincible. If Russia was his intended prize, he would stop at nothing to acquire it. Gerard was in all probability in mortal danger. She could not hope to see him soon—not unless she were to go to him.

"What terrible things are crossing your mind!" Clarissa cried, sensing from Mavreen's expression that some madness was afoot. "You must remain calm, my dear, and. . . ."

"Calm?" Mavreen interrupted, the bright spots of color high on her cheekbones. "Now that I know Gerard is alive, somewhere on this same earth? I cannot rest until I see him again. I love him, Aunt Clarrie. I have always loved him. Wherever he is, whatever he is doing, I have to be with him."

"Oh, my dear!" Clarissa said anxiously, convinced now that Mavreen had lost all reason. "Gerard must be several thousand miles away. He is fighting with England's enemy. You cannot hope to. . . ."

But Mavreen was not listening. She was pulling hard upon the bellrope. When Rose appeared, she sent her at once to find Dickon.

"Mavreen, of what are you thinking?" Clarissa begged. "I pray you, calm yourself! Do not be hasty!"

But Mavreen did not hear her words. No sooner had Dickon's carroty head appeared through the doorway than she ran to him and caught his arm.

"Dickon!" she said, her breath coming in short deep gasps. "Dickon, I have just heard that Monsieur le vicomte lives. I know that you of all people will understand that I have to go to him. It is a long, long road to travel. There will be many dangers."

Behind her, Clarissa cried out in protest. But Dickon was grinning.

"You beant going nowhere without me, surelye," he said. "I goes where you go. You know you have but to tell me."

"Very well," Mavreen said quietly. "Take me to Russia! For that, Dickon, is where I intend to go."

CHAPTER FORTY-FOUR
1812

Mavreen and Dickon were but three miles short of the river Niemen, the border between Prussia and Russia, when disaster all but overcame them. Fortunately, Mavreen was prepared for an attack, although they could not be certain when it might occur.

At the inn where they had spent the previous night, the landlord had warned them of the dangers of continuing their journey across the border.

"There's almost as many deserters as wounded wandering back from the battle front!" he informed the beautiful woman he believed to be a French lady from the town of Compiègne. "We've had a fair number of them in here this last week begging for food. When the Emperor Napoleon took his army through here last June he left the countryside behind him with little more than enough to survive on, so great was his requirement of supplies for that vast number of soldiers. Four hundred thousand, they say! And that many men need a deal of feeding not to mention their horses."

Mavreen had long since ascertained that, toward the end of June, Napoleon had established his headquarters at the old Lithuanian capital of Vilna, now part of the Russian empire, and its third largest city. She had also been told at a previous inn that the Russian armies had surprisingly refrained from engaging with the French invaders and retreated across the eastern plains as far as Smolensk. There were stories of the bombardment of the town by the French gunners and the terrible fire that raged when the wooden houses of the inner town were set alight, the wind fanning the flames so that they formed one vast blaze, whirling as it rose with a dismal roaring. Only now did she learn that the Russians had resisted for a day and a half, suffering great losses, and inflicting terrible casualties upon the invaders.

"If the French troops were victorious at Smolensk, why should so many be deserting?" she asked the innkeeper.

He shrugged.

"The men have come a long way from home. 'Twas a mighty long march for them before ever they reached Russia," he said. "And besides, only a third of the soldiers are Frenchmen. 'Tis not their war—our war. They've no heart for a campaign against the Russians! Most were battling *against* Bonaparte not so long ago!"

"Think you the Grand Army will be returning soon?" Mavreen asked, for the man seemed reasonably intelligent in his assessment of the situation.

"Who can say, milady. But one thing is for sure. The road to Moscow is no place for *you* to travel. There's starving, desperate bands of men as would not think twice to holding up your carriage and robbing you, maybe attacking your person. 'Twould be folly for you to go forward!"

But Mavreen would not be halted and to Dickon she recounted one of Gideon's stories which, at the time he told it, had caused her to laugh in delighted amusement but which now provided her with an idea that was to safeguard them both.

"And what be this famous plan that's a-going to save our necks?" Dickon asked, grinning as he sat perched on the coachman's seat, his new multiple caped box overcoat too warm for the wearing this September day but carefully folded beside him.

"Stop the horses and I'll show you!" Mavreen called out of the window, her eyes sparkling.

She climbed down from the carriage and careless of the dust that might dirty her stone-colored, beaver-trimmed habit, she sat upon the step, flinging her hat and muff onto the seat behind her but keeping her reticule on her lap.

From inside this, she withdrew her rouge pot and a prettily ornamented hand mirror.

"What be you doing?" Dickon asked, standing at the horses' heads, his face puzzled as he regarded her.

"Giving myself the Black Death!" Mavreen replied, "or at least, a pestilence just as horrible!"

As she daubed ugly red spots over her face, forehead, hands and wrists, she recounted Gideon's tale of the highwayman who had been cleverly outwitted by a lady travelling from London to Leicester in the previous century.

"She painted her face with spots and let it be thought she was suffering from the plague!" Mavreen said. "It was only later, when the highwayman happened to see her fit as a fiddle in Leicester a week later, that he realized he had been outwitted. So if we should be halted, Dickon, make no attempt to defend us and leave the matter to me!"

Dickon's uncertainty as to the wisdom for this charade dissolved as Mavreen completed her transformation. She did, indeed, look most horrible, the scarlet blobs upon her white skin looking most realistically alike to some terrible pox. He grinned as he climbed back onto his seat.

"Us will surelye not be well received in Vilna happen that red don't wash off afore we get there!" he said.

But there was no smile upon his face when, as they had been warned, a ragged band of brigandly men in the tattered remnants of their uniforms, straddled the dusty road, their muskets leveled as Dickon pulled the horses to a shuddering halt. He dared not look back as the men surged forward to drag open the door of the carriage.

From the interior came a series of low, gasping moans. Slowly, Dickon turned his head and was hard put to keep his face straight when he saw the varying expressions on the faces of the five men staring into the carriage. They began to jabber to one another in a tongue he could not understand. One took a pace backward, then another, until it was obvious that they were quite unnerved by the spectacle Mavreen presented.

One of them, dark skinned and ugly, motioned Dickon to get down from his seat. He did so obediently. But when a musket was jabbed in his side and he was prodded toward the door of the carriage he shook his head with a remarkably well-simulated expression of fear. He pointed to the inert figure of the sick woman lying in an attitude of collapse across the seat.

By signs, the men indicated that they wanted him to reach inside the carriage and bring out money, jewelery, a watch. But Dickon fell to his knees, staring up at the men in appeal as he jabbed his finger at his face where at any moment the ugly red spots might appear, all the while shaking his head.

By now, it occurred to the robbers that Dickon, too, might pass on to them the infection his passenger suffered. They backed away from him. Much as he longed to jump back onto the driver's seat and make a determined bolt for safety, Dickon remained where he was and the men discussed the situation at a safe distance. The dark-skinned soldier seemed unwilling to give up his prey, but the remainder were in favor of abandoning the hold-up. They had seen such infections rage like a fire through the ranks, leaving men dead in their wake. They had not deserted their regiments to save their lives only to lose them by slower, more tortuous ways than that of a musket shot.

" 'Twas risky, all the same!" Dickon said when they were at last free to go safely upon their way and Mavreen was congratulating him on his play-acting. "I'd not wish to see it happen a second time!"

They reached Vilna without further mishap despite the passing of many more deserters and wounded. In her guise of Madame de Valle, Mavreen took rooms in one of the largest coaching houses and set about the business of acquiring information as to the latest movements of the Grand Army.

Fortune favored her. Dining alone at a nearby table was a young French captain who responded eagerly to Mavreen's friendly overtures. Within a short while, they were drinking wine together and the captain was captivated as much by Mavreen's undoubted beauty as by her lavish compliments. Smiling prettily at him across the table, she told him how brave he was, how daring, how courageous, how strong and admirable! In such manner, she extracted a wealth of information from him.

Captain Louis de Rousseau had fought under the command of Marshal Murat at Smolensk and again at Borodino. On August fifteenth, he had watched the French bombardment of Smolensk.

"It was an awesome sight for those of us waiting to go forward," he told the attentive Mavreen. "But it must have been far more so for the Russians and the hapless inhabitants of the city. The French entered the city on the seventeenth of August but found little comfort there amongst the ruins. We had thought perhaps the war would be over now that we had the enemy beaten and Smolensk was ours, but our emperor, when he arrived on the eighteenth, decided we should press forward in pursuit of the enemy."

He described how they had caught up with the Russians at Borodino.

"The emperor was unwell, ill from acute dysuria. Perhaps this accounted for the fact that we seemed unable to defeat the Russians as decisively as we should have done. My own commander, Marshal Murat, called many times for reinforcements but they were not forthcoming and our casualties were most appalling. Our horsemen had already suffered very terribly from the Russian cannon at Shevardino on the outskirts of Borodino." He pulled himself up short as he realised that he was in female company. "It would be improper for me to describe the horrors of this battle to a lady such as yourself," he said smiling at her. "Suffice it to say that by the eighth of September, the Russians were once more in retreat!"

Mavreen did not hope for the near impossible chance that Rousseau had met with Gerard, or even knew him. Nevertheless, she asked if he had met with him. He shook his head. Upon hearing that Mavreen was going in search of her husband, his face took on an expression of horrified dismay.

"You must not entertain such an idea, my dear madame!" he said, looking deeply shocked. "Conditions upon the road are very bad and it would be a most dangerous enterprise for a lady to consider such a journey. Moreover, I have not yet informed you that our army has now captured Moscow. The city is ablaze and burns so fiercely, the emperor has had to leave the Kremlin and take refuge in Petrovsky palace outside the town. He is even now negotiating with the czar for peace. Hopefully, there is no need for you to go further for your husband may soon be returning with the victorious army."

"Perhaps I could travel to Moscow with you?" Mavreen suggested. But the captain regretfully shook his head.

"I am on my way from there to Paris," he said. "I carry important documents concerning the proposed treaty with Russia. Believe me, madame, you must abandon all thought of going to Moscow. You would find it quite impossible to go through Russia freely, even were I accompanying you and even were there no physical dangers. You have no papers!"

"Papers?" Mavreen repeated with an assumed stupidity. "What do you mean, mon capitaine? Why should I require papers?"

Patiently, he withdrew from a leather pouch some documents which guaranteed him and his servant safe passage to France and back to Moscow. They stated that he was Emperor Napoleon's emissary and that all possible assistance should be afforded him to expedite his journey.

"These alone could guarantee you safe passage through Smolensk, Borodino and into Moscow," he said. She shrugged her shoulders, saying that perhaps the captain was right and she should give up any idea of following her husband to Moscow.

"After all," she said, placing her hand nonchalantly over his, "there is no real necessity for me to risk my life. I had merely thought such a journey might prove entertaining for I have been told that the Russian aristocracy lead gay and amusing lives and have close personal links with our own people."

She hid her smile at the shocked expression on his face.

"Perhaps that is true in peacetime, but the Russians are at bay!" he said. "I dare not think what harm might befall you, madame, were so beautiful a lady as yourself to become the prisoner of the peasantry. In Russia there is much resentment of the rich by the poor."

"Then I shall take your advice and go home!" Mavreen replied. She affected a yawn and presently excused her-

self, going at once in search of Dickon who was curled up
on a bundle of straw in the stables.

"Dickon, I have work for you!" she cried, dragging
him to his feet. Quickly, she outlined to him the importance of carrying documents if they were to proceed
through Russia. She saw his face crease into a grin when
she told him that the French captain carried such papers.

"No need to tell me what to do!" he said simply. "If 'tis
papers we need, I'll get them, surelye."

"Do not kill him!" Mavreen commanded, "for he is a
harmless enough fellow and wished me well. But I want
his clothes as well as his papers, Dickon. It is my intention
to travel henceforth as a captain of the French army. And
you will be my servant. In which case you will need to rob
his man of his uniform, too. Think you such thefts can be
made without danger to your life, Dickon?"

"I'll do what's needed!" Dickon said. "It should not be
too difficult if your captain has consumed the quantity of
wine you say he swallowed this past two hours. Doubtless
his servant has also been refreshing himself likewise."

Robbing the captain and his manservant in the night as
they slept proved a simple matter. Disposing of the securely bound and gagged unfortunates was another matter. Dickon wished to bundle them into the carriage and
tumble them unceremoniously into the roadway somewhere out in the wilderness. But Mavreen was afraid for
their lives.

"We dursn't leave them here in Vilna," Dickon argued
reasonably. "T'would be only a matter of hours before
they took to their horses and came after us!"

So it was agreed to take them in the carriage, a three
days' march from Vilna. At this point they untied their
captives, unharnessed the horses and returned to the
shocked Capitaine de Rousseau his sword so that he could
defend himself if the need arose, on the walk back to
Vilna.

His face sullen and angry with humiliation, the French
officer stared at Mavreen. His uniform though large in
size for her, was nevertheless very becoming.

"You'll not get far in that disguise!" he muttered as
Dickon began to loosen the bonds securing him as Mav-

reen stood with her pistol leveled at him lest he make a sudden move. "You have the face and voice of a female no matter what clothing you wear or papers you carry to prove that you are an officer of the French army."

"I am well aware of it!" Mavreen said calmly, suddenly wishing that Gideon Morris were with her to enjoy this moment. She had already determined to disguise her white skin with a bandage over the lower part of her face. A wound in the jaw would enable her to avoid the necessity for speech and permit her to communicate, when required, by the written word. "*Adieu, mon capitaine,* and once again, my apologies and regrets!"

By now Dickon had released the captain's servant. Leaving the two men standing by the roadside, they mounted their horses and galloped away. When at last they deemed it safe to slow to a walk, Dickon looked at Mavreen and grinned.

"That uniform surelye does disguise you well!" he said. " 'Twas lucky the poor captain was no mountain of a man, though I'll warrant you'd not walk far in those boots. They're a deal too large for you!"

Mavreen laughed.

"We have been lucky!" she said. "I little imagined when I struck up conversation with the poor Capitaine de Rousseau last night, that today I would be masquerading in his name."

"And we have papers to prove it!" Dickon chuckled.

"And now to Moscow!" Mavreen cried, her cheeks aglow, her eyes brilliant with excitement.

But their good spirits were soon to become sorely tested. As day followed upon day, the weather constantly worsened. The rain soaked them to the skin despite their cloaks and the road fast became indistinguishable from the fields, so deep in mud was it. And more distressing than their own discomfort was the sight of the refugees they passed, women and children amongst them, homeless and starving.

In the ruins of Smolensk conditions were little better. There they learned that the czar had rejected Napoleon's demand for a peace treaty. The great fire of Moscow had burned for four days and destroyed three quarters of the city and the Russians believed the French had deliberately ravaged Holy Moscow. Their patriotic fervor was now fully aroused and peace was out of the question. The principal Russian army had moved southwest of Moscow toward Kaluga and was threatening Napoleon's communications with Smolensk and Vilna. Forty thousand reinforcements were on their way from the Turkish front, and the French had no such reinforcements and their army was becoming severely depleted, not only by the casualties and deserters, but by the need to garrison the strategic points they had captured along the five-hundred mile route from Germany. Winter was fast approaching and the loss of a further 2,500 men following a Russian cavalry raid at Winkovo near Tautino, decided Napoleon to leave Moscow and fall back on Smolensk.

But rather than lead his men through ravaged fields and villages along the old line of advance, he took a more southerly route intending to destroy the Russian arms factories and enemy concentration before wintering in Smolensk and Minsk. He left Moscow on October 19th.

Mavreen received this news with mixed feelings. It now looked possible that the army would be returning before long. But at the same time she had no way of knowing whether Gerard had survived the fighting or was among the ever-increasing number of casualties.

"We must find accommodation and consider the matter," she said to Dickon. She could see that he was as exhausted as herself and the horses, too, needed rest.

The city still had buildings left standing despite the terrible fire and French bombardment of the August battle. After some searching Mavreen and Dickon found an inn in which to rest. But there were no fresh horses and their own needed rest as much as they did. Moreover, Mavreen required time to bathe the dirt of travel from her; wash her hair and give her uniform to Dickon to brush the mud that caked it.

Wherever possible, they avoided contact or conversation with others. The Russian landlord, though far from friendly, was content to take Mavreen's gold coins and did not question her. In answer to her written question, he told her that the French were retreating towards Smolensk.

"If 'tis true, mayhap we should go no further but await the army here!" Mavreen said to Dickon in the privacy of her room. They had now been travelling for three months. It was mid-October and the weather was worsening daily although, as yet, there had been no snow. She was tired and dispirited. Although it now looked very possible that Bonaparte and his army were little more than three hundred kilometers distant, there was still no certainty that Gerard had survived the fighting at Smolensk, Borodino or Moscow and might even now be lying dead upon the battlefield at Winkovo.

Dickon sought to reassure her.

"Do you disremember how oft you've told me you'd know inside yourself if the vicomte weren't living? If you really think he be dead, howsomever we beant going home to England right now?"

Mavreen nodded.

"You're right, Dickon. I won't give up until I find him! If only we could meet with someone who knows him—or has seen him!"

"I reckon as how we should wait awhile here!" Dickon said. " 'Tis safe enough in this inn. If we venture back on the road, mayhap we'll meet with the Russian soldiers and those papers of the captain's won't do us no good nohow! Even with the Frenchies there's the danger one of 'em we meet might know Capitaine de Rousseau."

"A day or two longer, then!" Mavreen agreed. "Mayhap by then we shall discover whether the French army is really on its way back to Smolensk."

She tried not to think too much about the possibility that Gerard had been killed, but from her window, it was impossible not to see the miserable aftermath of battle as the wounded, most bandaged, many on crutches, passed by in misery. And despite the folly of such behavior, she searched the face of every wounded man praying that by some miracle it might be Gerard.

Gerard, no less dejected and exhausted, had left Moscow with Napoleon and was on his way southward to

Tula. But the plans he had helped to prepare to destroy the city were drawn up in vain. Following upon a fierce engagement between the French and Russian vanguards, the two main armies met once more in a battle for the town of Maloyaroslavets, which changed hands seven times, finally being taken by Eugene Beauharnais' corps. On the following day, October 25th, Napoleon was nearly captured by a patrol of Russian Tartar cavalry. The emperor then made his decision to head directly westward where the terrain did not so easily favor the sudden appearance of raiding horsemen. By the 26th of October, they were on their way back to Smolensk.

"Our uniforms were not designed for such cold!" Gerard remarked to Nikolai bitterly.

They were constantly harried by Cossack horsemen and partisan bands of guerillas seeking vengeance on the invaders. The rearguard, under Marshal Davout, was three days' march behind them and under heavy attack outside Vyazma.

Gerard, huddled in his greatcoat, rode close behind Napoleon's carriage. On November 4th, still some fifty miles east of Smolensk, the snow began to fall. Two nights later, the full rigor of the winter began. The blizzard was so bad that Napoleon himself was forced to leave his carriage and plod through the snow as his riders and escort sought to lead their horses around the deep drifts at the ill-defined sides of the road.

The snow fell in such vast flakes that Gerard could no longer see the sky, nor yet even the men in front of him. Nikolai reined in his horse alongside.

"If we don't find shelter soon, the army will freeze to death!" he said.

Gerard shivered, slapping his arms across his body in an effort to keep his circulation going. Nikolai grinned.

" 'Tis Russian vengeance!" he said through chattering teeth. "I've never known such cold so early in the winter!"

Mercifully, they found some shelter in a forest where men and horses rested for eighteen hours. By the 9th of November, they reached the comparative haven of Smolensk.

But such a vast number of men could not possibly be

accommodated in the few remaining buildings in the city. These were commandeered to house the sick. Despite the weather, the army had to remain under canvas. As the straggling columns in the rear arrived in ever-worsening conditions, it became clear that they could not remain in Smolensk for long. The Russians, though not harassing them, were following close upon their heels and food was in desperately short supply except for those who exchanged some of the loot they had brought with them from Moscow for food and liquor.

"At least there is no shortage of brandy in Smolensk!" Nikolai said cheerfully as he placed some bottles on the table in Gerard's tent.

Feeling as if the cold was visibly eating into his bones, Gerard gratefully swallowed some of the spirit before setting out upon his most immediate task—to ascertain from the musters the number of men still under Napoleon's command.

His expression, when finally he returned to his tent, told Nikolai that the news was far from good. Of the initial army of 400,000 men who had crossed the border into Russia, there were but 50,000 in retreat.

There was no further pretence that this was but a temporary tactical withdrawal.

"We are in danger of being encircled!" Gerard said to Nikolai as he studied the tattered remains of the map he carried everywhere with him. "And before we can get out of Russia, we must cross the river Berezina. If the Russians get there before us. . . ."

"The men are in bad heart!" Nikolai said. "Especially those in the rearguard who suffered a deal worse than us. And I don't say as how I blame them. The sight of all those corpses exposed by the ruins and floods at Borodino fair turned my stomach, and there's not much as can still affect an old campaigner like me!"

"Many of the soldiers had to abandon their loot and their personal possessions too, to keep up with the main body of men," Gerard said sighing. "And that was all they had to show for the long bitter days of marching and fighting."

"God help the prisoners; they'll get small mercy!"

Nikolai said. "And I pity the camp followers, too. They are all over the town seeking shelter. Which mention of my own visit to the city brings to mind something strange I have to tell you, Monsieur le vicomte."

"Then sit yourself down, Nikolai," Gerard ordered wearily. "You'll be long enough on your feet when we march tomorrow!"

He poured out a tumbler of brandy for his servant and leaned back against the bitterly cold canvas walls of the tent, huddling deeper into his greatcoat in an attempt to find some warmth.

" 'Twas the strangest thing happened today when I was in Smolensk. I was trying to scavenge something to eat and I stopped at this hostelry to see if the landlord had a smoked ham or suchlike I could purchase. Then up comes this young Frenchman, heavily bandaged about the face and he hands a note to the innkeeper. The captain had been badly wounded in the mouth, you see, and couldn't talk, poor devil. I'd not have given him a second thought but when he held out his hand with his note, a gentleman's hand for it was small and well cared for, I noticed a ring upon one of his fingers."

"And what of that, Nikolai!" Gerard asked, for he had now become accustomed to the Russian's love for spinning out a story. But this late hour of the night, he was half asleep and not inclined for concentration.

" 'Twas not the ring's value I noted!" Nikolai replied, "but the ring itself. I'll swear on my life that the crest upon it is the selfsame as your own, and I've seen that seal of yours times enough to know it when I see it! I'd have asked the man about it except he could not speak to reply to me, so I did not bother. Could he have been a relation of yours, for I'll wager my life it was the de Valle crest!"

Gerard sighed.

"You must have been mistaken. I have no relations and no signet ring. 'Tis true I owned one many years ago but I gave that to the Englishwoman I loved so dearly!"

He sighed again.

"Heaven knows what is become of her, Nikolai. I sometimes wonder if she has quite forgot me by now. 'Tis seven years since I saw her last in Vienna. 'Twas the greatest pity that you never met her for had you once seen her, you would understand why she is never far from my mind!"

Knowing full well that thoughts of his love invariably brought on one of Gerard's fits of deepest depression, Nikolai quickly changed the subject.

"The emperor has issued new orders," he said. "The army is to be split into four sections, each one to set out from Smolensk a day after the other."

Gerard was to go with Napoleon and the Imperial Guard in the second section; Marshal Ney was to bring up the rear; the advance guard to leave on the morrow.

"So we'll not be departing until the day after tomorrow!" Gerard said. "And none too soon in my opinion." Privately he had begun to wonder if the emperor had left his departure from Moscow too late.

Despite the icy roads and series of low hills heavy with snow, Napoleon covered sixteen miles on the first day's march. But without knowing it, the road he had chosen ran parallel with that chosen by the Russian commander, Kutuzov. On November 15th, they were only two miles apart. But although on the succeeding day Cossacks and cavalry attacked and raked the French columns, Kutuzov did not order a general attack. The Russian general Miloradovich was successful in blocking the French line of retreat before Marshal Ney and the rearguard arrived, so forcing the French to make a detour northward to the frozen river Dnieper. The army crossed the ice on all fours, the rank and file now in desperate state. They suffered at one and the same time from frostbite and dysentery and had hallucinations of food and drink and of warm fires. Soldiers were killing one another for the sake of a piece of horseflesh. The plight of the women and children seeking protection with the rearguard from the Cossacks and partisans was pitiful.

With them rode Dickon and Mavreen.

CHAPTER FORTY-FIVE

1812

Gerard was in the small town of Orsha with Napoleon. He was sick with worry. Nikolai had spoken a second time of the wounded Frenchman in Smolensk but on this occasion, he had further remarked upon the unusual carrot-colored hair of the captain's servant. Immediately, the memory of Dickon sprang to Gerard's mind, followed by the suspicion that the French captain might be his own beloved Mavreen in disguise.

In his heart of hearts, Gerard did not really believe that Dickon—far less Mavreen—could be in Russia. There was no conceivable reason why they, of English birth, should be in enemy territory in the midst of war. The very notion was absurd, yet he could not rid himself of the suspicion. It would not be the first time she had dressed as a man and faced untold dangers in wartime. Moreover, it would explain why Nikolai was so convinced the ring the Frenchman was wearing bore his crest.

If indeed it was Mavreen and Dickon, then they were in terrible danger. Yet he could not go back to search for them. There was no returning to Smolensk; and if Mavreen had departed the city with one or another of the French army sections, he had no way of knowing which one.

Terrible stories were filtering through as to the fate of Marshal Ney's rearguard. The emperor had received word that the Russian Admiral Pavel Chichagov had taken Minsk and was now on his way to the Berezina river. General Kutuzov was at their heels and Wittgenstein, who had re-taken Vitebsk, had cut off Napoleon's route to Vilna and the supplies from Prussia and Warsaw. He was now north of them also converging upon the river.

Napoleon ordered the reserves, under Marshal Oudinot,

to engage the Russians at Borisov but although the French took the town, the single bridge over the Berezina was fired and destroyed in the fighting. Gerard was ordered to go with a reconnaissance party to discover if pontoon bridges could be erected seven miles to the north at Studenka.

Between the 18th and the 23rd of November, the snow held off but when the main column of troops was still thirty miles from the river, the blizzard struck with such force that it took a terrible toll of the weak and hungry.

"But it has helped to thicken the ice!" Nikolai said comfortingly, as Gerard swayed on his feet from exhaustion. "If it thawed, there'd be no hope for anyone falling into those icy waters!"

By the 25th of November, the sappers had built two bridges at Studenka. Under fire from the Russian advance guard, Napoleon and most of his troops reached the right bank of the river. But although the bridges were packed tight day and night, as men, women, and children fought one another to cross over, by the 29th of November there were still 15,000 people remaining on the eastern bank of the river.

On the night of the 28th, Gerard absented himself from his section. With Nikolai at his side, he stood on the east bank of the river, searching with a stubborn kind of insanity for Mavreen's face among the desperate hordes fighting to cross to safety before the French rearguard destroyed the bridges.

"I know she is here. I feel it!" Gerard cried as Nikolai tried again and again to urge him to cross before it was too late. "I cannot leave her, Nikolai. Imagine to yourself the fate of those who are left behind!"

"It is madness to risk your life when you do not even know if she is amongst the refugees!" Nikolai protested.

But it was useless to reason with his master, he thought. Hunger, cold, exhaustion, had all taken their toll of Gerard and he was behaving irrationally, if not with downright insanity. It was not even as if the vicomte had one concrete reason to believe his English lady was really somewhere among the 15,000 still remaining, huddled around camp fires, seemingly resigned to their fate at the hands of the approaching Cossacks, and even were she there, there was no more hope of espying her than of finding a needle in a haystack.

He tried once more to talk reason into Gerard's head, now seriously concerned for his safety. When still he refused to move, Nikolai dealt him a swift blow upon the chin, felling him instantly. He picked up the pitifully undernourished body of his master, slung him unceremoniously over his shoulder and forced his way onto the bridge.

By the time Gerard fully recovered his senses, they were on their way to the comparative safety of Vilna. Gerard was now ill. The temperature continued to fall and at times there were twenty-five degrees of frost. Nikolai stole a pathetically emaciated cavalry horse and rode with Gerard to Vilna. The army, or those still fit enough to move, were already leaving for Niemen and the haven of the Prussian frontier. On December 5th, Napoleon left by carriage and sledge for Paris, 1,100 miles away. But Gerard, like several thousand others, was too ill to go further.

It was the beginning of December. Nikolai knew that it could not be long before the Russians reached the city. There was no hope that Gerard could be taken to safety; even a strong possibility that he would die before many days were past if he could not get proper medical care, warmth and food. But Nikolai would not leave him.

Thirteen days later, Kutuzov's army arrived.

There was little visible of Mavreen as she slipped and stumbled along the road. With one hand covered by her beaver muff, she clung to Dickon's leather-thonged belt as she followed blindly behind him. His broad back offered some protection from the snow falling like a curtain before them.

But for Dickon, Mavreen knew she would long since be dead. It was he who had insisted that they leave Smolensk the same day as he heard the French Army was on the march. In the four days that Napoleon had been in the city, Mavreen had not ceased in her search for Gerard. Dressed once more in woman's attire, she went out into the streets, pestering every French officer she encountered with her demands to be told where she must go for infor-

mation. Her dogged perseverance brought her finally to
army headquarters, where she was treated with civility
and promised that as soon as Gerard was located, she
would be informed. But for the time being, troops were
arriving in ever-increasing numbers and the administrative
problems of coping with the situation made it impossible
for the army authorities to advise her where exactly Gerard might be found.

For the whole of the ensuing day, Mavreen sat in a
fever of excited impatience as she awaited the promised
news. She now knew that Gerard was alive—or had been
so when he was in Moscow serving as one of Napoleon's
staff officers. Her face radiant, she hugged Dickon ecstati-
cally as she said over and over again, "I know the vicomte
is here, safe, in Smolensk. *I know it.* At any moment, I
may see him. Oh, Dickon, I am so happy I cannot believe it is all true and that our journey has not been in
vain. I care not one jot that the army is in retreat. Gerard
is alive and I shall see him soon . . . very soon!"

But no word came. In an agony of impatience, Mavreen
rode once more to headquarters. The confusion there was
appalling. The rearguard were only now beginning to arrive and the officers and men were in a terrible condition.
Many were wounded in the attacks inflicted upon them by
the Russians, who in bands of partisans or groups of Cossacks chased after the invaders as they retreated from
Moscow. She learned from one of Napoleon's aides that
the emperor planned to leave Smolensk within the next
few days. He had realized that the Russian army was encircling him and that all hopes of wintering in the city were
gone. The only chance of survival for his army lay in a
return to Vilna. To achieve this end, they must cross the
Berezina river before the Russians reached it.

"But surely you can tell me where I can find the
vicomte!" Mavreen begged. "Is he in Smolensk itself? Have
you no information for me?"

The not unsympathetic officer with whom she pleaded
so forcefully shook his head regretfully.

"I am sorry, madame, I know only that he is safely
arrived at Smolensk and was seen only yesterday by another of the emperor's staff officers. Meanwhile, may I

suggest that you yourself make plans to leave Smolensk? Food is becoming unobtainable and conditions are worsening every hour as ever more refugees arrive. You would do well to ride at once for Vilna before your horses are killed and eaten. I do not wish to frighten you but this is no place for a lady such as yourself!"

"And the officer is right, surelye!" Dickon said forcibly. "If the vicomte has reached Smolensk safely, then he, too, will be shortly on his way to Vilna. 'Twould be best for all concerned if we look for him there!"

But Mavreen would not leave the city until she realized that the army was already actually on the march. By this time, Dickon had made careful preparation for the journey, the possible dangers of which he now fully appreciated. Cold and hunger were their first enemies and he made provision for both. He persuaded Mavreen back into her soldier's uniform beneath which she wore her dress and pelisse for added warmth. All spare clothing they could find, he bound around their feet, legs, arms, until they were swathed like polar bears. He cleaned and primed the pistols; sharpened a sheath knife to a fine edge and tucked it into a leather thong around his thigh. He made two of the saddle bags into satchels which could be slung over their shoulders and filled them with food and a brandy flask. He did not believe that they would reach Vilna on horseback. When men were hungry, the horses were the first to be taken for food.

Although Mavreen shrugged indifferently at these elaborate preparations beforehand, she now realized how much she owed to Dickon's foresight. It was the 25th of November and they were still twenty miles from the river Berezina. Along with thousands of others, they had crossed the Dnieper some five days previously, slipping and sliding across the ice on all fours in the wake of Marshal Ney, who was commanding the rearguard of the French army. They had a narrowly missed encounter with the Russian cavalry, who was seeking to cut off their route to the Berezina.

The hunger of the masses pouring northward towards Borisov was such that Mavreen and Dickon would have been dragged from their horses and killed without deliberation, if they had not voluntarily dismounted and allowed the miserable beasts to be consumed. Those who were unable to find such means of sustenance died quickly of starvation and cold.

The blizzard which raged with terrible severity throughout the night of the 23rd of November killed thousands more. But for Dickon's innate country instinct for survival, they, too, would surely have frozen to death. As it was, he built a rough wall of snow between them and the prevailing wind and as the snow piled up behind it, and over their huddled bodies, they retained some measure of warmth within their freezing limbs.

" 'Tis not so much worser nor that night we spent in the sea twixt France and England!" he said, forcing Mavreen to take another tot of the carefully hoarded brandy. "If us could survive that night, we'll live through this, surelye!"

But not even Dickon could produce a note of optimism when finally they staggered to the pontoon bridges at Studenka on November 28th. Hundreds were camped upon the eastern bank of the river. Some, knowing the rearguard intended to destroy the bridges next day, had already given up all hope of crossing and sat pitifully huddled beside the dying embers of their campfires, awaiting their certain deaths at the point of the Cossack lances.

Many were already dead, drowned in the river as they fought to get onto the crowded bridges. Others were trampled to death beneath the hooves of the horses pulling the gun carriages. This was no orderly crossing, but a last desperate battle for survival. The shouts, cries, screams, of those still attempting to force a passage to safety echoed in their ears.

"Come!" Dickon said quietly to Mavreen. "We're going to try to get across, even if we do die in the attempt. Hold fast to me and don't let go nohow!"

But they were still some distance from the bridge, the mass of refugees forming a solid block between them and the shaky structure of the pontoon.

Night fell before they even reached the river's edge. Mavreen was by now so bruised that every part of her body ached that was not too numbed by the cold for feeling of any kind. She would have been trampled to death had not Dickon used his knife, plunging it without mercy into the throat of a massive, panic-stricken Croat who would otherwise have struck them both down with the barrel of his musket as he sought to clear a path for himself. Twice she lost her footing as those pressing behind her pushed her against those in front. She would most certainly have been parted from Dickon had he not tied their two bodies together with one of the leather reins he had thoughtfully retained when the animals were slaughtered and ravenously consumed.

Somehow, they made the crossing to the west bank. By now Mavreen was so weak with exhaustion she was but barely conscious as Dickon dragged her to safety. He would not permit her to stop and rest for more than a few minutes, fearing that the intense cold might kill them even more certainly than an enemy bayonet. It took them a further eleven days to stumble and stagger along the corpse-strewn road to Vilna. In a numb stupor they plodded forward, resting now and again, eating the last remains of the food in the saddlebags. Mavreen was asleep on her feet when finally they reached the haven of Vilna.

It was now the 10th of December. Those survivors of the French army who were fit enough to march had already left the city and were upon their way to the Niemen and the Prussian frontier. But for every man who left Vilna, there were nine who remained, too sick, too exhausted or too badly wounded to continue. Dickon and Mavreen, barely able to stand, were among those who could go no further. He therefore used the one argument which he knew would convince Mavreen they must abandon all thought of following the army to the Niemen.

"Since there's so many more soldiers left here in Vilna than has gone on to the border," he said quietly, "our chances of finding the vicomte must be the greater if we remain here. 'Tis a gamble of ten to one in our favor!" he said, with a parody of his old grin although the skin was now stretched so taut over his face that it looked more of a grimace to Mavreen. Seeing him, unaware that she herself looked every bit as skeletal, Mavreen burst into tears.

"Oh, Dickon!" she wept. "To think I brought all this upon you! And we still have not found Gerard!"

"But we will!" he comforted her, wishing as he spoke that he could feel more sure. "But before we begin searching, we'd best find somewhere warm to sleep and food to fill our stomachs."

The city was undamaged by the war and despite their ragged appearance they had no difficulty in obtaining rooms in a hotel, for Mavreen had stitched into the hem of her dress all her remaining gold coins. Most of the refugees were penniless as well as starving, but on seeing proof of Mavreen's ability to pay, the hotel quickly found rooms for the two of them.

They ate first and then slept for twenty-four hours and ate once more. Slowly, their energies began to return. A seamstress was called in to make Mavreen a dress and Dickon went out to find a tailor to provide him with coat and breeches.

He could not speak the native language so brought back no information to Mavreen except the unwelcome news that the city was filthy and stinking with bodies and carcasses of beasts.

"There is straw burning before every house," he said frowning, "though I know not why, and the smoke only adds to the foulness of the atmosphere! And the city is full of soldiers," he added. "Russian, I think!"

Mavreen hurried downstairs, where she quickly discovered that she and Dickon had slept through the most momentous days. On the 13th of December, three days behind them, Kutuzov's army had entered Vilna. The thousands of French soldiers remaining in the city were now prisoners. Many hundreds were dying; others were sick with a pestilence the physicians seemed unable to control.

"If Gerard is indeed in Vilna, he too will be a prisoner!" Mavreen said to Dickon. "I must go at once to the Russian authorities. At least I can now reveal my nationality. England is one of Russia's allies and mayhap they will be pleased to assist me!"

Her energies and hopes much restored, Mavreen at once hired a carriage and set out with Dickon to begin her search.

But a week later, despite all her efforts, she had still not discovered if Gerard was imprisoned. Now even the authorities declined her requests for interviews. They were, she was told, too busy preparing for the visit of their emperor, the Czar Alexander. He was coming himself to Vilna to celebrate the liberation of his empire from the invader.

"Mayhap when the celebrations and parades are over, I shall find the authorities more helpful!" Mavreen said. But she, like Dickon, had begun to lose hope. The prisoners were dying in not hundreds but thousands. The disease which ravaged them had now spread to the townspeople and to the Russian troops. There seemed no way of stopping it. On days when the temperature rose a few degrees above freezing point, the pestilence seemed to spread even more rapidly. The mountain of human bodies and carcasses was growing daily higher.

Dickon now feared for their lives, or more particularly, for Mavreen's. Had it been possible, he would have persuaded her to leave this city of death and begin the journey home without delay. But Mavreen would not consider the notion. She had been listening to the talk in the cafés in Vilna and knew that Emperor Alexander intended to ride around the town on the morrow, and her hopes were once more revived.

"The czar is but thirty-five years of age!" she said to Dickon. "I have heard he is not unsusceptible to women. Despite his marriage to the beautiful Elizabeth Alexeevna some nineteen years ago, he has a Polish countess for a mistress and 'tis said he has had two children by her. Mayhap if I can but bring myself to his attention, I can plead with him for Gerard's release!"

"If the vicomte do be a prisoner!" Dickon muttered doubtfully.

But Mavreen was too busy to listen to him as she planned the outfit she would wear.

"Between now and the morning, no matter what the cost, I shall have made for me a new riding dress," she told Dickon excitedly. "Let us go out at once so that I may select materials and find a seamstress. And I must employ a girl who can wash and coif my hair. And a milliner to make me a hat!"

Despite the shortage of time at their disposal, Mavreen achieved her designs by sheer will power. By morning, she was able to attire herself in a new bright green habit with high collar and military trimmings from the neckline to the knee. Perched on top of her golden curls was a new beaver riding hat with a huge green feather curving forward from forehead down to one shoulder. Her half-boots were laced with green and her hands warmly covered in tan York gloves.

Dickon grinned as she pirouetted before him.

"You surelye look a picture!" he said admiringly. "There's none as won't notice you today, surelye!"

Dickon, too, looked smart in the groom's livery she had purchased for him, fortunately discovering one already made that had found its way to the Jewish quarter of the town.

Dickon had not been idle. He had secured a magnificent mount for Mavreen—a beautiful white stallion that had once been a French cavalry officer's horse—and a less noble but sturdy animal for himself. He stayed up half the night grooming both beasts so that they and their saddles and harnesses shone in the pale December sunshine. There lacked but three days to the close of the year and the ground was white with frozen snow.

It proved no difficulty to discover the whereabouts of the Russian czar for the crowds gathered to cheer and applaud him in every street and square as he made his tour of the city. Mavreen waited until the emperor and his suite rode down the main street on their return to the castle. He was followed by General Kutuzov in a troika, wearing his full-dress uniform, proudly displaying his new decoration, the Order of St. George, and accompanied by some hundred generals and staff officers all in full parade uniforms.

"Now is the moment!" Mavreen whispered to Dickon as she watched the approach of the handsome young czar and his entourage.

She dug her heels sharply into her unsuspecting horse's flanks and whipped it hard across the rump. The stallion sprang forward. Deliberately, Mavreen refrained from reining in the great animal as it surged forward, its path from the side street where they had been waiting, leading them directly into the approaching parade.

As she had anticipated, the frightened stallion reared in sudden alarm as it saw the mass of horses and people blocking its path. With perfect timing, Mavreen let go her hold upon the reins and allowed herself to slip easily from the sidesaddle onto the soft heaps of snow beneath.

Her ruse worked to perfection. The czar and his party were forced to pull their own mounts to a halt, in order not to trample underfoot the unseated rider. One of the emperor's aides dismounted and ran to assist Dickon in helping Mavreen to her feet. The czar, not a little concerned by the incident, rode forward to inquire if the lady were hurt. Mavreen smiled ruefully at him and confessed to a badly sprained ankle. With yet another woeful but beguiling smile, she informed him that being an Englishwoman but newly arrived in a strange city, she knew not where to go for the attentions of a physician.

The presence of an English noblewoman in Vilna at such a time was remarkable enough for the czar to question her further. Her helplessness as much as her beauty intrigued him. Mavreen lost no time in playing upon his sympathy and advised him of her search for her fiancé.

"We must see what can be done to help the cause of love!" the czar said. "Meanwhile, dear lady, let me offer what assistance I can."

He ordered her to be helped into the carriage of General Kutuzov and further, that she was to be taken back to the castle of Vilna and accommodated there while inquiries were made as to the whereabouts of her fiancé, the vicomte de Valle.

"If the gentleman is imprisoned here in Vilna, I shall be so appraised," he said, and with a gallant bow he added, "It will be my pleasure, madame, to inform you personally of the facts arising from my inquiry!"

This last promise he did not keep, but Mavreen cared little that she was denied the honor of a personal visit from the czar of Russia, for true to his first promise, he did indeed discover Gerard's whereabouts. No more than twenty-four hours after her installation at the castle, he sent one of his aides to inform her that the vicomte de

Valle was alive and a guest at the villa of General Bennigsen on his estate at Zakret, some few miles outside Vilna.

Nearly incoherent with happiness, Mavreen plied her informant with questions. Was Gerard well? Had he been wounded? Was he imprisoned? But the aide was unable to give her any answers. Nevertheless, his next words were better than any such replies.

"I have orders to place a troika at your disposal, ma'am, so that you may visit the vicomte and ascertain his well-being for yourself! It is even now awaiting your convenience in the courtyard."

Her eyes brilliant with excitement, Mavreen beckoned one of the attendant footmen to her side.

"Go find my manservant, Dickon!" she commanded him. "Tell him that we shall be leaving at once for Zakret!"

CHAPTER FORTY-SIX

1812

Gerard was very weak. He lay in the big four-poster for the most part sleeping; waking intermittently when one of the servants came into the room or, as happened several times a day, when the Countess Helga von Heissen came to sit with him.

He had not at first grasped how or why this still beautiful fifty-year-old woman was at his bedside, supervising his nursing with tender care; urging him to try to eat; to get well again.

But as his strength began to return, he slowly pieced together the three weeks since Nikolai had brought him half dead on horseback to Vilna. He knew that he owed his life to the resourcefulness of his faithful servant. Upon entering Vilna, Nikolai realized that they were still far from reaching safety; that the Russian armies were not far behind them and Gerard, if not he, himself, would be promptly taken prisoner when they arrived at Vilna. Those of the French army in a fit state to continue the retreat had already departed for the border and no help could be expected from them. They were penniless, starving; and Gerard was very ill.

Nikolai decided at once not to remain in the city. One of his brothers had been for many years a forester on the estate of Count Bennigsen, not more than a few miles distant from Vilna. Exhausted though he was, and despite Gerard's now total collapse, Nikolai pressed onward carrying Gerard across his massive shoulders until they reached Zakret.

His brother, Andrei, greeted him warmly. He professed himself willing to conceal the vicomte in his simple homestead for Nikolai's sake, but doubted the necessity for it.

"There are many French émigrés of the nobility fighting for our country!" he pointed out to Nikolai as he put a vast bowl of rabbit stew before the starving man. "You need but refrain from letting it be known that your vicomte has been in Napoleon's army, then he will surely be given succor at Count Bennigsen's villa. The count is at present in Kaluga, retired there by General Kutuzov, so one of the household servants told me. But his mistress is in residence, awaiting his return from the war. She's an Austrian countess, a kindly lady, I'm told, and doubtless she will know best how to look after your vicomte! I'd say he needs a good physician—and quickly," he added, glancing at Gerard's unconscious form lying on the bearskin rug by the wood fire.

Gerard could not credit the stroke of good fortune that had brought the erstwhile Helga to this remote part of the world. She told him she had been under the protection of Count Bennigsen these past six years. When she first met the Russian general he was fighting for the Russian Empress Catherine, Alexander's grandmother, in the war against Poland. She, herself, was living then in Pultusk and when the French defeated the Russians in a battle fought there in 1806, General Bennigsen had taken her to live at his Russian estate in Zakret.

"I've been here ever since!" she told Gerard. "The count is a kindly man and I am well cared for. I never thought to see you again, *mon petit* Gerard!" she added, stroking the hair from his hot, feverish forehead.

She would not permit him to tell the long story of his own adventures covering the fourteen years since they had last been in communication.

"I have heard most already from your servant, Nikolai!" she told him, "so I will not allow you to tire yourself by recounting the details to me now." She smiled at him with affection. "I must confess, Gerard, that I never thought to hear that you, who fought so bravely with the émigrés during the revolution, would have ended by fighting for the Emperor Napoleon."

"I fought for my king!" Gerard explained. "And only when the Royalist cause seemed forever doomed, did I decide to fight for France. Besides, I am indebted to the emperor who personally effected my mother's release from captivity and restored our château to us in Compiègne."

It was not just illness and the debilitations of the three year-long campaigns that had brought Gerard to the state of mind where he cared not if he lived or died. Not even Helga's exhortations that he must make the effort to get well for her sake could revive him from his apathy. Only the belief, now abandoned, that he would see Mavreen again could restore his enthusiasm for life.

It was now seven years since he had last seen Mavreen in Vienna and given her his sacred oath that he would return to her as soon as he had completed his visit to Compiègne. Seven years! He could not himself believe that so much time had disappeared without one opportunity to make his way to her side. Yet the chance seemed never to have presented itself. On his return from Naples where he had felt obliged to go in search of his wife, he had been caught up against his will in the campaigns in Spain and Portugal. When at last he returned to France, he had been ordered by the emperor himself to take part in the planning of the Russian campaign, and now, well over a year from the start of those plans, the campaign was over, the French defeated and Napoleon, according to the news

Helga gave him, was back once more in Paris with nothing but the loss of a half-million soldiers to show for all the fighting. The triumphant czar of Russia was even now in Vilna and the French prisoners of war were dying by the thousands.

"And I, who still live, have nothing to live for!" Gerard thought, for he could not hope that Mavreen still loved him; still desired to share her life with him even if such were possible; and the likelihood was that by now she had settled down and adjusted to married life with James Pettigrew, nay, even had children by him! As for his only little daughter, Tamarisk would be fourteen years of age, approaching womanhood and older even than the child Mavreen had been when he first had met her. His daughter's childhood was lost to him, as inevitable a fact as that his own youth was gone forever.

Helga von Heissen, sensing Gerard's terrible depression, called Nikolai in to see him, begging him to find some means of reviving Gerard's will to live. Standing outside Gerard's sickroom, she looked at the man's anxious face and knew that he loved his master.

"If we cannot make him desire to live," she impressed on the trembling Nikolai, "the physician says he will never recover. Can you not talk to the vicomte of the Englishwoman he once loved? He will not speak of her to me, and yet I know he has talked of her to you!"

But before Nikolai could go to do her bidding, there was a vast commotion in the hallway downstairs.

"Mayhap 'tis the Count Bennigsen returned home!" Helga cried, leaning over the banister rail as the front door was pushed closed by the servant against the fierce flurry of snow beating inward on to the wood floors and settling upon the rugs in a white mantle.

But she did not recognize either of the two figures standing below her removing their fur-lined cloaks and handing them to the waiting servant. One was a burly, square-shouldered fellow with an unusual head of ginger colored hair; the other a fair-haired woman in her thirties, slender, beautiful, her cheeks flushed from the sudden entry to warmth from the bitter cold outside.

But Nikolai had no doubt as to Mavreen's identity. He had heard his master's description of the woman he loved so often that he had not the slightest difficulty in recognizing her in person. Moreover, on one of the slender hands drawn out for warmth to the blazing pine-log fire, he saw again the vicomte's signet ring.

"Methinks 'tis milady from England!" Nikolai said. "And the fellow with her is her servant, Dickon!"

Slowly, Helga von Heissen descended the stairway.

As Mavreen caught sight of her, she dropped a curtsy.

"Countess Bennigsen?" she inquired politely.

Helga shook her head.

"I am the Countess von Heissen!" she said. "Count Bennigsen is absent from home. May I know your name?"

Mavreen introduced herself and said breathlessly, "I am come in search of Monsieur le vicomte de Valle. I have been informed that he is here!"

"And rightly so!" Helga said gently. She now realized that here in person was the woman Gerard loved, and who loved him so deeply in return that she could not conceal her impatience to be near him. But she was afraid that the sudden shock of seeing Mavreen might be too much for Gerard in his weakened condition. She laid a restraining hand on Mavreen's arm.

"Before I take you to the vicomte, I pray you come with me into the salon so that I may prepare you. He has been very ill, you know, and is not yet recovered."

Mavreen curbed her impatience to ask a thousand questions. Silently, she waited restlessly as a servant brought glasses of tea for refreshment. Only when they were once more alone did the countess relax the formality of her behavior and address Mavreen as if she were an old friend. Indeed, the plump, bejeweled countess suddenly reminded her of Clarissa for she had the same motherly kindness of attitude.

"I doubt not that once Gerard sees you and realizes that you have come so far to be with him, his recovery will be rapid and total!" she said to Mavreen. "But though I understand that it is most probably your dearest wish to surprise him, I think it better if first I break the news to him that you are here. Do you understand, my dear? We do not want your sudden appearance to prove too great a shock to him."

"I will do anything you say that is for Gerard's good!" Mavreen cried, jumping to her feet and pacing the room restlessly. "Only hurry, madame, I pray you. I have waited so long already for this moment of our reunion."

Her eyes were now feverishly bright, her cheeks were flushed a soft pink. She looked no older than a girl of twenty, the countess thought, silently acknowledging Mavreen's beauty and the justification for Gerard's undying love for her.

"I have a wonderful idea!" Mavreen cried, pulling at the clasp of the tiny gold chain around her neck. "Give this to Gerard, madame. It is a locket. He will know at once that it is mine. When he asks you how you came by it, and he most surely will, you can advise him that I gave it to you in person. So he will come gradually to the realization that I am here!"

"I will do as you say, my dear!" the countess said, taking the locket from Mavreen and going at once from the room.

Mavreen was not mistaken. No sooner had Helga put the locket into Gerard's hands than his feverish color paled.

"For pity's sake, tell me, how came this into your possession?" he begged in a tight hoarse voice. He clasped the tiny gold locket to his heart. The countess was alarmed to see tears roll silently down his white, hollow cheeks.

"There is no need for sadness, Gerard!" she said quickly. "Indeed, it is good news I bring you, Gerard. The very best of news!"

Gerard attempted to raise himself from the pillows but he was too weak. He raised his hands in appeal.

"You have had word—of Mavreen?" he whispered.

The countess nodded.

"Yes, Gerard! Mavreen is alive and well, and most deeply concerned about you. If you will promise me to stay calm, I will give you further joyful tidings. Mavreen is here in Zakret."

Once again, Gerard tried to raise himself.

"Help me!" he cried. "Help me to get out of this bed. I must get up, Helga. I must go to her. Where is she? Where can I find her?"

Gently, the countess pushed him back onto the pillows.

"You have no need to bestir yourself, Gerard. Your brave and beautiful Mavreen is here, in this house. She awaits only my calling to come to you!"

Gerard let out his breath in a long, tremulous sigh.

"I must indeed be nearer to death even than I supposed!" he murmured. "I am most certainly dreaming. Helga, tell me at least that you are no dream, that you are here with me and that what you have just told me is the truth before God!"

"It is the truth before God!" Helga said, tears in her own eyes as she bent to kiss Gerard's cheek. "Come now, *mon ami,* you would not want your loved one to see you so disordered. Let me help you to a sitting position!"

Miraculously, Gerard now seemed to regain some strength. With the aid of Helga's arm, he succeeded in raising himself to a semi-upright position where he reclined against the pillows.

"There now!" Helga said, as she straightened the coverlet. "I will go myself and tell Mavreen that you are ready to receive her!"

It seemed to him an eternity before the door reopened and he saw Mavreen standing there. Wordlessly, she crossed the room toward him. A smoldering pine log burst into a shower of sparks in the grate and cast a golden shadow over her face. She had never looked more radiant or more beautiful to him.

Outside the casement window, a sudden gust of wind sent a curtain of white snow against the glass. Far away in the distant woods, a pack of wolves howled dismally. Below, in the driveway, a groom came to lead away the three horses which had brought Mavreen's troika to the villa.

But neither Mavreen nor Gerard were aware of anything but each other as she came to the bedside. Kneeling beside it, she laid her cheek on Gerard's frail hand.

"I had thought never to see you again!" he whispered. "Ah, Mavreen, *mon amour, mon petit écureuil!*"

Although her tears fell hot upon his hand, her eyes were shining with joy as she looked up at him.

"Oh, Gerard, my love!" she cried. "I never doubted that I should find you. But you are so thin! So pale! The countess told me you had been ill, but you must get well now. And quickly, Gerard. 'Tis time we returned to England together."

She rose to her feet, her tears dried, her face alive with excitement as she put her arms around him and hugged him.

"There is nothing in the world to stop us being together now, Gerard!" she cried rapturously. "You will not know of it, but poor James died several years ago. I am free to remain at your side. And Gerard, there will be no difficulties put in your way when you are fit enough to travel. The czar himself has placed you in my charge! Do you understand, Gerard? As soon as you are well, we may return to England together!"

"Yes, my love, I understand!" Gerard said tenderly, smiling at her radiance and her vitality, some of which already seemed to put new life into him. "And naturally, such prospects for my future fill me with happiness. But for the present, my Mavreen, I care nothing for tomorrow. It is enough for me that you are here, now, close beside me where I can kiss your lips, so! And touch your hair, so! And feel your soft cheek against mine. Ah, *mon amour,* if you but knew how much I loved you. *Je t'aime, je t'aime!*"

Downstairs in the kitchen, Nikolai and Dickon, their two loyal servants, raised their brimming glasses of vodka to one another in a toast.

"May they live happily ever after!" Nikolai said devoutly.

Dickon scratched his head and grinned.

"Leastways milady will be happy now!" he said, "for there beant no happiness for her without him. Nor never was!" He let out his breath in a long sigh. "Happen we'll be a-goin' home now," he said, "and none too soon. Reckon as how I've had enough of Frenchies, begging your pardon, Nikolai Kuragin. Happen I'm getting old and am justabout ready to settle down. Leastways, if the pair on 'em don't need me to go further adventuring!"

It was Nikolai's turn to smile.

"They'll still have me to take care of them!" he said proudly, "for I'm not leaving the vicomte's service, no matter what foreign country he chooses to live in."

"Furrin!" Dickon echoed, his face scarlet. " 'Taint England what's a furrin country; 'tis everywhere else in the world!"

"If you feel like that," Nikolai said craftily, "you'll not want your fine mistress marrying a foreign gentleman, then!"

The flush died down on Dickon's face and suddenly he was smiling again.

"My dad usened to tell me there's 'ceptions to every rule," he said, "so happen even if most Frenchies is furriners, the vicomte and you be English Frenchies. Howmsoever do that sound to you, eh?"

"Fair enough, comrade!" said Nikolai, who had not understood one word of it but sensed Dickon's friendliness. He poured out another two glasses of vodka and raised his own.

"A long life and happiness to the both of them and to the both of us!" he said in his own language, and draining his glass in one draft, he threw it over his shoulder. Hesitating only a moment, Dickon felt it was only polite to do likewise.

Upstairs, Gerard and Mavreen heard the faint sound of breaking glass. But they paid no attention. They lay side by side in perfect happiness, silently holding each other's hands.

"I cannot believe that this miracle has happened! What strange turn of fate can have brought you to Russia, to Zakret, whilst I, too, am here?" Gerard asked.

Mavreen's eyes sparkled with delight.

" 'Twas no matter of chance," she told him, "for it was I who turned the wheels of fate, Gerard. When the marquis de Guéridon wrote and told us that you were started out upon Napoleon's Russian campaign, I was overjoyed, for at long last I knew that you were alive. Until then, I could but doubt your existence. Moreover, I knew that however large the great continent of Europe, there would always be someone to give me news of the whereabouts of the Grand Army and that in time, I must find you. It was my search for you, my love, which brought me to Russia!"

Gerard was overcome. Wordlessly, he drew her closer against him.

"No man deserves a love as faithful and courageous as yours!" he murmured. "I least of all. Oh, Mavreen, if you but knew what pain it gives me to think of all the wasted years that were my doing! I should have had courage enough to marry you when first we fell in love—sixteen years ago. Sixteen years of life that we might have shared! How can you forgive me? How can you still love me?"

Mavreen smiled.

"I will always love you," she said simply. "As for forgiveness, none is needed, Gerard. Mayhap if we had married so young we would never have valued our love as now we do, knowing that there is no true happiness apart from one another. Moreover, I understood your duties and obligations to your family even whilst childishly I raged against fate for taking you from me."

Bit by bit, she persuaded him to recount his adventures since last they parted in Vienna. When finally he ended his account, she sighed.

"You have been near death so many times!" she said. "Yet you live, my Gerard, and we must thank God for sparing you."

"It is a miracle!" Gerard agreed. "If only my mother were alive to share our happiness!"

"She will know of it, I'm certain," Mavreen said. "No one understood better than the vicomtesse how deep was my love for you."

"Was?" Gerard echoed, smiling.

As he had expected, Mavreen threw her arms around him.

"Is, my darling!" she cried. "And ever will be. Have I not proved it, Gerard?"

As his memory reached backwards over the years, Gerard realized that there had been no occasion ever when her love had faltered. She was brave, fearless, undaunted, more beautiful than ever, and he knew himself the most fortunate of all men.

"Je t'aime! Je t'aime!" he whispered. *"Mon petit écureuil!"*

Barbara Cartland

The world's bestselling author of romantic fiction. Her stories are always captivating tales of intrigue, adventure and love.

☐	THE CRUEL COUNT	2128	$1.25
☐	CALL OF THE HEART	2140	$1.25
☐	AS EAGLES FLY	2147	$1.25
☐	THE MASK OF LOVE	2366	$1.25
☐	AN ARROW OF LOVE	2426	$1.25
☐	A GAMBLE WITH HEARTS	2430	$1.25
☐	A KISS FOR THE KING	2433	$1.25
☐	A FRAME OF DREAMS	2434	$1.25
☐	THE FRAGRANT FLOWER	2435	$1.25
☐	MOON OVER EDEN	2437	$1.25
☐	THE GOLDEN ILLUSION	2449	$1.25
☐	FIRE ON THE SNOW	2450	$1.25
☐	THE HUSBAND HUNTERS	2461	$1.25
☐	THE SHADOW OF SIN	6430	$1.25
☐	SAY YES, SAMANTHA	7834	$1.25
☐	THE KARMA OF LOVE	8106	$1.25
☐	BEWITCHED	8630	$1.25
☐	THE IMPETUOUS DUCHESS	8705	$1.25

Buy them at your local bookseller or use this handy coupon:

Catherine Cookson

For years a bestselling author in England, Catherine Cookson's readership today is worldwide. Now one of the most popular and best-loved writers of romantic fiction, her spellbinding novels are memorable stories of love, tragedy and courage.

☐	A GRAND MAN	2233	$1.50
☐	THE INVISIBLE CORD	2350	$1.75
☐	THE LORD AND MARY ANN	2432	$1.50
☐	THE MALLON LOT	6323	$1.50
☐	THE DWELLING PLACE	7246	$1.25
☐	FEATHERS IN THE FIRE	7289	$1.25
☐	OUR KATE	7599	$1.25
☐	THE MALLEN STREAK	7806	$1.50
☐	PURE AS THE LILY	8079	$1.25
☐	THE FIFTEEN STREETS	8174	$1.25
☐	THE MALLEN GIRL	8406	$1.50
☐	KATE HANNIGAN	8646	$1.25
☐	FENWICK HOUSES	8656	$1.25
☒	KATIE MULHOLLAND	10078	$1.50
☐	THE GLASS VIRGIN	10358	$1.50

ANGÉLIQUE

Bantam Book Catalog

It lists over a thousand money-saving best-sellers originally priced from $3.75 to $15.00 —bestsellers that are yours now for as little as 60¢ to $2.95!

The catalog gives you a great opportunity to build your own private library at huge savings!

So don't delay any longer—send us your name and address and 25¢ (to help defray postage and handling costs).